The Definitive
CHARLES DICKENS

Charles Dickens (1812-1870) was one of the foremost English authors of his time. He wrote both novels and short stories, most of which garnered widespread acclaim and continue to be widely read. His best known works include *David Copperfield, A Tale of Two Cities* and *Hard Times*.

The Definitive
CHARLES DICKENS

RUPA

Published by
Rupa Publications India Pvt. Ltd 2017
7/16, Ansari Road, Daryaganj
New Delhi 110002

Sales Centres:
Allahabad Bengaluru Chennai
Hyderabad Jaipur Kathmandu
Kolkata Mumbai

Edition Copyright © Rupa Publications India Pvt. Ltd 2017

This is a work of fiction. Names, characters, places and incidents are
either the product of the author's imagination or are used fictitiously,
and any resemblance to any actual persons, living or dead,
events or locales is entirely coincidental.

All rights reserved.
No part of this publication may be reproduced, transmitted, or stored in a
retrieval system, in any form or by any means, electronic, mechanical, photocopying,
recording or otherwise, without the prior permission of the publisher.

ISBN: 978-81-291-4882-7

First impression 2017

10 9 8 7 6 5 4 3 2 1

This edition is for sale in the Indian Subcontinent only.

Printed at Nutech Print Services, New Delhi

This book is sold subject to the condition that it shall not, by way of
trade or otherwise, be lent, resold, hired out, or otherwise circulated,
without the publisher's prior consent, in any form of binding
or cover other than that in which it is published.

CONTENTS

Great Expectations	1
Is She His Wife?	461
Master Humphrey's Clock	489
The Trial For Murder	605
The Letters	619

GREAT EXPECTATIONS

Chapter 1

My father's family name being Pirrip, and my Christian name Philip, my infant tongue could make of both names nothing longer or more explicit than Pip. So, I called myself Pip, and came to be called Pip.

I give Pirrip as my father's family name, on the authority of his tombstone and my sister,—Mrs Joe Gargery, who married the blacksmith. As I never saw my father or my mother, and never saw any likeness of either of them (for their days were long before the days of photographs), my first fancies regarding what they were like were unreasonably derived from their tombstones. The shape of the letters on my father's, gave me an odd idea that he was a square, stout, dark man, with curly black hair. From the character and turn of the inscription, '*Also Georgiana Wife of the Above*', I drew a childish conclusion that my mother was freckled and sickly. To five little stone lozenges, each about a foot and a half long, which were arranged in a neat row beside their grave, and were sacred to the memory of five little brothers of mine,—who gave up trying to get a living, exceedingly early in that universal struggle,—I am indebted for a belief I religiously entertained that they had all been born on their backs with their hands in their trousers-pockets, and had never taken them out in this state of existence.

Ours was the marsh country, down by the river, within, as the river wound, twenty miles of the sea. My first most vivid and broad impression of the identity of things seems to me to have been gained on a memorable raw afternoon towards evening. At such a time I found out for certain that this bleak place overgrown with nettles was the churchyard; and that Philip Pirrip, late of this parish, and also Georgiana wife of the above, were dead and buried; and that Alexander, Bartholomew, Abraham, Tobias, and Roger, infant children of the aforesaid, were also dead and buried; and that the dark flat wilderness beyond the churchyard, intersected with dikes and mounds and gates, with scattered cattle feeding on it, was the marshes; and that the low leaden line beyond was the river; and that the distant savage lair from which the wind was rushing was the sea; and that the small bundle of shivers growing afraid of it all and beginning to cry, was Pip.

'Hold your noise!' cried a terrible voice, as a man started up from among the graves at the side of the church porch. 'Keep still, you little devil, or I'll cut your throat!'

A fearful man, all in coarse grey, with a great iron on his leg. A man with no hat, and with broken shoes, and with an old rag tied round his head. A man who had been soaked in water, and smothered in mud, and lamed by stones, and cut by flints, and stung by nettles, and torn by briars; who limped, and shivered, and glared, and growled; and whose teeth chattered in his head as he seized me by the chin.

'Oh! Don't cut my throat, sir,' I pleaded in terror. 'Pray don't do it, sir.'

'Tell us your name!' said the man. 'Quick!'

'Pip, sir.'

'Once more,' said the man, staring at me. 'Give it mouth!'

'Pip. Pip, sir.'

'Show us where you live,' said the man. 'Pint out the place!'

I pointed to where our village lay, on the flat inshore among the alder trees and pollards, a mile or more from the church.

The man, after looking at me for a moment, turned me upside down, and emptied my pockets. There was nothing in them but a piece of bread. When the church came to itself,—for he was so sudden and strong that he made it go head over heels before me, and I saw the steeple under my feet,—when the church came to itself, I say, I was seated on a high tombstone, trembling while he ate the bread ravenously.

'You young dog,' said the man, licking his lips, 'what fat cheeks you ha' got.'

I believe they were fat, though I was at that time undersized for my years, and not strong.

'Darn me if I couldn't eat em,' said the man, with a threatening shake of his head, 'and if I han't half a mind to't!'

I earnestly expressed my hope that he wouldn't, and held tighter to the tombstone on which he had put me; partly, to keep myself upon it; partly, to keep myself from crying.

'Now lookee here!' said the man. 'Where's your mother?'

'There, sir!' said I.

He started, made a short run, and stopped and looked over his shoulder.

'There, sir!' I timidly explained. 'Also Georgiana. That's my mother.'

'Oh!' said he, coming back. 'And is that your father alonger your mother?'

'Yes, sir,' said I; 'him too; late of this parish.'

'Ha!' he muttered then, considering. 'Who d'ye live with,—supposin' you're kindly let to live, which I han't made up my mind about?'

'My sister, sir,—Mrs Joe Gargery,—wife of Joe Gargery, the blacksmith, sir.'

'Blacksmith, eh?' said he. And looked down at his leg.

After darkly looking at his leg and me several times, he came closer to my tombstone, took me by both arms, and tilted me back as far as he could hold me; so that his eyes looked most powerfully down into mine, and mine looked most helplessly up into his.

'Now lookee here,' he said, 'the question being whether you're to be let to live. You know what a file is?'

'Yes, sir.'

'And you know what wittles is?'

'Yes, sir.'

After each question he tilted me over a little more, so as to give me a greater sense of helplessness and danger.

'You get me a file.' He tilted me again. 'And you get me wittles.' He tilted me again. 'You bring 'em both to me.' He tilted me again. 'Or I'll have your heart and liver out.' He tilted me again.

I was dreadfully frightened, and so giddy that I clung to him with both hands, and said, 'If you would kindly please to let me keep upright, sir, perhaps I shouldn't be sick, and perhaps I could attend more.'

He gave me a most tremendous dip and roll, so that the church jumped over its own weathercock. Then, he held me by the arms, in an upright position on the top of the stone, and went on in these fearful terms:—

'You bring me, tomorrow morning early, that file and them wittles.

You bring the lot to me, at that old Battery over yonder. You do it, and you never dare to say a word or dare to make a sign concerning your having seen such a person as me, or any person sumever, and you shall be let to live. You fail, or you go from my words in any partickler, no matter how small it is, and your heart and your liver shall be tore out, roasted, and ate. Now, I ain't alone, as you may think I am. There's a young man hid with me, in comparison with which young man I am a Angel. That young man hears the words I speak. That young man has a secret way pecooliar to himself, of getting at a boy, and at his heart, and at his liver. It is in wain for a boy to attempt to hide himself from that young man. A boy may lock his door, may be warm in bed, may tuck himself up, may draw the clothes over his head, may think himself comfortable and safe, but that young man will softly creep and creep his way to him and tear him open. I am a keeping that young man from harming of you at the present moment, with great difficulty. I find it wery hard to hold that young man off of your inside. Now, what do you say?'

I said that I would get him the file, and I would get him what broken bits of food I could, and I would come to him at the Battery, early in the morning.

'Say Lord strike you dead if you don't!' said the man.

I said so, and he took me down.

'Now,' he pursued, 'you remember what you've undertook, and you remember that young man, and you get home!'

'Goo-goodnight, sir,' I faltered.

'Much of that!' said he, glancing about him over the cold wet flat. 'I wish I was a frog. Or a eel!'

At the same time, he hugged his shuddering body in both his arms,—clasping himself, as if to hold himself together,—and limped towards the low church wall. As I saw him go, picking his way among the nettles, and among the brambles that bound the green mounds, he looked in my young eyes as if he were eluding the hands of the dead people, stretching up cautiously out of their graves, to get a twist upon his ankle and pull him in.

When he came to the low church wall, he got over it, like a man whose legs were numbed and stiff, and then turned round to look for me. When I saw him turning, I set my face towards home, and made the best use of my legs. But presently I looked over my shoulder, and saw him going on again towards the river, still hugging himself in both arms, and picking his way with his sore feet among the great stones dropped into the marshes here and there, for stepping-places when the rains were heavy or the tide was in.

The marshes were just a long black horizontal line then, as I stopped to look after him; and the river was just another horizontal line, not nearly so broad nor yet so black; and the sky was just a row of long angry red lines and dense black lines intermixed. On the edge of the river I could faintly make out the only two black things in all the prospect that seemed to be standing upright; one of these was the beacon by which the sailors steered,—like an unhooped cask upon a pole,—an ugly thing when you were near it; the other, a gibbet, with some chains hanging to it which had once held a pirate. The man was limping on towards this latter, as if he were the pirate come to life, and come down, and going back to hook himself up again. It gave me a terrible turn when I thought so; and as I saw the cattle lifting their heads to gaze after him, I wondered whether they thought so too. I looked all round for the horrible young man, and could see no signs of him. But now I was frightened again, and ran home without stopping.

Chapter 2

My sister, Mrs Joe Gargery, was more than twenty years older than I, and had established a great reputation with herself and the neighbours because she had brought me up 'by hand'. Having at that time to find out for myself what the expression meant, and knowing her to have a hard and heavy hand, and to be much in the habit of laying it upon her husband as well as upon me, I supposed that Joe Gargery and I were both brought up by hand.

She was not a good-looking woman, my sister; and I had a general impression that she must have made Joe Gargery marry her by hand. Joe was a fair man, with curls of flaxen hair on each side of his smooth face, and with eyes of such a very undecided blue that they seemed to have somehow got mixed with their own whites. He was a mild, good-natured, sweet-tempered, easy-going, foolish, dear fellow,—a sort of Hercules in strength, and also in weakness.

My sister, Mrs Joe, with black hair and eyes, had such a prevailing redness of skin that I sometimes used to wonder whether it was possible she washed herself with a nutmeg-grater instead of soap. She was tall and bony, and almost always wore a coarse apron, fastened over her figure behind with two loops, and having a square impregnable bib in front, that was stuck full of pins and needles. She made it a powerful merit in herself, and a strong reproach against Joe, that she wore this apron so much. Though I really see no reason why she should have worn it at all; or why, if she did wear it at all, she should not have taken it off, every day of her life.

Joe's forge adjoined our house, which was a wooden house, as many of the dwellings in our country were,—most of them, at that time. When I ran home from the churchyard, the forge was shut up, and Joe was sitting alone in the kitchen. Joe and I being fellow-sufferers, and having confidences as such, Joe imparted a confidence to me, the moment I raised the latch of the door and peeped in at him opposite to it, sitting in the chimney corner.

'Mrs Joe has been out a dozen times, looking for you, Pip. And she's out now, making it a baker's dozen.'

'Is she?'

'Yes, Pip,' said Joe; 'and what's worse, she's got Tickler with her.'

At this dismal intelligence, I twisted the only button on my waistcoat round and round, and looked in great depression at the fire. Tickler was a wax-ended piece of cane, worn smooth by collision with my tickled frame.

'She sot down,' said Joe, 'and she got up, and she made a grab at Tickler, and she Ram-paged out. That's what she did,' said Joe, slowly clearing the fire between the lower bars with the poker, and looking at it; 'she Ram-paged out, Pip.'

'Has she been gone long, Joe?' I always treated him as a larger species of child, and as no more than my equal.

'Well,' said Joe, glancing up at the Dutch clock, 'she's been on the Ram-page, this last spell, about five minutes, Pip. She's a coming! Get behind the door, old chap, and have the jack-towel betwixt you.'

I took the advice. My sister, Mrs Joe, throwing the door wide open, and finding an obstruction behind it, immediately divined the cause, and applied Tickler to its further investigation. She concluded by throwing me—I often served as a connubial missile—at Joe, who, glad to get hold of me on any terms, passed me on into the chimney and quietly fenced me up there with his great leg.

'Where have you been, you young monkey?' said Mrs Joe, stamping her foot. 'Tell me directly what you've been doing to wear me away with fret and fright and worrit, or I'd have you out of that corner if you was fifty Pips, and he was five hundred Gargerys.'

'I have only been to the churchyard,' said I, from my stool, crying and rubbing myself.

'Churchyard!' repeated my sister. 'If it warn't for me you'd have been to the churchyard long ago, and stayed there. Who brought you up by hand?'

'You did,' said I.

'And why did I do it, I should like to know?' exclaimed my sister.

I whimpered, 'I don't know.'

'*I* don't!' said my sister. 'I'd never do it again! I know that. I may truly say I've never had this apron of mine off since born you were. It's bad enough to be a blacksmith's wife (and him a Gargery) without being your mother.'

My thoughts strayed from that question as I looked disconsolately at the fire. For the fugitive out on the marshes with the ironed leg, the mysterious young man, the file, the food, and the dreadful pledge I was under to commit a larceny on those sheltering premises, rose before me in the avenging coals.

'Hah!' said Mrs Joe, restoring Tickler to his station. 'Churchyard, indeed! You may well say churchyard, you two.' One of us, by the by, had not said it at all. 'You'll drive *me* to the churchyard betwixt you, one of these days, and O, a pr-r-recious pair you'd be without me!'

As she applied herself to set the tea-things, Joe peeped down at me over his leg, as if he were mentally casting me and himself up, and calculating what kind of pair we practically should make, under the grievous circumstances foreshadowed. After that, he sat feeling his right-side flaxen curls and whisker, and following Mrs Joe about with his blue eyes, as his manner always was at squally times.

My sister had a trenchant way of cutting our bread and butter for us, that never varied. First, with her left hand she jammed the loaf hard and fast against her bib,—where it sometimes got a pin into it, and sometimes a needle, which we afterwards got into our mouths. Then she took some butter (not too much) on a knife and spread it on the loaf, in an apothecary kind of way, as if she were making a plaster,—using both sides of the knife with a slapping dexterity, and trimming and moulding the butter off round the crust. Then, she gave the knife a final smart wipe on the edge of the plaster, and then sawed a very thick round off the loaf: which she finally, before separating from the loaf, hewed into two halves, of which Joe got one, and I the other.

On the present occasion, though I was hungry, I dared not eat my slice. I felt that I must have something in reserve for my dreadful acquaintance, and his ally the still more dreadful young man. I knew Mrs Joe's housekeeping to be of the strictest kind, and that my larcenous researches might find nothing available in the safe. Therefore, I resolved to put my hunk of bread and butter down the leg of my trousers.

The effort of resolution necessary to the achievement of this purpose I found to be quite awful. It was as if I had to make up my mind to leap from the top of a high house, or plunge into a great depth of water. And it was made the more difficult by the unconscious Joe. In our already-mentioned freemasonry as fellow-sufferers, and in his good-natured companionship with me, it was our evening habit to compare the way we bit through our slices, by silently holding them up to each other's admiration now and then,—which stimulated us to new exertions. Tonight, Joe several times invited me, by the display of his fast diminishing slice, to enter upon our usual friendly competition; but he found me, each time, with my yellow mug of tea on one knee, and my untouched bread and butter on the other. At last, I desperately considered that the thing I contemplated must be done, and that it had best be done in the least improbable manner consistent with the circumstances. I took advantage of a moment when Joe had just looked at me, and got my bread and butter down my leg.

Joe was evidently made uncomfortable by what he supposed to be my loss of appetite, and took a thoughtful bite out of his slice, which he didn't seem to enjoy. He turned it about in his mouth much longer than usual, pondering over it a good deal, and after all gulped it down like a pill. He was about to take another bite, and had just got his head on one side for a good purchase on it, when his eye fell on me, and he saw that my bread and butter was gone.

The wonder and consternation with which Joe stopped on the threshold of his bite and stared at me, were too evident to escape my sister's observation.

'What's the matter *now*?' said she, smartly, as she put down her cup.

'I say, you know!' muttered Joe, shaking his head at me in very serious remonstrance. 'Pip, old chap! You'll do yourself a mischief. It'll stick somewhere. You can't have chawed it, Pip.'

'What's the matter now?' repeated my sister, more sharply than before.

'If you can cough any trifle on it up, Pip, I'd recommend you to do it,' said Joe, all aghast. 'Manners is manners, but still your elth's your elth.'

By this time, my sister was quite desperate, so she pounced on Joe, and, taking him by the two whiskers, knocked his head for a little while against the wall behind him, while I sat in the corner, looking guiltily on.

'Now, perhaps you'll mention what's the matter,' said my sister, out of breath, 'you staring great stuck pig.'

Joe looked at her in a helpless way, then took a helpless bite, and looked at me again.

'You know, Pip,' said Joe, solemnly, with his last bite in his cheek, and speaking in a confidential voice, as if we two were quite alone, 'you and me is always friends, and I'd be the last to tell upon you, any time. But such a—' he moved his chair and looked about the floor between us, and then again at me—'such a most oncommon Bolt as that!'

'Been bolting his food, has he?' cried my sister.

'You know, old chap,' said Joe, looking at me, and not at

Mrs Joe, with his bite still in his cheek, 'I Bolted, myself, when I was your age—frequent—and as a boy I've been among a many Bolters; but I never see your Bolting equal yet, Pip, and it's a mercy you ain't Bolted dead.'

My sister made a dive at me, and fished me up by the hair, saying nothing more than the awful words, 'You come along and be dosed.'

Some medical beast had revived Tar-water in those days as a fine medicine, and Mrs Joe always kept a supply of it in the cupboard; having a belief in its virtues correspondent to its nastiness. At the best of times, so much of this elixir was administered to me as a choice restorative, that I was conscious of going about, smelling like a new fence. On this particular evening the urgency of my case demanded a pint of this mixture, which was poured down my throat, for my greater comfort, while Mrs Joe held my head under her arm, as a boot would be held in a bootjack. Joe got off with half a pint; but was made to swallow that (much to his disturbance, as he sat slowly munching and meditating before the fire), 'because he had had a turn.' Judging from myself, I should say he certainly had a turn afterwards, if he had had none before.

Conscience is a dreadful thing when it accuses man or boy; but when, in the case of a boy, that secret burden co-operates with another secret burden down the leg of his trousers, it is (as I can testify) a great punishment. The guilty knowledge that I was going to rob Mrs Joe—I never thought I was going to rob Joe, for I never thought of any of the housekeeping property as his—united to the necessity of always keeping one hand on my bread and butter as I sat, or when I was ordered about the kitchen on any small errand, almost drove me out of my mind. Then, as the marsh winds made the fire glow and flare, I thought I heard the voice outside, of the man with the iron on his leg who had sworn me to secrecy, declaring that he couldn't and wouldn't starve until tomorrow, but must be fed now. At other times, I thought, what if the young man who was with so much difficulty restrained from imbruing his hands in me should yield to a constitutional impatience, or should mistake the time, and should think himself accredited to my heart and liver tonight, instead of tomorrow! If ever anybody's hair stood on end with terror, mine must have done so then. But, perhaps, nobody's ever did?

It was Christmas Eve, and I had to stir the pudding for next day, with a copper-stick, from seven to eight by the Dutch clock. I tried it with the load upon my leg (and that made me think afresh of the man with the load on *his* leg), and found the tendency of exercise to bring the bread and butter out at my ankle, quite unmanageable. Happily I slipped away, and deposited that part of my conscience in my garret bedroom.

'Hark!' said I, when I had done my stirring, and was taking a final warm in the chimney corner before being sent up to bed; 'was that great guns, Joe?'

'Ah!' said Joe. 'There's another conwict off.'

'What does that mean, Joe?' said I.

Mrs Joe, who always took explanations upon herself, said, snappishly, 'Escaped. Escaped.' Administering the definition like Tar-water.

While Mrs Joe sat with her head bending over her needlework, I put my mouth into the forms of saying to Joe, 'What's a convict?' Joe put *his* mouth into the forms of returning such a highly elaborate answer, that I could make out nothing of it but the single word 'Pip.'

'There was a conwict off last night,' said Joe, aloud, 'after sunset-gun. And they fired warning of him. And now it appears they're firing warning of another.'

'*Who's* firing?' said I.

'Drat that boy,' interposed my sister, frowning at me over her work, 'what a questioner he is. Ask no questions, and you'll be told no lies.'

It was not very polite to herself, I thought, to imply that I should be told lies by her even if I did ask questions. But she never was polite unless there was company.

At this point Joe greatly augmented my curiosity by taking the utmost pains to open his mouth very wide, and to put it into the form of a word that looked to me like 'sulks.' Therefore, I naturally pointed to Mrs Joe, and put my mouth into the form of saying, 'her?' But Joe wouldn't hear of that, at all, and again opened his mouth very wide, and shook the form of a most emphatic word out of it. But I could make nothing of the word.

'Mrs Joe,' said I, as a last resort, 'I should like to know—if you wouldn't much mind—where the firing comes from?'

'Lord bless the boy!' exclaimed my sister, as if she didn't quite mean that but rather the contrary. 'From the Hulks!'

'Oh-h!' said I, looking at Joe. 'Hulks!'

Joe gave a reproachful cough, as much as to say, 'Well, I told you so.'

'And please, what's Hulks?' said I.

'That's the way with this boy!' exclaimed my sister, pointing me out with her needle and thread, and shaking her head at me. 'Answer him one question, and he'll ask you a dozen directly. Hulks are prison-ships, right 'cross th' meshes.' We always used that name for marshes, in our country.'

'I wonder who's put into prison-ships, and why they're put there?' said I, in a general way, and with quiet desperation.

It was too much for Mrs Joe, who immediately rose. 'I tell you what, young fellow,' said she, 'I didn't bring you up by hand to badger people's lives out. It would be blame to me and not praise, if I had. People are put in the Hulks because they murder, and because they rob, and forge, and do all sorts of bad; and they always begin by asking questions. Now, you get along to bed!'

I was never allowed a candle to light me to bed, and, as I went upstairs in the dark, with my head tingling,—from Mrs Joe's thimble having played the tambourine upon it, to accompany her last words,—I felt fearfully sensible of the great convenience that the hulks were handy for me. I was clearly on my way there. I had begun by asking questions, and I was going to rob Mrs Joe.

Since that time, which is far enough away now, I have often thought that few people know what secrecy there is in the young under terror. No matter how unreasonable the terror, so that it be terror. I was in mortal terror of the young man who wanted my heart and liver; I was in mortal terror of my interlocutor with the iron leg; I was in mortal terror of myself, from whom an awful promise had been extracted; I had no hope of deliverance through my all-powerful sister, who repulsed me at every turn; I am afraid to think of what I might have done on requirement, in the secrecy of my terror.

If I slept at all that night, it was only to imagine myself drifting down the river on a strong spring-tide, to the Hulks; a ghostly pirate calling out to me through a speaking-trumpet, as I passed the gibbet-station, that I had better come ashore and be hanged there at once, and not put it off. I was afraid to sleep, even if I had been inclined, for I knew that at the first faint dawn of morning I must rob the pantry. There was no doing it in the night, for there was no getting a light by easy friction then; to have got one I must have struck it out of flint and steel, and have made a noise like the very pirate himself rattling his chains.

As soon as the great black velvet pall outside my little window was shot with gray, I got up and went downstairs; every board upon the way, and every crack in every board calling after me, 'Stop thief!' and 'Get up, Mrs Joe!' In the pantry, which was far more abundantly supplied than usual, owing to the season, I was very much alarmed by a hare hanging up by the heels, whom I rather thought I caught, when my back was half turned, winking. I had no time for verification, no time for selection, no time for anything, for I had no time to spare. I stole some bread, some rind of cheese, about half a jar of mincemeat (which I tied up in my pocket-handkerchief with my last night's slice), some brandy from a stone bottle (which I decanted into a glass bottle I had secretly used for making that intoxicating fluid, Spanish-liquorice-water, up in my room: diluting the stone bottle from a jug in the kitchen cupboard), a meat bone with very little on it, and a beautiful round compact pork pie. I was nearly going away without the pie, but I was tempted to mount upon a shelf, to look what it was that was put away so carefully in a covered earthenware dish in a corner, and I found it was the pie, and I took it in the hope that it was not intended for early use, and would not be missed for some time.

There was a door in the kitchen, communicating with the forge; I unlocked and unbolted that door, and got a file from among Joe's tools. Then I put the fastenings as I had found them, opened the door at which I had entered when I ran home last night, shut it, and ran for the misty marshes.

Chapter 3

It was a rimy morning, and very damp. I had seen the damp lying on the outside of my little window, as if some goblin had been crying there all night, and using the window for a pocket-handkerchief. Now, I saw the damp lying on the bare hedges and spare grass, like a coarser sort of spiders' webs; hanging itself from twig to twig and blade to blade. On every rail and gate, wet lay clammy, and the marsh mist was so thick, that the wooden finger on the post directing people to our village—a direction which they never accepted, for they never came there—was invisible to me until I was quite close under it. Then, as I looked up at it, while it dripped, it seemed to my oppressed conscience like a phantom devoting me to the Hulks.

The mist was heavier yet when I got out upon the marshes, so that instead of my running at everything, everything seemed to run at me. This was very disagreeable to a guilty mind. The gates and dikes and banks came bursting at me through the mist, as if they cried as plainly as could be, 'A boy with somebody else's pork pie! Stop him!' The cattle came upon me with like suddenness, staring out of their eyes, and steaming out of their nostrils, 'Halloa, young thief!' One black ox, with a white cravat on,—who even had to my awakened conscience something of a clerical air,—fixed me so obstinately with his eyes, and moved his blunt head round in such an accusatory manner as I moved round, that I blubbered out to him, 'I couldn't help it, sir! It wasn't for myself I took it!' Upon which he put down his head, blew a cloud of smoke out of his nose, and vanished with a kick-up of his hind-legs and a flourish of his tail.

All this time, I was getting on towards the river; but however fast I went, I couldn't warm my feet, to which the damp cold seemed riveted, as the iron was riveted to the leg of the man I was running to meet. I knew my way to the Battery, pretty straight, for I had been down there on a Sunday with Joe, and Joe, sitting on an old gun, had told me that when I was 'prentice to him, regularly bound, we would have such Larks there! However, in the confusion of the mist, I found myself at last too far to the right, and consequently had to try back along the riverside, on the bank of loose stones above the mud and the stakes that staked the tide out. Making my way along here with all despatch, I had just crossed a ditch which I knew to be very near the Battery, and had just scrambled up the mound beyond the ditch, when I saw the man sitting before me. His back was towards me, and he had his arms folded, and was nodding forward, heavy with sleep.

I thought he would be more glad if I came upon him with his breakfast, in that unexpected manner, so I went forward softly and touched him on the shoulder. He instantly jumped up, and it was not the same man, but another man!

And yet this man was dressed in coarse grey, too, and had a great iron on his leg, and was lame, and hoarse, and cold, and was everything that the other man was; except that he had not the same face, and had a flat broad-brimmed low-crowned felt hat on. All this I saw in a moment, for I had only a moment to see it in: he swore an oath at me, made a hit at me,—it was a round weak blow that missed me and almost knocked himself down, for it made him stumble,—and then he ran into the mist, stumbling twice as he went, and I lost him.

'It's the young man!' I thought, feeling my heart shoot as I identified him. I dare say I should have felt a pain in my liver, too, if I had known where it was.

I was soon at the Battery after that, and there was the right man,—hugging himself and limping to and fro, as if he had never all night left off hugging and limping,—waiting for me. He was awfully cold, to be sure. I half expected to see him drop down before my face and die of deadly cold. His eyes looked so awfully hungry too, that when I handed him the file and he laid it down on the grass, it occurred to me he would have tried to eat it, if he had not seen my bundle. He did not turn me upside down this time to get at what I had, but left me right side upwards while I opened the bundle and emptied my pockets.

'What's in the bottle, boy?' said he.

'Brandy,' said I.

He was already handing mincemeat down his throat in the most curious manner,—more like a man who was putting it away somewhere in a violent hurry, than a man who was eating it,—but he left off to take some of the liquor. He shivered all the while so violently, that it was quite as much as he could do to keep the neck of the bottle between his teeth, without biting it off.

'I think you have got the ague,' said I.

'I'm much of your opinion, boy,' said he.

'It's bad about here,' I told him. 'You've been lying out on the meshes, and they're dreadful aguish. Rheumatic too.'

'I'll eat my breakfast afore they're the death of me,' said he. 'I'd do that, if I was going to be strung up to that there gallows as there is over there, directly afterwards. I'll beat the shivers so far, I'll bet you.'

He was gobbling mincemeat, meatbone, bread, cheese, and pork pie, all at once: staring distrustfully while he did so at the mist all round us, and often stopping—even stopping his jaws—to listen. Some real or fancied sound, some clink upon the river or breathing of beast upon the marsh, now gave him a start, and he said, suddenly,—

'You're not a deceiving imp? You brought no one with you?'

'No, sir! No!'

'Nor giv' no one the office to follow you?'

'No!'

'Well,' said he, 'I believe you. You'd be but a fierce young hound indeed, if at your time of life you could help to hunt a wretched warmint hunted as near death and dunghill as this poor wretched warmint is!'

Something clicked in his throat as if he had works in him like a clock, and was going to strike. And he smeared his ragged rough sleeve over his eyes.

Pitying his desolation, and watching him as he gradually settled down upon the pie, I made bold to say, 'I am glad you enjoy it.'

'Did you speak?'

'I said I was glad you enjoyed it.'

'Thankee, my boy. I do.'

I had often watched a large dog of ours eating his food; and I now noticed a decided similarity between the dog's way of eating, and the man's. The man took strong sharp sudden bites, just like the dog. He swallowed, or rather snapped up, every mouthful, too soon and too fast; and he looked sideways here and there while he ate, as if he thought there was danger in every direction of somebody's coming to take the pie away. He was altogether too unsettled in his mind over it, to appreciate it comfortably I thought, or to have anybody to dine with him, without making a chop with his jaws at the visitor. In all of which particulars he was very like the dog.

'I am afraid you won't leave any of it for him,' said I, timidly; after a silence during which I had hesitated as to the politeness of making the remark. 'There's no more to be got where that came from.' It was the certainty of this fact that impelled me to offer the hint.

'Leave any for him? Who's him?' said my friend, stopping in his crunching of pie-crust.

'The young man. That you spoke of. That was hid with you.'

'Oh ah!' he returned, with something like a gruff laugh. 'Him? Yes, yes! *He* don't want no wittles.'

'I thought he looked as if he did,' said I.

The man stopped eating, and regarded me with the keenest scrutiny and the greatest surprise.

'Looked? When?'

'Just now.'

'Where?'

'Yonder,' said I, pointing; 'over there, where I found him nodding asleep, and thought it was you.'

He held me by the collar and stared at me so, that I began to think his first idea about cutting my throat had revived.

'Dressed like you, you know, only with a hat,' I explained, trembling; 'and—and'—I was very anxious to put this delicately—'and with—the same reason for wanting to borrow a file. Didn't you hear the cannon last night?'

'Then there *was* firing!' he said to himself.

'I wonder you shouldn't have been sure of that,' I returned, 'for we heard it up at home, and that's farther away, and we were shut in besides.'

'Why, see now!' said he. 'When a man's alone on these flats, with a light head and a light stomach, perishing of cold and want, he hears nothin' all night, but guns firing, and voices calling. Hears? He sees the soldiers, with their red coats lighted up by the torches carried afore, closing in round him. Hears his number called, hears himself challenged, hears the rattle of the muskets, hears the orders 'Make ready! Present! Cover him steady, men!' and is laid hands on—and there's nothin'! Why, if I see one pursuing party last night—coming up in order, Damn 'em, with their tramp, tramp—I see a hundred. And as to firing! Why, I see the mist shake with the cannon, arter it was broad day,—But this man'; he had said all the rest, as if he had forgotten my being there; 'did you notice anything in him?'

'He had a badly bruised face,' said I, recalling what I hardly knew I knew.

'Not here?' exclaimed the man, striking his left cheek mercilessly, with the flat of his hand.

'Yes, there!'

'Where is he?' He crammed what little food was left, into the breast of his gray jacket. 'Show me the way he went. I'll pull him down, like a bloodhound. Curse this iron on my sore leg! Give us hold of the file, boy.'

I indicated in what direction the mist had shrouded the other man, and he looked up at it for an instant. But he was down on the rank wet grass, filing at his iron like a madman, and not minding me or minding his own leg, which had an old chafe upon it and was bloody, but which he handled as roughly as if it had no more feeling in it than the file. I was very much afraid of him again, now that he had worked himself into this fierce hurry, and I was likewise very much afraid of keeping away from home any longer. I told him I must go, but he took no notice, so I thought the best thing I could do was to slip off. The last I saw of him, his head was bent over his knee and he was working hard at his fetter, muttering impatient imprecations at it and at his leg. The last I heard of him, I stopped in the mist to listen, and the file was still going.

Chapter 4

I fully expected to find a Constable in the kitchen, waiting to take me up. But not only was there no Constable there, but no discovery had yet been made of the robbery. Mrs Joe was prodigiously busy in getting the house ready for the festivities of the day, and Joe had been put upon the kitchen doorstep to keep him out of the dustpan,—an article into which his destiny always led him, sooner or later, when my sister was vigorously reaping the floors of her establishment.

'And where the deuce ha' *you* been?' was Mrs Joe's Christmas salutation, when I and my conscience showed ourselves.

I said I had been down to hear the Carols. 'Ah! well!' observed Mrs Joe. 'You might ha' done worse.' Not a doubt of that I thought.

'Perhaps if I warn't a blacksmith's wife, and (what's the same thing) a slave with her apron never off, *I* should have been to hear the Carols,' said Mrs Joe. 'I'm rather partial to Carols, myself, and that's the best of reasons for my never hearing any.'

Joe, who had ventured into the kitchen after me as the dustpan had retired before us, drew the back of his hand across his nose with a conciliatory air, when Mrs Joe darted a look at him, and, when her eyes were withdrawn, secretly crossed his two forefingers, and exhibited them to me, as our token that Mrs Joe was in a cross temper. This was so much her normal state, that Joe and I would often, for weeks together, be, as to our fingers, like monumental Crusaders as to their legs.

We were to have a superb dinner, consisting of a leg of pickled pork and greens, and a pair of roast stuffed fowls. A handsome mince-pie had been made yesterday morning (which accounted for the mincemeat not being missed), and the pudding was already on the boil. These extensive arrangements occasioned us to be cut off unceremoniously in respect of breakfast; 'for I ain't,' said Mrs Joe,—'I ain't a going to have no formal cramming and busting and washing up now, with what I've got before me, I promise you!'

So, we had our slices served out, as if we were two thousand troops on a forced march instead of a man and boy at home; and we took gulps of milk and water, with apologetic countenances, from a jug on the dresser. In the meantime, Mrs Joe put clean white curtains up, and tacked a new flowered flounce across the wide chimney to replace the old one, and uncovered the little state parlour across the passage, which was never uncovered at any other time, but passed the rest of the year in a cool haze of silver paper, which even extended to the four little white crockery poodles on the mantel-shelf, each with a black nose and a basket of flowers in his mouth, and each the counterpart of the other. Mrs Joe was a very clean housekeeper, but had an exquisite art of making her cleanliness more uncomfortable and unacceptable than dirt itself. Cleanliness is next to Godliness, and some people do the same by their religion.

My sister, having so much to do, was going to church vicariously, that is to say, Joe and I were going. In his working-clothes, Joe was a well-knit characteristic-looking blacksmith; in his holiday clothes, he was more like a scarecrow in good circumstances, than anything else. Nothing that he wore then fitted him or seemed to belong to him; and everything that he wore then grazed him. On the present festive occasion he emerged from his room, when the blithe bells were going, the picture of misery, in a full suit of Sunday penitentials. As to me, I think my sister must have had some general idea that I was a young offender whom an Accoucheur Policeman had taken up (on my birthday) and delivered over to her, to be dealt with according to the outraged majesty of the law. I was always treated as if I had insisted on being born in opposition to the dictates of reason, religion, and morality, and against the dissuading arguments of my best friends. Even when I was taken to have a new suit of clothes, the tailor had orders to make them like a kind of Reformatory, and on no account to let me have the free use of my limbs.

Joe and I going to church, therefore, must have been a moving spectacle for compassionate minds. Yet, what I suffered outside was nothing to what I underwent within. The terrors that had assailed me whenever Mrs Joe had gone near the pantry, or out of the room, were only to be equalled by the remorse with which my mind dwelt on what my hands had done. Under the weight of my wicked secret, I pondered whether the Church would be powerful enough to shield me from the vengeance of the terrible young man, if I divulged to that establishment. I conceived the idea that the time when the banns were read and when the clergyman said, 'Ye are now to declare it!' would be the time for me to rise and propose a private conference in the vestry. I am far from being sure that I might not have astonished our small congregation by resorting to this extreme measure, but for its being Christmas Day and no Sunday.

Mr Wopsle, the clerk at church, was to dine with us; and Mr Hubble the wheelwright and Mrs Hubble; and Uncle Pumblechook (Joe's uncle, but Mrs Joe appropriated him), who was a well-to-do cornchandler in the nearest town, and drove his own chaise-cart. The dinner hour was half-past one. When Joe and I got home, we found the table laid, and Mrs Joe dressed, and the dinner dressing, and the front door unlocked (it never was at any other time) for the company to enter by, and everything most splendid. And still, not a word of the robbery.

The time came, without bringing with it any relief to my feelings, and the company came. Mr Wopsle, united to a Roman nose and a large shining bald forehead, had a deep voice which he was uncommonly proud of; indeed it was understood among his acquaintance that if you could only give him his head, he would read the clergyman into fits; he himself confessed that if the Church was 'thrown open,' meaning to competition, he would not despair of making his mark in it. The Church not being 'thrown open,' he was, as I have said, our clerk. But he punished the Amens tremendously; and when he gave out the psalm,—always giving the whole verse,—he looked all round the congregation first, as much as to say, 'You have heard my friend overhead; oblige me with your opinion of this style!'

I opened the door to the company,—making believe that it was a habit of ours to open that door,—and I opened it first to Mr Wopsle, next to Mr and Mrs Hubble, and last of all to Uncle Pumblechook. N.B. *I* was not allowed to call him uncle, under the severest penalties.

'Mrs Joe,' said Uncle Pumblechook, a large hard-breathing middle-aged slow man, with a mouth like a fish, dull staring eyes, and sandy hair standing upright on his head, so that he looked as if he had just been all but choked, and had that moment come to, 'I have brought you as the compliments of the season—I have brought you, Mum, a bottle of sherry wine—and I have brought you, Mum, a bottle of port wine.'

Every Christmas Day he presented himself, as a profound novelty, with exactly the same words, and carrying the two bottles like dumb-bells. Every Christmas Day, Mrs Joe replied, as she now replied, 'O, Un—cle Pum-ble—chook! This *is* kind!' Every Christmas Day, he retorted, as he now retorted, 'It's no more than your merits. And now are you all bobbish, and how's Sixpennorth of halfpence?' meaning me.

We dined on these occasions in the kitchen, and adjourned, for the nuts and oranges and apples to the parlor; which was a change very like Joe's change from his working-clothes to his Sunday dress. My sister was uncommonly lively on the present occasion, and indeed was generally more gracious in the society of Mrs Hubble than in other company. I remember Mrs Hubble as a little curly sharp-edged person in sky-blue, who held a conventionally juvenile position, because she had married Mr Hubble,—I don't know at what remote period,—when she was much younger than he. I remember Mr Hubble as a tough, high-shouldered, stooping old man, of a sawdusty fragrance, with his legs extraordinarily wide apart: so that in my short days I always saw some miles of open country between them when I met him coming up the lane.

Among this good company I should have felt myself, even if I hadn't robbed the pantry, in a false position. Not because I was squeezed in at an acute angle of the tablecloth, with the table in my chest, and the Pumblechookian elbow in my eye, nor because I was not allowed to speak (I didn't want to speak), nor because I was regaled with the scaly tips of the drumsticks of the fowls, and with those obscure corners of pork of which the pig, when living, had had the least reason to be vain. No; I should not have minded that, if they would only have left me alone. But they wouldn't leave me alone. They seemed to think the opportunity lost, if they failed to point the conversation at me, every now and then, and stick the point into me. I might have been an unfortunate little bull in a Spanish arena, I got so smartingly touched up by these moral goads.

It began the moment we sat down to dinner. Mr Wopsle said grace with theatrical declamation,—as it now appears to me, something like a religious cross of the Ghost in Hamlet with Richard the Third,—and ended with the very proper aspiration that we might be truly grateful. Upon which my sister fixed me with her eye, and said, in a low reproachful voice, 'Do you hear that? Be grateful.'

'Especially,' said Mr Pumblechook, 'be grateful, boy, to them which brought you up by hand.'

Mrs Hubble shook her head, and contemplating me with a mournful presentiment that I should come to no good, asked, 'Why is it that the young are never grateful?' This moral mystery seemed too much for the company until Mr Hubble tersely solved it by saying, 'Naterally wicious.' Everybody then murmured 'True!' and looked at me in a particularly unpleasant and personal manner.

Joe's station and influence were something feebler (if possible) when there was company than when there was none. But he always aided and comforted me when he could, in some way of his own, and he always did so at dinner-time by giving me gravy, if there were any. There being plenty of gravy today, Joe spooned into my plate, at this point, about half a pint.

A little later on in the dinner, Mr Wopsle reviewed the sermon with some severity, and intimated—in the usual hypothetical case of the Church being 'thrown open'—what kind of sermon *he* would have given them. After favouring them with some heads of that discourse, he remarked that he considered the subject of the day's homily, ill chosen; which was the less excusable, he added, when there were so many subjects 'going about.'

'True again,' said Uncle Pumblechook. 'You've hit it, sir! Plenty of subjects going about, for them that know how to put salt upon their tails. That's what's wanted. A man needn't go far to find a subject, if he's ready with his salt-box.' Mr Pumblechook added, after a short interval of reflection, 'Look at Pork alone. There's a subject! If you want a subject, look at Pork!'

'True, sir. Many a moral for the young,' returned Mr Wopsle,—and I knew he was going to lug me in, before he said it; 'might be deduced from that text.'

('You listen to this,' said my sister to me, in a severe parenthesis.)

Joe gave me some more gravy.

'Swine,' pursued Mr Wopsle, in his deepest voice, and pointing his fork at my blushes, as if he were mentioning my Christian name,—'swine were the companions of the prodigal. The gluttony of swine is put before us, as an example to the young.' (I thought this pretty well in him who had been praising up the pork for being so plump and juicy.) 'What is detestable in a pig is more detestable in a boy.'

'Or girl,' suggested Mr Hubble.

'Of course, or girl, Mr Hubble,' assented Mr Wopsle, rather irritably, 'but there is no girl present.'

'Besides,' said Mr Pumblechook, turning sharp on me, 'think what you've got to be grateful for. If you'd been born a Squeaker—'

'He *was*, if ever a child was,' said my sister, most emphatically.

Joe gave me some more gravy.

'Well, but I mean a four-footed Squeaker,' said Mr Pumblechook. 'If you had been born such, would you have been here now? Not you—'

'Unless in that form,' said Mr Wopsle, nodding towards the dish.

'But I don't mean in that form, sir,' returned Mr Pumblechook, who had an objection to being interrupted; 'I mean, enjoying himself with his elders and betters, and improving himself with their conversation, and rolling in the lap of luxury. Would he have been doing that? No, he wouldn't. And what would have been your destination?' turning on me again. 'You would have been disposed of for so many shillings according to the market price of the article, and Dunstable the butcher would have come up to you as you lay in your straw, and he would have whipped you under his left arm, and with his right he would have tucked up his frock to get a penknife from out of his waistcoat-pocket, and he would have shed your blood and had your life. No bringing up by hand then. Not a bit of it!'

Joe offered me more gravy, which I was afraid to take.

'He was a world of trouble to you, ma'am,' said Mrs Hubble, commiserating my sister.

'Trouble?' echoed my sister; 'trouble?' and then entered on a fearful catalogue of all the illnesses I had been guilty of, and all the acts of sleeplessness I had committed, and all the high places I had tumbled from, and all the low places I had tumbled into, and all the injuries I had done myself, and all the times she had wished me in my grave, and I had contumaciously refused to go there.

I think the Romans must have aggravated one another very much, with their noses. Perhaps, they became the restless people they were, in consequence. Anyhow, Mr Wopsle's Roman nose so aggravated me, during the recital of my misdemeanours, that I should have liked to pull it until he howled. But, all I had endured up to this time was nothing in comparison with the awful feelings that took possession of me when the pause was broken which ensued upon my sister's recital, and in which pause everybody had looked at me (as I felt painfully conscious) with indignation and abhorrence.

'Yet,' said Mr Pumblechook, leading the company gently back to the theme from which they had strayed, 'Pork—regarded as biled—is rich, too; ain't it?'

'Have a little brandy, uncle,' said my sister.

O Heavens, it had come at last! He would find it was weak, he would say it was weak, and I was lost! I held tight to the leg of the table under the cloth, with both hands, and awaited my fate.

My sister went for the stone bottle, came back with the stone bottle, and poured his brandy out: no one else taking any. The wretched man trifled with his glass,—took it up, looked at it through the light, put it down,—prolonged my misery. All this time Mrs Joe and Joe were briskly clearing the table for the pie and pudding.

I couldn't keep my eyes off him. Always holding tight by the leg of the table with my hands and feet, I saw the miserable creature finger his glass playfully, take it up, smile, throw his head back, and drink the brandy off. Instantly afterwards, the company were seized with unspeakable consternation, owing to his springing to his feet, turning round several times in an appalling spasmodic whooping-cough dance, and rushing out at the door; he then became visible through the window, violently plunging and expectorating, making the most hideous faces, and apparently out of his mind.

I held on tight, while Mrs Joe and Joe ran to him. I didn't know how I had done it, but I had no doubt I had murdered him somehow. In my dreadful situation, it was a relief when he was brought back, and surveying the company all round as if *they* had disagreed with him, sank down into his chair with the one significant gasp, 'Tar!'

I had filled up the bottle from the tar-water jug. I knew he would be worse by and by. I moved the table, like a Medium of the present day, by the vigour of my unseen hold upon it.

'Tar!' cried my sister, in amazement. 'Why, how ever could Tar come there?'

But, Uncle Pumblechook, who was omnipotent in that kitchen,

wouldn't hear the word, wouldn't hear of the subject, imperiously waved it all away with his hand, and asked for hot gin and water. My sister, who had begun to be alarmingly meditative, had to employ herself actively in getting the gin, the hot water, the sugar, and the lemon-peel, and mixing them. For the time being at least, I was saved. I still held on to the leg of the table, but clutched it now with the fervor of gratitude.

By degrees, I became calm enough to release my grasp and partake of pudding. Mr Pumblechook partook of pudding. All partook of pudding. The course terminated, and Mr Pumblechook had begun to beam under the genial influence of gin and water. I began to think I should get over the day, when my sister said to Joe, 'Clean plates,—cold.'

I clutched the leg of the table again immediately, and pressed it to my bosom as if it had been the companion of my youth and friend of my soul. I foresaw what was coming, and I felt that this time I really was gone.

'You must taste,' said my sister, addressing the guests with her best grace—'you must taste, to finish with, such a delightful and delicious present of Uncle Pumblechook's!'

Must they! Let them not hope to taste it!

'You must know,' said my sister, rising, 'it's a pie; a savory pork pie.'

The company murmured their compliments. Uncle Pumblechook, sensible of having deserved well of his fellow-creatures, said,—quite vivaciously, all things considered,—'Well, Mrs Joe, we'll do our best endeavours; let us have a cut at this same pie.'

My sister went out to get it. I heard her steps proceed to the pantry. I saw Mr Pumblechook balance his knife. I saw reawakening appetite in the Roman nostrils of Mr Wopsle. I heard Mr Hubble remark that 'a bit of savory pork pie would lay atop of anything you could mention, and do no harm,' and I heard Joe say, 'You shall have some, Pip.' I have never been absolutely certain whether I uttered a shrill yell of terror, merely in spirit, or in the bodily hearing of the company. I felt that I could bear no more, and that I must run away. I released the leg of the table, and ran for my life.

But I ran no farther than the house door, for there I ran

head-foremost into a party of soldiers with their muskets, one of whom held out a pair of handcuffs to me, saying, 'Here you are, look sharp, come on!'

Chapter 5

The apparition of a file of soldiers ringing down the but-ends of their loaded muskets on our door-step, caused the dinner-party to rise from table in confusion, and caused Mrs Joe re-entering the kitchen empty-handed, to stop short and stare, in her wondering lament of 'Gracious goodness gracious me, what's gone—with the—pie!'

The sergeant and I were in the kitchen when Mrs Joe stood staring; at which crisis I partially recovered the use of my senses. It was the sergeant who had spoken to me, and he was now looking round at the company, with his handcuffs invitingly extended towards them in his right hand, and his left on my shoulder.

'Excuse me, ladies and gentleman,' said the sergeant, 'but as I have mentioned at the door to this smart young shaver,' (which he hadn't), 'I am on a chase in the name of the king, and I want the blacksmith.'

'And pray what might you want with *him*?' retorted my sister, quick to resent his being wanted at all.

'Missis,' returned the gallant sergeant, 'speaking for myself, I should reply, the honour and pleasure of his fine wife's acquaintance; speaking for the king, I answer, a little job done.'

This was received as rather neat in the sergeant; insomuch that Mr Pumblechook cried audibly, 'Good again!'

'You see, blacksmith,' said the sergeant, who had by this time picked out Joe with his eye, 'we have had an accident with these, and I find the lock of one of 'em goes wrong, and the coupling don't act pretty. As they are wanted for immediate service, will you throw your eye over them?'

Joe threw his eye over them, and pronounced that the job would necessitate the lighting of his forge fire, and would take nearer two hours than one. 'Will it? Then will you set about it at once, blacksmith?' said the off-hand sergeant, 'as it's on His Majesty's service. And if my men can bear a hand anywhere, they'll make themselves useful.' With that, he called to his men, who came trooping into the kitchen one after another, and piled their arms in a corner. And then they stood about, as soldiers do; now, with their hands loosely clasped before them; now, resting a knee or a shoulder; now, easing a belt or a pouch; now, opening the door to spit stiffly over their high stocks, out into the yard.

All these things I saw without then knowing that I saw them, for I was in an agony of apprehension. But beginning to perceive that the handcuffs were not for me, and that the military had so far got the better of the pie as to put it in the background, I collected a little more of my scattered wits.

'Would you give me the time?' said the sergeant, addressing himself to Mr Pumblechook, as to a man whose appreciative powers justified the inference that he was equal to the time.

'It's just gone half past two.'

'That's not so bad,' said the sergeant, reflecting; 'even if I was forced to halt here nigh two hours, that'll do. How far might you call yourselves from the marshes, hereabouts? Not above a mile, I reckon?'

'Just a mile,' said Mrs Joe.

'That'll do. We begin to close in upon 'em about dusk. A little before dusk, my orders are. That'll do.'

'Convicts, sergeant?' asked Mr Wopsle, in a matter-of-course way.

'Ay!' returned the sergeant, 'two. They're pretty well known to be out on the marshes still, and they won't try to get clear of 'em before dusk. Anybody here seen anything of any such game?'

Everybody, myself excepted, said no, with confidence. Nobody thought of me.

'Well!' said the sergeant, 'they'll find themselves trapped in a circle, I expect, sooner than they count on. Now, blacksmith! If you're ready, His Majesty the King is.'

Joe had got his coat and waistcoat and cravat off, and his leather apron on, and passed into the forge. One of the soldiers opened its wooden windows, another lighted the fire, another turned to at the bellows, the rest stood round the blaze, which was soon roaring. Then Joe began to hammer and clink, hammer and clink, and we all looked on.

The interest of the impending pursuit not only absorbed the general attention, but even made my sister liberal. She drew a pitcher of beer from the cask for the soldiers, and invited the sergeant to take a glass of brandy. But Mr Pumblechook said, sharply, 'Give him wine, Mum. I'll engage there's no tar in that,' so, the sergeant thanked him and said that as he preferred his drink without tar, he would take wine, if it was equally convenient. When it was given him, he drank His Majesty's health and compliments of the season, and took it all at a mouthful and smacked his lips.

'Good stuff, eh, sergeant?' said Mr Pumblechook.

'I'll tell you something,' returned the sergeant; 'I suspect that stuff's of *your* providing.'

Mr Pumblechook, with a fat sort of laugh, said, 'Ay, ay? Why?'

'Because,' returned the sergeant, clapping him on the shoulder, 'you're a man that knows what's what.'

'D'ye think so?' said Mr Pumblechook, with his former laugh. 'Have another glass!'

'With you. Hob and nob,' returned the sergeant. 'The top of mine to the foot of yours,—the foot of yours to the top of mine,—Ring once, ring twice,—the best tune on the Musical Glasses! Your health. May you live a thousand years, and never be a worse judge of the right sort than you are at the present moment of your life!'

The sergeant tossed off his glass again and seemed quite ready for another glass. I noticed that Mr Pumblechook in his hospitality appeared to forget that he had made a present of the wine, but took the bottle from Mrs Joe and had all the credit of handing it about in a gush of joviality. Even I got some. And he was so very free of the wine that he even called for the other bottle, and handed that about with the same liberality, when the first was gone.

As I watched them while they all stood clustering about the forge, enjoying themselves so much, I thought what terrible good sauce for a dinner my fugitive friend on the marshes was. They had not enjoyed themselves a quarter so much, before the entertainment was brightened with the excitement he furnished. And now, when they were all in lively anticipation of 'the two villains' being taken, and when the bellows seemed to roar for the fugitives, the fire to flare for them, the smoke to hurry away in pursuit of them, Joe to hammer and clink for them, and all the murky shadows on the wall to shake at them in menace as the blaze rose and sank, and the red-hot sparks dropped and died, the pale afternoon outside almost seemed in my pitying young fancy to have turned pale on their account, poor wretches.

At last, Joe's job was done, and the ringing and roaring stopped. As Joe got on his coat, he mustered courage to propose that some of us should go down with the soldiers and see what came of the hunt. Mr Pumblechook and Mr Hubble declined, on the plea of a pipe and ladies' society; but Mr Wopsle said he would go, if Joe would. Joe said he was agreeable, and would take me, if Mrs Joe approved. We never should have got leave to go, I am sure, but for Mrs Joe's curiosity to know all about it and how it ended. As it was, she merely stipulated, 'If you bring the boy back with his head blown to bits by a musket, don't look to me to put it together again.'

The sergeant took a polite leave of the ladies, and parted from Mr Pumblechook as from a comrade; though I doubt if he were quite as fully sensible of that gentleman's merits under arid conditions, as when something moist was going. His men resumed their muskets and fell in. Mr Wopsle, Joe, and I, received strict charge to keep in the rear, and to speak no word after we reached the marshes. When we were all out in the raw air and were steadily moving towards our business, I treasonably whispered to Joe, 'I hope, Joe, we shan't find them,' and Joe whispered to me, 'I'd give a shilling if they had cut and run, Pip.'

We were joined by no stragglers from the village, for the weather was cold and threatening, the way dreary, the footing bad, darkness coming on, and the people had good fires indoors and were keeping the day. A few faces hurried to glowing windows and looked after us, but none came out. We passed the finger-post, and held straight on to the churchyard. There we were stopped a few minutes by a signal from the sergeant's hand, while two or three of his men dispersed themselves among the graves, and also examined the porch. They came in again without finding anything, and then we struck out on the open marshes, through the gate at the side of the churchyard. A bitter sleet came rattling against us here on the east wind, and Joe took me on his back.

Now that we were out upon the dismal wilderness where they little thought I had been within eight or nine hours and had seen both men hiding, I considered for the first time, with great dread, if we should come upon them, would my particular convict suppose that it was I who had brought the soldiers there? He had asked me if I was a deceiving imp, and he had said I should be a fierce young hound if I joined the hunt against him. Would he believe that I was both imp and hound in treacherous earnest, and had betrayed him?

It was of no use asking myself this question now. There I was, on Joe's back, and there was Joe beneath me, charging at the ditches like a hunter, and stimulating Mr Wopsle not to tumble on his Roman nose, and to keep up with us. The soldiers were in front of us, extending into a pretty wide line with an interval between man and man. We were taking the course I had begun with, and from which I had diverged in the mist. Either the mist was not out again yet, or the wind had dispelled it. Under the low red glare of sunset, the beacon, and the gibbet, and the mound of the Battery, and the opposite shore of the river, were plain, though all of a watery lead colour.

With my heart thumping like a blacksmith at Joe's broad shoulder, I looked all about for any sign of the convicts. I could see none, I could hear none. Mr Wopsle had greatly alarmed me more than once, by his blowing and hard breathing; but I knew the sounds by this time, and could dissociate them from the object of pursuit. I got a dreadful start, when I thought I heard the file still going; but it was only a sheep-bell. The sheep stopped in their eating and looked timidly at us; and the cattle, their heads turned from the wind and sleet, stared angrily as if they held us responsible for both annoyances; but, except these things, and the shudder of the dying day in every blade of grass, there was no break in the bleak stillness of the marshes.

The soldiers were moving on in the direction of the old Battery, and we were moving on a little way behind them, when, all of a sudden, we all stopped. For there had reached us on the wings of the wind and rain, a long shout. It was repeated. It was at a distance towards the east, but it was long and loud. Nay, there seemed to be two or more shouts raised together,—if one might judge from a confusion in the sound.

To this effect the sergeant and the nearest men were speaking under their breath, when Joe and I came up. After another moment's listening, Joe (who was a good judge) agreed, and Mr Wopsle (who was a bad judge) agreed. The sergeant, a decisive man, ordered that the sound should not be answered, but that the course should be changed, and that his men should make towards it 'at the double.' So we slanted to the right (where the East was), and Joe pounded away so wonderfully, that I had to hold on tight to keep my seat.

It was a run indeed now, and what Joe called, in the only two words he spoke all the time, 'a Winder.' Down banks and up banks, and over gates, and splashing into dikes, and breaking among coarse rushes: no man cared where he went. As we came nearer to the shouting, it became more and more apparent that it was made by more than one voice. Sometimes, it seemed to stop altogether, and then the soldiers stopped. When it broke out again, the soldiers made for it at a greater rate than ever, and we after them. After a while, we had so run it down, that we could hear one voice calling 'Murder!' and another voice, 'Convicts! Runaways! Guard! This way for the runaway convicts!' Then both voices would seem to be stifled in a struggle, and then would break out again. And when it had come to this, the soldiers ran like deer, and Joe too.

The sergeant ran in first, when we had run the noise quite down, and two of his men ran in close upon him. Their pieces were cocked and levelled when we all ran in.

'Here are both men!' panted the sergeant, struggling at the bottom of a ditch. 'Surrender, you two! And confound you for two wild beasts! Come asunder!'

Water was splashing, and mud was flying, and oaths were being sworn, and blows were being struck, when some more men went down into the ditch to help the sergeant, and dragged out, separately, my convict and the other one. Both were bleeding and panting and execrating and struggling; but of course I knew them both directly.

'Mind!' said my convict, wiping blood from his face with his ragged sleeves, and shaking torn hair from his fingers: '*I* took him! *I* give him up to you! Mind that!'

'It's not much to be particular about,' said the sergeant; 'it'll do you small good, my man, being in the same plight yourself. Handcuffs there!'

'I don't expect it to do me any good. I don't want it to do me more good than it does now,' said my convict, with a greedy laugh. 'I took him. He knows it. That's enough for me.'

The other convict was livid to look at, and, in addition to the old bruised left side of his face, seemed to be bruised and torn all over. He could not so much as get his breath to speak, until they were both separately handcuffed, but leaned upon a soldier to keep himself from falling.

'Take notice, guard,—he tried to murder me,' were his first words.

'Tried to murder him?' said my convict, disdainfully. 'Try, and not do it? I took him, and giv' him up; that's what I done. I not only prevented him getting off the marshes, but I dragged him here,— dragged him this far on his way back. He's a gentleman, if you please, this villain. Now, the Hulks has got its gentleman again, through me. Murder him? Worth my while, too, to murder him, when I could do worse and drag him back!'

The other one still gasped, 'He tried—he tried to—murder me. Bear—bear witness.'

'Lookee here!' said my convict to the sergeant. 'Single-handed I got clear of the prison-ship; I made a dash and I done it. I could ha' got clear of these death-cold flats likewise—look at my leg: you won't find much iron on it—if I hadn't made the discovery that *he* was here. Let *him* go free? Let *him* profit by the means as I found out? Let *him* make a tool of me afresh and again? Once more? No, no, no. If I had died at the bottom there,' and he made an emphatic swing at the ditch with his manacled hands, 'I'd have held to him with that grip, that you should have been safe to find him in my hold.'

The other fugitive, who was evidently in extreme horror of his companion, repeated, 'He tried to murder me. I should have been a dead man if you had not come up.'

'He lies!' said my convict, with fierce energy. 'He's a liar born, and he'll die a liar. Look at his face; ain't it written there? Let him turn those eyes of his on me. I defy him to do it.'

The other, with an effort at a scornful smile, which could not, however, collect the nervous working of his mouth into any set expression, looked at the soldiers, and looked about at the marshes and at the sky, but certainly did not look at the speaker.

'Do you see him?' pursued my convict. 'Do you see what a villain he is? Do you see those grovelling and wandering eyes? That's how he looked when we were tried together. He never looked at me.'

The other, always working and working his dry lips and turning his eyes restlessly about him far and near, did at last turn them for a moment on the speaker, with the words, 'You are not much to look at,' and with a half-taunting glance at the bound hands. At that point, my convict became so frantically exasperated, that he would have rushed upon him but for the interposition of the soldiers. 'Didn't I tell you,' said the other convict then, 'that he would murder me, if he could?' And anyone could see that he shook with fear, and that there broke out upon his lips curious white flakes, like thin snow.

'Enough of this parley,' said the sergeant. 'Light those torches.'

As one of the soldiers, who carried a basket in lieu of a gun, went down on his knee to open it, my convict looked round him for the first time, and saw me. I had alighted from Joe's back on the brink of the ditch when we came up, and had not moved since. I looked at him eagerly when he looked at me, and slightly moved my hands and shook my head. I had been waiting for him to see me that I might try to assure him of my innocence. It was not at all expressed to me that he even comprehended my intention, for he gave me a look that I did not understand, and it all passed in a moment. But if he had looked at me for an hour or for a day, I could not have remembered his face ever afterwards, as having been more attentive.

The soldier with the basket soon got a light, and lighted three or four torches, and took one himself and distributed the others. It had been almost dark before, but now it seemed quite dark, and soon afterwards very dark. Before we departed from that spot, four soldiers standing in a ring, fired twice into the air. Presently we saw other torches kindled at some distance behind us, and others on the marshes on the opposite bank of the river. 'All right,' said the sergeant. 'March.'

We had not gone far when three cannon were fired ahead of us with a sound that seemed to burst something inside my ear. 'You are expected on board,' said the sergeant to my convict; 'they know you are coming. Don't straggle, my man. Close up here.'

The two were kept apart, and each walked surrounded by a separate guard. I had hold of Joe's hand now, and Joe carried one of the torches. Mr Wopsle had been for going back, but Joe was resolved to see it out, so we went on with the party. There was a reasonably good path now, mostly on the edge of the river, with a divergence here and there where a dike came, with a miniature windmill on it and a muddy sluice-gate. When I looked round, I could see the other lights coming in after us. The torches we carried dropped great blotches of fire upon the track, and I could see those, too, lying smoking and flaring. I could see nothing else but black darkness. Our lights warmed the air about us with their pitchy blaze, and the two prisoners seemed rather to like that, as they limped along in the midst of the muskets. We could not go fast, because of their lameness; and they were so spent, that two or three times we had to halt while they rested.

After an hour or so of this travelling, we came to a rough wooden hut and a landing-place. There was a guard in the hut, and they challenged, and the sergeant answered. Then, we went into the hut, where there was a smell of tobacco and whitewash, and a bright fire, and a lamp, and a stand of muskets, and a drum, and a low wooden bedstead, like an overgrown mangle without the machinery, capable of holding about a dozen soldiers all at once. Three or four soldiers who lay upon it in their great-coats were not much interested in us, but just lifted their heads and took a sleepy stare, and then lay down again. The sergeant made some kind of report, and some entry in a book, and then the convict whom I call the other convict was drafted off with his guard, to go on board first.

My convict never looked at me, except that once. While we stood in the hut, he stood before the fire looking thoughtfully at it, or putting up his feet by turns upon the hob, and looking thoughtfully at them as if he pitied them for their recent adventures. Suddenly, he turned to the sergeant, and remarked,—

'I wish to say something respecting this escape. It may prevent some persons laying under suspicion alonger me.'

'You can say what you like,' returned the sergeant, standing coolly looking at him with his arms folded, 'but you have no call to say it here. You'll have opportunity enough to say about it, and hear about it, before it's done with, you know.'

'I know, but this is another pint, a separate matter. A man can't starve; at least *I* can't. I took some wittles, up at the willage over yonder,—where the church stands a'most out on the marshes.'

'You mean stole,' said the sergeant.

'And I'll tell you where from. From the blacksmith's.'

'Halloa!' said the sergeant, staring at Joe.

'Halloa, Pip!' said Joe, staring at me.

'It was some broken wittles—that's what it was—and a dram of liquor, and a pie.'

'Have you happened to miss such an article as a pie, blacksmith?' asked the sergeant, confidentially.

'My wife did, at the very moment when you came in. Don't you know, Pip?'

'So,' said my convict, turning his eyes on Joe in a moody manner, and without the least glance at me,—'so you're the blacksmith, are you? Than I'm sorry to say, I've eat your pie.'

'God knows you're welcome to it,—so far as it was ever mine,' returned Joe, with a saving remembrance of Mrs Joe. 'We don't know what you have done, but we wouldn't have you starved to death for it, poor miserable fellow-creatur.—Would us, Pip?'

The something that I had noticed before, clicked in the man's throat again, and he turned his back. The boat had returned, and his guard were ready, so we followed him to the landing-place made of rough stakes and stones, and saw him put into the boat, which was rowed by a crew of convicts like himself. No one seemed surprised to see him, or interested in seeing him, or glad to see him, or sorry to see him, or spoke a word, except that somebody in the boat growled as if to dogs, 'Give way, you!' which was the signal for the dip of the oars. By the light of the torches, we saw the black Hulk lying out a little way from the mud of the shore, like a wicked Noah's ark. Cribbed and barred and moored by massive rusty chains, the prison-ship seemed in my young eyes to be ironed like the prisoners. We saw the boat go alongside, and we saw him taken up the side and disappear. Then, the ends of the torches were flung hissing into the water, and went out, as if it were all over with him.

Chapter 6

My state of mind regarding the pilfering from which I had been so unexpectedly exonerated did not impel me to frank disclosure; but I hope it had some dregs of good at the bottom of it.

I do not recall that I felt any tenderness of conscience in reference to Mrs Joe, when the fear of being found out was lifted off me. But I loved Joe,—perhaps for no better reason in those early days than because the dear fellow let me love him,—and, as to him, my inner self was not so easily composed. It was much upon my mind (particularly when I first saw him looking about for his file) that I ought to tell Joe the whole truth. Yet I did not, and for the reason that I mistrusted that if I did, he would think me worse than I was. The fear of losing Joe's confidence, and of thenceforth sitting in the chimney corner at night staring drearily at my forever lost companion and friend, tied up my tongue. I morbidly represented to myself that if Joe knew it, I never afterwards could see him at the fireside feeling his fair whisker, without thinking that he was meditating on it. That, if Joe knew it, I never afterwards could see him glance, however casually, at yesterday's meat or pudding when it came on today's table, without thinking that he was debating whether I had been in the pantry. That, if Joe knew it, and at any subsequent period of our joint domestic life remarked that his beer was flat or thick, the conviction that he suspected tar in it, would bring a rush of blood to my face. In a word, I was too cowardly to do what I knew to be right, as I had been too cowardly to avoid doing what I knew to be wrong. I had had no intercourse with the world at that time, and I imitated none of its many inhabitants who act in this manner. Quite an untaught genius, I made the discovery of the line of action for myself.

As I was sleepy before we were faraway from the prison-ship, Joe took me on his back again and carried me home. He must have had a tiresome journey of it, for Mr Wopsle, being knocked up, was in such a very bad temper that if the Church had been thrown open, he would probably have excommunicated the whole expedition, beginning with Joe and myself. In his lay capacity, he persisted in sitting down in the damp to such an insane extent, that when his coat was taken off to be dried at the kitchen fire, the circumstantial evidence on his trousers would have hanged him, if it had been a capital offence.

By that time, I was staggering on the kitchen floor like a little drunkard, through having been newly set upon my feet, and through having been fast asleep, and through waking in the heat and lights and noise of tongues. As I came to myself (with the aid of a heavy thump between the shoulders, and the restorative exclamation 'Yah! Was there ever such a boy as this!' from my sister,) I found Joe telling them about the convict's confession, and all the visitors suggesting different ways by which he had got into the pantry. Mr Pumblechook made out, after carefully surveying the premises, that he had first got upon the roof of the forge, and had then got upon the roof of the house, and had then let himself down the kitchen chimney by a rope made of his bedding cut into strips; and as Mr Pumblechook was very positive and drove his own chaise-cart—over everybody—it was agreed that it must be so. Mr Wopsle, indeed, wildly cried out, 'No!' with the feeble malice of a tired man; but, as he had no theory, and no coat on, he was unanimously set at naught,—not to mention his smoking hard behind, as he stood with his back to the kitchen fire to draw the damp out: which was not calculated to inspire confidence.

This was all I heard that night before my sister clutched me, as a slumberous offence to the company's eyesight, and assisted me up to bed with such a strong hand that I seemed to have fifty boots on, and to be dangling them all against the edges of the stairs. My state of mind, as I have described it, began before I was up in the morning, and lasted long after the subject had died out, and had ceased to be mentioned saving on exceptional occasions.

Chapter 7

At the time when I stood in the churchyard reading the family tombstones, I had just enough learning to be able to spell them out. My construction even of their simple meaning was not very correct, for I read 'wife of the Above' as a complimentary reference to my father's exaltation to a better world; and if anyone of my deceased relations had been referred to as 'Below,' I have no doubt I should have formed the worst opinions of that member of the family. Neither were my notions of the theological positions to which my Catechism bound me, at all accurate; for, I have a lively remembrance that I supposed my declaration that I was to 'walk in the same all the days of my life,' laid me under an obligation always to go through the village from our house in one particular direction, and never to vary it by turning down by the wheelwright's or up by the mill.

When I was old enough, I was to be apprenticed to Joe, and until I could assume that dignity I was not to be what Mrs Joe called 'Pompeyed,' or (as I render it) pampered. Therefore, I was not only odd-boy about the forge, but if any neighbour happened to want an extra boy to frighten birds, or pick up stones, or do any such job, I was favoured with the employment. In order, however, that our superior position might not be compromised thereby, a money-box was kept on the kitchen mantel-shelf, into which it was publicly made known that all my earnings were dropped. I have an impression that they were to be contributed eventually towards the liquidation of the National Debt, but I know I had no hope of any personal participation in the treasure.

Mr Wopsle's great-aunt kept an evening school in the village; that is to say, she was a ridiculous old woman of limited means and unlimited infirmity, who used to go to sleep from six to seven every evening, in the society of youth who paid two pence per week each, for the improving opportunity of seeing her do it. She rented a small cottage, and Mr Wopsle had the room upstairs, where we students used to overhear him reading aloud in a most dignified and terrific manner, and occasionally bumping on the ceiling. There was a fiction that Mr Wopsle 'examined' the scholars once a quarter. What he did on those occasions was to turn up his cuffs, stick up his hair, and give us Mark Antony's oration over the body of Caesar. This was always followed by Collins's Ode on the Passions, wherein I particularly venerated Mr Wopsle as Revenge throwing his blood-stained sword in thunder down, and taking the war-denouncing trumpet with a withering look. It was not with me then, as it was in later life, when I fell into the society of the Passions, and compared them with Collins and Wopsle, rather to the disadvantage of both gentlemen.

Mr Wopsle's great-aunt, besides keeping this Educational Institution, kept in the same room—a little general shop. She had no idea what stock she had, or what the price of anything in it was; but there was a little greasy memorandum-book kept in a drawer, which served as a Catalogue of Prices, and by this oracle Biddy arranged all the shop transactions. Biddy was Mr Wopsle's great-aunt's granddaughter; I confess myself quite unequal to the working out of the problem, what relation she was to Mr Wopsle. She was an orphan like myself; like me, too, had been brought up by hand. She was most noticeable, I thought, in respect of her extremities; for, her hair always wanted brushing, her hands always wanted washing, and her shoes always wanted mending and pulling up at heel. This description must be received with a week-day limitation. On Sundays, she went to church elaborated.

Much of my unassisted self, and more by the help of Biddy than of Mr Wopsle's great-aunt, I struggled through the alphabet as if it had been a bramble-bush; getting considerably worried and scratched by every letter. After that I fell among those thieves, the nine figures, who seemed every evening to do something new to disguise themselves and baffle recognition. But, at last I began, in a purblind groping way, to read, write, and cipher, on the very smallest scale.

One night I was sitting in the chimney corner with my slate, expending great efforts on the production of a letter to Joe. I think it must have been a full year after our hunt upon the marshes, for it was a long time after, and it was winter and a hard frost. With an alphabet on the hearth at my feet for reference, I contrived in an hour or two to print and smear this epistle:—

There was no indispensable necessity for my communicating with Joe by letter, inasmuch as he sat beside me and we were alone. But I delivered this written communication (slate and all) with my own hand, and Joe received it as a miracle of erudition.

'I say, Pip, old chap!' cried Joe, opening his blue eyes wide, 'what a scholar you are! An't you?'

'I should like to be,' said I, glancing at the slate as he held it; with a misgiving that the writing was rather hilly.

'Why, here's a J,' said Joe, 'and a O equal to anythink! Here's a J and a O, Pip, and a J-O, Joe.'

I had never heard Joe read aloud to any greater extent than this monosyllable, and I had observed at church last Sunday, when I accidentally held our Prayer-Book upside down, that it seemed to suit his convenience quite as well as if it had been all right. Wishing to embrace the present occasion of finding out whether in teaching Joe, I should have to begin quite at the beginning, I said, 'Ah! But read the rest, Jo.'

'The rest, eh, Pip?' said Joe, looking at it with a slow, searching eye, 'One, two, three. Why, here's three Js, and three Os, and three J-O, Joes in it, Pip!'

I leaned over Joe, and, with the aid of my forefinger read him the whole letter.

'Astonishing!' said Joe, when I had finished. 'You ARE a scholar.'

'How do you spell Gargery, Joe?' I asked him, with a modest patronage.

'I don't spell it at all,' said Joe.

'But supposing you did?'

'It *can't* be supposed,' said Joe. 'Tho' I'm uncommon fond of reading, too.'

'Are you, Joe?'

'On-common. Give me,' said Joe, 'a good book, or a good newspaper, and sit me down afore a good fire, and I ask no better. Lord!' he continued, after rubbing his knees a little, 'when you *do* come to a J and a O, and says you, 'Here, at last, is a J-O, Joe,' how interesting reading is!'

I derived from this, that Joe's education, like Steam, was yet in its infancy. Pursuing the subject, I inquired,—

'Didn't you ever go to school, Joe, when you were as little as me?'

'No, Pip.'

'Why didn't you ever go to school, Joe, when you were as little as me?'

'Well, Pip,' said Joe, taking up the poker, and settling himself to his usual occupation when he was thoughtful, of slowly raking the fire between the lower bars; 'I'll tell you. My father, Pip, he were given to drink, and when he were overtook with drink, he hammered away at my mother, most onmerciful. It were a'most the only hammering he did, indeed, 'xcepting at myself. And he hammered at me with a wigor only to be equalled by the wigor with which he didn't hammer at his anwil.—You're a listening and understanding, Pip?'

'Yes, Joe.'

'Consequence, my mother and me, we ran away from my father several times; and then my mother she'd go out to work, and she'd say, "Joe," she'd say, "now, please God, you shall have some schooling, child," and she'd put me to school. But my father were that good in his hart that he couldn't abear to be without us. So, he'd come with a most tremenjous crowd and make such a row at the doors of the houses where we was, that they used to be obligated to have no more to do with us and to give us up to him. And then he took us home and hammered us. Which, you see, Pip,' said Joe, pausing in his meditative raking of the fire, and looking at me, 'were a drawback on my learning.'

'Certainly, poor Joe!'

'Though mind you, Pip,' said Joe, with a judicial touch or two of the poker on the top bar, 'rendering unto all their doo, and maintaining equal justice betwixt man and man, my father were that good in his hart, don't you see?'

I didn't see; but I didn't say so.

'Well!' Joe pursued, 'somebody must keep the pot a biling, Pip, or the pot won't bile, don't you know?'

I saw that, and said so.

'Consequence, my father didn't make objections to my going to work; so I went to work at my present calling, which were his too, if he would have followed it, and I worked tolerable hard, I assure *you*, Pip. In time I were able to keep him, and I kep him till he went off in a purple leptic fit. And it were my intentions to have had put upon his tombstone that, Whatsume'er the failings on his part, Remember reader he were that good in his heart.'

Joe recited this couplet with such manifest pride and careful perspicuity, that I asked him if he had made it himself.

'I made it,' said Joe, 'my own self. I made it in a moment. It was like striking out a horseshoe complete, in a single blow. I never was so much surprised in all my life,—couldn't credit my own ed,—to tell you the truth, hardly believed it *were* my own ed. As I was saying, Pip, it were my intentions to have had it cut over him; but poetry costs money, cut it how you will, small or large, and it were not done. Not to mention bearers, all the money that could be spared were wanted for my mother. She were in poor elth, and quite broke. She weren't long of following, poor soul, and her share of peace come round at last.'

Joe's blue eyes turned a little watery; he rubbed first one of them, and then the other, in a most uncongenial and uncomfortable manner, with the round knob on the top of the poker.

'It were but lonesome then,' said Joe, 'living here alone, and I got acquainted with your sister. Now, Pip,'—Joe looked firmly at me as if he knew I was not going to agree with him;—'your sister is a fine figure of a woman.'

I could not help looking at the fire, in an obvious state of doubt.

'Whatever family opinions, or whatever the world's opinions, on that subject may be, Pip, your sister is,' Joe tapped the top bar with the poker after every word following, 'a-fine-figure—of—a—woman!'

I could think of nothing better to say than 'I am glad you think so, Joe.'

'So am I,' returned Joe, catching me up. '*I* am glad I think so, Pip. A little redness or a little matter of bone, here or there, what does it signify to me?'

I sagaciously observed, if it didn't signify to him, to whom did it signify?

'Certainly!' assented Joe. 'That's it. You're right, old chap! When I got acquainted with your sister, it were the talk how she was bringing you up by hand. Very kind of her too, all the folks said, and I said, along with all the folks. As to you,' Joe pursued with a countenance expressive of seeing something very nasty indeed, 'if you could have been aware how small and flabby and mean you was, dear me, you'd have formed the most contemptible opinion of yourself!'

Not exactly relishing this, I said, 'Never mind me, Joe.'

'But I did mind you, Pip,' he returned with tender simplicity. 'When I offered to your sister to keep company, and to be asked in church at such times as she was willing and ready to come to the forge, I said to her, 'And bring the poor little child. God bless the poor little child,' I said to your sister, 'there's room for *him* at the forge!'"

I broke out crying and begging pardon, and hugged Joe round the neck: who dropped the poker to hug me, and to say, 'Ever the best of friends; an't us, Pip? Don't cry, old chap!'

When this little interruption was over, Joe resumed:—

'Well, you see, Pip, and here we are! That's about where it lights; here we are! Now, when you take me in hand in my learning, Pip (and I tell you beforehand I am awful dull, most awful dull), Mrs Joe mustn't see too much of what we're up to. It must be done, as I may say, on the sly. And why on the sly? I'll tell you why, Pip.'

He had taken up the poker again; without which, I doubt if he could have proceeded in his demonstration.

'Your sister is given to government.'

'Given to government, Joe?' I was startled, for I had some shadowy idea (and I am afraid I must add, hope) that Joe had divorced her in a favour of the Lords of the Admiralty, or Treasury.

'Given to government,' said Joe. 'Which I meantersay the government of you and myself.'

'Oh!'

'And she an't over partial to having scholars on the premises,' Joe continued, 'and in partickler would not be over partial to my being a scholar, for fear as I might rise. Like a sort of rebel, don't you see?'

I was going to retort with an inquiry, and had got as far as 'Why—' when Joe stopped me.

'Stay a bit. I know what you're a going to say, Pip; stay a bit! I don't deny that your sister comes the Mo-gul over us, now and again. I don't deny that she do throw us back-falls, and that she do drop down upon us heavy. At such times as when your sister is on the Ram-page, Pip,' Joe sank his voice to a whisper and glanced at the door, 'candor compels fur to admit that she is a Buster.'

Joe pronounced this word, as if it began with at least twelve capital Bs.

'Why don't I rise? That were your observation when I broke it off, Pip?'

'Yes, Joe.'

'Well,' said Joe, passing the poker into his left hand, that he might feel his whisker; and I had no hope of him whenever he took to that placid occupation; 'your sister's a master-mind. A master-mind.'

'What's that?' I asked, in some hope of bringing him to a stand. But Joe was readier with his definition than I had expected, and completely stopped me by arguing circularly, and answering with a fixed look, 'Her.'

'And I ain't a master-mind,' Joe resumed, when he had unfixed his look, and got back to his whisker. 'And last of all, Pip,—and this I want to say very serious to you, old chap,—I see so much in my poor mother, of a woman drudging and slaving and breaking her honest hart and never getting no peace in her mortal days, that I'm dead afeerd of going wrong in the way of not doing what's right by a woman, and I'd fur rather of the two go wrong the t'other way, and be a little ill-conwenienced myself. I wish it was only me that got put out, Pip; I wish there warn't no Tickler for you, old chap; I wish I could take it all on myself; but this is the up-and-down-and-straight on it, Pip, and I hope you'll overlook shortcomings.'

Young as I was, I believe that I dated a new admiration of Joe from that night. We were equals afterwards, as we had been before; but, afterwards at quiet times when I sat looking at Joe and thinking about him, I had a new sensation of feeling conscious that I was looking up to Joe in my heart.

'However,' said Joe, rising to replenish the fire; 'here's the Dutch-clock a working himself up to being equal to strike Eight of 'em, and she's not come home yet! I hope Uncle Pumblechook's mare mayn't have set a forefoot on a piece o' ice, and gone down.'

Mrs Joe made occasional trips with Uncle Pumblechook on market-days, to assist him in buying such household stuffs and goods as required a woman's judgment; Uncle Pumblechook being a bachelor and reposing no confidences in his domestic servant. This was market-day, and Mrs Joe was out on one of these expeditions.

Joe made the fire and swept the hearth, and then we went to the door to listen for the chaise-cart. It was a dry cold night, and the wind blew keenly, and the frost was white and hard. A man would die tonight of lying out on the marshes, I thought. And then I looked at the stars, and considered how awful it would be for a man to turn his face up to them as he froze to death, and see no help or pity in all the glittering multitude.

'Here comes the mare,' said Joe, 'ringing like a peal of bells!'

The sound of her iron shoes upon the hard road was quite musical, as she came along at a much brisker trot than usual. We got a chair out, ready for Mrs Joe's alighting, and stirred up the fire that they might see a bright window, and took a final survey of the kitchen that nothing might be out of its place. When we had completed these preparations, they drove up, wrapped to the eyes. Mrs Joe was soon landed, and Uncle Pumblechook was soon down too, covering the mare with a cloth, and we were soon all in the kitchen, carrying so much cold air in with us that it seemed to drive all the heat out of the fire.

'Now,' said Mrs Joe, unwrapping herself with haste and excitement, and throwing her bonnet back on her shoulders where it hung by the strings, 'if this boy ain't grateful this night, he never will be!'

I looked as grateful as any boy possibly could, who was wholly uninformed why he ought to assume that expression.

'It's only to be hoped,' said my sister, 'that he won't be Pompeyed. But I have my fears.'

'She ain't in that line, Mum,' said Mr Pumblechook. 'She knows better.'

She? I looked at Joe, making the motion with my lips and eyebrows, 'She?' Joe looked at me, making the motion with *his* lips and eyebrows, 'She?' My sister catching him in the act, he drew the back of his hand across his nose with his usual conciliatory air on such occasions, and looked at her.

'Well?' said my sister, in her snappish way. 'What are you staring at? Is the house afire?'

'—Which some individual,' Joe politely hinted, 'mentioned—she.'

'And she is a she, I suppose?' said my sister. 'Unless you call Miss Havisham a he. And I doubt if even you'll go so far as that.'

'Miss Havisham, up town?' said Joe.

'Is there any Miss Havisham down town?' returned my sister.

'She wants this boy to go and play there. And of course he's going.

And he had better play there,' said my sister, shaking her head at me as an encouragement to be extremely light and sportive, 'or I'll work him.'

I had heard of Miss Havisham up town,—everybody for miles round had heard of Miss Havisham up town,—as an immensely rich and grim lady who lived in a large and dismal house barricaded against robbers, and who led a life of seclusion.

'Well to be sure!' said Joe, astounded. 'I wonder how she come to know Pip!'

'Noodle!' cried my sister. 'Who said she knew him?'

'—Which some individual,' Joe again politely hinted, 'mentioned that she wanted him to go and play there.'

'And couldn't she ask Uncle Pumblechook if he knew of a boy to go and play there? Isn't it just barely possible that Uncle Pumblechook may be a tenant of hers, and that he may sometimes—we won't say quarterly or half-yearly, for that would be requiring too much of you—but sometimes—go there to pay his rent? And couldn't she then ask Uncle Pumblechook if he knew of a boy to go and play there? And couldn't Uncle Pumblechook, being always considerate and thoughtful for us—though you may not think it, Joseph,' in a tone of the deepest reproach, as if he were the most callous of nephews, 'then mention this boy, standing Prancing here'—which I solemnly declare I was not doing—'that I have forever been a willing slave to?'

'Good again!' cried Uncle Pumblechook. 'Well put! Prettily pointed! Good indeed! Now Joseph, you know the case.'

'No, Joseph,' said my sister, still in a reproachful manner, while Joe apologetically drew the back of his hand across and across his nose, 'you do not yet—though you may not think it—know the case. You may consider that you do, but you do *not*, Joseph. For you do not know that Uncle Pumblechook, being sensible that for anything we can tell, this boy's fortune may be made by his going to Miss Havisham's, has offered to take him into town tonight in his own chaise-cart, and to keep him tonight, and to take him with his own hands to Miss Havisham's tomorrow morning. And Lor-a-mussy me!' cried my sister, casting off her bonnet in sudden desperation, 'here I stand talking to mere Mooncalfs, with Uncle Pumblechook waiting, and the mare catching cold at the door, and the boy grimed with crock and dirt from the hair of his head to the sole of his foot!'

With that, she pounced upon me, like an eagle on a lamb, and my face was squeezed into wooden bowls in sinks, and my head was put under taps of water-butts, and I was soaped, and kneaded, and towelled, and thumped, and harrowed, and rasped, until I really was quite beside myself. (I may here remark that I suppose myself to be better acquainted than any living authority, with the ridgy effect of a wedding-ring, passing unsympathetically over the human countenance.)

When my ablutions were completed, I was put into clean linen of the stiffest character, like a young penitent into sackcloth, and was trussed up in my tightest and fearfullest suit. I was then delivered over to Mr Pumblechook, who formally received me as if he were the sheriff, and who let off upon me the speech that I knew he had been dying to make all along: 'Boy, be forever grateful to all friends, but especially unto them which brought you up by hand!'

'Goodbye, Joe!'

'God bless you, Pip, old chap!'

I had never parted from him before, and what with my feelings and what with soapsuds, I could at first see no stars from the chaise-cart. But they twinkled out one by one, without throwing any light on the questions why on earth I was going to play at Miss Havisham's, and what on earth I was expected to play at.

Chapter 8

Mr Pumblechook's premises in the High Street of the market town, were of a peppercorny and farinaceous character, as the premises of a cornchandler and seedsman should be. It appeared to me that he must be a very happy man indeed, to have so many little drawers in his shop; and I wondered when I peeped into one or two on the lower tiers, and saw the tied-up brown paper packets inside, whether the flower-seeds and bulbs ever wanted of a fine day to break out of those jails, and bloom.

It was in the early morning after my arrival that I entertained this speculation. On the previous night, I had been sent straight to bed in an attic with a sloping roof, which was so low in the corner where the bedstead was, that I calculated the tiles as being within a foot of my eyebrows. In the same early morning, I discovered a singular affinity between seeds and corduroys. Mr Pumblechook wore corduroys, and so did his shopman; and somehow, there was a general air and flavour about the corduroys, so much in the nature of seeds, and a general air and flavour about the seeds, so much in the nature of corduroys, that I hardly knew which was which. The same opportunity served me for noticing that Mr Pumblechook appeared to conduct his business by looking across the street at the saddler, who appeared to transact *his* business by keeping his eye on the coachmaker, who appeared to get on in life by putting his hands in his pockets and contemplating the baker, who in his turn folded his arms and stared at the grocer, who stood at his door and yawned at the chemist. The watchmaker, always poring over a little desk with a magnifying-glass at his eye, and always inspected by a group of smock-frocks poring over him through the glass of his shop-window, seemed to be about the only person in the High Street whose trade engaged his attention.

Mr Pumblechook and I breakfasted at eight o'clock in the parlor behind the shop, while the shopman took his mug of tea and hunch of bread and butter on a sack of peas in the front premises. I considered Mr Pumblechook a wretched company. Besides being possessed by my sister's idea that a mortifying and penitential character ought to be imparted to my diet,—besides giving me as much crumb as possible in combination with as little butter, and putting such a quantity of warm water into my milk that it would have been more candid to have left the milk out altogether,—his conversation consisted of nothing but arithmetic. On my politely bidding him good morning, he said, pompously, 'Seven times nine, boy?' And how should I be able to answer, dodged in that way, in a strange place, on an empty stomach! I was hungry, but before I had swallowed a morsel, he began a running sum that lasted all through the breakfast. 'Seven?' 'And four?' 'And eight?' 'And six?' 'And two?' 'And ten?' And so on. And after each figure was disposed of, it was as much as I could do to get a bite or a sup, before the next came; while he sat at his ease guessing nothing, and eating bacon and hot roll, in (if I may be allowed the expression) a gorging and gormandizing manner.

For such reasons, I was very glad when ten o'clock came and we started for Miss Havisham's; though I was not at all at my ease regarding the manner in which I should acquit myself under that lady's roof. Within a quarter of an hour we came to Miss Havisham's house, which was of old brick, and dismal, and had a great many iron bars to it. Some of the windows had been walled up; of those that remained, all the lower were rustily barred. There was a courtyard in front, and that was barred; so we had to wait, after ringing the bell, until some one should come to open it. While we waited at the gate, I peeped in (even then Mr Pumblechook said, 'And fourteen?' but I pretended not to hear him), and saw that at the side of the house there was a large brewery. No brewing was going on in it, and none seemed to have gone on for a long long time.

A window was raised, and a clear voice demanded 'What name?' To which my conductor replied, 'Pumblechook.' The voice returned, 'Quite right,' and the window was shut again, and a young lady came across the courtyard, with keys in her hand.

'This,' said Mr Pumblechook, 'is Pip.'

'This is Pip, is it?' returned the young lady, who was very pretty and seemed very proud; 'come in, Pip.'

Mr Pumblechook was coming in also, when she stopped him with the gate.

'Oh!' she said. 'Did you wish to see Miss Havisham?'

'If Miss Havisham wished to see me,' returned Mr Pumblechook, discomfited.

'Ah!' said the girl; 'but you see she don't.'

She said it so finally, and in such an undiscussible way, that Mr Pumblechook, though in a condition of ruffled dignity, could not protest. But he eyed me severely,—as if *I* had done anything to him!—and departed with the words reproachfully delivered: 'Boy! Let your behaviour here be a credit unto them which brought you up by hand!' I was not free from apprehension that he would come back to propound through the gate, 'And sixteen?' But he didn't.

My young conductress locked the gate, and we went across the courtyard. It was paved and clean, but grass was growing in every crevice. The brewery buildings had a little lane of communication with it, and the wooden gates of that lane stood open, and all the brewery beyond stood open, away to the high enclosing wall; and all was empty and disused. The cold wind seemed to blow colder there than outside the gate; and it made a shrill noise in howling in and out at the open sides of the brewery, like the noise of wind in the rigging of a ship at sea.

She saw me looking at it, and she said, 'You could drink without hurt all the strong beer that's brewed there now, boy.'

'I should think I could, miss,' said I, in a shy way.

'Better not try to brew beer there now, or it would turn out sour, boy; don't you think so?'

'It looks like it, miss.'

'Not that anybody means to try,' she added, 'for that's all done with, and the place will stand as idle as it is till it falls. As to strong beer, there's enough of it in the cellars already, to drown the Manor House.'

'Is that the name of this house, miss?'

'One of its names, boy.'

'It has more than one, then, miss?'

'One more. Its other name was Satis; which is Greek, or Latin, or Hebrew, or all three—or all one to me—for enough.'

'Enough House,' said I; 'that's a curious name, miss.'

'Yes,' she replied; 'but it meant more than it said. It meant, when it was given, that whoever had this house could want nothing else. They must have been easily satisfied in those days, I should think. But don't loiter, boy.'

Though she called me 'boy' so often, and with a carelessness that was far from complimentary, she was of about my own age. She seemed much older than I, of course, being a girl, and beautiful and self-possessed; and she was as scornful of me as if she had been one-and-twenty, and a queen.

We went into the house by a side door, the great front entrance had two chains across it outside,—and the first thing I noticed was, that the passages were all dark, and that she had left a candle burning there. She took it up, and we went through more passages and up a staircase, and still it was all dark, and only the candle lighted us.

At last we came to the door of a room, and she said, 'Go in.'

I answered, more in shyness than politeness, 'After you, miss.'

To this she returned: 'Don't be ridiculous, boy; I am not going in.' And scornfully walked away, and—what was worse—took the candle with her.

This was very uncomfortable, and I was half afraid. However, the only thing to be done being to knock at the door, I knocked, and was told from within to enter. I entered, therefore, and found myself in a pretty large room, well lighted with wax candles. No glimpse of daylight was to be seen in it. It was a dressing-room, as I supposed from the furniture, though much of it was of forms and uses then quite unknown to me. But prominent in it was a draped table with a gilded looking-glass, and that I made out at first sight to be a fine lady's dressing-table.

Whether I should have made out this object so soon if there had been no fine lady sitting at it, I cannot say. In an armchair, with an elbow resting on the table and her head leaning on that hand, sat the strangest lady I have ever seen, or shall ever see.

She was dressed in rich materials,—satins, and lace, and silks,—all of white. Her shoes were white. And she had a long white veil dependent from her hair, and she had bridal flowers in her hair, but her hair was white. Some bright jewels sparkled on her neck and on her hands, and some other jewels lay sparkling on the table. Dresses, less splendid than the dress she wore, and half-packed trunks, were scattered about. She had not quite finished dressing, for she had but one shoe on,—the other was on the table near her hand,—her veil was but half arranged, her watch and chain were not put on, and some lace for her bosom lay with those trinkets, and with her handkerchief, and gloves, and some flowers, and a Prayer-Book all confusedly heaped about the looking-glass.

It was not in the first few moments that I saw all these things, though I saw more of them in the first moments than might be supposed. But I saw that everything within my view which ought to be white, had been white long ago, and had lost its lustre and was faded and yellow. I saw that the bride within the bridal dress had withered like the dress, and like the flowers, and had no brightness left but the brightness of her sunken eyes. I saw that the dress had been put upon the rounded figure of a young woman, and that the figure upon which it now hung loose had shrunk to skin and bone. Once, I had been taken to see some ghastly waxwork at the Fair, representing I know not what impossible personage lying in state. Once, I had been taken to one of our old marsh churches to see a skeleton in the ashes of a rich dress that had been dug out of a vault under the church pavement. Now, waxwork and skeleton seemed to have dark eyes that moved and looked at me. I should have cried out, if I could.

'Who is it?' said the lady at the table.

'Pip, ma'am.'

'Pip?'

'Mr Pumblechook's boy, ma'am. Come—to play.'

'Come nearer; let me look at you. Come close.'

It was when I stood before her, avoiding her eyes, that I took note of the surrounding objects in detail, and saw that her watch had stopped at twenty minutes to nine, and that a clock in the room had stopped at twenty minutes to nine.

'Look at me,' said Miss Havisham. 'You are not afraid of a woman who has never seen the sun since you were born?'

I regret to state that I was not afraid of telling the enormous lie comprehended in the answer 'No.'

'Do you know what I touch here?' she said, laying her hands, one upon the other, on her left side.

'Yes, ma'am.' (It made me think of the young man.)

'What do I touch?'

'Your heart.'

'Broken!'

She uttered the word with an eager look, and with strong emphasis, and with a weird smile that had a kind of boast in it. Afterwards she kept her hands there for a little while, and slowly took them away as if they were heavy.

'I am tired,' said Miss Havisham. 'I want diversion, and I have done with men and women. Play.'

I think it will be conceded by my most disputatious reader, that she could hardly have directed an unfortunate boy to do anything in the wide world more difficult to be done under the circumstances.

'I sometimes have sick fancies,' she went on, 'and I have a sick fancy that I want to see some play. There, there!' with an impatient movement of the fingers of her right hand; 'play, play, play!'

For a moment, with the fear of my sister's working me before my eyes, I had a desperate idea of starting round the room in the assumed character of Mr Pumblechook's chaise-cart. But I felt myself so unequal to the performance that I gave it up, and stood looking at Miss Havisham in what I suppose she took for a dogged manner, inasmuch as she said, when we had taken a good look at each other,—

'Are you sullen and obstinate?'

'No, ma'am, I am very sorry for you, and very sorry I can't play just now. If you complain of me I shall get into trouble with my sister, so I would do it if I could; but it's so new here, and so strange, and so fine,—and melancholy—.' I stopped, fearing I might say too much, or had already said it, and we took another look at each other.

Before she spoke again, she turned her eyes from me, and looked at the dress she wore, and at the dressing-table, and finally at herself in the looking-glass.

'So new to him,' she muttered, 'so old to me; so strange to him, so familiar to me; so melancholy to both of us! Call Estella.'

As she was still looking at the reflection of herself, I thought she was still talking to herself, and kept quiet.

'Call Estella,' she repeated, flashing a look at me. 'You can do that. Call Estella. At the door.'

To stand in the dark in a mysterious passage of an unknown house, bawling Estella to a scornful young lady neither visible nor responsive, and feeling it a dreadful liberty so to roar out her name, was almost as bad as playing to order. But she answered at last, and her light came along the dark passage like a star.

Miss Havisham beckoned her to come close, and took up a jewel from the table, and tried its effect upon her fair young bosom and against her pretty brown hair. 'Your own, one day, my dear, and you will use it well. Let me see you play cards with this boy.'

'With this boy? Why, he is a common labouring boy!'

I thought I overheard Miss Havisham answer,—only it seemed so unlikely,—'Well? You can break his heart.'

'What do you play, boy?' asked Estella of myself, with the greatest disdain.

'Nothing but beggar my neighbour, miss.'

'Beggar him,' said Miss Havisham to Estella. So we sat down to cards.

It was then I began to understand that everything in the room had stopped, like the watch and the clock, a long time ago. I noticed that Miss Havisham put down the jewel exactly on the spot from which she had taken it up. As Estella dealt the cards, I glanced at the dressing-table again, and saw that the shoe upon it, once white, now yellow, had never been worn. I glanced down at the foot from which the shoe was absent, and saw that the silk stocking on it, once white, now yellow, had been trodden ragged. Without this arrest of everything, this standing still of all the pale decayed objects, not even the withered bridal dress on the collapsed form could have looked so like grave-clothes, or the long veil so like a shroud.

So she sat, corpse-like, as we played at cards; the frillings and trimmings on her bridal dress, looking like earthy paper. I knew nothing then of the discoveries that are occasionally made of bodies buried in ancient times, which fall to powder in the moment of being distinctly seen; but, I have often thought since, that she must have looked as if the admission of the natural light of day would have struck her to dust.

'He calls the knaves Jacks, this boy!' said Estella with disdain, before our first game was out. 'And what coarse hands he has! And what thick boots!'

I had never thought of being ashamed of my hands before; but I began to consider them a very indifferent pair. Her contempt for me was so strong, that it became infectious, and I caught it.

She won the game, and I dealt. I misdealt, as was only natural, when I knew she was lying in wait for me to do wrong; and she denounced me for a stupid, clumsy labouring-boy.

'You say nothing of her,' remarked Miss Havisham to me, as she looked on. 'She says many hard things of you, but you say nothing of her. What do you think of her?'

'I don't like to say,' I stammered.

'Tell me in my ear,' said Miss Havisham, bending down.
'I think she is very proud,' I replied, in a whisper.
'Anything else?'
'I think she is very pretty.'
'Anything else?'
'I think she is very insulting.' (She was looking at me then with a look of supreme aversion.)
'Anything else?'
'I think I should like to go home.'
'And never see her again, though she is so pretty?'
'I am not sure that I shouldn't like to see her again, but I should like to go home now.'
'You shall go soon,' said Miss Havisham, aloud. 'Play the game out.'

Saving for the one weird smile at first, I should have felt almost sure that Miss Havisham's face could not smile. It had dropped into a watchful and brooding expression,—most likely when all the things about her had become transfixed,—and it looked as if nothing could ever lift it up again. Her chest had dropped, so that she stooped; and her voice had dropped, so that she spoke low, and with a dead lull upon her; altogether, she had the appearance of having dropped body and soul, within and without, under the weight of a crushing blow.

I played the game to an end with Estella, and she beggared me. She threw the cards down on the table when she had won them all, as if she despised them for having been won of me.

'When shall I have you here again?' said Miss Havisham. 'Let me think.'

I was beginning to remind her that today was Wednesday, when she checked me with her former impatient movement of the fingers of her right hand.

'There, there! I know nothing of days of the week; I know nothing of weeks of the year. Come again after six days. You hear?'

'Yes, ma'am.'

'Estella, take him down. Let him have something to eat, and let him roam and look about him while he eats. Go, Pip.'

I followed the candle down, as I had followed the candle up, and she stood it in the place where we had found it. Until she opened the side entrance, I had fancied, without thinking about it, that it must necessarily be night-time. The rush of the daylight quite confounded me, and made me feel as if I had been in the candlelight of the strange room many hours.

'You are to wait here, you boy,' said Estella; and disappeared and closed the door.

I took the opportunity of being alone in the courtyard to look at my coarse hands and my common boots. My opinion of those accessories was not favourable. They had never troubled me before, but they troubled me now, as vulgar appendages. I determined to ask Joe why he had ever taught me to call those picture-cards Jacks, which ought to be called knaves. I wished Joe had been rather more genteelly brought up, and then I should have been so too.

She came back, with some bread and meat and a little mug of beer. She put the mug down on the stones of the yard, and gave me the bread and meat without looking at me, as insolently as if I were a dog in disgrace. I was so humiliated, hurt, spurned, offended, angry, sorry,—I cannot hit upon the right name for the smart—God knows what its name was,—that tears started to my eyes. The moment they sprang there, the girl looked at me with a quick delight in having been the cause of them. This gave me power to keep them back and to look at her: so, she gave a contemptuous toss—but with a sense, I thought, of having made too sure that I was so wounded—and left me.

But when she was gone, I looked about me for a place to hide my face in, and got behind one of the gates in the brewery-lane, and leaned my sleeve against the wall there, and leaned my forehead on it and cried. As I cried, I kicked the wall, and took a hard twist at my hair; so bitter were my feelings, and so sharp was the smart without a name, that needed counteraction.

My sister's bringing up had made me sensitive. In the little world in which children have their existence whosoever brings them up, there is nothing so finely perceived and so finely felt as injustice. It may be only small injustice that the child can be exposed to; but the child is small, and its world is small, and its rocking-horse stands as many hands high, according to scale, as a big-boned Irish hunter. Within myself, I had sustained, from my babyhood, a perpetual conflict with injustice. I had known, from the time when I could speak, that my sister, in her capricious and violent coercion, was unjust to me. I had cherished a profound conviction that her bringing me up by hand gave her no right to bring me up by jerks. Through all my punishments, disgraces, fasts, and vigils, and other penitential performances, I had nursed this assurance; and to my communing so much with it, in a solitary and unprotected way, I in great part refer the fact that I was morally timid and very sensitive.

I got rid of my injured feelings for the time by kicking them into the brewery wall, and twisting them out of my hair, and then I smoothed my face with my sleeve, and came from behind the gate. The bread and meat were acceptable, and the beer was warming and tingling, and I was soon in spirits to look about me.

To be sure, it was a deserted place, down to the pigeon-house in the brewery-yard, which had been blown crooked on its pole by some high wind, and would have made the pigeons think themselves at sea, if there had been any pigeons there to be rocked by it. But there were no pigeons in the dove-cot, no horses in the stable, no pigs in the sty, no malt in the storehouse, no smells of grains and beer in the copper or the vat. All the uses and scents of the brewery might have evaporated with its last reek of smoke. In a by-yard, there was a wilderness of empty casks, which had a certain sour remembrance of better days lingering about them; but it was too sour to be accepted as a sample of the beer that was gone,—and in this respect I remember those recluses as being like most others.

Behind the furthest end of the brewery, was a rank garden with an old wall; not so high but that I could struggle up and hold on long enough to look over it, and see that the rank garden was the garden of the house, and that it was overgrown with tangled weeds, but that there was a track upon the green and yellow paths, as if someone sometimes walked there, and that Estella was walking away from me even then. But she seemed to be everywhere. For when I yielded to the temptation presented by the casks, and began to walk on them, I saw *her* walking on them at the end of the yard of casks. She had her back towards me, and held her pretty brown hair spread out in her two hands, and never looked round, and passed out of my view directly. So, in the brewery itself,—by which I mean the large paved lofty place in which they used to make the beer, and where the brewing utensils still were. When I first went into it, and, rather oppressed by its gloom, stood near the door looking about me, I saw her pass among the extinguished fires, and ascend some light iron stairs, and go out by a gallery high overhead, as if she were going out into the sky.

It was in this place, and at this moment, that a strange thing happened to my fancy. I thought it a strange thing then, and I thought it a stranger thing long afterwards. I turned my eyes—a little dimmed by looking up at the frosty light—towards a great wooden beam in a low nook of the building near me on my right hand, and I saw a figure hanging there by the neck. A figure all in yellow white, with but one shoe to the feet; and it hung so, that I could see that the faded trimmings of the dress were like earthy paper, and that the face was Miss Havisham's, with a movement going over the whole countenance as if she were trying to call to me. In the terror of seeing the figure, and in the terror of being certain that it had not been there a moment before, I at first ran from it, and then ran towards it. And my terror was greatest of all when I found no figure there.

Nothing less than the frosty light of the cheerful sky, the sight of people passing beyond the bars of the courtyard gate, and the reviving influence of the rest of the bread and meat and beer, would have brought me round. Even with those aids, I might not have come to myself as soon as I did, but that I saw Estella approaching with the keys, to let me out. She would have some fair reason for looking down upon me, I thought, if she saw me frightened; and she would have no fair reason.

She gave me a triumphant glance in passing me, as if she rejoiced that my hands were so coarse and my boots were so thick, and she opened the gate, and stood holding it. I was passing out without looking at her, when she touched me with a taunting hand.

'Why don't you cry?'

'Because I don't want to.'

'You do,' said she. 'You have been crying till you are half blind, and you are near crying again now.'

She laughed contemptuously, pushed me out, and locked the gate upon me. I went straight to Mr Pumblechook's, and was immensely relieved to find him not at home. So, leaving word with the shopman on what day I was wanted at Miss Havisham's again, I set off on the four-mile walk to our forge; pondering, as I went along, on all I had seen, and deeply revolving that I was a common labouring-boy; that my hands were coarse; that my boots were thick; that I had fallen into a despicable habit of calling knaves Jacks; that I was much more ignorant than I had considered myself last night, and generally that I was in a low-lived bad way.

Chapter 9

When I reached home, my sister was very curious to know all about Miss Havisham's, and asked a number of questions. And I soon found myself getting heavily bumped from behind in the nape of the neck and the small of the back, and having my face ignominiously shoved against the kitchen wall, because I did not answer those questions at sufficient length.

If a dread of not being understood be hidden in the breasts of other young people to anything like the extent to which it used to be hidden in mine,—which I consider probable, as I have no particular reason to suspect myself of having been a monstrosity,—it is the key to many reservations. I felt convinced that if I described Miss Havisham's as my eyes had seen it, I should not be understood. Not only that, but I felt convinced that Miss Havisham too would not be understood; and although she was perfectly incomprehensible to me, I entertained an impression that there would be something coarse and treacherous in my dragging her as she really was (to say nothing of Miss Estella) before the contemplation of Mrs Joe. Consequently, I said as little as I could, and had my face shoved against the kitchen wall.

The worst of it was that that bullying old Pumblechook, preyed upon by a devouring curiosity to be informed of all I had seen and heard, came gaping over in his chaise-cart at tea-time, to have the details divulged to him. And the mere sight of the torment, with his fishy eyes and mouth open, his sandy hair inquisitively on end, and his waistcoat heaving with windy arithmetic, made me vicious in my reticence.

'Well, boy,' Uncle Pumblechook began, as soon as he was seated in the chair of honour by the fire. 'How did you get on up town?'

I answered, 'Pretty well, sir,' and my sister shook her fist at me.

'Pretty well?' Mr Pumblechook repeated. 'Pretty well is no answer. Tell us what you mean by pretty well, boy?'

Whitewash on the forehead hardens the brain into a state of obstinacy perhaps. Anyhow, with whitewash from the wall on my forehead, my obstinacy was adamantine. I reflected for some time, and then answered as if I had discovered a new idea, 'I mean pretty well.'

My sister with an exclamation of impatience was going to fly at me,—I had no shadow of defence, for Joe was busy in the forge,—when Mr Pumblechook interposed with 'No! Don't lose your temper. Leave this lad to me, ma'am; leave this lad to me.' Mr Pumblechook then turned me towards him, as if he were going to cut my hair, and said,—

'First (to get our thoughts in order): Forty-three pence?'

I calculated the consequences of replying 'Four Hundred Pound,' and finding them against me, went as near the answer as I could—which was somewhere about eightpence off. Mr Pumblechook then put me through my pence-table from 'twelve pence make one shilling,' up to 'forty pence make three and fourpence,' and then triumphantly demanded, as if he had done for me, '*Now!* How much is forty-three pence?' To which I replied, after a long interval of reflection, 'I don't know.' And I was so aggravated that I almost doubt if I did know.

Mr Pumblechook worked his head like a screw to screw it out of me, and said, 'Is forty-three pence seven and sixpence three fardens, for instance?'

'Yes!' said I. And although my sister instantly boxed my ears, it was highly gratifying to me to see that the answer spoilt his joke, and brought him to a dead stop.

'Boy! What like is Miss Havisham?' Mr Pumblechook began again when he had recovered; folding his arms tight on his chest and applying the screw.

'Very tall and dark,' I told him.

'Is she, uncle?' asked my sister.

Mr Pumblechook winked assent; from which I at once inferred that he had never seen Miss Havisham, for she was nothing of the kind.

'Good!' said Mr Pumblechook conceitedly. ('This is the way to have him! We are beginning to hold our own, I think, Mum?')

'I am sure, uncle,' returned Mrs Joe, 'I wish you had him always; you know so well how to deal with him.'

'Now, boy! What was she a doing of, when you went in today?' asked Mr Pumblechook.

'She was sitting,' I answered, 'in a black velvet coach.'

Mr Pumblechook and Mrs Joe stared at one another—as they well might—and both repeated, 'In a black velvet coach?'

'Yes,' said I. 'And Miss Estella—that's her niece, I think—handed her in cake and wine at the coach-window, on a gold plate. And we all had cake and wine on gold plates. And I got up behind the coach to eat mine, because she told me to.'

'Was anybody else there?' asked Mr Pumblechook.

'Four dogs,' said I.

'Large or small?'

'Immense,' said I. 'And they fought for veal-cutlets out of a silver basket.'

Mr Pumblechook and Mrs Joe stared at one another again, in utter amazement. I was perfectly frantic,—a reckless witness under the torture,—and would have told them anything.

'Where *was* this coach, in the name of gracious?' asked my sister.

'In Miss Havisham's room.' They stared again. 'But there weren't any horses to it.' I added this saving clause, in the moment of rejecting four richly caparisoned coursers which I had had wild thoughts of harnessing.

'Can this be possible, uncle?' asked Mrs Joe. 'What can the boy mean?'

'I'll tell you, Mum,' said Mr Pumblechook. 'My opinion is, it's a sedan-chair. She's flighty, you know,—very flighty,—quite flighty enough to pass her days in a sedan-chair.'

'Did you ever see her in it, uncle?' asked Mrs Joe.

'How could I,' he returned, forced to the admission, 'when I never see her in my life? Never clapped eyes upon her!'

'Goodness, uncle! And yet you have spoken to her?'

'Why, don't you know,' said Mr Pumblechook, testily, 'that when I have been there, I have been took up to the outside of her door, and the door has stood ajar, and she has spoke to me that way. Don't say you don't know *that*, Mum. Howsomever, the boy went there to play. What did you play at, boy?'

'We played with flags,' I said. (I beg to observe that I think of myself with amazement, when I recall the lies I told on this occasion.)

'Flags!' echoed my sister.

'Yes,' said I. 'Estella waved a blue flag, and I waved a red one, and Miss Havisham waved one sprinkled all over with little gold stars, out at the coach-window. And then we all waved our swords and hurrahed.'

'Swords!' repeated my sister. 'Where did you get swords from?'

'Out of a cupboard,' said I. 'And I saw pistols in it,—and jam,—and pills. And there was no daylight in the room, but it was all lighted up with candles.'

'That's true, Mum,' said Mr Pumblechook, with a grave nod. 'That's the state of the case, for that much I've seen myself.' And then they both stared at me, and I, with an obtrusive show of artlessness on my countenance, stared at them, and plaited the right leg of my trousers with my right hand.

If they had asked me any more questions, I should undoubtedly have betrayed myself, for I was even then on the point of mentioning that there was a balloon in the yard, and should have hazarded the statement but for my invention being divided between that phenomenon and a bear in the brewery. They were so much occupied, however, in discussing the marvels I had already presented for their consideration, that I escaped. The subject still held them when Joe came in from his work to have a cup of tea. To whom my sister, more for the relief of her own mind than for the gratification of his, related my pretended experiences.

Now, when I saw Joe open his blue eyes and roll them all round the kitchen in helpless amazement, I was overtaken by penitence; but only as regarded him,—not in the least as regarded the other two. Towards Joe, and Joe only, I considered myself a young monster, while they sat debating what results would come to me from Miss Havisham's acquaintance and favour. They had no doubt that Miss Havisham would 'do something' for me; their doubts related to the form that something would take. My sister stood out for 'property.' Mr Pumblechook was in favour of a handsome premium for binding me apprentice to some genteel trade,—say, the corn and seed trade, for instance. Joe fell into the deepest disgrace with both, for offering the bright suggestion that I might only be presented with one of the dogs who had fought for the veal-cutlets. 'If a fool's head can't express better opinions than that,' said my sister, 'and you have got any work to do, you had better go and do it.' So he went.

After Mr Pumblechook had driven off, and when my sister was washing up, I stole into the forge to Joe, and remained by him until he had done for the night. Then I said, 'Before the fire goes out, Joe, I should like to tell you something.'

'Should you, Pip?' said Joe, drawing his shoeing-stool near the forge. 'Then tell us. What is it, Pip?'

'Joe,' said I, taking hold of his rolled-up shirt sleeve, and twisting it between my finger and thumb, 'you remember all that about Miss Havisham's?'

'Remember?' said Joe. 'I believe you! Wonderful!'

'It's a terrible thing, Joe; it ain't true.'

'What are you telling of, Pip?' cried Joe, falling back in the greatest amazement. 'You don't mean to say it's—'

'Yes I do; it's lies, Joe.'

'But not all of it? Why sure you don't mean to say, Pip, that there was no black welwet co—eh?' For, I stood shaking my head. 'But at least there was dogs, Pip? Come, Pip,' said Joe, persuasively, 'if there warn't no weal-cutlets, at least there was dogs?'

'No, Joe.'

'A dog?' said Joe. 'A puppy? Come?'

'No, Joe, there was nothing at all of the kind.'

As I fixed my eyes hopelessly on Joe, Joe contemplated me in dismay. 'Pip, old chap! This won't do, old fellow! I say! Where do you expect to go to?'

'It's terrible, Joe; ain't it?'

'Terrible?' cried Joe. 'Awful! What possessed you?'

'I don't know what possessed me, Joe,' I replied, letting his shirt sleeve go, and sitting down in the ashes at his feet, hanging my head; 'but I wish you hadn't taught me to call Knaves at cards Jacks; and I wish my boots weren't so thick nor my hands so coarse.'

And then I told Joe that I felt very miserable, and that I hadn't been able to explain myself to Mrs Joe and Pumblechook, who were so rude to me, and that there had been a beautiful young lady at Miss Havisham's who was dreadfully proud, and that she had said I was common, and that I knew I was common, and that I wished I was not common, and that the lies had come of it somehow, though I didn't know how.

This was a case of metaphysics, at least as difficult for Joe to deal with as for me. But Joe took the case altogether out of the region of metaphysics, and by that means vanquished it.

'There's one thing you may be sure of, Pip,' said Joe, after some rumination, 'namely, that lies is lies. Howsever they come, they didn't ought to come, and they come from the father of lies, and work round to the same. Don't you tell no more of 'em, Pip. *That* ain't the way to get out of being common, old chap. And as to being common, I don't make it out at all clear. You are oncommon in some things. You're oncommon small. Likewise you're a oncommon scholar.'

'No, I am ignorant and backward, Joe.'

'Why, see what a letter you wrote last night! Wrote in print even! I've seen letters—Ah! And from gentlefolks!—that I'll swear weren't wrote in print,' said Joe.

'I have learnt next to nothing, Joe. You think much of me. It's only that.'

'Well, Pip,' said Joe, 'be it so or be it son't, you must be a common scholar afore you can be a oncommon one, I should hope! The king upon his throne, with his crown upon his ed, can't sit and write his acts of Parliament in print, without having begun, when he were a unpromoted Prince, with the alphabet.—Ah!' added Joe, with a shake of the head that was full of meaning, 'and begun at A too, and worked his way to Z. And *I* know what that is to do, though I can't say I've exactly done it.'

There was some hope in this piece of wisdom, and it rather encouraged me.

'Whether common ones as to callings and earnings,' pursued Joe, reflectively, 'mightn't be the better of continuing for to keep company with common ones, instead of going out to play with oncommon ones,—which reminds me to hope that there were a flag, perhaps?'

'No, Joe.'

'(I'm sorry there weren't a flag, Pip). Whether that might be or mightn't be, is a thing as can't be looked into now, without putting your sister on the Rampage; and that's a thing not to be thought of as being done intentional. Lookee here, Pip, at what is said to you by a true friend. Which this to you the true friend say. If you can't get to be oncommon through going straight, you'll never get to do it through going crooked. So don't tell no more on 'em, Pip, and live well and die happy.'

'You are not angry with me, Joe?'

'No, old chap. But bearing in mind that them were which I meantersay of a stunning and outdacious sort,—alluding to them which bordered on weal-cutlets and dog-fighting,—a sincere well-wisher would adwise, Pip, their being dropped into your meditations, when you go upstairs to bed. That's all, old chap, and don't never do it no more.'

When I got up to my little room and said my prayers, I did not forget Joe's recommendation, and yet my young mind was in that disturbed and unthankful state, that I thought long after I laid me down, how common Estella would consider Joe, a mere blacksmith; how thick his boots, and how coarse his hands. I thought how Joe and my sister were then sitting in the kitchen, and how I had come up to bed from the kitchen, and how Miss Havisham and Estella never sat in a kitchen, but were far above the level of such common doings. I fell asleep recalling what I 'used to do' when I was at Miss Havisham's; as though I had been there weeks or months, instead of hours; and as though it were quite an old subject of remembrance, instead of one that had arisen only that day.

That was a memorable day to me, for it made great changes in me. But it is the same with any life. Imagine one selected day struck out of it, and think how different its course would have been. Pause you who read this, and think for a moment of the long chain of iron or gold, of thorns or flowers, that would never have bound you, but for the formation of the first link on one memorable day.

Chapter 10

The felicitous idea occurred to me a morning or two later when I woke, that the best step I could take towards making myself uncommon was to get out of Biddy everything she knew. In pursuance of this luminous conception I mentioned to Biddy when I went to Mr Wopsle's great-aunt's at night, that I had a particular reason for wishing to get on in life, and that I should feel very much obliged to her if she would impart all her learning to me. Biddy, who was the most obliging of girls, immediately said she would, and indeed began to carry out her promise within five minutes.

The Educational scheme or Course established by Mr Wopsle's great-aunt may be resolved into the following synopsis. The pupils ate apples and put straws down one another's backs, until Mr Wopsle's great-aunt collected her energies, and made an indiscriminate totter at them with a birch-rod. After receiving the charge with every mark of derision, the pupils formed in line and buzzingly passed a ragged book from hand to hand. The book had an alphabet in it, some figures and tables, and a little spelling,—that is to say, it had had once. As soon as this volume began to circulate, Mr Wopsle's great-aunt fell into a state of coma, arising either from sleep or a rheumatic paroxysm. The pupils then entered among themselves upon a competitive examination on the subject of Boots, with the view of ascertaining who could tread the hardest upon whose toes. This mental exercise lasted until Biddy made a rush at them and distributed three defaced Bibles (shaped as if they had been unskilfully cut off the chump end of something), more illegibly printed at the best than any curiosities of literature I have since met with, speckled all over with ironmould, and having various specimens of the insect world smashed between their leaves. This part of the Course was usually lightened by several single combats between Biddy and refractory students. When the fights were over, Biddy gave out the number of a page, and then we all read aloud what we could,—or what we couldn't—in a frightful chorus; Biddy leading with a high, shrill, monotonous voice, and none of us having the least notion of, or reverence for, what we were reading about. When this horrible din had lasted a certain time, it mechanically awoke Mr Wopsle's great-aunt, who staggered at a boy fortuitously, and pulled his ears. This was understood to terminate the Course for the evening, and we emerged into the air with shrieks of intellectual victory. It is fair to remark that there was no prohibition against any pupil's entertaining himself with a slate or even with the ink (when there was any), but that it was not easy to pursue that branch of study in the winter season, on account of the little general shop in which the classes were holden—and which was also Mr Wopsle's great-aunt's sitting-room and bedchamber—being but faintly illuminated through the agency of one low-spirited dip-candle and no snuffers.

It appeared to me that it would take time to become uncommon, under these circumstances: nevertheless, I resolved to try it, and that very evening Biddy entered on our special agreement, by imparting some information from her little catalogue of prices, under the head of moist sugar, and lending me, to copy at home, a large old English D which she had imitated from the heading of some newspaper, and which I supposed, until she told me what it was, to be a design for a buckle.

Of course there was a public-house in the village, and of course Joe liked sometimes to smoke his pipe there. I had received strict orders from my sister to call for him at the Three Jolly Bargemen, that evening, on my way from school, and bring him home at my peril. To the Three Jolly Bargemen, therefore, I directed my steps.

There was a bar at the Jolly Bargemen, with some alarmingly long chalk scores in it on the wall at the side of the door, which seemed to me to be never paid off. They had been there ever since I could remember, and had grown more than I had. But there was a quantity of chalk about our country, and perhaps the people neglected no opportunity of turning it to account.

It being Saturday night, I found the landlord looking rather grimly at these records; but as my business was with Joe and not with him, I merely wished him good evening, and passed into the common room at the end of the passage, where there was a bright large kitchen fire, and where Joe was smoking his pipe in company with Mr Wopsle and a stranger. Joe greeted me as usual with 'Halloa, Pip, old chap!' and the moment he said that, the stranger turned his head and looked at me.

He was a secret-looking man whom I had never seen before. His head was all on one side, and one of his eyes was half shut up, as if he were taking aim at something with an invisible gun. He had a pipe in his mouth, and he took it out, and, after slowly blowing all his smoke away and looking hard at me all the time, nodded. So, I nodded, and then he nodded again, and made room on the settle beside him that I might sit down there.

But as I was used to sit beside Joe whenever I entered that place of resort, I said 'No, thank you, sir,' and fell into the space Joe made for me on the opposite settle. The strange man, after glancing at Joe, and seeing that his attention was otherwise engaged, nodded to me again when I had taken my seat, and then rubbed his leg—in a very odd way, as it struck me.

'You was saying,' said the strange man, turning to Joe, 'that you was a blacksmith.'

'Yes. I said it, you know,' said Joe.

'What'll you drink, Mr—? You didn't mention your name, by the bye.'

Joe mentioned it now, and the strange man called him by it. 'What'll you drink, Mr Gargery? At my expense? To top up with?'

'Well,' said Joe, 'to tell you the truth, I ain't much in the habit of drinking at anybody's expense but my own.'

'Habit? No,' returned the stranger, 'but once and away, and on a Saturday night too. Come! Put a name to it, Mr Gargery.'

'I wouldn't wish to be stiff company,' said Joe. 'Rum.'

'Rum,' repeated the stranger. 'And will the other gentleman originate a sentiment.'

'Rum,' said Mr Wopsle.

'Three Rums!' cried the stranger, calling to the landlord. 'Glasses round!'

'This other gentleman,' observed Joe, by way of introducing Mr Wopsle, 'is a gentleman that you would like to hear give it out. Our clerk at church.'

'Aha!' said the stranger, quickly, and cocking his eye at me. 'The lonely church, right out on the marshes, with graves round it!'

'That's it,' said Joe.

The stranger, with a comfortable kind of grunt over his pipe, put his legs up on the settle that he had to himself. He wore a flapping broad-brimmed traveller's hat, and under it a handkerchief tied over his head in the manner of a cap: so that he showed no hair. As he looked at the fire, I thought I saw a cunning expression, followed by a half-laugh, come into his face.

'I am not acquainted with this country, gentlemen, but it seems a solitary country towards the river.'

'Most marshes is solitary,' said Joe.

'No doubt, no doubt. Do you find any gypsies, now, or tramps, or vagrants of any sort, out there?'

'No,' said Joe; 'none but a runaway convict now and then. And we don't find *them*, easy. Eh, Mr Wopsle?'

Mr Wopsle, with a majestic remembrance of old discomfiture, assented; but not warmly.

'Seems you have been out after such?' asked the stranger.

'Once,' returned Joe. 'Not that we wanted to take them, you understand; we went out as lookers on; me, and Mr Wopsle, and Pip. Didn't us, Pip?'

'Yes, Joe.'

The stranger looked at me again,—still cocking his eye, as if he were expressly taking aim at me with his invisible gun,—and said, 'He's a likely young parcel of bones that. What is it you call him?'

'Pip,' said Joe.

'Christened Pip?'

'No, not christened Pip.'

'Surname Pip?'

'No,' said Joe, 'it's a kind of family name what he gave himself when a infant, and is called by.'

'Son of yours?'

'Well,' said Joe, meditatively, not, of course, that it could be in anywise necessary to consider about it, but because it was the way at the Jolly Bargemen to seem to consider deeply about everything that was discussed over pipes,—'well—no. No, he ain't.'

'Nevvy?' said the strange man.

'Well,' said Joe, with the same appearance of profound cogitation, 'he is not—no, not to deceive you, he is *not*—my nevvy.'

'What the Blue Blazes is he?' asked the stranger. Which appeared to me to be an inquiry of unnecessary strength.

Mr Wopsle struck in upon that; as one who knew all about relationships, having professional occasion to bear in mind what female relations a man might not marry; and expounded the ties between me and Joe. Having his hand in, Mr Wopsle finished off with a most terrifically snarling passage from Richard the Third, and seemed to think he had done quite enough to account for it when he added, '—as the poet says.'

And here I may remark that when Mr Wopsle referred to me, he considered it a necessary part of such reference to rumple my hair and poke it into my eyes. I cannot conceive why everybody of his standing who visited at our house should always have put me through the same inflammatory process under similar circumstances. Yet I do not call to mind that I was ever in my earlier youth the subject of remark in our social family circle, but some large-handed person took some such ophthalmic steps to patronize me.

All this while, the strange man looked at nobody but me, and looked at me as if he were determined to have a shot at me at last, and bring me down. But he said nothing after offering his Blue Blazes observation, until the glasses of rum and water were brought; and then he made his shot, and a most extraordinary shot it was.

It was not a verbal remark, but a proceeding in dumb-show, and was pointedly addressed to me. He stirred his rum and water pointedly at me, and he tasted his rum and water pointedly at me. And he stirred it and he tasted it; not with a spoon that was brought to him, but *with a file*.

He did this so that nobody but I saw the file; and when he had done it he wiped the file and put it in a breast-pocket. I knew it to be Joe's file, and I knew that he knew my convict, the moment I saw the instrument. I sat gazing at him, spell-bound. But he now reclined on his settle, taking very little notice of me, and talking principally about turnips.

There was a delicious sense of cleaning-up and making a quiet pause before going on in life afresh, in our village on Saturday nights, which stimulated Joe to dare to stay out half an hour longer on Saturdays than at other times. The half-hour and the rum and water running out together, Joe got up to go, and took me by the hand.

'Stop half a moment, Mr Gargery,' said the strange man. 'I think I've got a bright new shilling somewhere in my pocket, and if I have, the boy shall have it.'

He looked it out from a handful of small change, folded it in some crumpled paper, and gave it to me. 'Yours!' said he. 'Mind! Your own.'

I thanked him, staring at him far beyond the bounds of good manners, and holding tight to Joe. He gave Joe goodnight, and he gave Mr Wopsle goodnight (who went out with us), and he gave me only a look with his aiming eye,—no, not a look, for he shut it up, but wonders may be done with an eye by hiding it.

On the way home, if I had been in a humour for talking, the talk must have been all on my side, for Mr Wopsle parted from us at the door of the Jolly Bargemen, and Joe went all the way home with his mouth wide open, to rinse the rum out with as much air as possible. But I was in a manner stupefied by this turning up of my old misdeed and old acquaintance, and could think of nothing else.

My sister was not in a very bad temper when we presented ourselves in the kitchen, and Joe was encouraged by that unusual circumstance to tell her about the bright shilling. 'A bad un, I'll be bound,' said Mrs Joe triumphantly, 'or he wouldn't have given it to the boy! Let's look at it.'

I took it out of the paper, and it proved to be a good one. 'But what's this?' said Mrs Joe, throwing down the shilling and catching up the paper. 'Two One-Pound notes?'

Nothing less than two fat sweltering one-pound notes that seemed to have been on terms of the warmest intimacy with all the cattle-markets in the county. Joe caught up his hat again, and ran with them to the

Jolly Bargemen to restore them to their owner. While he was gone, I sat down on my usual stool and looked vacantly at my sister, feeling pretty sure that the man would not be there.

Presently, Joe came back, saying that the man was gone, but that he, Joe, had left word at the Three Jolly Bargemen concerning the notes. Then my sister sealed them up in a piece of paper, and put them under some dried rose-leaves in an ornamental teapot on the top of a press in the state parlor. There they remained, a nightmare to me, many and many a night and day.

I had sadly broken sleep when I got to bed, through thinking of the strange man taking aim at me with his invisible gun, and of the guiltily coarse and common thing it was, to be on secret terms of conspiracy with convicts,—a feature in my low career that I had previously forgotten. I was haunted by the file too. A dread possessed me that when I least expected it, the file would reappear. I coaxed myself to sleep by thinking of Miss Havisham's, next Wednesday; and in my sleep I saw the file coming at me out of a door, without seeing who held it, and I screamed myself awake.

Chapter 11

At the appointed time I returned to Miss Havisham's, and my hesitating ring at the gate brought out Estella. She locked it after admitting me, as she had done before, and again preceded me into the dark passage where her candle stood. She took no notice of me until she had the candle in her hand, when she looked over her shoulder, superciliously saying, 'You are to come this way today,' and took me to quite another part of the house.

The passage was a long one, and seemed to pervade the whole square basement of the Manor House. We traversed but one side of the square, however, and at the end of it she stopped, and put her candle down and opened a door. Here, the daylight reappeared, and I found myself in a small paved courtyard, the opposite side of which was formed by a detached dwelling-house, that looked as if it had once belonged to the manager or head clerk of the extinct brewery. There was a clock in the outer wall of this house. Like the clock in Miss Havisham's room, and like Miss Havisham's watch, it had stopped at twenty minutes to nine.

We went in at the door, which stood open, and into a gloomy room with a low ceiling, on the ground-floor at the back. There was some company in the room, and Estella said to me as she joined it, 'You are to go and stand there boy, till you are wanted.' 'There', being the window, I crossed to it, and stood 'there,' in a very uncomfortable state of mind, looking out.

It opened to the ground, and looked into a most miserable corner of the neglected garden, upon a rank ruin of cabbage-stalks, and one box-tree that had been clipped round long ago, like a pudding, and had a new growth at the top of it, out of shape and of a different colour, as if that part of the pudding had stuck to the saucepan and got burnt. This was my homely thought, as I contemplated the box-tree. There had been some light snow, overnight, and it lay nowhere else to my knowledge; but, it had not quite melted from the cold shadow of this bit of garden, and the wind caught it up in little eddies and threw it at the window, as if it pelted me for coming there.

I divined that my coming had stopped conversation in the room, and that its other occupants were looking at me. I could see nothing of the room except the shining of the fire in the window-glass, but I stiffened in all my joints with the consciousness that I was under close inspection.

There were three ladies in the room and one gentleman. Before I had been standing at the window five minutes, they somehow conveyed to me that they were all toadies and humbugs, but that each of them pretended not to know that the others were toadies and humbugs: because the admission that he or she did know it, would have made him or her out to be a toady and humbug.

They all had a listless and dreary air of waiting somebody's pleasure, and the most talkative of the ladies had to speak quite rigidly to repress a yawn. This lady, whose name was Camilla, very much reminded me of my sister, with the difference that she was older, and (as I found when I caught sight of her) of a blunter cast of features. Indeed, when I knew her better I began to think it was a mercy she had any features at all, so very blank and high was the dead wall of her face.

'Poor dear soul!' said this lady, with an abruptness of manner quite my sister's. 'Nobody's enemy but his own!'

'It would be much more commendable to be somebody else's enemy,' said the gentleman; 'far more natural.'

'Cousin Raymond,' observed another lady, 'we are to love our neighbour.'

'Sarah Pocket,' returned Cousin Raymond, 'if a man is not his own neighbour, who is?'

Miss Pocket laughed, and Camilla laughed and said (checking a yawn), 'The idea!' But I thought they seemed to think it rather a good idea too. The other lady, who had not spoken yet, said gravely and emphatically, '*Very* true!'

'Poor soul!' Camilla presently went on (I knew they had all been looking at me in the mean time), 'he is so very strange! Would anyone believe that when Tom's wife died, he actually could not be induced to see the importance of the children's having the deepest of trimmings to their mourning? 'Good Lord!' says he, 'Camilla, what can it signify so long as the poor bereaved little things are in black?' So like Matthew! The idea!'

'Good points in him, good points in him,' said Cousin Raymond; 'Heaven forbid I should deny good points in him; but he never had, and he never will have, any sense of the proprieties.'

'You know I was obliged,' said Camilla,—'I was obliged to be firm. I said, 'It WILL NOT DO, for the credit of the family.' I told him that, without deep trimmings, the family was disgraced. I cried about it from breakfast till dinner. I injured my digestion. And at last he flung out in his violent way, and said, with a D, 'Then do as you like.' Thank Goodness it will always be a consolation to me to know that I instantly went out in a pouring rain and bought the things.'

'*He* paid for them, did he not?' asked Estella.

'It's not the question, my dear child, who paid for them,' returned Camilla. '*I* bought them. And I shall often think of that with peace, when I wake up in the night.'

The ringing of a distant bell, combined with the echoing of some cry or call along the passage by which I had come, interrupted the conversation and caused Estella to say to me, 'Now, boy!' On my turning round, they all looked at me with the utmost contempt, and, as I went out, I heard Sarah Pocket say, 'Well I am sure! What next!' and Camilla add, with indignation, 'Was there ever such a fancy! The i-de-a!'

As we were going with our candle along the dark passage, Estella stopped all of a sudden, and, facing round, said in her taunting manner, with her face quite close to mine,—

'Well?'

'Well, miss?' I answered, almost falling over her and checking myself. She stood looking at me, and, of course, I stood looking at her.

'Am I pretty?'

'Yes; I think you are very pretty.'

'Am I insulting?'

'Not so much so as you were last time,' said I.

'Not so much so?'

'No.'

She fired when she asked the last question, and she slapped my face with such force as she had, when I answered it.

'Now?' said she. 'You little coarse monster, what do you think of me now?'

'I shall not tell you.'

'Because you are going to tell upstairs. Is that it?'

'No,' said I, 'that's not it.'

'Why don't you cry again, you little wretch?'

'Because I'll never cry for you again,' said I. Which was, I suppose, as false a declaration as ever was made; for I was inwardly crying for her then, and I know what I know of the pain she cost me afterwards.

We went on our way upstairs after this episode; and, as we were going up, we met a gentleman groping his way down.

'Whom have we here?' asked the gentleman, stopping and looking at me.

'A boy,' said Estella.

He was a burly man of an exceedingly dark complexion, with an exceedingly large head, and a corresponding large hand. He took my chin in his large hand and turned up my face to have a look at me by the light of the candle. He was prematurely bald on the top of his head, and had bushy black eyebrows that wouldn't lie down but stood up bristling. His eyes were set very deep in his head, and were disagreeably sharp and suspicious. He had a large watch-chain, and strong black dots where his beard and whiskers would have been if he had let them. He was nothing to me, and I could have had no foresight then, that he ever would be anything to me, but it happened that I had this opportunity of observing him well.

'Boy of the neighbourhood? Hey?' said he.

'Yes, sir,' said I.

'How do *you* come here?'

'Miss Havisham sent for me, sir,' I explained.

'Well! Behave yourself. I have a pretty large experience of boys, and you're a bad set of fellows. Now mind!' said he, biting the side of his great forefinger as he frowned at me, 'you behave yourself!'

With those words, he released me—which I was glad of, for his hand smelt of scented soap—and went his way downstairs. I wondered whether he could be a doctor; but no, I thought; he couldn't be a doctor, or he would have a quieter and more persuasive manner. There was not much time to consider the subject, for we were soon in Miss Havisham's room, where she and everything else were just as I had left them. Estella left me standing near the door, and I stood there until Miss Havisham cast her eyes upon me from the dressing-table.

'So!' she said, without being startled or surprised: 'the days have worn away, have they?'

'Yes, ma'am. Today is—'

'There, there, there!' with the impatient movement of her fingers. 'I don't want to know. Are you ready to play?'

I was obliged to answer in some confusion, 'I don't think I am, ma'am.'

'Not at cards again?' she demanded, with a searching look.

'Yes, ma'am; I could do that, if I was wanted.'

'Since this house strikes you old and grave, boy,' said Miss Havisham, impatiently, 'and you are unwilling to play, are you willing to work?'

I could answer this inquiry with a better heart than I had been able to find for the other question, and I said I was quite willing.

'Then go into that opposite room,' said she, pointing at the door behind me with her withered hand, 'and wait there till I come.'

I crossed the staircase landing, and entered the room she indicated. From that room, too, the daylight was completely excluded, and it had an airless smell that was oppressive. A fire had been lately kindled in the damp old-fashioned grate, and it was more disposed to go out than to burn up, and the reluctant smoke which hung in the room seemed colder than the clearer air,—like our own marsh mist. Certain wintry branches of candles on the high chimney-piece faintly lighted the chamber; or it would be more expressive to say, faintly troubled its darkness. It was spacious, and I dare say had once been handsome, but every discernible thing in it was covered with dust and mould, and dropping to pieces. The most prominent object was a long table with a tablecloth spread on it, as if a feast had been in preparation when the house and the clocks all stopped together. An epergne or centre-piece of some kind was in the middle of this cloth; it was so heavily overhung with cobwebs that its form was quite undistinguishable; and, as I looked along the yellow expanse out of which I remember its seeming to grow, like a black fungus, I saw speckle-legged spiders with blotchy bodies running home to it, and running out from it, as if some circumstances of the greatest public importance had just transpired in the spider community.

I heard the mice too, rattling behind the panels, as if the same occurrence were important to their interests. But the black beetles took no notice of the agitation, and groped about the hearth in a ponderous elderly way, as if they were short-sighted and hard of hearing, and not on terms with one another.

These crawling things had fascinated my attention, and I was watching them from a distance, when Miss Havisham laid a hand upon my shoulder. In her other hand she had a crutch-headed stick on which she leaned, and she looked like the Witch of the place.

'This,' said she, pointing to the long table with her stick, 'is where I will be laid when I am dead. They shall come and look at me here.'

With some vague misgiving that she might get upon the table then and there and die at once, the complete realization of the ghastly waxwork at the Fair, I shrank under her touch.

'What do you think that is?' she asked me, again pointing with her stick; 'that, where those cobwebs are?'

'I can't guess what it is, ma'am.'

'It's a great cake. A bride-cake. Mine!'

She looked all round the room in a glaring manner, and then said, leaning on me while her hand twitched my shoulder, 'Come, come, come! Walk me, walk me!'

I made out from this, that the work I had to do, was to walk Miss Havisham round and round the room. Accordingly, I started at once, and she leaned upon my shoulder, and we went away at a pace that might have been an imitation (founded on my first impulse under that roof) of Mr Pumblechook's chaise-cart.

She was not physically strong, and after a little time said, 'Slower!' Still, we went at an impatient fitful speed, and as we went, she twitched the hand upon my shoulder, and worked her mouth, and led me to believe that we were going fast because her thoughts went fast. After a while she said, 'Call Estella!' so I went out on the landing and roared that name as I had done on the previous occasion. When her light appeared, I returned to Miss Havisham, and we started away again round and round the room.

If only Estella had come to be a spectator of our proceedings, I should have felt sufficiently discontented; but as she brought with her the three ladies and the gentleman whom I had seen below, I didn't know what to do. In my politeness, I would have stopped; but Miss Havisham twitched my shoulder, and we posted on,—with a shame-faced consciousness on my part that they would think it was all my doing.

'Dear Miss Havisham,' said Miss Sarah Pocket. 'How well you look!'

'I do not,' returned Miss Havisham. 'I am yellow skin and bone.'

Camilla brightened when Miss Pocket met with this rebuff; and she murmured, as she plaintively contemplated Miss Havisham, 'Poor dear soul! Certainly not to be expected to look well, poor thing. The idea!'

'And how are *you*?' said Miss Havisham to Camilla. As we were close to Camilla then, I would have stopped as a matter of course, only Miss Havisham wouldn't stop. We swept on, and I felt that I was highly obnoxious to Camilla.

'Thank you, Miss Havisham,' she returned, 'I am as well as can be expected.'

'Why, what's the matter with you?' asked Miss Havisham, with exceeding sharpness.

'Nothing worth mentioning,' replied Camilla. 'I don't wish to make a display of my feelings, but I have habitually thought of you more in the night than I am quite equal to.'

'Then don't think of me,' retorted Miss Havisham.

'Very easily said!' remarked Camilla, amiably repressing a sob, while a hitch came into her upper lip, and her tears overflowed. 'Raymond is a witness what ginger and sal volatile I am obliged to take in the night. Raymond is a witness what nervous jerkings I have in my legs. Chokings and nervous jerkings, however, are nothing new to me when I think with anxiety of those I love. If I could be less affectionate and sensitive, I should have a better digestion and an iron set of nerves. I am sure I wish it could be so. But as to not thinking of you in the night—The idea!' Here, a burst of tears.

The Raymond referred to, I understood to be the gentleman present, and him I understood to be Mr Camilla. He came to the rescue at this point, and said in a consolatory and complimentary voice, 'Camilla, my dear, it is well known that your family feelings are gradually undermining you to the extent of making one of your legs shorter than the other.'

'I am not aware,' observed the grave lady whose voice I had heard but once, 'that to think of any person is to make a great claim upon that person, my dear.'

Miss Sarah Pocket, whom I now saw to be a little dry, brown, corrugated old woman, with a small face that might have been made of walnut-shells, and a large mouth like a cat's without the whiskers, supported this position by saying, 'No, indeed, my dear. Hem!'

'Thinking is easy enough,' said the grave lady.

'What is easier, you know?' assented Miss Sarah Pocket.

'Oh, yes, yes!' cried Camilla, whose fermenting feelings appeared to rise from her legs to her bosom. 'It's all very true! It's a weakness to be so affectionate, but I can't help it. No doubt my health would be much better if it was otherwise, still I wouldn't change my disposition if I could. It's the cause of much suffering, but it's a consolation to know I posses it, when I wake up in the night.' Here another burst of feeling.

Miss Havisham and I had never stopped all this time, but kept going round and round the room; now brushing against the skirts of the visitors, now giving them the whole length of the dismal chamber.

'There's Matthew!' said Camilla. 'Never mixing with any natural ties, never coming here to see how Miss Havisham is! I have taken to the sofa with my staylace cut, and have lain there hours insensible, with my head over the side, and my hair all down, and my feet I don't know where—'

('Much higher than your head, my love,' said Mr Camilla.)

'I have gone off into that state, hours and hours, on account of Matthew's strange and inexplicable conduct, and nobody has thanked me.'

'Really I must say I should think not!' interposed the grave lady.

'You see, my dear,' added Miss Sarah Pocket (a blandly vicious personage), 'the question to put to yourself is, who did you expect to thank you, my love?'

'Without expecting any thanks, or anything of the sort,' resumed Camilla, 'I have remained in that state, hours and hours, and Raymond is a witness of the extent to which I have choked, and what the total inefficacy of ginger has been, and I have been heard at the piano-forte tuner's across the street, where the poor mistaken children have even supposed it to be pigeons cooing at a distance,—and now to be told—' Here Camilla put her hand to her throat, and began to be quite chemical as to the formation of new combinations there.

When this same Matthew was mentioned, Miss Havisham stopped me and herself, and stood looking at the speaker. This change had a great influence in bringing Camilla's chemistry to a sudden end.

'Matthew will come and see me at last,' said Miss Havisham, sternly, 'when I am laid on that table. That will be his place,—there,' striking the table with her stick, 'at my head! And yours will be there! And your husband's there! And Sarah Pocket's there! And Georgiana's there! Now you all know where to take your stations when you come to feast upon me. And now go!'

At the mention of each name, she had struck the table with her stick in a new place. She now said, 'Walk me, walk me!' and we went on again.

'I suppose there's nothing to be done,' exclaimed Camilla, 'but comply and depart. It's something to have seen the object of one's love and duty for even so short a time. I shall think of it with a melancholy satisfaction when I wake up in the night. I wish Matthew could have that comfort, but he sets it at defiance. I am determined not to make a display of my feelings, but it's very hard to be told one wants to feast on one's relations,—as if one was a Giant,—and to be told to go. The bare idea!'

Mr Camilla interposing, as Mrs Camilla laid her hand upon her heaving bosom, that lady assumed an unnatural fortitude of manner which I supposed to be expressive of an intention to drop and choke when out of view, and kissing her hand to Miss Havisham, was escorted forth. Sarah Pocket and Georgiana contended who should remain last; but Sarah was too knowing to be outdone, and ambled round Georgiana with that artful slipperiness that the latter was obliged to take precedence. Sarah Pocket then made her separate effect of departing with, 'Bless you, Miss Havisham dear!' and with a smile of forgiving pity on her walnut-shell countenance for the weaknesses of the rest.

While Estella was away lighting them down, Miss Havisham still walked with her hand on my shoulder, but more and more slowly. At last she stopped before the fire, and said, after muttering and looking at it some seconds,—

'This is my birthday, Pip.'

I was going to wish her many happy returns, when she lifted her stick.

'I don't suffer it to be spoken of. I don't suffer those who were here just now, or any one to speak of it. They come here on the day, but they dare not refer to it.'

Of course *I* made no further effort to refer to it.

'On this day of the year, long before you were born, this heap of decay,' stabbing with her crutched stick at the pile of cobwebs on the table, but not touching it, 'was brought here. It and I have worn away together. The mice have gnawed at it, and sharper teeth than teeth of mice have gnawed at me.'

She held the head of her stick against her heart as she stood looking at the table; she in her once white dress, all yellow and withered; the once white cloth all yellow and withered; everything around in a state to crumble under a touch.

'When the ruin is complete,' said she, with a ghastly look, 'and when they lay me dead, in my bride's dress on the bride's table,—which shall be done, and which will be the finished curse upon him,—so much the better if it is done on this day!'

She stood looking at the table as if she stood looking at her own figure lying there. I remained quiet. Estella returned, and she too remained quiet. It seemed to me that we continued thus for a long time. In the heavy air of the room, and the heavy darkness that brooded in its remoter corners, I even had an alarming fancy that Estella and I might presently begin to decay.

At length, not coming out of her distraught state by degrees, but in an instant, Miss Havisham said, 'Let me see you two play cards; why have you not begun?' With that, we returned to her room, and sat down as before; I was beggared, as before; and again, as before, Miss Havisham watched us all the time, directed my attention to Estella's beauty, and made me notice it the more by trying her jewels on Estella's breast and hair.

Estella, for her part, likewise treated me as before, except that she did not condescend to speak. When we had played some half-dozen games, a day was appointed for my return, and I was taken down into the yard to be fed in the former dog-like manner. There, too, I was again left to wander about as I liked.

It is not much to the purpose whether a gate in that garden wall which I had scrambled up to peep over on the last occasion was, on that last occasion, open or shut. Enough that I saw no gate then, and that I saw one now. As it stood open, and as I knew that Estella had let the visitors out,—for she had returned with the keys in her hand,—I strolled into the garden, and strolled all over it. It was quite a wilderness, and there were old melon-frames and cucumber-frames in it, which seemed in their decline to have produced a spontaneous growth of weak attempts at pieces of old hats and boots, with now and then a weedy offshoot into the likeness of a battered saucepan.

When I had exhausted the garden and a greenhouse with nothing in it but a fallen-down grapevine and some bottles, I found myself in the dismal corner upon which I had looked out of the window. Never questioning for a moment that the house was now empty, I looked in at another window, and found myself, to my great surprise, exchanging a broad stare with a pale young gentleman with red eyelids and light hair.

This pale young gentleman quickly disappeared, and reappeared beside me. He had been at his books when I had found myself staring at him, and I now saw that he was inky.

'Halloa!' said he, 'young fellow!'

Halloa being a general observation which I had usually observed to be best answered by itself, *I* said, 'Halloa!' politely omitting young fellow.

'Who let *you* in?' said he.

'Miss Estella.'

'Who gave you leave to prowl about?'

'Miss Estella.'

'Come and fight,' said the pale young gentleman.

What could I do but follow him? I have often asked myself the question since; but what else could I do? His manner was so final, and I was so astonished, that I followed where he led, as if I had been under a spell.

'Stop a minute, though,' he said, wheeling round before we had gone many paces. 'I ought to give you a reason for fighting, too. There it is!' In a most irritating manner he instantly slapped his hands against one another, daintily flung one of his legs up behind him, pulled my hair, slapped his hands again, dipped his head, and butted it into my stomach.

The bull-like proceeding last mentioned, besides that it was unquestionably to be regarded in the light of a liberty, was particularly disagreeable just after bread and meat. I therefore hit out at him and was going to hit out again, when he said, 'Aha! Would you?' and began dancing backwards and forwards in a manner quite unparalleled within my limited experience.

'Laws of the game!' said he. Here, he skipped from his left leg on to his right. 'Regular rules!' Here, he skipped from his right leg on to his left. 'Come to the ground, and go through the preliminaries!' Here, he dodged backwards and forwards, and did all sorts of things while I looked helplessly at him.

I was secretly afraid of him when I saw him so dexterous; but I felt morally and physically convinced that his light head of hair could have had no business in the pit of my stomach, and that I had a right to consider it irrelevant when so obtruded on my attention. Therefore, I followed him without a word, to a retired nook of the garden, formed by the junction of two walls and screened by some rubbish. On his asking me if I was satisfied with the ground, and on my replying yes, he begged my leave to absent himself for a moment, and quickly returned with a bottle of water and a sponge dipped in vinegar. 'Available for both,' he said, placing these against the wall. And then fell to pulling off, not only his jacket and waistcoat, but his shirt too, in a manner at once light-hearted, business-like, and bloodthirsty.

Although he did not look very healthy,—having pimples on his face, and a breaking out at his mouth,—these dreadful preparations quite appalled me. I judged him to be about my own age, but he was much taller, and he had a way of spinning himself about that was full of appearance. For the rest, he was a young gentleman in a grey suit (when not denuded for battle), with his elbows, knees, wrists, and heels considerably in advance of the rest of him as to development.

My heart failed me when I saw him squaring at me with every demonstration of mechanical nicety, and eyeing my anatomy as if he were minutely choosing his bone. I never have been so surprised in my life, as I was when I let out the first blow, and saw him lying on his back, looking up at me with a bloody nose and his face exceedingly fore-shortened.

But, he was on his feet directly, and after sponging himself with a great show of dexterity began squaring again. The second greatest surprise I have ever had in my life was seeing him on his back again, looking up at me out of a black eye.

His spirit inspired me with great respect. He seemed to have no strength, and he never once hit me hard, and he was always knocked down; but he would be up again in a moment, sponging himself or drinking out of the water-bottle, with the greatest satisfaction in seconding himself according to form, and then came at me with an air and a show that made me believe he really was going to do for me at last. He got heavily bruised, for I am sorry to record that the more I hit him, the harder I hit him; but he came up again and again and again, until at last he got a bad fall with the back of his head against the wall. Even after that crisis in our affairs, he got up and turned round and round confusedly a few times, not knowing where I was; but finally went on his knees to his sponge and threw it up: at the same time panting out, 'That means you have won.'

He seemed so brave and innocent, that although I had not proposed the contest, I felt but a gloomy satisfaction in my victory. Indeed, I go so far as to hope that I regarded myself while dressing as a species of savage young wolf or other wild beast. However, I got dressed, darkly wiping my sanguinary face at intervals, and I said, 'Can I help you?' and he said 'No thankee,' and I said 'Good afternoon,' and *he* said 'Same to you.'

When I got into the courtyard, I found Estella waiting with the keys. But she neither asked me where I had been, nor why I had kept her waiting; and there was a bright flush upon her face, as though something had happened to delight her. Instead of going straight to the gate, too, she stepped back into the passage, and beckoned me.

'Come here! You may kiss me, if you like.'

I kissed her cheek as she turned it to me. I think I would have gone through a great deal to kiss her cheek. But I felt that the kiss was given to the coarse common boy as a piece of money might have been, and that it was worth nothing.

What with the birthday visitors, and what with the cards, and what with the fight, my stay had lasted so long, that when I neared home the light on the spit of sand off the point on the marshes was gleaming against a black night sky, and Joe's furnace was flinging a path of fire across the road.

Chapter 12

My mind grew very uneasy on the subject of the pale young gentleman. The more I thought of the fight, and recalled the pale young gentleman on his back in various stages of puffy and incrimsoned countenance, the more certain it appeared that something would be done to me. I felt that the pale young gentleman's blood was on my head, and that the law would avenge it. Without having any definite idea of the penalties I had incurred, it was clear to me that village boys could not go stalking about the country, ravaging the houses of gentlefolks and pitching into the studious youth of England, without laying themselves open to severe punishment. For some days, I even kept close at home, and looked out at the kitchen door with the greatest caution and trepidation before going on an errand, lest the officers of the County Jail should pounce upon me. The pale young gentleman's nose had stained my trousers, and I tried to wash out that evidence of my guilt in the dead of night. I had cut my knuckles against the pale young gentleman's teeth, and I twisted my imagination into a thousand tangles, as I devised incredible ways of accounting for that damnatory circumstance when I should be haled before the Judges.

When the day came round for my return to the scene of the deed of violence, my terrors reached their height. Whether myrmidons of justice, specially sent down from London, would be lying in ambush behind the gate;—whether Miss Havisham, preferring to take personal vengeance for an outrage done to her house, might rise in those grave-clothes of hers, draw a pistol, and shoot me dead:—whether suborned boys—a numerous band of mercenaries—might be engaged to fall upon me in the brewery, and cuff me until I was no more;—it was high testimony to my confidence in the spirit of the pale young gentleman, that I never imagined *him* accessory to these retaliations; they always came into my mind as the acts of injudicious relatives of his, goaded on by the state of his visage and an indignant sympathy with the family features.

However, go to Miss Havisham's I must, and go I did. And behold! nothing came of the late struggle. It was not alluded to in any way, and no pale young gentleman was to be discovered on the premises.

I found the same gate open, and I explored the garden, and even looked in at the windows of the detached house; but my view was suddenly stopped by the closed shutters within, and all was lifeless. Only in the corner where the combat had taken place could I detect any evidence of the young gentleman's existence. There were traces of his gore in that spot, and I covered them with garden-mould from the eye of man.

On the broad landing between Miss Havisham's own room and that other room in which the long table was laid out, I saw a garden-chair,—a light chair on wheels, that you pushed from behind. It had been placed there since my last visit, and I entered, that same day, on a regular occupation of pushing Miss Havisham in this chair (when she was tired of walking with her hand upon my shoulder) round her own room, and across the landing, and round the other room. Over and over and over again, we would make these journeys, and sometimes they would last as long as three hours at a stretch. I insensibly fall into a general mention of these journeys as numerous, because it was at once settled that I should return every alternate day at noon for these purposes, and because I am now going to sum up a period of at least eight or ten months.

As we began to be more used to one another, Miss Havisham talked more to me, and asked me such questions as what had I learnt and what was I going to be? I told her I was going to be apprenticed to Joe, I believed; and I enlarged upon my knowing nothing and wanting to know everything, in the hope that she might offer some help towards that desirable end. But she did not; on the contrary, she seemed to prefer my being ignorant. Neither did she ever give me any money,—or anything but my daily dinner,—nor ever stipulate that I should be paid for my services.

Estella was always about, and always let me in and out, but never told me I might kiss her again. Sometimes, she would coldly tolerate me; sometimes, she would condescend to me; sometimes, she would be quite familiar with me; sometimes, she would tell me energetically that she hated me. Miss Havisham would often ask me in a whisper, or when we were alone, 'Does she grow prettier and prettier, Pip?' And when I said yes (for indeed she did), would seem to enjoy it greedily. Also, when we played at cards Miss Havisham would look on, with a miserly relish of Estella's moods, whatever they were. And sometimes, when her moods were so many and so contradictory of one another that I was puzzled what to say or do, Miss Havisham would embrace her with lavish fondness, murmuring something in her ear that sounded like 'Break their hearts my pride and hope, break their hearts and have no mercy!'

There was a song Joe used to hum fragments of at the forge, of which the burden was Old Clem. This was not a very ceremonious way of rendering homage to a patron saint, but I believe Old Clem stood in that relation towards smiths. It was a song that imitated the measure of beating upon iron, and was a mere lyrical excuse for the introduction of Old Clem's respected name. Thus, you were to hammer boys round—Old Clem! With a thump and a sound—Old Clem! Beat it out, beat it out—Old Clem! With a clink for the stout—Old Clem! Blow the fire, blow the fire—Old Clem! Roaring dryer, soaring higher—Old Clem! One day soon after the appearance of the chair, Miss Havisham suddenly saying to me, with the impatient movement of her fingers, 'There, there, there! Sing!' I was surprised into crooning this ditty as I pushed her over the floor. It happened so to catch her fancy that she took it up in a low brooding voice as if she were singing in her sleep. After that, it became customary with us to have it as we moved about, and Estella would often join in; though the whole strain was so subdued, even when there were three of us, that it made less noise in the grim old house than the lightest breath of wind.

What could I become with these surroundings? How could my character fail to be influenced by them? Is it to be wondered at if my thoughts were dazed, as my eyes were, when I came out into the natural light from the misty yellow rooms?

Perhaps I might have told Joe about the pale young gentleman, if I had not previously been betrayed into those enormous inventions to which I had confessed. Under the circumstances, I felt that Joe could hardly fail to discern in the pale young gentleman, an appropriate passenger to be put into the black velvet coach; therefore, I said nothing of him. Besides, that shrinking from having Miss Havisham and Estella discussed, which had come upon me in the beginning, grew much more potent as time went on. I reposed complete confidence in no one but Biddy; but I told poor Biddy everything. Why it came natural to me to do so, and why Biddy had a deep concern in everything I told her, I did not know then, though I think I know now.

Meanwhile, councils went on in the kitchen at home, fraught with almost insupportable aggravation to my exasperated spirit. That ass, Pumblechook, used often to come over of a night for the purpose of discussing my prospects with my sister; and I really do believe (to this hour with less penitence than I ought to feel), that if these hands could have taken a linchpin out of his chaise-cart, they would have done it. The miserable man was a man of that confined stolidity of mind, that he could not discuss my prospects without having me before him,—as it were, to operate upon,—and he would drag me up from my stool (usually by the collar) where I was quiet in a corner, and, putting me before the fire as if I were going to be cooked, would begin by saying, 'Now, Mum, here is this boy! Here is this boy which you brought up by hand. Hold up your head, boy, and be forever grateful unto them which so did do. Now, Mum, with respections to this boy!' And then he would rumple my hair the wrong way,—which from my earliest remembrance, as already hinted, I have in my soul denied the right of any fellow-creature to do,—and would hold me before him by the sleeve,—a spectacle of imbecility only to be equalled by himself.

Then, he and my sister would pair off in such nonsensical speculations about Miss Havisham, and about what she would do with me and for me, that I used to want—quite painfully—to burst into spiteful tears, fly at Pumblechook, and pummel him all over. In these dialogues, my sister spoke to me as if she were morally wrenching one of my teeth out at every reference; while Pumblechook himself, self-constituted my patron, would sit supervising me with a depreciatory eye, like the architect of my fortunes who thought himself engaged on a very unremunerative job.

In these discussions, Joe bore no part. But he was often talked at, while they were in progress, by reason of Mrs Joe's perceiving that he was not favourable to my being taken from the forge. I was fully old enough now to be apprenticed to Joe; and when Joe sat with the poker on his knees thoughtfully raking out the ashes between the lower bars, my sister would so distinctly construe that innocent action into opposition on his part, that she would dive at him, take the poker out of his hands, shake him, and put it away. There was a most irritating end to every one of these debates. All in a moment, with nothing to lead up to it, my sister would stop herself in a yawn, and catching sight of me as it were incidentally, would swoop upon me with, 'Come! There's enough of *you*! *You* get along to bed; *you*'ve given trouble enough for one night, I hope!' As if I had besought them as a favour to bother my life out.

We went on in this way for a long time, and it seemed likely that we should continue to go on in this way for a long time, when one day Miss Havisham stopped short as she and I were walking, she leaning on my shoulder; and said with some displeasure,—

'You are growing tall, Pip!'

I thought it best to hint, through the medium of a meditative look, that this might be occasioned by circumstances over which I had no control.

She said no more at the time; but she presently stopped and looked at me again; and presently again; and after that, looked frowning and moody. On the next day of my attendance, when our usual exercise was over, and I had landed her at her dressing-table, she stayed me with a movement of her impatient fingers:—

'Tell me the name again of that blacksmith of yours.'

'Joe Gargery, ma'am.'

'Meaning the master you were to be apprenticed to?'

'Yes, Miss Havisham.'

'You had better be apprenticed at once. Would Gargery come here with you, and bring your indentures, do you think?'

I signified that I had no doubt he would take it as an honour to be asked.

'Then let him come.'

'At any particular time, Miss Havisham?'

'There, there! I know nothing about times. Let him come soon, and come along with you.'

When I got home at night, and delivered this message for Joe, my sister 'went on the Rampage,' in a more alarming degree than at any previous period. She asked me and Joe whether we supposed she was door-mats under our feet, and how we dared to use her so, and what company we graciously thought she *was* fit for? When she had exhausted a torrent of such inquiries, she threw a candlestick at Joe, burst into a loud sobbing, got out the dustpan,—which was always a very bad sign,—put on her coarse apron, and began cleaning up to a terrible extent. Not satisfied with a dry cleaning, she took to a pail and scrubbing-brush, and cleaned us out of house and home, so that we stood shivering in the backyard. It was ten o'clock at night before we ventured to creep in again, and then she asked Joe why he hadn't married a negress slave at once? Joe offered no answer, poor fellow, but stood feeling his whisker and looking dejectedly at me, as if he thought it really might have been a better speculation.

Chapter 13

It was a trial to my feelings, on the next day but one, to see Joe arraying himself in his Sunday clothes to accompany me to Miss Havisham's. However, as he thought his court-suit necessary to the occasion, it was not for me to tell him that he looked far better in his working-dress; the rather, because I knew he made himself so dreadfully uncomfortable, entirely on my account, and that it was for me he pulled up his shirt-collar so very high behind, that it made the hair on the crown of his head stand up like a tuft of feathers.

At breakfast time my sister declared her intention of going to town with us, and being left at Uncle Pumblechook's and called for 'when we had done with our fine ladies'—a way of putting the case, from which Joe appeared inclined to augur the worst. The forge was shut up for the day, and Joe inscribed in chalk upon the door (as it was his custom to do on the very rare occasions when he was not at work) the monosyllable HOUT, accompanied by a sketch of an arrow supposed to be flying in the direction he had taken.

We walked to town, my sister leading the way in a very large beaver bonnet, and carrying a basket like the Great Seal of England in plaited Straw, a pair of pattens, a spare shawl, and an umbrella, though it was a fine bright day. I am not quite clear whether these articles were carried penitentially or ostentatiously; but I rather think they were displayed as articles of property,—much as Cleopatra or any other sovereign lady on the Rampage might exhibit her wealth in a pageant or procession.

When we came to Pumblechook's, my sister bounced in and left us. As it was almost noon, Joe and I held straight on to Miss Havisham's house. Estella opened the gate as usual, and, the moment she appeared, Joe took his hat off and stood weighing it by the brim in both his hands; as if he had some urgent reason in his mind for being particular to half a quarter of an ounce.

Estella took no notice of either of us, but led us the way that I knew so well. I followed next to her, and Joe came last. When I looked back at Joe in the long passage, he was still weighing his hat with the greatest care, and was coming after us in long strides on the tips of his toes.

Estella told me we were both to go in, so I took Joe by the coat-cuff and conducted him into Miss Havisham's presence. She was seated at her dressing-table, and looked round at us immediately.

'Oh!' said she to Joe. 'You are the husband of the sister of this boy?'

I could hardly have imagined dear old Joe looking so unlike himself or so like some extraordinary bird; standing as he did speechless, with his tuft of feathers ruffled, and his mouth open as if he wanted a worm.

'You are the husband,' repeated Miss Havisham, 'of the sister of this boy?'

It was very aggravating; but, throughout the interview, Joe persisted in addressing me instead of Miss Havisham.

'Which I meantersay, Pip,' Joe now observed in a manner that was at once expressive of forcible argumentation, strict confidence, and great politeness, 'as I hup and married your sister, and I were at the time what you might call (if you was anyways inclined) a single man.'

'Well!' said Miss Havisham. 'And you have reared the boy, with the intention of taking him for your apprentice; is that so, Mr Gargery?'

'You know, Pip,' replied Joe, 'as you and me were ever friends, and it were looked for'ard to betwixt us, as being calc'lated to lead to larks. Not but what, Pip, if you had ever made objections to the business,—such as its being open to black and sut, or such-like,—not but what they would have been attended to, don't you see?'

'Has the boy,' said Miss Havisham, 'ever made any objection? Does he like the trade?'

'Which it is well beknown to yourself, Pip,' returned Joe, strengthening his former mixture of argumentation, confidence, and politeness, 'that it were the wish of your own hart.' (I saw the idea suddenly break upon him that he would adapt his epitaph to the occasion, before he went on to say) 'And there weren't no objection on your part, and Pip it were the great wish of your hart!'

It was quite in vain for me to endeavour to make him sensible that he ought to speak to Miss Havisham. The more I made faces and gestures to him to do it, the more confidential, argumentative, and polite, he persisted in being to me.

'Have you brought his indentures with you?' asked Miss Havisham.

'Well, Pip, you know,' replied Joe, as if that were a little unreasonable, 'you yourself see me put 'em in my 'at, and therefore you know as they are here.' With which he took them out, and gave them, not to Miss Havisham, but to me. I am afraid I was ashamed of the dear good fellow,—I *know* I was ashamed of him,—when I saw that Estella stood at the back of Miss Havisham's chair, and that her eyes laughed mischievously. I took the indentures out of his hand and gave them to Miss Havisham.

'You expected,' said Miss Havisham, as she looked them over, 'no premium with the boy?'

'Joe!' I remonstrated, for he made no reply at all. 'Why don't you answer—'

'Pip,' returned Joe, cutting me short as if he were hurt, 'which I meantersay that were not a question requiring a answer betwixt yourself and me, and which you know the answer to be full well No. You know it to be No, Pip, and wherefore should I say it?'

Miss Havisham glanced at him as if she understood what he really was better than I had thought possible, seeing what he was there; and took up a little bag from the table beside her.

'Pip has earned a premium here,' she said, 'and here it is. There are five-and-twenty guineas in this bag. Give it to your master, Pip.'

As if he were absolutely out of his mind with the wonder awakened in him by her strange figure and the strange room, Joe, even at this pass, persisted in addressing me.

'This is wery liberal on your part, Pip,' said Joe, 'and it is as such received and grateful welcome, though never looked for, far nor near, nor nowheres. And now, old chap,' said Joe, conveying to me a sensation, first of burning and then of freezing, for I felt as if that familiar expression were applied to Miss Havisham,—'and now, old chap, may we do our duty! May you and me do our duty, both on us, by one and another, and by them which your liberal present—have-conweyed—to be—for the satisfaction of mind-of—them as never—' here Joe showed that he felt he had fallen into frightful difficulties, until he triumphantly rescued himself with the words, 'and from myself far be it!' These words had such a round and convincing sound for him that he said them twice.

'Goodbye, Pip!' said Miss Havisham. 'Let them out, Estella.'

'Am I to come again, Miss Havisham?' I asked.

'No. Gargery is your master now. Gargery! One word!'

Thus calling him back as I went out of the door, I heard her say to Joe in a distinct emphatic voice, 'The boy has been a good boy here, and that is his reward. Of course, as an honest man, you will expect no other and no more.'

How Joe got out of the room, I have never been able to determine; but I know that when he did get out he was steadily proceeding upstairs instead of coming down, and was deaf to all remonstrances until I went after him and laid hold of him. In another minute we were outside the gate, and it was locked, and Estella was gone. When we stood in the daylight alone again, Joe backed up against a wall, and said to me, 'Astonishing!' And there he remained so long saying, 'Astonishing' at intervals, so often, that I began to think his senses were never coming back. At length he prolonged his remark into 'Pip, I do assure *you* this is as-TON-ishing!' and so, by degrees, became conversational and able to walk away.

I have reason to think that Joe's intellects were brightened by the encounter they had passed through, and that on our way to

Pumblechook's he invented a subtle and deep design. My reason is to be found in what took place in Mr Pumblechook's parlor: where, on our presenting ourselves, my sister sat in conference with that detested seedsman.

'Well?' cried my sister, addressing us both at once. 'And what's happened to *you*? I wonder you condescend to come back to such poor society as this, I am sure I do!'

'Miss Havisham,' said Joe, with a fixed look at me, like an effort of remembrance, 'made it wery partick'ler that we should give her—were it compliments or respects, Pip?'

'Compliments,' I said.

'Which that were my own belief,' answered Joe; 'her compliments to Mrs J. Gargery—'

'Much good they'll do me!' observed my sister; but rather gratified too.

'And wishing,' pursued Joe, with another fixed look at me, like another effort of remembrance, 'that the state of Miss Havisham's elth were sitch as would have—allowed, were it, Pip?'

'Of her having the pleasure,' I added.

'Of ladies' company,' said Joe. And drew a long breath.

'Well!' cried my sister, with a mollified glance at Mr Pumblechook. 'She might have had the politeness to send that message at first, but it's better late than never. And what did she give young Rantipole here?'

'She giv' him,' said Joe, 'nothing.'

Mrs Joe was going to break out, but Joe went on.

'What she giv',' said Joe, 'she giv' to his friends. "And by his friends," were her explanation, "I mean into the hands of his sister Mrs J. Gargery." Them were her words; "Mrs J. Gargery." She mayn't have know'd,' added Joe, with an appearance of reflection, 'whether it were Joe, or Jorge.'

My sister looked at Pumblechook: who smoothed the elbows of his wooden armchair, and nodded at her and at the fire, as if he had known all about it beforehand.

'And how much have you got?' asked my sister, laughing. Positively laughing!

'What would present company say to ten pound?' demanded Joe.

'They'd say,' returned my sister, curtly, 'pretty well. Not too much, but pretty well.'

'It's more than that, then,' said Joe.

That fearful impostor, Pumblechook, immediately nodded, and said, as he rubbed the arms of his chair, 'It's more than that, Mum.'

'Why, you don't mean to say—' began my sister.

'Yes I do, Mum,' said Pumblechook; 'but wait a bit. Go on, Joseph. Good in you! Go on!'

'What would present company say,' proceeded Joe, 'to twenty pound?'

'Handsome would be the word,' returned my sister.

'Well, then,' said Joe, 'It's more than twenty pound.'

That abject hypocrite, Pumblechook, nodded again, and said, with a patronizing laugh, 'It's more than that, Mum. Good again! Follow her up, Joseph!'

'Then to make an end of it,' said Joe, delightedly handing the bag to my sister; 'it's five-and-twenty pound.'

'It's five-and-twenty pound, Mum,' echoed that basest of swindlers, Pumblechook, rising to shake hands with her; 'and it's no more than your merits (as I said when my opinion was asked), and I wish you joy of the money!'

If the villain had stopped here, his case would have been sufficiently awful, but he blackened his guilt by proceeding to take me into custody, with a right of patronage that left all his former criminality far behind.

'Now you see, Joseph and wife,' said Pumblechook, as he took me by the arm above the elbow, 'I am one of them that always go right through with what they've begun. This boy must be bound, out of hand. That's *my* way. Bound out of hand.'

'Goodness knows, Uncle Pumblechook,' said my sister (grasping the money), 'we're deeply beholden to you.'

'Never mind me, Mum,' returned that diabolical cornchandler. 'A pleasure's a pleasure all the world over. But this boy, you know; we must have him bound. I said I'd see to it—to tell you the truth.'

The Justices were sitting in the Town Hall near at hand, and we at once went over to have me bound apprentice to Joe in the Magisterial presence. I say we went over, but I was pushed over by Pumblechook, exactly as if I had that moment picked a pocket or fired a rick; indeed, it was the general impression in Court that I had been taken red-handed; for, as Pumblechook shoved me before him through the crowd, I heard some people say, 'What's he done?' and others, 'He's a young 'un, too, but looks bad, don't he?' One person of mild and benevolent aspect even gave me a tract ornamented with a woodcut of a malevolent young man fitted up with a perfect sausage-shop of fetters, and entitled TO BE READ IN MY CELL.

The Hall was a queer place, I thought, with higher pews in it than a church,—and with people hanging over the pews looking on,—and with mighty Justices (one with a powdered head) leaning back in chairs, with folded arms, or taking snuff, or going to sleep, or writing, or reading the newspapers,—and with some shining black portraits on the walls, which my unartistic eye regarded as a composition of hardbake and sticking-plaster. Here, in a corner my indentures were duly signed and attested, and I was 'bound'; Mr Pumblechook holding me all the while as if we had looked in on our way to the scaffold, to have those little preliminaries disposed of.

When we had come out again, and had got rid of the boys who had been put into great spirits by the expectation of seeing me publicly tortured, and who were much disappointed to find that my friends were merely rallying round me, we went back to Pumblechook's. And there my sister became so excited by the twenty-five guineas, that nothing would serve her but we must have a dinner out of that windfall at the Blue Boar, and that Pumblechook must go over in his chaise-cart, and bring the Hubbles and Mr Wopsle.

It was agreed to be done; and a most melancholy day I passed. For, it inscrutably appeared to stand to reason, in the minds of the whole company, that I was an excrescence on the entertainment. And to make it worse, they all asked me from time to time,—in short, whenever they had nothing else to do,—why I didn't enjoy myself? And what could I possibly do then, but say I *was* enjoying myself,—when I wasn't!

However, they were grown up and had their own way, and they made the most of it. That swindling Pumblechook, exalted into the beneficent contriver of the whole occasion, actually took the top of the table; and, when he addressed them on the subject of my being bound, and had fiendishly congratulated them on my being liable to imprisonment if I played at cards, drank strong liquors, kept late hours or bad company, or indulged in other vagaries which the form of my indentures appeared to contemplate as next to inevitable, he placed me standing on a chair beside him to illustrate his remarks.

My only other remembrances of the great festival are, that they wouldn't let me go to sleep, but whenever they saw me dropping off, woke me up and told me to enjoy myself. That, rather late in the evening Mr Wopsle gave us Collins's ode, and threw his bloodstained sword in thunder down, with such effect, that a waiter came in and said, 'The Commercials underneath sent up their compliments, and it wasn't the Tumblers' Arms.' That, they were all in excellent spirits on the road home, and sang, "O Lady Fair!" Mr Wopsle taking the bass, and asserting with a tremendously strong voice (in reply to the inquisitive bore who leads that piece of music in a most impertinent manner, by wanting to know all about everybody's private affairs) that *he* was the man with his white locks flowing, and that he was upon the whole the weakest pilgrim going.

Finally, I remember that when I got into my little bedroom, I was truly wretched, and had a strong conviction on me that I should never like Joe's trade. I had liked it once, but once was not now.

Chapter 14

It is a most miserable thing to feel ashamed of home. There may be black ingratitude in the thing, and the punishment may be retributive and well deserved; but that it is a miserable thing, I can testify.

Home had never been a very pleasant place to me, because of my sister's temper. But, Joe had sanctified it, and I had believed in it. I had believed in the best parlor as a most elegant saloon; I had believed in the front door, as a mysterious portal of the Temple of State whose solemn opening was attended with a sacrifice of roast fowls; I had believed in the kitchen as a chaste though not magnificent apartment; I had believed in the forge as the glowing road to manhood and independence. Within a single year all this was changed. Now it was all coarse and common, and I would not have had Miss Havisham and Estella see it on any account.

How much of my ungracious condition of mind may have been my own fault, how much Miss Havisham's, how much my sister's, is now of no moment to me or to anyone. The change was made in me; the thing was done. Well or ill done, excusably or inexcusably, it was done.

Once, it had seemed to me that when I should at last roll up my shirt-sleeves and go into the forge, Joe's 'prentice, I should be distinguished and happy. Now the reality was in my hold, I only felt that I was dusty with the dust of small-coal, and that I had a weight upon my daily remembrance to which the anvil was a feather. There have been occasions in my later life (I suppose as in most lives) when I have felt for a time as if a thick curtain had fallen on all its interest and romance, to shut me out from anything save dull endurance any more. Never has that curtain dropped so heavy and blank, as when my way in life lay stretched out straight before me through the newly entered road of apprenticeship to Joe.

I remember that at a later period of my 'time,' I used to stand about the churchyard on Sunday evenings when night was falling, comparing my own perspective with the windy marsh view, and making out some likeness between them by thinking how flat and low both were, and how on both there came an unknown way and a dark mist and then the sea. I was quite as dejected on the first working-day of my apprenticeship as in that after-time; but I am glad to know that I never breathed a murmur to Joe while my indentures lasted. It is about the only thing I *am* glad to know of myself in that connection.

For, though it includes what I proceed to add, all the merit of what I proceed to add was Joe's. It was not because I was faithful, but because Joe was faithful, that I never ran away and went for a soldier or a sailor. It was not because I had a strong sense of the virtue of industry, but because Joe had a strong sense of the virtue of industry, that I worked with tolerable zeal against the grain. It is not possible to know how far the influence of any amiable honest-hearted duty-doing man flies out into the world; but it is very possible to know how it has touched one's self in going by, and I know right well that any good that intermixed itself with my apprenticeship came of plain contented Joe, and not of restlessly aspiring discontented me.

What I wanted, who can say? How can *I* say, when I never knew? What I dreaded was, that in some unlucky hour I, being at my grimiest and commonest, should lift up my eyes and see Estella looking in at one of the wooden windows of the forge. I was haunted by the fear that she would, sooner or later, find me out, with a black face and hands, doing the coarsest part of my work, and would exult over me and despise me. Often after dark, when I was pulling the bellows for Joe, and we were singing Old Clem, and when the thought how we used to sing it at Miss Havisham's would seem to show me Estella's face in the fire, with her pretty hair fluttering in the wind and her eyes scorning me,—often at such a time I would look towards those panels of black night in the wall which the wooden windows then were, and would fancy that I saw her just drawing her face away, and would believe that she had come at last.

After that, when we went in to supper, the place and the meal would have a more homely look than ever, and I would feel more ashamed of home than ever, in my own ungracious breast.

Chapter 15

As I was getting too big for Mr Wopsle's great-aunt's room, my education under that preposterous female terminated. Not, however, until Biddy had imparted to me everything she knew, from the little catalogue of prices, to a comic song she had once bought for a halfpenny. Although the only coherent part of the latter piece of literature were the opening lines,

> When I went to Lunnon town sirs,
> Too rul loo rul
> Too rul loo rul
> Wasn't I done very brown sirs?
> Too rul loo rul
> Too rul loo rul

—still, in my desire to be wiser, I got this composition by heart with the utmost gravity; nor do I recollect that I questioned its merit, except that I thought (as I still do) the amount of Too rul somewhat in excess of the poetry. In my hunger for information, I made proposals to Mr Wopsle to bestow some intellectual crumbs upon me, with which he kindly complied. As it turned out, however, that he only wanted me for a dramatic lay-figure, to be contradicted and embraced and wept over and bullied and clutched and stabbed and knocked about in a variety of ways, I soon declined that course of instruction; though not until Mr Wopsle in his poetic fury had severely mauled me.

Whatever I acquired, I tried to impart to Joe. This statement sounds so well, that I cannot in my conscience let it pass unexplained. I wanted to make Joe less ignorant and common, that he might be worthier of my society and less open to Estella's reproach.

The old Battery out on the marshes was our place of study, and a broken slate and a short piece of slate-pencil were our educational implements: to which Joe always added a pipe of tobacco. I never knew Joe to remember anything from one Sunday to another, or to acquire, under my tuition, any piece of information whatever. Yet he would smoke his pipe at the Battery with a far more sagacious air than anywhere else,—even with a learned air,—as if he considered himself to be advancing immensely. Dear fellow, I hope he did.

It was pleasant and quiet, out there with the sails on the river passing beyond the earthwork, and sometimes, when the tide was low, looking as if they belonged to sunken ships that were still sailing on at the bottom of the water. Whenever I watched the vessels standing out to sea with their white sails spread, I somehow thought of Miss Havisham and Estella; and whenever the light struck aslant, afar off, upon a cloud or sail or green hillside or water-line, it was just the same.—Miss Havisham and Estella and the strange house and the strange life appeared to have something to do with everything that was picturesque.

One Sunday when Joe, greatly enjoying his pipe, had so plumed himself on being 'most awful dull,' that I had given him up for the day, I lay on the earthwork for some time with my chin on my hand, descrying traces of Miss Havisham and Estella all over the prospect, in the sky and in the water, until at last I resolved to mention a thought concerning them that had been much in my head.

'Joe,' said I; 'don't you think I ought to make Miss Havisham a visit?'

'Well, Pip,' returned Joe, slowly considering. 'What for?'

'What for, Joe? What is any visit made for?'

'There is some wisits p'r'aps,' said Joe, 'as forever remains open to the question, Pip. But in regard to wisiting Miss Havisham. She might think you wanted something,—expected something of her.'

'Don't you think I might say that I did not, Joe?'

'You might, old chap,' said Joe. 'And she might credit it. Similarly she mightn't.'

Joe felt, as I did, that he had made a point there, and he pulled hard at his pipe to keep himself from weakening it by repetition.

'You see, Pip,' Joe pursued, as soon as he was past that danger, 'Miss Havisham done the handsome thing by you. When Miss Havisham done the handsome thing by you, she called me back to say to me as that were all.'

'Yes, Joe. I heard her.'

'ALL,' Joe repeated, very emphatically.

'Yes, Joe. I tell you, I heard her.'

'Which I meantersay, Pip, it might be that her meaning were,—Make a end on it!—As you was!—Me to the North, and you to the South!—Keep in sunders!'

I had thought of that too, and it was very far from comforting to me to find that he had thought of it; for it seemed to render it more probable.

'But, Joe.'

'Yes, old chap.'

'Here am I, getting on in the first year of my time, and, since the day of my being bound, I have never thanked Miss Havisham, or asked after her, or shown that I remember her.'

'That's true, Pip; and unless you was to turn her out a set of shoes all four round,—and which I meantersay as even a set of shoes all four round might not be acceptable as a present, in a total wacancy of hoofs—'

'I don't mean that sort of remembrance, Joe; I don't mean a present.'

But Joe had got the idea of a present in his head and must harp upon it. 'Or even,' said he, 'if you was helped to knocking her up a new chain for the front door,—or say a gross or two of sharkheaded screws for general use,—or some light fancy article, such as a toasting-fork when she took her muffins,—or a gridiron when she took a sprat or such like—'

'I don't mean any present at all, Joe,' I interposed.

'Well,' said Joe, still harping on it as though I had particularly pressed it, 'if I was yourself, Pip, I wouldn't. No, I would *not*. For what's a door-chain when she's got one always up? And shark-headers is open to misrepresentations. And if it was a toasting-fork, you'd go into brass and do yourself no credit. And the oncommonest workman can't show himself oncommon in a gridiron,—for a gridiron IS a gridiron,' said Joe, steadfastly impressing it upon me, as if he were endeavouring to rouse me from a fixed delusion, 'and you may haim at what you like, but a gridiron it will come out, either by your leave or again your leave, and you can't help yourself—'

'My dear Joe,' I cried, in desperation, taking hold of his coat, 'don't go on in that way. I never thought of making Miss Havisham any present.'

'No, Pip,' Joe assented, as if he had been contending for that, all along; 'and what I say to you is, you are right, Pip.'

'Yes, Joe; but what I wanted to say, was, that as we are rather slack just now, if you would give me a half-holiday tomorrow, I think I would go uptown and make a call on Miss Est—Havisham.'

'Which her name,' said Joe, gravely, 'ain't Estavisham, Pip, unless she have been rechris'ened.'

'I know, Joe, I know. It was a slip of mine. What do you think of it, Joe?'

In brief, Joe thought that if I thought well of it, he thought well of it. But, he was particular in stipulating that if I were not received with cordiality, or if I were not encouraged to repeat my visit as a visit which had no ulterior object but was simply one of gratitude for a favour received, then this experimental trip should have no successor. By these conditions I promised to abide.

Now, Joe kept a journeyman at weekly wages whose name was

Orlick. He pretended that his Christian name was Dolge,—a clear impossibility,—but he was a fellow of that obstinate disposition that I believe him to have been the prey of no delusion in this particular, but wilfully to have imposed that name upon the village as an affront to its understanding. He was a broadshouldered loose-limbed swarthy fellow of great strength, never in a hurry, and always slouching. He never even seemed to come to his work on purpose, but would slouch in as if by mere accident; and when he went to the Jolly Bargemen to eat his dinner, or went away at night, he would slouch out, like Cain or the Wandering Jew, as if he had no idea where he was going and no intention of ever coming back. He lodged at a sluice-keeper's out on the marshes, and on working-days would come slouching from his hermitage, with his hands in his pockets and his dinner loosely tied in a bundle round his neck and dangling on his back. On Sundays he mostly lay all day on the sluice-gates, or stood against ricks and barns. He always slouched, locomotively, with his eyes on the ground; and, when accosted or otherwise required to raise them, he looked up in a half-resentful, half-puzzled way, as though the only thought he ever had was, that it was rather an odd and injurious fact that he should never be thinking.

This morose journeyman had no liking for me. When I was very small and timid, he gave me to understand that the Devil lived in a black corner of the forge, and that he knew the fiend very well: also that it was necessary to make up the fire, once in seven years, with a live boy, and that I might consider myself fuel. When I became Joe's 'prentice, Orlick was perhaps confirmed in some suspicion that I should displace him; howbeit, he liked me still less. Not that he ever said anything, or did anything, openly importing hostility; I only noticed that he always beat his sparks in my direction, and that whenever I sang Old Clem, he came in out of time.

Dolge Orlick was at work and present, next day, when I reminded Joe of my half-holiday. He said nothing at the moment, for he and Joe had just got a piece of hot iron between them, and I was at the bellows; but by and by he said, leaning on his hammer,—

'Now, master! Sure you're not a going to favour only one of us. If Young Pip has a half-holiday, do as much for Old Orlick.' I suppose he was about five-and-twenty, but he usually spoke of himself as an ancient person.

'Why, what'll you do with a half-holiday, if you get it?' said Joe.

'What'll *I* do with it! What'll *he* do with it? I'll do as much with it as *him*,' said Orlick.

'As to Pip, he's going up town,' said Joe.

'Well then, as to Old Orlick, *he*'s a going up town,' retorted that worthy. 'Two can go up town. Tain't only one wot can go up town.'

'Don't lose your temper,' said Joe.

'Shall if I like,' growled Orlick. 'Some and their uptowning! Now, master! Come. No favouring in this shop. Be a man!'

The master refusing to entertain the subject until the journeyman was in a better temper, Orlick plunged at the furnace, drew out a red-hot bar, made at me with it as if he were going to run it through my body, whisked it round my head, laid it on the anvil, hammered it out,—as if it were I, I thought, and the sparks were my spirting blood,—and finally said, when he had hammered himself hot and the iron cold, and he again leaned on his hammer,—

'Now, master!'

'Are you all right now?' demanded Joe.

'Ah! I am all right,' said gruff Old Orlick.

'Then, as in general you stick to your work as well as most men,' said Joe, 'let it be a half-holiday for all.'

My sister had been standing silent in the yard, within hearing,—she was a most unscrupulous spy and listener,—and she instantly looked in at one of the windows.

'Like you, you fool!' said she to Joe, 'giving holidays to great idle hulkers like that. You are a rich man, upon my life, to waste wages in that way. I wish *I* was his master!'

'You'd be everybody's master, if you durst,' retorted Orlick, with an ill-favoured grin.

('Let her alone,' said Joe.)

'I'd be a match for all noodles and all rogues,' returned my sister, beginning to work herself into a mighty rage. 'And I couldn't be a match for the noodles, without being a match for your master, who's the dunder-headed king of the noodles. And I couldn't be a match for the rogues, without being a match for you, who are the blackest-looking and the worst rogue between this and France. Now!'

'You're a foul shrew, Mother Gargery,' growled the journeyman. 'If that makes a judge of rogues, you ought to be a good'un.'

('Let her alone, will you?' said Joe.)

'What did you say?' cried my sister, beginning to scream. 'What did you say? What did that fellow Orlick say to me, Pip? What did he call me, with my husband standing by? Oh! Oh! Oh!' Each of these exclamations was a shriek; and I must remark of my sister, what is equally true of all the violent women I have ever seen, that passion was no excuse for her, because it is undeniable that instead of lapsing into passion, she consciously and deliberately took extraordinary pains to force herself into it, and became blindly furious by regular stages; 'what was the name he gave me before the base man who swore to defend me? Oh! Hold me! Oh!'

'Ah-h-h!' growled the journeyman, between his teeth, 'I'd hold you, if you was my wife. I'd hold you under the pump, and choke it out of you.'

('I tell you, let her alone,' said Joe.)

'Oh! To hear him!' cried my sister, with a clap of her hands and a scream together,—which was her next stage. 'To hear the names he's giving me! That Orlick! In my own house! Me, a married woman! With my husband standing by! Oh! Oh!' Here my sister, after a fit of clappings and screamings, beat her hands upon her bosom and upon her knees, and threw her cap off, and pulled her hair down,—which were the last stages on her road to frenzy. Being by this time a perfect Fury and a complete success, she made a dash at the door which I had fortunately locked.

What could the wretched Joe do now, after his disregarded parenthetical interruptions, but stand up to his journeyman, and ask him what he meant by interfering betwixt himself and Mrs Joe; and further whether he was man enough to come on? Old Orlick felt that the situation admitted of nothing less than coming on, and was on his defence straightway; so, without so much as pulling off their singed and burnt aprons, they went at one another, like two giants. But, if any man in that neighbourhood could stand uplong against Joe, I never saw the man. Orlick, as if he had been of no more account than the pale young gentleman, was very soon among the coal-dust, and in no hurry to come out of it. Then Joe unlocked the door and picked up my sister, who had dropped insensible at the window (but who had seen the fight first, I think), and who was carried into the house and laid down, and who was recommended to revive, and would do nothing but struggle and clench her hands in Joe's hair. Then, came that singular calm and silence which succeed all uproars; and then, with the vague sensation which I have always connected with such a lull,—namely, that it was Sunday, and somebody was dead,—I went upstairs to dress myself.

When I came down again, I found Joe and Orlick sweeping up, without any other traces of discomposure than a slit in one of Orlick's nostrils, which was neither expressive nor ornamental. A pot of beer had appeared from the Jolly Bargemen, and they were sharing it by turns in a peaceable manner. The lull had a sedative and philosophical influence on Joe, who followed me out into the road to say, as a parting observation that might do me good, 'On the Rampage, Pip, and off the Rampage, Pip:—such is life!'

With what absurd emotions (for we think the feelings that are very serious in a man quite comical in a boy) I found myself again going to Miss Havisham's, matters little here. Nor, how I passed and repassed the gate many times before I could make up my mind to ring. Nor, how I debated whether I should go away without ringing; nor, how I should undoubtedly have gone, if my time had been my own, to come back.

Miss Sarah Pocket came to the gate. No Estella.

'How, then? You here again?' said Miss Pocket. 'What do you want?'

When I said that I only came to see how Miss Havisham was, Sarah evidently deliberated whether or no she should send me about my business. But unwilling to hazard the responsibility, she let me in, and presently brought the sharp message that I was to 'come up.'

Everything was unchanged, and Miss Havisham was alone.

'Well?' said she, fixing her eyes upon me. 'I hope you want nothing? You'll get nothing.'

'No indeed, Miss Havisham. I only wanted you to know that

I am doing very well in my apprenticeship, and am always much obliged to you.'

'There, there!' with the old restless fingers. 'Come now and then; come on your birthday.—Ay!' she cried suddenly, turning herself and her chair towards me, 'You are looking round for Estella? Hey?'

I had been looking round,—in fact, for Estella,—and I stammered that I hoped she was well.

'Abroad,' said Miss Havisham; 'educating for a lady; far out of reach; prettier than ever; admired by all who see her. Do you feel that you have lost her?'

There was such a malignant enjoyment in her utterance of the last words, and she broke into such a disagreeable laugh, that I was at a loss what to say. She spared me the trouble of considering, by dismissing me. When the gate was closed upon me by Sarah of the walnut-shell countenance, I felt more than ever dissatisfied with my home and with my trade and with everything; and that was all I took by *that* motion.

As I was loitering along the High Street, looking in disconsolately at the shop windows, and thinking what I would buy if I were a gentleman, who should come out of the bookshop but Mr Wopsle. Mr Wopsle had in his hand the affecting tragedy of George Barnwell, in which he had that moment invested sixpence, with the view of heaping every word of it on the head of Pumblechook, with whom he was going to drink tea. No sooner did he see me, than he appeared to consider that a special Providence had put a 'prentice in his way to be read at; and he laid hold of me, and insisted on my accompanying him to the Pumblechookian parlor. As I knew it would be miserable at home, and as the nights were dark and the way was dreary, and almost any companionship on the road was better than none, I made no great resistance; consequently, we turned into Pumblechook's just as the street and the shops were lighting up.

As I never assisted at any other representation of George Barnwell, I don't know how long it may usually take; but I know very well that it took until half-past nine o' clock that night, and that when Mr Wopsle got into Newgate, I thought he never would go to the scaffold, he became so much slower than at any former period of his disgraceful career. I thought it a little too much that he should complain of being cut short in his flower after all, as if he had not been running to seed, leaf after leaf, ever since his course began. This, however, was a mere question of length and wearisomeness. What stung me, was the identification of the whole affair with my unoffending self. When Barnwell began to go wrong, I declare that I felt positively apologetic, Pumblechook's indignant stare so taxed me with it. Wopsle, too, took pains to present me in the worst light. At once ferocious and maudlin, I was made to murder my uncle with no extenuating circumstances whatever; Millwood put me down in argument, on every occasion; it became sheer monomania in my master's daughter to care a button for me; and all I can say for my gasping and procrastinating conduct on the fatal morning, is, that it was worthy of the general feebleness of my character. Even after I was happily hanged and Wopsle had closed the book, Pumblechook sat staring at me, and shaking his head, and saying, 'Take warning, boy, take warning!' as if it were a well known fact that I contemplated murdering a near relation, provided I could only induce one to have the weakness to become my benefactor.

It was a very dark night when it was all over, and when I set out with Mr Wopsle on the walk home. Beyond town, we found a heavy mist out, and it fell wet and thick. The turnpike lamp was a blur, quite out of the lamp's usual place apparently, and its rays looked solid substance on the fog. We were noticing this, and saying how that the mist rose with a change of wind from a certain quarter of our marshes, when we came upon a man, slouching under the lee of the turnpike house.

'Halloa!' we said, stopping. 'Orlick there?'

'Ah!' he answered, slouching out. 'I was standing by a minute, on the chance of company.'

'You are late,' I remarked.

Orlick not unnaturally answered, 'Well? And *you*'re late.'

'We have been,' said Mr Wopsle, exalted with his late performance,—'we have been indulging, Mr Orlick, in an intellectual evening.'

Old Orlick growled, as if he had nothing to say about that, and we all went on together. I asked him presently whether he had been spending his half-holiday up and down town?

'Yes,' said he, 'all of it. I come in behind yourself. I didn't see you, but I must have been pretty close behind you. By the by, the guns is going again.'

'At the Hulks?' said I.

'Ay! There's some of the birds flown from the cages. The guns have been going since dark, about. You'll hear one presently.'

In effect, we had not walked many yards further, when the well-remembered boom came towards us, deadened by the mist, and heavily rolled away along the low grounds by the river, as if it were pursuing and threatening the fugitives.

'A good night for cutting off in,' said Orlick. 'We'd be puzzled how to bring down a jail-bird on the wing, tonight.'

The subject was a suggestive one to me, and I thought about it in silence. Mr Wopsle, as the ill-requited uncle of the evening's tragedy, fell to meditating aloud in his garden at Camberwell. Orlick, with his hands in his pockets, slouched heavily at my side. It was very dark, very wet, very muddy, and so we splashed along. Now and then, the sound of the signal cannon broke upon us again, and again rolled sulkily along the course of the river. I kept myself to myself and my thoughts. Mr Wopsle died amiably at Camberwell, and exceedingly game on Bosworth Field, and in the greatest agonies at Glastonbury. Orlick sometimes growled, 'Beat it out, beat it out,—Old Clem! With a clink for the stout,—Old Clem!' I thought he had been drinking, but he was not drunk.

Thus, we came to the village. The way by which we approached it took us past the Three Jolly Bargemen, which we were surprised to find—it being eleven o'clock—in a state of commotion, with the door wide open, and unwonted lights that had been hastily caught up and put down scattered about. Mr Wopsle dropped in to ask what was the matter (surmising that a convict had been taken), but came running out in a great hurry.

'There's something wrong,' said he, without stopping, 'up at your place, Pip. Run all!'

'What is it?' I asked, keeping up with him. So did Orlick, at my side.

'I can't quite understand. The house seems to have been violently entered when Joe Gargery was out. Supposed by convicts. Somebody has been attacked and hurt.'

We were running too fast to admit of more being said, and we made no stop until we got into our kitchen. It was full of people; the whole village was there, or in the yard; and there was a surgeon, and there was Joe, and there were a group of women, all on the floor in the midst of the kitchen. The unemployed bystanders drew back when they saw me, and so I became aware of my sister,—lying without sense or movement on the bare boards where she had been knocked down by a tremendous blow on the back of the head, dealt by some unknown hand when her face was turned towards the fire,—destined never to be on the Rampage again, while she was the wife of Joe.

Chapter 16

With my head full of George Barnwell, I was at first disposed to believe that *I* must have had some hand in the attack upon my sister, or at all events that as her near relation, popularly known to be under obligations to her, I was a more legitimate object of suspicion than anyone else. But when, in the clearer light of next morning, I began to reconsider the matter and to hear it discussed around me on all sides, I took another view of the case, which was more reasonable.

Joe had been at the Three Jolly Bargemen, smoking his pipe, from a quarter after eight o'clock to a quarter before ten. While he was there, my sister had been seen standing at the kitchen door, and had exchanged Goodnight with a farm-labourer going home. The man could not be more particular as to the time at which he saw her (he got into dense confusion when he tried to be), than that it must have been before nine. When Joe went home at five minutes before ten, he found her struck down on the floor, and promptly called in assistance. The fire had not then burnt unusually low, nor was the snuff of the candle very long; the candle, however, had been blown out.

Nothing had been taken away from any part of the house. Neither, beyond the blowing out of the candle,—which stood on a table between the door and my sister, and was behind her when she stood facing the fire and was struck,—was there any disarrangement of the kitchen, excepting such as she herself had made, in falling and bleeding. But, there was one remarkable piece of evidence on the spot. She had been struck with something blunt and heavy, on the head and spine; after the blows were dealt, something heavy had been thrown down at her with considerable violence, as she lay on her face. And on the ground beside her, when Joe picked her up, was a convict's leg-iron which had been filed asunder.

Now, Joe, examining this iron with a smith's eye, declared it to have been filed asunder some time ago. The hue and cry going off to the Hulks, and people coming thence to examine the iron, Joe's opinion was corroborated. They did not undertake to say when it had left the prison-ships to which it undoubtedly had once belonged; but they claimed to know for certain that that particular manacle had not been worn by either of the two convicts who had escaped last night. Further, one of those two was already retaken, and had not freed himself of his iron.

Knowing what I knew, I set up an inference of my own here. I believed the iron to be my convict's iron,—the iron I had seen and heard him filing at, on the marshes,—but my mind did not accuse him of having put it to its latest use. For I believed one of two other persons to have become possessed of it, and to have turned it to this cruel account. Either Orlick, or the strange man who had shown me the file.

Now, as to Orlick; he had gone to town exactly as he told us when we picked him up at the turnpike, he had been seen about town all the evening, he had been in divers companies in several public-houses, and he had come back with myself and Mr Wopsle. There was nothing against him, save the quarrel; and my sister had quarrelled with him, and with everybody else about her, ten thousand times. As to the strange man; if he had come back for his two bank-notes there could have been no dispute about them, because my sister was fully prepared to restore them. Besides, there had been no altercation; the assailant had come in so silently and suddenly, that she had been felled before she could look round.

It was horrible to think that I had provided the weapon, however undesignedly, but I could hardly think otherwise. I suffered unspeakable trouble while I considered and reconsidered whether I should at last dissolve that spell of my childhood and tell Joe all the story. For months afterwards, I every day settled the question finally in the negative, and reopened and reargued it next morning. The contention came, after all, to this;—the secret was such an old one now, had so grown into me and become a part of myself, that I could not tear it away. In addition to the dread that, having led up to so much mischief, it would be now more likely than ever to alienate Joe from me if he believed it, I had a further restraining dread that he would not believe it, but would assort it with the fabulous dogs and veal-cutlets as a monstrous invention. However, I temporized with myself, of course—for, was I not wavering between right and wrong, when the thing is always done?—and resolved to make a full disclosure if I should see any such new occasion as a new chance of helping in the discovery of the assailant.

The constables and the Bow Street men from London—for, this happened in the days of the extinct red-waistcoated police—were about the house for a week or two, and did pretty much what I have heard and read of like authorities doing in other such cases. They took up several obviously wrong people, and they ran their heads very hard against wrong ideas, and persisted in trying to fit the circumstances to the ideas, instead of trying to extract ideas from the circumstances. Also, they stood about the door of the Jolly Bargemen, with knowing and reserved looks that filled the whole neighbourhood with admiration; and they had a mysterious manner of taking their drink, that was almost as good as taking the culprit. But not quite, for they never did it.

Long after these constitutional powers had dispersed, my sister lay very ill in bed. Her sight was disturbed, so that she saw objects multiplied, and grasped at visionary teacups and wineglasses instead of the realities; her hearing was greatly impaired; her memory also; and her speech was unintelligible. When, at last, she came round so far as to be helped downstairs, it was still necessary to keep my slate always by her, that she might indicate in writing what she could not indicate in speech. As she was (very bad handwriting apart) a more than indifferent speller, and as Joe was a more than indifferent reader, extraordinary complications arose between them which I was always called in to solve. The administration of mutton instead of medicine, the substitution of Tea for Joe, and the baker for bacon, were among the mildest of my own mistakes.

However, her temper was greatly improved, and she was patient. A tremulous uncertainty of the action of all her limbs soon became a part of her regular state, and afterwards, at intervals of two or three months, she would often put her hands to her head, and would then remain for about a week at a time in some gloomy aberration of mind. We were at a loss to find a suitable attendant for her, until a circumstance happened conveniently to relieve us. Mr Wopsle's great-aunt conquered a confirmed habit of living into which she had fallen, and Biddy became a part of our establishment.

It may have been about a month after my sister's reappearance in the kitchen, when Biddy came to us with a small speckled box containing the whole of her worldly effects, and became a blessing to the household. Above all, she was a blessing to Joe, for the dear old fellow was sadly cut up by the constant contemplation of the wreck of his wife, and had been accustomed, while attending on her of an evening, to turn to me every now and then and say, with his blue eyes moistened, 'Such a fine figure of a woman as she once were, Pip!' Biddy instantly taking the cleverest charge of her as though she had studied her from infancy; Joe became able in some sort to appreciate the greater quiet of his life, and to get down to the Jolly Bargemen now and then for a change that did him good. It was characteristic of the police people that they had all more or less suspected poor Joe (though he never knew it), and that they had to a man concurred in regarding him as one of the deepest spirits they had ever encountered.

Biddy's first triumph in her new office, was to solve a difficulty that had completely vanquished me. I had tried hard at it, but had made nothing of it. Thus it was:—

Again and again and again, my sister had traced upon the slate, a character that looked like a curious T, and then with the utmost eagerness had called our attention to it as something she particularly wanted. I had in vain tried everything producible that began with a T, from tar to toast and tub. At length it had come into my head that the sign looked like a hammer, and on my lustily calling that word in my sister's ear, she had begun to hammer on the table and had expressed a qualified assent. Thereupon, I had brought in all our hammers, one after another, but without avail. Then I bethought me of a crutch, the shape being much the same, and I borrowed one in the village, and displayed it to my sister with considerable confidence. But she shook her head to that extent when she was shown it, that we were terrified lest in her weak and shattered state she should dislocate her neck.

When my sister found that Biddy was very quick to understand her, this mysterious sign reappeared on the slate. Biddy looked thoughtfully at it, heard my explanation, looked thoughtfully at my sister, looked thoughtfully at Joe (who was always represented on the slate by his initial letter), and ran into the forge, followed by Joe and me.

'Why, of course!' cried Biddy, with an exultant face. 'Don't you see? It's *him*!'

Orlick, without a doubt! She had lost his name, and could only signify him by his hammer. We told him why we wanted him to come into the kitchen, and he slowly laid down his hammer, wiped his brow with his arm, took another wipe at it with his apron, and came slouching out, with a curious loose vagabond bend in the knees that strongly distinguished him.

I confess that I expected to see my sister denounce him, and that I was disappointed by the different result. She manifested the greatest anxiety to be on good terms with him, was evidently much pleased by his being at length produced, and motioned that she would have him given something to drink. She watched his countenance as if she were particularly wishful to be assured that he took kindly to his reception, she showed every possible desire to conciliate him, and there was an air of humble propitiation in all she did, such as I have seen pervade the bearing of a child towards a hard master. After that day, a day rarely passed without her drawing the hammer on her slate, and without Orlick's slouching in and standing doggedly before her, as if he knew no more than I did what to make of it.

Chapter 17

I now fell into a regular routine of apprenticeship life, which was varied beyond the limits of the village and the marshes, by no more remarkable circumstance than the arrival of my birthday and my paying another visit to Miss Havisham. I found Miss Sarah Pocket still on duty at the gate; I found Miss Havisham just as I had left her, and she spoke of Estella in the very same way, if not in the very same words. The interview lasted but a few minutes, and she gave me a guinea when I was going, and told me to come again on my next birthday. I may mention at once that this became an annual custom. I tried to decline taking the guinea on the first occasion, but with no better effect than causing her to ask me very angrily, if I expected more? Then, and after that, I took it.

So unchanging was the dull old house, the yellow light in the darkened room, the faded spectre in the chair by the dressing-table glass, that I felt as if the stopping of the clocks had stopped time in that mysterious place, and, while I and everything else outside it grew older, it stood still. Daylight never entered the house as to my thoughts and remembrances of it, any more than as to the actual fact. It bewildered me, and under its influence I continued at heart to hate my trade and to be ashamed of home.

Imperceptibly I became conscious of a change in Biddy, however. Her shoes came up at the heel, her hair grew bright and neat, her hands were always clean. She was not beautiful,—she was common, and could not be like Estella,—but she was pleasant and wholesome and sweet-tempered. She had not been with us more than a year (I remember her being newly out of mourning at the time it struck me), when I observed to myself one evening that she had curiously thoughtful and attentive eyes; eyes that were very pretty and very good.

It came of my lifting up my own eyes from a task I was poring at—writing some passages from a book, to improve myself in two ways at once by a sort of stratagem—and seeing Biddy observant of what I was about. I laid down my pen, and Biddy stopped in her needlework without laying it down.

'Biddy,' said I, 'how do you manage it? Either I am very stupid, or you are very clever.'

'What is it that I manage? I don't know,' returned Biddy, smiling.

She managed our whole domestic life, and wonderfully too; but I did not mean that, though that made what I did mean more surprising.

'How do you manage, Biddy,' said I, 'to learn everything that I learn, and always to keep up with me?' I was beginning to be rather vain of my knowledge, for I spent my birthday guineas on it, and set aside the greater part of my pocket money for similar investment; though I have no doubt, now, that the little I knew was extremely dear at the price.

'I might as well ask you,' said Biddy, 'how *you* manage?'

'No; because when I come in from the forge of a night, anyone can see me turning to at it. But you never turn to at it, Biddy.'

'I suppose I must catch it like a cough,' said Biddy, quietly; and went on with her sewing.

Pursuing my idea as I leaned back in my wooden chair, and looked at Biddy sewing away with her head on one side, I began to think her rather an extraordinary girl. For I called to mind now, that she was equally accomplished in the terms of our trade, and the names of our different sorts of work, and our various tools. In short, whatever I knew, Biddy knew. Theoretically, she was already as good a blacksmith as I, or better.

'You are one of those, Biddy,' said I, 'who make the most of every chance. You never had a chance before you came here, and see how improved you are!'

Biddy looked at me for an instant, and went on with her sewing. 'I was your first teacher though; wasn't I?' said she, as she sewed.

'Biddy!' I exclaimed, in amazement. 'Why, you are crying!'

'No I am not,' said Biddy, looking up and laughing. 'What put that in your head?'

What could have put it in my head but the glistening of a tear as it dropped on her work? I sat silent, recalling what a drudge she had been until Mr Wopsle's great-aunt successfully overcame that bad habit of living, so highly desirable to be got rid of by some people. I recalled the hopeless circumstances by which she had been surrounded in the miserable little shop and the miserable little noisy evening school, with that miserable old bundle of incompetence always to be dragged and shouldered. I reflected that even in those untoward times there must have been latent in Biddy what was now developing, for, in my first uneasiness and discontent I had turned to her for help, as a matter of course. Biddy sat quietly sewing, shedding no more tears, and while I looked at her and thought about it all, it occurred to me that perhaps I had not been sufficiently grateful to Biddy. I might have been too reserved, and should have patronized her more (though I did not use that precise word in my meditations) with my confidence.

'Yes, Biddy,' I observed, when I had done turning it over, 'you were my first teacher, and that at a time when we little thought of ever being together like this, in this kitchen.'

'Ah, poor thing!' replied Biddy. It was like her self-forgetfulness to transfer the remark to my sister, and to get up and be busy about her, making her more comfortable; 'that's sadly true!'

'Well!' said I, 'we must talk together a little more, as we used to do. And I must consult you a little more, as I used to do. Let us have a quiet walk on the marshes next Sunday, Biddy, and a long chat.'

My sister was never left alone now; but Joe more than readily undertook the care of her on that Sunday afternoon, and Biddy and I went out together. It was summer time, and lovely weather. When we had passed the village and the church and the churchyard, and were out on the marshes and began to see the sails of the ships as they sailed on, I began to combine Miss Havisham and Estella with the prospect, in my usual way. When we came to the riverside and sat down on the bank, with the water rippling at our feet, making it all more quiet than it would have been without that sound, I resolved that it was a good time and place for the admission of Biddy into my inner confidence.

'Biddy,' said I, after binding her to secrecy, 'I want to be a gentleman.'

'O, I wouldn't, if I was you!' she returned. 'I don't think it would answer.'

'Biddy,' said I, with some severity, 'I have particular reasons for wanting to be a gentleman.'

'You know best, Pip; but don't you think you are happier as you are?'

'Biddy,' I exclaimed, impatiently, 'I am not at all happy as I am. I am disgusted with my calling and with my life. I have never taken to either, since I was bound. Don't be absurd.'

'Was I absurd?' said Biddy, quietly raising her eyebrows; 'I am sorry for that; I didn't mean to be. I only want you to do well, and to be comfortable.'

'Well, then, understand once for all that I never shall or can be comfortable—or anything but miserable—there, Biddy!—unless I can lead a very different sort of life from the life I lead now.'

'That's a pity!' said Biddy, shaking her head with a sorrowful air.

Now, I too had so often thought it a pity, that, in the singular kind of quarrel with myself which I was always carrying on, I was half inclined to shed tears of vexation and distress when Biddy gave utterance to her sentiment and my own. I told her she was right, and I knew it was much to be regretted, but still it was not to be helped.

'If I could have settled down,' I said to Biddy, plucking up the short grass within reach, much as I had once upon a time pulled my feelings out of my hair and kicked them into the brewery wall,—'if I could have settled down and been but half as fond of the forge as I was when I was little, I know it would have been much better for me. You and I and Joe would have wanted nothing then, and Joe and I would perhaps have gone partners when I was out of my time, and I might even have grown up to keep company with you, and we might have sat on this very bank on a fine Sunday, quite different people. I should have been good enough for *you*; shouldn't I, Biddy?'

Biddy sighed as she looked at the ships sailing on, and returned for answer, 'Yes; I am not over-particular.' It scarcely sounded flattering, but I knew she meant well.

'Instead of that,' said I, plucking up more grass and chewing a blade or two, 'see how I am going on. Dissatisfied, and uncomfortable, and—what would it signify to me, being coarse and common, if nobody had told me so!'

Biddy turned her face suddenly towards mine, and looked far more attentively at me than she had looked at the sailing ships.

'It was neither a very true nor a very polite thing to say,' she remarked, directing her eyes to the ships again. 'Who said it?'

I was disconcerted, for I had broken away without quite seeing where I was going to. It was not to be shuffled off now, however, and I answered, 'The beautiful young lady at Miss Havisham's, and she's more beautiful than anybody ever was, and I admire her dreadfully, and I want to be a gentleman on her account.' Having made this lunatic confession, I began to throw my torn-up grass into the river, as if I had some thoughts of following it.

'Do you want to be a gentleman, to spite her or to gain her over?' Biddy quietly asked me, after a pause.

'I don't know,' I moodily answered.

'Because, if it is to spite her,' Biddy pursued, 'I should think—but you know best—that might be better and more independently done by caring nothing for her words. And if it is to gain her over, I should think—but you know best—she was not worth gaining over.'

Exactly what I myself had thought, many times. Exactly what was perfectly manifest to me at the moment. But how could I, a poor dazed village lad, avoid that wonderful inconsistency into which the best and wisest of men fall every day?

'It may be all quite true,' said I to Biddy, 'but I admire her dreadfully.'

In short, I turned over on my face when I came to that, and got a good grasp on the hair on each side of my head, and wrenched it well. All the while knowing the madness of my heart to be so very mad and misplaced, that I was quite conscious it would have served my face right, if I had lifted it up by my hair, and knocked it against the pebbles as a punishment for belonging to such an idiot.

Biddy was the wisest of girls, and she tried to reason no more with me. She put her hand, which was a comfortable hand though roughened by work, upon my hands, one after another, and gently took them out of my hair. Then she softly patted my shoulder in a soothing way, while with my face upon my sleeve I cried a little,—exactly as I had done in the brewery yard,—and felt vaguely convinced that I was very much ill-used by somebody, or by everybody; I can't say which.

'I am glad of one thing,' said Biddy, 'and that is, that you have felt you could give me your confidence, Pip. And I am glad of another thing, and that is, that of course you know you may depend upon my keeping it and always so far deserving it. If your first teacher (dear!

such a poor one, and so much in need of being taught herself!) had been your teacher at the present time, she thinks she knows what lesson she would set. But it would be a hard one to learn, and you have got beyond her, and it's of no use now.' So, with a quiet sigh for me, Biddy rose from the bank, and said, with a fresh and pleasant change of voice, 'Shall we walk a little farther, or go home?'

'Biddy,' I cried, getting up, putting my arm round her neck, and giving her a kiss, 'I shall always tell you everything.'

'Till you're a gentleman,' said Biddy.

'You know I never shall be, so that's always. Not that I have any occasion to tell you anything, for you know everything I know,—as I told you at home the other night.'

'Ah!' said Biddy, quite in a whisper, as she looked away at the ships. And then repeated, with her former pleasant change, 'shall we walk a little farther, or go home?'

I said to Biddy we would walk a little farther, and we did so, and the summer afternoon toned down into the summer evening, and it was very beautiful. I began to consider whether I was not more naturally and wholesomely situated, after all, in these circumstances, than playing beggar my neighbour by candle-light in the room with the stopped clocks, and being despised by Estella. I thought it would be very good for me if I could get her out of my head, with all the rest of those remembrances and fancies, and could go to work determined to relish what I had to do, and stick to it, and make the best of it. I asked myself the question whether I did not surely know that if Estella were beside me at that moment instead of Biddy, she would make me miserable? I was obliged to admit that I did know it for a certainty, and I said to myself, 'Pip, what a fool you are!'

We talked a good deal as we walked, and all that Biddy said seemed right. Biddy was never insulting, or capricious, or Biddy today and somebody else tomorrow; she would have derived only pain, and no pleasure, from giving me pain; she would far rather have wounded her own breast than mine. How could it be, then, that I did not like her much the better of the two?

'Biddy,' said I, when we were walking homewards, 'I wish you could put me right.'

'I wish I could!' said Biddy.

'If I could only get myself to fall in love with you,—you don't mind my speaking so openly to such an old acquaintance?'

'Oh dear, not at all!' said Biddy. 'Don't mind me.'

'If I could only get myself to do it, *that* would be the thing for me.'

'But you never will, you see,' said Biddy.

It did not appear quite so unlikely to me that evening, as it would have done if we had discussed it a few hours before. I therefore observed I was not quite sure of that. But Biddy said she *was*, and she said it decisively. In my heart I believed her to be right; and yet I took it rather ill, too, that she should be so positive on the point.

When we came near the churchyard, we had to cross an embankment, and get over a stile near a sluice-gate. There started up, from the gate, or from the rushes, or from the ooze (which was quite in his stagnant way), Old Orlick.

'Halloa!' he growled, 'where are you two going?'

'Where should we be going, but home?'

'Well, then,' said he, 'I'm jiggered if I don't see you home!'

This penalty of being jiggered was a favourite supposititious case of his. He attached no definite meaning to the word that I am aware of, but used it, like his own pretended Christian name, to affront mankind, and convey an idea of something savagely damaging. When I was younger, I had had a general belief that if he had jiggered me personally, he would have done it with a sharp and twisted hook.

Biddy was much against his going with us, and said to me in a whisper, 'Don't let him come; I don't like him.' As I did not like him either, I took the liberty of saying that we thanked him, but we didn't want seeing home. He received that piece of information with a yell of laughter, and dropped back, but came slouching after us at a little distance.

Curious to know whether Biddy suspected him of having had a hand in that murderous attack of which my sister had never been able to give any account, I asked her why she did not like him.

'Oh!' she replied, glancing over her shoulder as he slouched after us, 'because I—I am afraid he likes me.'

'Did he ever tell you he liked you?' I asked indignantly.

'No,' said Biddy, glancing over her shoulder again, 'he never told me so; but he dances at me, whenever he can catch my eye.'

However novel and peculiar this testimony of attachment, I did not doubt the accuracy of the interpretation. I was very hot indeed upon Old Orlick's daring to admire her; as hot as if it were an outrage on myself.

'But it makes no difference to you, you know,' said Biddy, calmly.

'No, Biddy, it makes no difference to me; only I don't like it; I don't approve of it.'

'Nor I neither,' said Biddy. 'Though *that* makes no difference to you.'

'Exactly,' said I; 'but I must tell you I should have no opinion of you, Biddy, if he danced at you with your own consent.'

I kept an eye on Orlick after that night, and, whenever circumstances were favourable to his dancing at Biddy, got before him to obscure that demonstration. He had struck root in Joe's establishment, by reason of my sister's sudden fancy for him, or I should have tried to get him dismissed. He quite understood and reciprocated my good intentions, as I had reason to know thereafter.

And now, because my mind was not confused enough before, I complicated its confusion fifty thousand-fold, by having states and seasons when I was clear that Biddy was immeasurably better than Estella, and that the plain honest working life to which I was born had nothing in it to be ashamed of, but offered me sufficient means of self-respect and happiness. At those times, I would decide conclusively that my disaffection to dear old Joe and the forge was gone, and that I was growing up in a fair way to be partners with Joe and to keep company with Biddy,—when all in a moment some confounding remembrance of the Havisham days would fall upon me like a destructive missile, and scatter my wits again. Scattered wits take a long time picking up; and often before I had got them well together, they would be dispersed in all directions by one stray thought, that perhaps after all Miss Havisham was going to make my fortune when my time was out.

If my time had run out, it would have left me still at the height of my perplexities, I dare say. It never did run out, however, but was brought to a premature end, as I proceed to relate.

Chapter 18

It was in the fourth year of my apprenticeship to Joe, and it was a Saturday night. There was a group assembled round the fire at the Three Jolly Bargemen, attentive to Mr Wopsle as he read the newspaper aloud. Of that group I was one.

A highly popular murder had been committed, and Mr Wopsle was imbrued in blood to the eyebrows. He gloated over every abhorrent adjective in the description, and identified himself with every witness at the inquest. He faintly moaned, 'I am done for,' as the victim, and he barbarously bellowed, 'I'll serve you out,' as the murderer. He gave the medical testimony, in pointed imitation of our local practitioner; and he piped and shook, as the aged turnpike-keeper who had heard blows, to an extent so very paralytic as to suggest a doubt regarding the mental competency of that witness. The coroner, in Mr Wopsle's hands, became Timon of Athens; the beadle, Coriolanus. He enjoyed himself thoroughly, and we all enjoyed ourselves, and were delightfully comfortable. In this cosey state of mind we came to the verdict Wilful Murder.

Then, and not sooner, I became aware of a strange gentleman leaning over the back of the settle opposite me, looking on. There was an expression of contempt on his face, and he bit the side of a great forefinger as he watched the group of faces.

'Well!' said the stranger to Mr Wopsle, when the reading was done, 'you have settled it all to your own satisfaction, I have no doubt?'

Everybody started and looked up, as if it were the murderer. He looked at everybody coldly and sarcastically.

'Guilty, of course?' said he. 'Out with it. Come!'

'Sir,' returned Mr Wopsle, 'without having the honour of your acquaintance, I do say Guilty.' Upon this we all took courage to unite in a confirmatory murmur.

'I know you do,' said the stranger; 'I knew you would. I told you so. But now I'll ask you a question. Do you know, or do you not know, that the law of England supposes every man to be innocent, until he is proved—proved—to be guilty?'

'Sir,' Mr Wopsle began to reply, 'as an Englishman myself, I—'

'Come!' said the stranger, biting his forefinger at him. 'Don't evade the question. Either you know it, or you don't know it. Which is it to be?'

He stood with his head on one side and himself on one side, in a bullying, interrogative manner, and he threw his forefinger at Mr Wopsle,—as it were to mark him out—before biting it again.

'Now!' said he. 'Do you know it, or don't you know it?'

'Certainly I know it,' replied Mr Wopsle.

'Certainly you know it. Then why didn't you say so at first? Now, I'll ask you another question,'—taking possession of Mr Wopsle, as if he had a right to him,—'*do* you know that none of these witnesses have yet been cross-examined?'

Mr Wopsle was beginning, 'I can only say—' when the stranger stopped him.

'What? You won't answer the question, yes or no? Now, I'll try you again.' Throwing his finger at him again. 'Attend to me. Are you aware, or are you not aware, that none of these witnesses have yet been cross-examined? Come, I only want one word from you. Yes, or no?'

Mr Wopsle hesitated, and we all began to conceive rather a poor opinion of him.

'Come!' said the stranger, 'I'll help you. You don't deserve help, but I'll help you. Look at that paper you hold in your hand. What is it?'

'What is it?' repeated Mr Wopsle, eyeing it, much at a loss.

'Is it,' pursued the stranger in his most sarcastic and suspicious manner, 'the printed paper you have just been reading from?'

'Undoubtedly.'

'Undoubtedly. Now, turn to that paper, and tell me whether it distinctly states that the prisoner expressly said that his legal advisers instructed him altogether to reserve his defence?'

'I read that just now,' Mr Wopsle pleaded.

'Never mind what you read just now, sir; I don't ask you what you read just now. You may read the Lord's Prayer backwards, if you like,—and, perhaps, have done it before today. Turn to the paper. No, no, no my friend; not to the top of the column; you know better than that; to the bottom, to the bottom.' (We all began to think Mr Wopsle full of subterfuge.) 'Well? Have you found it?'

'Here it is,' said Mr Wopsle.

'Now, follow that passage with your eye, and tell me whether it distinctly states that the prisoner expressly said that he was instructed by his legal advisers wholly to reserve his defence? Come! Do you make that of it?'

Mr Wopsle answered, 'Those are not the exact words.'

'Not the exact words!' repeated the gentleman bitterly. 'Is that the exact substance?'

'Yes,' said Mr Wopsle.

'Yes,' repeated the stranger, looking round at the rest of the company with his right hand extended towards the witness, Wopsle. 'And now I ask you what you say to the conscience of that man who, with that passage before his eyes, can lay his head upon his pillow after having pronounced a fellow-creature guilty, unheard?'

We all began to suspect that Mr Wopsle was not the man we had thought him, and that he was beginning to be found out.

'And that same man, remember,' pursued the gentleman, throwing his finger at Mr Wopsle heavily,—'that same man might be summoned as a juryman upon this very trial, and, having thus deeply committed himself, might return to the bosom of his family and lay his head upon his pillow, after deliberately swearing that he would well and truly try the issue joined between Our Sovereign Lord the King and the prisoner at the bar, and would a true verdict give according to the evidence, so help him God!'

We were all deeply persuaded that the unfortunate Wopsle had gone too far, and had better stop in his reckless career while there was yet time.

The strange gentleman, with an air of authority not to be disputed, and with a manner expressive of knowing something secret about every one of us that would effectually do for each individual if he chose to disclose it, left the back of the settle, and came into the space between the two settles, in front of the fire, where he remained standing, his left hand in his pocket, and he biting the forefinger of his right.

'From information I have received,' said he, looking round at us as we all quailed before him, 'I have reason to believe there is a blacksmith among you, by name Joseph—or Joe—Gargery. Which is the man?'

'Here is the man,' said Joe.

The strange gentleman beckoned him out of his place, and Joe went.

'You have an apprentice,' pursued the stranger, 'commonly known as Pip? Is he here?'

'I am here!' I cried.

The stranger did not recognize me, but I recognized him as the gentleman I had met on the stairs, on the occasion of my second visit to Miss Havisham. I had known him the moment I saw him looking over the settle, and now that I stood confronting him with his hand upon my shoulder, I checked off again in detail his large head, his dark complexion, his deep-set eyes, his bushy black eyebrows, his large watch-chain, his strong black dots of beard and whisker, and even the smell of scented soap on his great hand.

'I wish to have a private conference with you two,' said he, when he had surveyed me at his leisure. 'It will take a little time. Perhaps we had better go to your place of residence. I prefer not to anticipate my communication here; you will impart as much or as little of it as you please to your friends afterwards; I have nothing to do with that.'

Amidst a wondering silence, we three walked out of the Jolly Bargemen, and in a wondering silence walked home. While going along, the strange gentleman occasionally looked at me, and occasionally bit the side of his finger. As we neared home, Joe vaguely acknowledging the occasion as an impressive and ceremonious one, went on ahead to open the front door. Our conference was held in the state parlor, which was feebly lighted by one candle.

It began with the strange gentleman's sitting down at the table, drawing the candle to him, and looking over some entries in his pocket-book. He then put up the pocket-book and set the candle a little aside, after peering round it into the darkness at Joe and me, to ascertain which was which.

'My name,' he said, 'is Jaggers, and I am a lawyer in London. I am pretty well known. I have unusual business to transact with you, and I commence by explaining that it is not of my originating. If my advice had been asked, I should not have been here. It was not asked, and you see me here. What I have to do as the confidential agent of another, I do. No less, no more.'

Finding that he could not see us very well from where he sat, he got up, and threw one leg over the back of a chair and leaned upon it; thus having one foot on the seat of the chair, and one foot on the ground.

'Now, Joseph Gargery, I am the bearer of an offer to relieve you of this young fellow, your apprentice. You would not object to cancel his indentures at his request and for his good? You would want nothing for so doing?'

'Lord forbid that I should want anything for not standing in Pip's way,' said Joe, staring.

'Lord forbidding is pious, but not to the purpose,' returned Mr Jaggers. 'The question is, Would you want anything? Do you want anything?'

'The answer is,' returned Joe, sternly, 'No.'

I thought Mr Jaggers glanced at Joe, as if he considered him a fool for his disinterestedness. But I was too much bewildered between breathless curiosity and surprise, to be sure of it.

'Very well,' said Mr Jaggers. 'Recollect the admission you have made, and don't try to go from it presently.'

'Who's a going to try?' retorted Joe.

'I don't say anybody is. Do you keep a dog?'

'Yes, I do keep a dog.'

'Bear in mind then, that Brag is a good dog, but Holdfast is a better. Bear that in mind, will you?' repeated Mr Jaggers, shutting his eyes and nodding his head at Joe, as if he were forgiving him something. 'Now, I return to this young fellow. And the communication I have got to make is, that he has great expectations.'

Joe and I gasped, and looked at one another.

'I am instructed to communicate to him,' said Mr Jaggers, throwing his finger at me sideways, 'that he will come into a handsome property. Further, that it is the desire of the present possessor of that property, that he be immediately removed from his present sphere of life and from this place, and be brought up as a gentleman,—in a word, as a young fellow of great expectations.'

My dream was out; my wild fancy was surpassed by sober reality; Miss Havisham was going to make my fortune on a grand scale.

'Now, Mr Pip,' pursued the lawyer, 'I address the rest of what I have to say, to you. You are to understand, first, that it is the request of the person from whom I take my instructions that you always bear the name of Pip. You will have no objection, I dare say, to your great expectations being encumbered with that easy condition. But if you have any objection, this is the time to mention it.'

My heart was beating so fast, and there was such a singing in my ears, that I could scarcely stammer I had no objection.

'I should think not! Now you are to understand, secondly, Mr Pip, that the name of the person who is your liberal benefactor remains a profound secret, until the person chooses to reveal it. I am empowered to mention that it is the intention of the person to reveal it at first hand by word of mouth to yourself. When or where that intention may be carried out, I cannot say; no one can say. It may be years hence. Now, you are distinctly to understand that you are most positively prohibited from making any inquiry on this head, or any allusion or reference, however distant, to any individual whomsoever as *the* individual, in all the communications you may have with me. If you have a suspicion in your own breast, keep that suspicion in your own breast. It is not the least to the purpose what the reasons of this prohibition are; they may be the strongest and gravest reasons, or they may be mere whim. This is not for you to inquire into. The condition is laid down. Your acceptance of it, and your observance of it as binding, is the only remaining condition that I am charged with, by the person from whom I take my instructions, and for whom I am not otherwise responsible. That person is the person from whom you derive your expectations, and the secret is solely held by that person and by me. Again, not a very difficult condition with which to encumber such a rise in fortune; but if you have any objection to it, this is the time to mention it. Speak out.'

Once more, I stammered with difficulty that I had no objection.

'I should think not! Now, Mr Pip, I have done with stipulations.' Though he called me Mr Pip, and began rather to make up to me, he still could not get rid of a certain air of bullying suspicion; and even now he occasionally shut his eyes and threw his finger at me while he spoke, as much as to express that he knew all kinds of things to my disparagement, if he only chose to mention them. 'We come next, to mere details of arrangement. You must know that, although I have used the term 'expectations' more than once, you are not endowed with expectations only. There is already lodged in my hands a sum of money amply sufficient for your suitable education and maintenance. You will please consider me your guardian. Oh!' for I was going to thank him, 'I tell you at once, I am paid for my services, or I shouldn't render them. It is considered that you must be better educated, in accordance with your altered position, and that you will be alive to the importance and necessity of at once entering on that advantage.'

I said I had always longed for it.

'Never mind what you have always longed for, Mr Pip,' he retorted; 'keep to the record. If you long for it now, that's enough. Am I answered that you are ready to be placed at once under some proper tutor? Is that it?'

I stammered yes, that was it.

'Good. Now, your inclinations are to be consulted. I don't think that wise, mind, but it's my trust. Have you ever heard of any tutor whom you would prefer to another?'

I had never heard of any tutor but Biddy and Mr Wopsle's great-aunt; so, I replied in the negative.

'There is a certain tutor, of whom I have some knowledge, who I think might suit the purpose,' said Mr Jaggers. 'I don't recommend him, observe; because I never recommend anybody. The gentleman I speak of is one Mr Matthew Pocket.'

Ah! I caught at the name directly. Miss Havisham's relation. The Matthew whom Mr and Mrs Camilla had spoken of. The Matthew whose place was to be at Miss Havisham's head, when she lay dead, in her bride's dress on the bride's table.

'You know the name?' said Mr Jaggers, looking shrewdly at me, and then shutting up his eyes while he waited for my answer.

My answer was, that I had heard of the name.

'Oh!' said he. 'You have heard of the name. But the question is, what do you say of it?'

I said, or tried to say, that I was much obliged to him for his recommendation—

'No, my young friend!' he interrupted, shaking his great head very slowly. 'Recollect yourself!'

Not recollecting myself, I began again that I was much obliged to him for his recommendation—

'No, my young friend,' he interrupted, shaking his head and frowning and smiling both at once,—'no, no, no; it's very well done, but it won't do; you are too young to fix me with it. Recommendation is not the word, Mr Pip. Try another.'

Correcting myself, I said that I was much obliged to him for his mention of Mr Matthew Pocket—

'*That*'s more like it!' cried Mr Jaggers.—And (I added), I would gladly try that gentleman.

'Good. You had better try him in his own house. The way shall be prepared for you, and you can see his son first, who is in London. When will you come to London?'

I said (glancing at Joe, who stood looking on, motionless), that I supposed I could come directly.

'First,' said Mr Jaggers, 'you should have some new clothes to come in, and they should not be working-clothes. Say this day week. You'll want some money. Shall I leave you twenty guineas?'

He produced a long purse, with the greatest coolness, and counted them out on the table and pushed them over to me. This was the first time he had taken his leg from the chair. He sat astride of the chair when he had pushed the money over, and sat swinging his purse and eyeing Joe.

'Well, Joseph Gargery? You look dumbfoundered?'

'I *am*!' said Joe, in a very decided manner.

'It was understood that you wanted nothing for yourself, remember?'

'It were understood,' said Joe. 'And it are understood. And it ever will be similar according.'

'But what,' said Mr Jaggers, swinging his purse,—'what if it was in my instructions to make you a present, as compensation?'

'As compensation what for?' Joe demanded.

'For the loss of his services.'

Joe laid his hand upon my shoulder with the touch of a woman. I have often thought him since, like the steam-hammer that can crush a man or pat an egg-shell, in his combination of strength with gentleness. 'Pip is that hearty welcome,' said Joe, 'to go free with his services, to honour and fortun', as no words can tell him. But if you think as money can make compensation to me for the loss of the little child—what come to the forge—and ever the best of friends!—'

O dear good Joe, whom I was so ready to leave and so unthankful to, I see you again, with your muscular blacksmith's arm before your eyes, and your broad chest heaving, and your voice dying away. O dear good faithful tender Joe, I feel the loving tremble of your hand upon my arm, as solemnly this day as if it had been the rustle of an angel's wing!

But I encouraged Joe at the time. I was lost in the mazes of my future fortunes, and could not retrace the by-paths we had trodden together. I begged Joe to be comforted, for (as he said) we had ever been the best of friends, and (as I said) we ever would be so. Joe scooped his eyes with his disengaged wrist, as if he were bent on gouging himself, but said not another word.

Mr Jaggers had looked on at this, as one who recognized in Joe the village idiot, and in me his keeper. When it was over, he said, weighing in his hand the purse he had ceased to swing:—

'Now, Joseph Gargery, I warn you this is your last chance. No half measures with me. If you mean to take a present that I have it in charge to make you, speak out, and you shall have it. If on the contrary you mean to say—' Here, to his great amazement, he was stopped by Joe's suddenly working round him with every demonstration of a fell pugilistic purpose.

'Which I meantersay,' cried Joe, 'that if you come into my place bull-baiting and badgering me, come out! Which I meantersay as sech if you're a man, come on! Which I meantersay that what I say, I meantersay and stand or fall by!'

I drew Joe away, and he immediately became placable; merely stating to me, in an obliging manner and as a polite expostulatory notice to any one whom it might happen to concern, that he were not a going to be bull-baited and badgered in his own place. Mr Jaggers had risen when Joe demonstrated, and had backed near the door. Without evincing any inclination to come in again, he there delivered his valedictory remarks. They were these.

'Well, Mr Pip, I think the sooner you leave here—as you are to be a gentleman—the better. Let it stand for this day week, and you shall receive my printed address in the meantime. You can take a hackney-coach at the stage-coach office in London, and come straight to me. Understand, that I express no opinion, one way or other, on the trust I undertake. I am paid for undertaking it, and I do so. Now, understand that, finally. Understand that!'

He was throwing his finger at both of us, and I think would have gone on, but for his seeming to think Joe dangerous, and going off.

Something came into my head which induced me to run after him, as he was going down to the Jolly Bargemen, where he had left a hired carriage.

'I beg your pardon, Mr Jaggers.'

'Halloa!' said he, facing round, 'what's the matter?'

'I wish to be quite right, Mr Jaggers, and to keep to your directions; so I thought I had better ask. Would there be any objection to my taking leave of anyone I know, about here, before I go away?'

'No,' said he, looking as if he hardly understood me.

'I don't mean in the village only, but up town?'

'No,' said he. 'No objection.'

I thanked him and ran home again, and there I found that Joe had already locked the front door and vacated the state parlor, and was seated by the kitchen fire with a hand on each knee, gazing intently at the burning coals. I too sat down before the fire and gazed at the coals, and nothing was said for a long time.

My sister was in her cushioned chair in her corner, and Biddy sat at her needle-work before the fire, and Joe sat next to Biddy, and I sat next to Joe in the corner opposite my sister. The more I looked into the glowing coals, the more incapable I became of looking at Joe; the longer the silence lasted, the more unable I felt to speak.

At length I got out, 'Joe, have you told Biddy?'

'No, Pip,' returned Joe, still looking at the fire, and holding his knees tight, as if he had private information that they intended to make off somewhere, 'which I left it to yourself, Pip.'

'I would rather you told, Joe.'

'Pip's a gentleman of fortun' then,' said Joe, 'and God bless him in it!'

Biddy dropped her work, and looked at me. Joe held his knees and looked at me. I looked at both of them. After a pause, they both heartily congratulated me; but there was a certain touch of sadness in their congratulations that I rather resented.

I took it upon myself to impress Biddy (and through Biddy, Joe) with the grave obligation I considered my friends under, to know nothing and say nothing about the maker of my fortune. It would all come out in good time, I observed, and in the meanwhile nothing was to be said, save that I had come into great expectations from a mysterious patron. Biddy nodded her head thoughtfully at the fire as she took up her work again, and said she would be very particular; and Joe, still detaining his knees, said, 'Ay, ay, I'll be ekervally partickler, Pip;' and then they congratulated me again, and went on to express so much wonder at the notion of my being a gentleman that I didn't half like it.

Infinite pains were then taken by Biddy to convey to my sister some idea of what had happened. To the best of my belief, those efforts entirely failed. She laughed and nodded her head a great many times, and even repeated after Biddy, the words 'Pip' and 'Property.' But I doubt if they had more meaning in them than an election cry, and I cannot suggest a darker picture of her state of mind.

I never could have believed it without experience, but as Joe and Biddy became more at their cheerful ease again, I became quite gloomy. Dissatisfied with my fortune, of course I could not be; but it is possible that I may have been, without quite knowing it, dissatisfied with myself.

Any how, I sat with my elbow on my knee and my face upon my hand, looking into the fire, as those two talked about my going away, and about what they should do without me, and all that. And whenever I caught one of them looking at me, though never so pleasantly (and they often looked at me,—particularly Biddy), I felt offended: as if they were expressing some mistrust of me. Though Heaven knows they never did by word or sign.

At those times I would get up and look out at the door; for our kitchen door opened at once upon the night, and stood open on summer evenings to air the room. The very stars to which I then raised my eyes, I am afraid I took to be but poor and humble stars for glittering on the rustic objects among which I had passed my life.

'Saturday night,' said I, when we sat at our supper of bread and cheese and beer. 'Five more days, and then the day before *the* day! They'll soon go.'

'Yes, Pip,' observed Joe, whose voice sounded hollow in his beer mug. 'They'll soon go.'

'Soon, soon go,' said Biddy.

'I have been thinking, Joe, that when I go down town on Monday, and order my new clothes, I shall tell the tailor that I'll come and put them on there, or that I'll have them sent to Mr Pumblechook's. It would be very disagreeable to be stared at by all the people here.'

'Mr and Mrs Hubble might like to see you in your new gen-teel figure too, Pip,' said Joe, industriously cutting his bread, with his cheese on it, in the palm of his left hand, and glancing at my untasted supper as if he thought of the time when we used to compare slices. 'So might Wopsle. And the Jolly Bargemen might take it as a compliment.'

'That's just what I don't want, Joe. They would make such a business of it,—such a coarse and common business,—that I couldn't bear myself.'

'Ah, that indeed, Pip!' said Joe. 'If you couldn't abear yourself—'

Biddy asked me here, as she sat holding my sister's plate, 'Have you thought about when you'll show yourself to Mr Gargery, and your sister and me? You will show yourself to us; won't you?'

'Biddy,' I returned with some resentment, 'you are so exceedingly quick that it's difficult to keep up with you.'

('She always were quick,' observed Joe.)

'If you had waited another moment, Biddy, you would have heard me say that I shall bring my clothes here in a bundle one evening,—most likely on the evening before I go away.'

Biddy said no more. Handsomely forgiving her, I soon exchanged an affectionate goodnight with her and Joe, and went up to bed. When I got into my little room, I sat down and took a long look at it, as a mean little room that I should soon be parted from and raised above, forever. It was furnished with fresh young remembrances too, and even at the same moment I fell into much the same confused division of mind between it and the better rooms to which I was going, as I had been in so often between the forge and Miss Havisham's, and Biddy and Estella.

The sun had been shining brightly all day on the roof of my attic, and the room was warm. As I put the window open and stood looking out, I saw Joe come slowly forth at the dark door, below, and take a turn or two in the air; and then I saw Biddy come, and bring him a pipe and light it for him. He never smoked so late, and it seemed to hint to me that he wanted comforting, for some reason or other.

He presently stood at the door immediately beneath me, smoking his pipe, and Biddy stood there too, quietly talking to him, and I knew that they talked of me, for I heard my name mentioned in an endearing tone by both of them more than once. I would not have listened for more, if I could have heard more; so I drew away from the window, and sat down in my one chair by the bedside, feeling it very sorrowful and strange that this first night of my bright fortunes should be the loneliest I had ever known.

Looking towards the open window, I saw light wreaths from Joe's pipe floating there, and I fancied it was like a blessing from Joe,—not obtruded on me or paraded before me, but pervading the air we shared together. I put my light out, and crept into bed; and it was an uneasy bed now, and I never slept the old sound sleep in it any more.

Chapter 19

Morning made a considerable difference in my general prospect of life, and brightened it so much that it scarcely seemed the same. What lay heaviest on my mind was, the consideration that six days intervened between me and the day of departure; for I could not divest myself of a misgiving that something might happen to London in the meanwhile, and that, when I got there, it would be either greatly deteriorated or clean gone.

Joe and Biddy were very sympathetic and pleasant when I spoke of our approaching separation; but they only referred to it when I did.

After breakfast, Joe brought out my indentures from the press in the best parlor, and we put them in the fire, and I felt that I was free. With all the novelty of my emancipation on me, I went to church with Joe, and thought perhaps the clergyman wouldn't have read that about the rich man and the kingdom of Heaven, if he had known all.

After our early dinner, I strolled out alone, purposing to finish off the marshes at once, and get them done with. As I passed the church, I felt (as I had felt during service in the morning) a sublime compassion for the poor creatures who were destined to go there, Sunday after Sunday, all their lives through, and to lie obscurely at last among the low green mounds. I promised myself that I would do something for them one of these days, and formed a plan in outline for bestowing a dinner of roast-beef and plum-pudding, a pint of ale, and a gallon of condescension, upon everybody in the village.

If I had often thought before, with something allied to shame, of my companionship with the fugitive whom I had once seen limping among those graves, what were my thoughts on this Sunday, when the place recalled the wretch, ragged and shivering, with his felon iron and badge! My comfort was, that it happened a long time ago, and that he had doubtless been transported a long way off, and that he was dead to me, and might be veritably dead into the bargain.

No more low, wet grounds, no more dikes and sluices, no more of these grazing cattle,—though they seemed, in their dull manner, to wear a more respectful air now, and to face round, in order that they might stare as long as possible at the possessor of such great expectations,—farewell, monotonous acquaintances of my childhood, henceforth I was for London and greatness; not for smith's work in general, and for you! I made my exultant way to the old Battery, and, lying down there to consider the question whether Miss Havisham intended me for Estella, fell asleep.

When I awoke, I was much surprised to find Joe sitting beside me, smoking his pipe. He greeted me with a cheerful smile on my opening my eyes, and said,—

'As being the last time, Pip, I thought I'd foller.'

'And Joe, I am very glad you did so.'

'Thankee, Pip.'

'You may be sure, dear Joe,' I went on, after we had shaken hands, 'that I shall never forget you.'

'No, no, Pip!' said Joe, in a comfortable tone, '*I*'m sure of that. Ay, ay, old chap! Bless you, it were only necessary to get it well round in a man's mind, to be certain on it. But it took a bit of time to get it well round, the change come so oncommon plump; didn't it?'

Somehow, I was not best pleased with Joe's being so mightily secure of me. I should have liked him to have betrayed emotion, or to have said, 'It does you credit, Pip,' or something of that sort. Therefore, I made no remark on Joe's first head; merely saying as to his second, that the tidings had indeed come suddenly, but that I had always wanted to be a gentleman, and had often and often speculated on what I would do, if I were one.

'Have you though?' said Joe. 'Astonishing!'

'It's a pity now, Joe,' said I, 'that you did not get on a little more, when we had our lessons here; isn't it?'

'Well, I don't know,' returned Joe. 'I'm so awful dull. I'm only master of my own trade. It were always a pity as I was so awful dull; but it's no more of a pity now, than it was—this day twelvemonth—don't you see?'

What I had meant was, that when I came into my property and was able to do something for Joe, it would have been much more agreeable if he had been better qualified for a rise in station. He was so perfectly innocent of my meaning, however, that I thought I would mention it to Biddy in preference.

So, when we had walked home and had had tea, I took Biddy into our little garden by the side of the lane, and, after throwing out in a general way for the elevation of her spirits, that I should never forget her, said I had a favour to ask of her.

'And it is, Biddy,' said I, 'that you will not omit any opportunity of helping Joe on, a little.'

'How helping him on?' asked Biddy, with a steady sort of glance.

'Well! Joe is a dear good fellow,—in fact, I think he is the dearest fellow that ever lived,—but he is rather backward in some things. For instance, Biddy, in his learning and his manners.'

Although I was looking at Biddy as I spoke, and although she opened her eyes very wide when I had spoken, she did not look at me.

'O, his manners! Won't his manners do then?' asked Biddy, plucking a black-currant leaf.

'My dear Biddy, they do very well here—'

'O! They *do* very well here?' interrupted Biddy, looking closely at the leaf in her hand.

'Hear me out,—but if I were to remove Joe into a higher sphere, as I shall hope to remove him when I fully come into my property, they would hardly do him justice.'

'And don't you think he knows that?' asked Biddy.

It was such a very provoking question (for it had never in the most distant manner occurred to me), that I said, snappishly,—

'Biddy, what do you mean?'

Biddy, having rubbed the leaf to pieces between her hands,—and the smell of a black-currant bush has ever since recalled to me that evening in the little garden by the side of the lane,—said, 'Have you never considered that he may be proud?'

'Proud?' I repeated, with disdainful emphasis.

'O! There are many kinds of pride,' said Biddy, looking full at me and shaking her head; 'pride is not all of one kind—'

'Well? What are you stopping for?' said I.

'Not all of one kind,' resumed Biddy. 'He may be too proud to let anyone take him out of a place that he is competent to fill, and fills well and with respect. To tell you the truth, I think he is; though it sounds bold in me to say so, for you must know him far better than I do.'

'Now, Biddy,' said I, 'I am very sorry to see this in you. I did not expect to see this in you. You are envious, Biddy, and grudging. You are dissatisfied on account of my rise in fortune, and you can't help showing it.'

'If you have the heart to think so,' returned Biddy, 'say so. Say so over and over again, if you have the heart to think so.'

'If you have the heart to be so, you mean, Biddy,' said I, in a virtuous and superior tone; 'don't put it off upon me. I am very sorry to see it, and it's a—it's a bad side of human nature. I did intend to ask you to use any little opportunities you might have after I was gone, of improving dear Joe. But after this I ask you nothing. I am extremely sorry to see this in you, Biddy,' I repeated. 'It's a—it's a bad side of human nature.'

'Whether you scold me or approve of me,' returned poor Biddy, 'you may equally depend upon my trying to do all that lies in my power, here, at all times. And whatever opinion you take away of me, shall make no difference in my remembrance of you. Yet a gentleman should not be unjust neither,' said Biddy, turning away her head.

I again warmly repeated that it was a bad side of human nature (in which sentiment, waiving its application, I have since seen reason to think I was right), and I walked down the little path away from Biddy, and Biddy went into the house, and I went out at the garden gate and took a dejected stroll until supper-time; again feeling it very sorrowful and strange that this, the second night of my bright fortunes, should be as lonely and unsatisfactory as the first.

But, morning once more brightened my view, and I extended my clemency to Biddy, and we dropped the subject. Putting on the best clothes I had, I went into town as early as I could hope to find the shops open, and presented myself before Mr Trabb, the tailor, who was having his breakfast in the parlor behind his shop, and who did not think it worth his while to come out to me, but called me in to him.

'Well!' said Mr Trabb, in a hail-fellow-well-met kind of way. 'How are you, and what can I do for you?'

Mr Trabb had sliced his hot roll into three feather-beds, and was slipping butter in between the blankets, and covering it up. He was a prosperous old bachelor, and his open window looked into a prosperous little garden and orchard, and there was a prosperous iron safe let into the wall at the side of his fireplace, and I did not doubt that heaps of his prosperity were put away in it in bags.

'Mr Trabb,' said I, 'it's an unpleasant thing to have to mention, because it looks like boasting; but I have come into a handsome property.'

A change passed over Mr Trabb. He forgot the butter in bed, got up from the bedside, and wiped his fingers on the tablecloth, exclaiming, 'Lord bless my soul!'

'I am going up to my guardian in London,' said I, casually drawing some guineas out of my pocket and looking at them; 'and I want a fashionable suit of clothes to go in. I wish to pay for them,' I added—otherwise I thought he might only pretend to make them, 'with ready money.'

'My dear sir,' said Mr Trabb, as he respectfully bent his body, opened his arms, and took the liberty of touching me on the outside of each elbow, 'don't hurt me by mentioning that. May I venture to congratulate you? Would you do me the favour of stepping into the shop?'

Mr Trabb's boy was the most audacious boy in all that countryside. When I had entered he was sweeping the shop, and he had sweetened his labours by sweeping over me. He was still sweeping when I came out into the shop with Mr Trabb, and he knocked the broom against all possible corners and obstacles, to express (as I understood it) equality with any blacksmith, alive or dead.

'Hold that noise,' said Mr Trabb, with the greatest sternness, 'or I'll knock your head off!—Do me the favour to be seated, sir. Now, this,' said Mr Trabb, taking down a roll of cloth, and tiding it out in a flowing manner over the counter, preparatory to getting his hand under it to show the gloss, 'is a very sweet article. I can recommend it for your purpose, sir, because it really is extra super. But you shall see some others. Give me Number Four, you!' (To the boy, and with a dreadfully severe stare; foreseeing the danger of that miscreant's brushing me with it, or making some other sign of familiarity.)

Mr Trabb never removed his stern eye from the boy until he had deposited number four on the counter and was at a safe distance again. Then he commanded him to bring number five, and number eight. 'And let me have none of your tricks here,' said Mr Trabb, 'or you shall repent it, you young scoundrel, the longest day you have to live.'

Mr Trabb then bent over number four, and in a sort of deferential confidence recommended it to me as a light article for summer wear, an article much in vogue among the nobility and gentry, an article that it would ever be an honour to him to reflect upon a distinguished fellow-townsman's (if he might claim me for a fellow-townsman) having worn. 'Are you bringing numbers five and eight, you vagabond,' said Mr Trabb to the boy after that, 'or shall I kick you out of the shop and bring them myself?'

I selected the materials for a suit, with the assistance of Mr Trabb's judgment, and re-entered the parlor to be measured. For although Mr Trabb had my measure already, and had previously been quite contented with it, he said apologetically that it 'wouldn't do under existing circumstances, sir,—wouldn't do at all.' So, Mr Trabb measured and calculated me in the parlor, as if I were an estate and he the finest species of surveyor, and gave himself such a world of trouble that I felt that no suit of clothes could possibly remunerate him for his pains. When he had at last done and had appointed to send the articles to Mr Pumblechook's on the Thursday evening, he said, with his hand upon the parlor lock, 'I know, sir, that London gentlemen cannot be expected to patronize local work, as a rule; but if you would give me a turn now and then in the quality of a townsman, I should greatly esteem it. Good morning, sir, much obliged.—Door!'

The last word was flung at the boy, who had not the least notion what it meant. But I saw him collapse as his master rubbed me out with his hands, and my first decided experience of the stupendous power of money was, that it had morally laid upon his back Trabb's boy.

After this memorable event, I went to the hatter's, and the bootmaker's, and the hosier's, and felt rather like Mother Hubbard's dog whose outfit required the services of so many trades. I also went to the coach-office and took my place for seven o'clock on Saturday morning. It was not necessary to explain everywhere that I had come into a handsome property; but whenever I said anything to that effect, it followed that the officiating tradesman ceased to have his attention diverted through the window by the High Street, and concentrated his mind upon me. When I had ordered everything I wanted, I directed my steps towards Pumblechook's, and, as I approached that gentleman's place of business, I saw him standing at his door.

He was waiting for me with great impatience. He had been out early with the chaise-cart, and had called at the forge and heard the news. He had prepared a collation for me in the Barnwell parlor, and he too ordered his shopman to 'come out of the gangway' as my sacred person passed.

'My dear friend,' said Mr Pumblechook, taking me by both hands, when he and I and the collation were alone, 'I give you joy of your good fortune. Well deserved, well deserved!'

This was coming to the point, and I thought it a sensible way of expressing himself.

'To think,' said Mr Pumblechook, after snorting admiration at me for some moments, 'that I should have been the humble instrument of leading up to this, is a proud reward.'

I begged Mr Pumblechook to remember that nothing was to be ever said or hinted, on that point.

'My dear young friend,' said Mr Pumblechook; 'if you will allow me to call you so—'

I murmured 'Certainly,' and Mr Pumblechook took me by both hands again, and communicated a movement to his waistcoat, which had an emotional appearance, though it was rather low down, 'My dear young friend, rely upon my doing my little all in your absence, by keeping the fact before the mind of Joseph.—Joseph!' said Mr Pumblechook, in the way of a compassionate adjuration. 'Joseph! Joseph!' Thereupon he shook his head and tapped it, expressing his sense of deficiency in Joseph.

'But my dear young friend,' said Mr Pumblechook, 'you must be hungry, you must be exhausted. Be seated. Here is a chicken had round from the Boar, here is a tongue had round from the Boar, here's one or two little things had round from the Boar, that I hope you may not despise. But do I,' said Mr Pumblechook, getting up again the moment after he had sat down, 'see afore me, him as I ever sported with in his times of happy infancy? And may I—*may* I—?'

This May I, meant might he shake hands? I consented, and he was fervent, and then sat down again.

'Here is wine,' said Mr Pumblechook. 'Let us drink, thanks to fortune, and may she ever pick out her favorites with equal judgment! And yet I cannot,' said Mr Pumblechook, getting up again, 'see afore me One—and likewise drink to One—without again expressing—May I—*may* I—?'

I said he might, and he shook hands with me again, and emptied his glass and turned it upside down. I did the same; and if I had turned myself upside down before drinking, the wine could not have gone more direct to my head.

Mr Pumblechook helped me to the liver wing, and to the best slice of tongue (none of those out-of-the-way No Thoroughfares of Pork now), and took, comparatively speaking, no care of himself at all. 'Ah! Poultry, poultry! You little thought,' said Mr Pumblechook, apostrophizing the fowl in the dish, 'when you was a young fledgling, what was in store for you. You little thought you was to be refreshment beneath this humble roof for one as—call it a weakness, if you will,' said Mr Pumblechook, getting up again, 'but may I? *may* I—?'

It began to be unnecessary to repeat the form of saying he might, so he did it at once. How he ever did it so often without wounding himself with my knife, I don't know.

'And your sister,' he resumed, after a little steady eating, 'which had the honour of bringing you up by hand! It's a sad picter, to reflect that she's no longer equal to fully understanding the honour. May—'

I saw he was about to come at me again, and I stopped him.

'We'll drink her health,' said I.

'Ah!' cried Mr Pumblechook, leaning back in his chair, quite flaccid with admiration, 'that's the way you know 'em, sir!' (I don't know who Sir was, but he certainly was not I, and there was no third person present); 'that's the way you know the noble-minded, sir! Ever forgiving and ever affable. It might,' said the servile Pumblechook, putting down his untasted glass in a hurry and getting up again, 'to a common person, have the appearance of repeating—but *may* I—?'

When he had done it, he resumed his seat and drank to my sister. 'Let us never be blind,' said Mr Pumblechook, 'to her faults of temper, but it is to be hoped she meant well.'

At about this time, I began to observe that he was getting flushed in the face; as to myself, I felt all face, steeped in wine and smarting.

I mentioned to Mr Pumblechook that I wished to have my new clothes sent to his house, and he was ecstatic on my so distinguishing him. I mentioned my reason for desiring to avoid observation in the village, and he lauded it to the skies. There was nobody but himself, he intimated, worthy of my confidence, and—in short, might he? Then he asked me tenderly if I remembered our boyish games at sums, and how we had gone together to have me bound apprentice, and, in effect, how he had ever been my favorite fancy and my chosen friend? If I had taken ten times as many glasses of wine as I had, I should have known that he never had stood in that relation towards me, and should in my heart of hearts have repudiated the idea. Yet for all that, I remember feeling convinced that I had been much mistaken in him, and that he was a sensible, practical, good-hearted prime fellow.

By degrees he fell to reposing such great confidence in me, as to ask my advice in reference to his own affairs. He mentioned that there was an opportunity for a great amalgamation and monopoly of the corn and seed trade on those premises, if enlarged, such as had never occurred before in that or any other neighbourhood. What alone was wanting to the realization of a vast fortune, he considered to be More Capital. Those were the two little words, more capital. Now it appeared to him (Pumblechook) that if that capital were got into the business, through a sleeping partner, sir,—which sleeping partner would have nothing to do but walk in, by self or deputy, whenever he pleased, and examine the books,—and walk in twice a year and take his profits away in his pocket, to the tune of fifty per cent,—it appeared to him that that might be an opening for a young gentleman of spirit combined with property, which would be worthy of his attention. But what did I think? He had great confidence in my opinion, and what did I think? I gave it as my opinion. 'Wait a bit!' The united vastness and distinctness of this view so struck him, that he no longer asked if he might shake hands with me, but said he really must,—and did.

We drank all the wine, and Mr Pumblechook pledged himself over and over again to keep Joseph up to the mark (I don't know what mark), and to render me efficient and constant service (I don't know what service). He also made known to me for the first time in my life, and certainly after having kept his secret wonderfully well, that he had always said of me, 'That boy is no common boy, and mark me, his fortun' will be no common fortun'.' He said with a tearful smile that it was a singular thing to think of now, and I said so too. Finally, I went out into the air, with a dim perception that there was something unwonted in the conduct of the sunshine, and found that I had slumberously got to the turnpike without having taken any account of the road.

There, I was roused by Mr Pumblechook's hailing me. He was a long way down the sunny street, and was making expressive gestures for me to stop. I stopped, and he came up breathless.

'No, my dear friend,' said he, when he had recovered wind for speech. 'Not if I can help it. This occasion shall not entirely pass without that affability on your part.—May I, as an old friend and well-wisher? *May* I?'

We shook hands for the hundredth time at least, and he ordered a young carter out of my way with the greatest indignation. Then, he blessed me and stood waving his hand to me until I had passed the crook in the road; and then I turned into a field and had a long nap under a hedge before I pursued my way home.

I had scant luggage to take with me to London, for little of the little I possessed was adapted to my new station. But I began packing that same afternoon, and wildly packed up things that I knew I should want next morning, in a fiction that there was not a moment to be lost.

So, Tuesday, Wednesday, and Thursday, passed; and on Friday morning I went to Mr Pumblechook's, to put on my new clothes and pay my visit to Miss Havisham. Mr Pumblechook's own room was given up to me to dress in, and was decorated with clean towels expressly for the event. My clothes were rather a disappointment, of course. Probably every new and eagerly expected garment ever put on since clothes came in, fell a trifle short of the wearer's expectation. But after I had had my new suit on some half an hour, and had gone through an immensity of posturing with Mr Pumblechook's very limited dressing-glass, in the futile endeavour to see my legs, it seemed to fit me better. It being market morning at a neighbouring town some ten miles off, Mr Pumblechook was not at home. I had not told him exactly when I meant to leave, and was not likely to shake hands with him again before departing. This was all as it should be, and I went out in my new array, fearfully ashamed of having to pass the shopman, and suspicious after all that I was at a personal disadvantage, something like Joe's in his Sunday suit.

I went circuitously to Miss Havisham's by all the back ways, and rang at the bell constrainedly, on account of the stiff long fingers of my gloves. Sarah Pocket came to the gate, and positively reeled back when she saw me so changed; her walnut-shell countenance likewise turned from brown to green and yellow.

'You?' said she. 'You? Good gracious! What do you want?'

'I am going to London, Miss Pocket,' said I, 'and want to say goodbye to Miss Havisham.'

I was not expected, for she left me locked in the yard, while she went to ask if I were to be admitted. After a very short delay, she returned and took me up, staring at me all the way.

Miss Havisham was taking exercise in the room with the long spread table, leaning on her crutch stick. The room was lighted as of yore, and at the sound of our entrance, she stopped and turned. She was then just abreast of the rotted bride-cake.

'Don't go, Sarah,' she said. 'Well, Pip?'

'I start for London, Miss Havisham, tomorrow,' I was exceedingly careful what I said, 'and I thought you would kindly not mind my taking leave of you.'

'This is a gay figure, Pip,' said she, making her crutch stick play round me, as if she, the fairy godmother who had changed me, were bestowing the finishing gift.

'I have come into such good fortune since I saw you last, Miss Havisham,' I murmured. 'And I am so grateful for it, Miss Havisham!'

'Ay, ay!' said she, looking at the discomfited and envious Sarah, with delight. 'I have seen Mr Jaggers. *I* have heard about it, Pip. So you go tomorrow?'

'Yes, Miss Havisham.'

'And you are adopted by a rich person?'

'Yes, Miss Havisham.'

'Not named?'

'No, Miss Havisham.'

'And Mr Jaggers is made your guardian?'

'Yes, Miss Havisham.'

She quite gloated on these questions and answers, so keen was her enjoyment of Sarah Pocket's jealous dismay. 'Well!' she went on; 'you have a promising career before you. Be good—deserve it—and abide by Mr Jaggers's instructions.' She looked at me, and looked at Sarah, and Sarah's countenance wrung out of her watchful face a cruel smile. 'Goodbye, Pip!—you will always keep the name of Pip, you know.'

'Yes, Miss Havisham.'

'Goodbye, Pip!'

She stretched out her hand, and I went down on my knee and put it to my lips. I had not considered how I should take leave of her; it came naturally to me at the moment to do this. She looked at Sarah Pocket with triumph in her weird eyes, and so I left my fairy godmother, with both her hands on her crutch stick, standing in the midst of the dimly lighted room beside the rotten bride-cake that was hidden in cobwebs.

Sarah Pocket conducted me down, as if I were a ghost who must be seen out. She could not get over my appearance, and was in the last degree confounded. I said 'Goodbye, Miss Pocket;' but she merely stared, and did not seem collected enough to know that I had spoken. Clear of the house, I made the best of my way back to Pumblechook's, took off my new clothes, made them into a bundle, and went back home in my older dress, carrying it—to speak the truth—much more at my ease too, though I had the bundle to carry.

And now, those six days which were to have run out so slowly, had run out fast and were gone, and tomorrow looked me in the face more steadily than I could look at it. As the six evenings had dwindled away, to five, to four, to three, to two, I had become more and more appreciative of the society of Joe and Biddy. On this last evening, I dressed my self out in my new clothes for their delight, and sat in my splendor until bedtime. We had a hot supper on the occasion, graced by the inevitable roast fowl, and we had some flip to finish with. We were all very low, and none the higher for pretending to be in spirits.

I was to leave our village at five in the morning, carrying my little hand-portmanteau, and I had told Joe that I wished to walk away all alone. I am afraid—sore afraid—that this purpose originated in my sense of the contrast there would be between me and Joe, if we went to the coach together. I had pretended with myself that there was nothing of this taint in the arrangement; but when I went up to my little room on this last night, I felt compelled to admit that it might be so, and had an impulse upon me to go down again and entreat

Joe to walk with me in the morning. I did not.

All night there were coaches in my broken sleep, going to wrong places instead of to London, and having in the traces, now dogs, now cats, now pigs, now men,—never horses. Fantastic failures of journeys occupied me until the day dawned and the birds were singing. Then, I got up and partly dressed, and sat at the window to take a last look out, and in taking it fell asleep.

Biddy was astir so early to get my breakfast, that, although I did not sleep at the window an hour, I smelt the smoke of the kitchen fire when I started up with a terrible idea that it must be late in the afternoon. But long after that, and long after I had heard the clinking of the teacups and was quite ready, I wanted the resolution to go downstairs. After all, I remained up there, repeatedly unlocking and unstrapping my small portmanteau and locking and strapping it up again, until Biddy called to me that I was late.

It was a hurried breakfast with no taste in it. I got up from the meal, saying with a sort of briskness, as if it had only just occurred to me, 'Well! I suppose I must be off!' and then I kissed my sister who was laughing and nodding and shaking in her usual chair, and kissed Biddy, and threw my arms around Joe's neck. Then I took up my little portmanteau and walked out. The last I saw of them was, when I presently heard a scuffle behind me, and looking back, saw Joe throwing an old shoe after me and Biddy throwing another old shoe. I stopped then, to wave my hat, and dear old Joe waved his strong right arm above his head, crying huskily 'Hooroar!' and Biddy put her apron to her face.

I walked away at a good pace, thinking it was easier to go than I had supposed it would be, and reflecting that it would never have done to have had an old shoe thrown after the coach, in sight of all the High Street. I whistled and made nothing of going. But the village was very peaceful and quiet, and the light mists were solemnly rising, as if to show me the world, and I had been so innocent and little there, and all beyond was so unknown and great, that in a moment with a strong heave and sob I broke into tears. It was by the finger-post at the end of the village, and I laid my hand upon it, and said, 'Goodbye, O my dear, dear friend!'

Heaven knows we need never be ashamed of our tears, for they are rain upon the blinding dust of earth, overlying our hard hearts. I was better after I had cried than before,—more sorry, more aware of my own ingratitude, more gentle. If I had cried before, I should have had Joe with me then.

So subdued I was by those tears, and by their breaking out again in the course of the quiet walk, that when I was on the coach, and it was clear of the town, I deliberated with an aching heart whether I would not get down when we changed horses and walk back, and have another evening at home, and a better parting. We changed, and I had not made up my mind, and still reflected for my comfort that it would be quite practicable to get down and walk back, when we changed again. And while I was occupied with these deliberations, I would fancy an exact resemblance to Joe in some man coming along the road towards us, and my heart would beat high.—As if he could possibly be there!

We changed again, and yet again, and it was now too late and too far to go back, and I went on. And the mists had all solemnly risen now, and the world lay spread before me.

This is the end of the first stage of Pip's expectations.

Chapter 20

The journey from our town to the metropolis was a journey of about five hours. It was a little past midday when the four-horse stage-coach by which I was a passenger, got into the ravel of traffic frayed out about the Cross Keys, Wood Street, Cheapside, London.

We Britons had at that time particularly settled that it was treasonable to doubt our having and our being the best of everything: otherwise, while I was scared by the immensity of London, I think I might have had some faint doubts whether it was not rather ugly, crooked, narrow, and dirty.

Mr Jaggers had duly sent me his address; it was, Little Britain, and he had written after it on his card, 'just out of Smithfield, and close by the coach-office.' Nevertheless, a hackney-coachman, who seemed to have as many capes to his greasy great-coat as he was years old, packed me up in his coach and hemmed me in with a folding and jingling barrier of steps, as if he were going to take me fifty miles. His getting on his box, which I remember to have been decorated with an old weather-stained pea-green hammercloth moth-eaten into rags, was quite a work of time. It was a wonderful equipage, with six great coronets outside, and ragged things behind for I don't know how many footmen to hold on by, and a harrow below them, to prevent amateur footmen from yielding to the temptation.

I had scarcely had time to enjoy the coach and to think how like a straw-yard it was, and yet how like a rag-shop, and to wonder why the horses' nose-bags were kept inside, when I observed the coachman beginning to get down, as if we were going to stop presently. And stop we presently did, in a gloomy street, at certain offices with an open door, whereon was painted Mr JAGGERS.

'How much?' I asked the coachman.

The coachman answered, 'A shilling—unless you wish to make it more.'

I naturally said I had no wish to make it more.

'Then it must be a shilling,' observed the coachman. 'I don't want to get into trouble. *I* know *him*!' He darkly closed an eye at Mr Jaggers's name, and shook his head.

When he had got his shilling, and had in course of time completed the ascent to his box, and had got away (which appeared to relieve his mind), I went into the front office with my little portmanteau in my hand and asked, Was Mr Jaggers at home?

'He is not,' returned the clerk. 'He is in Court at present. Am I addressing Mr Pip?'

I signified that he was addressing Mr Pip.

'Mr Jaggers left word, would you wait in his room. He couldn't say how long he might be, having a case on. But it stands to reason, his time being valuable, that he won't be longer than he can help.'

With those words, the clerk opened a door, and ushered me into an inner chamber at the back. Here, we found a gentleman with one eye, in a velveteen suit and knee-breeches, who wiped his nose with his sleeve on being interrupted in the perusal of the newspaper.

'Go and wait outside, Mike,' said the clerk.

I began to say that I hoped I was not interrupting, when the clerk shoved this gentleman out with as little ceremony as I ever saw used, and tossing his fur cap out after him, left me alone.

Mr Jaggers's room was lighted by a skylight only, and was a most dismal place; the skylight, eccentrically pitched like a broken head, and the distorted adjoining houses looking as if they had twisted themselves to peep down at me through it. There were not so many papers about, as I should have expected to see; and there were some odd objects about, that I should not have expected to see,—such as an old rusty pistol, a sword in a scabbard, several strange-looking boxes and packages, and two dreadful casts on a shelf, of faces peculiarly swollen, and twitchy about the nose. Mr Jaggers's own high-backed chair was of deadly black horsehair, with rows of brass nails round it, like a coffin; and I fancied I could see how he leaned back in it, and bit his forefinger at the clients. The room was but small, and the clients seemed to have had a habit of backing up against the wall; the wall, especially opposite to Mr Jaggers's chair, being greasy with shoulders. I recalled, too, that the one-eyed gentleman had shuffled forth against the wall when I was the innocent cause of his being turned out.

I sat down in the cliental chair placed over against Mr Jaggers's chair, and became fascinated by the dismal atmosphere of the place. I called to mind that the clerk had the same air of knowing something to everybody else's disadvantage, as his master had. I wondered how many other clerks there were upstairs, and whether they all claimed to have the same detrimental mastery of their fellow-creatures. I wondered what was the history of all the odd litter about the room, and how it came there. I wondered whether the two swollen faces were of Mr Jaggers's family, and, if he were so unfortunate as to have had a pair of such ill-looking relations, why he stuck them on that dusty perch for the blacks and flies to settle on, instead of giving them a place at home. Of course I had no experience of a London summer day, and my spirits may have been oppressed by the hot exhausted air, and by the dust and grit that lay thick on everything. But I sat wondering and waiting in Mr Jaggers's close room, until I really could not bear the two casts on the shelf above Mr Jaggers's chair, and got up and went out.

When I told the clerk that I would take a turn in the air while I waited, he advised me to go round the corner and I should come into Smithfield. So I came into Smithfield; and the shameful place, being all asmear with filth and fat and blood and foam, seemed to stick to me. So, I rubbed it off with all possible speed by turning into a street where I saw the great black dome of Saint Paul's bulging at me from behind a grim stone building which a bystander said was Newgate Prison. Following the wall of the jail, I found the roadway covered with straw to deaden the noise of passing vehicles; and from this, and from the quantity of people standing about smelling strongly of spirits and beer, I inferred that the trials were on.

While I looked about me here, an exceedingly dirty and partially drunk minister of justice asked me if I would like to step in and hear a trial or so: informing me that he could give me a front place for half a crown, whence I should command a full view of the Lord Chief Justice in his wig and robes,—mentioning that awful personage like waxwork, and presently offering him at the reduced price of eighteen-pence. As I declined the proposal on the plea of an appointment, he was so good as to take me into a yard and show me where the gallows was kept, and also where people were publicly whipped, and then he showed me the Debtors' Door, out of which culprits came to be hanged; heightening the interest of that dreadful portal by giving me to understand that 'four on 'em' would come out at that door the day after tomorrow at eight in the morning, to be killed in a row. This was horrible, and gave me a sickening idea of London; the more so as the Lord Chief Justice's proprietor wore (from his hat down to his boots and up again to his pocket-handkerchief inclusive) mildewed clothes which had evidently not belonged to him originally, and which I took it into my head he had bought cheap of the executioner. Under these circumstances I thought myself well rid of him for a shilling.

I dropped into the office to ask if Mr Jaggers had come in yet, and I found he had not, and I strolled out again. This time, I made the tour of Little Britain, and turned into Bartholomew Close; and now I became aware that other people were waiting about for Mr Jaggers, as well as I. There were two men of secret appearance lounging in Bartholomew Close, and thoughtfully fitting their feet into the cracks of the pavement as they talked together, one of whom said to the other when they first passed me, that 'Jaggers would do it if it was to be done.' There was a knot of three men and two women standing at a corner, and one of the women was crying on her dirty shawl, and the other comforted her by saying, as she pulled her own shawl over her shoulders, 'Jaggers is for him, 'Melia, and what more *could* you have?' There was a red-eyed little Jew who came into the Close while I was loitering there, in company with a second little Jew whom he sent upon an errand; and while the messenger was gone, I remarked this Jew, who was of a highly excitable temperament, performing a jig of anxiety under a lamp-post and accompanying himself, in a kind of frenzy, with the words, 'O Jaggerth, Jaggerth, Jaggerth! All otherth ith Cag-Maggerth, give me Jaggerth!' These testimonies to the popularity of my guardian made a deep impression on me, and I admired and wondered more than ever.

At length, as I was looking out at the iron gate of Bartholomew Close into Little Britain, I saw Mr Jaggers coming across the road towards me. All the others who were waiting saw him at the same time, and there was quite a rush at him. Mr Jaggers, putting a hand on my shoulder and walking me on at his side without saying anything to me, addressed himself to his followers.

First, he took the two secret men.

'Now, I have nothing to say to *you*,' said Mr Jaggers, throwing his finger at them. 'I want to know no more than I know. As to the result, it's a toss-up. I told you from the first it was a toss-up. Have you paid Wemmick?'

'We made the money up this morning, sir,' said one of the men, submissively, while the other perused Mr Jaggers's face.

'I don't ask you when you made it up, or where, or whether you made it up at all. Has Wemmick got it?'

'Yes, sir,' said both the men together.

'Very well; then you may go. Now, I won't have it!' said Mr Jaggers, waving his hand at them to put them behind him. 'If you say a word to me, I'll throw up the case.'

'We thought, Mr Jaggers—' one of the men began, pulling off his hat.

'That's what I told you not to do,' said Mr Jaggers. '*You* thought! I think for you; that's enough for you. If I want you, I know where to find you; I don't want you to find me. Now I won't have it. I won't hear a word.'

The two men looked at one another as Mr Jaggers waved them behind again, and humbly fell back and were heard no more.

'And now *you*!' said Mr Jaggers, suddenly stopping, and turning on the two women with the shawls, from whom the three men had meekly separated,—'Oh! Amelia, is it?'

'Yes, Mr Jaggers.'

'And do you remember,' retorted Mr Jaggers, 'that but for me you wouldn't be here and couldn't be here?'

'O yes, sir!' exclaimed both women together. 'Lord bless you, sir, well we knows that!'

'Then why,' said Mr Jaggers, 'do you come here?'

'My Bill, sir!' the crying woman pleaded.

'Now, I tell you what!' said Mr Jaggers. 'Once for all. If you don't know that your Bill's in good hands, I know it. And if you come here bothering about your Bill, I'll make an example of both your Bill and you, and let him slip through my fingers. Have you paid Wemmick?'

'O yes, sir! Every farden.'

'Very well. Then you have done all you have got to do. Say another word—one single word—and Wemmick shall give you your money back.'

This terrible threat caused the two women to fall off immediately. No one remained now but the excitable Jew, who had already raised the skirts of Mr Jaggers's coat to his lips several times.

'I don't know this man!' said Mr Jaggers, in the same devastating strain: 'What does this fellow want?'

'Ma thear Mithter Jaggerth. Hown brother to Habraham Latharuth?'

'Who's he?' said Mr Jaggers. 'Let go of my coat.'

The suitor, kissing the hem of the garment again before relinquishing it, replied, 'Habraham Latharuth, on thuthpithion of plate.'

'You're too late,' said Mr Jaggers. 'I am over the way.'

'Holy father, Mithter Jaggerth!' cried my excitable acquaintance, turning white, 'don't thay you're again Habraham Latharuth!'

'I am,' said Mr Jaggers, 'and there's an end of it. Get out of the way.'

'Mithter Jaggerth! Half a moment! My hown cuthen'th gone to Mithter Wemmick at thith prethent minute, to hoffer him hany termth. Mithter Jaggerth! Half a quarter of a moment! If you'd have the condethenthun to be bought off from the t'other thide—at hany thuperior prithe!—money no object!—Mithter Jaggerth—Mithter—!'

My guardian threw his supplicant off with supreme indifference, and left him dancing on the pavement as if it were red hot. Without further interruption, we reached the front office, where we found the clerk and the man in velveteen with the fur cap.

'Here's Mike,' said the clerk, getting down from his stool, and approaching Mr Jaggers confidentially.

'Oh!' said Mr Jaggers, turning to the man, who was pulling a lock of hair in the middle of his forehead, like the Bull in Cock Robin pulling at the bell-rope; 'your man comes on this afternoon. Well?'

'Well, Mas'r Jaggers,' returned Mike, in the voice of a sufferer from a constitutional cold; 'arter a deal o' trouble, I've found one, sir, as might do.'

'What is he prepared to swear?'

'Well, Mas'r Jaggers,' said Mike, wiping his nose on his fur cap this time; 'in a general way, anythink.'

Mr Jaggers suddenly became most irate. 'Now, I warned you before,' said he, throwing his forefinger at the terrified client, 'that if you ever presumed to talk in that way here, I'd make an example of you. You infernal scoundrel, how dare you tell ME that?'

The client looked scared, but bewildered too, as if he were unconscious what he had done.

'Spooney!' said the clerk, in a low voice, giving him a stir with his elbow. 'Soft Head! Need you say it face to face?'

'Now, I ask you, you blundering booby,' said my guardian, very sternly, 'once more and for the last time, what the man you have brought here is prepared to swear?'

Mike looked hard at my guardian, as if he were trying to learn a lesson from his face, and slowly replied, 'Ayther to character, or to having been in his company and never left him all the night in question.'

'Now, be careful. In what station of life is this man?'

Mike looked at his cap, and looked at the floor, and looked at the ceiling, and looked at the clerk, and even looked at me, before beginning to reply in a nervous manner, 'We've dressed him up like—' when my guardian blustered out,—

'What? You WILL, will you?'

('Spooney!' added the clerk again, with another stir.)

After some helpless casting about, Mike brightened and began again:—

'He is dressed like a 'spectable pieman. A sort of a pastry-cook.'

'Is he here?' asked my guardian.

'I left him,' said Mike, 'a setting on some doorsteps round the corner.'

'Take him past that window, and let me see him.'

The window indicated was the office window. We all three went to it, behind the wire blind, and presently saw the client go by in an accidental manner, with a murderous-looking tall individual, in a short suit of white linen and a paper cap. This guileless confectioner was not by any means sober, and had a black eye in the green stage of recovery, which was painted over.

'Tell him to take his witness away directly,' said my guardian to the clerk, in extreme disgust, 'and ask him what he means by bringing such a fellow as that.'

My guardian then took me into his own room, and while he lunched, standing, from a sandwich-box and a pocket-flask of sherry (he seemed to bully his very sandwich as he ate it), informed me what arrangements he had made for me. I was to go to 'Barnard's Inn,' to young Mr Pocket's rooms, where a bed had been sent in for my accommodation; I was to remain with young Mr Pocket until Monday; on Monday I was to go with him to his father's house on a visit, that I might try how I liked it. Also, I was told what my allowance was to be,—it was a very liberal one,—and had handed to me from one of my guardian's drawers, the cards of certain tradesmen with whom I was to deal for all kinds of clothes, and such other things as I could in reason want. 'You will find your credit good, Mr Pip,' said my guardian, whose flask of sherry smelt like a whole caskful, as he hastily refreshed himself, 'but I shall by this means be able to check your bills, and to pull you up if I find you outrunning the constable. Of course you'll go wrong somehow, but that's no fault of mine.'

After I had pondered a little over this encouraging sentiment, I asked Mr Jaggers if I could send for a coach? He said it was not worth while, I was so near my destination; Wemmick should walk round with me, if I pleased.

I then found that Wemmick was the clerk in the next room. Another clerk was rung down from upstairs to take his place while he was out, and I accompanied him into the street, after shaking hands with my guardian. We found a new set of people lingering outside, but Wemmick made a way among them by saying coolly yet decisively, 'I tell you it's no use; he won't have a word to say to one of you;' and we soon got clear of them, and went on side by side.

Chapter 21

Casting my eyes on Mr Wemmick as we went along, to see what he was like in the light of day, I found him to be a dry man, rather short in stature, with a square wooden face, whose expression seemed to have been imperfectly chipped out with a dull-edged chisel. There were some marks in it that might have been dimples, if the material had been softer and the instrument finer, but which, as it was, were only dints. The chisel had made three or four of these attempts at embellishment over his nose, but had given them up without an effort to smooth them off. I judged him to be a bachelor from the frayed condition of his linen, and he appeared to have sustained a good many bereavements; for he wore at least four mourning rings, besides a brooch representing a lady and a weeping willow at a tomb with an urn on it. I noticed, too, that several rings and seals hung at his watch-chain, as if he were quite laden with remembrances of departed friends. He had glittering eyes,—small, keen, and black,—and thin wide mottled lips. He had had them, to the best of my belief, from forty to fifty years.

'So you were never in London before?' said Mr Wemmick to me.
'No,' said I.
'*I* was new here once,' said Mr Wemmick. 'Rum to think of now!'
'You are well acquainted with it now?'
'Why, yes,' said Mr Wemmick. 'I know the moves of it.'
'Is it a very wicked place?' I asked, more for the sake of saying something than for information.

'You may get cheated, robbed, and murdered in London. But there are plenty of people anywhere, who'll do that for you.'

'If there is bad blood between you and them,' said I, to soften it off a little.

'O! I don't know about bad blood,' returned Mr Wemmick; 'there's not much bad blood about. They'll do it, if there's anything to be got by it.'

'That makes it worse.'

'You think so?' returned Mr Wemmick. 'Much about the same, I should say.'

He wore his hat on the back of his head, and looked straight before him: walking in a self-contained way as if there were nothing in the streets to claim his attention. His mouth was such a post-office of a mouth that he had a mechanical appearance of smiling. We had got to the top of Holborn Hill before I knew that it was merely a mechanical appearance, and that he was not smiling at all.

'Do you know where Mr Matthew Pocket lives?' I asked Mr Wemmick.

'Yes,' said he, nodding in the direction. 'At Hammersmith, west of London.'

'Is that far?'

'Well! Say five miles.'

'Do you know him?'

'Why, you're a regular cross-examiner!' said Mr Wemmick, looking at me with an approving air. 'Yes, I know him. *I* know him!'

There was an air of toleration or depreciation about his utterance of these words that rather depressed me; and I was still looking sideways at his block of a face in search of any encouraging note to the text, when he said here we were at Barnard's Inn. My depression was not alleviated by the announcement, for, I had supposed that establishment to be an hotel kept by Mr Barnard, to which the Blue Boar in our town was a mere public-house. Whereas I now found Barnard to be a disembodied spirit, or a fiction, and his inn the dingiest collection of shabby buildings ever squeezed together in a rank corner as a club for Tom-cats.

We entered this haven through a wicket-gate, and were disgorged by an introductory passage into a melancholy little square that looked to me like a flat burying-ground. I thought it had the most dismal trees in it, and the most dismal sparrows, and the most dismal cats, and the most dismal houses (in number half a dozen or so), that I had ever seen. I thought the windows of the sets of chambers into which those houses were divided were in every stage of dilapidated blind and curtain, crippled flower-pot, cracked glass, dusty decay, and miserable makeshift; while To Let, To Let, To Let, glared at me from empty rooms, as if no new wretches ever came there, and the vengeance of the soul of Barnard were being slowly appeased by the gradual suicide of the present occupants and their unholy interment under the gravel. A frowzy mourning of soot and smoke attired this forlorn creation of Barnard, and it had strewn ashes on its head, and was undergoing penance and humiliation as a mere dust-hole. Thus far my sense of sight; while dry rot and wet rot and all the silent rots that rot in neglected roof and cellar,—rot of rat and mouse and bug and coaching-stables near at hand besides—addressed themselves faintly to my sense of smell, and moaned, 'Try Barnard's Mixture.'

So imperfect was this realization of the first of my great expectations, that I looked in dismay at Mr Wemmick. 'Ah!' said he, mistaking me; 'the retirement reminds you of the country. So it does me.'

He led me into a corner and conducted me up a flight of stairs,— which appeared to me to be slowly collapsing into sawdust, so that one of those days the upper lodgers would look out at their doors and find themselves without the means of coming down,—to a set of chambers on the top floor. Mr POCKET, JUN., was painted on the door, and there was a label on the letter-box, 'Return shortly.'

'He hardly thought you'd come so soon,' Mr Wemmick explained. 'You don't want me any more?'

'No, thank you,' said I.

'As I keep the cash,' Mr Wemmick observed, 'we shall most likely meet pretty often. Good day.'

'Good day.'

I put out my hand, and Mr Wemmick at first looked at it as if he thought I wanted something. Then he looked at me, and said, correcting himself,—

'To be sure! Yes. You're in the habit of shaking hands?'

I was rather confused, thinking it must be out of the London fashion, but said yes.

'I have got so out of it!' said Mr Wemmick,—'except at last. Very glad, I'm sure, to make your acquaintance. Good day!'

When we had shaken hands and he was gone, I opened the staircase window and had nearly beheaded myself, for, the lines had rotted away, and it came down like the guillotine. Happily it was so quick that I had not put my head out. After this escape, I was content to take a foggy view of the inn through the window's encrusting dirt, and to stand dolefully looking out, saying to myself that London was decidedly overrated.

Mr Pocket, Junior's idea of Shortly was not mine, for I had nearly maddened myself with looking out for half an hour, and had written my name with my finger several times in the dirt of every pane in the window, before I heard footsteps on the stairs. Gradually there arose before me the hat, head, neckcloth, waistcoat, trousers, boots, of a member of society of about my own standing. He had a paper-bag under each arm and a pottle of strawberries in one hand, and was out of breath.

'Mr Pip?' said he.

'Mr Pocket?' said I.

'Dear me!' he exclaimed. 'I am extremely sorry; but I knew there was a coach from your part of the country at midday, and I thought you would come by that one. The fact is, I have been out on your account,—not that that is any excuse,—for I thought, coming from the country, you might like a little fruit after dinner, and I went to Covent Garden Market to get it good.'

For a reason that I had, I felt as if my eyes would start out of my head. I acknowledged his attention incoherently, and began to think this was a dream.

'Dear me!' said Mr Pocket, Junior. 'This door sticks so!'

As he was fast making jam of his fruit by wrestling with the door while the paper-bags were under his arms, I begged him to allow me to hold them. He relinquished them with an agreeable smile, and combated with the door as if it were a wild beast. It yielded so suddenly at last, that he staggered back upon me, and I staggered back upon the opposite door, and we both laughed. But still I felt as if my eyes must start out of my head, and as if this must be a dream.

'Pray come in,' said Mr Pocket, Junior. 'Allow me to lead the way. I am rather bare here, but I hope you'll be able to make out tolerably well till Monday. My father thought you would get on more agreeably through tomorrow with me than with him, and might like to take a walk about London. I am sure I shall be very happy to show London to you. As to our table, you won't find that bad, I hope, for it will be supplied from our coffee-house here, and (it is only right I should add) at your expense, such being Mr Jaggers's directions. As to our lodging, it's not by any means splendid, because I have my own bread to earn, and my father hasn't anything to give me, and I shouldn't be willing to take it, if he had. This is our sitting-room,—just such chairs and tables and carpet and so forth, you see, as they could spare from home. You mustn't give me credit for the tablecloth and spoons and castors, because they come for you from the coffee-house. This is my little bedroom; rather musty, but Barnard's *is* musty. This is your bedroom; the furniture's hired for the occasion, but I trust it will answer the purpose; if you should want anything, I'll go and fetch it. The chambers are retired, and we shall be alone together, but we shan't fight, I dare say. But dear me, I beg your pardon, you're holding the fruit all this time. Pray let me take these bags from you. I am quite ashamed.'

As I stood opposite to Mr Pocket, Junior, delivering him the bags, One, Two, I saw the starting appearance come into his own eyes that I knew to be in mine, and he said, falling back,—

'Lord bless me, you're the prowling boy!'

'And you,' said I, 'are the pale young gentleman!'

Chapter 22

The pale young gentleman and I stood contemplating one another in Barnard's Inn, until we both burst out laughing. 'The idea of its being you!' said he. 'The idea of its being *you*!' said I. And then we contemplated one another afresh, and laughed again. 'Well!' said the pale young gentleman, reaching out his hand good-humouredly, 'it's all over now, I hope, and it will be magnanimous in you if you'll forgive me for having knocked you about so.'

I derived from this speech that Mr Herbert Pocket (for Herbert was the pale young gentleman's name) still rather confounded his intention with his execution. But I made a modest reply, and we shook hands warmly.

'You hadn't come into your good fortune at that time?' said Herbert Pocket.

'No,' said I.

'No,' he acquiesced: 'I heard it had happened very lately. *I* was rather on the lookout for good fortune then.'

'Indeed?'

'Yes. Miss Havisham had sent for me, to see if she could take a fancy to me. But she couldn't,—at all events, she didn't.'

I thought it polite to remark that I was surprised to hear that.

'Bad taste,' said Herbert, laughing, 'but a fact. Yes, she had sent for me on a trial visit, and if I had come out of it successfully, I suppose I should have been provided for; perhaps I should have been what-you-may-called it to Estella.'

'What's that?' I asked, with sudden gravity.

He was arranging his fruit in plates while we talked, which divided his attention, and was the cause of his having made this lapse of a word. 'Affianced,' he explained, still busy with the fruit. 'Betrothed. Engaged. What's-his-named. Any word of that sort.'

'How did you bear your disappointment?' I asked.

'Pooh!' said he, 'I didn't care much for it. *She's* a Tartar.'

'Miss Havisham?'

'I don't say no to that, but I meant Estella. That girl's hard and haughty and capricious to the last degree, and has been brought up by Miss Havisham to wreak revenge on all the male sex.'

'What relation is she to Miss Havisham?'

'None,' said he. 'Only adopted.'

'Why should she wreak revenge on all the male sex? What revenge?'

'Lord, Mr Pip!' said he. 'Don't you know?'

'No,' said I.

'Dear me! It's quite a story, and shall be saved till dinner-time. And now let me take the liberty of asking you a question. How did you come there, that day?'

I told him, and he was attentive until I had finished, and then burst out laughing again, and asked me if I was sore afterwards? I didn't ask him if *he* was, for my conviction on that point was perfectly established.

'Mr Jaggers is your guardian, I understand?' he went on.

'Yes.'

'You know he is Miss Havisham's man of business and solicitor, and has her confidence when nobody else has?'

This was bringing me (I felt) towards dangerous ground. I answered with a constraint I made no attempt to disguise, that I had seen Mr Jaggers in Miss Havisham's house on the very day of our combat, but never at any other time, and that I believed he had no recollection of having ever seen me there.

'He was so obliging as to suggest my father for your tutor, and he called on my father to propose it. Of course he knew about my father from his connection with Miss Havisham. My father is Miss Havisham's cousin; not that that implies familiar intercourse between them, for he is a bad courtier and will not propitiate her.'

Herbert Pocket had a frank and easy way with him that was very taking. I had never seen anyone then, and I have never seen anyone since, who more strongly expressed to me, in every look and tone, a natural incapacity to do anything secret and mean. There was something wonderfully hopeful about his general air, and something that at the same time whispered to me he would never be very successful or rich. I don't know how this was. I became imbued with the notion on that first occasion before we sat down to dinner, but I cannot define by what means.

He was still a pale young gentleman, and had a certain conquered languor about him in the midst of his spirits and briskness, that did not seem indicative of natural strength. He had not a handsome face, but it was better than handsome: being extremely amiable and cheerful. His figure was a little ungainly, as in the days when my knuckles had taken such liberties with it, but it looked as if it would always be light and young. Whether Mr Trabb's local work would have sat more gracefully on him than on me, may be a question; but I am conscious that he carried off his rather old clothes much better than I carried off my new suit.

As he was so communicative, I felt that reserve on my part would be a bad return unsuited to our years. I therefore told him my small story, and laid stress on my being forbidden to inquire who my benefactor was. I further mentioned that as I had been brought up a blacksmith in a country place, and knew very little of the ways of politeness, I would take it as a great kindness in him if he would give me a hint whenever he saw me at a loss or going wrong.

'With pleasure,' said he, 'though I venture to prophesy that you'll want very few hints. I dare say we shall be often together, and I should like to banish any needless restraint between us. Will you do me the favour to begin at once to call me by my Christian name, Herbert?'

I thanked him and said I would. I informed him in exchange that my Christian name was Philip.

'I don't take to Philip,' said he, smiling, 'for it sounds like a moral boy out of the spelling-book, who was so lazy that he fell into a pond, or so fat that he couldn't see out of his eyes, or so avaricious that he locked up his cake till the mice ate it, or so determined to go a bird's-nesting that he got himself eaten by bears who lived handy in the neighbourhood. I tell you what I should like. We are so harmonious, and you have been a blacksmith,—would you mind it?'

'I shouldn't mind anything that you propose,' I answered, 'but I don't understand you.'

'Would you mind Handel for a familiar name? There's a charming piece of music by Handel, called the Harmonious Blacksmith.'

'I should like it very much.'

'Then, my dear Handel,' said he, turning round as the door opened, 'here is the dinner, and I must beg of you to take the top of the table, because the dinner is of your providing.'

This I would not hear of, so he took the top, and I faced him. It was a nice little dinner,—seemed to me then a very Lord Mayor's Feast,—and it acquired additional relish from being eaten under those independent circumstances, with no old people by, and with London all around us. This again was heightened by a certain gypsy character that set the banquet off; for while the table was, as Mr Pumblechook might have said, the lap of luxury,—being entirely furnished forth from the coffee-house,—the circumjacent region of sitting-room was of a comparatively pastureless and shifty character; imposing on the waiter the wandering habits of putting the covers on the floor (where he fell over them), the melted butter in the armchair, the bread on the bookshelves, the cheese in the coal-scuttle, and the boiled fowl into my bed in the next room,—where I found much of its parsley and butter in a state of congelation when I retired for the night. All this made the feast delightful, and when the waiter was not there to watch me, my pleasure was without alloy.

We had made some progress in the dinner, when I reminded Herbert of his promise to tell me about Miss Havisham.

'True,' he replied. 'I'll redeem it at once. Let me introduce the topic, Handel, by mentioning that in London it is not the custom to put the knife in the mouth,—for fear of accidents,—and that while the fork is reserved for that use, it is not put further in than necessary. It is scarcely worth mentioning, only it's as well to do as other people do. Also, the spoon is not generally used over-hand, but under. This has two advantages. You get at your mouth better (which after all is the object), and you save a good deal of the attitude of opening oysters, on the part of the right elbow.'

He offered these friendly suggestions in such a lively way, that we both laughed and I scarcely blushed.

'Now,' he pursued, 'concerning Miss Havisham. Miss Havisham, you must know, was a spoilt child. Her mother died when she was a baby, and her father denied her nothing. Her father was a country gentleman down in your part of the world, and was a brewer. I don't know why it should be a crack thing to be a brewer; but it is indisputable that while you cannot possibly be genteel and bake, you may be as genteel as never was and brew. You see it every day.'

'Yet a gentleman may not keep a public-house; may he?' said I.

'Not on any account,' returned Herbert; 'but a public-house may keep a gentleman. Well! Mr Havisham was very rich and very proud. So was his daughter.'

'Miss Havisham was an only child?' I hazarded.

'Stop a moment, I am coming to that. No, she was not an only child; she had a half-brother. Her father privately married again—his cook, I rather think.'

'I thought he was proud,' said I.

'My good Handel, so he was. He married his second wife privately, because he was proud, and in course of time *she* died. When she was dead, I apprehend he first told his daughter what he had done, and then the son became a part of the family, residing in the house you are acquainted with. As the son grew a young man, he turned out riotous, extravagant, undutiful,—altogether bad. At last his father disinherited him; but he softened when he was dying, and left him well off, though not nearly so well off as Miss Havisham.—Take another glass of wine, and excuse my mentioning that society as a body does not expect one to be so strictly conscientious in emptying one's glass, as to turn it bottom upwards with the rim on one's nose.'

I had been doing this, in an excess of attention to his recital. I thanked him, and apologized. He said, 'Not at all,' and resumed.

'Miss Havisham was now an heiress, and you may suppose was looked after as a great match. Her half-brother had now ample means again, but what with debts and what with new madness wasted them most fearfully again. There were stronger differences between him and her than there had been between him and his father, and it is suspected that he cherished a deep and mortal grudge against her as having influenced the father's anger. Now, I come to the cruel part of the story,—merely breaking off, my dear Handel, to remark that a dinner-napkin will not go into a tumbler.'

Why I was trying to pack mine into my tumbler, I am wholly unable to say. I only know that I found myself, with a perseverance worthy of a much better cause, making the most strenuous exertions to compress it within those limits. Again I thanked him and apologized, and again he said in the cheerfullest manner, 'Not at all, I am sure!' and resumed.

'There appeared upon the scene—say at the races, or the public balls, or anywhere else you like—a certain man, who made love to Miss Havisham. I never saw him (for this happened five-and-twenty years ago, before you and I were, Handel), but I have heard my father mention that he was a showy man, and the kind of man for the purpose. But that he was not to be, without ignorance or prejudice, mistaken for a gentleman, my father most strongly asseverates; because it is a principle of his that no man who was not a true gentleman at heart ever was, since the world began, a true gentleman in manner. He says, no varnish can hide the grain of the wood; and that the more varnish you put on, the more the grain will express itself. Well! This man pursued Miss Havisham closely, and professed to be devoted to her. I believe she had not shown much susceptibility up to that time; but all the susceptibility she possessed certainly came out then, and she passionately loved him. There is no doubt that she perfectly idolized him. He practised on her affection in that systematic way, that he got great sums of money from her, and he induced her to buy her brother out of a share in the brewery (which had been weakly left him by his father) at an immense price, on the plea that when he was her husband he must hold and manage it all. Your guardian was not at that time in Miss Havisham's counsels, and she was too haughty and too much in love to be advised by anyone. Her relations were poor and scheming, with the exception of my father; he was poor enough, but not time-serving or jealous. The only independent one among them, he warned her that she was doing too much for this man, and was placing herself too unreservedly in his power. She took the first opportunity of angrily ordering my father out of the house, in his presence, and my father has never seen her since.'

I thought of her having said, 'Matthew will come and see me at last when I am laid dead upon that table;' and I asked Herbert whether his father was so inveterate against her?

'It's not that,' said he, 'but she charged him, in the presence of her intended husband, with being disappointed in the hope of fawning upon her for his own advancement, and, if he were to go to her now, it would look true—even to him—and even to her. To return to the man and make an end of him. The marriage day was fixed, the wedding dresses were bought, the wedding tour was planned out, the wedding guests were invited. The day came, but not the bridegroom. He wrote her a letter—'

'Which she received,' I struck in, 'when she was dressing for her marriage? At twenty minutes to nine?'

'At the hour and minute,' said Herbert, nodding, 'at which she afterwards stopped all the clocks. What was in it, further than that it most heartlessly broke the marriage off, I can't tell you, because I don't know. When she recovered from a bad illness that she had, she laid the whole place waste, as you have seen it, and she has never since looked upon the light of day.'

'Is that all the story?' I asked, after considering it.

'All I know of it; and indeed I only know so much, through piecing it out for myself; for my father always avoids it, and, even when Miss Havisham invited me to go there, told me no more of it than it was absolutely requisite I should understand. But I have forgotten one thing. It has been supposed that the man to whom she gave her misplaced confidence acted throughout in concert with her half-brother; that it was a conspiracy between them; and that they shared the profits.'

'I wonder he didn't marry her and get all the property,' said I.

'He may have been married already, and her cruel mortification may have been a part of her half-brother's scheme,' said Herbert. 'Mind! I don't know that.'

'What became of the two men?' I asked, after again considering the subject.

'They fell into deeper shame and degradation—if there can be deeper—and ruin.'

'Are they alive now?'

'I don't know.'

'You said just now that Estella was not related to Miss Havisham, but adopted. When adopted?'

Herbert shrugged his shoulders. 'There has always been an Estella, since I have heard of a Miss Havisham. I know no more. And now, Handel,' said he, finally throwing off the story as it were, 'there is a perfectly open understanding between us. All that I know about Miss Havisham, you know.'

'And all that I know,' I retorted, 'you know.'

'I fully believe it. So there can be no competition or perplexity between you and me. And as to the condition on which you hold your advancement in life,—namely, that you are not to inquire or discuss to whom you owe it,—you may be very sure that it will never be encroached upon, or even approached, by me, or by any one belonging to me.'

In truth, he said this with so much delicacy, that I felt the subject done with, even though I should be under his father's roof for years and years to come. Yet he said it with so much meaning, too, that I felt he as perfectly understood Miss Havisham to be my benefactress, as I understood the fact myself.

It had not occurred to me before, that he had led up to the theme for the purpose of clearing it out of our way; but we were so much the lighter and easier for having broached it, that I now perceived this to be the case. We were very gay and sociable, and I asked him, in the course of conversation, what he was? He replied, 'A capitalist,—an Insurer of Ships.' I suppose he saw me glancing about the room in search of some tokens of Shipping, or capital, for he added, 'In the City.'

I had grand ideas of the wealth and importance of Insurers of Ships in the City, and I began to think with awe of having laid a young Insurer on his back, blackened his enterprising eye, and cut his responsible head open. But again there came upon me, for my relief, that odd impression that Herbert Pocket would never be very successful or rich.

'I shall not rest satisfied with merely employing my capital in insuring ships. I shall buy up some good Life Assurance shares, and cut into the direction. I shall also do a little in the mining way. None of these things will interfere with my chartering a few thousand tons on my own account. I think I shall trade,' said he, leaning back in his chair, 'to the East Indies, for silks, shawls, spices, dyes, drugs, and precious woods. It's an interesting trade.'

'And the profits are large?' said I.

'Tremendous!' said he.

I wavered again, and began to think here were greater expectations than my own.

'I think I shall trade, also,' said he, putting his thumbs in his waist-coat pockets, 'to the West Indies, for sugar, tobacco, and rum. Also to Ceylon, specially for elephants' tusks.'

'You will want a good many ships,' said I.

'A perfect fleet,' said he.

Quite overpowered by the magnificence of these transactions, I asked him where the ships he insured mostly traded to at present?

'I haven't begun insuring yet,' he replied. 'I am looking about me.'

Somehow, that pursuit seemed more in keeping with Barnard's Inn. I said (in a tone of conviction), 'Ah-h!'

'Yes. I am in a counting-house, and looking about me.'

'Is a counting-house profitable?' I asked.

'To—do you mean to the young fellow who's in it?' he asked, in reply.

'Yes; to you.'

'Why, n-no; not to me.' He said this with the air of one carefully reckoning up and striking a balance. 'Not directly profitable. That is, it doesn't pay me anything, and I have to—keep myself.'

This certainly had not a profitable appearance, and I shook my head as if I would imply that it would be difficult to lay by much accumulative capital from such a source of income.

'But the thing is,' said Herbert Pocket, 'that you look about you. *That's* the grand thing. You are in a counting-house, you know, and you look about you.'

It struck me as a singular implication that you couldn't be out of a counting-house, you know, and look about you; but I silently deferred to his experience.

'Then the time comes,' said Herbert, 'when you see your opening. And you go in, and you swoop upon it and you make your capital, and then there you are! When you have once made your capital, you have nothing to do but employ it.'

This was very like his way of conducting that encounter in the garden; very like. His manner of bearing his poverty, too, exactly corresponded to his manner of bearing that defeat. It seemed to me that he took all blows and buffets now with just the same air as he had taken mine then. It was evident that he had nothing around him but the simplest necessaries, for everything that I remarked upon turned out to have been sent in on my account from the coffee-house or somewhere else.

Yet, having already made his fortune in his own mind, he was so unassuming with it that I felt quite grateful to him for not being puffed up. It was a pleasant addition to his naturally pleasant ways, and we got on famously. In the evening we went out for a walk in the streets, and went half-price to the theatre; and next day we went to church at Westminster Abbey, and in the afternoon we walked in the parks; and I wondered who shod all the horses there, and wished Joe did.

On a moderate computation, it was many months, that Sunday, since I had left Joe and Biddy. The space interposed between myself and them partook of that expansion, and our marshes were any distance off. That I could have been at our old church in my old church-going clothes, on the very last Sunday that ever was, seemed a combination of impossibilities, geographical and social, solar and lunar. Yet in the London streets so crowded with people and so brilliantly lighted in the dusk of evening, there were depressing hints of reproaches for that I had put the poor old kitchen at home so far away; and in the dead of night, the footsteps of some incapable impostor of a porter mooning about Barnard's Inn, under pretence of watching it, fell hollow on my heart.

On the Monday morning at a quarter before nine, Herbert went to the counting-house to report himself,—to look about him, too, I suppose,—and I bore him company. He was to come away in an hour or two to attend me to Hammersmith, and I was to wait about for him. It appeared to me that the eggs from which young insurers were hatched were incubated in dust and heat, like the eggs of ostriches, judging from the places to which those incipient giants repaired on a Monday morning. Nor did the counting-house where Herbert assisted, show in my eyes as at all a good observatory; being a back second floor up a yard, of a grimy presence in all particulars, and with a look into another back second floor, rather than a look out.

I waited about until it was noon, and I went upon 'Change, and I saw fluey men sitting there under the bills about shipping, whom I took to be great merchants, though I couldn't understand why they should all be out of spirits. When Herbert came, we went and had lunch at a celebrated house which I then quite venerated, but now believe to have been the most abject superstition in Europe, and where I could not help noticing, even then, that there was much more gravy on the tablecloths and knives and waiters' clothes, than in the steaks. This collation disposed of at a moderate price (considering the grease, which was not charged for), we went back to Barnard's Inn and got my little portmanteau, and then took coach for Hammersmith. We arrived there at two or three o'clock in the afternoon, and had very little way to walk to Mr Pocket's house. Lifting the latch of a gate, we passed direct into a little garden overlooking the river, where Mr Pocket's children were playing about. And unless I deceive myself on a point where my interests or prepossessions are certainly not concerned, I saw that Mr and Mrs Pocket's children were not growing up or being brought up, but were tumbling up.

Mrs Pocket was sitting on a garden chair under a tree, reading, with her legs upon another garden chair; and Mrs Pocket's two nurse-maids were looking about them while the children played. 'Mamma,' said Herbert, 'this is young Mr Pip.' Upon which Mrs Pocket received me with an appearance of amiable dignity.

'Master Alick and Miss Jane,' cried one of the nurses to two of the children, 'if you go a bouncing up against them bushes you'll fall over into the river and be drownded, and what'll your pa say then?'

At the same time this nurse picked up Mrs Pocket's handkerchief, and said, 'If that don't make six times you've dropped it, Mum!' Upon which Mrs Pocket laughed and said, 'Thank you, Flopson,' and settling herself in one chair only, resumed her book. Her countenance immediately assumed a knitted and intent expression as if she had been reading for a week, but before she could have read half a dozen lines, she fixed her eyes upon me, and said, 'I hope your mamma is quite well?' This unexpected inquiry put me into such a difficulty that

I began saying in the absurdest way that if there had been any such person I had no doubt she would have been quite well and would have been very much obliged and would have sent her compliments, when the nurse came to my rescue.

'Well!' she cried, picking up the pocket-handkerchief, 'if that don't make seven times! What ARE you a doing of this afternoon, Mum!' Mrs Pocket received her property, at first with a look of unutterable surprise as if she had never seen it before, and then with a laugh of recognition, and said, 'Thank you, Flopson,' and forgot me, and went on reading.

I found, now I had leisure to count them, that there were no fewer than six little Pockets present, in various stages of tumbling up. I had scarcely arrived at the total when a seventh was heard, as in the region of air, wailing dolefully.

'If there ain't Baby!' said Flopson, appearing to think it most surprising. 'Make haste up, Millers.'

Millers, who was the other nurse, retired into the house, and by degrees the child's wailing was hushed and stopped, as if it were a young ventriloquist with something in its mouth. Mrs Pocket read all the time, and I was curious to know what the book could be.

We were waiting, I supposed, for Mr Pocket to come out to us; at any rate we waited there, and so I had an opportunity of observing the remarkable family phenomenon that whenever any of the children strayed near Mrs Pocket in their play, they always tripped themselves up and tumbled over her,—always very much to her momentary astonishment, and their own more enduring lamentation. I was at a loss to account for this surprising circumstance, and could not help giving my mind to speculations about it, until by and by Millers came down with the baby, which baby was handed to Flopson, which Flopson was handing it to Mrs Pocket, when she too went fairly head foremost over Mrs Pocket, baby and all, and was caught by Herbert and myself.

'Gracious me, Flopson!' said Mrs Pocket, looking off her book for a moment, 'everybody's tumbling!'

'Gracious you, indeed, Mum!' returned Flopson, very red in the face; 'what have you got there?'

'*I* got here, Flopson?' asked Mrs Pocket.

'Why, if it ain't your footstool!' cried Flopson. 'And if you keep it under your skirts like that, who's to help tumbling? Here! Take the baby, Mum, and give me your book.'

Mrs Pocket acted on the advice, and inexpertly danced the infant a little in her lap, while the other children played about it. This had lasted but a very short time, when Mrs Pocket issued summary orders that they were all to be taken into the house for a nap. Thus I made the second discovery on that first occasion, that the nurture of the little Pockets consisted of alternately tumbling up and lying down.

Under these circumstances, when Flopson and Millers had got the children into the house, like a little flock of sheep, and Mr Pocket came out of it to make my acquaintance, I was not much surprised to find that Mr Pocket was a gentleman with a rather perplexed expression of face, and with his very grey hair disordered on his head, as if he didn't quite see his way to putting anything straight.

Chapter 23

Mr Pocket said he was glad to see me, and he hoped I was not sorry to see him. 'For, I really am not,' he added, with his son's smile, 'an alarming personage.' He was a young-looking man, in spite of his perplexities and his very grey hair, and his manner seemed quite natural. I use the word natural, in the sense of its being unaffected; there was something comic in his distraught way, as though it would have been downright ludicrous but for his own perception that it was very near being so. When he had talked with me a little, he said to Mrs Pocket, with a rather anxious contraction of his eyebrows, which were black and handsome, 'Belinda, I hope you have welcomed Mr Pip?' And she looked up from her book, and said, 'Yes.' She then smiled upon me in an absent state of mind, and asked me if I liked the taste of orange-flower water? As the question had no bearing, near or remote, on any foregone or subsequent transaction, I consider it to have been thrown out, like her previous approaches, in general conversational condescension.

I found out within a few hours, and may mention at once, that Mrs Pocket was the only daughter of a certain quite accidental deceased Knight, who had invented for himself a conviction that his deceased father would have been made a Baronet but for somebody's determined opposition arising out of entirely personal motives,—I forget whose, if I ever knew,—the Sovereign's, the Prime Minister's, the Lord Chancellor's, the Archbishop of Canterbury's, anybody's,—and had tacked himself on to the nobles of the earth in right of this quite supposititious fact. I believe he had been knighted himself for storming the English grammar at the point of the pen, in a desperate address engrossed on vellum, on the occasion of the laying of the first stone of some building or other, and for handing some Royal Personage either the trowel or the mortar. Be that as it may, he had directed Mrs Pocket to be brought up from her cradle as one who in the nature of things must marry a title, and who was to be guarded from the acquisition of plebeian domestic knowledge.

So successful a watch and ward had been established over the young lady by this judicious parent, that she had grown up highly ornamental, but perfectly helpless and useless. With her character thus happily formed, in the first bloom of her youth she had encountered Mr Pocket: who was also in the first bloom of youth, and not quite decided whether to mount to the Woolsack, or to roof himself in with a mitre. As his doing the one or the other was a mere question of time, he and Mrs Pocket had taken time by the forelock (when, to judge from its length, it would seem to have wanted cutting), and had married without the knowledge of the judicious parent. The judicious parent, having nothing to bestow or withhold but his blessing, had handsomely settled that dower upon them after a short struggle, and had informed Mr Pocket that his wife was 'a treasure for a Prince.' Mr Pocket had invested the Prince's treasure in the ways of the world ever since, and it was supposed to have brought him in but indifferent interest. Still, Mrs Pocket was in general the object of a queer sort of respectful pity, because she had not married a title; while Mr Pocket was the object of a queer sort of forgiving reproach, because he had never got one.

Mr Pocket took me into the house and showed me my room:

which was a pleasant one, and so furnished as that I could use it with comfort for my own private sitting-room. He then knocked at the doors of two other similar rooms, and introduced me to their occupants, by name Drummle and Startop. Drummle, an old-looking young man of a heavy order of architecture, was whistling. Startop, younger in years and appearance, was reading and holding his head, as if he thought himself in danger of exploding it with too strong a charge of knowledge.

Both Mr and Mrs Pocket had such a noticeable air of being in somebody else's hands, that I wondered who really was in possession of the house and let them live there, until I found this unknown power to be the servants. It was a smooth way of going on, perhaps, in respect of saving trouble; but it had the appearance of being expensive, for the servants felt it a duty they owed to themselves to be nice in their eating and drinking, and to keep a deal of company downstairs. They allowed a very liberal table to Mr and Mrs Pocket, yet it always appeared to me that by far the best part of the house to have boarded in would have been the kitchen,—always supposing the boarder capable of self-defence, for, before I had been there a week, a neighbouring lady with whom the family were personally unacquainted, wrote in to say that she had seen Millers slapping the baby. This greatly distressed Mrs Pocket, who burst into tears on receiving the note, and said that it was an extraordinary thing that the neighbours couldn't mind their own business.

By degrees I learnt, and chiefly from Herbert, that Mr Pocket had been educated at Harrow and at Cambridge, where he had distinguished himself; but that when he had had the happiness of marrying Mrs Pocket very early in life, he had impaired his prospects and taken up the calling of a Grinder. After grinding a number of dull blades,—of whom it was remarkable that their fathers, when influential, were always going to help him to preferment, but always forgot to do it when the blades had left the Grindstone,—he had wearied of that poor work and had come to London. Here, after gradually failing in loftier hopes, he had 'read' with divers who had lacked opportunities or neglected them, and had refurbished divers others for special occasions, and had turned his acquirements to the account of literary compilation and correction, and on such means, added to some very moderate private resources, still maintained the house I saw.

Mr and Mrs Pocket had a toady neighbour; a widow lady of that highly sympathetic nature that she agreed with everybody, blessed everybody, and shed smiles and tears on everybody, according to circumstances. This lady's name was Mrs Coiler, and I had the honour of taking her down to dinner on the day of my installation. She gave me to understand on the stairs, that it was a blow to dear Mrs Pocket that dear Mr Pocket should be under the necessity of receiving gentlemen to read with him. That did not extend to me, she told me in a gush of love and confidence (at that time, I had known her something less than five minutes); if they were all like Me, it would be quite another thing.

'But dear Mrs Pocket,' said Mrs Coiler, 'after her early disappointment (not that dear Mr Pocket was to blame in that), requires so much luxury and elegance—'

'Yes, ma'am,' I said, to stop her, for I was afraid she was going to cry.

'And she is of so aristocratic a disposition—'

'Yes, ma'am,' I said again, with the same object as before.

'—That it *is* hard,' said Mrs Coiler, 'to have dear Mr Pocket's time and attention diverted from dear Mrs Pocket.'

I could not help thinking that it might be harder if the butcher's time and attention were diverted from dear Mrs Pocket; but I said nothing, and indeed had enough to do in keeping a bashful watch upon my company manners.

It came to my knowledge, through what passed between Mrs Pocket and Drummle while I was attentive to my knife and fork, spoon, glasses, and other instruments of self-destruction, that Drummle, whose Christian name was Bentley, was actually the next heir but one to a baronetcy. It further appeared that the book I had seen Mrs Pocket reading in the garden was all about titles, and that she knew the exact date at which her grandpapa would have come into the book, if he ever had come at all. Drummle didn't say much, but in his limited way (he struck me as a sulky kind of fellow) he spoke as one of the elect, and recognized Mrs Pocket as a woman and a sister. No one but themselves and Mrs Coiler the toady neighbour showed any interest in this part of the conversation, and it appeared to me that it was painful to Herbert; but it promised to last a long time, when the page came in with the announcement of a domestic affliction. It was, in effect, that the cook had mislaid the beef. To my unutterable amazement, I now, for the first time, saw Mr Pocket relieve his mind by going through a performance that struck me as very extraordinary, but which made no impression on anybody else, and with which I soon became as familiar as the rest. He laid down the carving-knife and fork,—being engaged in carving, at the moment,—put his two hands into his disturbed hair, and appeared to make an extraordinary effort to lift himself up by it. When he had done this, and had not lifted himself up at all, he quietly went on with what he was about.

Mrs Coiler then changed the subject and began to flatter me. I liked it for a few moments, but she flattered me so very grossly that the pleasure was soon over. She had a serpentine way of coming close at me when she pretended to be vitally interested in the friends and localities I had left, which was altogether snaky and fork-tongued; and when she made an occasional bounce upon Startop (who said very little to her), or upon Drummle (who said less), I rather envied them for being on the opposite side of the table.

After dinner the children were introduced, and Mrs Coiler made admiring comments on their eyes, noses, and legs,—a sagacious way of improving their minds. There were four little girls, and two little boys, besides the baby who might have been either, and the baby's next successor who was as yet neither. They were brought in by Flopson and Millers, much as though those two non-commissioned officers had been recruiting somewhere for children and had enlisted these, while Mrs Pocket looked at the young Nobles that ought to have been as if she rather thought she had had the pleasure of inspecting them before, but didn't quite know what to make of them.

'Here! Give me your fork, Mum, and take the baby,' said Flopson. 'Don't take it that way, or you'll get its head under the table.'

Thus advised, Mrs Pocket took it the other way, and got its head upon the table; which was announced to all present by a prodigious concussion.

'Dear, dear! Give it me back, Mum,' said Flopson; 'and Miss Jane, come and dance to baby, do!'

One of the little girls, a mere mite who seemed to have prematurely taken upon herself some charge of the others, stepped out of her place by me, and danced to and from the baby until it left off crying, and laughed. Then, all the children laughed, and Mr Pocket (who in the meantime had twice endeavoured to lift himself up by the hair) laughed, and we all laughed and were glad.

Flopson, by dint of doubling the baby at the joints like a Dutch doll, then got it safely into Mrs Pocket's lap, and gave it the nutcrackers to play with; at the same time recommending Mrs Pocket to take notice that the handles of that instrument were not likely to agree with its eyes, and sharply charging Miss Jane to look after the same. Then, the two nurses left the room, and had a lively scuffle on the staircase with a dissipated page who had waited at dinner, and who had clearly lost half his buttons at the gaming-table.

I was made very uneasy in my mind by Mrs Pocket's falling into a discussion with Drummle respecting two baronetcies, while she ate a sliced orange steeped in sugar and wine, and, forgetting all about the baby on her lap, who did most appalling things with the nutcrackers. At length little Jane, perceiving its young brains to be imperilled, softly left her place, and with many small artifices coaxed the dangerous weapon away. Mrs Pocket finishing her orange at about the same time, and not approving of this, said to Jane,—

'You naughty child, how dare you? Go and sit down this instant!'

'Mamma dear,' lisped the little girl, 'baby ood have put hith eyeth out.'

'How dare you tell me so?' retorted Mrs Pocket. 'Go and sit down in your chair this moment!'

Mrs Pocket's dignity was so crushing, that I felt quite abashed, as if I myself had done something to rouse it.

'Belinda,' remonstrated Mr Pocket, from the other end of the table, 'how can you be so unreasonable? Jane only interfered for the protection of baby.'

'I will not allow anybody to interfere,' said Mrs Pocket. 'I am surprised, Matthew, that you should expose me to the affront of interference.'

'Good God!' cried Mr Pocket, in an outbreak of desolate desperation. 'Are infants to be nutcrackered into their tombs, and is nobody to save them?'

'I will not be interfered with by Jane,' said Mrs Pocket, with a majestic glance at that innocent little offender. 'I hope I know my poor grandpapa's position. Jane, indeed!'

Mr Pocket got his hands in his hair again, and this time really did lift himself some inches out of his chair. 'Hear this!' he helplessly exclaimed to the elements. 'Babies are to be nutcrackered dead, for people's poor grandpapa's positions!' Then he let himself down again, and became silent.

We all looked awkwardly at the tablecloth while this was going on. A pause succeeded, during which the honest and irrepressible baby made a series of leaps and crows at little Jane, who appeared to me to be the only member of the family (irrespective of servants) with whom it had any decided acquaintance.

'Mr Drummle,' said Mrs Pocket, 'will you ring for Flopson? Jane, you undutiful little thing, go and lie down. Now, baby darling, come with ma!'

The baby was the soul of honour, and protested with all its might. It doubled itself up the wrong way over Mrs Pocket's arm, exhibited a pair of knitted shoes and dimpled ankles to the company in lieu of its soft face, and was carried out in the highest state of mutiny. And it gained its point after all, for I saw it through the window within a few minutes, being nursed by little Jane.

It happened that the other five children were left behind at the dinner-table, through Flopson's having some private engagement, and their not being anybody else's business. I thus became aware of the mutual relations between them and Mr Pocket, which were exemplified in the following manner. Mr Pocket, with the normal perplexity of his face heightened and his hair rumpled, looked at them for some minutes, as if he couldn't make out how they came to be boarding and lodging in that establishment, and why they hadn't been billeted by Nature on somebody else. Then, in a distant Missionary way he asked them certain questions,—as why little Joe had that hole in his frill, who said, Pa, Flopson was going to mend it when she had time,—and how little Fanny came by that whitlow, who said, Pa, Millers was going to poultice it when she didn't forget. Then, he melted into parental tenderness, and gave them a shilling apiece and told them to go and play; and then as they went out, with one very strong effort to lift himself up by the hair he dismissed the hopeless subject.

In the evening there was rowing on the river. As Drummle and Startop had each a boat, I resolved to set up mine, and to cut them both out. I was pretty good at most exercises in which country boys are adepts, but as I was conscious of wanting elegance of style for the Thames,—not to say for other waters,—I at once engaged to place myself under the tuition of the winner of a prize-wherry who plied at our stairs, and to whom I was introduced by my new allies. This practical authority confused me very much by saying I had the arm of a blacksmith. If he could have known how nearly the compliment lost him his pupil, I doubt if he would have paid it.

There was a supper-tray after we got home at night, and I think we should all have enjoyed ourselves, but for a rather disagreeable domestic occurrence. Mr Pocket was in good spirits, when a housemaid came in, and said, 'If you please, sir, I should wish to speak to you.'

'Speak to your master?' said Mrs Pocket, whose dignity was roused again. 'How can you think of such a thing? Go and speak to Flopson. Or speak to me—at some other time.'

'Begging your pardon, ma'am,' returned the housemaid, 'I should wish to speak at once, and to speak to master.'

Hereupon, Mr Pocket went out of the room, and we made the best of ourselves until he came back.

'This is a pretty thing, Belinda!' said Mr Pocket, returning with a countenance expressive of grief and despair. 'Here's the cook lying insensibly drunk on the kitchen floor, with a large bundle of fresh butter made up in the cupboard ready to sell for grease!'

Mrs Pocket instantly showed much amiable emotion, and said, 'This is that odious Sophia's doing!'

'What do you mean, Belinda?' demanded Mr Pocket.

'Sophia has told you,' said Mrs Pocket. 'Did I not see her with my own eyes and hear her with my own ears, come into the room just now and ask to speak to you?'

'But has she not taken me downstairs, Belinda,' returned Mr Pocket, 'and shown me the woman, and the bundle too?'

'And do you defend her, Matthew,' said Mrs Pocket, 'for making mischief?'

Mr Pocket uttered a dismal groan.

'Am I, grandpapa's granddaughter, to be nothing in the house?' said Mrs Pocket. 'Besides, the cook has always been a very nice respectful woman, and said in the most natural manner when she came to look after the situation, that she felt I was born to be a Duchess.'

There was a sofa where Mr Pocket stood, and he dropped upon it in the attitude of the Dying Gladiator. Still in that attitude he said, with a hollow voice, 'Goodnight, Mr Pip,' when I deemed it advisable to go to bed and leave him.

Chapter 24

After two or three days, when I had established myself in my room and had gone backwards and forwards to London several times, and had ordered all I wanted of my tradesmen, Mr Pocket and I had a long talk together. He knew more of my intended career than I knew myself, for he referred to his having been told by Mr Jaggers that I was not designed for any profession, and that I should be well enough educated for my destiny if I could 'hold my own' with the average of young men in prosperous circumstances. I acquiesced, of course, knowing nothing to the contrary.

He advised my attending certain places in London, for the acquisition of such mere rudiments as I wanted, and my investing him with the functions of explainer and director of all my studies. He hoped that with intelligent assistance I should meet with little to discourage me, and should soon be able to dispense with any aid but his. Through his way of saying this, and much more to similar purpose, he placed himself on confidential terms with me in an admirable manner; and I may state at once that he was always so zealous and honourable in fulfilling his compact with me, that he made me zealous and honourable in fulfilling mine with him. If he had shown indifference as a master, I have no doubt I should have returned the compliment as a pupil; he gave me no such excuse, and each of us did the other justice. Nor did I ever regard him as having anything ludicrous about him—or anything but what was serious, honest, and good—in his tutor communication with me.

When these points were settled, and so far carried out as that I had begun to work in earnest, it occurred to me that if I could retain my bedroom in Barnard's Inn, my life would be agreeably varied, while my manners would be none the worse for Herbert's society. Mr Pocket did not object to this arrangement, but urged that before any step could possibly be taken in it, it must be submitted to my guardian. I felt that this delicacy arose out of the consideration that the plan would save Herbert some expense, so I went off to Little Britain and imparted my wish to Mr Jaggers.

'If I could buy the furniture now hired for me,' said I, 'and one or two other little things, I should be quite at home there.'

'Go it!' said Mr Jaggers, with a short laugh. 'I told you you'd get on. Well! How much do you want?'

I said I didn't know how much.

'Come!' retorted Mr Jaggers. 'How much? Fifty pounds?'

'O, not nearly so much.'

'Five pounds?' said Mr Jaggers.

This was such a great fall, that I said in discomfiture, 'O, more than that.'

'More than that, eh!' retorted Mr Jaggers, lying in wait for me, with his hands in his pockets, his head on one side, and his eyes on the wall behind me; 'how much more?'

'It is so difficult to fix a sum,' said I, hesitating.

'Come!' said Mr Jaggers. 'Let's get at it. Twice five; will that do? Three times five; will that do? Four times five; will that do?'

I said I thought that would do handsomely.

'Four times five will do handsomely, will it?' said Mr Jaggers, knitting his brows. 'Now, what do you make of four times five?'

'What do I make of it?'

'Ah!' said Mr Jaggers; 'how much?'

'I suppose you make it twenty pounds,' said I, smiling.

'Never mind what *I* make it, my friend,' observed Mr Jaggers, with a knowing and contradictory toss of his head. 'I want to know what *you* make it.'

'Twenty pounds, of course.'

'Wemmick!' said Mr Jaggers, opening his office door. 'Take Mr Pip's written order, and pay him twenty pounds.'

This strongly marked way of doing business made a strongly marked impression on me, and that not of an agreeable kind. Mr Jaggers never laughed; but he wore great bright creaking boots, and, in poising himself on these boots, with his large head bent down and his eyebrows joined together, awaiting an answer, he sometimes caused the boots to creak, as if *they* laughed in a dry and suspicious way. As he happened to go out now, and as Wemmick was brisk and talkative, I said to Wemmick that I hardly knew what to make of Mr Jaggers's manner.

'Tell him that, and he'll take it as a compliment,' answered Wemmick; 'he don't mean that you *should* know what to make of it.—Oh!' for I looked surprised, 'it's not personal; it's professional: only professional.'

Wemmick was at his desk, lunching—and crunching—on a dry hard biscuit; pieces of which he threw from time to time into his slit of a mouth, as if he were posting them.

'Always seems to me,' said Wemmick, 'as if he had set a man-trap and was watching it. Suddenly-click—you're caught!'

Without remarking that man-traps were not among the amenities of life, I said I supposed he was very skilful?

'Deep,' said Wemmick, 'as Australia.' Pointing with his pen at the office floor, to express that Australia was understood, for the purposes of the figure, to be symmetrically on the opposite spot of the globe. 'If there was anything deeper,' added Wemmick, bringing his pen to paper, 'he'd be it.'

Then, I said I supposed he had a fine business, and Wemmick said, 'Ca-pi-tal!' Then I asked if there were many clerks? to which he replied,—

'We don't run much into clerks, because there's only one Jaggers, and people won't have him at second hand. There are only four of us. Would you like to see 'em? You are one of us, as I may say.'

I accepted the offer. When Mr Wemmick had put all the biscuit into the post, and had paid me my money from a cash box in a safe, the key of which safe he kept somewhere down his back and produced from his coat-collar like an iron-pigtail, we went upstairs. The house was dark and shabby, and the greasy shoulders that had left their mark in Mr Jaggers's room seemed to have been shuffling up and down the staircase for years. In the front first floor, a clerk who looked something between a publican and a rat-catcher—a large pale, puffed, swollen man—was attentively engaged with three or four people of shabby appearance, whom he treated as unceremoniously as everybody seemed to be treated who contributed to Mr Jaggers's coffers. 'Getting evidence together,' said Mr Wemmick, as we came out, 'for the Bailey.' In the room over that, a little flabby terrier of a clerk with dangling hair (his cropping seemed to have been forgotten when he was a puppy) was similarly engaged with a man with weak eyes, whom Mr Wemmick presented to me as a smelter who kept his pot always boiling, and who would melt me anything I pleased,—and who was in an excessive white-perspiration, as if he had been trying his art on himself. In a back room, a high-shouldered man with a face-ache tied up in dirty flannel, who was dressed in old black clothes that bore the appearance of having been waxed, was stooping over his work of making fair copies of the notes of the other two gentlemen, for Mr Jaggers's own use.

This was all the establishment. When we went downstairs again, Wemmick led me into my guardian's room, and said, 'This you've seen already.'

'Pray,' said I, as the two odious casts with the twitchy leer upon them caught my sight again, 'whose likenesses are those?'

'These?' said Wemmick, getting upon a chair, and blowing the dust off the horrible heads before bringing them down. 'These are two celebrated ones. Famous clients of ours that got us a world of credit. This chap (why you must have come down in the night and been peeping into the inkstand, to get this blot upon your eyebrow, you old rascal!) murdered his master, and, considering that he wasn't brought up to evidence, didn't plan it badly.'

'Is it like him?' I asked, recoiling from the brute, as Wemmick spat upon his eyebrow and gave it a rub with his sleeve.

'Like him? It's himself, you know. The cast was made in Newgate, directly after he was taken down. You had a particular fancy for me, hadn't you, Old Artful?' said Wemmick. He then explained this affectionate apostrophe, by touching his brooch representing the lady and the weeping willow at the tomb with the urn upon it, and saying, 'Had it made for me, express!'

'Is the lady anybody?' said I.

'No,' returned Wemmick. 'Only his game. (You liked your bit of game, didn't you?) No; deuce a bit of a lady in the case, Mr Pip, except one,—and she wasn't of this slender lady-like sort, and you wouldn't have caught *her* looking after this urn, unless there was something to drink in it.' Wemmick's attention being thus directed to his brooch, he put down the cast, and polished the brooch with his pocket-handkerchief.

'Did that other creature come to the same end?' I asked. 'He has the same look.'

'You're right,' said Wemmick; 'it's the genuine look. Much as if one nostril was caught up with a horse-hair and a little fish-hook. Yes, he came to the same end; quite the natural end here, I assure you. He forged wills, this blade did, if he didn't also put the supposed testators to sleep too. You were a gentlemanly Cove, though' (Mr Wemmick was again apostrophizing), 'and you said you could write Greek. Yah, Bounceable! What a liar you were! I never met such a liar as you!' Before putting his late friend on his shelf again, Wemmick touched the largest of his mourning rings and said, 'Sent out to buy it for me, only the day before.'

While he was putting up the other cast and coming down from the chair, the thought crossed my mind that all his personal jewelry was derived from like sources. As he had shown no diffidence on the subject, I ventured on the liberty of asking him the question, when he stood before me, dusting his hands.

'O yes,' he returned, 'these are all gifts of that kind. One brings another, you see; that's the way of it. I always take 'em. They're curiosities. And they're property. They may not be worth much, but, after all, they're property and portable. It don't signify to you with your brilliant lookout, but as to myself, my guiding-star always is, 'Get hold of portable property'.'

When I had rendered homage to this light, he went on to say, in a friendly manner:—

'If at any odd time when you have nothing better to do, you wouldn't mind coming over to see me at Walworth, I could offer you a bed, and I should consider it an honour. I have not much to show you; but such two or three curiosities as I have got you might like to look over; and I am fond of a bit of garden and a summer-house.'

I said I should be delighted to accept his hospitality.

'Thankee,' said he; 'then we'll consider that it's to come off, when convenient to you. Have you dined with Mr Jaggers yet?'

'Not yet.'

'Well,' said Wemmick, 'he'll give you wine, and good wine. I'll give you punch, and not bad punch. And now I'll tell you something. When you go to dine with Mr Jaggers, look at his housekeeper.'

'Shall I see something very uncommon?'

'Well,' said Wemmick, 'you'll see a wild beast tamed. Not so very uncommon, you'll tell me. I reply, that depends on the original wildness of the beast, and the amount of taming. It won't lower your opinion of Mr Jaggers's powers. Keep your eye on it.'

I told him I would do so, with all the interest and curiosity that his preparation awakened. As I was taking my departure, he asked me if I would like to devote five minutes to seeing Mr Jaggers 'at it?'

For several reasons, and not least because I didn't clearly know what Mr Jaggers would be found to be 'at,' I replied in the affirmative. We dived into the City, and came up in a crowded police-court, where a blood-relation (in the murderous sense) of the deceased, with the fanciful taste in brooches, was standing at the bar, uncomfortably chewing something; while my guardian had a woman under examination or cross-examination,—I don't know which,—and was striking her, and the bench, and everybody present, with awe. If anybody, of whatsoever degree, said a word that he didn't approve of, he instantly required to have it 'taken down.' If anybody wouldn't make an admission, he said, 'I'll have it out of you!' and if anybody made an admission, he said, 'Now I have got you!' The magistrates shivered under a single bite of his finger. Thieves and thief-takers hung in dread rapture on his words, and shrank when a hair of his eyebrows turned in their direction. Which side he was on I couldn't make out, for he seemed to me to be grinding the whole place in a mill; I only know that when I stole out on tiptoe, he was not on the side of the bench; for, he was making the legs of the old gentleman who presided, quite convulsive under the table, by his denunciations of his conduct as the representative of British law and justice in that chair that day.

Chapter 25

Bentley Drummle, who was so sulky a fellow that he even took up a book as if its writer had done him an injury, did not take up an acquaintance in a more agreeable spirit. Heavy in figure, movement, and comprehension,—in the sluggish complexion of his face, and in the large, awkward tongue that seemed to loll about in his mouth as he himself lolled about in a room,—he was idle, proud, niggardly, reserved, and suspicious. He came of rich people down in Somersetshire, who had nursed this combination of qualities until they made the discovery that it was just of age and a blockhead. Thus, Bentley Drummle had come to Mr Pocket when he was a head taller than that gentleman, and half a dozen heads thicker than most gentlemen.

Startop had been spoilt by a weak mother and kept at home when he ought to have been at school, but he was devotedly attached to her, and admired her beyond measure. He had a woman's delicacy of feature, and was—'as you may see, though you never saw her,' said Herbert to me—'exactly like his mother.' It was but natural that I should take to him much more kindly than to Drummle, and that, even in the earliest evenings of our boating, he and I should pull homewards abreast of one another, conversing from boat to boat, while Bentley Drummle came up in our wake alone, under the overhanging banks and among the rushes. He would always creep in-shore like some uncomfortable amphibious creature, even when the tide would have sent him fast upon his way; and I always think of him as coming after us in the dark or by the backwater, when our own two boats were breaking the sunset or the moonlight in midstream.

Herbert was my intimate companion and friend. I presented him with a half-share in my boat, which was the occasion of his often coming down to Hammersmith; and my possession of a half-share in his chambers often took me up to London. We used to walk between the two places at all hours. I have an affection for the road yet (though it is not so pleasant a road as it was then), formed in the impressibility of untried youth and hope.

When I had been in Mr Pocket's family a month or two, Mr and Mrs Camilla turned up. Camilla was Mr Pocket's sister. Georgiana, whom I had seen at Miss Havisham's on the same occasion, also turned up. She was a cousin,—an indigestive single woman, who called her rigidity religion, and her liver love. These people hated me with the hatred of cupidity and disappointment. As a matter of course, they fawned upon me in my prosperity with the basest meanness. Towards Mr Pocket, as a grown-up infant with no notion of his own interests, they showed the complacent forbearance I had heard them express. Mrs Pocket they held in contempt; but they allowed the poor soul to have been heavily disappointed in life, because that shed a feeble reflected light upon themselves.

These were the surroundings among which I settled down, and applied myself to my education. I soon contracted expensive habits, and began to spend an amount of money that within a few short months I should have thought almost fabulous; but through good and evil I stuck to my books. There was no other merit in this, than my having sense enough to feel my deficiencies. Between Mr Pocket and Herbert I got on fast; and, with one or the other always at my elbow to give me the start I wanted, and clear obstructions out of my road, I must have been as great a dolt as Drummle if I had done less.

I had not seen Mr Wemmick for some weeks, when I thought I would write him a note and propose to go home with him on a certain evening. He replied that it would give him much pleasure, and that he would expect me at the office at six o'clock. Thither I went, and there I found him, putting the key of his safe down his back as the clock struck.

'Did you think of walking down to Walworth?' said he.

'Certainly,' said I, 'if you approve.'

'Very much,' was Wemmick's reply, 'for I have had my legs under the desk all day, and shall be glad to stretch them. Now, I'll tell you what I have got for supper, Mr Pip. I have got a stewed steak,—which is of home preparation,—and a cold roast fowl,—which is from the cook's-shop. I think it's tender, because the master of the shop was a Juryman in some cases of ours the other day, and we let him down easy. I reminded him of it when I bought the fowl, and I said, "Pick us out a good one, old Briton, because if we had chosen to keep you in the box another day or two, we could easily have done it." He said to that, "Let me make you a present of the best fowl in the shop." I let him, of course. As far as it goes, it's property and portable. You don't object to an aged parent, I hope?'

I really thought he was still speaking of the fowl, until he added, 'Because I have got an aged parent at my place.' I then said what politeness required.

'So, you haven't dined with Mr Jaggers yet?' he pursued, as we walked along.

'Not yet.'

'He told me so this afternoon when he heard you were coming. I expect you'll have an invitation tomorrow. He's going to ask your pals, too. Three of 'em; ain't there?'

Although I was not in the habit of counting Drummle as one of my intimate associates, I answered, 'Yes.'

'Well, he's going to ask the whole gang,'—I hardly felt complimented by the word,—'and whatever he gives you, he'll give you good. Don't look forward to variety, but you'll have excellence. And there's another rum thing in his house,' proceeded Wemmick, after a moment's pause, as if the remark followed on the housekeeper understood; 'he never lets a door or window be fastened at night.'

'Is he never robbed?'

'That's it!' returned Wemmick. 'He says, and gives it out publicly, "I want to see the man who'll rob *me*." Lord bless you, I have heard him, a hundred times, if I have heard him once, say to regular cracksmen in our front office, "You know where I live; now, no bolt is ever drawn there; why don't you do a stroke of business with me? Come; can't I tempt you?' Not a man of them, sir, would be bold enough to try it on, for love or money.'

'They dread him so much?' said I.

'Dread him,' said Wemmick. 'I believe you they dread him. Not but what he's artful, even in his defiance of them. No silver, sir. Britannia metal, every spoon.'

'So they wouldn't have much,' I observed, 'even if they—'

'Ah! But *he* would have much,' said Wemmick, cutting me short, 'and they know it. He'd have their lives, and the lives of scores of 'em. He'd have all he could get. And it's impossible to say what he couldn't get, if he gave his mind to it.'

I was falling into meditation on my guardian's greatness, when Wemmick remarked:—

'As to the absence of plate, that's only his natural depth, you know. A river's its natural depth, and he's his natural depth. Look at his watch-chain. That's real enough.'

'It's very massive,' said I.

'Massive?' repeated Wemmick. 'I think so. And his watch is a gold repeater, and worth a hundred pound if it's worth a penny. Mr Pip, there are about seven hundred thieves in this town who know all about that watch; there's not a man, a woman, or a child, among them, who wouldn't identify the smallest link in that chain, and drop it as if it was red hot, if inveigled into touching it.'

At first with such discourse, and afterwards with conversation of a more general nature, did Mr Wemmick and I beguile the time and the road, until he gave me to understand that we had arrived in the district of Walworth.

It appeared to be a collection of back lanes, ditches, and little gardens, and to present the aspect of a rather dull retirement. Wemmick's house was a little wooden cottage in the midst of plots of garden, and the top of it was cut out and painted like a battery mounted with guns.

'My own doing,' said Wemmick. 'Looks pretty; don't it?'

I highly commended it, I think it was the smallest house I ever saw; with the queerest gothic windows (by far the greater part of them sham), and a gothic door almost too small to get in at.

'That's a real flagstaff, you see,' said Wemmick, 'and on Sundays I run up a real flag. Then look here. After I have crossed this bridge, I hoist it up—so—and cut off the communication.'

The bridge was a plank, and it crossed a chasm about four feet wide and two deep. But it was very pleasant to see the pride with which he hoisted it up and made it fast; smiling as he did so, with a relish and not merely mechanically.

'At nine o'clock every night, Greenwich time,' said Wemmick, 'the gun fires. There he is, you see! And when you hear him go, I think you'll say he's a Stinger.'

The piece of ordnance referred to, was mounted in a separate fortress, constructed of lattice-work. It was protected from the weather by an ingenious little tarpaulin contrivance in the nature of an umbrella.

'Then, at the back,' said Wemmick, 'out of sight, so as not to impede the idea of fortifications,—for it's a principle with me, if you have an idea, carry it out and keep it up,—I don't know whether that's your opinion—'

I said, decidedly.

'—At the back, there's a pig, and there are fowls and rabbits; then, I knock together my own little frame, you see, and grow cucumbers; and you'll judge at supper what sort of a salad I can raise. So, sir,' said Wemmick, smiling again, but seriously too, as he shook his head, 'if you can suppose the little place besieged, it would hold out a devil of a time in point of provisions.'

Then, he conducted me to a bower about a dozen yards off, but which was approached by such ingenious twists of path that it took quite a long time to get at; and in this retreat our glasses were already set forth. Our punch was cooling in an ornamental lake, on whose margin the bower was raised. This piece of water (with an island in the middle which might have been the salad for supper) was of a circular form, and he had constructed a fountain in it, which, when you set a little mill going and took a cork out of a pipe, played to that powerful extent that it made the back of your hand quite wet.

'I am my own engineer, and my own carpenter, and my own plumber, and my own gardener, and my own Jack of all Trades,' said Wemmick, in acknowledging my compliments. 'Well; it's a good thing, you know. It brushes the Newgate cobwebs away, and pleases the Aged. You wouldn't mind being at once introduced to the Aged, would you? It wouldn't put you out?'

I expressed the readiness I felt, and we went into the castle. There we found, sitting by a fire, a very old man in a flannel coat: clean, cheerful, comfortable, and well cared for, but intensely deaf.

'Well aged parent,' said Wemmick, shaking hands with him in a cordial and jocose way, 'how are you?'

'All right, John; all right!' replied the old man.

'Here's Mr Pip, aged parent,' said Wemmick, 'and I wish you could hear his name. Nod away at him, Mr Pip; that's what he likes. Nod away at him, if you please, like winking!'

'This is a fine place of my son's, sir,' cried the old man, while I nodded as hard as I possibly could. 'This is a pretty pleasure-ground, sir. This spot and these beautiful works upon it ought to be kept together by the Nation, after my son's time, for the people's enjoyment.'

'You're as proud of it as Punch; ain't you, Aged?' said Wemmick, contemplating the old man, with his hard face really softened; '*there's* a nod for you;' giving him a tremendous one; '*there's* another for you;' giving him a still more tremendous one; 'you like that, don't you? If you're not tired, Mr Pip—though I know it's tiring to strangers—will you tip him one more? You can't think how it pleases him.'

I tipped him several more, and he was in great spirits. We left him bestirring himself to feed the fowls, and we sat down to our punch in the arbor; where Wemmick told me, as he smoked a pipe, that it had taken him a good many years to bring the property up to its present pitch of perfection.

'Is it your own, Mr Wemmick?'

'O yes,' said Wemmick, 'I have got hold of it, a bit at a time. It's a freehold, by George!'

'Is it indeed? I hope Mr Jaggers admires it?'

'Never seen it,' said Wemmick. 'Never heard of it. Never seen the Aged. Never heard of him. No; the office is one thing, and private life is another. When I go into the office, I leave the Castle behind me, and when I come into the Castle, I leave the office behind me. If it's not in any way disagreeable to you, you'll oblige me by doing the same. I don't wish it professionally spoken about.'

Of course I felt my good faith involved in the observance of his request. The punch being very nice, we sat there drinking it and talking, until it was almost nine o'clock. 'Getting near gun-fire,' said Wemmick then, as he laid down his pipe; 'it's the Aged's treat.'

Proceeding into the Castle again, we found the Aged heating the poker, with expectant eyes, as a preliminary to the performance of this great nightly ceremony. Wemmick stood with his watch in his hand until the moment was come for him to take the red-hot poker from the Aged, and repair to the battery. He took it, and went out, and presently the Stinger went off with a Bang that shook the crazy little box of a cottage as if it must fall to pieces, and made every glass and teacup in it ring. Upon this, the Aged—who I believe would have been blown out of his armchair but for holding on by the elbows—cried out exultingly, 'He's fired! I heerd him!' and I nodded at the old gentleman until it is no figure of speech to declare that I absolutely could not see him.

The interval between that time and supper Wemmick devoted to showing me his collection of curiosities. They were mostly of a felonious character; comprising the pen with which a celebrated forgery had been committed, a distinguished razor or two, some locks of hair, and several manuscript confessions written under condemnation,—upon which Mr Wemmick set particular value as being, to use his own words, 'every one of 'em Lies, sir.' These were agreeably dispersed among small specimens of china and glass, various neat trifles made by the proprietor of the museum, and some tobacco-stoppers carved by the Aged. They were all displayed in that chamber of the Castle into which I had been first inducted, and which served, not only as the general sitting-room but as the kitchen too, if I might judge from a saucepan on the hob, and a brazen bijou over the fireplace designed for the suspension of a roasting-jack.

There was a neat little girl in attendance, who looked after the Aged in the day. When she had laid the supper-cloth, the bridge was lowered to give her means of egress, and she withdrew for the night. The supper was excellent; and though the Castle was rather subject to dry-rot insomuch that it tasted like a bad nut, and though the pig might have been farther off, I was heartily pleased with my whole entertainment. Nor was there any drawback on my little turret bedroom, beyond there being such a very thin ceiling between me and the flagstaff, that when I lay down on my back in bed, it seemed as if I had to balance that pole on my forehead all night.

Wemmick was up early in the morning, and I am afraid I heard him cleaning my boots. After that, he fell to gardening, and I saw him from my gothic window pretending to employ the Aged, and nodding at him in a most devoted manner. Our breakfast was as good as the supper, and at half-past eight precisely we started for Little Britain. By degrees, Wemmick got dryer and harder as we went along, and his mouth tightened into a post-office again. At last, when we got to his place of business and he pulled out his key from his coat-collar, he looked as unconscious of his Walworth property as if the Castle and the drawbridge and the arbor and the lake and the fountain and the Aged, had all been blown into space together by the last discharge of the Stinger.

Chapter 26

It fell out as Wemmick had told me it would, that I had an early opportunity of comparing my guardian's establishment with that of his cashier and clerk. My guardian was in his room, washing his hands with his scented soap, when I went into the office from Walworth; and he called me to him, and gave me the invitation for myself and friends which Wemmick had prepared me to receive. 'No ceremony,' he stipulated, 'and no dinner dress, and say tomorrow.' I asked him where we should come to (for I had no idea where he lived), and I believe it was in his general objection to make anything like an admission, that he replied, 'Come here, and I'll take you home with me.' I embrace this opportunity of remarking that he washed his clients off, as if he were a surgeon or a dentist. He had a closet in his room, fitted up for the purpose, which smelt of the scented soap like a perfumer's shop. It had an unusually large jack-towel on a roller inside the door, and he would wash his hands, and wipe them and dry them all over this towel, whenever he came in from a police court or dismissed a client from his room. When I and my friends repaired to him at six o'clock next day, he seemed to have been engaged on a case of a darker complexion than usual, for we found him with his head butted into this closet, not only washing his hands, but laving his face and gargling his throat. And even when he had done all that, and had gone all round the jack-towel, he took out his penknife and scraped the case out of his nails before he put his coat on.

There were some people slinking about as usual when we passed out into the street, who were evidently anxious to speak with him; but there was something so conclusive in the halo of scented soap which encircled his presence, that they gave it up for that day. As we walked along westward, he was recognized ever and again by some face in the crowd of the streets, and whenever that happened he talked louder to me; but he never otherwise recognized anybody, or took notice that anybody recognized him.

He conducted us to Gerrard Street, Soho, to a house on the south side of that street. Rather a stately house of its kind, but dolefully in want of painting, and with dirty windows. He took out his key and opened the door, and we all went into a stone hall, bare, gloomy, and little used. So, up a dark brown staircase into a series of three dark brown rooms on the first floor. There were carved garlands on the panelled walls, and as he stood among them giving us welcome, I know what kind of loops I thought they looked like.

Dinner was laid in the best of these rooms; the second was his dressing-room; the third, his bedroom. He told us that he held the whole house, but rarely used more of it than we saw. The table was comfortably laid—no silver in the service, of course—and at the side of his chair was a capacious dumb-waiter, with a variety of bottles and decanters on it, and four dishes of fruit for dessert. I noticed throughout, that he kept everything under his own hand, and distributed everything himself.

There was a bookcase in the room; I saw from the backs of the books, that they were about evidence, criminal law, criminal biography, trials, acts of Parliament, and such things. The furniture was all very solid and good, like his watch-chain. It had an official look, however, and there was nothing merely ornamental to be seen. In a corner was a little table of papers with a shaded lamp: so that he seemed to bring the office home with him in that respect too, and to wheel it out of an evening and fall to work.

As he had scarcely seen my three companions until now,—for he and I had walked together,—he stood on the hearth-rug, after ringing the bell, and took a searching look at them. To my surprise, he seemed at once to be principally if not solely interested in Drummle.

'Pip,' said he, putting his large hand on my shoulder and moving me to the window, 'I don't know one from the other. Who's the Spider?'

'The spider?' said I.

'The blotchy, sprawly, sulky fellow.'

'That's Bentley Drummle,' I replied; 'the one with the delicate face is Startop.'

Not making the least account of 'the one with the delicate face,' he returned, 'Bentley Drummle is his name, is it? I like the look of that fellow.'

He immediately began to talk to Drummle: not at all deterred by his replying in his heavy reticent way, but apparently led on by it to screw discourse out of him. I was looking at the two, when there came between me and them the housekeeper, with the first dish for the table.

She was a woman of about forty, I supposed,—but I may have thought her younger than she was. Rather tall, of a lithe nimble figure, extremely pale, with large faded eyes, and a quantity of streaming hair. I cannot say whether any diseased affection of the heart caused her lips to be parted as if she were panting, and her face to bear a curious expression of suddenness and flutter; but I know that I had been to see Macbeth at the theatre, a night or two before, and that her face looked to me as if it were all disturbed by fiery air, like the faces I had seen rise out of the Witches' caldron.

She set the dish on, touched my guardian quietly on the arm with a finger to notify that dinner was ready, and vanished. We took our seats at the round table, and my guardian kept Drummle on one side of him, while Startop sat on the other. It was a noble dish of fish that the housekeeper had put on table, and we had a joint of equally choice mutton afterwards, and then an equally choice bird. Sauces, wines, all the accessories we wanted, and all of the best, were given out by our host from his dumb-waiter; and when they had made the circuit of the table, he always put them back again. Similarly, he dealt us clean plates and knives and forks, for each course, and dropped those just disused into two baskets on the ground by his chair. No other attendant than the housekeeper appeared. She set on every dish; and I always saw in her face, a face rising out of the caldron. Years afterwards, I made a dreadful likeness of that woman, by causing a face that had no other natural resemblance to it than it derived from flowing hair to pass behind a bowl of flaming spirits in a dark room.

Induced to take particular notice of the housekeeper, both by her own striking appearance and by Wemmick's preparation, I observed that whenever she was in the room she kept her eyes attentively on my guardian, and that she would remove her hands from any dish she put before him, hesitatingly, as if she dreaded his calling her back, and wanted him to speak when she was nigh, if he had anything to say. I fancied that I could detect in his manner a consciousness of this, and a purpose of always holding her in suspense.

Dinner went off gayly, and although my guardian seemed to follow rather than originate subjects, I knew that he wrenched the weakest part of our dispositions out of us. For myself, I found that I was expressing my tendency to lavish expenditure, and to patronize Herbert, and to boast of my great prospects, before I quite knew that I had opened my lips. It was so with all of us, but with no one more than Drummle: the development of whose inclination to gird in a grudging and suspicious way at the rest, was screwed out of him before the fish was taken off.

It was not then, but when we had got to the cheese, that our conversation turned upon our rowing feats, and that Drummle was rallied for coming up behind of a night in that slow amphibious way of his. Drummle upon this, informed our host that he much preferred our room to our company, and that as to skill he was more than our master, and that as to strength he could scatter us like chaff. By some invisible agency, my guardian wound him up to a pitch little short of ferocity about this trifle; and he fell to baring and spanning his arm to show how muscular it was, and we all fell to baring and spanning our arms in a ridiculous manner.

Now the housekeeper was at that time clearing the table; my guardian, taking no heed of her, but with the side of his face turned from her, was leaning back in his chair biting the side of his forefinger and showing an interest in Drummle, that, to me, was quite inexplicable. Suddenly, he clapped his large hand on the housekeeper's, like a trap, as she stretched it across the table. So suddenly and smartly did he do this, that we all stopped in our foolish contention.

'If you talk of strength,' said Mr Jaggers, '*I*'ll show you a wrist. Molly, let them see your wrist.'

Her entrapped hand was on the table, but she had already put her other hand behind her waist. 'Master,' she said, in a low voice, with her eyes attentively and entreatingly fixed upon him. 'Don't.'

'*I*'ll show you a wrist,' repeated Mr Jaggers, with an immovable determination to show it. 'Molly, let them see your wrist.'

'Master,' she again murmured. 'Please!'

'Molly,' said Mr Jaggers, not looking at her, but obstinately looking at the opposite side of the room, 'let them see *both* your wrists. Show them. Come!'

He took his hand from hers, and turned that wrist up on the table. She brought her other hand from behind her, and held the two out side by side. The last wrist was much disfigured,—deeply scarred and scarred across and across. When she held her hands out she took her eyes from Mr Jaggers, and turned them watchfully on every one of the rest of us in succession.

'There's power here,' said Mr Jaggers, coolly tracing out the sinews with his forefinger. 'Very few men have the power of wrist that this woman has. It's remarkable what mere force of grip there is in these hands. I have had occasion to notice many hands; but I never saw stronger in that respect, man's or woman's, than these.'

While he said these words in a leisurely, critical style, she continued to look at every one of us in regular succession as we sat. The moment he ceased, she looked at him again. 'That'll do, Molly,' said Mr Jaggers, giving her a slight nod; 'you have been admired, and can go.' She withdrew her hands and went out of the room, and Mr Jaggers, putting the decanters on from his dumb-waiter, filled his glass and passed round the wine.

'At half-past nine, gentlemen,' said he, 'we must break up. Pray make the best use of your time. I am glad to see you all. Mr Drummle, I drink to you.'

If his object in singling out Drummle were to bring him out still more, it perfectly succeeded. In a sulky triumph, Drummle showed his morose depreciation of the rest of us, in a more and more offensive degree, until he became downright intolerable. Through all his stages, Mr Jaggers followed him with the same strange interest. He actually seemed to serve as a zest to Mr Jaggers's wine.

In our boyish want of discretion I dare say we took too much to drink, and I know we talked too much. We became particularly hot upon some boorish sneer of Drummle's, to the effect that we were too free with our money. It led to my remarking, with more zeal than discretion, that it came with a bad grace from him, to whom Startop had lent money in my presence but a week or so before.

'Well,' retorted Drummle; 'he'll be paid.'

'I don't mean to imply that he won't,' said I, 'but it might make you hold your tongue about us and our money, I should think.'

'*You* should think!' retorted Drummle. 'Oh Lord!'

'I dare say,' I went on, meaning to be very severe, 'that you wouldn't lend money to any of us if we wanted it.'

'You are right,' said Drummle. 'I wouldn't lend one of you a sixpence. I wouldn't lend anybody a sixpence.'

'Rather mean to borrow under those circumstances, I should say.'

'*You* should say,' repeated Drummle. 'Oh Lord!'

This was so very aggravating—the more especially as I found myself making no way against his surly obtuseness—that I said, disregarding Herbert's efforts to check me,—

'Come, Mr Drummle, since we are on the subject, I'll tell you what passed between Herbert here and me, when you borrowed that money.'

'*I* don't want to know what passed between Herbert there and you,' growled Drummle. And I think he added in a lower growl, that we might both go to the devil and shake ourselves.

'I'll tell you, however,' said I, 'whether you want to know or not.

We said that as you put it in your pocket very glad to get it, you seemed to be immensely amused at his being so weak as to lend it.'

Drummle laughed outright, and sat laughing in our faces, with his hands in his pockets and his round shoulders raised; plainly signifying that it was quite true, and that he despised us as asses all.

Hereupon Startop took him in hand, though with a much better grace than I had shown, and exhorted him to be a little more agreeable. Startop, being a lively, bright young fellow, and Drummle being the exact opposite, the latter was always disposed to resent him as a direct personal affront. He now retorted in a coarse, lumpish way, and Startop tried to turn the discussion aside with some small pleasantry that made us all laugh. Resenting this little success more than anything, Drummle, without any threat or warning, pulled his hands out of his pockets, dropped his round shoulders, swore, took up a large glass, and would have flung it at his adversary's head, but for our entertainer's dexterously seizing it at the instant when it was raised for that purpose.

'Gentlemen,' said Mr Jaggers, deliberately putting down the glass, and hauling out his gold repeater by its massive chain, 'I am exceedingly sorry to announce that it's half past nine.'

On this hint we all rose to depart. Before we got to the street door, Startop was cheerily calling Drummle 'old boy,' as if nothing had happened. But the old boy was so far from responding, that he would not even walk to Hammersmith on the same side of the way; so Herbert and I, who remained in town, saw them going down the street on opposite sides; Startop leading, and Drummle lagging behind in the shadow of the houses, much as he was wont to follow in his boat.

As the door was not yet shut, I thought I would leave Herbert there for a moment, and run upstairs again to say a word to my guardian. I found him in his dressing-room surrounded by his stock of boots, already hard at it, washing his hands of us.

I told him I had come up again to say how sorry I was that anything disagreeable should have occurred, and that I hoped he would not blame me much.

'Pooh!' said he, sluicing his face, and speaking through the water-drops; 'it's nothing, Pip. I like that Spider though.'

He had turned towards me now, and was shaking his head, and

blowing, and towelling himself.

'I am glad you like him, sir,' said I—'but I don't.'

'No, no,' my guardian assented; 'don't have too much to do with him. Keep as clear of him as you can. But I like the fellow, Pip; he is one of the true sort. Why, if I was a fortune-teller—'

Looking out of the towel, he caught my eye.

'But I am not a fortune-teller,' he said, letting his head drop into a festoon of towel, and towelling away at his two ears. 'You know what I am, don't you? Goodnight, Pip.'

'Goodnight, sir.'

In about a month after that, the Spider's time with Mr Pocket was up for good, and, to the great relief of all the house but Mrs Pocket, he went home to the family hole.

Chapter 27

'MY DEAR MR PIP:—

'I write this by request of Mr Gargery, for to let you know that he is going to London in company with Mr Wopsle and would be glad if agreeable to be allowed to see you. He would call at Barnard's Hotel Tuesday morning at nine o'clock, when if not agreeable please leave word. Your poor sister is much the same as when you left. We talk of you in the kitchen every night, and wonder what you are saying and doing. If now considered in the light of a liberty, excuse it for the love of poor old days. No more, dear Mr Pip, from your ever obliged, and affectionate servant,

'BIDDY.'

'P.S. He wishes me most particular to write *what larks*. He says you will understand. I hope and do not doubt it will be agreeable to see him, even though a gentleman, for you had ever a good heart, and he is a worthy, worthy man. I have read him all, excepting only the last little sentence, and he wishes me most particular to write again *what larks*.'

I received this letter by the post on Monday morning, and therefore its appointment was for next day. Let me confess exactly with what feelings I looked forward to Joe's coming.

Not with pleasure, though I was bound to him by so many ties; no; with considerable disturbance, some mortification, and a keen sense of incongruity. If I could have kept him away by paying money, I certainly would have paid money. My greatest reassurance was that he was coming to Barnard's Inn, not to Hammersmith, and consequently would not fall in Bentley Drummle's way. I had little objection to his being seen by Herbert or his father, for both of whom I had a respect; but I had the sharpest sensitiveness as to his being seen by Drummle, whom I held in contempt. So, throughout life, our worst weaknesses and meannesses are usually committed for the sake of the people whom we most despise.

I had begun to be always decorating the chambers in some quite unnecessary and inappropriate way or other, and very expensive those wrestles with Barnard proved to be. By this time, the rooms were vastly different from what I had found them, and I enjoyed the honour of occupying a few prominent pages in the books of a neighbouring upholsterer. I had got on so fast of late, that I had even started a boy in boots,—top boots,—in bondage and slavery to whom I might have been said to pass my days. For, after I had made the monster (out of the refuse of my washerwoman's family), and had clothed him with a blue coat, canary waistcoat, white cravat, creamy breeches, and the boots already mentioned, I had to find him a little to do and a great deal to eat; and with both of those horrible requirements he haunted my existence.

This avenging phantom was ordered to be on duty at eight on Tuesday morning in the hall, (it was two feet square, as charged for floorcloth,) and Herbert suggested certain things for breakfast that he thought Joe would like. While I felt sincerely obliged to him for being so interested and considerate, I had an odd half-provoked sense of suspicion upon me, that if Joe had been coming to see *him*, he wouldn't have been quite so brisk about it.

However, I came into town on the Monday night to be ready for Joe, and I got up early in the morning, and caused the sitting-room and breakfast-table to assume their most splendid appearance. Unfortunately the morning was drizzly, and an angel could not have concealed the fact that Barnard was shedding sooty tears outside the window, like some weak giant of a Sweep.

As the time approached I should have liked to run away, but the Avenger pursuant to orders was in the hall, and presently I heard Joe on the staircase. I knew it was Joe, by his clumsy manner of coming upstairs,—his state boots being always too big for him,—and by the time it took him to read the names on the other floors in the course of his ascent. When at last he stopped outside our door, I could hear his finger tracing over the painted letters of my name, and I afterwards distinctly heard him breathing in at the keyhole. Finally he gave a faint single rap, and Pepper—such was the compromising name of the avenging boy—announced 'Mr Gargery!' I thought he never would have done wiping his feet, and that I must have gone out to lift him off the mat, but at last he came in.

'Joe, how are you, Joe?'

'Pip, how AIR you, Pip?'

With his good honest face all glowing and shining, and his hat put down on the floor between us, he caught both my hands and worked them straight up and down, as if I had been the last-patented Pump.

'I am glad to see you, Joe. Give me your hat.'

But Joe, taking it up carefully with both hands, like a bird's-nest with eggs in it, wouldn't hear of parting with that piece of property, and persisted in standing talking over it in a most uncomfortable way.

'Which you have that growed,' said Joe, 'and that swelled, and that gentle-folked;' Joe considered a little before he discovered this word; 'as to be sure you are a honour to your king and country.'

'And you, Joe, look wonderfully well.'

'Thank God,' said Joe, 'I'm ekerval to most. And your sister, she's no worse than she were. And Biddy, she's ever right and ready. And all friends is no backerder, if not no forarder. 'Ceptin Wopsle; he's had a drop.'

All this time (still with both hands taking great care of the bird's-nest), Joe was rolling his eyes round and round the room, and round and round the flowered pattern of my dressing-gown.

'Had a drop, Joe?'

'Why yes,' said Joe, lowering his voice, 'he's left the Church and went into the playacting. Which the playacting have likeways brought him to London along with me. And his wish were,' said Joe, getting the bird's-nest under his left arm for the moment, and groping in it for an egg with his right; 'if no offence, as I would 'and you that.'

I took what Joe gave me, and found it to be the crumpled play-bill of a small metropolitan theatre, announcing the first appearance, in that very week, of 'the celebrated Provincial Amateur of Roscian renown, whose unique performance in the highest tragic walk of our National Bard has lately occasioned so great a sensation in local dramatic circles.'

'Were you at his performance, Joe?' I inquired.

'I *were*,' said Joe, with emphasis and solemnity.

'Was there a great sensation?'

'Why,' said Joe, 'yes, there certainly were a peck of orange-peel. Partickler when he see the ghost. Though I put it to yourself, sir, whether it were calc'lated to keep a man up to his work with a good hart, to be continiwally cutting in betwixt him and the Ghost with "Amen!" A man may have had a misfortun' and been in the Church,' said Joe, lowering his voice to an argumentative and feeling tone, 'but that is no reason why you should put him out at such a time. Which I meantersay, if the ghost of a man's own father cannot be allowed to claim his attention, what can, Sir? Still more, when his mourning 'at is unfortunately made so small as that the weight of the black feathers brings it off, try to keep it on how you may.'

A ghost-seeing effect in Joe's own countenance informed me that Herbert had entered the room. So, I presented Joe to Herbert, who held out his hand; but Joe backed from it, and held on by the bird's-nest.

'Your servant, Sir,' said Joe, 'which I hope as you and Pip'—here his eye fell on the Avenger, who was putting some toast on table, and so plainly denoted an intention to make that young gentleman one of the family, that I frowned it down and confused him more—'I meantersay, you two gentlemen,—which I hope as you get your elths in this close spot? For the present may be a werry good inn, according to London opinions,' said Joe, confidentially, 'and I believe its character do stand it; but I wouldn't keep a pig in it myself,—not in the case that I wished him to fatten wholesome and to eat with a meller flavour on him.'

Having borne this flattering testimony to the merits of our

dwelling-place, and having incidentally shown this tendency to call me 'sir,' Joe, being invited to sit down to table, looked all round the room for a suitable spot on which to deposit his hat,—as if it were only on some very few rare substances in nature that it could find a resting place,—and ultimately stood it on an extreme corner of the chimney-piece, from which it ever afterwards fell off at intervals.

'Do you take tea, or coffee, Mr Gargery?' asked Herbert, who always presided of a morning.

'Thankee, Sir,' said Joe, stiff from head to foot, 'I'll take whichever is most agreeable to yourself.'

'What do you say to coffee?'

'Thankee, Sir,' returned Joe, evidently dispirited by the proposal, 'since you *are* so kind as make chice of coffee, I will not run contrairy to your own opinions. But don't you never find it a little 'eating?'

'Say tea then,' said Herbert, pouring it out.

Here Joe's hat tumbled off the mantel-piece, and he started out of his chair and picked it up, and fitted it to the same exact spot. As if it were an absolute point of good breeding that it should tumble off again soon.

'When did you come to town, Mr Gargery?'

'Were it yesterday afternoon?' said Joe, after coughing behind his hand, as if he had had time to catch the whooping-cough since he came. 'No it were not. Yes it were. Yes. It were yesterday afternoon' (with an appearance of mingled wisdom, relief, and strict impartiality).

'Have you seen anything of London yet?'

'Why, yes, Sir,' said Joe, 'me and Wopsle went off straight to look at the Blacking Ware'us. But we didn't find that it come up to its likeness in the red bills at the shop doors; which I meantersay,' added Joe, in an explanatory manner, 'as it is there drawd too architectooralooral.'

I really believe Joe would have prolonged this word (mightily expressive to my mind of some architecture that I know) into a perfect Chorus, but for his attention being providentially attracted by his hat, which was toppling. Indeed, it demanded from him a constant attention, and a quickness of eye and hand, very like that exacted by wicket-keeping. He made extraordinary play with it, and showed the greatest skill; now, rushing at it and catching it neatly as it dropped;

now, merely stopping it midway, beating it up, and humouring it in various parts of the room and against a good deal of the pattern of the paper on the wall, before he felt it safe to close with it; finally splashing it into the slop-basin, where I took the liberty of laying hands upon it.

As to his shirt-collar, and his coat-collar, they were perplexing to reflect upon,—insoluble mysteries both. Why should a man scrape himself to that extent, before he could consider himself full dressed? Why should he suppose it necessary to be purified by suffering for his holiday clothes? Then he fell into such unaccountable fits of meditation, with his fork midway between his plate and his mouth; had his eyes attracted in such strange directions; was afflicted with such remarkable coughs; sat so far from the table, and dropped so much more than he ate, and pretended that he hadn't dropped it; that I was heartily glad when Herbert left us for the City.

I had neither the good sense nor the good feeling to know that this was all my fault, and that if I had been easier with Joe, Joe would have been easier with me. I felt impatient of him and out of temper with him; in which condition he heaped coals of fire on my head.

'Us two being now alone, sir,'—began Joe.

'Joe,' I interrupted, pettishly, 'how can you call me, sir?'

Joe looked at me for a single instant with something faintly like reproach. Utterly preposterous as his cravat was, and as his collars were, I was conscious of a sort of dignity in the look.

'Us two being now alone,' resumed Joe, 'and me having the intentions and abilities to stay not many minutes more, I will now conclude—leastways begin—to mention what have led to my having had the present honour. For was it not,' said Joe, with his old air of lucid exposition, 'that my only wish were to be useful to you, I should not have had the honour of breaking wittles in the company and abode of gentlemen.'

I was so unwilling to see the look again, that I made no remonstrance against this tone.

'Well, sir,' pursued Joe, 'this is how it were. I were at the Bargemen t'other night, Pip;'—whenever he subsided into affection, he called me Pip, and whenever he relapsed into politeness he called me sir;

'when there come up in his shay-cart, Pumblechook. Which that same identical,' said Joe, going down a new track, 'do comb my 'air the wrong way sometimes, awful, by giving out up and down town as it were him which ever had your infant companionation and were looked upon as a playfellow by yourself.'

'Nonsense. It was you, Joe.'

'Which I fully believed it were, Pip,' said Joe, slightly tossing his head, 'though it signify little now, sir. Well, Pip; this same identical, which his manners is given to blusterous, come to me at the Bargemen (wot a pipe and a pint of beer do give refreshment to the workingman, sir, and do not over stimilate), and his word were, 'Joseph, Miss Havisham she wish to speak to you."

'Miss Havisham, Joe?'

"She wish,' were Pumblechook's word, 'to speak to you." Joe sat and rolled his eyes at the ceiling.

'Yes, Joe? Go on, please.'

'Next day, sir,' said Joe, looking at me as if I were a long way off, 'having cleaned myself, I go and I see Miss A.'

'Miss A., Joe? Miss Havisham?'

'Which I say, sir,' replied Joe, with an air of legal formality, as if he were making his will, 'Miss A., or otherways Havisham. Her expression air then as follering: 'Mr Gargery. You air in correspondence with Mr Pip?' Having had a letter from you, I were able to say 'I am.' (When I married your sister, sir, I said 'I will;' and when I answered your friend, Pip, I said 'I am.') 'Would you tell him, then,' said she, 'that which Estella has come home and would be glad to see him."

I felt my face fire up as I looked at Joe. I hope one remote cause of its firing may have been my consciousness that if I had known his errand, I should have given him more encouragement.

'Biddy,' pursued Joe, 'when I got home and asked her fur to write the message to you, a little hung back. Biddy says, 'I know he will be very glad to have it by word of mouth, it is holiday time, you want to see him, go!' I have now concluded, sir,' said Joe, rising from his chair, 'and, Pip, I wish you ever well and ever prospering to a greater and a greater height.'

'But you are not going now, Joe?'

'Yes I am,' said Joe.

'But you are coming back to dinner, Joe?'

'No I am not,' said Joe.

Our eyes met, and all the 'Sir' melted out of that manly heart as he gave me his hand.

'Pip, dear old chap, life is made of ever so many partings welded together, as I may say, and one man's a blacksmith, and one's a whitesmith, and one's a goldsmith, and one's a coppersmith. Diwisions among such must come, and must be met as they come. If there's been any fault at all today, it's mine. You and me is not two figures to be together in London; nor yet anywheres else but what is private, and beknown, and understood among friends. It ain't that I am proud, but that I want to be right, as you shall never see me no more in these clothes. I'm wrong in these clothes. I'm wrong out of the forge, the kitchen, or off th' meshes. You won't find half so much fault in me if you think of me in my forge dress, with my hammer in my hand, or even my pipe. You won't find half so much fault in me if, supposing as you should ever wish to see me, you come and put your head in at the forge window and see Joe the blacksmith, there, at the old anvil, in the old burnt apron, sticking to the old work. I'm awful dull, but I hope I've beat out something nigh the rights of this at last. And so GOD bless you, dear old Pip, old chap, GOD bless you!'

I had not been mistaken in my fancy that there was a simple dignity in him. The fashion of his dress could no more come in its way when he spoke these words than it could come in its way in Heaven. He touched me gently on the forehead, and went out. As soon as I could recover myself sufficiently, I hurried out after him and looked for him in the neighbouring streets; but he was gone.

Chapter 28

It was clear that I must repair to our town next day, and in the first flow of my repentance, it was equally clear that I must stay at Joe's. But, when I had secured my box-place by tomorrow's coach, and had been down to Mr Pocket's and back, I was not by any means convinced on the last point, and began to invent reasons and make excuses for putting up at the Blue Boar. I should be an inconvenience at Joe's; I was not expected, and my bed would not be ready; I should be too far from Miss Havisham's, and she was exacting and mightn't like it. All other swindlers upon earth are nothing to the self-swindlers, and with such pretences did I cheat myself. Surely a curious thing. That I should innocently take a bad half-crown of somebody else's manufacture is reasonable enough; but that I should knowingly reckon the spurious coin of my own make as good money! An obliging stranger, under pretence of compactly folding up my bank-notes for security's sake, abstracts the notes and gives me nutshells; but what is his sleight of hand to mine, when I fold up my own nutshells and pass them on myself as notes!

Having settled that I must go to the Blue Boar, my mind was much disturbed by indecision whether or not to take the Avenger. It was tempting to think of that expensive Mercenary publicly airing his boots in the archway of the Blue Boar's posting-yard; it was almost solemn to imagine him casually produced in the tailor's shop, and confounding the disrespectful senses of Trabb's boy. On the other hand, Trabb's boy might worm himself into his intimacy and tell him things; or, reckless and desperate wretch as I knew he could be, might hoot him in the High Street. My patroness, too, might hear of him, and not approve. On the whole, I resolved to leave the Avenger behind.

It was the afternoon coach by which I had taken my place, and, as winter had now come round, I should not arrive at my destination until two or three hours after dark. Our time of starting from the Cross Keys was two o'clock. I arrived on the ground with a quarter of an hour to spare, attended by the Avenger,—if I may connect that expression with one who never attended on me if he could possibly help it.

At that time it was customary to carry convicts down to the dockyards by stage-coach. As I had often heard of them in the capacity of outside passengers, and had more than once seen them on the high road dangling their ironed legs over the coach roof, I had no cause to be surprised when Herbert, meeting me in the yard, came up and told me there were two convicts going down with me. But I had a reason that was an old reason now for constitutionally faltering whenever I heard the word 'convict.'

'You don't mind them, Handel?' said Herbert.

'O no!'

'I thought you seemed as if you didn't like them?'

'I can't pretend that I do like them, and I suppose you don't particularly. But I don't mind them.'

'See! There they are,' said Herbert, 'coming out of the Tap. What a degraded and vile sight it is!'

They had been treating their guard, I suppose, for they had a gaoler with them, and all three came out wiping their mouths on their hands. The two convicts were handcuffed together, and had irons on their legs,—irons of a pattern that I knew well. They wore the dress that I likewise knew well. Their keeper had a brace of pistols, and carried a thick-knobbed bludgeon under his arm; but he was on terms of good understanding with them, and stood with them beside him, looking on at the putting-to of the horses, rather with an air as if the convicts were an interesting exhibition not formally open at the moment, and he the curator. One was a taller and stouter man than the other, and appeared as a matter of course, according to the mysterious ways of the world, both convict and free, to have had allotted to him the smaller suit of clothes. His arms and legs were like great pincushions of those shapes, and his attire disguised him absurdly; but I knew his half-closed eye at one glance. There stood the man whom I had seen on the settle at the Three Jolly Bargemen on a Saturday night, and who had brought me down with his invisible gun!

It was easy to make sure that as yet he knew me no more than if he had never seen me in his life. He looked across at me, and his eye appraised my watch-chain, and then he incidentally spat and said something to the other convict, and they laughed and slued themselves round with a clink of their coupling manacle, and looked at something else. The great numbers on their backs, as if they were street doors; their coarse mangy ungainly outer surface, as if they were lower animals; their ironed legs, apologetically garlanded with pocket-handkerchiefs; and the way in which all present looked at them and kept from them; made them (as Herbert had said) a most disagreeable and degraded spectacle.

But this was not the worst of it. It came out that the whole of the back of the coach had been taken by a family removing from London, and that there were no places for the two prisoners but on the seat in front behind the coachman. Hereupon, a choleric gentleman, who had taken the fourth place on that seat, flew into a most violent passion, and said that it was a breach of contract to mix him up with such villainous company, and that it was poisonous, and pernicious, and infamous, and shameful, and I don't know what else. At this time the coach was ready and the coachman impatient, and we were all preparing to get up, and the prisoners had come over with their keeper,—bringing with them that curious flavour of bread-poultice, baize, rope-yarn, and hearthstone, which attends the convict presence.

'Don't take it so much amiss, sir,' pleaded the keeper to the angry passenger; 'I'll sit next you myself. I'll put 'em on the outside of the row. They won't interfere with you, sir. You needn't know they're there.'

'And don't blame *me*,' growled the convict I had recognized. '*I* don't want to go. *I* am quite ready to stay behind. As fur as I am concerned anyone's welcome to *my* place.'

'Or mine,' said the other, gruffly. 'I wouldn't have incommoded none of you, if I'd had *my* way.' Then they both laughed, and began cracking nuts, and spitting the shells about.—As I really think I should have liked to do myself, if I had been in their place and so despised.

At length, it was voted that there was no help for the angry gentleman, and that he must either go in his chance company or remain behind. So he got into his place, still making complaints, and the keeper got into the place next him, and the convicts hauled themselves up as well as they could, and the convict I had recognized sat behind me with his breath on the hair of my head.

'Goodbye, Handel!' Herbert called out as we started. I thought what a blessed fortune it was, that he had found another name for me than Pip.

It is impossible to express with what acuteness I felt the convict's breathing, not only on the back of my head, but all along my spine. The sensation was like being touched in the marrow with some pungent and searching acid, it set my very teeth on edge. He seemed to have more breathing business to do than another man, and to make more noise in doing it; and I was conscious of growing high-shouldered on one side, in my shrinking endeavours to fend him off.

The weather was miserably raw, and the two cursed the cold. It made us all lethargic before we had gone far, and when we had left the Half-way House behind, we habitually dozed and shivered and were silent. I dozed off, myself, in considering the question whether I ought to restore a couple of pounds sterling to this creature before losing sight of him, and how it could best be done. In the act of dipping forward as if I were going to bathe among the horses, I woke in a fright and took the question up again.

But I must have lost it longer than I had thought, since, although I could recognize nothing in the darkness and the fitful lights and shadows of our lamps, I traced marsh country in the cold damp wind that blew at us. Cowering forward for warmth and to make me a screen against the wind, the convicts were closer to me than before. The very first words I heard them interchange as I became conscious, were the words of my own thought, 'Two One Pound notes.'

'How did he get 'em?' said the convict I had never seen.

'How should I know?' returned the other. 'He had 'em stowed away somehows. Giv him by friends, I expect.'

'I wish,' said the other, with a bitter curse upon the cold, 'that I had 'em here.'

'Two one pound notes, or friends?'

'Two one pound notes. I'd sell all the friends I ever had for one, and think it a blessed good bargain. Well? So he says—?'

'So he says,' resumed the convict I had recognized,—'it was all said and done in half a minute, behind a pile of timber in the Dock-yard,—"You're a going to be discharged?" Yes, I was. Would I find out that boy that had fed him and kep his secret, and give him them two one pound notes? Yes, I would. And I did.'

'More fool you,' growled the other. 'I'd have spent 'em on a Man, in wittles and drink. He must have been a green one. Mean to say he knowed nothing of you?'

'Not a ha'porth. Different gangs and different ships. He was tried again for prison breaking, and got made a Lifer.'

'And was that— Honour!—the only time you worked out, in this part of the country?'

'The only time.'

'What might have been your opinion of the place?'

'A most beastly place. Mudbank, mist, swamp, and work; work, swamp, mist, and mudbank.'

They both execrated the place in very strong language, and gradually growled themselves out, and had nothing left to say.

After overhearing this dialogue, I should assuredly have got down and been left in the solitude and darkness of the highway, but for feeling certain that the man had no suspicion of my identity. Indeed, I was not only so changed in the course of nature, but so differently dressed and so differently circumstanced, that it was not at all likely he could have known me without accidental help. Still, the coincidence of our being together on the coach, was sufficiently strange to fill me with a dread that some other coincidence might at any moment connect me, in his hearing, with my name. For this reason, I resolved to alight as soon as we touched the town, and put myself out of his hearing. This device I executed successfully. My little portmanteau was in the boot under my feet; I had but to turn a hinge to get it out; I threw it down before me, got down after it, and was left at the first lamp on the first stones of the town pavement. As to the convicts, they went their way with the coach, and I knew at what point they would be spirited off to the river. In my fancy, I saw the boat with its convict crew waiting for them at the slime-washed stairs,—again heard the gruff 'Give way, you!' like and order to dogs,—again saw the wicked Noah's Ark lying out on the black water.

I could not have said what I was afraid of, for my fear was altogether undefined and vague, but there was great fear upon me. As I walked on to the hotel, I felt that a dread, much exceeding the mere apprehension of a painful or disagreeable recognition, made me tremble. I am confident that it took no distinctness of shape, and that it was the revival for a few minutes of the terror of childhood.

The coffee-room at the Blue Boar was empty, and I had not only ordered my dinner there, but had sat down to it, before the waiter knew me. As soon as he had apologized for the remissness of his memory, he asked me if he should send Boots for Mr Pumblechook?

'No,' said I, 'certainly not.'

The waiter (it was he who had brought up the Great Remonstrance from the Commercials, on the day when I was bound) appeared surprised, and took the earliest opportunity of putting a dirty old copy of a local newspaper so directly in my way, that I took it up and read this paragraph:—

Our readers will learn, not altogether without interest, in reference to the recent romantic rise in fortune of a young artificer in iron of this neighbourhood (what a theme, by the way, for the magic pen of our as yet not universally acknowledged townsman TOOBY, the poet of our columns!) that the youth's earliest patron, companion, and friend, was a highly respected individual not entirely unconnected with the corn and seed trade, and whose eminently convenient and commodious business premises are situate within a hundred miles of the High Street. It is not wholly irrespective of our personal feelings that we record HIM as the Mentor of our young Telemachus, for it is good to know that our town produced the founder of the latter's fortunes. Does the thought-contracted brow of the local Sage or the lustrous eye of local Beauty inquire whose fortunes? We believe that Quintin Matsys was the BLACKSMITH of Antwerp. VERB. SAP.

I entertain a conviction, based upon large experience, that if in the days of my prosperity I had gone to the North Pole, I should have met somebody there, wandering Esquimaux or civilized man, who would have told me that Pumblechook was my earliest patron and the founder of my fortunes.

Chapter 29

Betimes in the morning I was up and out. It was too early yet to go to Miss Havisham's, so I loitered into the country on Miss Havisham's side of town,—which was not Joe's side; I could go there tomorrow,—thinking about my patroness, and painting brilliant pictures of her plans for me.

She had adopted Estella, she had as good as adopted me, and it could not fail to be her intention to bring us together. She reserved it for me to restore the desolate house, admit the sunshine into the dark rooms, set the clocks a-going and the cold hearths a-blazing, tear down the cobwebs, destroy the vermin,—in short, do all the shining deeds of the young Knight of romance, and marry the Princess. I had stopped to look at the house as I passed; and its seared red brick walls, blocked windows, and strong green ivy clasping even the stacks of chimneys with its twigs and tendons, as if with sinewy old arms, had made up a rich attractive mystery, of which I was the hero. Estella was the inspiration of it, and the heart of it, of course. But, though she had taken such strong possession of me, though my fancy and my hope were so set upon her, though her influence on my boyish life and character had been all-powerful, I did not, even that romantic morning, invest her with any attributes save those she possessed. I mention this in this place, of a fixed purpose, because it is the clew by which I am to be followed into my poor labyrinth. According to my experience, the conventional notion of a lover cannot be always true. The unqualified truth is, that when I loved Estella with the love of a man, I loved her simply because I found her irresistible. Once for all; I knew to my sorrow, often and often, if not always, that I loved her against reason, against promise, against peace, against hope, against happiness, against all discouragement that could be. Once for all; I loved her none the less because I knew it, and it had no more influence in restraining me than if I had devoutly believed her to be human perfection.

I so shaped out my walk as to arrive at the gate at my old time. When I had rung at the bell with an unsteady hand, I turned my back upon the gate, while I tried to get my breath and keep the beating of my heart moderately quiet. I heard the side-door open, and steps come across the courtyard; but I pretended not to hear, even when the gate swung on its rusty hinges.

Being at last touched on the shoulder, I started and turned. I started much more naturally then, to find myself confronted by a man in a sober grey dress. The last man I should have expected to see in that place of porter at Miss Havisham's door.

'Orlick!'

'Ah, young master, there's more changes than yours. But come in, come in. It's opposed to my orders to hold the gate open.'

I entered and he swung it, and locked it, and took the key out. 'Yes!' said he, facing round, after doggedly preceding me a few steps towards the house. 'Here I am!'

'How did you come here?'

'I come her,' he retorted, 'on my legs. I had my box brought alongside me in a barrow.'

'Are you here for good?'

'I ain't here for harm, young master, I suppose?'

I was not so sure of that. I had leisure to entertain the retort in my mind, while he slowly lifted his heavy glance from the pavement, up my legs and arms, to my face.

'Then you have left the forge?' I said.

'Do this look like a forge?' replied Orlick, sending his glance all round him with an air of injury. 'Now, do it look like it?'

I asked him how long he had left Gargery's forge?

'One day is so like another here,' he replied, 'that I don't know without casting it up. However, I come here some time since you left.'

'I could have told you that, Orlick.'

'Ah!' said he, dryly. 'But then you've got to be a scholar.'

By this time we had come to the house, where I found his room to be one just within the side-door, with a little window in it looking on the courtyard. In its small proportions, it was not unlike the kind of place usually assigned to a gate-porter in Paris. Certain keys were hanging on the wall, to which he now added the gate key; and his patchwork-covered bed was in a little inner division or recess. The whole had a slovenly, confined, and sleepy look, like a cage for a human dormouse; while he, looming dark and heavy in the shadow of a corner by the window, looked like the human dormouse for whom it was fitted up,—as indeed he was.

'I never saw this room before,' I remarked; 'but there used to be no Porter here.'

'No,' said he; 'not till it got about that there was no protection on the premises, and it come to be considered dangerous, with convicts and Tag and Rag and Bobtail going up and down. And then I was recommended to the place as a man who could give another man as good as he brought, and I took it. It's easier than bellowsing and hammering.—That's loaded, that is.'

My eye had been caught by a gun with a brass-bound stock over the chimney-piece, and his eye had followed mine.

'Well,' said I, not desirous of more conversation, 'shall I go up to Miss Havisham?'

'Burn me, if I know!' he retorted, first stretching himself and then shaking himself; 'my orders ends here, young master. I give this here bell a rap with this here hammer, and you go on along the passage till you meet somebody.'

'I am expected, I believe?'

'Burn me twice over, if I can say!' said he.

Upon that, I turned down the long passage which I had first trodden in my thick boots, and he made his bell sound. At the end of the passage, while the bell was still reverberating, I found Sarah Pocket, who appeared to have now become constitutionally green and yellow by reason of me.

'Oh!' said she. 'You, is it, Mr Pip?'

'It is, Miss Pocket. I am glad to tell you that Mr Pocket and family are all well.'

'Are they any wiser?' said Sarah, with a dismal shake of the head; 'they had better be wiser, than well. Ah, Matthew, Matthew! You know your way, sir?'

Tolerably, for I had gone up the staircase in the dark, many a time. I ascended it now, in lighter boots than of yore, and tapped in my old way at the door of Miss Havisham's room. 'Pip's rap,' I heard her say, immediately; 'come in, Pip.'

She was in her chair near the old table, in the old dress, with her two hands crossed on her stick, her chin resting on them, and her eyes on the fire. Sitting near her, with the white shoe, that had never been worn, in her hand, and her head bent as she looked at it, was an elegant lady whom I had never seen.

'Come in, Pip,' Miss Havisham continued to mutter, without looking round or up; 'come in, Pip, how do you do, Pip? So you kiss my hand as if I were a queen, eh?—Well?'

She looked up at me suddenly, only moving her eyes, and repeated in a grimly playful manner,—

'Well?'

'I heard, Miss Havisham,' said I, rather at a loss, 'that you were so kind as to wish me to come and see you, and I came directly.'

'Well?'

The lady whom I had never seen before, lifted up her eyes and looked archly at me, and then I saw that the eyes were Estella's eyes. But she was so much changed, was so much more beautiful, so much more womanly, in all things winning admiration, had made such wonderful advance, that I seemed to have made none. I fancied, as I looked at her, that I slipped hopelessly back into the coarse and common boy again. O the sense of distance and disparity that came upon me, and the inaccessibility that came about her!

She gave me her hand. I stammered something about the pleasure I felt in seeing her again, and about my having looked forward to it, for a long, long time.

'Do you find her much changed, Pip?' asked Miss Havisham, with her greedy look, and striking her stick upon a chair that stood between them, as a sign to me to sit down there.

'When I came in, Miss Havisham, I thought there was nothing of Estella in the face or figure; but now it all settles down so curiously into the old—'

'What? You are not going to say into the old Estella?' Miss Havisham interrupted. 'She was proud and insulting, and you wanted to go away from her. Don't you remember?'

I said confusedly that that was long ago, and that I knew no better then, and the like. Estella smiled with perfect composure, and said she had no doubt of my having been quite right, and of her having been very disagreeable.

'Is *he* changed?' Miss Havisham asked her.

'Very much,' said Estella, looking at me.

'Less coarse and common?' said Miss Havisham, playing with Estella's hair.

Estella laughed, and looked at the shoe in her hand, and laughed again, and looked at me, and put the shoe down. She treated me as a boy still, but she lured me on.

We sat in the dreamy room among the old strange influences which had so wrought upon me, and I learnt that she had but just come home from France, and that she was going to London. Proud and wilful as of old, she had brought those qualities into such subjection to her beauty that it was impossible and out of nature—or I thought so—to separate them from her beauty. Truly it was impossible to dissociate her presence from all those wretched hankerings after money and gentility that had disturbed my boyhood,—from all those ill-regulated aspirations that had first made me ashamed of home and Joe,—from all those visions that had raised her face in the glowing fire, struck it out of the iron on the anvil, extracted it from the darkness of night to look in at the wooden window of the forge, and flit away. In a word, it was impossible for me to separate her, in the past or in the present, from the innermost life of my life.

It was settled that I should stay there all the rest of the day, and return to the hotel at night, and to London tomorrow. When we had conversed for a while, Miss Havisham sent us two out to walk in the neglected garden: on our coming in by and by, she said, I should wheel her about a little, as in times of yore.

So, Estella and I went out into the garden by the gate through which I had strayed to my encounter with the pale young gentleman, now Herbert; I, trembling in spirit and worshipping the very hem of her dress; she, quite composed and most decidedly not worshipping the hem of mine. As we drew near to the place of encounter, she stopped and said,—

'I must have been a singular little creature to hide and see that fight that day; but I did, and I enjoyed it very much.'

'You rewarded me very much.'

'Did I?' she replied, in an incidental and forgetful way. 'I remember I entertained a great objection to your adversary, because I took it ill that he should be brought here to pester me with his company.'

'He and I are great friends now.'

'Are you? I think I recollect though, that you read with his father?'

'Yes.'

I made the admission with reluctance, for it seemed to have a boyish look, and she already treated me more than enough like a boy.

'Since your change of fortune and prospects, you have changed your companions,' said Estella.

'Naturally,' said I.

'And necessarily,' she added, in a haughty tone; 'what was fit company for you once, would be quite unfit company for you now.'

In my conscience, I doubt very much whether I had any lingering intention left of going to see Joe; but if I had, this observation put it to flight.

'You had no idea of your impending good fortune, in those times?' said Estella, with a slight wave of her hand, signifying in the fighting times.

'Not the least.'

The air of completeness and superiority with which she walked at my side, and the air of youthfulness and submission with which I walked at hers, made a contrast that I strongly felt. It would have rankled in me more than it did, if I had not regarded myself as eliciting it by being so set apart for her and assigned to her.

The garden was too overgrown and rank for walking in with ease, and after we had made the round of it twice or thrice, we came out again into the brewery yard. I showed her to a nicety where I had seen her walking on the casks, that first old day, and she said, with a cold and careless look in that direction, 'Did I?' I reminded her where she had come out of the house and given me my meat and drink, and she said, 'I don't remember.' 'Not remember that you made me cry?' said I. 'No,' said she, and shook her head and looked about her. I verily believe that her not remembering and not minding in the least, made me cry again, inwardly,—and that is the sharpest crying of all.

'You must know,' said Estella, condescending to me as a brilliant and beautiful woman might, 'that I have no heart,—if that has anything to do with my memory.'

I got through some jargon to the effect that I took the liberty of doubting that. That I knew better. That there could be no such beauty without it.

'Oh! I have a heart to be stabbed in or shot in, I have no doubt,' said Estella, 'and of course if it ceased to beat I should cease to be.

But you know what I mean. I have no softness there, no—sympathy—sentiment—nonsense.'

What *was* it that was borne in upon my mind when she stood still and looked attentively at me? Anything that I had seen in Miss Havisham? No. In some of her looks and gestures there was that tinge of resemblance to Miss Havisham which may often be noticed to have been acquired by children, from grown person with whom they have been much associated and secluded, and which, when childhood is passed, will produce a remarkable occasional likeness of expression between faces that are otherwise quite different. And yet I could not trace this to Miss Havisham. I looked again, and though she was still looking at me, the suggestion was gone.

What *was* it?

'I am serious,' said Estella, not so much with a frown (for her brow was smooth) as with a darkening of her face; 'if we are to be thrown much together, you had better believe it at once. No!' imperiously stopping me as I opened my lips. 'I have not bestowed my tenderness anywhere. I have never had any such thing.'

In another moment we were in the brewery, so long disused, and she pointed to the high gallery where I had seen her going out on that same first day, and told me she remembered to have been up there, and to have seen me standing scared below. As my eyes followed her white hand, again the same dim suggestion that I could not possibly grasp crossed me. My involuntary start occasioned her to lay her hand upon my arm. Instantly the ghost passed once more and was gone.

What *was* it?

'What is the matter?' asked Estella. 'Are you scared again?'

'I should be, if I believed what you said just now,' I replied, to turn it off.

'Then you don't? Very well. It is said, at any rate. Miss Havisham will soon be expecting you at your old post, though I think that might be laid aside now, with other old belongings. Let us make one more round of the garden, and then go in. Come! You shall not shed tears for my cruelty today; you shall be my Page, and give me your shoulder.'

Her handsome dress had trailed upon the ground. She held it in one hand now, and with the other lightly touched my shoulder as we walked. We walked round the ruined garden twice or thrice more, and it was all in bloom for me. If the green and yellow growth of weed in the chinks of the old wall had been the most precious flowers that ever blew, it could not have been more cherished in my remembrance.

There was no discrepancy of years between us to remove her far from me; we were of nearly the same age, though of course the age told for more in her case than in mine; but the air of inaccessibility which her beauty and her manner gave her, tormented me in the midst of my delight, and at the height of the assurance I felt that our patroness had chosen us for one another. Wretched boy!

At last we went back into the house, and there I heard, with surprise, that my guardian had come down to see Miss Havisham on business, and would come back to dinner. The old wintry branches of chandeliers in the room where the mouldering table was spread had been lighted while we were out, and Miss Havisham was in her chair and waiting for me.

It was like pushing the chair itself back into the past, when we began the old slow circuit round about the ashes of the bridal feast. But, in the funereal room, with that figure of the grave fallen back in the chair fixing its eyes upon her, Estella looked more bright and beautiful than before, and I was under stronger enchantment.

The time so melted away, that our early dinner-hour drew close at hand, and Estella left us to prepare herself. We had stopped near the centre of the long table, and Miss Havisham, with one of her withered arms stretched out of the chair, rested that clenched hand upon the yellow cloth. As Estella looked back over her shoulder before going out at the door, Miss Havisham kissed that hand to her, with a ravenous intensity that was of its kind quite dreadful.

Then, Estella being gone and we two left alone, she turned to me, and said in a whisper,—

'Is she beautiful, graceful, well-grown? Do you admire her?'

'Everybody must who sees her, Miss Havisham.'

She drew an arm round my neck, and drew my head close down to hers as she sat in the chair. 'Love her, love her, love her! How does she use you?'

Before I could answer (if I could have answered so difficult a question at all) she repeated, 'Love her, love her, love her! If she favours you, love her. If she wounds you, love her. If she tears your heart to pieces,—and as it gets older and stronger it will tear deeper,—love her, love her, love her!'

Never had I seen such passionate eagerness as was joined to her utterance of these words. I could feel the muscles of the thin arm round my neck swell with the vehemence that possessed her.

'Hear me, Pip! I adopted her, to be loved. I bred her and educated her, to be loved. I developed her into what she is, that she might be loved. Love her!'

She said the word often enough, and there could be no doubt that she meant to say it; but if the often repeated word had been hate instead of love—despair—revenge—dire death—it could not have sounded from her lips more like a curse.

'I'll tell you,' said she, in the same hurried passionate whisper, 'what real love is. It is blind devotion, unquestioning self-humiliation, utter submission, trust and belief against yourself and against the whole world, giving up your whole heart and soul to the smiter—as I did!'

When she came to that, and to a wild cry that followed that, I caught her round the waist. For she rose up in the chair, in her shroud of a dress, and struck at the air as if she would as soon have struck herself against the wall and fallen dead.

All this passed in a few seconds. As I drew her down into her chair, I was conscious of a scent that I knew, and turning, saw my guardian in the room.

He always carried (I have not yet mentioned it, I think) a pocket-handkerchief of rich silk and of imposing proportions, which was of great value to him in his profession. I have seen him so terrify a client or a witness by ceremoniously unfolding this pocket-handkerchief as if he were immediately going to blow his nose, and then pausing, as if he knew he should not have time to do it before such client or witness committed himself, that the self-committal has followed directly, quite as a matter of course. When I saw him in the room he had this expressive pocket-handkerchief in both hands, and was looking at us. On meeting my eye, he said plainly, by a momentary and silent pause in that attitude, 'Indeed? Singular!' and then put the handkerchief to its right use with wonderful effect.

Miss Havisham had seen him as soon as I, and was (like everybody else) afraid of him. She made a strong attempt to compose herself, and stammered that he was as punctual as ever.

'As punctual as ever,' he repeated, coming up to us. '(How do you do, Pip? Shall I give you a ride, Miss Havisham? Once round?) And so you are here, Pip?'

I told him when I had arrived, and how Miss Havisham had wished me to come and see Estella. To which he replied, 'Ah! Very fine young lady!' Then he pushed Miss Havisham in her chair before him, with one of his large hands, and put the other in his trousers-pocket as if the pocket were full of secrets.

'Well, Pip! How often have you seen Miss Estella before?' said he, when he came to a stop.

'How often?'

'Ah! How many times? Ten thousand times?'

'Oh! Certainly not so many.'

'Twice?'

'Jaggers,' interposed Miss Havisham, much to my relief, 'leave my Pip alone, and go with him to your dinner.'

He complied, and we groped our way down the dark stairs together. While we were still on our way to those detached apartments across the paved yard at the back, he asked me how often I had seen Miss Havisham eat and drink; offering me a breadth of choice, as usual, between a hundred times and once.

I considered, and said, 'Never.'

'And never will, Pip,' he retorted, with a frowning smile. 'She has never allowed herself to be seen doing either, since she lived this present life of hers. She wanders about in the night, and then lays hands on such food as she takes.'

'Pray, sir,' said I, 'may I ask you a question?'

'You may,' said he, 'and I may decline to answer it. Put your question.'

'Estella's name. Is it Havisham or—?' I had nothing to add.

'Or what?' said he.

'Is it Havisham?'

'It is Havisham.'

This brought us to the dinner-table, where she and Sarah Pocket awaited us. Mr Jaggers presided, Estella sat opposite to him, I faced my green and yellow friend. We dined very well, and were waited on by a maidservant whom I had never seen in all my comings and goings, but who, for anything I know, had been in that mysterious house the whole time. After dinner a bottle of choice old port was placed before my guardian (he was evidently well acquainted with the vintage), and the two ladies left us.

Anything to equal the determined reticence of Mr Jaggers under that roof I never saw elsewhere, even in him. He kept his very looks to himself, and scarcely directed his eyes to Estella's face once during dinner. When she spoke to him, he listened, and in due course answered, but never looked at her, that I could see. On the other hand, she often looked at him, with interest and curiosity, if not distrust, but his face never showed the least consciousness. Throughout dinner he took a dry delight in making Sarah Pocket greener and yellower, by often referring in conversation with me to my expectations; but here, again, he showed no consciousness, and even made it appear that he extorted—and even did extort, though I don't know how—those references out of my innocent self.

And when he and I were left alone together, he sat with an air upon him of general lying by in consequence of information he possessed, that really was too much for me. He cross-examined his very wine when he had nothing else in hand. He held it between himself and the candle, tasted the port, rolled it in his mouth, swallowed it, looked at his glass again, smelt the port, tried it, drank it, filled again, and cross-examined the glass again, until I was as nervous as if I had known the wine to be telling him something to my disadvantage. Three or four times I feebly thought I would start conversation; but whenever he saw me going to ask him anything, he looked at me with his glass in his hand, and rolling his wine about in his mouth, as if requesting me to take notice that it was of no use, for he couldn't answer.

I think Miss Pocket was conscious that the sight of me involved her in the danger of being goaded to madness, and perhaps tearing off her cap,—which was a very hideous one, in the nature of a muslin mop,—and strewing the ground with her hair,—which assuredly had never grown on *her* head. She did not appear when we afterwards went up to Miss Havisham's room, and we four played at whist. In the interval, Miss Havisham, in a fantastic way, had put some of the most beautiful jewels from her dressing-table into Estella's hair, and about her bosom and arms; and I saw even my guardian look at her from under his thick eyebrows, and raise them a little, when her loveliness was before him, with those rich flushes of glitter and colour in it.

Of the manner and extent to which he took our trumps into custody, and came out with mean little cards at the ends of hands, before which the glory of our Kings and Queens was utterly abased, I say nothing; nor, of the feeling that I had, respecting his looking upon us personally in the light of three very obvious and poor riddles that he had found out long ago. What I suffered from, was the incompatibility between his cold presence and my feelings towards Estella. It was not that I knew I could never bear to speak to him about her, that I knew I could never bear to hear him creak his boots at her, that I knew I could never bear to see him wash his hands of her; it was, that my admiration should be within a foot or two of him,—it was, that my feelings should be in the same place with him,—*that*, was the agonizing circumstance.

We played until nine o'clock, and then it was arranged that when Estella came to London I should be forewarned of her coming and should meet her at the coach; and then I took leave of her, and touched her and left her.

My guardian lay at the Boar in the next room to mine. Far into the night, Miss Havisham's words, 'Love her, love her, love her!' sounded in my ears. I adapted them for my own repetition, and said to my pillow, 'I love her, I love her, I love her!' hundreds of times. Then, a burst of gratitude came upon me, that she should be destined for me, once the blacksmith's boy. Then I thought if she were, as I feared, by no means rapturously grateful for that destiny yet, when would she begin to be interested in me? When should I awaken the heart within her that was mute and sleeping now?

Ah me! I thought those were high and great emotions. But I never thought there was anything low and small in my keeping away from

Joe, because I knew she would be contemptuous of him. It was but a day gone, and Joe had brought the tears into my eyes; they had soon dried, God forgive me! Soon dried.

Chapter 30

After well considering the matter while I was dressing at the Blue Boar in the morning, I resolved to tell my guardian that I doubted Orlick's being the right sort of man to fill a post of trust at Miss Havisham's. 'Why of course he is not the right sort of man, Pip,' said my guardian, comfortably satisfied beforehand on the general head, 'because the man who fills the post of trust never is the right sort of man.' It seemed quite to put him into spirits to find that this particular post was not exceptionally held by the right sort of man, and he listened in a satisfied manner while I told him what knowledge I had of Orlick. 'Very good, Pip,' he observed, when I had concluded, 'I'll go round presently, and pay our friend off.' Rather alarmed by this summary action, I was for a little delay, and even hinted that our friend himself might be difficult to deal with. 'Oh no he won't,' said my guardian, making his pocket-handkerchief-point, with perfect confidence; 'I should like to see him argue the question with *me*.'

As we were going back together to London by the midday coach, and as I breakfasted under such terrors of Pumblechook that I could scarcely hold my cup, this gave me an opportunity of saying that I wanted a walk, and that I would go on along the London road while Mr Jaggers was occupied, if he would let the coachman know that I would get into my place when overtaken. I was thus enabled to fly from the Blue Boar immediately after breakfast. By then making a loop of about a couple of miles into the open country at the back of Pumblechook's premises, I got round into the High Street again, a little beyond that pitfall, and felt myself in comparative security.

It was interesting to be in the quiet old town once more, and it was not disagreeable to be here and there suddenly recognized and stared after. One or two of the tradespeople even darted out of their shops and went a little way down the street before me, that they might turn, as if they had forgotten something, and pass me face to face,—on which occasions I don't know whether they or I made the worse pretence; they of not doing it, or I of not seeing it. Still my position was a distinguished one, and I was not at all dissatisfied with it, until Fate threw me in the way of that unlimited miscreant, Trabb's boy.

Casting my eyes along the street at a certain point of my progress, I beheld Trabb's boy approaching, lashing himself with an empty blue bag. Deeming that a serene and unconscious contemplation of him would best beseem me, and would be most likely to quell his evil mind, I advanced with that expression of countenance, and was rather congratulating myself on my success, when suddenly the knees of Trabb's boy smote together, his hair uprose, his cap fell off, he trembled violently in every limb, staggered out into the road, and crying to the populace, 'Hold me! I'm so frightened!' feigned to be in a paroxysm of terror and contrition, occasioned by the dignity of my appearance. As I passed him, his teeth loudly chattered in his head, and with every mark of extreme humiliation, he prostrated himself in the dust.

This was a hard thing to bear, but this was nothing. I had not advanced another two hundred yards when, to my inexpressible terror, amazement, and indignation, I again beheld Trabb's boy approaching. He was coming round a narrow corner. His blue bag was slung over his shoulder, honest industry beamed in his eyes, a determination to proceed to Trabb's with cheerful briskness was indicated in his gait. With a shock he became aware of me, and was severely visited as before; but this time his motion was rotatory, and he staggered round and round me with knees more afflicted, and with uplifted hands as if beseeching for mercy. His sufferings were hailed with the greatest joy by a knot of spectators, and I felt utterly confounded.

I had not got as much further down the street as the post-office, when I again beheld Trabb's boy shooting round by a back way. This time, he was entirely changed. He wore the blue bag in the manner of my great-coat, and was strutting along the pavement towards me on the opposite side of the street, attended by a company of delighted young friends to whom he from time to time exclaimed, with a wave of his hand, 'Don't know yah!' Words cannot state the amount of aggravation and injury wreaked upon me by Trabb's boy, when passing abreast of me, he pulled up his shirt-collar, twined his side-hair, stuck an arm akimbo, and smirked extravagantly by, wriggling his elbows and body, and drawling to his attendants, 'Don't know yah, don't know yah, 'pon my soul don't know yah!' The disgrace attendant on his immediately afterwards taking to crowing and pursuing me across the bridge with crows, as from an exceedingly dejected fowl who had known me when I was a blacksmith, culminated the disgrace with which I left the town, and was, so to speak, ejected by it into the open country.

But unless I had taken the life of Trabb's boy on that occasion, I really do not even now see what I could have done save endure. To have struggled with him in the street, or to have exacted any lower recompense from him than his heart's best blood, would have been futile and degrading. Moreover, he was a boy whom no man could hurt; an invulnerable and dodging serpent who, when chased into a corner, flew out again between his captor's legs, scornfully yelping. I wrote, however, to Mr Trabb by next day's post, to say that Mr Pip must decline to deal further with one who could so far forget what he owed to the best interests of society, as to employ a boy who excited loathing in every respectable mind.

The coach, with Mr Jaggers inside, came up in due time, and I took my box-seat again, and arrived in London safe,—but not sound, for my heart was gone. As soon as I arrived, I sent a penitential codfish and barrel of oysters to Joe (as reparation for not having gone myself), and then went on to Barnard's Inn.

I found Herbert dining on cold meat, and delighted to welcome me back. Having despatched The Avenger to the coffee-house for an addition to the dinner, I felt that I must open my breast that very evening to my friend and chum. As confidence was out of the question with The Avenger in the hall, which could merely be regarded in the light of an antechamber to the keyhole, I sent him to the Play. A better proof of the severity of my bondage to that taskmaster could scarcely be afforded, than the degrading shifts to which I was constantly driven to find him employment. So mean is extremity, that I sometimes sent him to Hyde Park corner to see what o'clock it was.

Dinner done and we sitting with our feet upon the fender, I said to Herbert, 'My dear Herbert, I have something very particular to tell you.'

'My dear Handel,' he returned, 'I shall esteem and respect your confidence.'

'It concerns myself, Herbert,' said I, 'and one other person.'

Herbert crossed his feet, looked at the fire with his head on one side, and having looked at it in vain for some time, looked at me because I didn't go on.

'Herbert,' said I, laying my hand upon his knee, 'I love—I adore—Estella.'

Instead of being transfixed, Herbert replied in an easy matter-of-course way, 'Exactly. Well?'

'Well, Herbert? Is that all you say? Well?'

'What next, I mean?' said Herbert. 'Of course I know *that*.'

'How do you know it?' said I.

'How do I know it, Handel? Why, from you.'

'I never told you.'

'Told me! You have never told me when you have got your hair cut, but I have had senses to perceive it. You have always adored her, ever since I have known you. You brought your adoration and your portmanteau here together. Told me! Why, you have always told me all day long. When you told me your own story, you told me plainly that you began adoring her the first time you saw her, when you were very young indeed.'

'Very well, then,' said I, to whom this was a new and not unwelcome light, 'I have never left off adoring her. And she has come back, a most beautiful and most elegant creature. And I saw her yesterday. And if I adored her before, I now doubly adore her.'

'Lucky for you then, Handel,' said Herbert, 'that you are picked out for her and allotted to her. Without encroaching on forbidden ground, we may venture to say that there can be no doubt between ourselves of that fact. Have you any idea yet, of Estella's views on the adoration question?'

I shook my head gloomily. 'Oh! She is thousands of miles away, from me,' said I.

'Patience, my dear Handel: time enough, time enough. But you have something more to say?'

'I am ashamed to say it,' I returned, 'and yet it's no worse to say it than to think it. You call me a lucky fellow. Of course, I am. I was a blacksmith's boy but yesterday; I am—what shall I say I am—today?'

'Say a good fellow, if you want a phrase,' returned Herbert, smiling, and clapping his hand on the back of mine—'a good fellow, with impetuosity and hesitation, boldness and diffidence, action and dreaming, curiously mixed in him.'

I stopped for a moment to consider whether there really was this mixture in my character. On the whole, I by no means recognized the analysis, but thought it not worth disputing.

'When I ask what I am to call myself today, Herbert,' I went on, 'I suggest what I have in my thoughts. You say I am lucky. I know I have done nothing to raise myself in life, and that Fortune alone has raised me; that is being very lucky. And yet, when I think of Estella—'

('And when don't you, you know?' Herbert threw in, with his eyes on the fire; which I thought kind and sympathetic of him.)

'—Then, my dear Herbert, I cannot tell you how dependent and uncertain I feel, and how exposed to hundreds of chances. Avoiding forbidden ground, as you did just now, I may still say that on the constancy of one person (naming no person) all my expectations depend. And at the best, how indefinite and unsatisfactory, only to know so vaguely what they are!' In saying this, I relieved my mind of what had always been there, more or less, though no doubt most since yesterday.

'Now, Handel,' Herbert replied, in his gay, hopeful way, 'it seems to me that in the despondency of the tender passion, we are looking into our gift-horse's mouth with a magnifying-glass. Likewise, it seems to me that, concentrating our attention on the examination, we altogether overlook one of the best points of the animal. Didn't you tell me that your guardian, Mr Jaggers, told you in the beginning, that you were not endowed with expectations only? And even if he had not told you so,—though that is a very large If, I grant,—could you believe that of all men in London, Mr Jaggers is the man to hold his present relations towards you unless he were sure of his ground?'

I said I could not deny that this was a strong point. I said it (people often do so, in such cases) like a rather reluctant concession to truth and justice;—as if I wanted to deny it!

'I should think it *was* a strong point,' said Herbert, 'and I should think you would be puzzled to imagine a stronger; as to the rest, you must bide your guardian's time, and he must bide his client's time. You'll be one-and-twenty before you know where you are, and then perhaps you'll get some further enlightenment. At all events, you'll be nearer getting it, for it must come at last.'

'What a hopeful disposition you have!' said I, gratefully admiring his cheery ways.

'I ought to have,' said Herbert, 'for I have not much else. I must acknowledge, by the by, that the good sense of what I have just said is not my own, but my father's. The only remark I ever heard him make on your story, was the final one, "The thing is settled and done, or Mr Jaggers would not be in it." And now before I say anything more about my father, or my father's son, and repay confidence with confidence, I want to make myself seriously disagreeable to you for a moment,—positively repulsive.'

'You won't succeed,' said I.

'O yes I shall!' said he. 'One, two, three, and now I am in for it. Handel, my good fellow;'—though he spoke in this light tone, he was very much in earnest,—'I have been thinking since we have been talking with our feet on this fender, that Estella surely cannot be a condition of your inheritance, if she was never referred to by your guardian. Am I right in so understanding what you have told me, as that he never referred to her, directly or indirectly, in any way? Never even hinted, for instance, that your patron might have views as to your marriage ultimately?'

'Never.'

'Now, Handel, I am quite free from the flavour of sour grapes, upon my soul and honour! Not being bound to her, can you not detach yourself from her?—I told you I should be disagreeable.'

I turned my head aside, for, with a rush and a sweep, like the old marsh winds coming up from the sea, a feeling like that which had subdued me on the morning when I left the forge, when the mists were solemnly rising, and when I laid my hand upon the village finger-post, smote upon my heart again. There was silence between us for a little while.

'Yes; but my dear Handel,' Herbert went on, as if we had been talking, instead of silent, 'its having been so strongly rooted in the breast of a boy whom nature and circumstances made so romantic, renders it very serious. Think of her bringing-up, and think of Miss Havisham. Think of what she is herself (now I am repulsive and you abominate me). This may lead to miserable things.'

'I know it, Herbert,' said I, with my head still turned away, 'but I can't help it.'

'You can't detach yourself?'

'No. Impossible!'

'You can't try, Handel?'

'No. Impossible!'

'Well!' said Herbert, getting up with a lively shake as if he had been asleep, and stirring the fire, 'now I'll endeavour to make myself agreeable again!'

So he went round the room and shook the curtains out, put the chairs in their places, tidied the books and so forth that were lying about, looked into the hall, peeped into the letter-box, shut the door, and came back to his chair by the fire: where he sat down, nursing his left leg in both arms.

'I was going to say a word or two, Handel, concerning my father and my father's son. I am afraid it is scarcely necessary for my father's son to remark that my father's establishment is not particularly brilliant in its housekeeping.'

'There is always plenty, Herbert,' said I, to say something encouraging.

'O yes! and so the dustman says, I believe, with the strongest approval, and so does the marine-store shop in the back street. Gravely, Handel, for the subject is grave enough, you know how it is as well as I do. I suppose there was a time once when my father had not given matters up; but if ever there was, the time is gone. May I ask you if you have ever had an opportunity of remarking, down in your part of the country, that the children of not exactly suitable marriages are always most particularly anxious to be married?'

This was such a singular question, that I asked him in return, 'Is it so?'

'I don't know,' said Herbert, 'that's what I want to know. Because it is decidedly the case with us. My poor sister Charlotte, who was next me and died before she was fourteen, was a striking example. Little Jane is the same. In her desire to be matrimonially established, you might suppose her to have passed her short existence in the perpetual contemplation of domestic bliss. Little Alick in a frock has already made arrangements for his union with a suitable young person at Kew. And indeed, I think we are all engaged, except the baby.'

'Then you are?' said I.

'I am,' said Herbert; 'but it's a secret.'

I assured him of my keeping the secret, and begged to be favoured with further particulars. He had spoken so sensibly and feelingly of my weakness that I wanted to know something about his strength.

'May I ask the name?' I said.

'Name of Clara,' said Herbert.

'Live in London?'

'Yes, perhaps I ought to mention,' said Herbert, who had become curiously crestfallen and meek, since we entered on the interesting theme, 'that she is rather below my mother's nonsensical family notions. Her father had to do with the victualling of passenger-ships. I think he was a species of purser.'

'What is he now?' said I.

'He's an invalid now,' replied Herbert.

'Living on—?'

'On the first floor,' said Herbert. Which was not at all what I meant, for I had intended my question to apply to his means. 'I have never seen him, for he has always kept his room overhead, since I have known Clara. But I have heard him constantly. He makes tremendous rows,—roars, and pegs at the floor with some frightful instrument.' In looking at me and then laughing heartily, Herbert for the time recovered his usual lively manner.

'Don't you expect to see him?' said I.

'O yes, I constantly expect to see him,' returned Herbert, 'because I never hear him, without expecting him to come tumbling through the ceiling. But I don't know how long the rafters may hold.'

When he had once more laughed heartily, he became meek again, and told me that the moment he began to realize Capital, it was his intention to marry this young lady. He added as a self-evident proposition, engendering low spirits, 'But you *can't* marry, you know, while you're looking about you.'

As we contemplated the fire, and as I thought what a difficult vision to realize this same Capital sometimes was, I put my hands in my pockets. A folded piece of paper in one of them attracting my attention, I opened it and found it to be the play-bill I had received from Joe, relative to the celebrated provincial amateur of Roscian renown. 'And bless my heart,' I involuntarily added aloud, 'it's tonight!'

This changed the subject in an instant, and made us hurriedly resolve to go to the play. So, when I had pledged myself to comfort and abet Herbert in the affair of his heart by all practicable and impracticable means, and when Herbert had told me that his affianced already knew me by reputation and that I should be presented to her, and when we had warmly shaken hands upon our mutual confidence, we blew out our candles, made up our fire, locked our door, and issued forth in quest of Mr Wopsle and Denmark.

Chapter 31

On our arrival in Denmark, we found the king and queen of that country elevated in two armchairs on a kitchen-table, holding a Court. The whole of the Danish nobility were in attendance; consisting of a noble boy in the wash-leather boots of a gigantic ancestor, a venerable Peer with a dirty face who seemed to have risen from the people late in life, and the Danish chivalry with a comb in its hair and a pair of white silk legs, and presenting on the whole a feminine appearance. My gifted townsman stood gloomily apart, with folded arms, and I could have wished that his curls and forehead had been more probable.

Several curious little circumstances transpired as the action proceeded. The late king of the country not only appeared to have been troubled with a cough at the time of his decease, but to have taken it with him to the tomb, and to have brought it back. The royal phantom also carried a ghostly manuscript round its truncheon, to which it had the appearance of occasionally referring, and that too, with an air of anxiety and a tendency to lose the place of reference which were suggestive of a state of mortality. It was this, I conceive, which led to the Shade's being advised by the gallery to 'turn over!'—a recommendation which it took extremely ill. It was likewise to be noted of this majestic spirit, that whereas it always appeared with an air of having been out a long time and walked an immense distance, it perceptibly came from a closely contiguous wall. This occasioned its terrors to be received derisively. The Queen of Denmark, a very buxom lady, though no doubt historically brazen, was considered by the public to have too much brass about her; her chin being attached to her diadem by a broad band of that metal (as if she had a gorgeous toothache), her waist being encircled by another, and each of her arms by another, so that she was openly mentioned as 'the kettle-drum.' The noble boy in the ancestral boots was inconsistent, representing himself, as it were in one breath, as an able seaman, a strolling actor, a grave-digger, a clergyman, and a person of the utmost importance at a court fencing-match, on the authority of whose practised eye and nice discrimination the finest strokes were judged. This gradually led to a want of toleration for him, and even—on his being detected in holy orders, and declining to perform the funeral service—to the general indignation taking the form of nuts. Lastly, Ophelia was a prey to such slow musical madness, that when, in course of time, she had taken off her white muslin scarf, folded it up, and buried it, a sulky man who had been long cooling his impatient nose against an iron bar in the front row of the gallery, growled, 'Now the baby's put to bed let's have supper!' Which, to say the least of it, was out of keeping.

Upon my unfortunate townsman all these incidents accumulated with playful effect. Whenever that undecided Prince had to ask a question or state a doubt, the public helped him out with it. As for example; on the question whether 'twas nobler in the mind to suffer, some roared yes, and some no, and some inclining to both opinions said 'Toss up for it;' and quite a Debating Society arose. When he asked what should such fellows as he do crawling between earth and heaven, he was encouraged with loud cries of 'Hear, hear!' When he appeared with his stocking disordered (its disorder expressed, according to usage, by one very neat fold in the top, which I suppose to be always got up with a flat iron), a conversation took place in the gallery respecting the paleness of his leg, and whether it was occasioned by the turn the ghost had given him. On his taking the recorders,—very like a little black flute that had just been played in the orchestra and handed out at the door,—he was called upon unanimously for Rule Britannia. When he recommended the player not to saw the air thus, the sulky man said, 'And don't *you* do it, neither; you're a deal worse than *him*!' And I grieve to add that peals of laughter greeted Mr Wopsle on every one of these occasions.

But his greatest trials were in the churchyard, which had the appearance of a primeval forest, with a kind of small ecclesiastical wash-house on one side, and a turnpike gate on the other. Mr Wopsle in a comprehensive black cloak, being descried entering at the turnpike, the gravedigger was admonished in a friendly way, 'Look out! Here's the undertaker a coming, to see how you're a getting on with your work!' I believe it is well known in a constitutional country that Mr Wopsle could not possibly have returned the skull, after moralizing over it, without dusting his fingers on a white napkin taken from his breast; but even that innocent and indispensable action did not pass without the comment, 'Wai-ter!' The arrival of the body for interment (in an empty black box with the lid tumbling open), was the signal for a general joy, which was much enhanced by the discovery, among the bearers, of an individual obnoxious to identification. The joy attended Mr Wopsle through his struggle with Laertes on the brink of the orchestra and the grave, and slackened no more until he had tumbled the king off the kitchen-table, and had died by inches from the ankles upward.

We had made some pale efforts in the beginning to applaud Mr Wopsle; but they were too hopeless to be persisted in. Therefore we had sat, feeling keenly for him, but laughing, nevertheless, from ear to ear. I laughed in spite of myself all the time, the whole thing was so droll; and yet I had a latent impression that there was something decidedly fine in Mr Wopsle's elocution,—not for old associations' sake, I am afraid, but because it was very slow, very dreary, very uphill and downhill, and very unlike any way in which any man in any natural circumstances of life or death ever expressed himself about anything. When the tragedy was over, and he had been called for and hooted, I said to Herbert, 'Let us go at once, or perhaps we shall meet him.'

We made all the haste we could downstairs, but we were not quick enough either. Standing at the door was a Jewish man with an unnatural heavy smear of eyebrow, who caught my eyes as we advanced, and said, when we came up with him,—

'Mr Pip and friend?'

Identity of Mr Pip and friend confessed.

'Mr Waldengarver,' said the man, 'would be glad to have the honour.'

'Waldengarver?' I repeated—when Herbert murmured in my ear, 'Probably Wopsle.'

'Oh!' said I. 'Yes. Shall we follow you?'

'A few steps, please.' When we were in a side alley, he turned and asked, 'How did you think he looked?—I dressed him.'

I don't know what he had looked like, except a funeral; with the addition of a large Danish sun or star hanging round his neck by a blue ribbon, that had given him the appearance of being insured in some extraordinary Fire Office. But I said he had looked very nice.

'When he come to the grave,' said our conductor, 'he showed his cloak beautiful. But, judging from the wing, it looked to me that when he see the ghost in the queen's apartment, he might have made more of his stockings.'

I modestly assented, and we all fell through a little dirty swing door, into a sort of hot packing-case immediately behind it. Here Mr Wopsle was divesting himself of his Danish garments, and here there was just room for us to look at him over one another's shoulders, by keeping the packing-case door, or lid, wide open.

'Gentlemen,' said Mr Wopsle, 'I am proud to see you. I hope, Mr Pip, you will excuse my sending round. I had the happiness to know you in former times, and the Drama has ever had a claim which has ever been acknowledged, on the noble and the affluent.'

Meanwhile, Mr Waldengarver, in a frightful perspiration, was trying to get himself out of his princely sables.

'Skin the stockings off Mr Waldengarver,' said the owner of that property, 'or you'll bust 'em. Bust 'em, and you'll bust five-and-thirty shillings. Shakspeare never was complimented with a finer pair. Keep quiet in your chair now, and leave 'em to me.'

With that, he went upon his knees, and began to flay his victim; who, on the first stocking coming off, would certainly have fallen over backward with his chair, but for there being no room to fall anyhow.

I had been afraid until then to say a word about the play. But then, Mr Waldengarver looked up at us complacently, and said,—

'Gentlemen, how did it seem to you, to go, in front?'

Herbert said from behind (at the same time poking me), 'Capitally.' So I said 'Capitally.'

'How did you like my reading of the character, gentlemen?' said Mr Waldengarver, almost, if not quite, with patronage.

Herbert said from behind (again poking me), 'Massive and concrete.' So I said boldly, as if I had originated it, and must beg to insist upon it, 'Massive and concrete.'

'I am glad to have your approbation, gentlemen,' said Mr Waldengarver, with an air of dignity, in spite of his being ground against the wall at the time, and holding on by the seat of the chair.

'But I'll tell you one thing, Mr Waldengarver,' said the man who was on his knees, 'in which you're out in your reading. Now mind! I don't care who says contrairy; I tell you so. You're out in your reading of Hamlet when you get your legs in profile. The last Hamlet as I dressed, made the same mistakes in his reading at rehearsal, till I got him to put a large red wafer on each of his shins, and then at that rehearsal (which was the last) I went in front, sir, to the back of the pit, and whenever his reading brought him into profile, I called out "I don't see no wafers!" And at night his reading was lovely.'

Mr Waldengarver smiled at me, as much as to say 'a faithful dependent—I overlook his folly;' and then said aloud, 'My view is a little classic and thoughtful for them here; but they will improve, they will improve.'

Herbert and I said together, O, no doubt they would improve.

'Did you observe, gentlemen,' said Mr Waldengarver, 'that there was a man in the gallery who endeavoured to cast derision on the service,—I mean, the representation?'

We basely replied that we rather thought we had noticed such a man. I added, 'He was drunk, no doubt.'

'O dear no, sir,' said Mr Wopsle, 'not drunk. His employer would see to that, sir. His employer would not allow him to be drunk.'

'You know his employer?' said I.

Mr Wopsle shut his eyes, and opened them again; performing both ceremonies very slowly. 'You must have observed, gentlemen,' said he, 'an ignorant and a blatant ass, with a rasping throat and a countenance expressive of low malignity, who went through—I will not say sustained—the rôle (if I may use a French expression) of Claudius, King of Denmark. That is his employer, gentlemen. Such is the profession!'

Without distinctly knowing whether I should have been more sorry for Mr Wopsle if he had been in despair, I was so sorry for him as it was, that I took the opportunity of his turning round to have his braces put on,—which jostled us out at the doorway,—to ask Herbert what he thought of having him home to supper? Herbert said he thought it would be kind to do so; therefore I invited him, and he went to Barnard's with us, wrapped up to the eyes, and we did our best for him, and he sat until two o'clock in the morning, reviewing his success and developing his plans. I forget in detail what they were, but I have a general recollection that he was to begin with reviving the Drama, and to end with crushing it; inasmuch as his decease would leave it utterly bereft and without a chance or hope.

Miserably I went to bed after all, and miserably thought of Estella, and miserably dreamed that my expectations were all cancelled, and that I had to give my hand in marriage to Herbert's Clara, or play Hamlet to Miss Havisham's Ghost, before twenty thousand people, without knowing twenty words of it.

Chapter 32

One day when I was busy with my books and Mr Pocket, I received a note by the post, the mere outside of which threw me into a great flutter; for, though I had never seen the handwriting in which it was addressed, I divined whose hand it was. It had no set beginning, as

Dear Mr Pip, or Dear Pip, or Dear Sir, or Dear Anything, but ran thus:—

'I am to come to London the day after tomorrow by the midday coach. I believe it was settled you should meet me? At all events Miss Havisham has that impression, and I write in obedience to it. She sends you her regard.

'Yours, ESTELLA.'

If there had been time, I should probably have ordered several suits of clothes for this occasion; but as there was not, I was fain to be content with those I had. My appetite vanished instantly, and I knew no peace or rest until the day arrived. Not that its arrival brought me either; for, then I was worse than ever, and began haunting the coach-office in Wood Street, Cheapside, before the coach had left the Blue Boar in our town. For all that I knew this perfectly well, I still felt as if it were not safe to let the coach-office be out of my sight longer than five minutes at a time; and in this condition of unreason I had performed the first half-hour of a watch of four or five hours, when Wemmick ran against me.

'Halloa, Mr Pip,' said he; 'how do you do? I should hardly have thought this was *your* beat.'

I explained that I was waiting to meet somebody who was coming up by coach, and I inquired after the Castle and the Aged.

'Both flourishing thankye,' said Wemmick, 'and particularly the Aged. He's in wonderful feather. He'll be eighty-two next birthday. I have a notion of firing eighty-two times, if the neighbourhood shouldn't complain, and that cannon of mine should prove equal to the pressure. However, this is not London talk. Where do you think I am going to?'

'To the office?' said I, for he was tending in that direction.

'Next thing to it,' returned Wemmick, 'I am going to Newgate. We are in a banker's-parcel case just at present, and I have been down the road taking a squint at the scene of action, and thereupon must have a word or two with our client.'

'Did your client commit the robbery?' I asked.

'Bless your soul and body, no,' answered Wemmick, very drily. 'But he is accused of it. So might you or I be. Either of us might be accused of it, you know.'

'Only neither of us is,' I remarked.

'Yah!' said Wemmick, touching me on the breast with his forefinger; 'you're a deep one, Mr Pip! Would you like to have a look at Newgate? Have you time to spare?'

I had so much time to spare, that the proposal came as a relief, notwithstanding its irreconcilability with my latent desire to keep my eye on the coach-office. Muttering that I would make the inquiry whether I had time to walk with him, I went into the office, and ascertained from the clerk with the nicest precision and much to the trying of his temper, the earliest moment at which the coach could be expected,—which I knew beforehand, quite as well as he. I then rejoined Mr Wemmick, and affecting to consult my watch, and to be surprised by the information I had received, accepted his offer.

We were at Newgate in a few minutes, and we passed through the lodge where some fetters were hanging up on the bare walls among the prison rules, into the interior of the jail. At that time jails were much neglected, and the period of exaggerated reaction consequent on all public wrongdoing—and which is always its heaviest and longest punishment—was still far off. So, felons were not lodged and fed better than soldiers (to say nothing of paupers), and seldom set fire to their prisons with the excusable object of improving the flavour of their soup. It was visiting time when Wemmick took me in, and a potman was going his rounds with beer; and the prisoners, behind bars in yards, were buying beer, and talking to friends; and a frowzy, ugly, disorderly, depressing scene it was.

It struck me that Wemmick walked among the prisoners much as a gardener might walk among his plants. This was first put into my head by his seeing a shoot that had come up in the night, and saying, 'What, Captain Tom? Are *you* there? Ah, indeed!' and also, 'Is that Black Bill behind the cistern? Why I didn't look for you these two months; how do you find yourself?' Equally in his stopping at the bars and attending to anxious whisperers,—always singly,—Wemmick with his post-office in an immovable state, looked at them while in conference, as if he were taking particular notice of the advance they had made, since last observed, towards coming out in full blow at their trial.

He was highly popular, and I found that he took the familiar department of Mr Jaggers's business; though something of the state of Mr Jaggers hung about him too, forbidding approach beyond certain limits. His personal recognition of each successive client was comprised in a nod, and in his settling his hat a little easier on his head with both hands, and then tightening the post-office, and putting his hands in his pockets. In one or two instances there was a difficulty respecting the raising of fees, and then Mr Wemmick, backing as far as possible from the insufficient money produced, said, 'it's no use, my boy. I'm only a subordinate. I can't take it. Don't go on in that way with a subordinate. If you are unable to make up your quantum, my boy, you had better address yourself to a principal; there are plenty of principals in the profession, you know, and what is not worth the while of one, may be worth the while of another; that's my recommendation to you, speaking as a subordinate. Don't try on useless measures. Why should you? Now, who's next?'

Thus, we walked through Wemmick's greenhouse, until he turned to me and said, 'Notice the man I shall shake hands with.' I should have done so, without the preparation, as he had shaken hands with no one yet.

Almost as soon as he had spoken, a portly upright man (whom I can see now, as I write) in a well-worn olive-coloured frock-coat, with a peculiar pallor overspreading the red in his complexion, and eyes that went wandering about when he tried to fix them, came up to a corner of the bars, and put his hand to his hat—which had a greasy and fatty surface like cold broth—with a half-serious and half-jocose military salute.

'Colonel, to you!' said Wemmick; 'how are you, Colonel?'

'All right, Mr Wemmick.'

'Everything was done that could be done, but the evidence was too strong for us, Colonel.'

'Yes, it was too strong, sir,—but *I* don't care.'

'No, no,' said Wemmick, coolly, '*you* don't care.' Then, turning to me, 'Served His Majesty this man. Was a soldier in the line and bought his discharge.'

I said, 'Indeed?' and the man's eyes looked at me, and then looked over my head, and then looked all round me, and then he drew his hand across his lips and laughed.

'I think I shall be out of this on Monday, sir,' he said to Wemmick.

'Perhaps,' returned my friend, 'but there's no knowing.'

'I am glad to have the chance of bidding you goodbye, Mr Wemmick,' said the man, stretching out his hand between two bars.

'Thankye,' said Wemmick, shaking hands with him. 'Same to you, Colonel.'

'If what I had upon me when taken had been real, Mr Wemmick,' said the man, unwilling to let his hand go, 'I should have asked the favour of your wearing another ring—in acknowledgment of your attentions.'

'I'll accept the will for the deed,' said Wemmick. 'By the by; you were quite a pigeon-fancier.' The man looked up at the sky. 'I am told you had a remarkable breed of tumblers. *Could* you commission any friend of yours to bring me a pair, if you've no further use for 'em?'

'It shall be done, sir.'

'All right,' said Wemmick, 'they shall be taken care of. Good afternoon, Colonel. Goodbye!' They shook hands again, and as we walked away Wemmick said to me, 'A Coiner, a very good workman. The Recorder's report is made today, and he is sure to be executed on Monday. Still you see, as far as it goes, a pair of pigeons are portable property all the same.' With that, he looked back, and nodded at this dead plant, and then cast his eyes about him in walking out of the yard, as if he were considering what other pot would go best in its place.

As we came out of the prison through the lodge, I found that the great importance of my guardian was appreciated by the turnkeys, no less than by those whom they held in charge. 'Well, Mr Wemmick,' said the turnkey, who kept us between the two studded and spiked lodge gates, and who carefully locked one before he unlocked the other, 'what's Mr Jaggers going to do with that water-side murder? Is he going to make it manslaughter, or what's he going to make of it?'

'Why don't you ask him?' returned Wemmick.

'O yes, I dare say!' said the turnkey.

'Now, that's the way with them here, Mr Pip,' remarked Wemmick, turning to me with his post-office elongated. 'They don't mind what they ask of me, the subordinate; but you'll never catch 'em asking any questions of my principal.'

'Is this young gentleman one of the 'prentices or articled ones of your office?' asked the turnkey, with a grin at Mr Wemmick's humour.

'There he goes again, you see!' cried Wemmick, 'I told you so! Asks another question of the subordinate before his first is dry! Well, supposing Mr Pip is one of them?'

'Why then,' said the turnkey, grinning again, 'he knows what Mr Jaggers is.'

'Yah!' cried Wemmick, suddenly hitting out at the turnkey in a facetious way, 'you're dumb as one of your own keys when you have to do with my principal, you know you are. Let us out, you old fox, or I'll get him to bring an action against you for false imprisonment.'

The turnkey laughed, and gave us good day, and stood laughing at us over the spikes of the wicket when we descended the steps into the street.

'Mind you, Mr Pip,' said Wemmick, gravely in my ear, as he took my arm to be more confidential; 'I don't know that Mr Jaggers does a better thing than the way in which he keeps himself so high. He's always so high. His constant height is of a piece with his immense abilities. That Colonel durst no more take leave of *him*, than that turnkey durst ask him his intentions respecting a case. Then, between his height and them, he slips in his subordinate,—don't you see?—and so he has 'em, soul and body.'

I was very much impressed, and not for the first time, by my guardian's subtlety. To confess the truth, I very heartily wished, and not for the first time, that I had had some other guardian of minor abilities.

Mr Wemmick and I parted at the office in Little Britain, where suppliants for Mr Jaggers's notice were lingering about as usual, and I returned to my watch in the street of the coach-office, with some three hours on hand. I consumed the whole time in thinking how strange it was that I should be encompassed by all this taint of prison and crime; that, in my childhood out on our lonely marshes on a winter evening, I should have first encountered it; that, it should have reappeared on two occasions, starting out like a stain that was faded but not gone; that, it should in this new way pervade my fortune and advancement. While my mind was thus engaged, I thought of the beautiful young Estella, proud and refined, coming towards me, and I thought with absolute abhorrence of the contrast between the jail and her. I wished that Wemmick had not met me, or that I had not yielded to him and gone with him, so that, of all days in the year on this day, I might not have had Newgate in my breath and on my clothes. I beat the prison dust off my feet as I sauntered to and fro, and I shook it out of my dress, and I exhaled its air from my lungs. So contaminated did I feel, remembering who was coming, that the coach came quickly after all, and I was not yet free from the soiling consciousness of Mr Wemmick's conservatory, when I saw her face at the coach window and her hand waving to me.

What *was* the nameless shadow which again in that one instant had passed?

Chapter 33

In her furred travelling-dress, Estella seemed more delicately beautiful than she had ever seemed yet, even in my eyes. Her manner was more winning than she had cared to let it be to me before, and I thought I saw Miss Havisham's influence in the change.

We stood in the Inn Yard while she pointed out her luggage to me, and when it was all collected I remembered—having forgotten everything but herself in the meanwhile—that I knew nothing of her destination.

'I am going to Richmond,' she told me. 'Our lesson is, that there are two Richmonds, one in Surrey and one in Yorkshire, and that mine is the Surrey Richmond. The distance is ten miles. I am to have a carriage, and you are to take me. This is my purse, and you are to pay my charges out of it. O, you must take the purse! We have no choice, you and I, but to obey our instructions. We are not free to follow our own devices, you and I.'

As she looked at me in giving me the purse, I hoped there was an inner meaning in her words. She said them slightingly, but not with displeasure.

'A carriage will have to be sent for, Estella. Will you rest here a little?'

'Yes, I am to rest here a little, and I am to drink some tea, and you are to take care of me the while.'

She drew her arm through mine, as if it must be done, and I requested a waiter who had been staring at the coach like a man who had never seen such a thing in his life, to show us a private sitting-room. Upon that, he pulled out a napkin, as if it were a magic clew without which he couldn't find the way upstairs, and led us to the black hole of the establishment, fitted up with a diminishing mirror (quite a superfluous article, considering the hole's proportions), an anchovy sauce-cruet, and somebody's pattens. On my objecting to this retreat, he took us into another room with a dinner-table for thirty, and in the grate a scorched leaf of a copy-book under a bushel of coal-dust. Having looked at this extinct conflagration and shaken his head, he took my order; which, proving to be merely, 'Some tea for the lady,' sent him out of the room in a very low state of mind.

I was, and I am, sensible that the air of this chamber, in its strong combination of stable with soup-stock, might have led one to infer that the coaching department was not doing well, and that the enterprising proprietor was boiling down the horses for the refreshment department. Yet the room was all in all to me, Estella being in it. I thought that with her I could have been happy there for life. (I was not at all happy there at the time, observe, and I knew it well.)

'Where are you going to, at Richmond?' I asked Estella.

'I am going to live,' said she, 'at a great expense, with a lady there, who has the power—or says she has—of taking me about, and introducing me, and showing people to me and showing me to people.'

'I suppose you will be glad of variety and admiration?'

'Yes, I suppose so.'

She answered so carelessly, that I said, 'You speak of yourself as if you were someone else.'

'Where did you learn how I speak of others? Come, come,' said Estella, smiling delightfully, 'you must not expect me to go to school to *you*; I must talk in my own way. How do you thrive with Mr Pocket?'

'I live quite pleasantly there; at least—' It appeared to me that I was losing a chance.

'At least?' repeated Estella.

'As pleasantly as I could anywhere, away from you.'

'You silly boy,' said Estella, quite composedly, 'how can you talk such nonsense? Your friend Mr Matthew, I believe, is superior to the rest of his family?'

'Very superior indeed. He is nobody's enemy—'

'Don't add but his own,' interposed Estella, 'for I hate that class of man. But he really is disinterested, and above small jealousy and spite, I have heard?'

'I am sure I have every reason to say so.'

'You have not every reason to say so of the rest of his people,' said Estella, nodding at me with an expression of face that was at once grave and rallying, 'for they beset Miss Havisham with reports and insinuations to your disadvantage. They watch you, misrepresent you, write letters about you (anonymous sometimes), and you are the torment and the occupation of their lives. You can scarcely realize to yourself the hatred those people feel for you.'

'They do me no harm, I hope?'

Instead of answering, Estella burst out laughing. This was very singular to me, and I looked at her in considerable perplexity. When she left off—and she had not laughed languidly, but with real enjoyment—I said, in my diffident way with her,—

'I hope I may suppose that you would not be amused if they did me any harm.'

'No, no you may be sure of that,' said Estella. 'You may be certain that I laugh because they fail. O, those people with Miss Havisham, and the tortures they undergo!' She laughed again, and even now when she had told me why, her laughter was very singular to me, for I could not doubt its being genuine, and yet it seemed too much for the occasion. I thought there must really be something more here than I knew; she saw the thought in my mind, and answered it.

'It is not easy for even you.' said Estella, 'to know what satisfaction it gives me to see those people thwarted, or what an enjoyable sense of the ridiculous I have when they are made ridiculous. For you were not brought up in that strange house from a mere baby. I was. You had not your little wits sharpened by their intriguing against you, suppressed and defenceless, under the mask of sympathy and pity and what not that is soft and soothing. I had. You did not gradually open your round childish eyes wider and wider to the discovery of that impostor of a woman who calculates her stores of peace of mind for when she wakes up in the night. I did.'

It was no laughing matter with Estella now, nor was she summoning these remembrances from any shallow place. I would not have been the cause of that look of hers for all my expectations in a heap.

'Two things I can tell you,' said Estella. 'First, notwithstanding the proverb that constant dropping will wear away a stone, you may set your mind at rest that these people never will—never would, in hundred years—impair your ground with Miss Havisham, in any particular, great or small. Second, I am beholden to you as the cause of their being so busy and so mean in vain, and there is my hand upon it.'

As she gave it to me playfully,—for her darker mood had been but momentary,—I held it and put it to my lips. 'You ridiculous boy,' said Estella, 'will you never take warning? Or do you kiss my hand in the same spirit in which I once let you kiss my cheek?'

'What spirit was that?' said I.

'I must think a moment. A spirit of contempt for the fawners and plotters.'

'If I say yes, may I kiss the cheek again?'

'You should have asked before you touched the hand. But, yes, if you like.'

I leaned down, and her calm face was like a statue's. 'Now,' said Estella, gliding away the instant I touched her cheek, 'you are to take care that I have some tea, and you are to take me to Richmond.'

Her reverting to this tone as if our association were forced upon us, and we were mere puppets, gave me pain; but everything in our intercourse did give me pain. Whatever her tone with me happened to be, I could put no trust in it, and build no hope on it; and yet I went on against trust and against hope. Why repeat it a thousand times? So it always was.

I rang for the tea, and the waiter, reappearing with his magic clew, brought in by degrees some fifty adjuncts to that refreshment, but of tea not a glimpse. A teaboard, cups and saucers, plates, knives and forks (including carvers), spoons (various), saltcellars, a meek little muffin confined with the utmost precaution under a strong iron cover, Moses in the bulrushes typified by a soft bit of butter in a quantity of parsley, a pale loaf with a powdered head, two proof impressions of the bars of the kitchen fireplace on triangular bits of bread, and ultimately a fat family urn; which the waiter staggered in with, expressing in his countenance burden and suffering. After a prolonged absence at this stage of the entertainment, he at length came back with a casket of precious appearance containing twigs. These I steeped in hot water, and so from the whole of these appliances extracted one cup of I don't know what for Estella.

The bill paid, and the waiter remembered, and the ostler not forgotten, and the chambermaid taken into consideration,—in a word, the whole house bribed into a state of contempt and animosity, and Estella's purse much lightened,—we got into our post-coach and drove away. Turning into Cheapside and rattling up Newgate Street, we were soon under the walls of which I was so ashamed.

'What place is that?' Estella asked me.

I made a foolish pretence of not at first recognizing it, and then told her. As she looked at it, and drew in her head again, murmuring, 'Wretches!' I would not have confessed to my visit for any consideration.

'Mr Jaggers,' said I, by way of putting it neatly on somebody else, 'has the reputation of being more in the secrets of that dismal place than any man in London.'

'He is more in the secrets of every place, I think,' said Estella, in a low voice.

'You have been accustomed to see him often, I suppose?'

'I have been accustomed to see him at uncertain intervals, ever since I can remember. But I know him no better now, than I did before I could speak plainly. What is your own experience of him? Do you advance with him?'

'Once habituated to his distrustful manner,' said I, 'I have done very well.'

'Are you intimate?'

'I have dined with him at his private house.'

'I fancy,' said Estella, shrinking 'that must be a curious place.'

'It is a curious place.'

I should have been chary of discussing my guardian too freely even with her; but I should have gone on with the subject so far as to describe the dinner in Gerrard Street, if we had not then come into a sudden glare of gas. It seemed, while it lasted, to be all alight and alive with that inexplicable feeling I had had before; and when we were out of it, I was as much dazed for a few moments as if I had been in lightning.

So we fell into other talk, and it was principally about the way by which we were travelling, and about what parts of London lay on this side of it, and what on that. The great city was almost new to her, she told me, for she had never left Miss Havisham's neighbourhood until she had gone to France, and she had merely passed through London then in going and returning. I asked her if my guardian had any charge of her while she remained here? To that she emphatically said 'God forbid!' and no more.

It was impossible for me to avoid seeing that she cared to attract me; that she made herself winning, and would have won me even if the task had needed pains. Yet this made me none the happier, for even if she had not taken that tone of our being disposed of by others, I should have felt that she held my heart in her hand because she wilfully chose to do it, and not because it would have wrung any tenderness in her to crush it and throw it away.

When we passed through Hammersmith, I showed her where Mr Matthew Pocket lived, and said it was no great way from Richmond, and that I hoped I should see her sometimes.

'O yes, you are to see me; you are to come when you think proper; you are to be mentioned to the family; indeed you are already mentioned.'

I inquired was it a large household she was going to be a member of?

'No; there are only two; mother and daughter. The mother is a lady of some station, though not averse to increasing her income.'

'I wonder Miss Havisham could part with you again so soon.'

'It is a part of Miss Havisham's plans for me, Pip,' said Estella, with a sigh, as if she were tired; 'I am to write to her constantly and see her regularly and report how I go on,—I and the jewels,—for they are nearly all mine now.'

It was the first time she had ever called me by my name. Of course she did so purposely, and knew that I should treasure it up.

We came to Richmond all too soon, and our destination there was a house by the green,—a staid old house, where hoops and powder and patches, embroidered coats, rolled stockings, ruffles and swords, had had their court days many a time. Some ancient trees before the house were still cut into fashions as formal and unnatural as the hoops and wigs and stiff skirts; but their own allotted places in the great procession of the dead were not far off, and they would soon drop into them and go the silent way of the rest.

A bell with an old voice—which I dare say in its time had often said to the house, here is the green farthingale, here is the diamond-hilted sword, here are the shoes with red heels and the blue solitaire—sounded gravely in the moonlight, and two cherry-coloured maids came fluttering out to receive Estella. The doorway soon absorbed her boxes, and she gave me her hand and a smile, and said goodnight, and was absorbed likewise. And still I stood looking at the house, thinking how happy I should be if I lived there with her, and knowing that I never was happy with her, but always miserable.

I got into the carriage to be taken back to Hammersmith, and I got in with a bad heartache, and I got out with a worse heartache. At our own door, I found little Jane Pocket coming home from a little party escorted by her little lover; and I envied her little lover, in spite of his being subject to Flopson.

Mr Pocket was out lecturing; for, he was a most delightful lecturer on domestic economy, and his treatises on the management of children and servants were considered the very best textbooks on those themes. But Mrs Pocket was at home, and was in a little difficulty, on account of the baby's having been accommodated with a needle-case to keep him quiet during the unaccountable absence (with a relative in the Foot Guards) of Millers. And more needles were missing than it could be regarded as quite wholesome for a patient of such tender years either to apply externally or to take as a tonic.

Mr Pocket being justly celebrated for giving most excellent practical advice, and for having a clear and sound perception of things and a highly judicious mind, I had some notion in my heartache of begging him to accept my confidence. But happening to look up at Mrs Pocket as she sat reading her book of dignities after prescribing bed as a sovereign remedy for baby, I thought—Well—No, I wouldn't.

Chapter 34

As I had grown accustomed to my expectations, I had insensibly begun to notice their effect upon myself and those around me. Their influence on my own character I disguised from my recognition as much as possible, but I knew very well that it was not all good. I lived in a state of chronic uneasiness respecting my behaviour to Joe. My conscience was not by any means comfortable about Biddy. When I woke up in the night,—like Camilla,—I used to think, with a weariness on my spirits, that I should have been happier and better if I had never seen Miss Havisham's face, and had risen to manhood content to be partners with Joe in the honest old forge. Many a time of an evening, when I sat alone looking at the fire, I thought, after all there was no fire like the forge fire and the kitchen fire at home.

Yet Estella was so inseparable from all my restlessness and disquiet of mind, that I really fell into confusion as to the limits of my own part in its production. That is to say, supposing I had had no expectations, and yet had had Estella to think of, I could not make out to my satisfaction that I should have done much better. Now, concerning the influence of my position on others, I was in no such difficulty, and so I perceived—though dimly enough perhaps—that it was not beneficial to anybody, and, above all, that it was not beneficial to Herbert. My lavish habits led his easy nature into expenses that he could not afford, corrupted the simplicity of his life, and disturbed his peace with anxieties and regrets. I was not at all remorseful for having unwittingly set those other branches of the Pocket family to the poor arts they practised; because such littlenesses were their natural bent, and would have been evoked by anybody else, if I had left them slumbering. But Herbert's was a very different case, and it often caused me a twinge to think that I had done him evil service in crowding his sparely furnished chambers with incongruous upholstery work, and placing the Canary-breasted Avenger at his disposal.

So now, as an infallible way of making little ease great ease, I began to contract a quantity of debt. I could hardly begin but Herbert must begin too, so he soon followed. At Startop's suggestion, we put ourselves down for election into a club called The Finches of the Grove: the object of which institution I have never divined, if it were not that the members should dine expensively once a fortnight, to quarrel among themselves as much as possible after dinner, and to cause six waiters to get drunk on the stairs. I know that these gratifying social ends were so invariably accomplished, that Herbert and I understood nothing else to be referred to in the first standing toast of the society: which ran 'Gentlemen, may the present promotion of good feeling ever reign predominant among the Finches of the Grove.'

The Finches spent their money foolishly (the hotel we dined at was in Covent Garden), and the first Finch I saw when I had the honour of joining the Grove was Bentley Drummle, at that time floundering about town in a cab of his own, and doing a great deal of damage to the posts at the street corners. Occasionally, he shot himself out of his equipage headforemost over the apron; and I saw him on one occasion deliver himself at the door of the Grove in this unintentional way—like coals. But here I anticipate a little, for I was not a Finch, and could not be, according to the sacred laws of the society, until I came of age.

In my confidence in my own resources, I would willingly have taken Herbert's expenses on myself; but Herbert was proud, and I could make no such proposal to him. So he got into difficulties in every direction, and continued to look about him. When we gradually fell into keeping late hours and late company, I noticed that he looked about him with a desponding eye at breakfast-time; that he began to look about him more hopefully about midday; that he drooped when he came into dinner; that he seemed to descry Capital in the distance, rather clearly, after dinner; that he all but realized Capital towards midnight; and that at about two o'clock in the morning, he became so deeply despondent again as to talk of buying a rifle and going to America, with a general purpose of compelling buffaloes to make his fortune.

I was usually at Hammersmith about half the week, and when I was at Hammersmith I haunted Richmond, whereof separately by and by. Herbert would often come to Hammersmith when I was there, and I think at those seasons his father would occasionally have some passing perception that the opening he was looking for, had not appeared yet. But in the general tumbling up of the family, his tumbling out in life somewhere, was a thing to transact itself somehow. In the meantime Mr Pocket grew greyer, and tried oftener to lift himself out of his perplexities by the hair. While Mrs Pocket tripped up the family with her footstool, read her book of dignities, lost her pocket-handkerchief, told us about her grandpapa, and taught the young idea how to shoot, by shooting it into bed whenever it attracted her notice.

As I am now generalizing a period of my life with the object of clearing my way before me, I can scarcely do so better than by at once completing the description of our usual manners and customs at Barnard's Inn.

We spent as much money as we could, and got as little for it as people could make up their minds to give us. We were always more or less miserable, and most of our acquaintance were in the same condition. There was a gay fiction among us that we were constantly enjoying ourselves, and a skeleton truth that we never did. To the best of my belief, our case was in the last aspect a rather common one.

Every morning, with an air ever new, Herbert went into the city to look about him. I often paid him a visit in the dark back-room in which he consorted with an ink-jar, a hat-peg, a coal-box, a string-box, an almanac, a desk and stool, and a ruler; and I do not remember that I ever saw him do anything else but look about him. If we all did what we undertake to do, as faithfully as Herbert did, we might live in a Republic of the Virtues. He had nothing else to do, poor fellow, except at a certain hour of every afternoon to 'go to Lloyd's'—in observance of a ceremony of seeing his principal, I think. He never did anything else in connection with Lloyd's that I could find out, except come back again. When he felt his case unusually serious, and that he positively must find an opening, he would go on 'Change at a busy time, and walk in and out, in a kind of gloomy country dance figure, among the assembled magnates. 'For,' says Herbert to me, coming home to dinner on one of those special occasions, 'I find the truth to be, Handel, that an opening won't come to one, but one must go to it,—so I have been.'

If we had been less attached to one another, I think we must have hated one another regularly every morning. I detested the chambers beyond expression at that period of repentance, and could not endure the sight of the Avenger's livery; which had a more expensive and a less remunerative appearance then than at any other time in the four-and-twenty hours. As we got more and more into debt, breakfast became a hollower and hollower form, and, being on one occasion at breakfast-time threatened (by letter) with legal proceedings, 'not unwholly unconnected,' as my local paper might put it, 'with jewelery,' I went so far as to seize the Avenger by his blue collar and shake him off his feet,—so that he was actually in the air, like a booted Cupid,—for presuming to suppose that we wanted a roll.

At certain times—meaning at uncertain times, for they depended on our humour—I would say to Herbert, as if it were a remarkable discovery,—

'My dear Herbert, we are getting on badly.'

'My dear Handel,' Herbert would say to me, in all sincerity, 'if you will believe me, those very words were on my lips, by a strange coincidence.'

'Then, Herbert,' I would respond, 'let us look into our affairs.'

We always derived profound satisfaction from making an appointment for this purpose. I always thought this was business, this was the way to confront the thing, this was the way to take the foe by the throat. And I know Herbert thought so too.

We ordered something rather special for dinner, with a bottle of something similarly out of the common way, in order that our minds might be fortified for the occasion, and we might come well up to the mark. Dinner over, we produced a bundle of pens, a copious supply of ink, and a goodly show of writing and blotting paper. For there was something very comfortable in having plenty of stationery.

I would then take a sheet of paper, and write across the top of it, in a neat hand, the heading, 'Memorandum of Pip's debts'; with Barnard's Inn and the date very carefully added. Herbert would also take a sheet of paper, and write across it with similar formalities, 'Memorandum of Herbert's debts.'

Each of us would then refer to a confused heap of papers at his side, which had been thrown into drawers, worn into holes in pockets, half burnt in lighting candles, stuck for weeks into the looking-glass, and otherwise damaged. The sound of our pens going refreshed us exceedingly, insomuch that I sometimes found it difficult to distinguish between this edifying business proceeding and actually paying the money. In point of meritorious character, the two things seemed about equal.

When we had written a little while, I would ask Herbert how he got on? Herbert probably would have been scratching his head in a most rueful manner at the sight of his accumulating figures.

'They are mounting up, Handel,' Herbert would say; 'upon my life, they are mounting up.'

'Be firm, Herbert,' I would retort, plying my own pen with great assiduity. 'Look the thing in the face. Look into your affairs. Stare them out of countenance.'

'So I would, Handel, only they are staring *me* out of countenance.'

However, my determined manner would have its effect, and Herbert would fall to work again. After a time he would give up once more, on the plea that he had not got Cobbs's bill, or Lobbs's, or Nobbs's, as the case might be.

'Then, Herbert, estimate; estimate it in round numbers, and put it down.'

'What a fellow of resource you are!' my friend would reply, with admiration. 'Really your business powers are very remarkable.'

I thought so too. I established with myself, on these occasions, the reputation of a first-rate man of business,—prompt, decisive, energetic, clear, cool-headed. When I had got all my responsibilities down upon my list, I compared each with the bill, and ticked it off. My self-approval when I ticked an entry was quite a luxurious sensation. When I had no more ticks to make, I folded all my bills up uniformly, docketed each on the back, and tied the whole into a symmetrical bundle. Then I did the same for Herbert (who modestly said he had not my administrative genius), and felt that I had brought his affairs into a focus for him.

My business habits had one other bright feature, which I called 'leaving a Margin.' For example; supposing Herbert's debts to be one hundred and sixty-four pounds four-and-twopence, I would say, 'Leave a margin, and put them down at two hundred.' Or, supposing my own to be four times as much, I would leave a margin, and put them down at seven hundred. I had the highest opinion of the wisdom of this same Margin, but I am bound to acknowledge that on looking back, I deem it to have been an expensive device. For, we always ran into new debt immediately, to the full extent of the margin, and sometimes, in the sense of freedom and solvency it imparted, got pretty far on into another margin.

But there was a calm, a rest, a virtuous hush, consequent on these examinations of our affairs that gave me, for the time, an admirable opinion of myself. Soothed by my exertions, my method, and Herbert's compliments, I would sit with his symmetrical bundle and my own on the table before me among the stationary, and feel like a Bank of some sort, rather than a private individual.

We shut our outer door on these solemn occasions, in order that we might not be interrupted. I had fallen into my serene state one evening, when we heard a letter dropped through the slit in the said door, and fall on the ground. 'It's for you, Handel,' said Herbert, going out and coming back with it, 'and I hope there is nothing the matter.' This was in allusion to its heavy black seal and border.

The letter was signed Trabb & Co., and its contents were simply, that I was an honoured sir, and that they begged to inform me that Mrs J. Gargery had departed this life on Monday last at twenty minutes past six in the evening, and that my attendance was requested at the interment on Monday next at three o'clock in the afternoon.

Chapter 35

It was the first time that a grave had opened in my road of life, and the gap it made in the smooth ground was wonderful. The figure of my sister in her chair by the kitchen fire, haunted me night and day. That the place could possibly be, without her, was something my mind seemed unable to compass; and whereas she had seldom or never been in my thoughts of late, I had now the strangest ideas that she was coming towards me in the street, or that she would presently knock at the door. In my rooms too, with which she had never been at all associated, there was at once the blankness of death and a perpetual suggestion of the sound of her voice or the turn of her face or figure, as if she were still alive and had been often there.

Whatever my fortunes might have been, I could scarcely have recalled my sister with much tenderness. But I suppose there is a shock of regret which may exist without much tenderness. Under its influence (and perhaps to make up for the want of the softer feeling) I was seized with a violent indignation against the assailant from whom she had suffered so much; and I felt that on sufficient proof I could have revengefully pursued Orlick, or anyone else, to the last extremity.

Having written to Joe, to offer him consolation, and to assure him that I would come to the funeral, I passed the intermediate days in the curious state of mind I have glanced at. I went down early in the morning, and alighted at the Blue Boar in good time to walk over to the forge.

It was fine summer weather again, and, as I walked along, the times when I was a little helpless creature, and my sister did not spare me, vividly returned. But they returned with a gentle tone upon them that softened even the edge of Tickler. For now, the very breath of the beans and clover whispered to my heart that the day must come when it would be well for my memory that others walking in the sunshine should be softened as they thought of me.

At last I came within sight of the house, and saw that Trabb and Co. had put in a funereal execution and taken possession. Two dismally absurd persons, each ostentatiously exhibiting a crutch done up in a black bandage,—as if that instrument could possibly communicate any comfort to anybody,—were posted at the front door; and in one of them I recognized a postboy discharged from the Boar for turning a young couple into a sawpit on their bridal morning, in consequence of intoxication rendering it necessary for him to ride his horse clasped round the neck with both arms. All the children of the village, and most of the women, were admiring these sable warders and the closed windows of the house and forge; and as I came up, one of the two warders (the postboy) knocked at the door,—implying that I was far too much exhausted by grief to have strength remaining to knock for myself.

Another sable warder (a carpenter, who had once eaten two geese for a wager) opened the door, and showed me into the best parlor. Here, Mr Trabb had taken unto himself the best table, and had got all the leaves up, and was holding a kind of black Bazaar, with the aid of a quantity of black pins. At the moment of my arrival, he had just finished putting somebody's hat into black long-clothes, like an African baby; so he held out his hand for mine. But I, misled by the action, and confused by the occasion, shook hands with him with every testimony of warm affection.

Poor dear Joe, entangled in a little black cloak tied in a large bow under his chin, was seated apart at the upper end of the room; where, as chief mourner, he had evidently been stationed by Trabb. When I bent down and said to him, 'Dear Joe, how are you?' he said, 'Pip, old chap, you knowed her when she were a fine figure of a—' and clasped my hand and said no more.

Biddy, looking very neat and modest in her black dress, went quietly here and there, and was very helpful. When I had spoken to Biddy, as I thought it not a time for talking I went and sat down near Joe, and there began to wonder in what part of the house it—she—my sister—was. The air of the parlor being faint with the smell of sweet-cake, I looked about for the table of refreshments; it was scarcely visible until one had got accustomed to the gloom, but there was a cut-up plum cake upon it, and there were cut-up oranges, and sandwiches, and biscuits, and two decanters that I knew very well as ornaments, but had never seen used in all my life; one full of port, and one of sherry. Standing at this table, I became conscious of the servile Pumblechook in a black cloak and several yards of hatband, who was alternately stuffing himself, and making obsequious movements to catch my attention. The moment he succeeded, he came over to me (breathing sherry and crumbs), and said in a subdued voice, 'May I, dear sir?' and did. I then descried Mr and Mrs Hubble; the last-named in a decent speechless paroxysm in a corner. We were all going to 'follow,' and were all in course of being tied up separately (by Trabb) into ridiculous bundles.

'Which I meantersay, Pip,' Joe whispered to me, as we were being what Mr Trabb called 'formed' in the parlor, two and two,—and it was dreadfully like a preparation for some grim kind of dance; 'which I meantersay, sir, as I would in preference have carried her to the church myself, along with three or four friendly ones wot come to it with willing harts and arms, but it were considered wot the neighbours would look down on such and would be of opinions as it were wanting in respect.'

'Pocket-handkerchiefs out, all!' cried Mr Trabb at this point, in a depressed business-like voice. 'Pocket-handkerchiefs out! We are ready!'

So we all put our pocket-handkerchiefs to our faces, as if our noses were bleeding, and filed out two and two; Joe and I; Biddy and Pumblechook; Mr and Mrs Hubble. The remains of my poor sister had been brought round by the kitchen door, and, it being a point of undertaking ceremony that the six bearers must be stifled and blinded under a horrible black velvet housing with a white border, the whole looked like a blind monster with twelve human legs, shuffling and blundering along, under the guidance of two keepers,—the postboy and his comrade.

The neighbourhood, however, highly approved of these arrangements, and we were much admired as we went through the village; the more youthful and vigorous part of the community making dashes now and then to cut us off, and lying in wait to intercept us at points of vantage. At such times the more exuberant among them called out in an excited manner on our emergence round some corner of expectancy, '*Here* they come!' '*Here* they are!' and we were all but cheered. In this progress I was much annoyed by the abject Pumblechook, who, being behind me, persisted all the way as a delicate attention in arranging my streaming hatband, and smoothing my cloak. My thoughts were further distracted by the excessive pride of Mr and Mrs Hubble, who were surpassingly conceited and vainglorious in being members of so distinguished a procession.

And now the range of marshes lay clear before us, with the sails of the ships on the river growing out of it; and we went into the churchyard, close to the graves of my unknown parents, Philip Pirrip, late of this parish, and Also Georgiana, Wife of the Above. And there, my sister was laid quietly in the earth, while the larks sang high above it, and the light wind strewed it with beautiful shadows of clouds and trees.

Of the conduct of the worldly minded Pumblechook while this was doing, I desire to say no more than it was all addressed to me; and that even when those noble passages were read which remind humanity how it brought nothing into the world and can take nothing out, and how it fleeth like a shadow and never continueth long in one stay, I heard him cough a reservation of the case of a young gentleman who came unexpectedly into large property. When we got back, he had the hardihood to tell me that he wished my sister could have known I had done her so much honour, and to hint that she would have considered it reasonably purchased at the price of her death. After that, he drank all the rest of the sherry, and Mr Hubble drank the port, and the two talked (which I have since observed to be customary in such cases) as if they were of quite another race from the deceased, and were notoriously immortal. Finally, he went away with Mr and Mrs Hubble,—to make an evening of it, I felt sure, and to tell the Jolly Bargemen that he was the founder of my fortunes and my earliest benefactor.

When they were all gone, and when Trabb and his men—but not his Boy; I looked for him—had crammed their mummery into bags, and were gone too, the house felt wholesomer. Soon afterwards, Biddy, Joe, and I, had a cold dinner together; but we dined in the best parlor, not in the old kitchen, and Joe was so exceedingly particular what he did with his knife and fork and the saltcellar and what not, that there was great restraint upon us. But after dinner, when I made him take his pipe, and when I had loitered with him about the forge, and when we sat down together on the great block of stone outside it, we got on better. I noticed that after the funeral Joe changed his clothes so far, as to make a compromise between his Sunday dress and working dress; in which the dear fellow looked natural, and like the Man he was.

He was very much pleased by my asking if I might sleep in my own little room, and I was pleased too; for I felt that I had done rather a great thing in making the request. When the shadows of evening were closing in, I took an opportunity of getting into the garden with Biddy for a little talk.

'Biddy,' said I, 'I think you might have written to me about these sad matters.'

'Do you, Mr Pip?' said Biddy. 'I should have written if I had thought that.'

'Don't suppose that I mean to be unkind, Biddy, when I say I consider that you ought to have thought that.'

'Do you, Mr Pip?'

She was so quiet, and had such an orderly, good, and pretty way with her, that I did not like the thought of making her cry again. After looking a little at her downcast eyes as she walked beside me, I gave up that point.

'I suppose it will be difficult for you to remain here now, Biddy dear?'

'Oh! I can't do so, Mr Pip,' said Biddy, in a tone of regret but still of quiet conviction. 'I have been speaking to Mrs Hubble, and I am going to her tomorrow. I hope we shall be able to take some care of Mr Gargery, together, until he settles down.'

'How are you going to live, Biddy? If you want any mo—'

'How am I going to live?' repeated Biddy, striking in, with a momentary flush upon her face. 'I'll tell you, Mr Pip. I am going to try to get the place of mistress in the new school nearly finished here. I can be well recommended by all the neighbours, and I hope I can be industrious and patient, and teach myself while I teach others. You know, Mr Pip,' pursued Biddy, with a smile, as she raised her eyes to my face, 'the new schools are not like the old, but I learnt a good deal from you after that time, and have had time since then to improve.'

'I think you would always improve, Biddy, under any circumstances.'

'Ah! Except in my bad side of human nature,' murmured Biddy.

It was not so much a reproach as an irresistible thinking aloud. Well! I thought I would give up that point too. So, I walked a little further with Biddy, looking silently at her downcast eyes.

'I have not heard the particulars of my sister's death, Biddy.'

'They are very slight, poor thing. She had been in one of her bad states—though they had got better of late, rather than worse—for four days, when she came out of it in the evening, just at tea-time, and said quite plainly, "Joe." As she had never said any word for a long while, I ran and fetched in Mr Gargery from the forge. She made signs to me that she wanted him to sit down close to her, and wanted me to put her arms round his neck. So I put them round his neck, and she laid her head down on his shoulder quite content and satisfied. And so she presently said "Joe" again, and once "Pardon," and once "Pip." And so she never lifted her head up any more, and it was just an hour later when we laid it down on her own bed, because we found she was gone.'

Biddy cried; the darkening garden, and the lane, and the stars that were coming out, were blurred in my own sight.

'Nothing was ever discovered, Biddy?'

'Nothing.'

'Do you know what is become of Orlick?'

'I should think from the colour of his clothes that he is working in the quarries.'

'Of course you have seen him then?—Why are you looking at that dark tree in the lane?'

'I saw him there, on the night she died.'

'That was not the last time either, Biddy?'

'No; I have seen him there, since we have been walking here.—It is of no use,' said Biddy, laying her hand upon my arm, as I was for running out, 'you know I would not deceive you; he was not there a minute, and he is gone.'

It revived my utmost indignation to find that she was still pursued by this fellow, and I felt inveterate against him. I told her so, and told her that I would spend any money or take any pains to drive him out of that country. By degrees she led me into more temperate talk, and she told me how Joe loved me, and how Joe never complained of anything,—she didn't say, of me; she had no need; I knew what she meant,—but ever did his duty in his way of life, with a strong hand, a quiet tongue, and a gentle heart.

'Indeed, it would be hard to say too much for him,' said I; 'and

Biddy, we must often speak of these things, for of course I shall be often down here now. I am not going to leave poor Joe alone.'

Biddy said never a single word.

'Biddy, don't you hear me?'

'Yes, Mr Pip.'

'Not to mention your calling me Mr Pip,—which appears to me to be in bad taste, Biddy,—what do you mean?'

'What do I mean?' asked Biddy, timidly.

'Biddy,' said I, in a virtuously self-asserting manner, 'I must request to know what you mean by this?'

'By this?' said Biddy.

'Now, don't echo,' I retorted. 'You used not to echo, Biddy.'

'Used not!' said Biddy. 'O Mr Pip! Used!'

Well! I rather thought I would give up that point too. After another silent turn in the garden, I fell back on the main position.

'Biddy,' said I, 'I made a remark respecting my coming down here often, to see Joe, which you received with a marked silence. Have the goodness, Biddy, to tell me why.'

'Are you quite sure, then, that you WILL come to see him often?' asked Biddy, stopping in the narrow garden walk, and looking at me under the stars with a clear and honest eye.

'O dear me!' said I, as if I found myself compelled to give up Biddy in despair. 'This really is a very bad side of human nature! Don't say any more, if you please, Biddy. This shocks me very much.'

For which cogent reason I kept Biddy at a distance during supper, and when I went up to my own old little room, took as stately a leave of her as I could, in my murmuring soul, deem reconcilable with the churchyard and the event of the day. As often as I was restless in the night, and that was every quarter of an hour, I reflected what an unkindness, what an injury, what an injustice, Biddy had done me.

Early in the morning I was to go. Early in the morning I was out, and looking in, unseen, at one of the wooden windows of the forge. There I stood, for minutes, looking at Joe, already at work with a glow of health and strength upon his face that made it show as if the bright sun of the life in store for him were shining on it.

'Goodbye, dear Joe!—No, don't wipe it off—for God's sake, give me your blackened hand!—I shall be down soon and often.'

'Never too soon, sir,' said Joe, 'and never too often, Pip!'

Biddy was waiting for me at the kitchen door, with a mug of new milk and a crust of bread. 'Biddy,' said I, when I gave her my hand at parting, 'I am not angry, but I am hurt.'

'No, don't be hurt,' she pleaded quite pathetically; 'let only me be hurt, if I have been ungenerous.'

Once more, the mists were rising as I walked away. If they disclosed to me, as I suspect they did, that I should not come back, and that Biddy was quite right, all I can say is,—they were quite right too.

Chapter 36

Herbert and I went on from bad to worse, in the way of increasing our debts, looking into our affairs, leaving Margins, and the like exemplary transactions; and time went on, whether or no, as he has a way of doing; and I came of age,—in fulfilment of Herbert's prediction, that I should do so before I knew where I was.

Herbert himself had come of age eight months before me. As he had nothing else than his majority to come into, the event did not make a profound sensation in Barnard's Inn. But we had looked forward to my one-and-twentieth birthday, with a crowd of speculations and anticipations, for we had both considered that my guardian could hardly help saying something definite on that occasion.

I had taken care to have it well understood in Little Britain when my birthday was. On the day before it, I received an official note from Wemmick, informing me that Mr Jaggers would be glad if I would call upon him at five in the afternoon of the auspicious day. This convinced us that something great was to happen, and threw me into an unusual flutter when I repaired to my guardian's office, a model of punctuality.

In the outer office Wemmick offered me his congratulations, and incidentally rubbed the side of his nose with a folded piece of tissue-paper that I liked the look of. But he said nothing respecting it, and motioned me with a nod into my guardian's room. It was November, and my guardian was standing before his fire leaning his back against the chimney-piece, with his hands under his coattails.

'Well, Pip,' said he, 'I must call you Mr Pip today. Congratulations, Mr Pip.'

We shook hands,—he was always a remarkably short shaker,—and I thanked him.

'Take a chair, Mr Pip,' said my guardian.

As I sat down, and he preserved his attitude and bent his brows at his boots, I felt at a disadvantage, which reminded me of that old time when I had been put upon a tombstone. The two ghastly casts on the shelf were not far from him, and their expression was as if they were making a stupid apoplectic attempt to attend to the conversation.

'Now my young friend,' my guardian began, as if I were a witness in the box, 'I am going to have a word or two with you.'

'If you please, sir.'

'What do you suppose,' said Mr Jaggers, bending forward to look at the ground, and then throwing his head back to look at the ceiling,—'what do you suppose you are living at the rate of?'

'At the rate of, sir?'

'At,' repeated Mr Jaggers, still looking at the ceiling, 'the—rate—of?' And then looked all round the room, and paused with his pocket-handkerchief in his hand, halfway to his nose.

I had looked into my affairs so often, that I had thoroughly destroyed any slight notion I might ever have had of their bearings. Reluctantly, I confessed myself quite unable to answer the question. This reply seemed agreeable to Mr Jaggers, who said, 'I thought so!' and blew his nose with an air of satisfaction.

'Now, I have asked *you* a question, my friend,' said Mr Jaggers. 'Have you anything to ask *me*?'

'Of course it would be a great relief to me to ask you several questions, sir; but I remember your prohibition.'

'Ask one,' said Mr Jaggers.

'Is my benefactor to be made known to me today?'

'No. Ask another.'

'Is that confidence to be imparted to me soon?'

'Waive that, a moment,' said Mr Jaggers, 'and ask another.'

I looked about me, but there appeared to be now no possible

escape from the inquiry, 'Have-I—anything to receive, sir?' On that, Mr Jaggers said, triumphantly, 'I thought we should come to it!' and called to Wemmick to give him that piece of paper. Wemmick appeared, handed it in, and disappeared.

'Now, Mr Pip,' said Mr Jaggers, 'attend, if you please. You have been drawing pretty freely here; your name occurs pretty often in Wemmick's cash-book; but you are in debt, of course?'

'I am afraid I must say yes, sir.'

'You know you must say yes; don't you?' said Mr Jaggers.

'Yes, sir.'

'I don't ask you what you owe, because you don't know; and if you did know, you wouldn't tell me; you would say less. Yes, yes, my friend,' cried Mr Jaggers, waving his forefinger to stop me as I made a show of protesting: 'it's likely enough that you think you wouldn't, but you would. You'll excuse me, but I know better than you. Now, take this piece of paper in your hand. You have got it? Very good. Now, unfold it and tell me what it is.'

'This is a bank-note,' said I, 'for five hundred pounds.'

'That is a bank-note,' repeated Mr Jaggers, 'for five hundred pounds. And a very handsome sum of money too, I think. You consider it so?'

'How could I do otherwise!'

'Ah! But answer the question,' said Mr Jaggers.

'Undoubtedly.'

'You consider it, undoubtedly, a handsome sum of money. Now, that handsome sum of money, Pip, is your own. It is a present to you on this day, in earnest of your expectations. And at the rate of that handsome sum of money per annum, and at no higher rate, you are to live until the donor of the whole appears. That is to say, you will now take your money affairs entirely into your own hands, and you will draw from Wemmick one hundred and twenty-five pounds per quarter, until you are in communication with the fountainhead, and no longer with the mere agent. As I have told you before, I am the mere agent. I execute my instructions, and I am paid for doing so. I think them injudicious, but I am not paid for giving any opinion on their merits.'

I was beginning to express my gratitude to my benefactor for the great liberality with which I was treated, when Mr Jaggers stopped me. 'I am not paid, Pip,' said he, coolly, 'to carry your words to any one;' and then gathered up his coat-tails, as he had gathered up the subject, and stood frowning at his boots as if he suspected them of designs against him.

After a pause, I hinted,—

'There was a question just now, Mr Jaggers, which you desired me to waive for a moment. I hope I am doing nothing wrong in asking it again?'

'What is it?' said he.

I might have known that he would never help me out; but it took me aback to have to shape the question afresh, as if it were quite new. 'Is it likely,' I said, after hesitating, 'that my patron, the fountainhead you have spoken of, Mr Jaggers, will soon—' there I delicately stopped.

'Will soon what?' asked Mr Jaggers. 'That's no question as it stands, you know.'

'Will soon come to London,' said I, after casting about for a precise form of words, 'or summon me anywhere else?'

'Now, here,' replied Mr Jaggers, fixing me for the first time with his dark deep-set eyes, 'we must revert to the evening when we first encountered one another in your village. What did I tell you then, Pip?'

'You told me, Mr Jaggers, that it might be years hence when that person appeared.'

'Just so,' said Mr Jaggers, 'that's my answer.'

As we looked full at one another, I felt my breath come quicker in my strong desire to get something out of him. And as I felt that it came quicker, and as I felt that he saw that it came quicker, I felt that I had less chance than ever of getting anything out of him.

'Do you suppose it will still be years hence, Mr Jaggers?'

Mr Jaggers shook his head,—not in negativing the question, but in altogether negativing the notion that he could anyhow be got to answer it,—and the two horrible casts of the twitched faces looked, when my eyes strayed up to them, as if they had come to a crisis in their suspended attention, and were going to sneeze.

'Come!' said Mr Jaggers, warming the backs of his legs with the backs of his warmed hands, 'I'll be plain with you, my friend Pip.

That's a question I must not be asked. You'll understand that better, when I tell you it's a question that might compromise *me*. Come! I'll go a little further with you; I'll say something more.'

He bent down so low to frown at his boots, that he was able to rub the calves of his legs in the pause he made.

'When that person discloses,' said Mr Jaggers, straightening himself, 'you and that person will settle your own affairs. When that person discloses, my part in this business will cease and determine. When that person discloses, it will not be necessary for me to know anything about it. And that's all I have got to say.'

We looked at one another until I withdrew my eyes, and looked thoughtfully at the floor. From this last speech I derived the notion that Miss Havisham, for some reason or no reason, had not taken him into her confidence as to her designing me for Estella; that he resented this, and felt a jealousy about it; or that he really did object to that scheme, and would have nothing to do with it. When I raised my eyes again, I found that he had been shrewdly looking at me all the time, and was doing so still.

'If that is all you have to say, sir,' I remarked, 'there can be nothing left for me to say.'

He nodded assent, and pulled out his thief-dreaded watch, and asked me where I was going to dine? I replied at my own chambers, with Herbert. As a necessary sequence, I asked him if he would favour us with his company, and he promptly accepted the invitation. But he insisted on walking home with me, in order that I might make no extra preparation for him, and first he had a letter or two to write, and (of course) had his hands to wash. So I said I would go into the outer office and talk to Wemmick.

The fact was, that when the five hundred pounds had come into my pocket, a thought had come into my head which had been often there before; and it appeared to me that Wemmick was a good person to advise with concerning such thought.

He had already locked up his safe, and made preparations for going home. He had left his desk, brought out his two greasy office candlesticks and stood them in line with the snuffers on a slab near the door, ready to be extinguished; he had raked his fire low, put his hat and great-coat ready, and was beating himself all over the chest with his safe-key, as an athletic exercise after business.

'Mr Wemmick,' said I, 'I want to ask your opinion. I am very desirous to serve a friend.'

Wemmick tightened his post-office and shook his head, as if his opinion were dead against any fatal weakness of that sort.

'This friend,' I pursued, 'is trying to get on in commercial life, but has no money, and finds it difficult and disheartening to make a beginning. Now I want somehow to help him to a beginning.'

'With money down?' said Wemmick, in a tone drier than any sawdust.

'With *some* money down,' I replied, for an uneasy remembrance shot across me of that symmetrical bundle of papers at home—'with *some* money down, and perhaps some anticipation of my expectations.'

'Mr Pip,' said Wemmick, 'I should like just to run over with you on my fingers, if you please, the names of the various bridges up as high as Chelsea Reach. Let's see; there's London, one; Southwark, two; Blackfriars, three; Waterloo, four; Westminster, five; Vauxhall, six.' He had checked off each bridge in its turn, with the handle of his safe-key on the palm of his hand. 'There's as many as six, you see, to choose from.'

'I don't understand you,' said I.

'Choose your bridge, Mr Pip,' returned Wemmick, 'and take a walk upon your bridge, and pitch your money into the Thames over the centre arch of your bridge, and you know the end of it. Serve a friend with it, and you may know the end of it too,—but it's a less pleasant and profitable end.'

I could have posted a newspaper in his mouth, he made it so wide after saying this.

'This is very discouraging,' said I.

'Meant to be so,' said Wemmick.

'Then is it your opinion,' I inquired, with some little indignation, 'that a man should never—'

'—Invest portable property in a friend?' said Wemmick. 'Certainly he should not. Unless he wants to get rid of the friend,—and then it becomes a question how much portable property it may be worth to get rid of him.'

'And that,' said I, 'is your deliberate opinion, Mr Wemmick?'

'That,' he returned, 'is my deliberate opinion in this office.'

'Ah!' said I, pressing him, for I thought I saw him near a loophole here; 'but would that be your opinion at Walworth?'

'Mr Pip,' he replied, with gravity, 'Walworth is one place, and this office is another. Much as the Aged is one person, and Mr Jaggers is another. They must not be confounded together. My Walworth sentiments must be taken at Walworth; none but my official sentiments can be taken in this office.'

'Very well,' said I, much relieved, 'then I shall look you up at Walworth, you may depend upon it.'

'Mr Pip,' he returned, 'you will be welcome there, in a private and personal capacity.'

We had held this conversation in a low voice, well knowing my guardian's ears to be the sharpest of the sharp. As he now appeared in his doorway, towelling his hands, Wemmick got on his great-coat and stood by to snuff out the candles. We all three went into the street together, and from the doorstep Wemmick turned his way, and Mr Jaggers and I turned ours.

I could not help wishing more than once that evening, that Mr Jaggers had had an Aged in Gerrard Street, or a Stinger, or a Something, or a Somebody, to unbend his brows a little. It was an uncomfortable consideration on a twenty-first birthday, that coming of age at all seemed hardly worth while in such a guarded and suspicious world as he made of it. He was a thousand times better informed and cleverer than Wemmick, and yet I would a thousand times rather have had Wemmick to dinner. And Mr Jaggers made not me alone intensely melancholy, because, after he was gone, Herbert said of himself, with his eyes fixed on the fire, that he thought he must have committed a felony and forgotten the details of it, he felt so dejected and guilty.

Chapter 37

Deeming Sunday the best day for taking Mr Wemmick's Walworth sentiments, I devoted the next ensuing Sunday afternoon to a pilgrimage to the Castle. On arriving before the battlements, I found the Union Jack flying and the drawbridge up; but undeterred by this show of defiance and resistance, I rang at the gate, and was admitted in a most pacific manner by the Aged.

'My son, sir,' said the old man, after securing the drawbridge, 'rather had it in his mind that you might happen to drop in, and he left word that he would soon be home from his afternoon's walk. He is very regular in his walks, is my son. Very regular in everything, is my son.'

I nodded at the old gentleman as Wemmick himself might have nodded, and we went in and sat down by the fireside.

'You made acquaintance with my son, sir,' said the old man, in his chirping way, while he warmed his hands at the blaze, 'at his office, I expect?' I nodded. 'Hah! I have heerd that my son is a wonderful hand at his business, sir?' I nodded hard. 'Yes; so they tell me. His business is the Law?' I nodded harder. 'Which makes it more surprising in my son,' said the old man, 'for he was not brought up to the Law, but to the Wine-Coopering.'

Curious to know how the old gentleman stood informed concerning the reputation of Mr Jaggers, I roared that name at him. He threw me into the greatest confusion by laughing heartily and replying in a very sprightly manner, 'No, to be sure; you're right.' And to this hour I have not the faintest notion what he meant, or what joke he thought I had made.

As I could not sit there nodding at him perpetually, without making some other attempt to interest him, I shouted at inquiry whether his own calling in life had been 'the Wine-Coopering.' By dint of straining that term out of myself several times and tapping the old gentleman on the chest to associate it with him, I at last succeeded in making my meaning understood.

'No,' said the old gentleman; 'the warehousing, the warehousing. First, over yonder;' he appeared to mean up the chimney, but I believe he intended to refer me to Liverpool; 'and then in the City of London here. However, having an infirmity—for I am hard of hearing, sir—'

I expressed in pantomime the greatest astonishment.

'—Yes, hard of hearing; having that infirmity coming upon me, my son he went into the Law, and he took charge of me, and he by little and little made out this elegant and beautiful property. But returning to what you said, you know,' pursued the old man, again laughing heartily, 'what I say is, No to be sure; you're right.'

I was modestly wondering whether my utmost ingenuity would have enabled me to say anything that would have amused him half as much as this imaginary pleasantry, when I was startled by a sudden click in the wall on one side of the chimney, and the ghostly tumbling open of a little wooden flap with 'JOHN' upon it. The old man, following my eyes, cried with great triumph, 'My son's come home!' and we both went out to the drawbridge.

It was worth any money to see Wemmick waving a salute to me from the other side of the moat, when we might have shaken hands across it with the greatest ease. The Aged was so delighted to work the drawbridge, that I made no offer to assist him, but stood quiet until Wemmick had come across, and had presented me to Miss Skiffins; a lady by whom he was accompanied.

Miss Skiffins was of a wooden appearance, and was, like her escort, in the post-office branch of the service. She might have been some two or three years younger than Wemmick, and I judged her to stand possessed of portable property. The cut of her dress from the waist upward, both before and behind, made her figure very like a boy's kite; and I might have pronounced her gown a little too decidedly orange, and her gloves a little too intensely green. But she seemed to be a good sort of fellow, and showed a high regard for the Aged. I was not long in discovering that she was a frequent visitor at the Castle; for, on our going in, and my complimenting Wemmick on his ingenious contrivance for announcing himself to the Aged, he begged me to give my attention for a moment to the other side of the chimney, and disappeared. Presently another click came, and another little door tumbled open with 'Miss Skiffins' on it; then Miss Skiffins shut up and John tumbled open; then Miss Skiffins and John both tumbled open together, and finally shut up together. On Wemmick's return from working these mechanical appliances, I expressed the great admiration with which I regarded them, and he said, 'Well, you know, they're both pleasant and useful to the Aged. And by George, sir, it's a thing worth mentioning, that of all the people who come to this gate, the secret of those pulls is only known to the Aged, Miss Skiffins, and me!'

'And Mr Wemmick made them,' added Miss Skiffins, 'with his own hands out of his own head.'

While Miss Skiffins was taking off her bonnet (she retained her green gloves during the evening as an outward and visible sign that there was company), Wemmick invited me to take a walk with him round the property, and see how the island looked in wintertime. Thinking that he did this to give me an opportunity of taking his Walworth sentiments, I seized the opportunity as soon as we were out of the Castle.

Having thought of the matter with care, I approached my subject as if I had never hinted at it before. I informed Wemmick that I was anxious in behalf of Herbert Pocket, and I told him how we had first met, and how we had fought. I glanced at Herbert's home, and at his character, and at his having no means but such as he was dependent on his father for; those, uncertain and unpunctual. I alluded to the advantages I had derived in my first rawness and ignorance from his society, and I confessed that I feared I had but ill repaid them, and that he might have done better without me and my expectations. Keeping Miss Havisham in the background at a great distance, I still hinted at the possibility of my having competed with him in his prospects, and at the certainty of his possessing a generous soul, and being far above any mean distrusts, retaliations, or designs. For all these reasons (I told Wemmick), and because he was my young companion and friend, and I had a great affection for him, I wished my own good fortune to reflect some rays upon him, and therefore I sought advice from Wemmick's experience and knowledge of men and affairs, how I could best try with my resources to help Herbert to some present income,—say of a hundred a year, to keep him in good hope and heart,—and gradually to buy him on to some small partnership. I begged Wemmick, in conclusion, to understand that my help must always be rendered without Herbert's knowledge or suspicion, and that there was no one else in the world with whom I could advise. I wound up by laying my hand upon his shoulder, and saying, 'I can't help confiding in you, though I know it must be troublesome to you; but that is your fault, in having ever brought me here.'

Wemmick was silent for a little while, and then said with a kind of start, 'Well you know, Mr Pip, I must tell you one thing. This is devilish good of you.'

'Say you'll help me to be good then,' said I.

'Ecod,' replied Wemmick, shaking his head, 'that's not my trade.'

'Nor is this your trading-place,' said I.

'You are right,' he returned. 'You hit the nail on the head. Mr Pip, I'll put on my considering-cap, and I think all you want to do may be done by degrees. Skiffins (that's her brother) is an accountant and agent. I'll look him up and go to work for you.'

'I thank you ten thousand times.'

'On the contrary,' said he, 'I thank you, for though we are strictly in our private and personal capacity, still it may be mentioned that there *are* Newgate cobwebs about, and it brushes them away.'

After a little further conversation to the same effect, we returned into the Castle where we found Miss Skiffins preparing tea. The responsible duty of making the toast was delegated to the Aged, and that excellent old gentleman was so intent upon it that he seemed to me in some danger of melting his eyes. It was no nominal meal that we were going to make, but a vigorous reality. The Aged prepared such a hay-stack of buttered toast, that I could scarcely see him over it as it simmered on an iron stand hooked on to the top-bar; while Miss Skiffins brewed such a jorum of tea, that the pig in the back premises became strongly excited, and repeatedly expressed his desire to participate in the entertainment.

The flag had been struck, and the gun had been fired, at the right moment of time, and I felt as snugly cut off from the rest of Walworth as if the moat were thirty feet wide by as many deep. Nothing disturbed the tranquillity of the Castle, but the occasional tumbling open of John and Miss Skiffins: which little doors were a prey to some spasmodic infirmity that made me sympathetically uncomfortable until I got used to it. I inferred from the methodical nature of Miss Skiffins's arrangements that she made tea there every Sunday night; and I rather suspected that a classic brooch she wore, representing the profile of an undesirable female with a very straight nose and a very new moon, was a piece of portable property that had been given her by Wemmick.

We ate the whole of the toast, and drank tea in proportion, and it was delightful to see how warm and greasy we all got after it. The Aged especially, might have passed for some clean old chief of a savage tribe, just oiled. After a short pause of repose, Miss Skiffins—in the absence of the little servant who, it seemed, retired to the bosom of her family on Sunday afternoons—washed up the tea-things, in a trifling lady-like amateur manner that compromised none of us. Then, she put on her gloves again, and we drew round the fire, and Wemmick said, 'Now, Aged Parent, tip us the paper.'

Wemmick explained to me while the Aged got his spectacles out, that this was according to custom, and that it gave the old gentleman infinite satisfaction to read the news aloud. 'I won't offer an apology,' said Wemmick, 'for he isn't capable of many pleasures—are you, Aged P.?'

'All right, John, all right,' returned the old man, seeing himself spoken to.

'Only tip him a nod every now and then when he looks off his paper,' said Wemmick, 'and he'll be as happy as a king. We are all attention, Aged One.'

'All right, John, all right!' returned the cheerful old man, so busy and so pleased, that it really was quite charming.

The Aged's reading reminded me of the classes at Mr Wopsle's great-aunt's, with the pleasanter peculiarity that it seemed to come through a keyhole. As he wanted the candles close to him, and as he was always on the verge of putting either his head or the newspaper into them, he required as much watching as a powder-mill. But Wemmick was equally untiring and gentle in his vigilance, and the Aged read on, quite unconscious of his many rescues. Whenever he looked at us, we all expressed the greatest interest and amazement, and nodded until he resumed again.

As Wemmick and Miss Skiffins sat side by side, and as I sat in a shadowy corner, I observed a slow and gradual elongation of Mr Wemmick's mouth, powerfully suggestive of his slowly and gradually stealing his arm round Miss Skiffins's waist. In course of time I saw his hand appear on the other side of Miss Skiffins; but at that moment Miss Skiffins neatly stopped him with the green glove, unwound his arm again as if it were an article of dress, and with the greatest deliberation laid it on the table before her. Miss Skiffins's composure while she did this was one of the most remarkable sights I have ever seen, and if I could have thought the act consistent with abstraction of mind, I should have deemed that Miss Skiffins performed it mechanically.

By and by, I noticed Wemmick's arm beginning to disappear again, and gradually fading out of view. Shortly afterwards, his mouth began to widen again. After an interval of suspense on my part that was quite enthralling and almost painful, I saw his hand appear on the other side of Miss Skiffins. Instantly, Miss Skiffins stopped it with the neatness of a placid boxer, took off that girdle or cestus as before, and laid it on the table. Taking the table to represent the path of virtue, I am justified in stating that during the whole time of the Aged's reading, Wemmick's arm was straying from the path of virtue and being recalled to it by Miss Skiffins.

At last, the Aged read himself into a light slumber. This was the time for Wemmick to produce a little kettle, a tray of glasses, and a black bottle with a porcelain-topped cork, representing some clerical dignitary of a rubicund and social aspect. With the aid of these appliances we all had something warm to drink, including the Aged, who was soon awake again. Miss Skiffins mixed, and I observed that she and Wemmick drank out of one glass. Of course I knew better than to offer to see Miss Skiffins home, and under the circumstances I thought I had best go first; which I did, taking a cordial leave of the Aged, and having passed a pleasant evening.

Before a week was out, I received a note from Wemmick, dated Walworth, stating that he hoped he had made some advance in that matter appertaining to our private and personal capacities, and that he would be glad if I could come and see him again upon it. So, I went out to Walworth again, and yet again, and yet again, and I saw him by appointment in the City several times, but never held any communication with him on the subject in or near Little Britain. The upshot was, that we found a worthy young merchant or shipping-broker, not long established in business, who wanted intelligent help, and who wanted capital, and who in due course of time and receipt would want a partner. Between him and me, secret articles were signed of which Herbert was the subject, and I paid him half of my five hundred pounds down, and engaged for sundry other payments: some, to fall due at certain dates out of my income: some, contingent on my coming into my property. Miss Skiffins's brother conducted the negotiation. Wemmick pervaded it throughout, but never appeared in it.

The whole business was so cleverly managed, that Herbert had not the least suspicion of my hand being in it. I never shall forget the radiant face with which he came home one afternoon, and told me, as a mighty piece of news, of his having fallen in with one Clarriker (the young merchant's name), and of Clarriker's having shown an extraordinary inclination towards him, and of his belief that the opening had come at last. Day by day as his hopes grew stronger and his face brighter, he must have thought me a more and more affectionate friend, for I had the greatest difficulty in restraining my tears of triumph when I saw him so happy. At length, the thing being done, and he having that day entered Clarriker's House, and he having talked to me for a whole evening in a flush of pleasure and success, I did really cry in good earnest when I went to bed, to think that my expectations had done some good to somebody.

A great event in my life, the turning point of my life, now opens on my view. But, before I proceed to narrate it, and before I pass on to all the changes it involved, I must give one chapter to Estella. It is not much to give to the theme that so long filled my heart.

Chapter 38

If that staid old house near the Green at Richmond should ever come to be haunted when I am dead, it will be haunted, surely, by my ghost. O the many, many nights and days through which the unquiet spirit within me haunted that house when Estella lived there! Let my body be where it would, my spirit was always wandering, wandering, wandering, about that house.

The lady with whom Estella was placed, Mrs Brandley by name, was a widow, with one daughter several years older than Estella. The mother looked young, and the daughter looked old; the mother's complexion was pink, and the daughter's was yellow; the mother set up for frivolity, and the daughter for theology. They were in what is called a good position, and visited, and were visited by, numbers of people. Little, if any, community of feeling subsisted between them and Estella, but the understanding was established that they were necessary to her, and that she was necessary to them. Mrs Brandley had been a friend of Miss Havisham's before the time of her seclusion.

In Mrs Brandley's house and out of Mrs Brandley's house, I suffered every kind and degree of torture that Estella could cause me. The nature of my relations with her, which placed me on terms of familiarity without placing me on terms of favour, conduced to my distraction. She made use of me to tease other admirers, and she turned the very familiarity between herself and me to the account of putting a constant slight on my devotion to her. If I had been her secretary, steward, half-brother, poor relation,—if I had been a younger brother of her appointed husband,—I could not have seemed to myself further from my hopes when I was nearest to her. The privilege of calling her by her name and hearing her call me by mine became, under the circumstances an aggravation of my trials; and while I think it likely that it almost maddened her other lovers, I know too certainly that it almost maddened me.

She had admirers without end. No doubt my jealousy made an admirer of every one who went near her; but there were more than enough of them without that.

I saw her often at Richmond, I heard of her often in town, and I used often to take her and the Brandleys on the water; there were picnics, fête days, plays, operas, concerts, parties, all sorts of pleasures, through which I pursued her,—and they were all miseries to me. I never had one hour's happiness in her society, and yet my mind all round the four-and-twenty hours was harping on the happiness of having her with me unto death.

Throughout this part of our intercourse,—and it lasted, as will presently be seen, for what I then thought a long time,—she habitually reverted to that tone which expressed that our association was forced upon us. There were other times when she would come to a sudden check in this tone and in all her many tones, and would seem to pity me.

'Pip, Pip,' she said one evening, coming to such a check, when we sat apart at a darkening window of the house in Richmond; 'will you never take warning?'

'Of what?'

'Of me.'

'Warning not to be attracted by you, do you mean, Estella?'

'Do I mean! If you don't know what I mean, you are blind.'

I should have replied that Love was commonly reputed blind, but for the reason that I always was restrained—and this was not the least of my miseries—by a feeling that it was ungenerous to press myself upon her, when she knew that she could not choose but obey Miss Havisham. My dread always was, that this knowledge on her part laid me under a heavy disadvantage with her pride, and made me the subject of a rebellious struggle in her bosom.

'At any rate,' said I, 'I have no warning given me just now, for you wrote to me to come to you, this time.'

'That's true,' said Estella, with a cold careless smile that always chilled me.

After looking at the twilight without, for a little while, she went on to say:—

'The time has come round when Miss Havisham wishes to have me for a day at Satis. You are to take me there, and bring me back, if you will. She would rather I did not travel alone, and objects to receiving my maid, for she has a sensitive horror of being talked of by such people. Can you take me?'

'Can I take you, Estella!'

'You can then? The day after tomorrow, if you please. You are to pay all charges out of my purse, You hear the condition of your going?'

'And must obey,' said I.

This was all the preparation I received for that visit, or for others like it; Miss Havisham never wrote to me, nor had I ever so much as seen her handwriting. We went down on the next day but one, and we found her in the room where I had first beheld her, and it is needless to add that there was no change in Satis House.

She was even more dreadfully fond of Estella than she had been when I last saw them together; I repeat the word advisedly, for there was something positively dreadful in the energy of her looks and embraces. She hung upon Estella's beauty, hung upon her words, hung upon her gestures, and sat mumbling her own trembling fingers while she looked at her, as though she were devouring the beautiful creature she had reared.

From Estella she looked at me, with a searching glance that seemed to pry into my heart and probe its wounds. 'How does she use you, Pip; how does she use you?' she asked me again, with her witch-like eagerness, even in Estella's hearing. But, when we sat by her flickering fire at night, she was most weird; for then, keeping Estella's hand drawn through her arm and clutched in her own hand, she extorted from her, by dint of referring back to what Estella had told her in her regular letters, the names and conditions of the men whom she had fascinated; and as Miss Havisham dwelt upon this roll, with the intensity of a mind mortally hurt and diseased, she sat with her other hand on her crutch stick, and her chin on that, and her wan bright eyes glaring at me, a very spectre.

I saw in this, wretched though it made me, and bitter the sense of dependence and even of degradation that it awakened,—I saw in this that Estella was set to wreak Miss Havisham's revenge on men, and that she was not to be given to me until she had gratified it for a term. I saw in this, a reason for her being beforehand assigned to me. Sending her out to attract and torment and do mischief, Miss Havisham sent her with the malicious assurance that she was beyond the reach of all admirers, and that all who staked upon that cast were secured to lose. I saw in this that I, too, was tormented by a perversion of ingenuity, even while the prize was reserved for me. I saw in this the reason for my being staved off so long and the reason for my late guardian's declining to commit himself to the formal knowledge of such a scheme. In a word, I saw in this Miss Havisham as I had her then and there before my eyes, and always had had her before my eyes; and I saw in this, the distinct shadow of the darkened and unhealthy house in which her life was hidden from the sun.

The candles that lighted that room of hers were placed in sconces on the wall. They were high from the ground, and they burnt with the steady dulness of artificial light in air that is seldom renewed. As I looked round at them, and at the pale gloom they made, and at the stopped clock, and at the withered articles of bridal dress upon the table and the ground, and at her own awful figure with its ghostly reflection thrown large by the fire upon the ceiling and the wall, I saw in everything the construction that my mind had come to, repeated and thrown back to me. My thoughts passed into the great room across the landing where the table was spread, and I saw it written, as it were, in the falls of the cobwebs from the centre-piece, in the crawlings of the spiders on the cloth, in the tracks of the mice as they betook their little quickened hearts behind the panels, and in the gropings and pausings of the beetles on the floor.

It happened on the occasion of this visit that some sharp words arose between Estella and Miss Havisham. It was the first time I had ever seen them opposed.

We were seated by the fire, as just now described, and Miss Havisham still had Estella's arm drawn through her own, and still clutched Estella's hand in hers, when Estella gradually began to detach herself. She had shown a proud impatience more than once before, and had rather endured that fierce affection than accepted or returned it.

'What!' said Miss Havisham, flashing her eyes upon her, 'are you tired of me?'

'Only a little tired of myself,' replied Estella, disengaging her arm, and moving to the great chimney-piece, where she stood looking down at the fire.

'Speak the truth, you ingrate!' cried Miss Havisham, passionately striking her stick upon the floor; 'you are tired of me.'

Estella looked at her with perfect composure, and again looked down at the fire. Her graceful figure and her beautiful face expressed a self-possessed indifference to the wild heat of the other, that was almost cruel.

'You stock and stone!' exclaimed Miss Havisham. 'You cold, cold heart!'

'What?' said Estella, preserving her attitude of indifference as she leaned against the great chimney-piece and only moving her eyes; 'do you reproach me for being cold? You?'

'Are you not?' was the fierce retort.

'You should know,' said Estella. 'I am what you have made me. Take all the praise, take all the blame; take all the success, take all the failure; in short, take me.'

'O, look at her, look at her!' cried Miss Havisham, bitterly; 'Look at her so hard and thankless, on the hearth where she was reared! Where I took her into this wretched breast when it was first bleeding from its stabs, and where I have lavished years of tenderness upon her!'

'At least I was no party to the compact,' said Estella, 'for if I could walk and speak, when it was made, it was as much as I could do. But what would you have? You have been very good to me, and I owe everything to you. What would you have?'

'Love,' replied the other.

'You have it.'

'I have not,' said Miss Havisham.

'Mother by adoption,' retorted Estella, never departing from the easy grace of her attitude, never raising her voice as the other did, never yielding either to anger or tenderness,—'mother by adoption, I have said that I owe everything to you. All I possess is freely yours. All that you have given me, is at your command to have again. Beyond that, I have nothing. And if you ask me to give you, what you never gave me, my gratitude and duty cannot do impossibilities.'

'Did I never give her love!' cried Miss Havisham, turning wildly to me. 'Did I never give her a burning love, inseparable from jealousy at all times, and from sharp pain, while she speaks thus to me! Let her call me mad, let her call me mad!'

'Why should I call you mad,' returned Estella, 'I, of all people? Does any one live, who knows what set purposes you have, half as well as I do? Does any one live, who knows what a steady memory you have, half as well as I do? I who have sat on this same hearth on the little stool that is even now beside you there, learning your lessons and looking up into your face, when your face was strange and frightened me!'

'Soon forgotten!' moaned Miss Havisham. 'Times soon forgotten!'

'No, not forgotten,' retorted Estella,—'not forgotten, but treasured up in my memory. When have you found me false to your teaching? When have you found me unmindful of your lessons? When have you found me giving admission here,' she touched her bosom with her hand, 'to anything that you excluded? Be just to me.'

'So proud, so proud!' moaned Miss Havisham, pushing away her grey hair with both her hands.

'Who taught me to be proud?' returned Estella. 'Who praised me when I learnt my lesson?'

'So hard, so hard!' moaned Miss Havisham, with her former action.

'Who taught me to be hard?' returned Estella. 'Who praised me when I learnt my lesson?'

'But to be proud and hard to *me*!' Miss Havisham quite shrieked, as she stretched out her arms. 'Estella, Estella, Estella, to be proud and hard to *me*!'

Estella looked at her for a moment with a kind of calm wonder, but was not otherwise disturbed; when the moment was past, she looked down at the fire again.

'I cannot think,' said Estella, raising her eyes after a silence 'why you should be so unreasonable when I come to see you after a separation. I have never forgotten your wrongs and their causes. I have never been unfaithful to you or your schooling. I have never shown any weakness that I can charge myself with.'

'Would it be weakness to return my love?' exclaimed Miss Havisham. 'But yes, yes, she would call it so!'

'I begin to think,' said Estella, in a musing way, after another moment of calm wonder, 'that I almost understand how this comes about. If you had brought up your adopted daughter wholly in the dark confinement of these rooms, and had never let her know that there was such a thing as the daylight by which she had never once seen your face,—if you had done that, and then, for a purpose had wanted her to understand the daylight and know all about it, you would have been disappointed and angry?'

Miss Havisham, with her head in her hands, sat making a low moaning, and swaying herself on her chair, but gave no answer.

'Or,' said Estella,—'which is a nearer case,—if you had taught her, from the dawn of her intelligence, with your utmost energy and might, that there was such a thing as daylight, but that it was made to be her enemy and destroyer, and she must always turn against it, for it had blighted you and would else blight her;—if you had done this, and then, for a purpose, had wanted her to take naturally to the daylight and she could not do it, you would have been disappointed and angry?'

Miss Havisham sat listening (or it seemed so, for I could not see her face), but still made no answer.

'So,' said Estella, 'I must be taken as I have been made. The success is not mine, the failure is not mine, but the two together make me.'

Miss Havisham had settled down, I hardly knew how, upon the floor, among the faded bridal relics with which it was strewn. I took advantage of the moment—I had sought one from the first—to leave the room, after beseeching Estella's attention to her, with a movement of my hand. When I left, Estella was yet standing by the great chimney-piece, just as she had stood throughout. Miss Havisham's grey hair was all adrift upon the ground, among the other bridal wrecks, and was a miserable sight to see.

It was with a depressed heart that I walked in the starlight for an hour and more, about the courtyard, and about the brewery, and about the ruined garden. When I at last took courage to return to the room, I found Estella sitting at Miss Havisham's knee, taking up some stitches in one of those old articles of dress that were dropping to pieces, and of which I have often been reminded since by the faded tatters of old banners that I have seen hanging up in cathedrals. Afterwards, Estella and I played at cards, as of yore,—only we were skilful now, and played French games,—and so the evening wore away, and I went to bed.

I lay in that separate building across the courtyard. It was the first time I had ever lain down to rest in Satis House, and sleep refused to come near me. A thousand Miss Havishams haunted me. She was on this side of my pillow, on that, at the head of the bed, at the foot, behind the half-opened door of the dressing-room, in the dressing-room, in the room overhead, in the room beneath,—everywhere. At last, when the night was slow to creep on towards two o'clock, I felt that I absolutely could no longer bear the place as a place to lie down in, and that I must get up. I therefore got up and put on my clothes, and went out across the yard into the long stone passage, designing to gain the outer courtyard and walk there for the relief of my mind. But I was no sooner in the passage than I extinguished my candle; for I saw Miss Havisham going along it in a ghostly manner, making a low cry. I followed her at a distance, and saw her go up the staircase. She carried a bare candle in her hand, which she had probably taken from one of the sconces in her own room, and was a most unearthly object by its light. Standing at the bottom of the staircase, I felt the mildewed air of the feast-chamber, without seeing her open the door, and I heard her walking there, and so across into her own room, and so across again into that, never ceasing the low cry. After a time, I tried in the dark both to get out, and to go back, but I could do neither until some streaks of day strayed in and showed me where to lay my hands. During the whole interval, whenever I went to the bottom of the staircase, I heard her footstep, saw her light pass above, and heard her ceaseless low cry.

Before we left next day, there was no revival of the difference between her and Estella, nor was it ever revived on any similar occasion; and there were four similar occasions, to the best of my remembrance. Nor, did Miss Havisham's manner towards Estella in anywise change, except that I believed it to have something like fear infused among its former characteristics.

It is impossible to turn this leaf of my life, without putting Bentley Drummle's name upon it; or I would, very gladly.

On a certain occasion when the Finches were assembled in force, and when good feeling was being promoted in the usual manner by nobody's agreeing with anybody else, the presiding Finch called the Grove to order, forasmuch as Mr Drummle had not yet toasted a lady; which, according to the solemn constitution of the society, it was the brute's turn to do that day. I thought I saw him leer in an ugly way at me while the decanters were going round, but as there was no love lost between us, that might easily be. What was my indignant surprise when he called upon the company to pledge him to 'Estella!'

'Estella who?' said I.

'Never you mind,' retorted Drummle.

'Estella of where?' said I. 'You are bound to say of where.' Which he was, as a Finch.

'Of Richmond, gentlemen,' said Drummle, putting me out of the question, 'and a peerless beauty.'

Much he knew about peerless beauties, a mean, miserable idiot! I whispered Herbert.

'I know that lady,' said Herbert, across the table, when the toast had been honoured.

'*Do* you?' said Drummle.

'And so do I,' I added, with a scarlet face.

'*Do* you?' said Drummle. '*O*, Lord!'

This was the only retort—except glass or crockery—that the heavy creature was capable of making; but, I became as highly incensed by it as if it had been barbed with wit, and I immediately rose in my place and said that I could not but regard it as being like the honourable Finch's impudence to come down to that Grove,—we always talked about coming down to that Grove, as a neat Parliamentary turn of expression,—down to that Grove, proposing a lady of whom he knew nothing. Mr Drummle, upon this, starting up, demanded what I meant by that? Whereupon I made him the extreme reply that I believed he knew where I was to be found.

Whether it was possible in a Christian country to get on without blood, after this, was a question on which the Finches were divided. The debate upon it grew so lively, indeed, that at least six more honourable members told six more, during the discussion, that they believed *they* knew where *they* were to be found. However, it was decided at last (the Grove being a Court of Honour) that if Mr Drummle would bring never so slight a certificate from the lady, importing that he had the honour of her acquaintance, Mr Pip must express his regret, as a gentleman and a Finch, for 'having been betrayed into a warmth which.' Next day was appointed for the production (lest our honour should take cold from delay), and next day Drummle appeared with a polite little avowal in Estella's hand, that she had had the honour of dancing with him several times. This left me no course but to regret that I had been 'betrayed into a warmth which,' and on the whole to repudiate, as untenable, the idea that I was to be found anywhere. Drummle and I then sat snorting at one another for an hour, while the Grove engaged in indiscriminate contradiction, and finally the promotion of good feeling was declared to have gone ahead at an amazing rate.

I tell this lightly, but it was no light thing to me. For, I cannot adequately express what pain it gave me to think that Estella should show any favour to a contemptible, clumsy, sulky booby, so very far below the average. To the present moment, I believe it to have been referable to some pure fire of generosity and disinterestedness in my love for her, that I could not endure the thought of her stooping to that hound. No doubt I should have been miserable whomsoever she had favoured; but a worthier object would have caused me a different kind and degree of distress.

It was easy for me to find out, and I did soon find out, that Drummle had begun to follow her closely, and that she allowed him to do it. A little while, and he was always in pursuit of her, and he and I crossed one another every day. He held on, in a dull persistent way, and Estella held him on; now with encouragement, now with discouragement, now almost flattering him, now openly despising him, now knowing him very well, now scarcely remembering who he was.

The Spider, as Mr Jaggers had called him, was used to lying in wait, however, and had the patience of his tribe. Added to that, he had a blockhead confidence in his money and in his family greatness, which sometimes did him good service,—almost taking the place of concentration and determined purpose. So, the Spider, doggedly watching Estella, outwatched many brighter insects, and would often uncoil himself and drop at the right nick of time.

At a certain Assembly Ball at Richmond (there used to be Assembly Balls at most places then), where Estella had outshone all other beauties, this blundering Drummle so hung about her, and with so much toleration on her part, that I resolved to speak to her concerning him. I took the next opportunity; which was when she was waiting for Mrs Blandley to take her home, and was sitting apart among some flowers, ready to go. I was with her, for I almost always accompanied them to and from such places.

'Are you tired, Estella?'

'Rather, Pip.'

'You should be.'

'Say rather, I should not be; for I have my letter to Satis House to write, before I go to sleep.'

'Recounting tonight's triumph?' said I. 'Surely a very poor one, Estella.'

'What do you mean? I didn't know there had been any.'

'Estella,' said I, 'do look at that fellow in the corner yonder, who is looking over here at us.'

'Why should I look at him?' returned Estella, with her eyes on me instead. 'What is there in that fellow in the corner yonder,—to use your words,—that I need look at?'

'Indeed, that is the very question I want to ask you,' said I. 'For he has been hovering about you all night.'

'Moths, and all sorts of ugly creatures,' replied Estella, with a glance towards him, 'hover about a lighted candle. Can the candle help it?'

'No,' I returned; 'but cannot the Estella help it?'

'Well!' said she, laughing, after a moment, 'perhaps. Yes. Anything you like.'

'But, Estella, do hear me speak. It makes me wretched that you should encourage a man so generally despised as Drummle. You know he is despised.'

'Well?' said she.

'You know he is as ungainly within as without. A deficient, ill-tempered, lowering, stupid fellow.'

'Well?' said she.

'You know he has nothing to recommend him but money and a ridiculous roll of addle-headed predecessors; now, don't you?'

'Well?' said she again; and each time she said it, she opened her lovely eyes the wider.

To overcome the difficulty of getting past that monosyllable, I took it from her, and said, repeating it with emphasis, 'Well! Then, that is why it makes me wretched.'

Now, if I could have believed that she favoured Drummle with any idea of making me—wretched, I should have been in better heart about it; but in that habitual way of hers, she put me so entirely out of the question, that I could believe nothing of the kind.

'Pip,' said Estella, casting her glance over the room, 'don't be foolish about its effect on you. It may have its effect on others, and may be meant to have. It's not worth discussing.'

'Yes it is,' said I, 'because I cannot bear that people should say, "she throws away her graces and attractions on a mere boor, the lowest in the crowd."'

'I can bear it,' said Estella.

'Oh! Don't be so proud, Estella, and so inflexible.'

'Calls me proud and inflexible in this breath!' said Estella, opening her hands. 'And in his last breath reproached me for stooping to a boor!'

'There is no doubt you do,' said I, something hurriedly, 'for I have seen you give him looks and smiles this very night, such as you never give to—me.'

'Do you want me then,' said Estella, turning suddenly with a fixed and serious, if not angry, look, 'to deceive and entrap you?'

'Do you deceive and entrap him, Estella?'

'Yes, and many others,—all of them but you. Here is Mrs Brandley. I'll say no more.'

And now that I have given the one chapter to the theme that so filled my heart, and so often made it ache and ache again, I pass on unhindered, to the event that had impended over me longer yet; the event that had begun to be prepared for, before I knew that the world held Estella, and in the days when her baby intelligence was receiving its first distortions from Miss Havisham's wasting hands.

In the Eastern story, the heavy slab that was to fall on the bed of state in the flush of conquest was slowly wrought out of the quarry, the tunnel for the rope to hold it in its place was slowly carried through the leagues of rock, the slab was slowly raised and fitted in the roof, the rope was rove to it and slowly taken through the miles of hollow to the great iron ring. All being made ready with much labour, and the hour come, the sultan was aroused in the dead of the night, and the sharpened axe that was to sever the rope from the great iron ring was put into his hand, and he struck with it, and the rope parted and rushed away, and the ceiling fell. So, in my case; all the work, near and afar, that tended to the end, had been accomplished; and in an instant the blow was struck, and the roof of my stronghold dropped upon me.

Chapter 39

I was three-and-twenty years of age. Not another word had I heard to enlighten me on the subject of my expectations, and my twenty-third birthday was a week gone. We had left Barnard's Inn more than a year, and lived in the Temple. Our chambers were in Garden-court, down by the river.

Mr Pocket and I had for some time parted company as to our original relations, though we continued on the best terms. Notwithstanding my inability to settle to anything,—which I hope arose out of the restless and incomplete tenure on which I held my means,—I had a taste for reading, and read regularly so many hours a day. That matter of Herbert's was still progressing, and everything with me was as I have brought it down to the close of the last preceding chapter.

Business had taken Herbert on a journey to Marseilles. I was alone, and had a dull sense of being alone. Dispirited and anxious, long hoping that tomorrow or next week would clear my way, and long disappointed, I sadly missed the cheerful face and ready response of my friend.

It was wretched weather; stormy and wet, stormy and wet; and mud, mud, mud, deep in all the streets. Day after day, a vast heavy veil had been driving over London from the East, and it drove still, as if in the East there were an Eternity of cloud and wind. So furious had been the gusts, that high buildings in town had had the lead stripped off their roofs; and in the country, trees had been torn up, and sails of windmills carried away; and gloomy accounts had come in from the coast, of shipwreck and death. Violent blasts of rain had accompanied these rages of wind, and the day just closed as I sat down to read had been the worst of all.

Alterations have been made in that part of the Temple since that time, and it has not now so lonely a character as it had then, nor is it so exposed to the river. We lived at the top of the last house, and the wind rushing up the river shook the house that night, like discharges of cannon, or breakings of a sea. When the rain came with it and dashed against the windows, I thought, raising my eyes to them as they rocked, that I might have fancied myself in a storm-beaten lighthouse. Occasionally, the smoke came rolling down the chimney as though it could not bear to go out into such a night; and when I set the doors open and looked down the staircase, the staircase lamps were blown out; and when I shaded my face with my hands and looked through the black windows (opening them ever so little was out of the question in the teeth of such wind and rain), I saw that the lamps in the court were blown out, and that the lamps on the bridges and the shore were shuddering, and that the coal-fires in barges on the river were being carried away before the wind like red-hot splashes in the rain.

I read with my watch upon the table, purposing to close my book at eleven o'clock. As I shut it, Saint Paul's, and all the many church-clocks in the City—some leading, some accompanying, some following—struck that hour. The sound was curiously flawed by the wind; and I was listening, and thinking how the wind assailed and tore it, when I heard a footstep on the stair.

What nervous folly made me start, and awfully connect it with the footstep of my dead sister, matters not. It was past in a moment, and I listened again, and heard the footstep stumble in coming on. Remembering then, that the staircase-lights were blown out, I took up my reading-lamp and went out to the stair-head. Whoever was below had stopped on seeing my lamp, for all was quiet.

'There is some one down there, is there not?' I called out, looking down.

'Yes,' said a voice from the darkness beneath.

'What floor do you want?'

'The top. Mr Pip.'

'That is my name.—There is nothing the matter?'

'Nothing the matter,' returned the voice. And the man came on.

I stood with my lamp held out over the stair-rail, and he came slowly within its light. It was a shaded lamp, to shine upon a book, and its circle of light was very contracted; so that he was in it for a mere instant, and then out of it. In the instant, I had seen a face that was strange to me, looking up with an incomprehensible air of being touched and pleased by the sight of me.

Moving the lamp as the man moved, I made out that he was substantially dressed, but roughly, like a voyager by sea. That he had long iron-grey hair. That his age was about sixty. That he was a muscular man, strong on his legs, and that he was browned and hardened by exposure to weather. As he ascended the last stair or two, and the light of my lamp included us both, I saw, with a stupid kind of amazement, that he was holding out both his hands to me.

'Pray what is your business?' I asked him.

'My business?' he repeated, pausing. 'Ah! Yes. I will explain my business, by your leave.'

'Do you wish to come in?'

'Yes,' he replied; 'I wish to come in, master.'

I had asked him the question inhospitably enough, for I resented the sort of bright and gratified recognition that still shone in his face. I resented it, because it seemed to imply that he expected me to respond to it. But I took him into the room I had just left, and, having set the lamp on the table, asked him as civilly as I could to explain himself.

He looked about him with the strangest air,—an air of wondering pleasure, as if he had some part in the things he admired,—and he pulled off a rough outer coat, and his hat. Then, I saw that his head was furrowed and bald, and that the long iron-grey hair grew only on its sides. But, I saw nothing that in the least explained him. On the contrary, I saw him next moment, once more holding out both his hands to me.

'What do you mean?' said I, half suspecting him to be mad.

He stopped in his looking at me, and slowly rubbed his right hand over his head. 'It's disapinting to a man,' he said, in a coarse broken voice, 'arter having looked for'ard so distant, and come so fur; but you're not to blame for that,—neither on us is to blame for that. I'll speak in half a minute. Give me half a minute, please.'

He sat down on a chair that stood before the fire, and covered his forehead with his large brown veinous hands. I looked at him attentively then, and recoiled a little from him; but I did not know him.

'There's no one nigh,' said he, looking over his shoulder; 'is there?'

'Why do you, a stranger coming into my rooms at this time of the night, ask that question?' said I.

'You're a game one,' he returned, shaking his head at me with a deliberate affection, at once most unintelligible and most exasperating; 'I'm glad you've grow'd up, a game one! But don't catch hold of me. You'd be sorry arterwards to have done it.'

I relinquished the intention he had detected, for I knew him! Even yet I could not recall a single feature, but I knew him! If the wind and the rain had driven away the intervening years, had scattered all the intervening objects, had swept us to the churchyard where we first stood face to face on such different levels, I could not have known my convict more distinctly than I knew him now as he sat in the chair before the fire. No need to take a file from his pocket and show it to me; no need to take the handkerchief from his neck and twist it round his head; no need to hug himself with both his arms, and take a shivering turn across the room, looking back at me for recognition. I knew him before he gave me one of those aids, though, a moment before, I had not been conscious of remotely suspecting his identity.

He came back to where I stood, and again held out both his hands. Not knowing what to do,—for, in my astonishment I had lost my self-possession,—I reluctantly gave him my hands. He grasped them heartily, raised them to his lips, kissed them, and still held them.

'You acted noble, my boy,' said he. 'Noble, Pip! And I have never forgot it!'

At a change in his manner as if he were even going to embrace me, I laid a hand upon his breast and put him away.

'Stay!' said I. 'Keep off! If you are grateful to me for what I did when I was a little child, I hope you have shown your gratitude by mending your way of life. If you have come here to thank me, it was not necessary. Still, however you have found me out, there must be something good in the feeling that has brought you here, and I will not repulse you; but surely you must understand that—I—'

My attention was so attracted by the singularity of his fixed look at me, that the words died away on my tongue.

'You was a saying,' he observed, when we had confronted one another in silence, 'that surely I must understand. What, surely must I understand?'

'That I cannot wish to renew that chance intercourse with you of long ago, under these different circumstances. I am glad to believe you have repented and recovered yourself. I am glad to tell you so. I am glad that, thinking I deserve to be thanked, you have come to thank me. But our ways are different ways, none the less. You are wet, and you look weary. Will you drink something before you go?'

He had replaced his neckerchief loosely, and had stood, keenly observant of me, biting a long end of it. 'I think,' he answered, still with the end at his mouth and still observant of me, 'that I *will* drink (I thank you) afore I go.'

There was a tray ready on a side-table. I brought it to the table near the fire, and asked him what he would have? He touched one of the bottles without looking at it or speaking, and I made him some hot rum and water. I tried to keep my hand steady while I did so, but his look at me as he leaned back in his chair with the long draggled end of his neckerchief between his teeth—evidently forgotten—made my hand very difficult to master. When at last I put the glass to him, I saw with amazement that his eyes were full of tears.

Up to this time I had remained standing, not to disguise that I wished him gone. But I was softened by the softened aspect of the man, and felt a touch of reproach. 'I hope,' said I, hurriedly putting something into a glass for myself, and drawing a chair to the table, 'that you will not think I spoke harshly to you just now. I had no intention of doing it, and I am sorry for it if I did. I wish you well and happy!'

As I put my glass to my lips, he glanced with surprise at the end of his neckerchief, dropping from his mouth when he opened it, and stretched out his hand. I gave him mine, and then he drank, and drew his sleeve across his eyes and forehead.

'How are you living?' I asked him.

'I've been a sheep-farmer, stock-breeder, other trades besides, away in the new world,' said he; 'many a thousand mile of stormy water off from this.'

'I hope you have done well?'

'I've done wonderfully well. There's others went out alonger me as has done well too, but no man has done nigh as well as me. I'm famous for it.'

'I am glad to hear it.'

'I hope to hear you say so, my dear boy.'

Without stopping to try to understand those words or the tone in which they were spoken, I turned off to a point that had just come into my mind.

'Have you ever seen a messenger you once sent to me,' I inquired, 'since he undertook that trust?'

'Never set eyes upon him. I warn't likely to it.'

'He came faithfully, and he brought me the two one-pound notes. I was a poor boy then, as you know, and to a poor boy they were a little fortune. But, like you, I have done well since, and you must let me pay them back. You can put them to some other poor boy's use.' I took out my purse.

He watched me as I laid my purse upon the table and opened it, and he watched me as I separated two one-pound notes from its contents. They were clean and new, and I spread them out and handed them over to him. Still watching me, he laid them one upon the other, folded them long-wise, gave them a twist, set fire to them at the lamp, and dropped the ashes into the tray.

'May I make so bold,' he said then, with a smile that was like a frown, and with a frown that was like a smile, 'as ask you *how* you have done well, since you and me was out on them lone shivering marshes?'

'How?'

'Ah!'

He emptied his glass, got up, and stood at the side of the fire, with his heavy brown hand on the mantel-shelf. He put a foot up to the bars, to dry and warm it, and the wet boot began to steam; but, he neither looked at it, nor at the fire, but steadily looked at me. It was only now that I began to tremble.

When my lips had parted, and had shaped some words that were without sound, I forced myself to tell him (though I could not do it distinctly), that I had been chosen to succeed to some property.

'Might a mere warmint ask what property?' said he.

I faltered, 'I don't know.'

'Might a mere warmint ask whose property?' said he.

I faltered again, 'I don't know.'

'Could I make a guess, I wonder,' said the Convict, 'at your income since you come of age! As to the first figure now. Five?'

With my heart beating like a heavy hammer of disordered action, I rose out of my chair, and stood with my hand upon the back of it, looking wildly at him.

'Concerning a guardian,' he went on. 'There ought to have been some guardian, or such-like, whiles you was a minor. Some lawyer, maybe. As to the first letter of that lawyer's name now. Would it be J?'

All the truth of my position came flashing on me; and its disappointments, dangers, disgraces, consequences of all kinds, rushed in such a multitude that I was borne down by them and had to struggle for every breath I drew.

'Put it,' he resumed, 'as the employer of that lawyer whose name begun with a J, and might be Jaggers,—put it as he had come over sea to Portsmouth, and had landed there, and had wanted to come on to you. 'However, you have found me out,' you says just now. Well! However, did I find you out? Why, I wrote from Portsmouth to a person in London, for particulars of your address. That person's name? Why, Wemmick.'

I could not have spoken one word, though it had been to save my life. I stood, with a hand on the chair-back and a hand on my breast, where I seemed to be suffocating,—I stood so, looking wildly at him, until I grasped at the chair, when the room began to surge and turn. He caught me, drew me to the sofa, put me up against the cushions, and bent on one knee before me, bringing the face that I now well remembered, and that I shuddered at, very near to mine.

'Yes, Pip, dear boy, I've made a gentleman on you! It's me wot has done it! I swore that time, sure as ever I earned a guinea, that guinea should go to you. I swore arterwards, sure as ever I spec'lated and got rich, you should get rich. I lived rough, that you should live smooth; I worked hard, that you should be above work. What odds, dear boy? Do I tell it, fur you to feel a obligation? Not a bit. I tell it, fur you to know as that there hunted dunghill dog wot you kep life in, got his head so high that he could make a gentleman,—and, Pip, you're him!'

The abhorrence in which I held the man, the dread I had of him, the repugnance with which I shrank from him, could not have been exceeded if he had been some terrible beast.

'Look'ee here, Pip. I'm your second father. You're my son,—more to me nor any son. I've put away money, only for you to spend. When I was a hired-out shepherd in a solitary hut, not seeing no faces but faces of sheep till I half forgot wot men's and women's faces wos like, I see yourn. I drops my knife many a time in that hut when I was a-eating my dinner or my supper, and I says, 'Here's the boy again, a looking at me whiles I eats and drinks!' I see you there a many times, as plain as ever I see you on them misty marshes. 'Lord strike me dead!' I says each time,—and I goes out in the air to say it under the open heavens,—'but wot, if I gets liberty and money, I'll make that boy a gentleman!' And I done it. Why, look at you, dear boy! Look at these here lodgings o'yourn, fit for a lord! A lord? Ah! You shall show money with lords for wagers, and beat 'em!'

In his heat and triumph, and in his knowledge that I had been nearly fainting, he did not remark on my reception of all this. It was the one grain of relief I had.

'Look'ee here!' he went on, taking my watch out of my pocket, and turning towards him a ring on my finger, while I recoiled from his touch as if he had been a snake, 'a gold 'un and a beauty: *that's* a gentleman's, I hope! A diamond all set round with rubies; *that's* a gentleman's, I hope! Look at your linen; fine and beautiful! Look at your clothes; better ain't to be got! And your books too,' turning his eyes round the room, 'mounting up, on their shelves, by hundreds! And you read 'em; don't you? I see you'd been a reading of 'em when I come in. Ha, ha, ha! You shall read 'em to me, dear boy! And if they're in foreign languages wot I don't understand, I shall be just as proud as if I did.'

Again he took both my hands and put them to his lips, while my blood ran cold within me.

'Don't you mind talking, Pip,' said he, after again drawing his sleeve over his eyes and forehead, as the click came in his throat which I well remembered,—and he was all the more horrible to me that he was so much in earnest; 'you can't do better nor keep quiet, dear boy. You ain't looked slowly forward to this as I have; you wosn't prepared for this as I wos. But didn't you never think it might be me?'

'O no, no, no,' I returned, 'Never, never!'

'Well, you see it *wos* me, and single-handed. Never a soul in it but my own self and Mr Jaggers.'

'Was there no one else?' I asked.

'No,' said he, with a glance of surprise: 'who else should there be? And, dear boy, how good looking you have growed! There's bright eyes somewheres—eh? Isn't there bright eyes somewheres, wot you love the thoughts on?'

O Estella, Estella!

'They shall be yourn, dear boy, if money can buy 'em. Not that a gentleman like you, so well set up as you, can't win 'em off of his own game; but money shall back you! Let me finish wot I was a telling you, dear boy. From that there hut and that there hiring-out, I got money left me by my master (which died, and had been the same as me), and got my liberty and went for myself. In every single thing I went for, I went for you. 'Lord strike a blight upon it,' I says, wotever it was I went for, 'if it ain't for him!' It all prospered wonderful. As I giv' you to understand just now, I'm famous for it. It was the money left me, and the gains of the first few year wot I sent home to Mr Jaggers—all for you—when he first come arter you, agreeable to my letter.'

O that he had never come! That he had left me at the forge,—far from contented, yet, by comparison happy!

'And then, dear boy, it was a recompense to me, look'ee here, to know in secret that I was making a gentleman. The blood horses of them colonists might fling up the dust over me as I was walking; what do I say? I says to myself, 'I'm making a better gentleman nor ever *you*'ll be!' When one of 'em says to another, "He was a convict, a few year ago, and is a ignorant common fellow now, for all he's lucky," what do I say? I says to myself, 'If I ain't a gentleman, nor yet ain't got no learning, I'm the owner of such. All on you owns stock and land; which on you owns a brought-up London gentleman?' This way I kep myself a going. And this way I held steady afore my mind that I would for certain come one day and see my boy, and make myself known to him, on his own ground.'

He laid his hand on my shoulder. I shuddered at the thought that for anything I knew, his hand might be stained with blood.

'It warn't easy, Pip, for me to leave them parts, nor yet it warn't safe. But I held to it, and the harder it was, the stronger I held, for I was determined, and my mind firm made up. At last I done it. Dear boy, I done it!'

I tried to collect my thoughts, but I was stunned. Throughout, I had seemed to myself to attend more to the wind and the rain than to him; even now, I could not separate his voice from those voices, though those were loud and his was silent.

'Where will you put me?' he asked, presently. 'I must be put somewheres, dear boy.'

'To sleep?' said I.

'Yes. And to sleep long and sound,' he answered; 'for I've been sea-tossed and sea-washed, months and months.'

'My friend and companion,' said I, rising from the sofa, 'is absent; you must have his room.'

'He won't come back tomorrow; will he?'

'No,' said I, answering almost mechanically, in spite of my utmost efforts; 'not tomorrow.'

'Because, look'ee here, dear boy,' he said, dropping his voice, and laying a long finger on my breast in an impressive manner, 'caution is necessary.'

'How do you mean? Caution?'

'By G——, it's Death!'

'What's death?'

'I was sent for life. It's death to come back. There's been overmuch coming back of late years, and I should of a certainty be hanged if took.'

Nothing was needed but this; the wretched man, after loading wretched me with his gold and silver chains for years, had risked his life to come to me, and I held it there in my keeping! If I had loved him instead of abhorring him; if I had been attracted to him by the strongest admiration and affection, instead of shrinking from him with the strongest repugnance; it could have been no worse. On the contrary, it would have been better, for his preservation would then have naturally and tenderly addressed my heart.

My first care was to close the shutters, so that no light might be seen from without, and then to close and make fast the doors. While I did so, he stood at the table drinking rum and eating biscuit; and when I saw him thus engaged, I saw my convict on the marshes at his meal again. It almost seemed to me as if he must stoop down presently, to file at his leg.

When I had gone into Herbert's room, and had shut off any other communication between it and the staircase than through the room in which our conversation had been held, I asked him if he would go to bed? He said yes, but asked me for some of my 'gentleman's linen' to put on in the morning. I brought it out, and laid it ready for him, and my blood again ran cold when he again took me by both hands to give me goodnight.

I got away from him, without knowing how I did it, and mended the fire in the room where we had been together, and sat down by it, afraid to go to bed. For an hour or more, I remained too stunned to think; and it was not until I began to think, that I began fully to know how wrecked I was, and how the ship in which I had sailed was gone to pieces.

Miss Havisham's intentions towards me, all a mere dream; Estella not designed for me; I only suffered in Satis House as a convenience, a sting for the greedy relations, a model with a mechanical heart to practise on when no other practice was at hand; those were the first smarts I had. But, sharpest and deepest pain of all,—it was for the convict, guilty of I knew not what crimes, and liable to be taken out of those rooms where I sat thinking, and hanged at the Old Bailey door, that I had deserted Joe.

I would not have gone back to Joe now, I would not have gone back to Biddy now, for any consideration; simply, I suppose, because my sense of my own worthless conduct to them was greater than every consideration. No wisdom on earth could have given me the comfort that I should have derived from their simplicity and fidelity; but I could never, never, undo what I had done.

In every rage of wind and rush of rain, I heard pursuers. Twice, I could have sworn there was a knocking and whispering at the outer door. With these fears upon me, I began either to imagine or recall that I had had mysterious warnings of this man's approach. That, for weeks gone by, I had passed faces in the streets which I had thought like his. That these likenesses had grown more numerous, as he, coming over the sea, had drawn nearer. That his wicked spirit had somehow sent these messengers to mine, and that now on this stormy night he was as good as his word, and with me.

Crowding up with these reflections came the reflection that I had seen him with my childish eyes to be a desperately violent man; that I had heard that other convict reiterate that he had tried to murder him; that I had seen him down in the ditch tearing and fighting like a wild beast. Out of such remembrances I brought into the light of the fire a half-formed terror that it might not be safe to be shut up there with him in the dead of the wild solitary night. This dilated until it filled the room, and impelled me to take a candle and go in and look at my dreadful burden.

He had rolled a handkerchief round his head, and his face was set and lowering in his sleep. But he was asleep, and quietly too, though he had a pistol lying on the pillow. Assured of this, I softly removed the key to the outside of his door, and turned it on him before I again sat down by the fire. Gradually I slipped from the chair and lay on the floor. When I awoke without having parted in my sleep with the perception of my wretchedness, the clocks of the Eastward churches were striking five, the candles were wasted out, the fire was dead, and the wind and rain intensified the thick black darkness.

THIS IS THE END OF THE SECOND STAGE OF PIP'S EXPECTATIONS.

Chapter 40

It was fortunate for me that I had to take precautions to ensure (so far as I could) the safety of my dreaded visitor; for, this thought pressing on me when I awoke, held other thoughts in a confused concourse at a distance.

The impossibility of keeping him concealed in the chambers was self-evident. It could not be done, and the attempt to do it would inevitably engender suspicion. True, I had no Avenger in my service now, but I was looked after by an inflammatory old female, assisted by an animated rag-bag whom she called her niece, and to keep a room secret from them would be to invite curiosity and exaggeration. They both had weak eyes, which I had long attributed to their chronically looking in at keyholes, and they were always at hand when not wanted; indeed that was their only reliable quality besides larceny. Not to get up a mystery with these people, I resolved to announce in the morning that my uncle had unexpectedly come from the country.

This course I decided on while I was yet groping about in the darkness for the means of getting a light. Not stumbling on the means after all, I was fain to go out to the adjacent Lodge and get the watchman there to come with his lantern. Now, in groping my way down the black staircase I fell over something, and that something was a man crouching in a corner.

As the man made no answer when I asked him what he did there, but eluded my touch in silence, I ran to the Lodge and urged the watchman to come quickly; telling him of the incident on the way back. The wind being as fierce as ever, we did not care to endanger the light in the lantern by rekindling the extinguished lamps on the staircase, but we examined the staircase from the bottom to the top and found no one there. It then occurred to me as possible that the man might have slipped into my rooms; so, lighting my candle at the watchman's, and leaving him standing at the door, I examined them carefully, including the room in which my dreaded guest lay asleep. All was quiet, and assuredly no other man was in those chambers.

It troubled me that there should have been a lurker on the stairs, on that night of all nights in the year, and I asked the watchman, on the chance of eliciting some hopeful explanation as I handed him a dram at the door, whether he had admitted at his gate any gentleman who had perceptibly been dining out? Yes, he said; at different times of the night, three. One lived in Fountain Court, and the other two lived in the Lane, and he had seen them all go home. Again, the only other man who dwelt in the house of which my chambers formed a part had been in the country for some weeks, and he certainly had not returned in the night, because we had seen his door with his seal on it as we came upstairs.

'The night being so bad, sir,' said the watchman, as he gave me back my glass, 'uncommon few have come in at my gate. Besides them three gentlemen that I have named, I don't call to mind another since about eleven o'clock, when a stranger asked for you.'

'My uncle,' I muttered. 'Yes.'

'You saw him, sir?'

'Yes. Oh yes.'

'Likewise the person with him?'

'Person with him!' I repeated.

'I judged the person to be with him,' returned the watchman. 'The person stopped, when he stopped to make inquiry of me, and the person took this way when he took this way.'

'What sort of person?'

The watchman had not particularly noticed; he should say a working person; to the best of his belief, he had a dust-coloured kind of clothes on, under a dark coat. The watchman made more light of the matter than I did, and naturally; not having my reason for attaching weight to it.

When I had got rid of him, which I thought it well to do without prolonging explanations, my mind was much troubled by these two circumstances taken together. Whereas they were easy of innocent solution apart,—as, for instance, some diner out or diner at home, who had not gone near this watchman's gate, might have strayed to my staircase and dropped asleep there,—and my nameless visitor might have brought some one with him to show him the way,—still, joined, they had an ugly look to one as prone to distrust and fear as the changes of a few hours had made me.

I lighted my fire, which burnt with a raw pale flare at that time of the morning, and fell into a doze before it. I seemed to have been dozing a whole night when the clocks struck six. As there was full an hour and a half between me and daylight, I dozed again; now, waking up uneasily, with prolix conversations about nothing, in my ears; now, making thunder of the wind in the chimney; at length, falling off into a profound sleep from which the daylight woke me with a start.

All this time I had never been able to consider my own situation, nor could I do so yet. I had not the power to attend to it. I was greatly dejected and distressed, but in an incoherent wholesale sort of way. As to forming any plan for the future, I could as soon have formed an elephant. When I opened the shutters and looked out at the wet wild morning, all of a leaden hue; when I walked from room to room; when I sat down again shivering, before the fire, waiting for my laundress to appear; I thought how miserable I was, but hardly knew why, or how long I had been so, or on what day of the week I made the reflection, or even who I was that made it.

At last, the old woman and the niece came in,—the latter with a head not easily distinguishable from her dusty broom,—and testified surprise at sight of me and the fire. To whom I imparted how my uncle had come in the night and was then asleep, and how the breakfast preparations were to be modified accordingly. Then I washed and dressed while they knocked the furniture about and made a dust; and so, in a sort of dream or sleep-waking, I found myself sitting by the fire again, waiting for—Him—to come to breakfast.

By and by, his door opened and he came out. I could not bring myself to bear the sight of him, and I thought he had a worse look by daylight.

'I do not even know,' said I, speaking low as he took his seat at the table, 'by what name to call you. I have given out that you are my uncle.'

'That's it, dear boy! Call me uncle.'

'You assumed some name, I suppose, on board ship?'

'Yes, dear boy. I took the name of Provis.'

'Do you mean to keep that name?'

'Why, yes, dear boy, it's as good as another,—unless you'd like another.'

'What is your real name?' I asked him in a whisper.

'Magwitch,' he answered, in the same tone; 'chrisen'd Abel.'

'What were you brought up to be?'

'A warmint, dear boy.'

He answered quite seriously, and used the word as if it denoted some profession.

'When you came into the Temple last night—' said I, pausing to wonder whether that could really have been last night, which seemed so long ago.

'Yes, dear boy?'

'When you came in at the gate and asked the watchman the way here, had you any one with you?'

'With me? No, dear boy.'

'But there was some one there?'

'I didn't take particular notice,' he said, dubiously, 'not knowing the ways of the place. But I think there *was* a person, too, come in alonger me.'

'Are you known in London?'

'I hope not!' said he, giving his neck a jerk with his forefinger that made me turn hot and sick.

'Were you known in London, once?'

'Not over and above, dear boy. I was in the provinces mostly.'

'Were you—tried—in London?'

'Which time?' said he, with a sharp look.

'The last time.'

He nodded. 'First knowed Mr Jaggers that way. Jaggers was for me.'

It was on my lips to ask him what he was tried for, but he took up a knife, gave it a flourish, and with the words, 'And what I done is worked out and paid for!' fell to at his breakfast.

He ate in a ravenous way that was very disagreeable, and all his actions were uncouth, noisy, and greedy. Some of his teeth had failed him since I saw him eat on the marshes, and as he turned his food in his mouth, and turned his head sideways to bring his strongest fangs to bear upon it, he looked terribly like a hungry old dog. If I had begun with any appetite, he would have taken it away, and I should have sat much as I did,—repelled from him by an insurmountable aversion, and gloomily looking at the cloth.

'I'm a heavy grubber, dear boy,' he said, as a polite kind of apology when he made an end of his meal, 'but I always was. If it had been in my constitution to be a lighter grubber, I might ha' got into lighter trouble. Similarly, I must have my smoke. When I was first hired out as shepherd t'other side the world, it's my belief I should ha' turned into a molloncolly-mad sheep myself, if I hadn't a had my smoke.'

As he said so, he got up from table, and putting his hand into the breast of the pea-coat he wore, brought out a short black pipe, and a handful of loose tobacco of the kind that is called Negro-head. Having filled his pipe, he put the surplus tobacco back again, as if his pocket were a drawer. Then, he took a live coal from the fire with the tongs, and lighted his pipe at it, and then turned round on the hearth-rug with his back to the fire, and went through his favourite action of holding out both his hands for mine.

'And this,' said he, dandling my hands up and down in his, as he puffed at his pipe,—'and this is the gentleman what I made! The real genuine One! It does me good fur to look at you, Pip. All I stip'late, is, to stand by and look at you, dear boy!'

I released my hands as soon as I could, and found that I was beginning slowly to settle down to the contemplation of my condition. What I was chained to, and how heavily, became intelligible to me, as I heard his hoarse voice, and sat looking up at his furrowed bald head with its iron grey hair at the sides.

'I mustn't see my gentleman a footing it in the mire of the streets; there mustn't be no mud on *his* boots. My gentleman must have horses, Pip! Horses to ride, and horses to drive, and horses for his servant to ride and drive as well. Shall colonists have their horses (and blood 'uns, if you please, good Lord!) and not my London gentleman? No, no. We'll show 'em another pair of shoes than that, Pip; won't us?'

He took out of his pocket a great thick pocket-book, bursting with papers, and tossed it on the table.

'There's something worth spending in that there book, dear boy. It's yourn. All I've got ain't mine; it's yourn. Don't you be afeerd on it. There's more where that come from. I've come to the old country fur to see my gentleman spend his money *like* a gentleman. That'll be *my* pleasure. *My* pleasure 'ull be fur to see him do it. And blast you all!' he wound up, looking round the room and snapping his fingers once with a loud snap, 'blast you every one, from the judge in his wig, to the colonist a stirring up the dust, I'll show a better gentleman than the whole kit on you put together!'

'Stop!' said I, almost in a frenzy of fear and dislike, 'I want to speak to you. I want to know what is to be done. I want to know how you are to be kept out of danger, how long you are going to stay, what projects you have.'

'Look'ee here, Pip,' said he, laying his hand on my arm in a suddenly altered and subdued manner; 'first of all, look'ee here. I forgot myself half a minute ago. What I said was low; that's what it was; low. Look'ee here, Pip. Look over it. I ain't a going to be low.'

'First,' I resumed, half groaning, 'what precautions can be taken against your being recognized and seized?'

'No, dear boy,' he said, in the same tone as before, 'that don't go first. Lowness goes first. I ain't took so many year to make a gentleman, not without knowing what's due to him. Look'ee here, Pip. I was low; that's what I was; low. Look over it, dear boy.'

Some sense of the grimly-ludicrous moved me to a fretful laugh, as I replied, 'I *have* looked over it. In Heaven's name, don't harp upon it!'

'Yes, but look'ee here,' he persisted. 'Dear boy, I ain't come so fur, not fur to be low. Now, go on, dear boy. You was a saying—'

'How are you to be guarded from the danger you have incurred?'

'Well, dear boy, the danger ain't so great. Without I was informed agen, the danger ain't so much to signify. There's Jaggers, and there's Wemmick, and there's you. Who else is there to inform?'

'Is there no chance person who might identify you in the street?' said I.

'Well,' he returned, 'there ain't many. Nor yet I don't intend to advertise myself in the newspapers by the name of A.M. come back from Botany Bay; and years have rolled away, and who's to gain by it? Still, look'ee here, Pip. If the danger had been fifty times as great, I should ha' come to see you, mind you, just the same.'

'And how long do you remain?'

'How long?' said he, taking his black pipe from his mouth, and dropping his jaw as he stared at me. 'I'm not a going back. I've come for good.'

'Where are you to live?' said I. 'What is to be done with you? Where will you be safe?'

'Dear boy,' he returned, 'there's disguising wigs can be bought for money, and there's hair powder, and spectacles, and black clothes,—shorts and what not. Others has done it safe afore, and what others has done afore, others can do agen. As to the where and how of living, dear boy, give me your own opinions on it.'

'You take it smoothly now,' said I, 'but you were very serious last night, when you swore it was Death.'

'And so I swear it is Death,' said he, putting his pipe back in his mouth, 'and Death by the rope, in the open street not fur from this, and it's serious that you should fully understand it to be so. What then, when that's once done? Here I am. To go back now 'ud be as bad as to stand ground—worse. Besides, Pip, I'm here, because I've meant it by you, years and years. As to what I dare, I'm a old bird now, as has dared all manner of traps since first he was fledged, and I'm not afeerd to perch upon a scarecrow. If there's Death hid inside of it, there is, and let him come out, and I'll face him, and then I'll believe in him and not afore. And now let me have a look at my gentleman agen.'

Once more, he took me by both hands and surveyed me with an air of admiring proprietorship: smoking with great complacency all the while.

It appeared to me that I could do no better than secure him some quiet lodging hard by, of which he might take possession when Herbert returned: whom I expected in two or three days. That the secret must be confided to Herbert as a matter of unavoidable necessity, even if I could have put the immense relief I should derive from sharing it with him out of the question, was plain to me. But it was by no means so plain to Mr Provis (I resolved to call him by that name), who reserved his consent to Herbert's participation until he should have seen him and formed a favourable judgment of his physiognomy.

'And even then, dear boy,' said he, pulling a greasy little clasped black Testament out of his pocket, 'we'll have him on his oath.'

To state that my terrible patron carried this little black book about the world solely to swear people on in cases of emergency, would be to state what I never quite established; but this I can say, that I never knew him put it to any other use. The book itself had the appearance of having been stolen from some court of justice, and perhaps his knowledge of its antecedents, combined with his own experience in that wise, gave him a reliance on its powers as a sort of legal spell or charm. On this first occasion of his producing it, I recalled how he had made me swear fidelity in the churchyard long ago, and how he had described himself last night as always swearing to his resolutions in his solitude.

As he was at present dressed in a seafaring slop suit, in which he looked as if he had some parrots and cigars to dispose of, I next discussed with him what dress he should wear. He cherished an extraordinary belief in the virtues of 'shorts' as a disguise, and had in his own mind sketched a dress for himself that would have made him something between a dean and a dentist. It was with considerable difficulty that I won him over to the assumption of a dress more like a prosperous farmer's; and we arranged that he should cut his hair close, and wear a little powder. Lastly, as he had not yet been seen by the laundress or her niece, he was to keep himself out of their view until his change of dress was made.

It would seem a simple matter to decide on these precautions; but in my dazed, not to say distracted, state, it took so long, that I did not get out to further them until two or three in the afternoon. He was to remain shut up in the chambers while I was gone, and was on no account to open the door.

There being to my knowledge a respectable lodging-house in Essex Street, the back of which looked into the Temple, and was almost within hail of my windows, I first of all repaired to that house, and was so fortunate as to secure the second floor for my uncle, Mr Provis. I then went from shop to shop, making such purchases as were necessary to the change in his appearance. This business transacted, I turned my face, on my own account, to Little Britain. Mr Jaggers was at his desk, but, seeing me enter, got up immediately and stood before his fire.

'Now, Pip,' said he, 'be careful.'

'I will, sir,' I returned. For, coming along I had thought well of what I was going to say.

'Don't commit yourself,' said Mr Jaggers, 'and don't commit any one. You understand—any one. Don't tell me anything: I don't want to know anything; I am not curious.'

Of course I saw that he knew the man was come.

'I merely want, Mr Jaggers,' said I, 'to assure myself that what I have been told is true. I have no hope of its being untrue, but at least I may verify it.'

Mr Jaggers nodded. 'But did you say "told" or "informed"?' he asked me, with his head on one side, and not looking at me, but looking in a listening way at the floor. 'Told would seem to imply verbal communication. You can't have verbal communication with a man in New South Wales, you know.'

'I will say, informed, Mr Jaggers.'

'Good.'

'I have been informed by a person named Abel Magwitch, that he is the benefactor so long unknown to me.'

'That is the man,' said Mr Jaggers, 'in New South Wales.'

'And only he?' said I.

'And only he,' said Mr Jaggers.

'I am not so unreasonable, sir, as to think you at all responsible for my mistakes and wrong conclusions; but I always supposed it was Miss Havisham.'

'As you say, Pip,' returned Mr Jaggers, turning his eyes upon me coolly, and taking a bite at his forefinger, 'I am not at all responsible for that.'

'And yet it looked so like it, sir,' I pleaded with a downcast heart.

'Not a particle of evidence, Pip,' said Mr Jaggers, shaking his head and gathering up his skirts. 'Take nothing on its looks; take everything on evidence. There's no better rule.'

'I have no more to say,' said I, with a sigh, after standing silent for a little while. 'I have verified my information, and there's an end.'

'And Magwitch—in New South Wales—having at last disclosed himself,' said Mr Jaggers, 'you will comprehend, Pip, how rigidly throughout my communication with you, I have always adhered to the strict line of fact. There has never been the least departure from the strict line of fact. You are quite aware of that?'

'Quite, sir.'

'I communicated to Magwitch—in New South Wales—when he first wrote to me—from New South Wales—the caution that he must not expect me ever to deviate from the strict line of fact. I also communicated to him another caution. He appeared to me to have obscurely hinted in his letter at some distant idea he had of seeing you in England here. I cautioned him that I must hear no more of that; that he was not at all likely to obtain a pardon; that he was expatriated for the term of his natural life; and that his presenting himself in this country would be an act of felony, rendering him liable to the extreme penalty of the law. I gave Magwitch that caution,' said Mr Jaggers, looking hard at me; 'I wrote it to New South Wales. He guided himself by it, no doubt.'

'No doubt,' said I.

'I have been informed by Wemmick,' pursued Mr Jaggers, still looking hard at me, 'that he has received a letter, under date Portsmouth, from a colonist of the name of Purvis, or—'

'Or Provis,' I suggested.

'Or Provis—thank you, Pip. Perhaps it *is* Provis? Perhaps you know it's Provis?'

'Yes,' said I.

'You know it's Provis. A letter, under date Portsmouth, from a colonist of the name of Provis, asking for the particulars of your address, on behalf of Magwitch. Wemmick sent him the particulars, I understand, by return of post. Probably it is through Provis that you have received the explanation of Magwitch—in New South Wales?'

'It came through Provis,' I replied.

'Good day, Pip,' said Mr Jaggers, offering his hand; 'glad to have seen you. In writing by post to Magwitch—in New South Wales—or in communicating with him through Provis, have the goodness to mention that the particulars and vouchers of our long account shall be sent to you, together with the balance; for there is still a balance remaining. Good day, Pip!'

We shook hands, and he looked hard at me as long as he could see me. I turned at the door, and he was still looking hard at me, while the two vile casts on the shelf seemed to be trying to get their eyelids open, and to force out of their swollen throats, 'O, what a man he is!'

Wemmick was out, and though he had been at his desk he could have done nothing for me. I went straight back to the Temple, where I found the terrible Provis drinking rum and water and smoking negro-head, in safety.

Next day the clothes I had ordered all came home, and he put them on. Whatever he put on, became him less (it dismally seemed to me) than what he had worn before. To my thinking, there was something in him that made it hopeless to attempt to disguise him. The more I dressed him and the better I dressed him, the more he looked like the slouching fugitive on the marshes. This effect on my anxious fancy was partly referable, no doubt, to his old face and manner growing more familiar to me; but I believe too that he dragged one of his legs as if there were still a weight of iron on it, and that from head to foot there was convict in the very grain of the man.

The influences of his solitary hut-life were upon him besides, and gave him a savage air that no dress could tame; added to these were the influences of his subsequent branded life among men, and, crowning all, his consciousness that he was dodging and hiding now. In all his ways of sitting and standing, and eating and drinking,—of brooding about in a high-shouldered reluctant style,—of taking out his great horn-handled jackknife and wiping it on his legs and cutting his food,—of lifting light glasses and cups to his lips, as if they were clumsy pannikins,—of chopping a wedge off his bread, and soaking up with it the last fragments of gravy round and round his plate, as if to make the most of an allowance, and then drying his finger-ends on it, and then swallowing it,—in these ways and a thousand other small nameless instances arising every minute in the day, there was Prisoner, Felon, Bondsman, plain as plain could be.

It had been his own idea to wear that touch of powder, and I had conceded the powder after overcoming the shorts. But I can compare the effect of it, when on, to nothing but the probable effect of rouge upon the dead; so awful was the manner in which everything in him that it was most desirable to repress, started through that thin layer of pretence, and seemed to come blazing out at the crown of his head. It was abandoned as soon as tried, and he wore his grizzled hair cut short.

Words cannot tell what a sense I had, at the same time, of the dreadful mystery that he was to me. When he fell asleep of an evening, with his knotted hands clenching the sides of the easy-chair, and his bald head tattooed with deep wrinkles falling forward on his breast, I would sit and look at him, wondering what he had done, and loading him with all the crimes in the calendar, until the impulse was powerful on me to start up and fly from him. Every hour so increased my abhorrence of him, that I even think I might have yielded to this impulse in the first agonies of being so haunted, notwithstanding all he had done for me and the risk he ran, but for the knowledge that Herbert must soon come back. Once, I actually did start out of bed in the night, and begin to dress myself in my worst clothes, hurriedly intending to leave him there with everything else I possessed, and enlist for India as a private soldier.

I doubt if a ghost could have been more terrible to me, up in those lonely rooms in the long evenings and long nights, with the wind and the rain always rushing by. A ghost could not have been taken and hanged on my account, and the consideration that he could be, and the dread that he would be, were no small addition to my horrors. When he was not asleep, or playing a complicated kind of Patience with a ragged pack of cards of his own,—a game that I never saw before or since, and in which he recorded his winnings by sticking his jackknife into the table,—when he was not engaged in either of these pursuits, he would ask me to read to him,—'Foreign language, dear boy!' While I complied, he, not comprehending a single word, would stand before the fire surveying me with the air of an Exhibitor, and I would see him, between the fingers of the hand with which I shaded my face, appealing in dumb show to the furniture to take notice of my proficiency. The imaginary student pursued by the misshapen creature he had impiously made, was not more wretched than I, pursued by the creature who had made me, and recoiling from him with a stronger repulsion, the more he admired me and the fonder he was of me.

This is written of, I am sensible, as if it had lasted a year. It lasted about five days. Expecting Herbert all the time, I dared not go out, except when I took Provis for an airing after dark. At length, one evening when dinner was over and I had dropped into a slumber quite worn out,—for my nights had been agitated and my rest broken by fearful dreams,—I was roused by the welcome footstep on the staircase. Provis, who had been asleep too, staggered up at the noise I made, and in an instant I saw his jackknife shining in his hand.

'Quiet! It's Herbert!' I said; and Herbert came bursting in, with the airy freshness of six hundred miles of France upon him.

'Handel, my dear fellow, how are you, and again how are you, and again how are you? I seem to have been gone a twelvemonth! Why, so I must have been, for you have grown quite thin and pale! Handel, my—Halloa! I beg your pardon.'

He was stopped in his running on and in his shaking hands with me, by seeing Provis. Provis, regarding him with a fixed attention, was slowly putting up his jackknife, and groping in another pocket for something else.

'Herbert, my dear friend,' said I, shutting the double doors, while Herbert stood staring and wondering, 'something very strange has happened. This is—a visitor of mine.'

'It's all right, dear boy!' said Provis coming forward, with his little clasped black book, and then addressing himself to Herbert. 'Take it in your right hand. Lord strike you dead on the spot, if ever you split in any way sumever! Kiss it!'

'Do so, as he wishes it,' I said to Herbert. So, Herbert, looking at me with a friendly uneasiness and amazement, complied, and Provis immediately shaking hands with him, said, 'Now you're on your oath, you know. And never believe me on mine, if Pip shan't make a gentleman on you!'

Chapter 41

In vain should I attempt to describe the astonishment and disquiet of Herbert, when he and I and Provis sat down before the fire, and I recounted the whole of the secret. Enough, that I saw my own feelings reflected in Herbert's face, and not least among them, my repugnance towards the man who had done so much for me.

What would alone have set a division between that man and us, if there had been no other dividing circumstance, was his triumph in my story. Saving his troublesome sense of having been 'low' on one occasion since his return,—on which point he began to hold forth to Herbert, the moment my revelation was finished,—he had no perception of the possibility of my finding any fault with my good fortune. His boast that he had made me a gentleman, and that he had come to see me support the character on his ample resources, was made for me quite as much as for himself. And that it was a highly agreeable boast to both of us, and that we must both be very proud of it, was a conclusion quite established in his own mind.

'Though, look'ee here, Pip's comrade,' he said to Herbert, after having discoursed for some time, 'I know very well that once since I come back—for half a minute—I've been low. I said to Pip, I knowed as I had been low. But don't you fret yourself on that score. I ain't made Pip a gentleman, and Pip ain't a going to make you a gentleman, not fur me not to know what's due to ye both. Dear boy, and Pip's comrade, you two may count upon me always having a gen-teel muzzle on. Muzzled I have been since that half a minute when I was betrayed into lowness, muzzled I am at the present time, muzzled I ever will be.'

Herbert said, 'Certainly,' but looked as if there were no specific consolation in this, and remained perplexed and dismayed. We were anxious for the time when he would go to his lodging and leave us together, but he was evidently jealous of leaving us together, and sat late. It was midnight before I took him round to Essex Street, and saw him safely in at his own dark door. When it closed upon him, I experienced the first moment of relief I had known since the night of his arrival.

Never quite free from an uneasy remembrance of the man on the stairs, I had always looked about me in taking my guest out after dark, and in bringing him back; and I looked about me now. Difficult as it is in a large city to avoid the suspicion of being watched, when the mind is conscious of danger in that regard, I could not persuade myself that any of the people within sight cared about my movements. The few who were passing passed on their several ways, and the street was empty when I turned back into the Temple. Nobody had come out at the gate with us, nobody went in at the gate with me. As I crossed by the fountain, I saw his lighted back windows looking bright and quiet, and, when I stood for a few moments in the doorway of the building where I lived, before going up the stairs, Garden Court was as still and lifeless as the staircase was when I ascended it.

Herbert received me with open arms, and I had never felt before so blessedly what it is to have a friend. When he had spoken some sound words of sympathy and encouragement, we sat down to consider the question, What was to be done?

The chair that Provis had occupied still remaining where it had stood,—for he had a barrack way with him of hanging about one spot, in one unsettled manner, and going through one round of observances with his pipe and his negro-head and his jackknife and his pack of cards, and what not, as if it were all put down for him on a slate,—I say his chair remaining where it had stood, Herbert unconsciously took it, but next moment started out of it, pushed it away, and took another. He had no occasion to say after that that he had conceived an aversion for my patron, neither had I occasion to confess my own. We interchanged that confidence without shaping a syllable.

'What,' said I to Herbert, when he was safe in another chair,—'what is to be done?'

'My poor dear Handel,' he replied, holding his head, 'I am too stunned to think.'

'So was I, Herbert, when the blow first fell. Still, something must be done. He is intent upon various new expenses,—horses, and carriages, and lavish appearances of all kinds. He must be stopped somehow.'

'You mean that you can't accept—'

'How can I?' I interposed, as Herbert paused. 'Think of him! Look at him!'

An involuntary shudder passed over both of us.

'Yet I am afraid the dreadful truth is, Herbert, that he is attached to me, strongly attached to me. Was there ever such a fate!'

'My poor dear Handel,' Herbert repeated.

'Then,' said I, 'after all, stopping short here, never taking another penny from him, think what I owe him already! Then again: I am heavily in debt,—very heavily for me, who have now no expectations,—and I have been bred to no calling, and I am fit for nothing.'

'Well, well, well!' Herbert remonstrated. 'Don't say fit for nothing.'

'What am I fit for? I know only one thing that I am fit for, and that is, to go for a soldier. And I might have gone, my dear Herbert, but for the prospect of taking counsel with your friendship and affection.'

Of course I broke down there: and of course Herbert, beyond seizing a warm grip of my hand, pretended not to know it.

'Anyhow, my dear Handel,' said he presently, 'soldiering won't do. If you were to renounce this patronage and these favours, I suppose you would do so with some faint hope of one day repaying what you have already had. Not very strong, that hope, if you went soldiering! Besides, it's absurd. You would be infinitely better in Clarriker's house, small as it is. I am working up towards a partnership, you know.'

Poor fellow! He little suspected with whose money.

'But there is another question,' said Herbert. 'This is an ignorant, determined man, who has long had one fixed idea. More than that, he seems to me (I may misjudge him) to be a man of a desperate and fierce character.'

'I know he is,' I returned. 'Let me tell you what evidence I have seen of it.' And I told him what I had not mentioned in my narrative, of that encounter with the other convict.

'See, then,' said Herbert; 'think of this! He comes here at the peril of his life, for the realization of his fixed idea. In the moment of realization, after all his toil and waiting, you cut the ground from under his feet, destroy his idea, and make his gains worthless to him. Do you see nothing that he might do, under the disappointment?'

'I have seen it, Herbert, and dreamed of it, ever since the fatal night of his arrival. Nothing has been in my thoughts so distinctly as his putting himself in the way of being taken.'

'Then you may rely upon it,' said Herbert, 'that there would be great danger of his doing it. That is his power over you as long as he remains in England, and that would be his reckless course if you forsook him.'

I was so struck by the horror of this idea, which had weighed upon me from the first, and the working out of which would make me regard myself, in some sort, as his murderer, that I could not rest in my chair, but began pacing to and fro. I said to Herbert, meanwhile, that even if Provis were recognized and taken, in spite of himself, I should be wretched as the cause, however innocently. Yes; even though I was so wretched in having him at large and near me, and even though I would far rather have worked at the forge all the days of my life than I would ever have come to this!

But there was no staving off the question, What was to be done?

'The first and the main thing to be done,' said Herbert, 'is to get him out of England. You will have to go with him, and then he may be induced to go.'

'But get him where I will, could I prevent his coming back?'

'My good Handel, is it not obvious that with Newgate in the next street, there must be far greater hazard in your breaking your mind to him and making him reckless, here, than elsewhere? If a pretext to get him away could be made out of that other convict, or out of anything else in his life, now.'

'There, again!' said I, stopping before Herbert, with my open hands held out, as if they contained the desperation of the case. 'I know nothing of his life. It has almost made me mad to sit here of a night and see him before me, so bound up with my fortunes and misfortunes, and yet so unknown to me, except as the miserable wretch who terrified me two days in my childhood!'

Herbert got up, and linked his arm in mine, and we slowly walked to and fro together, studying the carpet.

'Handel,' said Herbert, stopping, 'you feel convinced that you can take no further benefits from him; do you?'

'Fully. Surely you would, too, if you were in my place?'

'And you feel convinced that you must break with him?'

'Herbert, can you ask me?'

'And you have, and are bound to have, that tenderness for the life he has risked on your account, that you must save him, if possible, from throwing it away. Then you must get him out of England before you stir a finger to extricate yourself. That done, extricate yourself, in Heaven's name, and we'll see it out together, dear old boy.'

It was a comfort to shake hands upon it, and walk up and down again, with only that done.

'Now, Herbert,' said I, 'with reference to gaining some knowledge of his history. There is but one way that I know of. I must ask him point blank.'

'Yes. Ask him,' said Herbert, 'when we sit at breakfast in the morning.' For he had said, on taking leave of Herbert, that he would come to breakfast with us.

With this project formed, we went to bed. I had the wildest dreams concerning him, and woke unrefreshed; I woke, too, to recover the fear which I had lost in the night, of his being found out as a returned transport. Waking, I never lost that fear.

He came round at the appointed time, took out his jackknife, and sat down to his meal. He was full of plans 'for his gentleman's coming out strong, and like a gentleman,' and urged me to begin speedily upon the pocket-book which he had left in my possession. He considered the chambers and his own lodging as temporary residences, and advised me to look out at once for a 'fashionable crib' near Hyde Park, in which he could have 'a shake-down.' When he had made an end of his breakfast, and was wiping his knife on his leg, I said to him, without a word of preface,—

'After you were gone last night, I told my friend of the struggle that the soldiers found you engaged in on the marshes, when we came up. You remember?'

'Remember!' said he. 'I think so!'

'We want to know something about that man—and about you. It is strange to know no more about either, and particularly you, than I was able to tell last night. Is not this as good a time as another for our knowing more?'

'Well!' he said, after consideration. 'You're on your oath, you know, Pip's comrade?'

'Assuredly,' replied Herbert.

'As to anything I say, you know,' he insisted. 'The oath applies to all.'

'I understand it to do so.'

'And look'ee here! Wotever I done is worked out and paid for,' he insisted again.

'So be it.'

He took out his black pipe and was going to fill it with negro-head, when, looking at the tangle of tobacco in his hand, he seemed to think it might perplex the thread of his narrative. He put it back again, stuck his pipe in a button-hole of his coat, spread a hand on each knee, and after turning an angry eye on the fire for a few silent moments, looked round at us and said what follows.

Chapter 42

'Dear boy and Pip's comrade. I am not a going fur to tell you my life like a song, or a story-book. But to give it you short and handy, I'll put it at once into a mouthful of English. In jail and out of jail, in jail and out of jail, in jail and out of jail. There, you've got it. That's *my* life pretty much, down to such times as I got shipped off, arter Pip stood my friend.

'I've been done everything to, pretty well—except hanged. I've been locked up as much as a silver tea-kittle. I've been carted here and carted there, and put out of this town, and put out of that town, and stuck in the stocks, and whipped and worried and drove. I've no more notion where I was born than you have—if so much. I first become aware of myself down in Essex, a thieving turnips for my living. Summun had run away from me—a man—a tinker—and he'd took the fire with him, and left me wery cold.

'I know'd my name to be Magwitch, chrisen'd Abel. How did I know it? Much as I know'd the birds' names in the hedges to be chaffinch, sparrer, thrush. I might have thought it was all lies together, only as the birds' names come out true, I supposed mine did.

'So fur as I could find, there warn't a soul that see young Abel Magwitch, with us little on him as in him, but wot caught fright at him, and either drove him off, or took him up. I was took up, took up, took up, to that extent that I reg'larly grow'd up took up.

'This is the way it was, that when I was a ragged little creetur as much to be pitied as ever I see (not that I looked in the glass, for there warn't many insides of furnished houses known to me), I got the name of being hardened. 'This is a terrible hardened one,' they says to prison wisitors, picking out me. 'May be said to live in jails, this boy.' Then they looked at me, and I looked at them, and they measured my head, some on 'em,—they had better a measured my stomach,—and others on 'em giv me tracts what I couldn't read, and made me speeches what I couldn't understand. They always went on agen me about the Devil. But what the Devil was I to do? I must put something into my stomach, mustn't I?—Howsomever, I'm a getting low, and I know what's due. Dear boy and Pip's comrade, don't you be afeerd of me being low.

'Tramping, begging, thieving, working sometimes when I could,—though that warn't as often as you may think, till you put the question whether you would ha' been over-ready to give me work yourselves,—a bit of a poacher, a bit of a labourer, a bit of a wagoner, a bit of a haymaker, a bit of a hawker, a bit of most things that don't pay and lead to trouble, I got to be a man. A deserting soldier in a Traveller's Rest, what lay hid up to the chin under a lot of taturs, learnt me to read; and a travelling Giant what signed his name at a penny a time learnt me to write. I warn't locked up as often now as formerly, but I wore out my good share of key-metal still.

'At Epsom races, a matter of over twenty years ago, I got acquainted wi' a man whose skull I'd crack wi' this poker, like the claw of a lobster, if I'd got it on this hob. His right name was Compeyson; and that's the man, dear boy, what you see me a pounding in the ditch, according to what you truly told your comrade arter I was gone last night.

'He set up fur a gentleman, this Compeyson, and he'd been to a public boarding-school and had learning. He was a smooth one to talk, and was a dab at the ways of gentlefolks. He was good-looking too. It was the night afore the great race, when I found him on the heath, in a booth that I know'd on. Him and some more was a sitting among the tables when I went in, and the landlord (which had a knowledge of me, and was a sporting one) called him out, and said, 'I think this is a man that might suit you,'—meaning I was.

'Compeyson, he looks at me very noticing, and I look at him. He has a watch and a chain and a ring and a breast-pin and a handsome suit of clothes.

"To judge from appearances, you're out of luck," says Compeyson to me.

"Yes, master, and I've never been in it much." (I had come out of Kingston Jail last on a vagrancy committal. Not but what it might have been for something else; but it warn't.)

"Luck changes," says Compeyson; "perhaps yours is going to change."

'I says, "I hope it may be so. There's room."

"What can you do?" says Compeyson.

"Eat and drink," I says; "if you'll find the materials."

'Compeyson laughed, looked at me again very noticing, giv me five shillings, and appointed me for next night. Same place.

'I went to Compeyson next night, same place, and Compeyson took me on to be his man and pardner. And what was Compeyson's business in which we was to go pardners? Compeyson's business was the swindling, handwriting forging, stolen bank-note passing, and such-like. All sorts of traps as Compeyson could set with his head, and keep his own legs out of and get the profits from and let another man in for, was Compeyson's business. He'd no more heart than a iron file, he was as cold as death, and he had the head of the Devil afore mentioned.

'There was another in with Compeyson, as was called Arthur,—not as being so chrisen'd, but as a surname. He was in a Decline, and was a shadow to look at. Him and Compeyson had been in a bad thing with a rich lady some years afore, and they'd made a pot of money by it; but Compeyson betted and gamed, and he'd have run through the king's taxes. So, Arthur was a dying, and a dying poor and with the horrors on him, and Compeyson's wife (which Compeyson kicked mostly) was a having pity on him when she could, and Compeyson was a having pity on nothing and nobody.

'I might a took warning by Arthur, but I didn't; and I won't pretend I was partick'ler—for where 'ud be the good on it, dear boy and comrade? So I begun wi' Compeyson, and a poor tool I was in his hands. Arthur lived at the top of Compeyson's house (over nigh Brentford it was), and Compeyson kept a careful account agen him for board and lodging, in case he should ever get better to work it out. But Arthur soon settled the account. The second or third time as ever I see him, he come a tearing down into Compeyson's parlor late at night, in only a flannel gown, with his hair all in a sweat, and he says to Compeyson's wife, "Sally, she really is upstairs alonger me, now, and I can't get rid of her. She's all in white," he says, "wi' white flowers in her hair, and she's awful mad, and she's got a shroud hanging over her arm, and she says she'll put it on me at five in the morning."

'Says Compeyson: "Why, you fool, don't you know she's got a living body? And how should she be up there, without coming through the door, or in at the window, and up the stairs?"

"I don't know how she's there," says Arthur, shivering dreadful with the horrors, "but she's standing in the corner at the foot of the bed, awful mad. And over where her heart's broke—*you* broke it!—there's drops of blood."

'Compeyson spoke hardy, but he was always a coward. "Go up alonger this drivelling sick man," he says to his wife, "and Magwitch, lend her a hand, will you?" But he never come nigh himself.

'Compeyson's wife and me took him up to bed agen, and he raved most dreadful. "Why look at her!" he cries out. "She's a shaking the shroud at me! Don't you see her? Look at her eyes! Ain't it awful to see her so mad?" Next he cries, "She'll put it on me, and then I'm done for! Take it away from her, take it away!" And then he catched hold of us, and kep on a talking to her, and answering of her, till I half believed I see her myself.

'Compeyson's wife, being used to him, giv him some liquor to get the horrors off, and by and by he quieted. "O, she's gone! Has her keeper been for her?" he says. "Yes," says Compeyson's wife. "Did you tell him to lock her and bar her in?" "Yes." "And to take that ugly thing away from her?" "Yes, yes, all right." "You're a good creetur," he says, "don't leave me, whatever you do, and thank you!"

'He rested pretty quiet till it might want a few minutes of five, and then he starts up with a scream, and screams out, "Here she is! She's got the shroud again. She's unfolding it. She's coming out of the corner. She's coming to the bed. Hold me, both on you—one of each side—don't let her touch me with it. Hah! she missed me that time. Don't let her throw it over my shoulders. Don't let her lift me up to get it round me. She's lifting me up. Keep me down!" Then he lifted himself up hard, and was dead.

'Compeyson took it easy as a good riddance for both sides. Him and me was soon busy, and first he swore me (being ever artful) on my own book,—this here little black book, dear boy, what I swore your comrade on.

'Not to go into the things that Compeyson planned, and I done— which 'ud take a week—I'll simply say to you, dear boy, and Pip's comrade, that that man got me into such nets as made me his black slave. I was always in debt to him, always under his thumb, always a working, always a getting into danger. He was younger than me, but he'd got craft, and he'd got learning, and he overmatched me five hundred times told and no mercy. My Missis as I had the hard time wi'—Stop though! I ain't brought *her* in—'

He looked about him in a confused way, as if he had lost his place in the book of his remembrance; and he turned his face to the fire, and spread his hands broader on his knees, and lifted them off and put them on again.

"There ain't no need to go into it," he said, looking round once more. "The time wi' Compeyson was a'most as hard a time as ever I had; that said, all's said. Did I tell you as I was tried, alone, for misdemeanor, while with Compeyson?"

I answered, No.

"Well!" he said, "I *was*, and got convicted. As to took up on suspicion, that was twice or three times in the four or five year that it lasted; but evidence was wanting. At last, me and Compeyson was both committed for felony,—on a charge of putting stolen notes in circulation,—and there was other charges behind. Compeyson says to me, "Separate defences, no communication," and that was all. And I was so miserable poor, that I sold all the clothes I had, except what hung on my back, afore I could get Jaggers.

'When we was put in the dock, I noticed first of all what a gentleman Compeyson looked, wi' his curly hair and his black clothes and his white pocket-handkercher, and what a common sort of a wretch I looked. When the prosecution opened and the evidence was put short, aforehand, I noticed how heavy it all bore on me, and how light on him. When the evidence was giv in the box, I noticed how it was always me that had come for'ard, and could be swore to, how it was always me that the money had been paid to, how it was always me that had seemed to work the thing and get the profit. But when the defence come on, then I see the plan plainer; for, says the counsellor for Compeyson, "My lord and gentlemen, here you has afore you, side by side, two persons as your eyes can separate wide; one, the younger, well brought up, who will be spoke to as such; one, the elder, ill brought up, who will be spoke to as such; one, the younger, seldom if ever seen in these here transactions, and only suspected; t'other, the elder, always seen in 'em and always wi' his guilt brought home. Can you doubt, if there is but one in it, which is the one, and, if there is two in it, which is much the worst one?" And such-like. And when it come to character, warn't it Compeyson as had been to the school, and warn't it his schoolfellows as was in this position and in that, and warn't it him as had been know'd by witnesses in such clubs and societies, and nowt to his disadvantage? And warn't it me as had been tried afore, and as had been know'd up hill and down dale in Bridewells and Lock-Ups! And when it come to speech-making, warn't it Compeyson as could speak to 'em wi' his face dropping every now and then into his white pocket-handkercher,—ah! and wi' verses in his speech, too,—and warn't it me as could only say, "Gentlemen, this man at my side is a most precious rascal?" And when the verdict come, warn't it Compeyson as was recommended to mercy on account of good character and bad company, and giving up all the information he could agen me, and warn't it me as got never a word but Guilty? And when I says to Compeyson, "Once out of this court, I'll smash that face of yourn!" ain't it Compeyson as prays the Judge to be protected, and gets two turnkeys stood betwixt us? And when we're sentenced, ain't it him as gets seven year, and me fourteen, and ain't it him as the Judge is sorry for, because he might a done so well, and ain't it me as the Judge perceives to be a old offender of wiolent passion, likely to come to worse?'

He had worked himself into a state of great excitement, but he checked it, took two or three short breaths, swallowed as often, and stretching out his hand towards me said, in a reassuring manner, 'I ain't a going to be low, dear boy!'

He had so heated himself that he took out his handkerchief and wiped his face and head and neck and hands, before he could go on.

'I had said to Compeyson that I'd smash that face of his, and I swore Lord smash mine! to do it. We was in the same prison-ship, but I couldn't get at him for long, though I tried. At last I come behind him and hit him on the cheek to turn him round and get a smashing one at him, when I was seen and seized. The black-hole of that ship warn't a strong one, to a judge of black-holes that could swim and dive. I escaped to the shore, and I was a hiding among the graves there, envying them as was in 'em and all over, when I first see my boy!'

He regarded me with a look of affection that made him almost abhorrent to me again, though I had felt great pity for him.

'By my boy, I was giv to understand as Compeyson was out on them marshes too. Upon my soul, I half believe he escaped in his terror, to get quit of me, not knowing it was me as had got ashore. I hunted him down. I smashed his face. "And now," says I "as the worst thing I can do, caring nothing for myself, I'll drag you back." And I'd have swum off, towing him by the hair, if it had come to that, and I'd a got him aboard without the soldiers.

'Of course he'd much the best of it to the last,—his character was so good. He had escaped when he was made half wild by me and my murderous intentions; and his punishment was light. I was put in irons, brought to trial again, and sent for life. I didn't stop for life, dear boy and Pip's comrade, being here.'

He wiped himself again, as he had done before, and then slowly took his tangle of tobacco from his pocket, and plucked his pipe from his button-hole, and slowly filled it, and began to smoke.

'Is he dead?' I asked, after a silence.

'Is who dead, dear boy?'

'Compeyson.'

'He hopes *I* am, if he's alive, you may be sure,' with a fierce look. 'I never heerd no more of him.'

Herbert had been writing with his pencil in the cover of a book. He softly pushed the book over to me, as Provis stood smoking with his eyes on the fire, and I read in it:—

'Young Havisham's name was Arthur. Compeyson is the man who professed to be Miss Havisham's lover.'

I shut the book and nodded slightly to Herbert, and put the book by; but we neither of us said anything, and both looked at Provis as he stood smoking by the fire.

Chapter 43

Why should I pause to ask how much of my shrinking from Provis might be traced to Estella? Why should I loiter on my road, to compare the state of mind in which I had tried to rid myself of the stain of the prison before meeting her at the coach-office, with the state of mind in which I now reflected on the abyss between Estella in her pride and beauty, and the returned transport whom I harbored? The road would be none the smoother for it, the end would be none the better for it, he would not be helped, nor I extenuated.

A new fear had been engendered in my mind by his narrative; or rather, his narrative had given form and purpose to the fear that was already there. If Compeyson were alive and should discover his return, I could hardly doubt the consequence. That Compeyson stood in mortal fear of him, neither of the two could know much better than I; and that any such man as that man had been described to be would hesitate to release himself for good from a dreaded enemy by the safe means of becoming an informer was scarcely to be imagined.

Never had I breathed, and never would I breathe—or so I resolved—a word of Estella to Provis. But, I said to Herbert that, before I could go abroad, I must see both Estella and Miss Havisham. This was when we were left alone on the night of the day when Provis told us his story. I resolved to go out to Richmond next day, and I went.

On my presenting myself at Mrs Brandley's, Estella's maid was called to tell that Estella had gone into the country. Where? To Satis House, as usual. Not as usual, I said, for she had never yet gone there without me; when was she coming back? There was an air of reservation in the answer which increased my perplexity, and the answer was, that her maid believed she was only coming back at all for a little while. I could make nothing of this, except that it was meant that I should make nothing of it, and I went home again in complete discomfiture.

Another night consultation with Herbert after Provis was gone home (I always took him home, and always looked well about me), led us to the conclusion that nothing should be said about going abroad until I came back from Miss Havisham's. In the mean time, Herbert and I were to consider separately what it would be best to say; whether we should devise any pretence of being afraid that he was under suspicious observation; or whether I, who had never yet been abroad, should propose an expedition. We both knew that I had but to propose anything, and he would consent. We agreed that his remaining many days in his present hazard was not to be thought of.

Next day I had the meanness to feign that I was under a binding promise to go down to Joe; but I was capable of almost any meanness towards Joe or his name. Provis was to be strictly careful while I was gone, and Herbert was to take the charge of him that I had taken. I was to be absent only one night, and, on my return, the gratification of his impatience for my starting as a gentleman on a greater scale was to be begun. It occurred to me then, and as I afterwards found to Herbert also, that he might be best got away across the water, on that pretence,—as, to make purchases, or the like.

Having thus cleared the way for my expedition to Miss Havisham's, I set off by the early morning coach before it was yet light, and was out on the open country road when the day came creeping on, halting and whimpering and shivering, and wrapped in patches of cloud and rags of mist, like a beggar. When we drove up to the Blue Boar after a drizzly ride, whom should I see come out under the gateway, toothpick in hand, to look at the coach, but Bentley Drummle!

As he pretended not to see me, I pretended not to see him. It was a very lame pretence on both sides; the lamer, because we both went into the coffee-room, where he had just finished his breakfast, and where I ordered mine. It was poisonous to me to see him in the town, for I very well knew why he had come there.

Pretending to read a smeary newspaper long out of date, which had nothing half so legible in its local news, as the foreign matter of coffee, pickles, fish sauces, gravy, melted butter, and wine with which it was sprinkled all over, as if it had taken the measles in a highly irregular form, I sat at my table while he stood before the fire. By degrees it became an enormous injury to me that he stood before the fire. And I got up, determined to have my share of it. I had to put my hand behind his legs for the poker when I went up to the fireplace to stir the fire, but still pretended not to know him.

'Is this a cut?' said Mr Drummle.

'Oh!' said I, poker in hand; 'it's you, is it? How do you do? I was wondering who it was, who kept the fire off.'

With that, I poked tremendously, and having done so, planted myself side by side with Mr Drummle, my shoulders squared and my back to the fire.

'You have just come down?' said Mr Drummle, edging me a little away with his shoulder.

'Yes,' said I, edging *him* a little away with *my* shoulder.

'Beastly place,' said Drummle. 'Your part of the country, I think?'

'Yes,' I assented. 'I am told it's very like your Shropshire.'

'Not in the least like it,' said Drummle.

Here Mr Drummle looked at his boots and I looked at mine, and then Mr Drummle looked at my boots, and I looked at his.

'Have you been here long?' I asked, determined not to yield an inch of the fire.

'Long enough to be tired of it,' returned Drummle, pretending to yawn, but equally determined.

'Do you stay here long?'

'Can't say,' answered Mr Drummle. 'Do you?'

'Can't say,' said I.

I felt here, through a tingling in my blood, that if Mr Drummle's shoulder had claimed another hair's breadth of room, I should have jerked him into the window; equally, that if my own shoulder had urged a similar claim, Mr Drummle would have jerked me into the nearest box. He whistled a little. So did I.

'Large tract of marshes about here, I believe?' said Drummle.

'Yes. What of that?' said I.

Mr Drummle looked at me, and then at my boots, and then said, 'Oh!' and laughed.

'Are you amused, Mr Drummle?'

'No,' said he, 'not particularly. I am going out for a ride in the saddle. I mean to explore those marshes for amusement. Out-of-the-way villages there, they tell me. Curious little public-houses—and smithies—and that. Waiter!'

'Yes, sir.'

'Is that horse of mine ready?'

'Brought round to the door, sir.'

'I say. Look here, you sir. The lady won't ride today; the weather won't do.'

'Very good, sir.'

'And I don't dine, because I'm going to dine at the lady's.'

'Very good, sir.'

Then, Drummle glanced at me, with an insolent triumph on his great-jowled face that cut me to the heart, dull as he was, and so exasperated me, that I felt inclined to take him in my arms (as the robber in the story-book is said to have taken the old lady) and seat him on the fire.

One thing was manifest to both of us, and that was, that until relief came, neither of us could relinquish the fire. There we stood, well squared up before it, shoulder to shoulder and foot to foot, with our hands behind us, not budging an inch. The horse was visible outside in the drizzle at the door, my breakfast was put on the table, Drummle's was cleared away, the waiter invited me to begin, I nodded, we both stood our ground.

'Have you been to the Grove since?' said Drummle.

'No,' said I, 'I had quite enough of the Finches the last time I was there.'

'Was that when we had a difference of opinion?'

'Yes,' I replied, very shortly.

'Come, come! They let you off easily enough,' sneered Drummle. 'You shouldn't have lost your temper.'

'Mr Drummle,' said I, 'you are not competent to give advice on that subject. When I lose my temper (not that I admit having done so on that occasion), I don't throw glasses.'

'I do,' said Drummle.

After glancing at him once or twice, in an increased state of smouldering ferocity, I said,—

'Mr Drummle, I did not seek this conversation, and I don't think it an agreeable one.'

'I am sure it's not,' said he, superciliously over his shoulder; 'I don't think anything about it.'

'And therefore,' I went on, 'with your leave, I will suggest that we hold no kind of communication in future.'

'Quite my opinion,' said Drummle, 'and what I should have suggested myself, or done—more likely—without suggesting. But don't lose your temper. Haven't you lost enough without that?'

'What do you mean, sir?'

'Waiter!' said Drummle, by way of answering me.

The waiter reappeared.

'Look here, you sir. You quite understand that the young lady don't ride today, and that I dine at the young lady's?'

'Quite so, sir!'

When the waiter had felt my fast-cooling teapot with the palm of his hand, and had looked imploringly at me, and had gone out, Drummle, careful not to move the shoulder next me, took a cigar from his pocket and bit the end off, but showed no sign of stirring. Choking and boiling as I was, I felt that we could not go a word further, without introducing Estella's name, which I could not endure to hear him utter; and therefore I looked stonily at the opposite wall, as if there were no one present, and forced myself to silence. How long we might have remained in this ridiculous position it is impossible to say, but for the incursion of three thriving farmers—laid on by the waiter, I think—who came into the coffee-room unbuttoning their great-coats and rubbing their hands, and before whom, as they charged at the fire, we were obliged to give way.

I saw him through the window, seizing his horse's mane, and mounting in his blundering brutal manner, and sidling and backing away. I thought he was gone, when he came back, calling for a light for the cigar in his mouth, which he had forgotten. A man in a dust-coloured dress appeared with what was wanted,—I could not have said from where: whether from the inn yard, or the street, or where not,—and as Drummle leaned down from the saddle and lighted his cigar and laughed, with a jerk of his head towards the coffee-room windows, the slouching shoulders and ragged hair of this man whose back was towards me reminded me of Orlick.

Too heavily out of sorts to care much at the time whether it were he or no, or after all to touch the breakfast, I washed the weather and the journey from my face and hands, and went out to the memorable old house that it would have been so much the better for me never to have entered, never to have seen.

Chapter 44

In the room where the dressing-table stood, and where the wax-candles burnt on the wall, I found Miss Havisham and Estella; Miss Havisham seated on a settee near the fire, and Estella on a cushion at her feet. Estella was knitting, and Miss Havisham was looking on. They both raised their eyes as I went in, and both saw an alteration in me. I derived that, from the look they interchanged.

'And what wind,' said Miss Havisham, 'blows you here, Pip?'

Though she looked steadily at me, I saw that she was rather confused. Estella, pausing a moment in her knitting with her eyes upon me, and then going on, I fancied that I read in the action of her fingers, as plainly as if she had told me in the dumb alphabet, that she perceived I had discovered my real benefactor.

'Miss Havisham,' said I, 'I went to Richmond yesterday, to speak to Estella; and finding that some wind had blown *her* here, I followed.'

Miss Havisham motioning to me for the third or fourth time to sit down, I took the chair by the dressing-table, which I had often seen her occupy. With all that ruin at my feet and about me, it seemed a natural place for me, that day.

'What I had to say to Estella, Miss Havisham, I will say before you, presently—in a few moments. It will not surprise you, it will not displease you. I am as unhappy as you can ever have meant me to be.'

Miss Havisham continued to look steadily at me. I could see in the action of Estella's fingers as they worked that she attended to what I said; but she did not look up.

'I have found out who my patron is. It is not a fortunate discovery, and is not likely ever to enrich me in reputation, station, fortune, anything. There are reasons why I must say no more of that. It is not my secret, but another's.'

As I was silent for a while, looking at Estella and considering how to go on, Miss Havisham repeated, 'It is not your secret, but another's. Well?'

'When you first caused me to be brought here, Miss Havisham, when I belonged to the village over yonder, that I wish I had never left, I suppose I did really come here, as any other chance boy might have come,—as a kind of servant, to gratify a want or a whim, and to be paid for it?'

'Ay, Pip,' replied Miss Havisham, steadily nodding her head; 'you did.'

'And that Mr Jaggers—'

'Mr Jaggers,' said Miss Havisham, taking me up in a firm tone, 'had nothing to do with it, and knew nothing of it. His being my lawyer, and his being the lawyer of your patron is a coincidence. He holds the same relation towards numbers of people, and it might easily arise. Be that as it may, it did arise, and was not brought about by anyone.'

Anyone might have seen in her haggard face that there was no suppression or evasion so far.

'But when I fell into the mistake I have so long remained in, at least you led me on?' said I.

'Yes,' she returned, again nodding steadily, 'I let you go on.'

'Was that kind?'

'Who am I,' cried Miss Havisham, striking her stick upon the floor and flashing into wrath so suddenly that Estella glanced up at her in surprise,—'who am I, for God's sake, that I should be kind?'

It was a weak complaint to have made, and I had not meant to make it. I told her so, as she sat brooding after this outburst.

'Well, well, well!' she said. 'What else?'

'I was liberally paid for my old attendance here,' I said, to soothe her, 'in being apprenticed, and I have asked these questions only for my own information. What follows has another (and I hope more disinterested) purpose. In humouring my mistake, Miss Havisham, you punished—practised on—perhaps you will supply whatever term expresses your intention, without offence—your self-seeking relations?'

'I did. Why, they would have it so! So would you. What has been my history, that I should be at the pains of entreating either them or you not to have it so! You made your own snares. *I* never made them.'

Waiting until she was quiet again,—for this, too, flashed out of her in a wild and sudden way,—I went on.

'I have been thrown among one family of your relations, Miss Havisham, and have been constantly among them since I went to London. I know them to have been as honestly under my delusion as I myself. And I should be false and base if I did not tell you, whether it is acceptable to you or no, and whether you are inclined to give credence to it or no, that you deeply wrong both Mr Matthew Pocket and his son Herbert, if you suppose them to be otherwise than generous, upright, open, and incapable of anything designing or mean.'

'They are your friends,' said Miss Havisham.

'They made themselves my friends,' said I, 'when they supposed me to have superseded them; and when Sarah Pocket, Miss Georgiana, and Mistress Camilla were not my friends, I think.'

This contrasting of them with the rest seemed, I was glad to see, to do them good with her. She looked at me keenly for a little while, and then said quietly,—

'What do you want for them?'

'Only,' said I, 'that you would not confound them with the others. They may be of the same blood, but, believe me, they are not of the same nature.'

Still looking at me keenly, Miss Havisham repeated,—

'What do you want for them?'

'I am not so cunning, you see,' I said, in answer, conscious that I reddened a little, 'as that I could hide from you, even if I desired, that I do want something. Miss Havisham, if you would spare the money to do my friend Herbert a lasting service in life, but which from the nature of the case must be done without his knowledge, I could show you how.'

'Why must it be done without his knowledge?' she asked, settling her hands upon her stick, that she might regard me the more attentively.

'Because,' said I, 'I began the service myself, more than two years ago, without his knowledge, and I don't want to be betrayed. Why I fail in my ability to finish it, I cannot explain. It is a part of the secret which is another person's and not mine.'

She gradually withdrew her eyes from me, and turned them on the fire. After watching it for what appeared in the silence and by the light of the slowly wasting candles to be a long time, she was roused by the collapse of some of the red coals, and looked towards me again—at first, vacantly—then, with a gradually concentrating attention. All this time Estella knitted on. When Miss Havisham had fixed her attention on me, she said, speaking as if there had been no lapse in our dialogue,—

'What else?'

'Estella,' said I, turning to her now, and trying to command my trembling voice, 'you know I love you. You know that I have loved you long and dearly.'

She raised her eyes to my face, on being thus addressed, and her fingers plied their work, and she looked at me with an unmoved countenance. I saw that Miss Havisham glanced from me to her, and from her to me.

'I should have said this sooner, but for my long mistake. It induced me to hope that Miss Havisham meant us for one another. While I thought you could not help yourself, as it were, I refrained from saying it. But I must say it now.'

Preserving her unmoved countenance, and with her fingers still going, Estella shook her head.

'I know,' said I, in answer to that action,—'I know. I have no hope that I shall ever call you mine, Estella. I am ignorant what may become of me very soon, how poor I may be, or where I may go. Still, I love you. I have loved you ever since I first saw you in this house.'

Looking at me perfectly unmoved and with her fingers busy, she shook her head again.

'It would have been cruel in Miss Havisham, horribly cruel, to practise on the susceptibility of a poor boy, and to torture me through all these years with a vain hope and an idle pursuit, if she had reflected on the gravity of what she did. But I think she did not. I think that, in the endurance of her own trial, she forgot mine, Estella.'

I saw Miss Havisham put her hand to her heart and hold it there, as she sat looking by turns at Estella and at me.

'It seems,' said Estella, very calmly, 'that there are sentiments, fancies,—I don't know how to call them,—which I am not able to comprehend. When you say you love me, I know what you mean, as a form of words; but nothing more. You address nothing in my breast, you touch nothing there. I don't care for what you say at all. I have tried to warn you of this; now, have I not?'

I said in a miserable manner, 'Yes.'

'Yes. But you would not be warned, for you thought I did not mean it. Now, did you not think so?'

'I thought and hoped you could not mean it. You, so young, untried, and beautiful, Estella! Surely it is not in Nature.'

'It is in *my* nature,' she returned. And then she added, with a stress upon the words, 'It is in the nature formed within me. I make a great difference between you and all other people when I say so much. I can do no more.'

'Is it not true,' said I, 'that Bentley Drummle is in town here, and pursuing you?'

'It is quite true,' she replied, referring to him with the indifference of utter contempt.

'That you encourage him, and ride out with him, and that he dines with you this very day?'

She seemed a little surprised that I should know it, but again replied, 'Quite true.'

'You cannot love him, Estella!'

Her fingers stopped for the first time, as she retorted rather angrily, 'What have I told you? Do you still think, in spite of it, that I do not mean what I say?'

'You would never marry him, Estella?'

She looked towards Miss Havisham, and considered for a moment with her work in her hands. Then she said, 'Why not tell you the truth? I am going to be married to him.'

I dropped my face into my hands, but was able to control myself better than I could have expected, considering what agony it gave me to hear her say those words. When I raised my face again, there was such a ghastly look upon Miss Havisham's, that it impressed me, even in my passionate hurry and grief.

'Estella, dearest Estella, do not let Miss Havisham lead you into this fatal step. Put me aside forever,—you have done so, I well know,—but bestow yourself on some worthier person than Drummle. Miss Havisham gives you to him, as the greatest slight and injury that could be done to the many far better men who admire you, and to the few who truly love you. Among those few there may be one who loves you even as dearly, though he has not loved you as long, as I. Take him, and I can bear it better, for your sake!'

My earnestness awoke a wonder in her that seemed as if it would have been touched with compassion, if she could have rendered me at all intelligible to her own mind.

'I am going,' she said again, in a gentler voice, 'to be married to him. The preparations for my marriage are making, and I shall be married soon. Why do you injuriously introduce the name of my mother by adoption? It is my own act.'

'Your own act, Estella, to fling yourself away upon a brute?'

'On whom should I fling myself away?' she retorted, with a smile. 'Should I fling myself away upon the man who would the soonest feel (if people do feel such things) that I took nothing to him? There! It is done. I shall do well enough, and so will my husband. As to leading me into what you call this fatal step, Miss Havisham would have had me wait, and not marry yet; but I am tired of the life I have led, which has very few charms for me, and I am willing enough to change it. Say no more. We shall never understand each other.'

'Such a mean brute, such a stupid brute!' I urged, in despair.

'Don't be afraid of my being a blessing to him,' said Estella; 'I shall not be that. Come! Here is my hand. Do we part on this, you visionary boy—or man?'

'O Estella!' I answered, as my bitter tears fell fast on her hand, do what I would to restrain them; 'even if I remained in England and could hold my head up with the rest, how could I see you Drummle's wife?'

'Nonsense,' she returned,—'nonsense. This will pass in no time.'

'Never, Estella!'

'You will get me out of your thoughts in a week.'

'Out of my thoughts! You are part of my existence, part of myself. You have been in every line I have ever read since I first came here, the rough common boy whose poor heart you wounded even then. You have been in every prospect I have ever seen since,—on the river, on the sails of the ships, on the marshes, in the clouds, in the light, in the darkness, in the wind, in the woods, in the sea, in the streets. You have been the embodiment of every graceful fancy that my mind has ever become acquainted with. The stones of which the strongest London buildings are made are not more real, or more impossible to be displaced by your hands, than your presence and influence have been to me, there and everywhere, and will be. Estella, to the last hour of my life, you cannot choose but remain part of my character, part of the little good in me, part of the evil. But, in this separation, I associate you only with the good; and I will faithfully hold you to that always, for you must have done me far more good than harm, let me feel now what sharp distress I may. O God bless you, God forgive you!'

In what ecstasy of unhappiness I got these broken words out of myself, I don't know. The rhapsody welled up within me, like blood from an inward wound, and gushed out. I held her hand to my lips some lingering moments, and so I left her. But ever afterwards, I remembered,—and soon afterwards with stronger reason,—that while Estella looked at me merely with incredulous wonder, the spectral figure of Miss Havisham, her hand still covering her heart, seemed all resolved into a ghastly stare of pity and remorse.

All done, all gone! So much was done and gone, that when I went out at the gate, the light of the day seemed of a darker colour than when I went in. For a while, I hid myself among some lanes and by-paths, and then struck off to walk all the way to London. For, I had by that time come to myself so far as to consider that I could not go back to the inn and see Drummle there; that I could not bear to sit upon the coach and be spoken to; that I could do nothing half so good for myself as tire myself out.

It was past midnight when I crossed London Bridge. Pursuing the narrow intricacies of the streets which at that time tended westward near the Middlesex shore of the river, my readiest access to the Temple was close by the riverside, through Whitefriars. I was not expected till tomorrow; but I had my keys, and, if Herbert were gone to bed, could get to bed myself without disturbing him.

As it seldom happened that I came in at that Whitefriars gate after the Temple was closed, and as I was very muddy and weary, I did not take it ill that the night-porter examined me with much attention as he held the gate a little way open for me to pass in. To help his memory I mentioned my name.

'I was not quite sure, sir, but I thought so. Here's a note, sir. The messenger that brought it, said would you be so good as read it by my lantern?'

Much surprised by the request, I took the note. It was directed to Philip Pip, Esquire, and on the top of the superscription were the words, 'PLEASE READ THIS, HERE.' I opened it, the watchman holding up his light, and read inside, in Wemmick's writing,—

'DON'T GO HOME.'

Chapter 45

Turning from the Temple gate as soon as I had read the warning, I made the best of my way to Fleet Street, and there got a late hackney chariot and drove to the Hummums in Covent Garden. In those times a bed was always to be got there at any hour of the night, and the chamberlain, letting me in at his ready wicket, lighted the candle next in order on his shelf, and showed me straight into the bedroom next in order on his list. It was a sort of vault on the ground floor at the back, with a despotic monster of a four-post bedstead in it, straddling over the whole place, putting one of his arbitrary legs into the fireplace and another into the doorway, and squeezing the wretched little washing-stand in quite a divinely righteous manner.

As I had asked for a night-light, the chamberlain had brought me in, before he left me, the good old constitutional rushlight of those virtuous days—an object like the ghost of a walking-cane, which instantly broke its back if it were touched, which nothing could ever be lighted at, and which was placed in solitary confinement at the bottom of a high tin tower, perforated with round holes that made a staringly wide-awake pattern on the walls. When I had got into bed, and lay there footsore, weary, and wretched, I found that I could no more close my own eyes than I could close the eyes of this foolish Argus. And thus, in the gloom and death of the night, we stared at one another.

What a doleful night! How anxious, how dismal, how long! There was an inhospitable smell in the room, of cold soot and hot dust; and, as I looked up into the corners of the tester over my head, I thought what a number of blue-bottle flies from the butchers', and earwigs from the market, and grubs from the country, must be holding on up there, lying by for next summer. This led me to speculate whether any of them ever tumbled down, and then I fancied that I felt light falls on my face,—a disagreeable turn of thought, suggesting other and more objectionable approaches up my back. When I had lain awake a little while, those extraordinary voices with which silence teems began to make themselves audible. The closet whispered, the fireplace sighed, the little washing-stand ticked, and one guitar-string played occasionally in the chest of drawers. At about the same time, the eyes on the wall acquired a new expression, and in every one of those staring rounds I saw written, DON'T GO HOME.

Whatever night-fancies and night-noises crowded on me, they never warded off this DON'T GO HOME. It plaited itself into whatever I thought of, as a bodily pain would have done. Not long before, I had read in the newspapers, how a gentleman unknown had come to the Hummums in the night, and had gone to bed, and had destroyed himself, and had been found in the morning weltering in blood. It came into my head that he must have occupied this very vault of mine, and I got out of bed to assure myself that there were no red marks about; then opened the door to look out into the passages, and cheer myself with the companionship of a distant light, near which I knew the chamberlain to be dozing. But all this time, why I was not to go home, and what had happened at home, and when I should go home, and whether Provis was safe at home, were questions occupying my mind so busily, that one might have supposed there could be no more room in it for any other theme. Even when I thought of Estella, and how we had parted that day forever, and when I recalled all the circumstances of our parting, and all her looks and tones, and the action of her fingers while she knitted,—even then I was pursuing, here and there and everywhere, the caution, Don't go home. When at last I dozed, in sheer exhaustion of mind and body, it became a vast shadowy verb which I had to conjugate. Imperative mood, present tense: Do not thou go home, let him not go home, let us not go home, do not ye or you go home, let not them go home. Then potentially: I may not and I cannot go home; and I might not, could not, would not, and should not go home; until I felt that I was going distracted, and rolled over on the pillow, and looked at the staring rounds upon the wall again.

I had left directions that I was to be called at seven; for it was plain that I must see Wemmick before seeing anyone else, and equally plain that this was a case in which his Walworth sentiments only could be taken. It was a relief to get out of the room where the night had been so miserable, and I needed no second knocking at the door to startle me from my uneasy bed.

The Castle battlements arose upon my view at eight o'clock. The little servant happening to be entering the fortress with two hot rolls, I passed through the postern and crossed the drawbridge in her company, and so came without announcement into the presence of Wemmick as he was making tea for himself and the Aged. An open door afforded a perspective view of the Aged in bed.

'Halloa, Mr Pip!' said Wemmick. 'You did come home, then?'

'Yes,' I returned; 'but I didn't go home.'

'That's all right,' said he, rubbing his hands. 'I left a note for you at each of the Temple gates, on the chance. Which gate did you come to?'

I told him.

'I'll go round to the others in the course of the day and destroy the notes,' said Wemmick; 'it's a good rule never to leave documentary evidence if you can help it, because you don't know when it may be put in. I'm going to take a liberty with you. *Would* you mind toasting this sausage for the Aged P.?'

I said I should be delighted to do it.

'Then you can go about your work, Mary Anne,' said Wemmick to the little servant; 'which leaves us to ourselves, don't you see, Mr Pip?' he added, winking, as she disappeared.

I thanked him for his friendship and caution, and our discourse proceeded in a low tone, while I toasted the Aged's sausage and he buttered the crumb of the Aged's roll.

'Now, Mr Pip, you know,' said Wemmick, 'you and I understand one another. We are in our private and personal capacities, and we have been engaged in a confidential transaction before today. Official sentiments are one thing. We are extra official.'

I cordially assented. I was so very nervous, that I had already lighted the Aged's sausage like a torch, and been obliged to blow it out.

'I accidentally heard, yesterday morning,' said Wemmick, 'being in a certain place where I once took you,—even between you and me, it's as well not to mention names when avoidable—'

'Much better not,' said I. 'I understand you.'

'I heard there by chance, yesterday morning,' said Wemmick, 'that a certain person not altogether of uncolonial pursuits, and not unpossessed of portable property,—I don't know who it may really be,—we won't name this person—'

'Not necessary,' said I.

'—Had made some little stir in a certain part of the world where a good many people go, not always in gratification of their own inclinations, and not quite irrespective of the government expense—'

In watching his face, I made quite a firework of the Aged's sausage, and greatly discomposed both my own attention and Wemmick's; for which I apologized.

'—By disappearing from such place, and being no more heard of thereabouts. From which,' said Wemmick, 'conjectures had been raised and theories formed. I also heard that you at your chambers in Garden Court, Temple, had been watched, and might be watched again.'

'By whom?' said I.

'I wouldn't go into that,' said Wemmick, evasively, 'it might clash with official responsibilities. I heard it, as I have in my time heard other curious things in the same place. I don't tell it you on information received. I heard it.'

He took the toasting-fork and sausage from me as he spoke, and set forth the Aged's breakfast neatly on a little tray. Previous to placing it before him, he went into the Aged's room with a clean white cloth, and tied the same under the old gentleman's chin, and propped him up, and put his nightcap on one side, and gave him quite a rakish air. Then he placed his breakfast before him with great care, and said, 'All right, ain't you, Aged P.?' To which the cheerful Aged replied, 'All right, John, my boy, all right!' As there seemed to be a tacit understanding that the Aged was not in a presentable state, and was therefore to be considered invisible, I made a pretence of being in complete ignorance of these proceedings.

'This watching of me at my chambers (which I have once had reason to suspect),' I said to Wemmick when he came back, 'is inseparable from the person to whom you have adverted; is it?'

Wemmick looked very serious. 'I couldn't undertake to say that, of my own knowledge. I mean, I couldn't undertake to say it was at first. But it either is, or it will be, or it's in great danger of being.'

As I saw that he was restrained by fealty to Little Britain from saying as much as he could, and as I knew with thankfulness to him how far out of his way he went to say what he did, I could not press him. But I told him, after a little meditation over the fire, that I would like to ask him a question, subject to his answering or not answering, as he deemed right, and sure that his course would be right. He paused in his breakfast, and crossing his arms, and pinching his shirt-sleeves (his notion of indoor comfort was to sit without any coat), he nodded to me once, to put my question.

'You have heard of a man of bad character, whose true name is Compeyson?'

He answered with one other nod.

'Is he living?'

One other nod.

'Is he in London?'

He gave me one other nod, compressed the post-office exceedingly, gave me one last nod, and went on with his breakfast.

'Now,' said Wemmick, 'questioning being over,' which he emphasized and repeated for my guidance, 'I come to what I did, after hearing what I heard. I went to Garden Court to find you; not finding you, I went to Clarriker's to find Mr Herbert.'

'And him you found?' said I, with great anxiety.

'And him I found. Without mentioning any names or going into any details, I gave him to understand that if he was aware of anybody—Tom, Jack, or Richard—being about the chambers, or about the immediate neighbourhood, he had better get Tom, Jack, or Richard out of the way while you were out of the way.'

'He would be greatly puzzled what to do?'

'He *was* puzzled what to do; not the less, because I gave him my opinion that it was not safe to try to get Tom, Jack, or Richard too far out of the way at present. Mr Pip, I'll tell you something. Under existing circumstances, there is no place like a great city when you are once in it. Don't break cover too soon. Lie close. Wait till things slacken, before you try the open, even for foreign air.'

I thanked him for his valuable advice, and asked him what Herbert had done?

'Mr Herbert,' said Wemmick, 'after being all of a heap for half an hour, struck out a plan. He mentioned to me as a secret, that he is courting a young lady who has, as no doubt you are aware, a bedridden Pa. Which Pa, having been in the Purser line of life, lies a-bed in a bow-window where he can see the ships sail up and down the river. You are acquainted with the young lady, most probably?'

'Not personally,' said I.

The truth was, that she had objected to me as an expensive companion who did Herbert no good, and that, when Herbert had first proposed to present me to her, she had received the proposal with such very moderate warmth, that Herbert had felt himself obliged to confide the state of the case to me, with a view to the lapse of a little time before I made her acquaintance. When I had begun to advance Herbert's prospects by stealth, I had been able to bear this with cheerful philosophy: he and his affianced, for their part, had naturally not been very anxious to introduce a third person into their interviews;

and thus, although I was assured that I had risen in Clara's esteem, and although the young lady and I had long regularly interchanged messages and remembrances by Herbert, I had never seen her. However, I did not trouble Wemmick with these particulars.

'The house with the bow-window,' said Wemmick, 'being by the riverside, down the Pool there between Limehouse and Greenwich, and being kept, it seems, by a very respectable widow who has a furnished upper floor to let, Mr Herbert put it to me, what did I think of that as a temporary tenement for Tom, Jack, or Richard? Now, I thought very well of it, for three reasons I'll give you. That is to say: *Firstly*. It's altogether out of all your beats, and is well away from the usual heap of streets great and small. *Secondly*. Without going near it yourself, you could always hear of the safety of Tom, Jack, or Richard, through Mr Herbert. *Thirdly*. After a while and when it might be prudent, if you should want to slip Tom, Jack, or Richard on board a foreign packet-boat, there he is—ready.'

Much comforted by these considerations, I thanked Wemmick again and again, and begged him to proceed.

'Well, sir! Mr Herbert threw himself into the business with a will, and by nine o'clock last night he housed Tom, Jack, or Richard,—whichever it may be,—you and I don't want to know,—quite successfully. At the old lodgings it was understood that he was summoned to Dover, and, in fact, he was taken down the Dover road and cornered out of it. Now, another great advantage of all this is, that it was done without you, and when, if anyone was concerning himself about your movements, you must be known to be ever so many miles off and quite otherwise engaged. This diverts suspicion and confuses it; and for the same reason I recommended that, even if you came back last night, you should not go home. It brings in more confusion, and you want confusion.'

Wemmick, having finished his breakfast, here looked at his watch, and began to get his coat on.

'And now, Mr Pip,' said he, with his hands still in the sleeves, 'I have probably done the most I can do; but if I can ever do more,—from a Walworth point of view, and in a strictly private and personal capacity,—I shall be glad to do it. Here's the address. There can be no harm in your going here tonight, and seeing for yourself that all is well with Tom, Jack, or Richard, before you go home,—which is another reason for your not going home last night. But, after you have gone home, don't go back here. You are very welcome, I am sure, Mr Pip'; his hands were now out of his sleeves, and I was shaking them; 'and let me finally impress one important point upon you.' He laid his hands upon my shoulders, and added in a solemn whisper: 'Avail yourself of this evening to lay hold of his portable property. You don't know what may happen to him. Don't let anything happen to the portable property.'

Quite despairing of making my mind clear to Wemmick on this point, I forbore to try.

'Time's up,' said Wemmick, 'and I must be off. If you had nothing more pressing to do than to keep here till dark, that's what I should advise. You look very much worried, and it would do you good to have a perfectly quiet day with the Aged,—he'll be up presently,—and a little bit of—you remember the pig?'

'Of course,' said I.

'Well; and a little bit of *him*. That sausage you toasted was his, and he was in all respects a first-rater. Do try him, if it is only for old acquaintance sake. Goodbye, Aged Parent!' in a cheery shout.

'All right, John; all right, my boy!' piped the old man from within.

I soon fell asleep before Wemmick's fire, and the Aged and I enjoyed one another's society by falling asleep before it more or less all day. We had loin of pork for dinner, and greens grown on the estate; and I nodded at the Aged with a good intention whenever I failed to do it drowsily. When it was quite dark, I left the Aged preparing the fire for toast; and I inferred from the number of teacups, as well as from his glances at the two little doors in the wall, that Miss Skiffins was expected.

Chapter 46

Eight o'clock had struck before I got into the air, that was scented, not disagreeably, by the chips and shavings of the long-shore boat-builders, and mast, oar, and block makers. All that water-side region of the upper and lower Pool below Bridge was unknown ground to me; and when I struck down by the river, I found that the spot I wanted was not where I had supposed it to be, and was anything but easy to find. It was called Mill Pond Bank, Chinks's Basin; and I had no other guide to Chinks's Basin than the Old Green Copper Rope-walk.

It matters not what stranded ships repairing in dry docks I lost myself among, what old hulls of ships in course of being knocked to pieces, what ooze and slime and other dregs of tide, what yards of ship-builders and ship-breakers, what rusty anchors blindly biting into the ground, though for years off duty, what mountainous country of accumulated casks and timber, how many rope-walks that were not the Old Green Copper. After several times falling short of my destination and as often overshooting it, I came unexpectedly round a corner, upon Mill Pond Bank. It was a fresh kind of place, all circumstances considered, where the wind from the river had room to turn itself round; and there were two or three trees in it, and there was the stump of a ruined windmill, and there was the Old Green Copper Rope-walk,—whose long and narrow vista I could trace in the moonlight, along a series of wooden frames set in the ground, that looked like superannuated haymaking-rakes which had grown old and lost most of their teeth.

Selecting from the few queer houses upon Mill Pond Bank a house with a wooden front and three stories of bow-window (not bay-window, which is another thing), I looked at the plate upon the door, and read there, Mrs Whimple. That being the name I wanted, I knocked, and an elderly woman of a pleasant and thriving appearance responded. She was immediately deposed, however, by Herbert, who silently led me into the parlor and shut the door. It was an odd sensation to see his very familiar face established quite at home in that very unfamiliar room and region; and I found myself looking at him, much as I looked at the corner-cupboard with the glass and china, the shells upon the chimney-piece, and the coloured engravings on the wall, representing the death of Captain Cook, a ship-launch, and his Majesty King George the Third in a state coachman's wig, leather-breeches, and top-boots, on the terrace at Windsor.

'All is well, Handel,' said Herbert, 'and he is quite satisfied, though eager to see you. My dear girl is with her father; and if you'll wait till she comes down, I'll make you known to her, and then we'll go upstairs. *That's* her father.'

I had become aware of an alarming growling overhead, and had probably expressed the fact in my countenance.

'I am afraid he is a sad old rascal,' said Herbert, smiling, 'but I have never seen him. Don't you smell rum? He is always at it.'

'At rum?' said I.

'Yes,' returned Herbert, 'and you may suppose how mild it makes his gout. He persists, too, in keeping all the provisions upstairs in his room, and serving them out. He keeps them on shelves over his head, and *will* weigh them all. His room must be like a chandler's shop.'

While he thus spoke, the growling noise became a prolonged roar, and then died away.

'What else can be the consequence,' said Herbert, in explanation, 'if he *will* cut the cheese? A man with the gout in his right hand—and everywhere else—can't expect to get through a Double Gloucester without hurting himself.'

He seemed to have hurt himself very much, for he gave another furious roar.

'To have Provis for an upper lodger is quite a godsend to Mrs Whimple,' said Herbert, 'for of course people in general won't stand that noise. A curious place, Handel; isn't it?'

It was a curious place, indeed; but remarkably well kept and clean.

'Mrs Whimple,' said Herbert, when I told him so, 'is the best of housewives, and I really do not know what my Clara would do without her motherly help. For, Clara has no mother of her own, Handel, and no relation in the world but old Gruffandgrim.'

'Surely that's not his name, Herbert?'

'No, no,' said Herbert, 'that's my name for him. His name is Mr Barley. But what a blessing it is for the son of my father and mother to love a girl who has no relations, and who can never bother herself or anybody else about her family!'

Herbert had told me on former occasions, and now reminded me, that he first knew Miss Clara Barley when she was completing her education at an establishment at Hammersmith, and that on her being recalled home to nurse her father, he and she had confided their affection to the motherly Mrs Whimple, by whom it had been fostered and regulated with equal kindness and discretion, ever since. It was understood that nothing of a tender nature could possibly be confided to old Barley, by reason of his being totally unequal to the consideration of any subject more psychological than Gout, Rum, and Purser's stores.

As we were thus conversing in a low tone while Old Barley's sustained growl vibrated in the beam that crossed the ceiling, the room door opened, and a very pretty, slight, dark-eyed girl of twenty or so came in with a basket in her hand: whom Herbert tenderly relieved of the basket, and presented, blushing, as 'Clara.' She really was a most charming girl, and might have passed for a captive fairy, whom that truculent Ogre, Old Barley, had pressed into his service.

'Look here,' said Herbert, showing me the basket, with a compassionate and tender smile, after we had talked a little; 'here's poor Clara's supper, served out every night. Here's her allowance of bread, and here's her slice of cheese, and here's her rum,—which I drink. This is Mr Barley's breakfast for tomorrow, served out to be cooked. Two mutton-chops, three potatoes, some split peas, a little flour, two ounces of butter, a pinch of salt, and all this black pepper. It's stewed up together, and taken hot, and it's a nice thing for the gout, I should think!'

There was something so natural and winning in Clara's resigned way of looking at these stores in detail, as Herbert pointed them out; and something so confiding, loving, and innocent in her modest manner of yielding herself to Herbert's embracing arm; and something so gentle in her, so much needing protection on Mill Pond Bank, by Chinks's Basin, and the Old Green Copper Rope-walk, with Old Barley growling in the beam,—that I would not have undone the engagement between her and Herbert for all the money in the pocket-book I had never opened.

I was looking at her with pleasure and admiration, when suddenly the growl swelled into a roar again, and a frightful bumping noise was heard above, as if a giant with a wooden leg were trying to bore it through the ceiling to come at us. Upon this Clara said to Herbert,

'Papa wants me, darling!' and ran away.

'There is an unconscionable old shark for you!' said Herbert. 'What do you suppose he wants now, Handel?'

'I don't know,' said I. 'Something to drink?'

'That's it!' cried Herbert, as if I had made a guess of extraordinary merit. 'He keeps his grog ready mixed in a little tub on the table. Wait a moment, and you'll hear Clara lift him up to take some. There he goes!' Another roar, with a prolonged shake at the end. 'Now,' said Herbert, as it was succeeded by silence, 'he's drinking. Now,' said Herbert, as the growl resounded in the beam once more, 'he's down again on his back!'

Clara returned soon afterwards, and Herbert accompanied me upstairs to see our charge. As we passed Mr Barley's door, he was heard hoarsely muttering within, in a strain that rose and fell like wind, the following Refrain, in which I substitute good wishes for something quite the reverse:—

'Ahoy! Bless your eyes, here's old Bill Barley. Here's old Bill Barley, bless your eyes. Here's old Bill Barley on the flat of his back, by the Lord. Lying on the flat of his back like a drifting old dead flounder, here's your old Bill Barley, bless your eyes. Ahoy! Bless you.'

In this strain of consolation, Herbert informed me the invisible Barley would commune with himself by the day and night together; Often, while it was light, having, at the same time, one eye at a telescope which was fitted on his bed for the convenience of sweeping the river.

In his two cabin rooms at the top of the house, which were fresh and airy, and in which Mr Barley was less audible than below, I found Provis comfortably settled. He expressed no alarm, and seemed to feel none that was worth mentioning; but it struck me that he was softened,—indefinably, for I could not have said how, and could never afterwards recall how when I tried, but certainly.

The opportunity that the day's rest had given me for reflection had resulted in my fully determining to say nothing to him respecting Compeyson. For anything I knew, his animosity towards the man might otherwise lead to his seeking him out and rushing on his own destruction. Therefore, when Herbert and I sat down with him by his fire, I asked him first of all whether he relied on Wemmick's judgment and sources of information?

'Ay, ay, dear boy!' he answered, with a grave nod, 'Jaggers knows.'

'Then, I have talked with Wemmick,' said I, 'and have come to tell you what caution he gave me and what advice.'

This I did accurately, with the reservation just mentioned; and I told him how Wemmick had heard, in Newgate prison (whether from officers or prisoners I could not say), that he was under some suspicion, and that my chambers had been watched; how Wemmick had recommended his keeping close for a time, and my keeping away from him; and what Wemmick had said about getting him abroad. I added, that of course, when the time came, I should go with him, or should follow close upon him, as might be safest in Wemmick's judgment. What was to follow that I did not touch upon; neither, indeed, was I at all clear or comfortable about it in my own mind, now that I saw him in that softer condition, and in declared peril for my sake. As to altering my way of living by enlarging my expenses, I put it to him whether in our present unsettled and difficult circumstances, it would not be simply ridiculous, if it were no worse?

He could not deny this, and indeed was very reasonable throughout. His coming back was a venture, he said, and he had always known it to be a venture. He would do nothing to make it a desperate venture, and he had very little fear of his safety with such good help.

Herbert, who had been looking at the fire and pondering, here said that something had come into his thoughts arising out of Wemmick's suggestion, which it might be worth while to pursue. 'We are both good watermen, Handel, and could take him down the river ourselves when the right time comes. No boat would then be hired for the purpose, and no boatmen; that would save at least a chance of suspicion, and any chance is worth saving. Never mind the season; don't you think it might be a good thing if you began at once to keep a boat at the Temple stairs, and were in the habit of rowing up and down the river? You fall into that habit, and then who notices or minds? Do it twenty or fifty times, and there is nothing special in your doing it the twenty-first or fifty-first.'

I liked this scheme, and Provis was quite elated by it. We agreed that it should be carried into execution, and that Provis should never recognize us if we came below Bridge, and rowed past Mill Pond Bank. But we further agreed that he should pull down the blind in that part of his window which gave upon the east, whenever he saw us and all was right.

Our conference being now ended, and everything arranged, I rose to go; remarking to Herbert that he and I had better not go home together, and that I would take half an hour's start of him. 'I don't like to leave you here,' I said to Provis, 'though I cannot doubt your being safer here than near me. Goodbye!'

'Dear boy,' he answered, clasping my hands, 'I don't know when we may meet again, and I don't like goodbye. Say goodnight!'

'Goodnight! Herbert will go regularly between us, and when the time comes you may be certain I shall be ready. Goodnight, goodnight!'

We thought it best that he should stay in his own rooms; and we left him on the landing outside his door, holding a light over the stair-rail to light us downstairs. Looking back at him, I thought of the first night of his return, when our positions were reversed, and when I little supposed my heart could ever be as heavy and anxious at parting from him as it was now.

Old Barley was growling and swearing when we repassed his door, with no appearance of having ceased or of meaning to cease. When we got to the foot of the stairs, I asked Herbert whether he had preserved the name of Provis. He replied, certainly not, and that the lodger was Mr Campbell. He also explained that the utmost known of Mr Campbell there was, that he (Herbert) had Mr Campbell consigned to him, and felt a strong personal interest in his being well cared for, and living a secluded life. So, when we went into the parlor where Mrs Whimple and Clara were seated at work, I said nothing of my own interest in Mr Campbell, but kept it to myself.

When I had taken leave of the pretty, gentle, dark-eyed girl, and of the motherly woman who had not outlived her honest sympathy with a little affair of true love, I felt as if the Old Green Copper Rope-walk had grown quite a different place. Old Barley might be as old as the hills, and might swear like a whole field of troopers, but there were redeeming youth and trust and hope enough in Chinks's Basin to fill it to overflowing. And then I thought of Estella, and of our parting, and went home very sadly.

All things were as quiet in the Temple as ever I had seen them. The windows of the rooms on that side, lately occupied by Provis, were dark and still, and there was no lounger in Garden Court. I walked past the fountain twice or thrice before I descended the steps that were between me and my rooms, but I was quite alone. Herbert, coming to my bedside when he came in,—for I went straight to bed, dispirited and fatigued,—made the same report. Opening one of the windows after that, he looked out into the moonlight, and told me that the pavement was as solemnly empty as the pavement of any cathedral at that same hour.

Next day I set myself to get the boat. It was soon done, and the boat was brought round to the Temple stairs, and lay where I could reach her within a minute or two. Then, I began to go out as for training and practice: sometimes alone, sometimes with Herbert. I was often out in cold, rain, and sleet, but nobody took much note of me after I had been out a few times. At first, I kept above Blackfriars Bridge; but as the hours of the tide changed, I took towards London Bridge. It was Old London Bridge in those days, and at certain states of the tide there was a race and fall of water there which gave it a bad reputation. But I knew well enough how to 'shoot' the bridge after seeing it done, and so began to row about among the shipping in the Pool, and down to Erith. The first time I passed Mill Pond Bank, Herbert and I were pulling a pair of oars; and, both in going and returning, we saw the blind towards the east come down. Herbert was rarely there less frequently than three times in a week, and he never brought me a single word of intelligence that was at all alarming. Still, I knew that there was cause for alarm, and I could not get rid of the notion of being watched. Once received, it is a haunting idea; how many undesigning persons I suspected of watching me, it would be hard to calculate.

In short, I was always full of fears for the rash man who was in hiding. Herbert had sometimes said to me that he found it pleasant to stand at one of our windows after dark, when the tide was running down, and to think that it was flowing, with everything it bore, towards Clara. But I thought with dread that it was flowing towards Magwitch, and that any black mark on its surface might be his pursuers, going swiftly, silently, and surely, to take him.

Chapter 47

Some weeks passed without bringing any change. We waited for Wemmick, and he made no sign. If I had never known him out of Little Britain, and had never enjoyed the privilege of being on a familiar footing at the Castle, I might have doubted him; not so for a moment, knowing him as I did.

My worldly affairs began to wear a gloomy appearance, and I was pressed for money by more than one creditor. Even I myself began to know the want of money (I mean of ready money in my own pocket), and to relieve it by converting some easily spared articles of jewelry into cash. But I had quite determined that it would be a heartless fraud to take more money from my patron in the existing state of my uncertain thoughts and plans. Therefore, I had sent him the unopened pocket-book by Herbert, to hold in his own keeping, and I felt a kind of satisfaction—whether it was a false kind or a true, I hardly know—in not having profited by his generosity since his revelation of himself.

As the time wore on, an impression settled heavily upon me that Estella was married. Fearful of having it confirmed, though it was all but a conviction, I avoided the newspapers, and begged Herbert (to whom I had confided the circumstances of our last interview) never to speak of her to me. Why I hoarded up this last wretched little rag of the robe of hope that was rent and given to the winds, how do I know? Why did you who read this, commit that not dissimilar inconsistency of your own last year, last month, last week?

It was an unhappy life that I lived; and its one dominant anxiety, towering over all its other anxieties, like a high mountain above a range of mountains, never disappeared from my view. Still, no new cause for fear arose. Let me start from my bed as I would, with the terror fresh upon me that he was discovered; let me sit listening, as I would with dread, for Herbert's returning step at night, lest it should be fleeter than ordinary, and winged with evil news,—for all that, and much more to like purpose, the round of things went on. Condemned to inaction and a state of constant restlessness and suspense, I rowed about in my boat, and waited, waited, waited, as I best could.

There were states of the tide when, having been down the river, I could not get back through the eddy-chafed arches and starlings of old London Bridge; then, I left my boat at a wharf near the Custom House, to be brought up afterwards to the Temple stairs. I was not averse to doing this, as it served to make me and my boat a commoner incident among the water-side people there. From this slight occasion sprang two meetings that I have now to tell of.

One afternoon, late in the month of February, I came ashore at the wharf at dusk. I had pulled down as far as Greenwich with the ebb tide, and had turned with the tide. It had been a fine bright day, but had become foggy as the sun dropped, and I had had to feel my way back among the shipping, pretty carefully. Both in going and returning, I had seen the signal in his window, All well.

As it was a raw evening, and I was cold, I thought I would comfort myself with dinner at once; and as I had hours of dejection and solitude before me if I went home to the Temple, I thought I would afterwards go to the play. The theatre where Mr Wopsle had achieved his questionable triumph was in that water-side neighbourhood (it is nowhere now), and to that theatre I resolved to go. I was aware that Mr Wopsle had not succeeded in reviving the Drama, but, on the contrary, had rather partaken of its decline. He had been ominously heard of, through the play-bills, as a faithful Black, in connection with a little girl of noble birth, and a monkey. And Herbert had seen him as a predatory Tartar of comic propensities, with a face like a red brick, and an outrageous hat all over bells.

I dined at what Herbert and I used to call a geographical chop-house, where there were maps of the world in porter-pot rims on every half-yard of the tablecloths, and charts of gravy on every one of the knives,—to this day there is scarcely a single chop-house within the Lord Mayor's dominions which is not geographical,—and wore out the time in dozing over crumbs, staring at gas, and baking in a hot blast of dinners. By and by, I roused myself, and went to the play.

There, I found a virtuous boatswain in His Majesty's service,—a most excellent man, though I could have wished his trousers not quite so tight in some places, and not quite so loose in others,—who knocked all the little men's hats over their eyes, though he was very generous and brave, and who wouldn't hear of anybody's paying taxes, though he was very patriotic. He had a bag of money in his pocket, like a pudding in the cloth, and on that property married a young person in bed-furniture, with great rejoicings; the whole population of Portsmouth (nine in number at the last census) turning out on the beach to rub their own hands and shake everybody else's, and sing 'Fill, fill!' A certain dark-complexioned Swab, however, who wouldn't fill, or do anything else that was proposed to him, and whose heart was openly stated (by the boatswain) to be as black as his figure-head, proposed to two other Swabs to get all mankind into difficulties; which was so effectually done (the Swab family having considerable political influence) that it took half the evening to set things right, and then it was only brought about through an honest little grocer with a white hat, black gaiters, and red nose, getting into a clock, with a gridiron, and listening, and coming out, and knocking everybody down from behind with the gridiron whom he couldn't confute with what he had overheard. This led to Mr Wopsle's (who had never been heard of before) coming in with a star and garter on, as a plenipotentiary of great power direct from the Admiralty, to say that the Swabs were all to go to prison on the spot, and that he had brought the boatswain down the Union Jack, as a slight acknowledgment of his public services. The boatswain, unmanned for the first time, respectfully dried his eyes on the Jack, and then cheering up, and addressing Mr Wopsle as Your Honour, solicited permission to take him by the fin. Mr Wopsle, conceding his fin with a gracious dignity, was immediately shoved into a dusty corner, while everybody danced a hornpipe; and from that corner, surveying the public with a discontented eye, became aware of me.

The second piece was the last new grand comic Christmas pantomime, in the first scene of which, it pained me to suspect that I detected Mr Wopsle with red worsted legs under a highly magnified phosphoric countenance and a shock of red curtain-fringe for his hair, engaged in the manufacture of thunderbolts in a mine, and displaying great cowardice when his gigantic master came home (very hoarse) to dinner. But he presently presented himself under worthier circumstances; for, the Genius of Youthful Love being in want of assistance,—on account of the parental brutality of an ignorant farmer who opposed the choice of his daughter's heart, by purposely falling upon the object, in a flour-sack, out of the first-floor window,—summoned a sententious enchanter; and he, coming up from the antipodes rather unsteadily, after an apparently violent journey, proved to be Mr Wopsle in a high-crowned hat, with a necromantic work in one volume under his arm. The business of this enchanter on earth being principally to be talked at, sung at, butted at, danced at, and flashed at with fires of various colours, he had a good deal of time on his hands. And I observed, with great surprise, that he devoted it to staring in my direction as if he were lost in amazement.

There was something so remarkable in the increasing glare of Mr Wopsle's eye, and he seemed to be turning so many things over in his mind and to grow so confused, that I could not make it out. I sat thinking of it long after he had ascended to the clouds in a large watch-case, and still I could not make it out. I was still thinking of it when I came out of the theatre an hour afterwards, and found him waiting for me near the door.

'How do you do?' said I, shaking hands with him as we turned down the street together. 'I saw that you saw me.'

'Saw you, Mr Pip!' he returned. 'Yes, of course I saw you. But who else was there?'

'Who else?'

'It is the strangest thing,' said Mr Wopsle, drifting into his lost look again; 'and yet I could swear to him.'

Becoming alarmed, I entreated Mr Wopsle to explain his meaning.

'Whether I should have noticed him at first but for your being there,' said Mr Wopsle, going on in the same lost way, 'I can't be positive; yet I think I should.'

Involuntarily I looked round me, as I was accustomed to look round me when I went home; for these mysterious words gave me a chill.

'Oh! He can't be in sight,' said Mr Wopsle. 'He went out before I went off. I saw him go.'

Having the reason that I had for being suspicious, I even suspected this poor actor. I mistrusted a design to entrap me into some admission. Therefore I glanced at him as we walked on together, but said nothing.

'I had a ridiculous fancy that he must be with you, Mr Pip, till I saw that you were quite unconscious of him, sitting behind you there like a ghost.'

My former chill crept over me again, but I was resolved not to speak yet, for it was quite consistent with his words that he might be set on to induce me to connect these references with Provis. Of course, I was perfectly sure and safe that Provis had not been there.

'I dare say you wonder at me, Mr Pip; indeed, I see you do. But it is so very strange! You'll hardly believe what I am going to tell you. I could hardly believe it myself, if you told me.'

'Indeed?' said I.

'No, indeed. Mr Pip, you remember in old times a certain Christmas Day, when you were quite a child, and I dined at Gargery's, and some soldiers came to the door to get a pair of handcuffs mended?'

'I remember it very well.'

'And you remember that there was a chase after two convicts, and that we joined in it, and that Gargery took you on his back, and that I took the lead, and you kept up with me as well as you could?'

'I remember it all very well.' Better than he thought,—except the last clause.

'And you remember that we came up with the two in a ditch, and that there was a scuffle between them, and that one of them had been severely handled and much mauled about the face by the other?'

'I see it all before me.'

'And that the soldiers lighted torches, and put the two in the centre, and that we went on to see the last of them, over the black marshes, with the torchlight shining on their faces,—I am particular about that,—with the torchlight shining on their faces, when there was an outer ring of dark night all about us?'

'Yes,' said I. 'I remember all that.'

'Then, Mr Pip, one of those two prisoners sat behind you tonight. I saw him over your shoulder.'

'Steady!' I thought. I asked him then, 'Which of the two do you suppose you saw?'

'The one who had been mauled,' he answered readily, 'and I'll swear I saw him! The more I think of him, the more certain I am of him.'

'This is very curious!' said I, with the best assumption I could put on of its being nothing more to me. 'Very curious indeed!'

I cannot exaggerate the enhanced disquiet into which this conversation threw me, or the special and peculiar terror I felt at Compeyson's having been behind me 'like a ghost.' For if he had ever been out of my thoughts for a few moments together since the hiding had begun, it was in those very moments when he was closest to me; and to think that I should be so unconscious and off my guard after all my care was as if I had shut an avenue of a hundred doors to keep him out, and then had found him at my elbow. I could not doubt, either, that he was there, because I was there, and that, however slight an appearance of danger there might be about us, danger was always near and active.

I put such questions to Mr Wopsle as, When did the man come in? He could not tell me that; he saw me, and over my shoulder he saw the man. It was not until he had seen him for some time that he began to identify him; but he had from the first vaguely associated him with me, and known him as somehow belonging to me in the old village time. How was he dressed? Prosperously, but not noticeably otherwise; he thought, in black. Was his face at all disfigured? No, he believed not. I believed not too, for, although in my brooding state I had taken no especial notice of the people behind me, I thought it likely that a face at all disfigured would have attracted my attention.

When Mr Wopsle had imparted to me all that he could recall or I extract, and when I had treated him to a little appropriate refreshment, after the fatigues of the evening, we parted. It was between twelve and one o'clock when I reached the Temple, and the gates were shut. No one was near me when I went in and went home.

Herbert had come in, and we held a very serious council by the fire. But there was nothing to be done, saving to communicate to Wemmick what I had that night found out, and to remind him that we waited for his hint. As I thought that I might compromise him if

I went too often to the Castle, I made this communication by letter. I wrote it before I went to bed, and went out and posted it; and again no one was near me. Herbert and I agreed that we could do nothing else but be very cautious. And we were very cautious indeed,—more cautious than before, if that were possible,—and I for my part never went near Chinks's Basin, except when I rowed by, and then I only looked at Mill Pond Bank as I looked at anything else.

Chapter 48

The second of the two meetings referred to in the last chapter occurred about a week after the first. I had again left my boat at the wharf below Bridge; the time was an hour earlier in the afternoon; and, undecided where to dine, I had strolled up into Cheapside, and was strolling along it, surely the most unsettled person in all the busy concourse, when a large hand was laid upon my shoulder by someone overtaking me. It was Mr Jaggers's hand, and he passed it through my arm.

'As we are going in the same direction, Pip, we may walk together. Where are you bound for?'

'For the Temple, I think,' said I.

'Don't you know?' said Mr Jaggers.

'Well,' I returned, glad for once to get the better of him in cross-examination, 'I do *not* know, for I have not made up my mind.'

'You are going to dine?' said Mr Jaggers. 'You don't mind admitting that, I suppose?'

'No,' I returned, 'I don't mind admitting that.'

'And are not engaged?'

'I don't mind admitting also that I am not engaged.'

'Then,' said Mr Jaggers, 'come and dine with me.'

I was going to excuse myself, when he added, 'Wemmick's coming.' So I changed my excuse into an acceptance,—the few words I had uttered, serving for the beginning of either,—and we went along Cheapside and slanted off to Little Britain, while the lights were springing up brilliantly in the shop windows, and the street lamp-lighters, scarcely finding ground enough to plant their ladders on in the midst of the afternoon's bustle, were skipping up and down and running in and out, opening more red eyes in the gathering fog than my rushlight tower at the Hummums had opened white eyes in the ghostly wall.

At the office in Little Britain there was the usual letter-writing, hand-washing, candle-snuffing, and safe-locking, that closed the business of the day. As I stood idle by Mr Jaggers's fire, its rising and falling flame made the two casts on the shelf look as if they were playing a diabolical game at bo-peep with me; while the pair of coarse, fat office candles that dimly lighted Mr Jaggers as he wrote in a corner were decorated with dirty winding-sheets, as if in remembrance of a host of hanged clients.

We went to Gerrard Street, all three together, in a hackney-coach: And, as soon as we got there, dinner was served. Although I should not have thought of making, in that place, the most distant reference by so much as a look to Wemmick's Walworth sentiments, yet I should have had no objection to catching his eye now and then in a friendly way. But it was not to be done. He turned his eyes on Mr Jaggers whenever he raised them from the table, and was as dry and distant to me as if there were twin Wemmicks, and this was the wrong one.

'Did you send that note of Miss Havisham's to Mr Pip, Wemmick?' Mr Jaggers asked, soon after we began dinner.

'No, sir,' returned Wemmick; 'it was going by post, when you brought Mr Pip into the office. Here it is.' He handed it to his principal instead of to me.

'It's a note of two lines, Pip,' said Mr Jaggers, handing it on, 'sent up to me by Miss Havisham on account of her not being sure of your address. She tells me that she wants to see you on a little matter of business you mentioned to her. You'll go down?'

'Yes,' said I, casting my eyes over the note, which was exactly in those terms.

'When do you think of going down?'

'I have an impending engagement,' said I, glancing at Wemmick, who was putting fish into the post-office, 'that renders me rather uncertain of my time. At once, I think.'

'If Mr Pip has the intention of going at once,' said Wemmick to

Mr Jaggers, 'he needn't write an answer, you know.'

Receiving this as an intimation that it was best not to delay, I settled that I would go tomorrow, and said so. Wemmick drank a glass of wine, and looked with a grimly satisfied air at Mr Jaggers, but not at me.

'So, Pip! Our friend the Spider,' said Mr Jaggers, 'has played his cards. He has won the pool.'

It was as much as I could do to assent.

'Hah! He is a promising fellow—in his way—but he may not have it all his own way. The stronger will win in the end, but the stronger has to be found out first. If he should turn to, and beat her—'

'Surely,' I interrupted, with a burning face and heart, 'you do not seriously think that he is scoundrel enough for that, Mr Jaggers?'

'I didn't say so, Pip. I am putting a case. If he should turn to and beat her, he may possibly get the strength on his side; if it should be a question of intellect, he certainly will not. It would be chance work to give an opinion how a fellow of that sort will turn out in such circumstances, because it's a toss-up between two results.'

'May I ask what they are?'

'A fellow like our friend the Spider,' answered Mr Jaggers, 'either beats or cringes. He may cringe and growl, or cringe and not growl; but he either beats or cringes. Ask Wemmick *his* opinion.'

'Either beats or cringes,' said Wemmick, not at all addressing himself to me.

'So here's to Mrs Bentley Drummle,' said Mr Jaggers, taking a decanter of choicer wine from his dumb-waiter, and filling for each of us and for himself, 'and may the question of supremacy be settled to the lady's satisfaction! To the satisfaction of the lady *and* the gentleman, it never will be. Now, Molly, Molly, Molly, Molly, how slow you are today!'

She was at his elbow when he addressed her, putting a dish upon the table. As she withdrew her hands from it, she fell back a step or two, nervously muttering some excuse. And a certain action of her fingers, as she spoke, arrested my attention.

'What's the matter?' said Mr Jaggers.

'Nothing. Only the subject we were speaking of,' said I, 'was rather painful to me.'

The action of her fingers was like the action of knitting. She stood looking at her master, not understanding whether she was free to go, or whether he had more to say to her and would call her back if she did go. Her look was very intent. Surely, I had seen exactly such eyes and such hands on a memorable occasion very lately!

He dismissed her, and she glided out of the room. But she remained before me as plainly as if she were still there. I looked at those hands, I looked at those eyes, I looked at that flowing hair; and I compared them with other hands, other eyes, other hair, that I knew of, and with what those might be after twenty years of a brutal husband and a stormy life. I looked again at those hands and eyes of the housekeeper, and thought of the inexplicable feeling that had come over me when I last walked—not alone—in the ruined garden, and through the deserted brewery. I thought how the same feeling had come back when I saw a face looking at me, and a hand waving to me from a stage-coach window; and how it had come back again and had flashed about me like lightning, when I had passed in a carriage—not alone—through a sudden glare of light in a dark street. I thought how one link of association had helped that identification in the theatre, and how such a link, wanting before, had been riveted for me now, when I had passed by a chance swift from Estella's name to the fingers with their knitting action, and the attentive eyes. And I felt absolutely certain that this woman was Estella's mother.

Mr Jaggers had seen me with Estella, and was not likely to have missed the sentiments I had been at no pains to conceal. He nodded when I said the subject was painful to me, clapped me on the back, put round the wine again, and went on with his dinner.

Only twice more did the housekeeper reappear, and then her stay in the room was very short, and Mr Jaggers was sharp with her. But her hands were Estella's hands, and her eyes were Estella's eyes, and if she had reappeared a hundred times I could have been neither more sure nor less sure that my conviction was the truth.

It was a dull evening, for Wemmick drew his wine, when it came round, quite as a matter of business,—just as he might have drawn his salary when that came round,—and with his eyes on his chief, sat in a state of perpetual readiness for cross-examination. As to the quantity of wine, his post-office was as indifferent and ready as any other post-office for its quantity of letters. From my point of view, he was the wrong twin all the time, and only externally like the Wemmick of Walworth.

We took our leave early, and left together. Even when we were groping among Mr Jaggers's stock of boots for our hats, I felt that the right twin was on his way back; and we had not gone half a dozen yards down Gerrard Street in the Walworth direction, before I found that I was walking arm in arm with the right twin, and that the wrong twin had evaporated into the evening air.

'Well!' said Wemmick, 'that's over! He's a wonderful man, without his living likeness; but I feel that I have to screw myself up when I dine with him,—and I dine more comfortably unscrewed.'

I felt that this was a good statement of the case, and told him so.

'Wouldn't say it to anybody but yourself,' he answered. 'I know that what is said between you and me goes no further.'

I asked him if he had ever seen Miss Havisham's adopted daughter, Mrs Bentley Drummle. He said no. To avoid being too abrupt, I then spoke of the Aged and of Miss Skiffins. He looked rather sly when I mentioned Miss Skiffins, and stopped in the street to blow his nose, with a roll of the head, and a flourish not quite free from latent boastfulness.

'Wemmick,' said I, 'do you remember telling me, before I first went to Mr Jaggers's private house, to notice that housekeeper?'

'Did I?' he replied. 'Ah, I dare say I did. Deuce take me,' he added, suddenly, 'I know I did. I find I am not quite unscrewed yet.'

'A wild beast tamed, you called her.'

'And what do *you* call her?'

'The same. How did Mr Jaggers tame her, Wemmick?'

'That's his secret. She has been with him many a long year.'

'I wish you would tell me her story. I feel a particular interest in being acquainted with it. You know that what is said between you and me goes no further.'

'Well!' Wemmick replied, 'I don't know her story,—that is, I don't know all of it. But what I do know I'll tell you. We are in our private and personal capacities, of course.'

'Of course.'

'A score or so of years ago, that woman was tried at the Old Bailey for murder, and was acquitted. She was a very handsome young woman, and I believe had some gypsy blood in her. Anyhow, it was hot enough when it was up, as you may suppose.'

'But she was acquitted.'

'Mr Jaggers was for her,' pursued Wemmick, with a look full of meaning, 'and worked the case in a way quite astonishing. It was a desperate case, and it was comparatively early days with him then, and he worked it to general admiration; in fact, it may almost be said to have made him. He worked it himself at the police-office, day after day for many days, contending against even a committal; and at the trial where he couldn't work it himself, sat under counsel, and—every one knew—put in all the salt and pepper. The murdered person was a woman,—a woman a good ten years older, very much larger, and very much stronger. It was a case of jealousy. They both led tramping lives, and this woman in Gerrard Street here had been married very young, over the broomstick (as we say), to a tramping man, and was a perfect fury in point of jealousy. The murdered woman,—more a match for the man, certainly, in point of years—was found dead in a barn near Hounslow Heath. There had been a violent struggle, perhaps a fight. She was bruised and scratched and torn, and had been held by the throat, at last, and choked. Now, there was no reasonable evidence to implicate any person but this woman, and on the improbabilities of her having been able to do it Mr Jaggers principally rested his case. 'You may be sure,' said Wemmick, touching me on the sleeve, 'that he never dwelt upon the strength of her hands then, though he sometimes does now.'

I had told Wemmick of his showing us her wrists, that day of the dinner party.

'Well, sir!' Wemmick went on; 'it happened—happened, don't you see?—that this woman was so very artfully dressed from the time of her apprehension, that she looked much slighter than she really was; in particular, her sleeves are always remembered to have been so skilfully contrived that her arms had quite a delicate look. She had only a bruise or two about her,—nothing for a tramp,—but the backs of her hands were lacerated, and the question was, Was it with finger-nails? Now, Mr Jaggers showed that she had struggled through a great lot of brambles which were not as high as her face; but which she could not have got through and kept her hands out of; and bits of those brambles were actually found in her skin and put in evidence, as well as the fact that the brambles in question were found on examination to have been broken through, and to have little shreds of her dress and little spots of blood upon them here and there. But the boldest point he made was this: it was attempted to be set up, in proof of her jealousy, that she was under strong suspicion of having, at about the time of the murder, frantically destroyed her child by this man—some three years old—to revenge herself upon him. Mr Jaggers worked that in this way: 'We say these are not marks of finger-nails, but marks of brambles, and we show you the brambles. You say they are marks of finger-nails, and you set up the hypothesis that she destroyed her child. You must accept all consequences of that hypothesis. For anything we know, she may have destroyed her child, and the child in clinging to her may have scratched her hands. What then? You are not trying her for the murder of her child; why don't you? As to this case, if you *will* have scratches, we say that, for anything we know, you may have accounted for them, assuming for the sake of argument that you have not invented them?' 'To sum up, sir,' said Wemmick, 'Mr Jaggers was altogether too many for the jury, and they gave in.'

'Has she been in his service ever since?'

'Yes; but not only that,' said Wemmick, 'she went into his service immediately after her acquittal, tamed as she is now. She has since been taught one thing and another in the way of her duties, but she was tamed from the beginning.'

'Do you remember the sex of the child?'

'Said to have been a girl.'

'You have nothing more to say to me tonight?'

'Nothing. I got your letter and destroyed it. Nothing.'

We exchanged a cordial goodnight, and I went home, with new matter for my thoughts, though with no relief from the old.

Chapter 49

Putting Miss Havisham's note in my pocket, that it might serve as my credentials for so soon reappearing at Satis House, in case her waywardness should lead her to express any surprise at seeing me, I went down again by the coach next day. But I alighted at the Halfway House, and breakfasted there, and walked the rest of the distance; for I sought to get into the town quietly by the unfrequented ways, and to leave it in the same manner.

The best light of the day was gone when I passed along the quiet echoing courts behind the High Street. The nooks of ruin where the old monks had once had their refectories and gardens, and where the strong walls were now pressed into the service of humble sheds and stables, were almost as silent as the old monks in their graves. The cathedral chimes had at once a sadder and a more remote sound to me, as I hurried on avoiding observation, than they had ever had before; so, the swell of the old organ was borne to my ears like funeral music; and the rooks, as they hovered about the grey tower and swung in the bare high trees of the priory garden, seemed to call to me that the place was changed, and that Estella was gone out of it forever.

An elderly woman, whom I had seen before as one of the servants who lived in the supplementary house across the back courtyard, opened the gate. The lighted candle stood in the dark passage within, as of old, and I took it up and ascended the staircase alone. Miss Havisham was not in her own room, but was in the larger room across the landing. Looking in at the door, after knocking in vain, I saw her sitting on the hearth in a ragged chair, close before, and lost in the contemplation of, the ashy fire.

Doing as I had often done, I went in, and stood touching the old chimney-piece, where she could see me when she raised her eyes. There was an air of utter loneliness upon her, that would have moved me to pity though she had wilfully done me a deeper injury than I could charge her with. As I stood compassionating her, and thinking how, in the progress of time, I too had come to be a part of the wrecked fortunes of that house, her eyes rested on me. She stared, and said in a low voice, 'Is it real?'

'It is I, Pip. Mr Jaggers gave me your note yesterday, and I have lost no time.'

'Thank you. Thank you.'

As I brought another of the ragged chairs to the hearth and sat down, I remarked a new expression on her face, as if she were afraid of me.

'I want,' she said, 'to pursue that subject you mentioned to me when you were last here, and to show you that I am not all stone. But perhaps you can never believe, now, that there is anything human in my heart?'

When I said some reassuring words, she stretched out her tremulous right hand, as though she was going to touch me; but she recalled it again before I understood the action, or knew how to receive it.

'You said, speaking for your friend, that you could tell me how to do something useful and good. Something that you would like done, is it not?'

'Something that I would like done very much.'

'What is it?'

I began explaining to her that secret history of the partnership. I had not got far into it, when I judged from her looks that she was thinking in a discursive way of me, rather than of what I said. It seemed to be so; for, when I stopped speaking, many moments passed before she showed that she was conscious of the fact.

'Do you break off,' she asked then, with her former air of being afraid of me, 'because you hate me too much to bear to speak to me?'

'No, no,' I answered, 'how can you think so, Miss Havisham! I stopped because I thought you were not following what I said.'

'Perhaps I was not,' she answered, putting a hand to her head. 'Begin again, and let me look at something else. Stay! Now tell me.'

She set her hand upon her stick in the resolute way that sometimes was habitual to her, and looked at the fire with a strong expression of forcing herself to attend. I went on with my explanation, and told her how I had hoped to complete the transaction out of my means, but how in this I was disappointed. That part of the subject (I reminded her) involved matters which could form no part of my explanation, for they were the weighty secrets of another.

'So!' said she, assenting with her head, but not looking at me. 'And how much money is wanting to complete the purchase?'

I was rather afraid of stating it, for it sounded a large sum. 'Nine hundred pounds.'

'If I give you the money for this purpose, will you keep my secret as you have kept your own?'

'Quite as faithfully.'

'And your mind will be more at rest?'

'Much more at rest.'

'Are you very unhappy now?'

She asked this question, still without looking at me, but in an unwonted tone of sympathy. I could not reply at the moment, for my voice failed me. She put her left arm across the head of her stick, and softly laid her forehead on it.

'I am far from happy, Miss Havisham; but I have other causes of disquiet than any you know of. They are the secrets I have mentioned.'

After a little while, she raised her head, and looked at the fire again.

'It is noble in you to tell me that you have other causes of unhappiness. Is it true?'

'Too true.'

'Can I only serve you, Pip, by serving your friend? Regarding that as done, is there nothing I can do for you yourself?'

'Nothing. I thank you for the question. I thank you even more for the tone of the question. But there is nothing.'

She presently rose from her seat, and looked about the blighted room for the means of writing. There were none there, and she took from her pocket a yellow set of ivory tablets, mounted in tarnished gold, and wrote upon them with a pencil in a case of tarnished gold that hung from her neck.

'You are still on friendly terms with Mr Jaggers?'

'Quite. I dined with him yesterday.'

'This is an authority to him to pay you that money, to lay out at your irresponsible discretion for your friend. I keep no money here; but if you would rather Mr Jaggers knew nothing of the matter, I will send it to you.'

'Thank you, Miss Havisham; I have not the least objection to receiving it from him.'

She read me what she had written; and it was direct and clear, and evidently intended to absolve me from any suspicion of profiting by the receipt of the money. I took the tablets from her hand, and it trembled again, and it trembled more as she took off the chain to which the pencil was attached, and put it in mine. All this she did without looking at me.

'My name is on the first leaf. If you can ever write under my name, 'I forgive her,' though ever so long after my broken heart is dust pray do it!'

'O Miss Havisham,' said I, 'I can do it now. There have been sore mistakes; and my life has been a blind and thankless one; and I want forgiveness and direction far too much, to be bitter with you.'

She turned her face to me for the first time since she had averted it, and, to my amazement, I may even add to my terror, dropped on her knees at my feet; with her folded hands raised to me in the manner in which, when her poor heart was young and fresh and whole, they must often have been raised to heaven from her mother's side.

To see her with her white hair and her worn face kneeling at my feet gave me a shock through all my frame. I entreated her to rise, and got my arms about her to help her up; but she only pressed that hand of mine which was nearest to her grasp, and hung her head over it and wept. I had never seen her shed a tear before, and, in the hope that the relief might do her good, I bent over her without speaking. She was not kneeling now, but was down upon the ground.

'O!' she cried, despairingly. 'What have I done! What have I done!'

'If you mean, Miss Havisham, what have you done to injure me, let me answer. Very little. I should have loved her under any circumstances. Is she married?'

'Yes.'

It was a needless question, for a new desolation in the desolate house had told me so.

'What have I done! What have I done!' She wrung her hands, and crushed her white hair, and returned to this cry over and over again. 'What have I done!'

I knew not how to answer, or how to comfort her. That she had done a grievous thing in taking an impressionable child to mould into the form that her wild resentment, spurned affection, and wounded pride found vengeance in, I knew full well. But that, in shutting out the light of day, she had shut out infinitely more; that, in seclusion, she had secluded herself from a thousand natural and healing influences; that, her mind, brooding solitary, had grown diseased, as all minds do and must and will that reverse the appointed order of their Maker, I knew equally well. And could I look upon her without compassion, seeing her punishment in the ruin she was, in her profound unfitness for this earth on which she was placed, in the vanity of sorrow which had become a master mania, like the vanity of penitence, the vanity of remorse, the vanity of unworthiness, and other monstrous vanities that have been curses in this world?

'Until you spoke to her the other day, and until I saw in you a looking-glass that showed me what I once felt myself, I did not know what I had done. What have I done! What have I done!' And so again, twenty, fifty times over, What had she done!

'Miss Havisham,' I said, when her cry had died away, 'you may dismiss me from your mind and conscience. But Estella is a different case, and if you can ever undo any scrap of what you have done amiss in keeping a part of her right nature away from her, it will be better to do that than to bemoan the past through a hundred years.'

'Yes, yes, I know it. But, Pip—my dear!' There was an earnest womanly compassion for me in her new affection. 'My dear! Believe this: when she first came to me, I meant to save her from misery like my own. At first, I meant no more.'

'Well, well!' said I. 'I hope so.'

'But as she grew, and promised to be very beautiful, I gradually did worse, and with my praises, and with my jewels, and with my teachings, and with this figure of myself always before her, a warning to back and point my lessons, I stole her heart away, and put ice in its place.'

'Better,' I could not help saying, 'to have left her a natural heart, even to be bruised or broken.'

With that, Miss Havisham looked distractedly at me for a while, and then burst out again, What had she done!

'If you knew all my story,' she pleaded, 'you would have some compassion for me and a better understanding of me.'

'Miss Havisham,' I answered, as delicately as I could, 'I believe I may say that I do know your story, and have known it ever since I first left this neighbourhood. It has inspired me with great commiseration, and I hope I understand it and its influences. Does what has passed between us give me any excuse for asking you a question relative to Estella? Not as she is, but as she was when she first came here?'

She was seated on the ground, with her arms on the ragged chair, and her head leaning on them. She looked full at me when I said this, and replied, 'Go on.'

'Whose child was Estella?'

She shook her head.

'You don't know?'

She shook her head again.

'But Mr Jaggers brought her here, or sent her here?'

'Brought her here.'

'Will you tell me how that came about?'

She answered in a low whisper and with caution: 'I had been shut up in these rooms a long time (I don't know how long; you know what time the clocks keep here), when I told him that I wanted a little girl to rear and love, and save from my fate. I had first seen him when I sent for him to lay this place waste for me; having read of him in the newspapers, before I and the world parted. He told me that he would look about him for such an orphan child. One night he brought her here asleep, and I called her Estella.'

'Might I ask her age then?'

'Two or three. She herself knows nothing, but that she was left an orphan and I adopted her.'

So convinced I was of that woman's being her mother, that I wanted no evidence to establish the fact in my own mind. But, to any mind, I thought, the connection here was clear and straight.

What more could I hope to do by prolonging the interview? I had succeeded on behalf of Herbert, Miss Havisham had told me all she knew of Estella, I had said and done what I could to ease her mind. No matter with what other words we parted; we parted.

Twilight was closing in when I went downstairs into the natural air. I called to the woman who had opened the gate when I entered, that I would not trouble her just yet, but would walk round the place before leaving. For I had a presentiment that I should never be there again, and I felt that the dying light was suited to my last view of it.

By the wilderness of casks that I had walked on long ago, and on which the rain of years had fallen since, rotting them in many places, and leaving miniature swamps and pools of water upon those that stood on end, I made my way to the ruined garden. I went all round it; round by the corner where Herbert and I had fought our battle; round by the paths where Estella and I had walked. So cold, so lonely, so dreary all!

Taking the brewery on my way back, I raised the rusty latch of a little door at the garden end of it, and walked through. I was going out at the opposite door,—not easy to open now, for the damp wood had started and swelled, and the hinges were yielding, and the threshold was encumbered with a growth of fungus,—when I turned my head to look back. A childish association revived with wonderful force in the moment of the slight action, and I fancied that I saw Miss Havisham hanging to the beam. So strong was the impression, that I stood under the beam shuddering from head to foot before I knew it was a fancy,—though to be sure I was there in an instant.

The mournfulness of the place and time, and the great terror of this illusion, though it was but momentary, caused me to feel an indescribable awe as I came out between the open wooden gates where I had once wrung my hair after Estella had wrung my heart. Passing on into the front courtyard, I hesitated whether to call the woman to let me out at the locked gate of which she had the key, or first to go upstairs and assure myself that Miss Havisham was as safe and well as I had left her. I took the latter course and went up.

I looked into the room where I had left her, and I saw her seated in the ragged chair upon the hearth close to the fire, with her back towards me. In the moment when I was withdrawing my head to go quietly away, I saw a great flaming light spring up. In the same moment I saw her running at me, shrieking, with a whirl of fire blazing all about her, and soaring at least as many feet above her head as she was high.

I had a double-caped great-coat on, and over my arm another thick coat. That I got them off, closed with her, threw her down, and got them over her; that I dragged the great cloth from the table for the same purpose, and with it dragged down the heap of rottenness in the midst, and all the ugly things that sheltered there; that we were on the ground struggling like desperate enemies, and that the closer I covered her, the more wildly she shrieked and tried to free herself,—that this occurred I knew through the result, but not through anything I felt, or thought, or knew I did. I knew nothing until I knew that we were on the floor by the great table, and that patches of tinder yet alight were floating in the smoky air, which, a moment ago, had been her faded bridal dress.

Then, I looked round and saw the disturbed beetles and spiders running away over the floor, and the servants coming in with breathless cries at the door. I still held her forcibly down with all my strength, like a prisoner who might escape; and I doubt if I even knew who she was, or why we had struggled, or that she had been in flames, or that the flames were out, until I saw the patches of tinder that had been her garments no longer alight but falling in a black shower around us.

She was insensible, and I was afraid to have her moved, or even touched. Assistance was sent for, and I held her until it came, as if I unreasonably fancied (I think I did) that, if I let her go, the fire would break out again and consume her. When I got up, on the surgeon's coming to her with other aid, I was astonished to see that both my hands were burnt; for, I had no knowledge of it through the sense of feeling.

On examination it was pronounced that she had received serious hurts, but that they of themselves were far from hopeless; the danger lay mainly in the nervous shock. By the surgeon's directions, her bed was carried into that room and laid upon the great table, which happened to be well suited to the dressing of her injuries. When I saw her again, an hour afterwards, she lay, indeed, where I had seen her strike her stick, and had heard her say that she would lie one day.

Though every vestige of her dress was burnt, as they told me, she still had something of her old ghastly bridal appearance; for, they had covered her to the throat with white cotton-wool, and as she lay with a white sheet loosely overlying that, the phantom air of something that had been and was changed was still upon her.

I found, on questioning the servants, that Estella was in Paris, and I got a promise from the surgeon that he would write to her by the next post. Miss Havisham's family I took upon myself; intending to communicate with Mr Matthew Pocket only, and leave him to do as he liked about informing the rest. This I did next day, through Herbert, as soon as I returned to town.

There was a stage, that evening, when she spoke collectedly of what had happened, though with a certain terrible vivacity. Towards midnight she began to wander in her speech; and after that it gradually set in that she said innumerable times in a low solemn voice, 'What have I done!' And then, 'When she first came, I meant to save her from misery like mine.' And then, 'Take the pencil and write under my name, 'I forgive her!"' She never changed the order of these three sentences, but she sometimes left out a word in one or other of them; never putting in another word, but always leaving a blank and going on to the next word.

As I could do no service there, and as I had, nearer home, that pressing reason for anxiety and fear which even her wanderings could not drive out of my mind, I decided, in the course of the night that I would return by the early morning coach, walking on a mile or so, and being taken up clear of the town. At about six o'clock of the morning, therefore, I leaned over her and touched her lips with mine, just as they said, not stopping for being touched, 'Take the pencil and write under my name, 'I forgive her.'

Chapter 50

My hands had been dressed twice or thrice in the night, and again in the morning. My left arm was a good deal burned to the elbow, and, less severely, as high as the shoulder; it was very painful, but the flames had set in that direction, and I felt thankful it was no worse. My right hand was not so badly burnt but that I could move the fingers. It was bandaged, of course, but much less inconveniently than my left hand and arm; those I carried in a sling; and I could only wear my coat like a cloak, loose over my shoulders and fastened at the neck. My hair had been caught by the fire, but not my head or face.

When Herbert had been down to Hammersmith and seen his father, he came back to me at our chambers, and devoted the day to attending on me. He was the kindest of nurses, and at stated times took off the bandages, and steeped them in the cooling liquid that was kept ready, and put them on again, with a patient tenderness that I was deeply grateful for.

At first, as I lay quiet on the sofa, I found it painfully difficult, I might say impossible, to get rid of the impression of the glare of the flames, their hurry and noise, and the fierce burning smell. If I dozed for a minute, I was awakened by Miss Havisham's cries, and by her running at me with all that height of fire above her head. This pain of the mind was much harder to strive against than any bodily pain I suffered; and Herbert, seeing that, did his utmost to hold my attention engaged.

Neither of us spoke of the boat, but we both thought of it. That was made apparent by our avoidance of the subject, and by our agreeing—without agreement—to make my recovery of the use of my hands a question of so many hours, not of so many weeks.

My first question when I saw Herbert had been of course, whether all was well down the river? As he replied in the affirmative, with perfect confidence and cheerfulness, we did not resume the subject until the day was wearing away. But then, as Herbert changed the bandages, more by the light of the fire than by the outer light, he went back to it spontaneously.

'I sat with Provis last night, Handel, two good hours.'

'Where was Clara?'

'Dear little thing!' said Herbert. 'She was up and down with Gruffandgrim all the evening. He was perpetually pegging at the floor the moment she left his sight. I doubt if he can hold out long, though. What with rum and pepper,—and pepper and rum,—I should think his pegging must be nearly over.'

'And then you will be married, Herbert?'

'How can I take care of the dear child otherwise?—Lay your arm out upon the back of the sofa, my dear boy, and I'll sit down here, and get the bandage off so gradually that you shall not know when it comes. I was speaking of Provis. Do you know, Handel, he improves?'

'I said to you I thought he was softened when I last saw him.'

'So you did. And so he is. He was very communicative last night, and told me more of his life. You remember his breaking off here about some woman that he had had great trouble with.—Did I hurt you?'

I had started, but not under his touch. His words had given me a start.

'I had forgotten that, Herbert, but I remember it now you speak of it.'

'Well! He went into that part of his life, and a dark wild part it is. Shall I tell you? Or would it worry you just now?'

'Tell me by all means. Every word.'

Herbert bent forward to look at me more nearly, as if my reply had been rather more hurried or more eager than he could quite account for. 'Your head is cool?' he said, touching it.

'Quite,' said I. 'Tell me what Provis said, my dear Herbert.'

'It seems,' said Herbert, '—there's a bandage off most charmingly, and now comes the cool one,—makes you shrink at first, my poor dear fellow, don't it? But it will be comfortable presently,—it seems that the woman was a young woman, and a jealous woman, and a revengeful woman; revengeful, Handel, to the last degree.'

'To what last degree?'

'Murder.—Does it strike too cold on that sensitive place?'

'I don't feel it. How did she murder? Whom did she murder?'

'Why, the deed may not have merited quite so terrible a name,' said Herbert, 'but, she was tried for it, and Mr Jaggers defended her, and the reputation of that defence first made his name known to Provis. It was another and a stronger woman who was the victim, and there had been a struggle—in a barn. Who began it, or how fair it was, or how unfair, may be doubtful; but how it ended is certainly not doubtful, for the victim was found throttled.'

'Was the woman brought in guilty?'

'No; she was acquitted.—My poor Handel, I hurt you!'

'It is impossible to be gentler, Herbert. Yes? What else?'

'This acquitted young woman and Provis had a little child; a little child of whom Provis was exceedingly fond. On the evening of the very night when the object of her jealousy was strangled as I tell you, the young woman presented herself before Provis for one moment, and swore that she would destroy the child (which was in her possession), and he should never see it again; then she vanished.—There's the worst arm comfortably in the sling once more, and now there remains but the right hand, which is a far easier job. I can do it better by this light than by a stronger, for my hand is steadiest when I don't see the poor blistered patches too distinctly.—You don't think your breathing is affected, my dear boy? You seem to breathe quickly.'

'Perhaps I do, Herbert. Did the woman keep her oath?'

'There comes the darkest part of Provis's life. She did.'

'That is, he says she did.'

'Why, of course, my dear boy,' returned Herbert, in a tone of surprise, and again bending forward to get a nearer look at me. 'He says it all. I have no other information.'

'No, to be sure.'

'Now, whether,' pursued Herbert, 'he had used the child's mother ill, or whether he had used the child's mother well, Provis doesn't say; but she had shared some four or five years of the wretched life he described to us at this fireside, and he seems to have felt pity for her, and forbearance towards her. Therefore, fearing he should be called upon to depose about this destroyed child, and so be the cause of her death, he hid himself (much as he grieved for the child), kept himself dark, as he says, out of the way and out of the trial, and was only vaguely talked of as a certain man called Abel, out of whom the jealousy arose. After the acquittal she disappeared, and thus he lost the child and the child's mother.'

'I want to ask—'

'A moment, my dear boy, and I have done. That evil genius, Compeyson, the worst of scoundrels among many scoundrels, knowing of his keeping out of the way at that time and of his reasons for doing so, of course afterwards held the knowledge over his head as a means of keeping him poorer and working him harder. It was clear last night that this barbed the point of Provis's animosity.'

'I want to know,' said I, 'and particularly, Herbert, whether he told you when this happened?'

'Particularly? Let me remember, then, what he said as to that. His expression was, "a round score o' year ago, and a'most directly after I took up wi' Compeyson." How old were you when you came upon him in the little churchyard?'

'I think in my seventh year.'

'Ay. It had happened some three or four years then, he said, and you brought into his mind the little girl so tragically lost, who would have been about your age.'

'Herbert,' said I, after a short silence, in a hurried way, 'can you see me best by the light of the window, or the light of the fire?'

'By the firelight,' answered Herbert, coming close again.

'Look at me.'

'I do look at you, my dear boy.'

'Touch me.'

'I do touch you, my dear boy.'

'You are not afraid that I am in any fever, or that my head is much disordered by the accident of last night?'

'N-no, my dear boy,' said Herbert, after taking time to examine me. 'You are rather excited, but you are quite yourself.'

'I know I am quite myself. And the man we have in hiding down the river, is Estella's Father.'

Chapter 51

What purpose I had in view when I was hot on tracing out and proving Estella's parentage, I cannot say. It will presently be seen that the question was not before me in a distinct shape until it was put before me by a wiser head than my own.

But when Herbert and I had held our momentous conversation, I was seized with a feverish conviction that I ought to hunt the matter down,—that I ought not to let it rest, but that I ought to see Mr Jaggers, and come at the bare truth. I really do not know whether I felt that I did this for Estella's sake, or whether I was glad to transfer to the man in whose preservation I was so much concerned some rays of the romantic interest that had so long surrounded me. Perhaps the latter possibility may be the nearer to the truth.

Any way, I could scarcely be withheld from going out to Gerrard Street that night. Herbert's representations that, if I did, I should probably be laid up and stricken useless, when our fugitive's safety would depend upon me, alone restrained my impatience. On the understanding, again and again reiterated, that, come what would, I was to go to Mr Jaggers tomorrow, I at length submitted to keep quiet, and to have my hurts looked after, and to stay at home. Early next morning we went out together, and at the corner of Giltspur Street by Smithfield, I left Herbert to go his way into the city, and took my way to Little Britain.

There were periodical occasions when Mr Jaggers and Wemmick went over the office accounts, and checked off the vouchers, and put all things straight. On these occasions, Wemmick took his books and papers into Mr Jaggers's room, and one of the upstairs clerks came down into the outer office. Finding such clerk on Wemmick's post that morning, I knew what was going on; but I was not sorry to have Mr Jaggers and Wemmick together, as Wemmick would then hear for himself that I said nothing to compromise him.

My appearance, with my arm bandaged and my coat loose over my shoulders, favoured my object. Although I had sent Mr Jaggers a brief account of the accident as soon as I had arrived in town, yet I had to give him all the details now; and the speciality of the occasion caused our talk to be less dry and hard, and less strictly regulated by the rules of evidence, than it had been before. While I described the disaster, Mr Jaggers stood, according to his wont, before the fire. Wemmick leaned back in his chair, staring at me, with his hands in the pockets of his trousers, and his pen put horizontally into the post. The two brutal casts, always inseparable in my mind from the official proceedings, seemed to be congestively considering whether they didn't smell fire at the present moment.

My narrative finished, and their questions exhausted, I then produced Miss Havisham's authority to receive the nine hundred pounds for Herbert. Mr Jaggers's eyes retired a little deeper into his head when I handed him the tablets, but he presently handed them over to Wemmick, with instructions to draw the check for his signature. While that was in course of being done, I looked on at Wemmick as he wrote, and Mr Jaggers, poising and swaying himself on his well-polished boots, looked on at me. 'I am sorry, Pip,' said he, as I put the check in my pocket, when he had signed it, 'that we do nothing for *you*.'

'Miss Havisham was good enough to ask me,' I returned, 'whether she could do nothing for me, and I told her No.'

'Everybody should know his own business,' said Mr Jaggers. And I saw Wemmick's lips form the words 'portable property.'

'I should *not* have told her No, if I had been you,' said Mr Jaggers; 'but every man ought to know his own business best.'

'Every man's business,' said Wemmick, rather reproachfully towards me, 'is portable property.'

As I thought the time was now come for pursuing the theme I had at heart, I said, turning on Mr Jaggers:—

'I did ask something of Miss Havisham, however, sir. I asked her to give me some information relative to her adopted daughter, and she gave me all she possessed.'

'Did she?' said Mr Jaggers, bending forward to look at his boots and then straightening himself. 'Hah! I don't think I should have done so, if I had been Miss Havisham. But *she* ought to know her own business best.'

'I know more of the history of Miss Havisham's adopted child than Miss Havisham herself does, sir. I know her mother.'

Mr Jaggers looked at me inquiringly, and repeated, 'Mother?'

'I have seen her mother within these three days.'

'Yes?' said Mr Jaggers.

'And so have you, sir. And you have seen her still more recently.'

'Yes?' said Mr Jaggers.

'Perhaps I know more of Estella's history than even you do,' said I. 'I know her father too.'

A certain stop that Mr Jaggers came to in his manner—he was too self-possessed to change his manner, but he could not help its being brought to an indefinably attentive stop—assured me that he did not know who her father was. This I had strongly suspected from Provis's account (as Herbert had repeated it) of his having kept himself dark; which I pieced on to the fact that he himself was not Mr Jaggers's client until some four years later, and when he could have no reason for claiming his identity. But, I could not be sure of this unconsciousness on Mr Jaggers's part before, though I was quite sure of it now.

'So! You know the young lady's father, Pip?' said Mr Jaggers.

'Yes,' I replied, 'and his name is Provis—from New South Wales.'

Even Mr Jaggers started when I said those words. It was the slightest start that could escape a man, the most carefully repressed and the sooner checked, but he did start, though he made it a part of the action of taking out his pocket-handkerchief. How Wemmick received the announcement I am unable to say; for I was afraid to look at him just then, lest Mr Jaggers's sharpness should detect that there had been some communication unknown to him between us.

'And on what evidence, Pip,' asked Mr Jaggers, very coolly, as he paused with his handkerchief halfway to his nose, 'does Provis make this claim?'

'He does not make it,' said I, 'and has never made it, and has no knowledge or belief that his daughter is in existence.'

For once, the powerful pocket-handkerchief failed. My reply was so unexpected, that Mr Jaggers put the handkerchief back into his pocket without completing the usual performance, folded his arms, and looked with stern attention at me, though with an immovable face.

Then I told him all I knew, and how I knew it; with the one reservation that I left him to infer that I knew from Miss Havisham what I in fact knew from Wemmick. I was very careful indeed as to that. Nor did I look towards Wemmick until I had finished all I had to tell, and had been for some time silently meeting Mr Jaggers's look. When I did at last turn my eyes in Wemmick's direction, I found that he had unposted his pen, and was intent upon the table before him.

'Hah!' said Mr Jaggers at last, as he moved towards the papers on the table. 'What item was it you were at, Wemmick, when Mr Pip came in?'

But I could not submit to be thrown off in that way, and I made a passionate, almost an indignant appeal, to him to be more frank and manly with me. I reminded him of the false hopes into which

I had lapsed, the length of time they had lasted, and the discovery I had made: and I hinted at the danger that weighed upon my spirits. I represented myself as being surely worthy of some little confidence from him, in return for the confidence I had just now imparted. I said that I did not blame him, or suspect him, or mistrust him, but I wanted assurance of the truth from him. And if he asked me why I wanted it, and why I thought I had any right to it, I would tell him, little as he cared for such poor dreams, that I had loved Estella dearly and long, and that although I had lost her, and must live a bereaved life, whatever concerned her was still nearer and dearer to me than anything else in the world. And seeing that Mr Jaggers stood quite still and silent, and apparently quite obdurate, under this appeal, I turned to Wemmick, and said, 'Wemmick, I know you to be a man with a gentle heart. I have seen your pleasant home, and your old father, and all the innocent, cheerful playful ways with which you refresh your business life. And I entreat you to say a word for me to Mr Jaggers, and to represent to him that, all circumstances considered, he ought to be more open with me!'

I have never seen two men look more oddly at one another than Mr Jaggers and Wemmick did after this apostrophe. At first, a misgiving crossed me that Wemmick would be instantly dismissed from his employment; but it melted as I saw Mr Jaggers relax into something like a smile, and Wemmick become bolder.

'What's all this?' said Mr Jaggers. 'You with an old father, and you with pleasant and playful ways?'

'Well!' returned Wemmick. 'If I don't bring 'em here, what does it matter?'

'Pip,' said Mr Jaggers, laying his hand upon my arm, and smiling openly, 'this man must be the most cunning impostor in all London.'

'Not a bit of it,' returned Wemmick, growing bolder and bolder. 'I think you're another.'

Again they exchanged their former odd looks, each apparently still distrustful that the other was taking him in.

'*You* with a pleasant home?' said Mr Jaggers.

'Since it don't interfere with business,' returned Wemmick, 'let it be so. Now, I look at you, sir, I shouldn't wonder if *you* might be planning and contriving to have a pleasant home of your own one of these days, when you're tired of all this work.'

Mr Jaggers nodded his head retrospectively two or three times, and actually drew a sigh. 'Pip,' said he, 'we won't talk about 'poor dreams;' you know more about such things than I, having much fresher experience of that kind. But now about this other matter. I'll put a case to you. Mind! I admit nothing.'

He waited for me to declare that I quite understood that he expressly said that he admitted nothing.

'Now, Pip,' said Mr Jaggers, 'put this case. Put the case that a woman, under such circumstances as you have mentioned, held her child concealed, and was obliged to communicate the fact to her legal adviser, on his representing to her that he must know, with an eye to the latitude of his defence, how the fact stood about that child. Put the case that, at the same time he held a trust to find a child for an eccentric rich lady to adopt and bring up.'

'I follow you, sir.'

'Put the case that he lived in an atmosphere of evil, and that all he saw of children was their being generated in great numbers for certain destruction. Put the case that he often saw children solemnly tried at a criminal bar, where they were held up to be seen; put the case that he habitually knew of their being imprisoned, whipped, transported, neglected, cast out, qualified in all ways for the hangman, and growing up to be hanged. Put the case that pretty nigh all the children he saw in his daily business life he had reason to look upon as so much spawn, to develop into the fish that were to come to his net,—to be prosecuted, defended, forsworn, made orphans, bedevilled somehow.'

'I follow you, sir.'

'Put the case, Pip, that here was one pretty little child out of the heap who could be saved; whom the father believed dead, and dared make no stir about; as to whom, over the mother, the legal adviser had this power: "I know what you did, and how you did it. You came so and so, you did such and such things to divert suspicion. I have tracked you through it all, and I tell it you all. Part with the child, unless it should be necessary to produce it to clear you, and then it shall be produced. Give the child into my hands, and I will do my best to bring you off. If you are saved, your child is saved too; if you are lost, your child is still saved." Put the case that this was done, and that the woman was cleared.'

'I understand you perfectly.'

'But that I make no admissions?'

'That you make no admissions.' And Wemmick repeated, 'No admissions.'

'Put the case, Pip, that passion and the terror of death had a little shaken the woman's intellects, and that when she was set at liberty, she was scared out of the ways of the world, and went to him to be sheltered. Put the case that he took her in, and that he kept down the old, wild, violent nature whenever he saw an inkling of its breaking out, by asserting his power over her in the old way. Do you comprehend the imaginary case?'

'Quite.'

'Put the case that the child grew up, and was married for money. That the mother was still living. That the father was still living. That the mother and father, unknown to one another, were dwelling within so many miles, furlongs, yards if you like, of one another. That the secret was still a secret, except that you had got wind of it. Put that last case to yourself very carefully.'

'I do.'

'I ask Wemmick to put it to *him*self very carefully.'

And Wemmick said, 'I do.'

'For whose sake would you reveal the secret? For the father's? I think he would not be much the better for the mother. For the mother's? I think if she had done such a deed she would be safer where she was. For the daughter's? I think it would hardly serve her to establish her parentage for the information of her husband, and to drag her back to disgrace, after an escape of twenty years, pretty secure to last for life. But add the case that you had loved her, Pip, and had made her the subject of those 'poor dreams' which have, at one time or another, been in the heads of more men than you think likely, then I tell you that you had better—and would much sooner when you had thought well of it—chop off that bandaged left hand of yours with your bandaged right hand, and then pass the chopper on to Wemmick there, to cut *that* off too.'

I looked at Wemmick, whose face was very grave. He gravely touched his lips with his forefinger. I did the same. Mr Jaggers did the same. 'Now, Wemmick,' said the latter then, resuming his usual manner, 'what item was it you were at when Mr Pip came in?'

Standing by for a little, while they were at work, I observed that the odd looks they had cast at one another were repeated several times: with this difference now, that each of them seemed suspicious, not to say conscious, of having shown himself in a weak and unprofessional light to the other. For this reason, I suppose, they were now inflexible with one another; Mr Jaggers being highly dictatorial, and Wemmick obstinately justifying himself whenever there was the smallest point in abeyance for a moment. I had never seen them on such ill terms; for generally they got on very well indeed together.

But they were both happily relieved by the opportune appearance of Mike, the client with the fur cap and the habit of wiping his nose on his sleeve, whom I had seen on the very first day of my appearance within those walls. This individual, who, either in his own person or in that of some member of his family, seemed to be always in trouble (which in that place meant Newgate), called to announce that his eldest daughter was taken up on suspicion of shoplifting. As he imparted this melancholy circumstance to Wemmick, Mr Jaggers standing magisterially before the fire and taking no share in the proceedings, Mike's eye happened to twinkle with a tear.

'What are you about?' demanded Wemmick, with the utmost indignation. 'What do you come snivelling here for?'

'I didn't go to do it, Mr Wemmick.'

'You did,' said Wemmick. 'How dare you? You're not in a fit state to come here, if you can't come here without spluttering like a bad pen. What do you mean by it?'

'A man can't help his feelings, Mr Wemmick,' pleaded Mike.

'His what?' demanded Wemmick, quite savagely. 'Say that again!'

'Now look here my man,' said Mr Jaggers, advancing a step, and pointing to the door. 'Get out of this office. I'll have no feelings here. Get out.'

'It serves you right,' said Wemmick, 'Get out.'

So, the unfortunate Mike very humbly withdrew, and Mr Jaggers and Wemmick appeared to have re-established their good understanding, and went to work again with an air of refreshment upon them as if they had just had lunch.

Chapter 52

From Little Britain I went, with my check in my pocket, to Miss Skiffins's brother, the accountant; and Miss Skiffins's brother, the accountant, going straight to Clarriker's and bringing Clarriker to me, I had the great satisfaction of concluding that arrangement. It was the only good thing I had done, and the only completed thing I had done, since I was first apprised of my great expectations.

Clarriker informing me on that occasion that the affairs of the House were steadily progressing, that he would now be able to establish a small branch-house in the East which was much wanted for the extension of the business, and that Herbert in his new partnership capacity would go out and take charge of it, I found that I must have prepared for a separation from my friend, even though my own affairs had been more settled. And now, indeed, I felt as if my last anchor were loosening its hold, and I should soon be driving with the winds and waves.

But there was recompense in the joy with which Herbert would come home of a night and tell me of these changes, little imagining that he told me no news, and would sketch airy pictures of himself conducting Clara Barley to the land of the Arabian Nights, and of me going out to join them (with a caravan of camels, I believe), and of our all going up the Nile and seeing wonders. Without being sanguine as to my own part in those bright plans, I felt that Herbert's way was clearing fast, and that old Bill Barley had but to stick to his pepper and rum, and his daughter would soon be happily provided for.

We had now got into the month of March. My left arm, though it presented no bad symptoms, took, in the natural course, so long to heal that I was still unable to get a coat on. My right arm was tolerably restored; disfigured, but fairly serviceable.

On a Monday morning, when Herbert and I were at breakfast, I received the following letter from Wemmick by the post.

'Walworth. Burn this as soon as read. Early in the week, or say Wednesday, you might do what you know of, if you felt disposed to try it. Now burn.'

When I had shown this to Herbert and had put it in the fire—but not before we had both got it by heart—we considered what to do. For, of course my being disabled could now be no longer kept out of view.

'I have thought it over again and again,' said Herbert, 'and I think I know a better course than taking a Thames waterman. Take Startop. A good fellow, a skilled hand, fond of us, and enthusiastic and honourable.'

I had thought of him more than once.

'But how much would you tell him, Herbert?'

'It is necessary to tell him very little. Let him suppose it a mere freak, but a secret one, until the morning comes: then let him know that there is urgent reason for your getting Provis aboard and away. You go with him?'

'No doubt.'

'Where?'

It had seemed to me, in the many anxious considerations I had given the point, almost indifferent what port we made for,—Hamburg, Rotterdam, Antwerp,—the place signified little, so that he was out of England. Any foreign steamer that fell in our way and would take us up would do. I had always proposed to myself to get him well down the river in the boat; certainly well beyond Gravesend, which was a critical place for search or inquiry if suspicion were afoot. As foreign steamers would leave London at about the time of high-water, our plan would be to get down the river by a previous ebb-tide, and lie by in some quiet spot until we could pull off to one. The time when one would be due where we lay, wherever that might be, could be calculated pretty nearly, if we made inquiries beforehand.

Herbert assented to all this, and we went out immediately after breakfast to pursue our investigations. We found that a steamer for Hamburg was likely to suit our purpose best, and we directed our thoughts chiefly to that vessel. But we noted down what other foreign steamers would leave London with the same tide, and we satisfied ourselves that we knew the build and colour of each. We then separated for a few hours: I, to get at once such passports as were necessary; Herbert, to see Startop at his lodgings. We both did what we had to do without any hindrance, and when we met again at one o'clock reported it done. I, for my part, was prepared with passports; Herbert had seen Startop, and he was more than ready to join.

Those two should pull a pair of oars, we settled, and I would steer; our charge would be sitter, and keep quiet; as speed was not our object, we should make way enough. We arranged that Herbert should not come home to dinner before going to Mill Pond Bank that evening; that he should not go there at all tomorrow evening, Tuesday; that he should prepare Provis to come down to some stairs hard by the house, on Wednesday, when he saw us approach, and not sooner; that all the arrangements with him should be concluded that Monday night; and that he should be communicated with no more in any way, until we took him on board.

These precautions well understood by both of us, I went home.

On opening the outer door of our chambers with my key, I found a letter in the box, directed to me; a very dirty letter, though not ill-written. It had been delivered by hand (of course, since I left home), and its contents were these:—

'If you are not afraid to come to the old marshes tonight or tomorrow night at nine, and to come to the little sluice-house by the limekiln, you had better come. If you want information regarding *your uncle Provis*, you had much better come and tell no one, and lose no time. *You must come alone.* Bring this with you.'

I had had load enough upon my mind before the receipt of this strange letter. What to do now, I could not tell. And the worst was, that I must decide quickly, or I should miss the afternoon coach, which would take me down in time for tonight. Tomorrow night I could not think of going, for it would be too close upon the time of the flight. And again, for anything I knew, the proffered information might have some important bearing on the flight itself.

If I had had ample time for consideration, I believe I should still have gone. Having hardly any time for consideration,—my watch showing me that the coach started within half an hour,—I resolved to go. I should certainly not have gone, but for the reference to my Uncle Provis. That, coming on Wemmick's letter and the morning's busy preparation, turned the scale.

It is so difficult to become clearly possessed of the contents of almost any letter, in a violent hurry, that I had to read this mysterious epistle again twice, before its injunction to me to be secret got mechanically into my mind. Yielding to it in the same mechanical kind of way, I left a note in pencil for Herbert, telling him that as I should be so soon going away, I knew not for how long, I had decided to hurry down and back, to ascertain for myself how Miss Havisham was faring. I had then barely time to get my great-coat, lock up the chambers, and make for the coach-office by the short by-ways. If I had taken a hackney-chariot and gone by the streets, I should have missed my aim; going as I did, I caught the coach just as it came out of the yard. I was the only inside passenger, jolting away knee-deep in straw, when I came to myself.

For I really had not been myself since the receipt of the letter; it had so bewildered me, ensuing on the hurry of the morning. The morning hurry and flutter had been great; for, long and anxiously as I had waited for Wemmick, his hint had come like a surprise at last. And now I began to wonder at myself for being in the coach, and to doubt whether I had sufficient reason for being there, and to consider whether I should get out presently and go back, and to argue against ever heeding an anonymous communication, and, in short, to pass through all those phases of contradiction and indecision to which I suppose very few hurried people are strangers. Still, the reference to Provis by name mastered everything. I reasoned as I had reasoned already without knowing it,—if that be reasoning,—in case any harm should befall him through my not going, how could I ever forgive myself!

It was dark before we got down, and the journey seemed long and dreary to me, who could see little of it inside, and who could not go outside in my disabled state. Avoiding the Blue Boar, I put up at an inn of minor reputation down the town, and ordered some dinner. While it was preparing, I went to Satis House and inquired for Miss Havisham; she was still very ill, though considered something better.

My inn had once been a part of an ancient ecclesiastical house, and I dined in a little octagonal common-room, like a font. As I was not able to cut my dinner, the old landlord with a shining bald head did it for me. This bringing us into conversation, he was so good as to entertain me with my own story,—of course with the popular feature that Pumblechook was my earliest benefactor and the founder of my fortunes.

'Do you know the young man?' said I.

'Know him!' repeated the landlord. 'Ever since he was—no height at all.'

'Does he ever come back to this neighbourhood?'

'Ay, he comes back,' said the landlord, 'to his great friends, now and again, and gives the cold shoulder to the man that made him.'

'What man is that?'

'Him that I speak of,' said the landlord. 'Mr Pumblechook.'

'Is he ungrateful to no one else?'

'No doubt he would be, if he could,' returned the landlord, 'but he can't. And why? Because Pumblechook done everything for him.'

'Does Pumblechook say so?'

'Say so!' replied the landlord. 'He han't no call to say so.'

'But does he say so?'

'It would turn a man's blood to white wine winegar to hear him tell of it, sir,' said the landlord.

I thought, 'Yet Joe, dear Joe, *you* never tell of it. Long-suffering and loving Joe, *you* never complain. Nor you, sweet-tempered Biddy!'

'Your appetite's been touched like by your accident,' said the landlord, glancing at the bandaged arm under my coat. 'Try a tenderer bit.'

'No, thank you,' I replied, turning from the table to brood over the fire. 'I can eat no more. Please take it away.'

I had never been struck at so keenly, for my thanklessness to Joe, as through the brazen impostor Pumblechook. The falser he, the truer Joe; the meaner he, the nobler Joe.

My heart was deeply and most deservedly humbled as I mused over the fire for an hour or more. The striking of the clock aroused me, but not from my dejection or remorse, and I got up and had my coat fastened round my neck, and went out. I had previously sought in my pockets for the letter, that I might refer to it again; but I could not find it, and was uneasy to think that it must have been dropped in the straw of the coach. I knew very well, however, that the appointed place was the little sluice-house by the limekiln on the marshes, and the hour nine. Towards the marshes I now went straight, having no time to spare.

Chapter 53

It was a dark night, though the full moon rose as I left the enclosed lands, and passed out upon the marshes. Beyond their dark line there was a ribbon of clear sky, hardly broad enough to hold the red large moon. In a few minutes she had ascended out of that clear field, in among the piled mountains of cloud.

There was a melancholy wind, and the marshes were very dismal. A stranger would have found them insupportable, and even to me they were so oppressive that I hesitated, half inclined to go back. But I knew them well, and could have found my way on a far darker night, and had no excuse for returning, being there. So, having come there against my inclination, I went on against it.

The direction that I took was not that in which my old home lay, nor that in which we had pursued the convicts. My back was turned towards the distant Hulks as I walked on, and, though I could see the old lights away on the spits of sand, I saw them over my shoulder. I knew the limekiln as well as I knew the old Battery, but they were miles apart; so that, if a light had been burning at each point that night, there would have been a long strip of the blank horizon between the two bright specks.

At first, I had to shut some gates after me, and now and then to stand still while the cattle that were lying in the banked-up pathway arose and blundered down among the grass and reeds. But after a little while I seemed to have the whole flats to myself.

It was another half-hour before I drew near to the kiln. The lime was burning with a sluggish stifling smell, but the fires were made up and left, and no workmen were visible. Hard by was a small stone-quarry.

It lay directly in my way, and had been worked that day, as I saw by the tools and barrows that were lying about.

Coming up again to the marsh level out of this excavation,—for the rude path lay through it,—I saw a light in the old sluice-house. I quickened my pace, and knocked at the door with my hand. Waiting for some reply, I looked about me, noticing how the sluice was abandoned and broken, and how the house—of wood with a tiled roof—would not be proof against the weather much longer, if it were so even now, and how the mud and ooze were coated with lime, and how the choking vapour of the kiln crept in a ghostly way towards me. Still there was no answer, and I knocked again. No answer still, and I tried the latch.

It rose under my hand, and the door yielded. Looking in, I saw a lighted candle on a table, a bench, and a mattress on a truckle bedstead. As there was a loft above, I called, 'Is there anyone here?' but no voice answered. Then I looked at my watch, and, finding that it was past nine, called again, 'Is there anyone here?' There being still no answer, I went out at the door, irresolute what to do.

It was beginning to rain fast. Seeing nothing save what I had seen already, I turned back into the house, and stood just within the shelter of the doorway, looking out into the night. While I was considering that someone must have been there lately and must soon be coming back, or the candle would not be burning, it came into my head to look if the wick were long. I turned round to do so, and had taken up the candle in my hand, when it was extinguished by some violent shock; and the next thing I comprehended was, that I had been caught in a strong running noose, thrown over my head from behind.

'Now,' said a suppressed voice with an oath, 'I've got you!'

'What is this?' I cried, struggling. 'Who is it? Help, help, help!'

Not only were my arms pulled close to my sides, but the pressure on my bad arm caused me exquisite pain. Sometimes, a strong man's hand, sometimes a strong man's breast, was set against my mouth to deaden my cries, and with a hot breath always close to me, I struggled ineffectually in the dark, while I was fastened tight to the wall. 'And now,' said the suppressed voice with another oath, 'call out again, and I'll make short work of you!'

Faint and sick with the pain of my injured arm, bewildered by the surprise, and yet conscious how easily this threat could be put in execution, I desisted, and tried to ease my arm were it ever so little. But, it was bound too tight for that. I felt as if, having been burnt before, it were now being boiled.

The sudden exclusion of the night, and the substitution of black darkness in its place, warned me that the man had closed a shutter. After groping about for a little, he found the flint and steel he wanted, and began to strike a light. I strained my sight upon the sparks that fell among the tinder, and upon which he breathed and breathed, match in hand, but I could only see his lips, and the blue point of the match; even those but fitfully. The tinder was damp,—no wonder there,—and one after another the sparks died out.

The man was in no hurry, and struck again with the flint and steel. As the sparks fell thick and bright about him, I could see his hands, and touches of his face, and could make out that he was seated and bending over the table; but nothing more. Presently I saw his blue lips again, breathing on the tinder, and then a flare of light flashed up, and showed me Orlick.

Whom I had looked for, I don't know. I had not looked for him. Seeing him, I felt that I was in a dangerous strait indeed, and I kept my eyes upon him.

He lighted the candle from the flaring match with great deliberation, and dropped the match, and trod it out. Then he put the candle away from him on the table, so that he could see me, and sat with his arms folded on the table and looked at me. I made out that I was fastened to a stout perpendicular ladder a few inches from the wall,—a fixture there,—the means of ascent to the loft above.

'Now,' said he, when we had surveyed one another for some time, 'I've got you.'

'Unbind me. Let me go!'

'Ah!' he returned, '*I*'ll let you go. I'll let you go to the moon, I'll let you go to the stars. All in good time.'

'Why have you lured me here?'

'Don't you know?' said he, with a deadly look.

'Why have you set upon me in the dark?'

'Because I mean to do it all myself. One keeps a secret better than two. O you enemy, you enemy!'

His enjoyment of the spectacle I furnished, as he sat with his arms folded on the table, shaking his head at me and hugging himself, had a malignity in it that made me tremble. As I watched him in silence, he put his hand into the corner at his side, and took up a gun with a brass-bound stock.

'Do you know this?' said he, making as if he would take aim at me. 'Do you know where you saw it afore? Speak, wolf!'

'Yes,' I answered.

'You cost me that place. You did. Speak!'

'What else could I do?'

'You did that, and that would be enough, without more. How dared you to come betwixt me and a young woman I liked?'

'When did I?'

'When didn't you? It was you as always give Old Orlick a bad name to her.'

'You gave it to yourself; you gained it for yourself. I could have done you no harm, if you had done yourself none.'

'You're a liar. And you'll take any pains, and spend any money, to drive me out of this country, will you?' said he, repeating my words to Biddy in the last interview I had with her. 'Now, I'll tell you a piece of information. It was never so well worth your while to get me out of this country as it is tonight. Ah! If it was all your money twenty times told, to the last brass farden!' As he shook his heavy hand at me, with his mouth snarling like a tiger's, I felt that it was true.

'What are you going to do to me?'

'I'm a going,' said he, bringing his fist down upon the table with a heavy blow, and rising as the blow fell to give it greater force,—'I'm a going to have your life!'

He leaned forward staring at me, slowly unclenched his hand and drew it across his mouth as if his mouth watered for me, and sat down again.

'You was always in Old Orlick's way since ever you was a child. You goes out of his way this present night. He'll have no more on you. You're dead.'

I felt that I had come to the brink of my grave. For a moment I looked wildly round my trap for any chance of escape; but there was none.

'More than that,' said he, folding his arms on the table again, 'I won't have a rag of you, I won't have a bone of you, left on earth. I'll put your body in the kiln,—I'd carry two such to it, on my shoulders,—and, let people suppose what they may of you, they shall never know nothing.'

My mind, with inconceivable rapidity followed out all the consequences of such a death. Estella's father would believe I had deserted him, would be taken, would die accusing me; even Herbert would doubt me, when he compared the letter I had left for him with the fact that I had called at Miss Havisham's gate for only a moment; Joe and Biddy would never know how sorry I had been that night, none would ever know what I had suffered, how true I had meant to be, what an agony I had passed through. The death close before me was terrible, but far more terrible than death was the dread of being misremembered after death. And so quick were my thoughts, that I saw myself despised by unborn generations,—Estella's children, and their children,—while the wretch's words were yet on his lips.

'Now, wolf,' said he, 'afore I kill you like any other beast,—which is wot I mean to do and wot I have tied you up for,—I'll have a good look at you and a good goad at you. O you enemy!'

It had passed through my thoughts to cry out for help again; though few could know better than I, the solitary nature of the spot, and the hopelessness of aid. But as he sat gloating over me, I was supported by a scornful detestation of him that sealed my lips. Above all things, I resolved that I would not entreat him, and that I would die making some last poor resistance to him. Softened as my thoughts of all the rest of men were in that dire extremity; humbly beseeching pardon, as I did, of Heaven; melted at heart, as I was, by the thought that I had taken no farewell, and never now could take farewell of those who were dear to me, or could explain myself to them, or ask for their compassion on my miserable errors,—still, if I could have killed him, even in dying, I would have done it.

He had been drinking, and his eyes were red and bloodshot. Around his neck was slung a tin bottle, as I had often seen his meat and drink slung about him in other days. He brought the bottle to his lips, and took a fiery drink from it; and I smelt the strong spirits that I saw flash into his face.

'Wolf!' said he, folding his arms again, 'Old Orlick's a going to tell you somethink. It was you as did for your shrew sister.'

Again my mind, with its former inconceivable rapidity, had exhausted the whole subject of the attack upon my sister, her illness, and her death, before his slow and hesitating speech had formed these words.

'It was you, villain,' said I.

'I tell you it was your doing,—I tell you it was done through you,' he retorted, catching up the gun, and making a blow with the stock at the vacant air between us. 'I come upon her from behind, as I come upon you tonight. *I* giv' it her! I left her for dead, and if there had been a limekiln as nigh her as there is now nigh you, she shouldn't have come to life again. But it warn't Old Orlick as did it; it was you. You was favoured, and he was bullied and beat. Old Orlick bullied and beat, eh? Now you pays for it. You done it; now you pays for it.'

He drank again, and became more ferocious. I saw by his tilting of the bottle that there was no great quantity left in it. I distinctly understood that he was working himself up with its contents to make an end of me. I knew that every drop it held was a drop of my life. I knew that when I was changed into a part of the vapour that had crept towards me but a little while before, like my own warning ghost, he would do as he had done in my sister's case,—make all haste to the town, and be seen slouching about there drinking at the alehouses. My rapid mind pursued him to the town, made a picture of the street with him in it, and contrasted its lights and life with the lonely marsh and the white vapour creeping over it, into which I should have dissolved.

It was not only that I could have summed up years and years and years while he said a dozen words, but that what he did say presented pictures to me, and not mere words. In the excited and exalted state of my brain, I could not think of a place without seeing it, or of persons without seeing them. It is impossible to overstate the vividness of these images, and yet I was so intent, all the time, upon him himself,—who would not be intent on the tiger crouching to spring!—that I knew of the slightest action of his fingers.

When he had drunk this second time, he rose from the bench on which he sat, and pushed the table aside. Then, he took up the candle, and, shading it with his murderous hand so as to throw its light on me, stood before me, looking at me and enjoying the sight.

'Wolf, I'll tell you something more. It was Old Orlick as you tumbled over on your stairs that night.'

I saw the staircase with its extinguished lamps. I saw the shadows of the heavy stair-rails, thrown by the watchman's lantern on the wall. I saw the rooms that I was never to see again; here, a door half open; there, a door closed; all the articles of furniture around.

'And why was Old Orlick there? I'll tell you something more, wolf. You and her *have* pretty well hunted me out of this country, so far as getting a easy living in it goes, and I've took up with new companions, and new masters. Some of 'em writes my letters when I wants 'em wrote,—do you mind?—writes my letters, wolf! They writes fifty hands; they're not like sneaking you, as writes but one. I've had a firm mind and a firm will to have your life, since you was down here at your sister's burying. I han't seen a way to get you safe, and I've looked arter you to know your ins and outs. For, says Old Orlick to himself, 'Somehow or another I'll have him!' What! When I looks for you, I finds your Uncle Provis, eh?'

Mill Pond Bank, and Chinks's Basin, and the Old Green Copper Rope-walk, all so clear and plain! Provis in his rooms, the signal whose use was over, pretty Clara, the good motherly woman, old Bill Barley on his back, all drifting by, as on the swift stream of my life fast running out to sea!

'*You* with a uncle too! Why, I know'd you at Gargery's when you was so small a wolf that I could have took your weazen betwixt this finger and thumb and chucked you away dead (as I'd thoughts o' doing, odd times, when I see you loitering amongst the pollards on a Sunday), and you hadn't found no uncles then. No, not you! But when Old Orlick come for to hear that your Uncle Provis had most like wore the leg-iron wot Old Orlick had picked up, filed asunder, on these meshes ever so many year ago, and wot he kep by him till he dropped your sister with it, like a bullock, as he means to drop you—hey?—when he come for to hear that—hey?'

In his savage taunting, he flared the candle so close at me that I turned my face aside to save it from the flame.

'Ah!' he cried, laughing, after doing it again, 'the burnt child dreads the fire! Old Orlick knowed you was burnt, Old Orlick knowed you was smuggling your Uncle Provis away, Old Orlick's a match for you and know'd you'd come tonight! Now I'll tell you something more, wolf, and this ends it. There's them that's as good a match for your Uncle Provis as Old Orlick has been for you. Let him 'ware them, when he's lost his nevvy! Let him 'ware them, when no man can't find a rag of his dear relation's clothes, nor yet a bone of his body. There's them that can't and that won't have Magwitch,—yes, *I* know the name!— Alive in the same land with them, and that's had such sure information of him when he was alive in another land, as that he couldn't and shouldn't leave it unbeknown and put them in danger. P'raps it's them that writes fifty hands, and that's not like sneaking you as writes but one. 'Ware Compeyson, Magwitch, and the gallows!'

He flared the candle at me again, smoking my face and hair, and for an instant blinding me, and turned his powerful back as he replaced the light on the table. I had thought a prayer, and had been with Joe and Biddy and Herbert, before he turned towards me again.

There was a clear space of a few feet between the table and the opposite wall. Within this space, he now slouched backwards and forwards. His great strength seemed to sit stronger upon him than ever before, as he did this with his hands hanging loose and heavy at his sides, and with his eyes scowling at me. I had no grain of hope left. Wild as my inward hurry was, and wonderful the force of the pictures that rushed by me instead of thoughts, I could yet clearly understand that, unless he had resolved that I was within a few moments of surely perishing out of all human knowledge, he would never have told me what he had told.

Of a sudden, he stopped, took the cork out of his bottle, and tossed it away. Light as it was, I heard it fall like a plummet. He swallowed slowly, tilting up the bottle by little and little, and now he looked at me no more. The last few drops of liquor he poured into the palm of his hand, and licked up. Then, with a sudden hurry of violence and swearing horribly, he threw the bottle from him, and stooped; and I saw in his hand a stone-hammer with a long heavy handle.

The resolution I had made did not desert me, for, without uttering one vain word of appeal to him, I shouted out with all my might, and struggled with all my might. It was only my head and my legs that I could move, but to that extent I struggled with all the force, until then unknown, that was within me. In the same instant I heard responsive shouts, saw figures and a gleam of light dash in at the door, heard voices and tumult, and saw Orlick emerge from a struggle of men, as if it were tumbling water, clear the table at a leap, and fly out into the night.

After a blank, I found that I was lying unbound, on the floor, in the same place, with my head on some one's knee. My eyes were fixed on the ladder against the wall, when I came to myself,—had opened on it before my mind saw it,—and thus as I recovered consciousness, I knew that I was in the place where I had lost it.

Too indifferent at first, even to look round and ascertain who supported me, I was lying looking at the ladder, when there came between me and it a face. The face of Trabb's boy!

'I think he's all right!' said Trabb's boy, in a sober voice; 'but ain't he just pale though!'

At these words, the face of him who supported me looked over into mine, and I saw my supporter to be—

'Herbert! Great Heaven!'

'Softly,' said Herbert. 'Gently, Handel. Don't be too eager.'

'And our old comrade, Startop!' I cried, as he too bent over me.

'Remember what he is going to assist us in,' said Herbert, 'and be calm.'

The allusion made me spring up; though I dropped again from the pain in my arm. 'The time has not gone by, Herbert, has it? What night is tonight? How long have I been here?' For, I had a strange and strong misgiving that I had been lying there a long time—a day and a night,—two days and nights,—more.

'The time has not gone by. It is still Monday night.'

'Thank God!'

'And you have all tomorrow, Tuesday, to rest in,' said Herbert. 'But you can't help groaning, my dear Handel. What hurt have you got? Can you stand?'

'Yes, yes,' said I, 'I can walk. I have no hurt but in this throbbing arm.'

They laid it bare, and did what they could. It was violently swollen and inflamed, and I could scarcely endure to have it touched. But, they tore up their handkerchiefs to make fresh bandages, and carefully replaced it in the sling, until we could get to the town and obtain some cooling lotion to put upon it. In a little while we had shut the door of the dark and empty sluice-house, and were passing through the quarry on our way back. Trabb's boy—Trabb's overgrown young man now—went before us with a lantern, which was the light I had seen come in at the door. But, the moon was a good two hours higher than when I had last seen the sky, and the night, though rainy, was much lighter. The white vapour of the kiln was passing from us as we went by, and as I had thought a prayer before, I thought a thanksgiving now.

Entreating Herbert to tell me how he had come to my rescue,—which at first he had flatly refused to do, but had insisted on my remaining quiet,—I learnt that I had in my hurry dropped the letter, open, in our chambers, where he, coming home to bring with him Startop whom he had met in the street on his way to me, found it, very soon after I was gone. Its tone made him uneasy, and the more so because of the inconsistency between it and the hasty letter I had left for him. His uneasiness increasing instead of subsiding, after a quarter of an hour's consideration, he set off for the coach-office with Startop, who volunteered his company, to make inquiry when the next coach went down. Finding that the afternoon coach was gone, and finding that his uneasiness grew into positive alarm, as obstacles came in his way, he resolved to follow in a post-chaise. So he and Startop arrived at the Blue Boar, fully expecting there to find me, or tidings of me; but, finding neither, went on to Miss Havisham's, where they lost me. Hereupon they went back to the hotel (doubtless at about the time when I was hearing the popular local version of my own story) to refresh themselves and to get someone to guide them out upon the marshes. Among the loungers under the Boar's archway happened to be Trabb's Boy,—true to his ancient habit of happening to be everywhere where he had no business,—and Trabb's boy had seen me passing from Miss Havisham's in the direction of my dining-place. Thus Trabb's boy became their guide, and with him they went out to the sluice-house, though by the town way to the marshes, which I had avoided. Now, as they went along, Herbert reflected, that I might, after all, have been brought there on some genuine and serviceable errand tending to Provis's safety, and, bethinking himself that in that case interruption must be mischievous, left his guide and Startop on the edge of the quarry, and went on by himself, and stole round the house two or three times, endeavouring to ascertain whether all was right within. As he could hear nothing but indistinct sounds of one deep rough voice (this was while my mind was so busy), he even at last began to doubt whether I was there, when suddenly I cried out loudly, and he answered the cries, and rushed in, closely followed by the other two.

When I told Herbert what had passed within the house, he was for our immediately going before a magistrate in the town, late at night as it was, and getting out a warrant. But, I had already considered that such a course, by detaining us there, or binding us to come back, might be fatal to Provis. There was no gainsaying this difficulty, and we relinquished all thoughts of pursuing Orlick at that time. For the present, under the circumstances, we deemed it prudent to make rather light of the matter to Trabb's boy; who, I am convinced, would have been much affected by disappointment, if he had known that his intervention saved me from the limekiln. Not that Trabb's boy was of a malignant nature, but that he had too much spare vivacity, and that it was in his constitution to want variety and excitement at anybody's expense. When we parted, I presented him with two guineas (which seemed to meet his views), and told him that I was sorry ever to have had an ill opinion of him (which made no impression on him at all).

Wednesday being so close upon us, we determined to go back to London that night, three in the post-chaise; the rather, as we should then be clear away before the night's adventure began to be talked of. Herbert got a large bottle of stuff for my arm; and by dint of having this stuff dropped over it all the night through, I was just able to bear its pain on the journey. It was daylight when we reached the Temple, and I went at once to bed, and lay in bed all day.

My terror, as I lay there, of falling ill, and being unfitted for tomorrow, was so besetting, that I wonder it did not disable me of itself. It would have done so, pretty surely, in conjunction with the mental wear and tear I had suffered, but for the unnatural strain upon me that tomorrow was. So anxiously looked forward to, charged with such consequences, its results so impenetrably hidden, though so near.

No precaution could have been more obvious than our refraining from communication with him that day; yet this again increased my restlessness. I started at every footstep and every sound, believing that he was discovered and taken, and this was the messenger to tell me so. I persuaded myself that I knew he was taken; that there was something more upon my mind than a fear or a presentiment; that the fact had occurred, and I had a mysterious knowledge of it. As the days wore on, and no ill news came, as the day closed in and darkness fell, my overshadowing dread of being disabled by illness before tomorrow morning altogether mastered me. My burning arm throbbed, and my burning head throbbed, and I fancied I was beginning to wander. I counted up to high numbers, to make sure of myself, and repeated passages that I knew in prose and verse. It happened sometimes that in the mere escape of a fatigued mind, I dozed for some moments or forgot; then I would say to myself with a start, 'Now it has come, and I am turning delirious!'

They kept me very quiet all day, and kept my arm constantly dressed, and gave me cooling drinks. Whenever I fell asleep, I awoke with the notion I had had in the sluice-house, that a long time had elapsed and the opportunity to save him was gone. About midnight I got out of bed and went to Herbert, with the conviction that I had been asleep for four-and-twenty hours, and that Wednesday was past. It was the last self-exhausting effort of my fretfulness, for after that I slept soundly.

Wednesday morning was dawning when I looked out of window.

The winking lights upon the bridges were already pale, the coming sun was like a marsh of fire on the horizon. The river, still dark and mysterious, was spanned by bridges that were turning coldly grey, with here and there at top a warm touch from the burning in the sky. As I looked along the clustered roofs, with church-towers and spires shooting into the unusually clear air, the sun rose up, and a veil seemed to be drawn from the river, and millions of sparkles burst out upon its waters. From me too, a veil seemed to be drawn, and I felt strong and well.

Herbert lay asleep in his bed, and our old fellow-student lay asleep on the sofa. I could not dress myself without help; but I made up the fire, which was still burning, and got some coffee ready for them. In good time they too started up strong and well, and we admitted the sharp morning air at the windows, and looked at the tide that was still flowing towards us.

'When it turns at nine o'clock,' said Herbert, cheerfully, 'look out for us, and stand ready, you over there at Mill Pond Bank!'

Chapter 54

It was one of those March days when the sun shines hot and the wind blows cold: when it is summer in the light, and winter in the shade. We had our pea-coats with us, and I took a bag. Of all my worldly possessions I took no more than the few necessaries that filled the bag. Where I might go, what I might do, or when I might return, were questions utterly unknown to me; nor did I vex my mind with them, for it was wholly set on Provis's safety. I only wondered for the passing moment, as I stopped at the door and looked back, under what altered circumstances I should next see those rooms, if ever.

We loitered down to the Temple stairs, and stood loitering there, as if we were not quite decided to go upon the water at all. Of course, I had taken care that the boat should be ready and everything in order. After a little show of indecision, which there were none to see but the two or three amphibious creatures belonging to our Temple stairs, we went on board and cast off; Herbert in the bow, I steering. It was then about high-water,—half-past eight.

Our plan was this. The tide, beginning to run down at nine, and being with us until three, we intended still to creep on after it had turned, and row against it until dark. We should then be well in those long reaches below Gravesend, between Kent and Essex, where the river is broad and solitary, where the water-side inhabitants are very few, and where lone public-houses are scattered here and there, of which we could choose one for a resting-place. There, we meant to lie by all night. The steamer for Hamburg and the steamer for Rotterdam would start from London at about nine on Thursday morning. We should know at what time to expect them, according to where we were, and would hail the first; so that, if by any accident we were not taken abroad, we should have another chance. We knew the distinguishing marks of each vessel.

The relief of being at last engaged in the execution of the purpose was so great to me that I felt it difficult to realize the condition in which I had been a few hours before. The crisp air, the sunlight, the movement on the river, and the moving river itself,—the road that ran with us, seeming to sympathize with us, animate us, and encourage us on,—freshened me with new hope. I felt mortified to be of so little use in the boat; but, there were few better oarsmen than my two friends, and they rowed with a steady stroke that was to last all day.

At that time, the steam-traffic on the Thames was far below its present extent, and watermen's boats were far more numerous. Of barges, sailing colliers, and coasting-traders, there were perhaps, as many as now; but of steam-ships, great and small, not a tithe or a twentieth part so many. Early as it was, there were plenty of scullers going here and there that morning, and plenty of barges dropping down with the tide; the navigation of the river between bridges, in an open boat, was a much easier and commoner matter in those days than it is in these; and we went ahead among many skiffs and wherries briskly.

Old London Bridge was soon passed, and old Billingsgate Market with its oyster-boats and Dutchmen, and the White Tower and Traitor's Gate, and we were in among the tiers of shipping. Here were the Leith, Aberdeen, and Glasgow steamers, loading and unloading goods, and looking immensely high out of the water as we passed alongside; here, were colliers by the score and score, with the coal-whippers plunging off stages on deck, as counterweights to measures of coal swinging up, which were then rattled over the side into barges; here, at her moorings was tomorrow's steamer for Rotterdam, of which we took good notice; and here tomorrow's for Hamburg, under whose bowsprit we crossed. And now I, sitting in the stern, could see, with a faster beating heart, Mill Pond Bank and Mill Pond stairs.

'Is he there?' said Herbert.

'Not yet.'

'Right! He was not to come down till he saw us. Can you see his signal?'

'Not well from here; but I think I see it.—Now I see him! Pull both. Easy, Herbert. Oars!'

We touched the stairs lightly for a single moment, and he was on board, and we were off again. He had a boat-cloak with him, and a black canvas bag; and he looked as like a river-pilot as my heart could have wished.

'Dear boy!' he said, putting his arm on my shoulder, as he took his seat. 'Faithful dear boy, well done. Thankye, thankye!'

Again among the tiers of shipping, in and out, avoiding rusty chain-cables frayed hempen hawsers and bobbing buoys, sinking for the moment floating broken baskets, scattering floating chips of wood and shaving, cleaving floating scum of coal, in and out, under the figure-head of the *John of Sunderland* making a speech to the winds (as is done by many Johns), and the *Betsy of Yarmouth* with a firm formality of bosom and her knobby eyes starting two inches out of her head; in and out, hammers going in ship-builders' yards, saws going at timber, clashing engines going at things unknown, pumps going in leaky ships, capstans going, ships going out to sea, and unintelligible sea-creatures roaring curses over the bulwarks at respondent lightermen, in and out,—out at last upon the clearer river, where the ships' boys might take their fenders in, no longer fishing in troubled waters with them over the side, and where the festooned sails might fly out to the wind.

At the stairs where we had taken him abroad, and ever since, I had looked warily for any token of our being suspected. I had seen none. We certainly had not been, and at that time as certainly we were not either attended or followed by any boat. If we had been waited on by any boat, I should have run in to shore, and have obliged her to go on, or to make her purpose evident. But we held our own without any appearance of molestation.

He had his boat-cloak on him, and looked, as I have said, a natural part of the scene. It was remarkable (but perhaps the wretched life he had led accounted for it) that he was the least anxious of any of us. He was not indifferent, for he told me that he hoped to live to see his gentleman one of the best of gentlemen in a foreign country; he was not disposed to be passive or resigned, as I understood it; but he had no notion of meeting danger halfway. When it came upon him, he confronted it, but it must come before he troubled himself.

'If you knowed, dear boy,' he said to me, 'what it is to sit here alonger my dear boy and have my smoke, arter having been day by day betwixt four walls, you'd envy me. But you don't know what it is.'

'I think I know the delights of freedom,' I answered.

'Ah,' said he, shaking his head gravely. 'But you don't know it equal to me. You must have been under lock and key, dear boy, to know it equal to me,—but I ain't a going to be low.'

It occurred to me as inconsistent, that, for any mastering idea, he should have endangered his freedom, and even his life. But I reflected that perhaps freedom without danger was too much apart from all the habit of his existence to be to him what it would be to another man. I was not far out, since he said, after smoking a little:—

'You see, dear boy, when I was over yonder, t'other side the world, I was always a looking to this side; and it come flat to be there, for all I was a growing rich. Everybody knowed Magwitch, and Magwitch could come, and Magwitch could go, and nobody's head would be troubled about him. They ain't so easy concerning me here, dear boy,—wouldn't be, leastwise, if they knowed where I was.'

'If all goes well,' said I, 'you will be perfectly free and safe again within a few hours.'

'Well,' he returned, drawing a long breath, 'I hope so.'

'And think so?'

He dipped his hand in the water over the boat's gunwale, and said, smiling with that softened air upon him which was not new to me:—

'Ay, I s'pose I think so, dear boy. We'd be puzzled to be more quiet and easy-going than we are at present. But—it's a flowing so soft and pleasant through the water, p'raps, as makes me think it—I was a thinking through my smoke just then, that we can no more see to the bottom of the next few hours than we can see to the bottom of this river what I catches hold of. Nor yet we can't no more hold their tide than I can hold this. And it's run through my fingers and gone, you see!' holding up his dripping hand.

'But for your face I should think you were a little despondent,' said I.

'Not a bit on it, dear boy! It comes of flowing on so quiet, and of that there rippling at the boat's head making a sort of a Sunday tune. Maybe I'm a growing a trifle old besides.'

He put his pipe back in his mouth with an undisturbed expression of face, and sat as composed and contented as if we were already out of England. Yet he was as submissive to a word of advice as if he had been in constant terror; for, when we ran ashore to get some bottles of beer into the boat, and he was stepping out, I hinted that I thought he would be safest where he was, and he said. 'Do you, dear boy?' and quietly sat down again.

The air felt cold upon the river, but it was a bright day, and the sunshine was very cheering. The tide ran strong, I took care to lose none of it, and our steady stroke carried us on thoroughly well. By imperceptible degrees, as the tide ran out, we lost more and more of the nearer woods and hills, and dropped lower and lower between the muddy banks, but the tide was yet with us when we were off Gravesend. As our charge was wrapped in his cloak, I purposely passed within a boat or two's length of the floating Custom House, and so out to catch the stream, alongside of two emigrant ships, and under the bows of a large transport with troops on the forecastle looking down at us. And soon the tide began to slacken, and the craft lying at anchor to swing, and presently they had all swung round, and the ships that were taking advantage of the new tide to get up to the Pool began to crowd upon us in a fleet, and we kept under the shore, as much out of the strength of the tide now as we could, standing carefully off from low shallows and mudbanks.

Our oarsmen were so fresh, by dint of having occasionally let her drive with the tide for a minute or two, that a quarter of an hour's rest proved full as much as they wanted. We got ashore among some slippery stones while we ate and drank what we had with us, and looked about. It was like my own marsh country, flat and monotonous, and with a dim horizon; while the winding river turned and turned, and the great floating buoys upon it turned and turned, and everything else seemed stranded and still. For now the last of the fleet of ships was round the last low point we had headed; and the last green barge, straw-laden, with a brown sail, had followed; and some ballast-lighters, shaped like a child's first rude imitation of a boat, lay low in the mud; and a little squat shoal-lighthouse on open piles stood crippled in the mud on stilts and crutches; and slimy stakes stuck out of the mud, and slimy stones stuck out of the mud, and red landmarks and tidemarks stuck out of the mud, and an old landing-stage and an old roofless building slipped into the mud, and all about us was stagnation and mud.

We pushed off again, and made what way we could. It was much harder work now, but Herbert and Startop persevered, and rowed and rowed and rowed until the sun went down. By that time the river had lifted us a little, so that we could see above the bank. There was the red sun, on the low level of the shore, in a purple haze, fast deepening into black; and there was the solitary flat marsh; and faraway there were the rising grounds, between which and us there seemed to be no life, save here and there in the foreground a melancholy gull.

As the night was fast falling, and as the moon, being past the full, would not rise early, we held a little council; a short one, for clearly our course was to lie by at the first lonely tavern we could find. So, they plied their oars once more, and I looked out for anything like a house. Thus we held on, speaking little, for four or five dull miles. It was very cold, and, a collier coming by us, with her galley-fire smoking and flaring, looked like a comfortable home. The night was as dark by this time as it would be until morning; and what light we had, seemed to come more from the river than the sky, as the oars in their dipping struck at a few reflected stars.

At this dismal time we were evidently all possessed by the idea that we were followed. As the tide made, it flapped heavily at irregular intervals against the shore; and whenever such a sound came, one or other of us was sure to start, and look in that direction. Here and there, the set of the current had worn down the bank into a little creek, and we were all suspicious of such places, and eyed them nervously. Sometimes, 'What was that ripple?' one of us would say in a low voice. Or another, 'Is that a boat yonder?' And afterwards we would fall into a dead silence, and I would sit impatiently thinking with what an unusual amount of noise the oars worked in the thowels.

At length we descried a light and a roof, and presently afterwards ran alongside a little causeway made of stones that had been picked up hard by. Leaving the rest in the boat, I stepped ashore, and found the light to be in a window of a public-house. It was a dirty place enough, and I dare say not unknown to smuggling adventurers; but there was a good fire in the kitchen, and there were eggs and bacon to eat, and various liquors to drink. Also, there were two double-bedded rooms,—'such as they were,' the landlord said. No other company was in the house than the landlord, his wife, and a grizzled male creature, the 'Jack' of the little causeway, who was as slimy and smeary as if he had been low-water mark too.

With this assistant, I went down to the boat again, and we all came ashore, and brought out the oars, and rudder and boat-hook, and all else, and hauled her up for the night. We made a very good meal by the kitchen fire, and then apportioned the bedrooms: Herbert and Startop were to occupy one; I and our charge the other. We found the air as carefully excluded from both, as if air were fatal to life; and there were more dirty clothes and bandboxes under the beds than I should have thought the family possessed. But we considered ourselves well off, notwithstanding, for a more solitary place we could not have found.

While we were comforting ourselves by the fire after our meal, the Jack—who was sitting in a corner, and who had a bloated pair of shoes on, which he had exhibited while we were eating our eggs and bacon, as interesting relics that he had taken a few days ago from the feet of a drowned seaman washed ashore—asked me if we had seen a four-oared galley going up with the tide? When I told him No, he said she must have gone down then, and yet she 'took up too,' when she left there.

'They must ha' thought better on't for some reason or another,' said the Jack, 'and gone down.'

'A four-oared galley, did you say?' said I.

'A four,' said the Jack, 'and two sitters.'

'Did they come ashore here?'

'They put in with a stone two-gallon jar for some beer. I'd ha' been glad to pison the beer myself,' said the Jack, 'or put some rattling physic in it.'

'Why?'

'*I* know why,' said the Jack. He spoke in a slushy voice, as if much mud had washed into his throat.

'He thinks,' said the landlord, a weakly meditative man with a pale eye, who seemed to rely greatly on his Jack,—'he thinks they was, what they wasn't.'

'*I* knows what I thinks,' observed the Jack.

'*You* thinks Custum 'Us, Jack?' said the landlord.

'I do,' said the Jack.

'Then you're wrong, Jack.'

'AM I!'

In the infinite meaning of his reply and his boundless confidence in his views, the Jack took one of his bloated shoes off, looked into it, knocked a few stones out of it on the kitchen floor, and put it on again. He did this with the air of a Jack who was so right that he could afford to do anything.

'Why, what do you make out that they done with their buttons then, Jack?' asked the landlord, vacillating weakly.

'Done with their buttons?' returned the Jack. 'Chucked 'em overboard. Swallered 'em. Sowed 'em, to come up small salad. Done with their buttons!'

'Don't be cheeky, Jack,' remonstrated the landlord, in a melancholy and pathetic way.

'A Custum 'Us officer knows what to do with his Buttons,' said the Jack, repeating the obnoxious word with the greatest contempt, 'when they comes betwixt him and his own light. A four and two sitters don't go hanging and hovering, up with one tide and down with another, and both with and against another, without there being

Custum 'Us at the bottom of it.' Saying which he went out in disdain; and the landlord, having no one to reply upon, found it impracticable to pursue the subject.

This dialogue made us all uneasy, and me very uneasy. The dismal wind was muttering round the house, the tide was flapping at the shore, and I had a feeling that we were caged and threatened. A four-oared galley hovering about in so unusual a way as to attract this notice was an ugly circumstance that I could not get rid of. When I had induced Provis to go up to bed, I went outside with my two companions (Startop by this time knew the state of the case), and held another council. Whether we should remain at the house until near the steamer's time, which would be about one in the afternoon, or whether we should put off early in the morning, was the question we discussed. On the whole we deemed it the better course to lie where we were, until within an hour or so of the steamer's time, and then to get out in her track, and drift easily with the tide. Having settled to do this, we returned into the house and went to bed.

I lay down with the greater part of my clothes on, and slept well for a few hours. When I awoke, the wind had risen, and the sign of the house (the Ship) was creaking and banging about, with noises that startled me. Rising softly, for my charge lay fast asleep, I looked out of the window. It commanded the causeway where we had hauled up our boat, and, as my eyes adapted themselves to the light of the clouded moon, I saw two men looking into her. They passed by under the window, looking at nothing else, and they did not go down to the landing-place which I could discern to be empty, but struck across the marsh in the direction of the Nore.

My first impulse was to call up Herbert, and show him the two men going away. But reflecting, before I got into his room, which was at the back of the house and adjoined mine, that he and Startop had had a harder day than I, and were fatigued, I forbore. Going back to my window, I could see the two men moving over the marsh. In that light, however, I soon lost them, and, feeling very cold, lay down to think of the matter, and fell asleep again.

We were up early. As we walked to and fro, all four together, before breakfast, I deemed it right to recount what I had seen. Again our charge was the least anxious of the party. It was very likely that the men belonged to the Custom House, he said quietly, and that they had no thought of us. I tried to persuade myself that it was so,—as, indeed, it might easily be. However, I proposed that he and I should walk away together to a distant point we could see, and that the boat should take us aboard there, or as near there as might prove feasible, at about noon. This being considered a good precaution, soon after breakfast he and I set forth, without saying anything at the tavern.

He smoked his pipe as we went along, and sometimes stopped to clap me on the shoulder. One would have supposed that it was I who was in danger, not he, and that he was reassuring me. We spoke very little. As we approached the point, I begged him to remain in a sheltered place, while I went on to reconnoitre; for it was towards it that the men had passed in the night. He complied, and I went on alone. There was no boat off the point, nor any boat drawn up anywhere near it, nor were there any signs of the men having embarked there. But, to be sure, the tide was high, and there might have been some footpints under water.

When he looked out from his shelter in the distance, and saw that I waved my hat to him to come up, he rejoined me, and there we waited; sometimes lying on the bank, wrapped in our coats, and sometimes moving about to warm ourselves, until we saw our boat coming round. We got aboard easily, and rowed out into the track of the steamer. By that time it wanted but ten minutes of one o'clock, and we began to look out for her smoke.

But, it was half-past one before we saw her smoke, and soon afterwards we saw behind it the smoke of another steamer. As they were coming on at full speed, we got the two bags ready, and took that opportunity of saying goodbye to Herbert and Startop. We had all shaken hands cordially, and neither Herbert's eyes nor mine were quite dry, when I saw a four-oared galley shoot out from under the bank but a little way ahead of us, and row out into the same track.

A stretch of shore had been as yet between us and the steamer's smoke, by reason of the bend and wind of the river; but now she was visible, coming head on. I called to Herbert and Startop to keep before the tide, that she might see us lying by for her, and I adjured Provis to sit quite still, wrapped in his cloak. He answered cheerily, 'Trust to me, dear boy,' and sat like a statue. Meantime the galley, which was very skilfully handled, had crossed us, let us come up with her, and fallen alongside. Leaving just room enough for the play of the oars, she kept alongside, drifting when we drifted, and pulling a stroke or two when we pulled. Of the two sitters one held the rudder-lines, and looked at us attentively,—as did all the rowers; the other sitter was wrapped up, much as Provis was, and seemed to shrink, and whisper some instruction to the steerer as he looked at us. Not a word was spoken in either boat.

Startop could make out, after a few minutes, which steamer was first, and gave me the word 'Hamburg,' in a low voice, as we sat face to face. She was nearing us very fast, and the beating of her peddles grew louder and louder. I felt as if her shadow were absolutely upon us, when the galley hailed us. I answered.

'You have a returned Transport there,' said the man who held the lines. 'That's the man, wrapped in the cloak. His name is Abel Magwitch, otherwise Provis. I apprehend that man, and call upon him to surrender, and you to assist.'

At the same moment, without giving any audible direction to his crew, he ran the galley abroad of us. They had pulled one sudden stroke ahead, had got their oars in, had run athwart us, and were holding on to our gunwale, before we knew what they were doing. This caused great confusion on board the steamer, and I heard them calling to us, and heard the order given to stop the paddles, and heard them stop, but felt her driving down upon us irresistibly. In the same moment, I saw the steersman of the galley lay his hand on his prisoner's shoulder, and saw that both boats were swinging round with the force of the tide, and saw that all hands on board the steamer were running forward quite frantically. Still, in the same moment, I saw the prisoner start up, lean across his captor, and pull the cloak from the neck of the shrinking sitter in the galley. Still in the same moment, I saw that the face disclosed, was the face of the other convict of long ago. Still, in the same moment, I saw the face tilt backward with a white terror on it that I shall never forget, and heard a great cry on board the steamer, and a loud splash in the water, and felt the boat sink from under me.

It was but for an instant that I seemed to struggle with a thousand mill-weirs and a thousand flashes of light; that instant past, I was taken on board the galley. Herbert was there, and Startop was there; but our boat was gone, and the two convicts were gone.

What with the cries aboard the steamer, and the furious blowing off of her steam, and her driving on, and our driving on, I could not at first distinguish sky from water or shore from shore; but the crew of the galley righted her with great speed, and, pulling certain swift strong strokes ahead, lay upon their oars, every man looking silently and eagerly at the water astern. Presently a dark object was seen in it, bearing towards us on the tide. No man spoke, but the steersman held up his hand, and all softly backed water, and kept the boat straight and true before it. As it came nearer, I saw it to be Magwitch, swimming, but not swimming freely. He was taken on board, and instantly manacled at the wrists and ankles.

The galley was kept steady, and the silent, eager look-out at the water was resumed. But, the Rotterdam steamer now came up, and apparently not understanding what had happened, came on at speed. By the time she had been hailed and stopped, both steamers were drifting away from us, and we were rising and falling in a troubled wake of water. The look-out was kept, long after all was still again and the two steamers were gone; but everybody knew that it was hopeless now.

At length we gave it up, and pulled under the shore towards the tavern we had lately left, where we were received with no little surprise. Here I was able to get some comforts for Magwitch,—Provis no longer,—who had received some very severe injury in the Chest, and a deep cut in the head.

He told me that he believed himself to have gone under the keel of the steamer, and to have been struck on the head in rising. The injury to his chest (which rendered his breathing extremely painful) he thought he had received against the side of the galley. He added that he did not pretend to say what he might or might not have done to Compeyson, but that, in the moment of his laying his hand on his cloak to identify him, that villain had staggered up and staggered back, and they had both gone overboard together, when the sudden wrenching of him (Magwitch) out of our boat, and the endeavour of his captor to keep him in it, had capsized us. He told me in a whisper that they had gone down fiercely locked in each other's arms, and that there had been a struggle under water, and that he had disengaged himself, struck out, and swum away.

I never had any reason to doubt the exact truth of what he thus told me. The officer who steered the galley gave the same account of their going overboard.

When I asked this officer's permission to change the prisoner's wet clothes by purchasing any spare garments I could get at the public-house, he gave it readily: merely observing that he must take charge of everything his prisoner had about him. So the pocket-book which had once been in my hands passed into the officer's. He further gave me leave to accompany the prisoner to London; but declined to accord that grace to my two friends.

The Jack at the Ship was instructed where the drowned man had gone down, and undertook to search for the body in the places where it was likeliest to come ashore. His interest in its recovery seemed to me to be much heightened when he heard that it had stockings on. Probably, it took about a dozen drowned men to fit him out completely; and that may have been the reason why the different articles of his dress were in various stages of decay.

We remained at the public-house until the tide turned, and then Magwitch was carried down to the galley and put on board. Herbert and Startop were to get to London by land, as soon as they could. We had a doleful parting, and when I took my place by Magwitch's side, I felt that that was my place henceforth while he lived.

For now, my repugnance to him had all melted away; and in the hunted, wounded, shackled creature who held my hand in his, I only saw a man who had meant to be my benefactor, and who had felt affectionately, gratefully, and generously, towards me with great constancy through a series of years. I only saw in him a much better man than I had been to Joe.

His breathing became more difficult and painful as the night drew on, and often he could not repress a groan. I tried to rest him on the arm I could use, in any easy position; but it was dreadful to think that I could not be sorry at heart for his being badly hurt, since it was unquestionably best that he should die. That there were, still living, people enough who were able and willing to identify him, I could not doubt. That he would be leniently treated, I could not hope. He who had been presented in the worst light at his trial, who had since broken prison and had been tried again, who had returned from transportation under a life sentence, and who had occasioned the death of the man who was the cause of his arrest.

As we returned towards the setting sun we had yesterday left behind us, and as the stream of our hopes seemed all running back, I told him how grieved I was to think that he had come home for my sake.

'Dear boy,' he answered, 'I'm quite content to take my chance. I've seen my boy, and he can be a gentleman without me.'

No. I had thought about that, while we had been there side by side. No. Apart from any inclinations of my own, I understood Wemmick's hint now. I foresaw that, being convicted, his possessions would be forfeited to the Crown.

'Lookee here, dear boy,' said he 'It's best as a gentleman should not be knowed to belong to me now. Only come to see me as if you come by chance alonger Wemmick. Sit where I can see you when I am swore to, for the last o' many times, and I don't ask no more.'

'I will never stir from your side,' said I, 'when I am suffered to be near you. Please God, I will be as true to you as you have been to me!'

I felt his hand tremble as it held mine, and he turned his face away as he lay in the bottom of the boat, and I heard that old sound in his throat,—softened now, like all the rest of him. It was a good thing that he had touched this point, for it put into my mind what I might not otherwise have thought of until too late,—that he need never know how his hopes of enriching me had perished.

Chapter 55

He was taken to the Police Court next day, and would have been immediately committed for trial, but that it was necessary to send down for an old officer of the prison-ship from which he had once escaped, to speak to his identity. Nobody doubted it; but Compeyson, who had meant to depose to it, was tumbling on the tides, dead, and it happened that there was not at that time any prison officer in London who could give the required evidence. I had gone direct to Mr Jaggers at his private house, on my arrival over night, to retain his assistance, and Mr Jaggers on the prisoner's behalf would admit nothing. It was the sole resource; for he told me that the case must be over in five minutes when the witness was there, and that no power on earth could prevent its going against us.

I imparted to Mr Jaggers my design of keeping him in ignorance of the fate of his wealth. Mr Jaggers was querulous and angry with me for having 'let it slip through my fingers,' and said we must memorialize by and by, and try at all events for some of it. But he did not conceal from me that, although there might be many cases in which the forfeiture would not be exacted, there were no circumstances in this case to make it one of them. I understood that very well. I was not related to the outlaw, or connected with him by any recognizable tie; he had put his hand to no writing or settlement in my favour before his apprehension, and to do so now would be idle. I had no claim, and I finally resolved, and ever afterwards abided by the resolution, that my heart should never be sickened with the hopeless task of attempting to establish one.

There appeared to be reason for supposing that the drowned informer had hoped for a reward out of this forfeiture, and had obtained some accurate knowledge of Magwitch's affairs. When his body was found, many miles from the scene of his death, and so horribly disfigured that he was only recognizable by the contents of his pockets, notes were still legible, folded in a case he carried. Among these were the name of a banking-house in New South Wales, where a sum of money was, and the designation of certain lands of considerable value. Both these heads of information were in a list that Magwitch, while in prison, gave to Mr Jaggers, of the possessions he supposed I should inherit. His ignorance, poor fellow, at last served him; he never mistrusted but that my inheritance was quite safe, with Mr Jaggers's aid.

After three days' delay, during which the crown prosecution stood over for the production of the witness from the prison-ship, the witness came, and completed the easy case. He was committed to take his trial at the next Sessions, which would come on in a month.

It was at this dark time of my life that Herbert returned home one evening, a good deal cast down, and said,—

'My dear Handel, I fear I shall soon have to leave you.'

His partner having prepared me for that, I was less surprised than he thought.

'We shall lose a fine opportunity if I put off going to Cairo, and I am very much afraid I must go, Handel, when you most need me.'

'Herbert, I shall always need you, because I shall always love you; but my need is no greater now than at another time.'

'You will be so lonely.'

'I have not leisure to think of that,' said I. 'You know that I am always with him to the full extent of the time allowed, and that I should be with him all day long, if I could. And when I come away from him, you know that my thoughts are with him.'

The dreadful condition to which he was brought, was so appalling to both of us, that we could not refer to it in plainer words.

'My dear fellow,' said Herbert, 'let the near prospect of our separation—for, it is very near—be my justification for troubling you about yourself. Have you thought of your future?'

'No, for I have been afraid to think of any future.'

'But yours cannot be dismissed; indeed, my dear dear Handel, it must not be dismissed. I wish you would enter on it now, as far as a few friendly words go, with me.'

'I will,' said I.

'In this branch house of ours, Handel, we must have a—'

I saw that his delicacy was avoiding the right word, so I said, 'A clerk.'

'A clerk. And I hope it is not at all unlikely that he may expand (as a clerk of your acquaintance has expanded) into a partner. Now, Handel,—in short, my dear boy, will you come to me?'

There was something charmingly cordial and engaging in the manner in which after saying 'Now, Handel,' as if it were the grave beginning of a portentous business exordium, he had suddenly given up that tone, stretched out his honest hand, and spoken like a schoolboy.

'Clara and I have talked about it again and again,' Herbert pursued, 'and the dear little thing begged me only this evening, with tears in her eyes, to say to you that, if you will live with us when we come together, she will do her best to make you happy, and to convince her husband's friend that he is her friend too. We should get on so well, Handel!'

I thanked her heartily, and I thanked him heartily, but said I could not yet make sure of joining him as he so kindly offered. Firstly, my mind was too preoccupied to be able to take in the subject clearly. Secondly,—Yes! Secondly, there was a vague something lingering in my thoughts that will come out very near the end of this slight narrative.

'But if you thought, Herbert, that you could, without doing any injury to your business, leave the question open for a little while—'

'For any while,' cried Herbert. 'Six months, a year!'

'Not so long as that,' said I. 'Two or three months at most.'

Herbert was highly delighted when we shook hands on this arrangement, and said he could now take courage to tell me that he believed he must go away at the end of the week.

'And Clara?' said I.

'The dear little thing,' returned Herbert, 'holds dutifully to her father as long as he lasts; but he won't last long. Mrs Whimple confides to me that he is certainly going.'

'Not to say an unfeeling thing,' said I, 'he cannot do better than go.'

'I am afraid that must be admitted,' said Herbert; 'and then I shall come back for the dear little thing, and the dear little thing and I will walk quietly into the nearest church. Remember! The blessed darling comes of no family, my dear Handel, and never looked into the red book, and hasn't a notion about her grandpapa. What a fortune for the son of my mother!'

On the Saturday in that same week, I took my leave of Herbert,—full of bright hope, but sad and sorry to leave me,—as he sat on one of the seaport mail coaches. I went into a coffee-house to write a little note to Clara, telling her he had gone off, sending his love to her over and over again, and then went to my lonely home,—if it deserved the name; for it was now no home to me, and I had no home anywhere.

On the stairs I encountered Wemmick, who was coming down,

after an unsuccessful application of his knuckles to my door. I had not seen him alone since the disastrous issue of the attempted flight; and he had come, in his private and personal capacity, to say a few words of explanation in reference to that failure.

'The late Compeyson,' said Wemmick, 'had by little and little got at the bottom of half of the regular business now transacted; and it was from the talk of some of his people in trouble (some of his people being always in trouble) that I heard what I did. I kept my ears open, seeming to have them shut, until I heard that he was absent, and I thought that would be the best time for making the attempt. I can only suppose now, that it was a part of his policy, as a very clever man, habitually to deceive his own instruments. You don't blame me, I hope, Mr Pip? I am sure I tried to serve you, with all my heart.'

'I am as sure of that, Wemmick, as you can be, and I thank you most earnestly for all your interest and friendship.'

'Thank you, thank you very much. It's a bad job,' said Wemmick, scratching his head, 'and I assure you I haven't been so cut up for a long time. What I look at is the sacrifice of so much portable property. Dear me!'

'What *I* think of, Wemmick, is the poor owner of the property.'

'Yes, to be sure,' said Wemmick. 'Of course, there can be no objection to your being sorry for him, and I'd put down a five-pound note myself to get him out of it. But what I look at is this. The late Compeyson having been beforehand with him in intelligence of his return, and being so determined to bring him to book, I do not think he could have been saved. Whereas, the portable property certainly could have been saved. That's the difference between the property and the owner, don't you see?'

I invited Wemmick to come upstairs, and refresh himself with a glass of grog before walking to Walworth. He accepted the invitation. While he was drinking his moderate allowance, he said, with nothing to lead up to it, and after having appeared rather fidgety,—

'What do you think of my meaning to take a holiday on Monday, Mr Pip?'

'Why, I suppose you have not done such a thing these twelve months.'

'These twelve years, more likely,' said Wemmick. 'Yes. I'm going to take a holiday. More than that; I'm going to take a walk. More than that; I'm going to ask you to take a walk with me.'

I was about to excuse myself, as being but a bad companion just then, when Wemmick anticipated me.

'I know your engagements,' said he, 'and I know you are out of sorts, Mr Pip. But if you *could* oblige me, I should take it as a kindness. It ain't a long walk, and it's an early one. Say it might occupy you (including breakfast on the walk) from eight to twelve. Couldn't you stretch a point and manage it?'

He had done so much for me at various times, that this was very little to do for him. I said I could manage it,—would manage it,—and he was so very much pleased by my acquiescence, that I was pleased too. At his particular request, I appointed to call for him at the Castle at half past eight on Monday morning, and so we parted for the time.

Punctual to my appointment, I rang at the Castle gate on the Monday morning, and was received by Wemmick himself, who struck me as looking tighter than usual, and having a sleeker hat on. Within, there were two glasses of rum and milk prepared, and two biscuits. The Aged must have been stirring with the lark, for, glancing into the perspective of his bedroom, I observed that his bed was empty.

When we had fortified ourselves with the rum and milk and biscuits, and were going out for the walk with that training preparation on us, I was considerably surprised to see Wemmick take up a fishing-rod, and put it over his shoulder. 'Why, we are not going fishing!' said I. 'No,' returned Wemmick, 'but I like to walk with one.'

I thought this odd; however, I said nothing, and we set off. We went towards Camberwell Green, and when we were thereabouts, Wemmick said suddenly,—

'Halloa! Here's a church!'

There was nothing very surprising in that; but again, I was rather surprised, when he said, as if he were animated by a brilliant idea,—

'Let's go in!'

We went in, Wemmick leaving his fishing-rod in the porch, and looked all round. In the mean time, Wemmick was diving into his coat-pockets, and getting something out of paper there.

'Halloa!' said he. 'Here's a couple of pair of gloves! Let's put 'em on!'

As the gloves were white kid gloves, and as the post-office was widened to its utmost extent, I now began to have my strong suspicions. They were strengthened into certainty when I beheld the Aged enter at a side door, escorting a lady.

'Halloa!' said Wemmick. 'Here's Miss Skiffins! Let's have a wedding.'

That discreet damsel was attired as usual, except that she was now engaged in substituting for her green kid gloves a pair of white. The Aged was likewise occupied in preparing a similar sacrifice for the altar of Hymen. The old gentleman, however, experienced so much difficulty in getting his gloves on, that Wemmick found it necessary to put him with his back against a pillar, and then to get behind the pillar himself and pull away at them, while I for my part held the old gentleman round the waist, that he might present an equal and safe resistance. By dint of this ingenious scheme, his gloves were got on to perfection.

The clerk and clergyman then appearing, we were ranged in order at those fatal rails. True to his notion of seeming to do it all without preparation, I heard Wemmick say to himself, as he took something out of his waistcoat-pocket before the service began, 'Halloa! Here's a ring!'

I acted in the capacity of backer, or best-man, to the bridegroom; while a little limp pew-opener in a soft bonnet like a baby's, made a feint of being the bosom friend of Miss Skiffins. The responsibility of giving the lady away devolved upon the Aged, which led to the clergyman's being unintentionally scandalized, and it happened thus. When he said, 'Who giveth this woman to be married to this man?' the old gentleman, not in the least knowing what point of the ceremony we had arrived at, stood most amiably beaming at the ten commandments. Upon which, the clergyman said again, 'WHO giveth this woman to be married to this man?' The old gentleman being still in a state of most estimable unconsciousness, the bridegroom cried out in his accustomed voice, 'Now Aged P. you know; who giveth?' To which the Aged replied with great briskness, before saying that *he* gave, 'All right, John, all right, my boy!' And the clergyman came to so gloomy a pause upon it, that I had doubts for the moment whether we should get completely married that day.

It was completely done, however, and when we were going out of church Wemmick took the cover off the font, and put his white gloves in it, and put the cover on again. Mrs Wemmick, more heedful of the future, put her white gloves in her pocket and assumed her green. '*Now*, Mr Pip,' said Wemmick, triumphantly shouldering the fishing-rod as we came out, 'let me ask you whether anybody would suppose this to be a wedding-party!'

Breakfast had been ordered at a pleasant little tavern, a mile or so away upon the rising ground beyond the green; and there was a bagatelle board in the room, in case we should desire to unbend our minds after the solemnity. It was pleasant to observe that Mrs Wemmick no longer unwound Wemmick's arm when it adapted itself to her figure, but sat in a high-backed chair against the wall, like a violoncello in its case, and submitted to be embraced as that melodious instrument might have done.

We had an excellent breakfast, and when anyone declined anything on table, Wemmick said, 'Provided by contract, you know; don't be afraid of it!' I drank to the new couple, drank to the Aged, drank to the Castle, saluted the bride at parting, and made myself as agreeable as I could.

Wemmick came down to the door with me, and I again shook hands with him, and wished him joy.

'Thankee!' said Wemmick, rubbing his hands. 'She's such a manager of fowls, you have no idea. You shall have some eggs, and judge for yourself. I say, Mr Pip!' calling me back, and speaking low. 'This is altogether a Walworth sentiment, please.'

'I understand. Not to be mentioned in Little Britain,' said I.

Wemmick nodded. 'After what you let out the other day, Mr Jaggers may as well not know of it. He might think my brain was softening, or something of the kind.'

Chapter 56

He lay in prison very ill, during the whole interval between his committal for trial and the coming round of the Sessions. He had broken two ribs, they had wounded one of his lungs, and he breathed with great pain and difficulty, which increased daily. It was a consequence of his hurt that he spoke so low as to be scarcely audible; therefore he spoke very little. But he was ever ready to listen to me; and it became the first duty of my life to say to him, and read to him, what I knew he ought to hear.

Being far too ill to remain in the common prison, he was removed, after the first day or so, into the infirmary. This gave me opportunities of being with him that I could not otherwise have had. And but for his illness he would have been put in irons, for he was regarded as a determined prison-breaker, and I know not what else.

Although I saw him every day, it was for only a short time; hence, the regularly recurring spaces of our separation were long enough to record on his face any slight changes that occurred in his physical state. I do not recollect that I once saw any change in it for the better; he wasted, and became slowly weaker and worse, day by day, from the day when the prison door closed upon him.

The kind of submission or resignation that he showed was that of a man who was tired out. I sometimes derived an impression, from his manner or from a whispered word or two which escaped him, that he pondered over the question whether he might have been a better man under better circumstances. But he never justified himself by a hint tending that way, or tried to bend the past out of its eternal shape.

It happened on two or three occasions in my presence, that his desperate reputation was alluded to by one or other of the people in attendance on him. A smile crossed his face then, and he turned his eyes on me with a trustful look, as if he were confident that I had seen some small redeeming touch in him, even so long ago as when I was a little child. As to all the rest, he was humble and contrite, and I never knew him complain.

When the Sessions came round, Mr Jaggers caused an application to be made for the postponement of his trial until the following Sessions. It was obviously made with the assurance that he could not live so long, and was refused. The trial came on at once, and, when he was put to the bar, he was seated in a chair. No objection was made to my getting close to the dock, on the outside of it, and holding the hand that he stretched forth to me.

The trial was very short and very clear. Such things as could be said for him were said,—how he had taken to industrious habits, and had thriven lawfully and reputably. But nothing could unsay the fact that he had returned, and was there in presence of the Judge and Jury. It was impossible to try him for that, and do otherwise than find him guilty.

At that time, it was the custom (as I learnt from my terrible experience of that Sessions) to devote a concluding day to the passing of Sentences, and to make a finishing effect with the Sentence of Death. But for the indelible picture that my remembrance now holds before me, I could scarcely believe, even as I write these words, that I saw two-and-thirty men and women put before the Judge to receive that sentence together. Foremost among the two-and-thirty was he; seated, that he might get breath enough to keep life in him.

The whole scene starts out again in the vivid colours of the moment, down to the drops of April rain on the windows of the court, glittering in the rays of April sun. Penned in the dock, as I again stood outside it at the corner with his hand in mine, were the two-and-thirty men and women; some defiant, some stricken with terror, some sobbing and weeping, some covering their faces, some staring gloomily about. There had been shrieks from among the women convicts; but they had been stilled, and a hush had succeeded. The sheriffs with their great chains and nosegays, other civic gewgaws and monsters, criers, ushers, a great gallery full of people,—a large theatrical audience,—looked on, as the two-and-thirty and the Judge were solemnly confronted. Then the Judge addressed them. Among the wretched creatures before him whom he must single out for special address was one who almost from his infancy had been an offender against the laws; who, after repeated imprisonments and punishments, had been at length sentenced to exile for a term of years; and who, under circumstances of great violence and daring, had made his escape and been re-sentenced to exile for life. That miserable man would seem for a time to have become convinced of his errors, when far removed from the scenes of his old offences, and to have lived a peaceable and honest life. But in a fatal moment, yielding to those propensities and passions, the indulgence of which had so long rendered him a scourge to society, he had quitted his haven of rest and repentance, and had come back to the country where he was proscribed. Being here presently denounced, he had for a time succeeded in evading the officers of Justice, but being at length seized while in the act of flight, he had resisted them, and had—he best knew whether by express design, or in the blindness of his hardihood—caused the death of his denouncer, to whom his whole career was known. The appointed punishment for his return to the land that had cast him out, being death, and his case being this aggravated case, he must prepare himself to die.

The sun was striking in at the great windows of the court, through the glittering drops of rain upon the glass, and it made a broad shaft of light between the two-and-thirty and the Judge, linking both together, and perhaps reminding some among the audience how both were passing on, with absolute equality, to the greater Judgment that knoweth all things, and cannot err. Rising for a moment, a distinct speck of face in this way of light, the prisoner said, 'My Lord, I have received my sentence of death from the Almighty, but I bow to yours,' and sat down again. There was some hushing, and the Judge went on with what he had to say to the rest. Then they were all formally doomed, and some of them were supported out, and some of them sauntered out with a haggard look of bravery, and a few nodded to the gallery, and two or three shook hands, and others went out chewing the fragments of herb they had taken from the sweet herbs lying about. He went last of all, because of having to be helped from his chair, and to go very slowly; and he held my hand while all the others were removed, and while the audience got up (putting their dresses right, as they might at church or elsewhere), and pointed down at this criminal or at that, and most of all at him and me.

I earnestly hoped and prayed that he might die before the Recorder's Report was made; but, in the dread of his lingering on, I began that night to write out a petition to the Home Secretary of State, setting forth my knowledge of him, and how it was that he had come back for my sake. I wrote it as fervently and pathetically as I could; and when I had finished it and sent it in, I wrote out other petitions to such men in authority as I hoped were the most merciful, and drew up one to the Crown itself. For several days and nights after he was sentenced I took no rest except when I fell asleep in my chair, but was wholly absorbed in these appeals. And after I had sent them in, I could not keep away from the places where they were, but felt as if they were more hopeful and less desperate when I was near them. In this unreasonable restlessness and pain of mind I would roam the streets of an evening, wandering by those offices and houses where I had left the petitions. To the present hour, the weary western streets of London on a cold, dusty spring night, with their ranges of stern, shut-up mansions, and their long rows of lamps, are melancholy to me from this association.

The daily visits I could make him were shortened now, and he was more strictly kept. Seeing, or fancying, that I was suspected of an intention of carrying poison to him, I asked to be searched before I sat down at his bedside, and told the officer who was always there, that I was willing to do anything that would assure him of the singleness of my designs. Nobody was hard with him or with me. There was duty to be done, and it was done, but not harshly. The officer always gave me the assurance that he was worse, and some other sick prisoners in the room, and some other prisoners who attended on them as sick nurses, (malefactors, but not incapable of kindness, God be thanked!) always joined in the same report.

As the days went on, I noticed more and more that he would lie placidly looking at the white ceiling, with an absence of light in his face until some word of mine brightened it for an instant, and then it would subside again. Sometimes he was almost or quite unable to speak, then he would answer me with slight pressures on my hand, and I grew to understand his meaning very well.

The number of the days had risen to ten, when I saw a greater change in him than I had seen yet. His eyes were turned towards the door, and lighted up as I entered.

'Dear boy,' he said, as I sat down by his bed: 'I thought you was late. But I knowed you couldn't be that.'

'It is just the time,' said I. 'I waited for it at the gate.'

'You always waits at the gate; don't you, dear boy?'

'Yes. Not to lose a moment of the time.'

'Thank'ee dear boy, thank'ee. God bless you! You've never deserted me, dear boy.'

I pressed his hand in silence, for I could not forget that I had once meant to desert him.

'And what's the best of all,' he said, 'you've been more comfortable alonger me, since I was under a dark cloud, than when the sun shone. That's best of all.'

He lay on his back, breathing with great difficulty. Do what he would, and love me though he did, the light left his face ever and again, and a film came over the placid look at the white ceiling.

'Are you in much pain today?'

'I don't complain of none, dear boy.'

'You never do complain.'

He had spoken his last words. He smiled, and I understood his touch to mean that he wished to lift my hand, and lay it on his breast. I laid it there, and he smiled again, and put both his hands upon it.

The allotted time ran out, while we were thus; but, looking round, I found the governor of the prison standing near me, and he whispered, 'You needn't go yet.' I thanked him gratefully, and asked, 'Might I speak to him, if he can hear me?'

The governor stepped aside, and beckoned the officer away. The change, though it was made without noise, drew back the film from the placid look at the white ceiling, and he looked most affectionately at me.

'Dear Magwitch, I must tell you now, at last. You understand what I say?'

A gentle pressure on my hand.

'You had a child once, whom you loved and lost.'

A stronger pressure on my hand.

'She lived, and found powerful friends. She is living now. She is a lady and very beautiful. And I love her!'

With a last faint effort, which would have been powerless but for my yielding to it and assisting it, he raised my hand to his lips. Then, he gently let it sink upon his breast again, with his own hands lying on it. The placid look at the white ceiling came back, and passed away, and his head dropped quietly on his breast.

Mindful, then, of what we had read together, I thought of the two men who went up into the Temple to pray, and I knew there were no better words that I could say beside his bed, than 'O Lord, be merciful to him a sinner!'

Chapter 57

Now that I was left wholly to myself, I gave notice of my intention to quit the chambers in the Temple as soon as my tenancy could legally determine, and in the meanwhile to underlet them. At once I put bills up in the windows; for, I was in debt, and had scarcely any money, and began to be seriously alarmed by the state of my affairs. I ought rather to write that I should have been alarmed if I had had energy and concentration enough to help me to the clear perception of any truth beyond the fact that I was falling very ill. The late stress upon me had enabled me to put off illness, but not to put it away; I knew that it was coming on me now, and I knew very little else, and was even careless as to that.

For a day or two, I lay on the sofa, or on the floor,—anywhere, according as I happened to sink down,—with a heavy head and aching limbs, and no purpose, and no power. Then there came, one night which appeared of great duration, and which teemed with anxiety and horror; and when in the morning I tried to sit up in my bed and think of it, I found I could not do so.

Whether I really had been down in Garden Court in the dead of the night, groping about for the boat that I supposed to be there; whether I had two or three times come to myself on the staircase with great terror, not knowing how I had got out of bed; whether I had found myself lighting the lamp, possessed by the idea that he was coming up the stairs, and that the lights were blown out; whether I had been inexpressibly harassed by the distracted talking, laughing, and groaning of someone, and had half suspected those sounds to be of my own making; whether there had been a closed iron furnace in a dark corner of the room, and a voice had called out, over and over again, that Miss Havisham was consuming within it,—these were things that I tried to settle with myself and get into some order, as

I lay that morning on my bed. But the vapour of a limekiln would come between me and them, disordering them all, and it was through the vapour at last that I saw two men looking at me.

'What do you want?' I asked, starting; 'I don't know you.'

'Well, sir,' returned one of them, bending down and touching me on the shoulder, 'this is a matter that you'll soon arrange, I dare say, but you're arrested.'

'What is the debt?'

'Hundred and twenty-three pound, fifteen, six. Jeweller's account, I think.'

'What is to be done?'

'You had better come to my house,' said the man. 'I keep a very nice house.'

I made some attempt to get up and dress myself. When I next attended to them, they were standing a little off from the bed, looking at me. I still lay there.

'You see my state,' said I. 'I would come with you if I could; but indeed I am quite unable. If you take me from here, I think I shall die by the way.'

Perhaps they replied, or argued the point, or tried to encourage me to believe that I was better than I thought. Forasmuch as they hang in my memory by only this one slender thread, I don't know what they did, except that they forbore to remove me.

That I had a fever and was avoided, that I suffered greatly, that I often lost my reason, that the time seemed interminable, that I confounded impossible existences with my own identity; that I was a brick in the house-wall, and yet entreating to be released from the giddy place where the builders had set me; that I was a steel beam of a vast engine, clashing and whirling over a gulf, and yet that I implored in my own person to have the engine stopped, and my part in it hammered off; that I passed through these phases of disease, I know of my own remembrance, and did in some sort know at the time. That I sometimes struggled with real people, in the belief that they were murderers, and that I would all at once comprehend that they meant to do me good, and would then sink exhausted in their arms, and suffer them to lay me down, I also knew at the time. But, above all, I knew that there was a constant tendency in all these people,—who, when I was very ill, would present all kinds of extraordinary transformations of the human face, and would be much dilated in size,—above all, I say, I knew that there was an extraordinary tendency in all these people, sooner or later, to settle down into the likeness of Joe.

After I had turned the worst point of my illness, I began to notice that while all its other features changed, this one consistent feature did not change. Whoever came about me, still settled down into Joe. I opened my eyes in the night, and I saw, in the great chair at the bedside, Joe. I opened my eyes in the day, and, sitting on the window-seat, smoking his pipe in the shaded open window, still I saw Joe. I asked for cooling drink, and the dear hand that gave it me was Joe's. I sank back on my pillow after drinking, and the face that looked so hopefully and tenderly upon me was the face of Joe.

At last, one day, I took courage, and said, '*Is* it Joe?'

And the dear old home-voice answered, 'Which it air, old chap.'

'O Joe, you break my heart! Look angry at me, Joe. Strike me, Joe. Tell me of my ingratitude. Don't be so good to me!'

For Joe had actually laid his head down on the pillow at my side, and put his arm round my neck, in his joy that I knew him.

'Which dear old Pip, old chap,' said Joe, 'you and me was ever friends. And when you're well enough to go out for a ride—what larks!'

After which, Joe withdrew to the window, and stood with his back towards me, wiping his eyes. And as my extreme weakness prevented me from getting up and going to him, I lay there, penitently whispering, 'O God bless him! O God bless this gentle Christian man!'

Joe's eyes were red when I next found him beside me; but I was holding his hand, and we both felt happy.

'How long, dear Joe?'

'Which you meantersay, Pip, how long have your illness lasted, dear old chap?'

'Yes, Joe.'

'It's the end of May, Pip. Tomorrow is the first of June.'

'And have you been here all that time, dear Joe?'

'Pretty nigh, old chap. For, as I says to Biddy when the news of your being ill were brought by letter, which it were brought by the post, and being formerly single he is now married though underpaid for a deal of walking and shoe-leather, but wealth were not a object on his part, and marriage were the great wish of his hart—'

'It is so delightful to hear you, Joe! But I interrupt you in what you said to Biddy.'

'Which it were,' said Joe, 'that how you might be amongst strangers, and that how you and me having been ever friends, a wisit at such a moment might not prove unacceptabobble. And Biddy, her word were, "Go to him, without loss of time." That,' said Joe, summing up with his judicial air, 'were the word of Biddy. "Go to him," Biddy say, "without loss of time." In short, I shouldn't greatly deceive you,' Joe added, after a little grave reflection, 'if I represented to you that the word of that young woman were, "without a minute's loss of time."'

There Joe cut himself short, and informed me that I was to be talked to in great moderation, and that I was to take a little nourishment at stated frequent times, whether I felt inclined for it or not, and that I was to submit myself to all his orders. So I kissed his hand, and lay quiet, while he proceeded to indite a note to Biddy, with my love in it.

Evidently Biddy had taught Joe to write. As I lay in bed looking at him, it made me, in my weak state, cry again with pleasure to see the pride with which he set about his letter. My bedstead, divested of its curtains, had been removed, with me upon it, into the sitting-room, as the airiest and largest, and the carpet had been taken away, and the room kept always fresh and wholesome night and day. At my own writing-table, pushed into a corner and cumbered with little bottles, Joe now sat down to his great work, first choosing a pen from the pen-tray as if it were a chest of large tools, and tucking up his sleeves as if he were going to wield a crow-bar or sledgehammer. It was necessary for Joe to hold on heavily to the table with his left elbow, and to get his right leg well out behind him, before he could begin; and when he did begin he made every downstroke so slowly that it might have been six feet long, while at every upstroke I could hear his pen spluttering extensively. He had a curious idea that the inkstand was on the side of him where it was not, and constantly dipped his pen into space, and seemed quite satisfied with the result. Occasionally, he was tripped up by some orthographical stumbling-block; but on the whole he got on very well indeed; and when he had signed his name, and had removed a finishing blot from the paper to the crown of his head with his two forefingers, he got up and hovered about the table, trying the effect of his performance from various points of view, as it lay there, with unbounded satisfaction.

Not to make Joe uneasy by talking too much, even if I had been able to talk much, I deferred asking him about Miss Havisham until next day. He shook his head when I then asked him if she had recovered.

'Is she dead, Joe?'

'Why you see, old chap,' said Joe, in a tone of remonstrance, and by way of getting at it by degrees, 'I wouldn't go so far as to say that, for that's a deal to say; but she ain't—'

'Living, Joe?'

'That's nigher where it is,' said Joe; 'she ain't living.'

'Did she linger long, Joe?'

'Arter you was took ill, pretty much about what you might call (if you was put to it) a week,' said Joe; still determined, on my account, to come at everything by degrees.

'Dear Joe, have you heard what becomes of her property?'

'Well, old chap,' said Joe, 'it do appear that she had settled the most of it, which I meantersay tied it up, on Miss Estella. But she had wrote out a little coddleshell in her own hand a day or two afore the accident, leaving a cool four thousand to Mr Matthew Pocket. And why, do you suppose, above all things, Pip, she left that cool four thousand unto him? "Because of Pip's account of him, the said Matthew." I am told by Biddy, that air the writing,' said Joe, repeating the legal turn as if it did him infinite good, '"account of him the said Matthew." And a cool four thousand, Pip!'

I never discovered from whom Joe derived the conventional temperature of the four thousand pounds; but it appeared to make the sum of money more to him, and he had a manifest relish in insisting on its being cool.

This account gave me great joy, as it perfected the only good thing

I had done. I asked Joe whether he had heard if any of the other relations had any legacies?

'Miss Sarah,' said Joe, 'she have twenty-five pound perannium fur to buy pills, on account of being bilious. Miss Georgiana, she have twenty pound down. Mrs—what's the name of them wild beasts with humps, old chap?'

'Camels?' said I, wondering why he could possibly want to know.

Joe nodded. 'Mrs Camels,' by which I presently understood he meant Camilla, 'she have five pound fur to buy rushlights to put her in spirits when she wake up in the night.'

The accuracy of these recitals was sufficiently obvious to me, to give me great confidence in Joe's information. 'And now,' said Joe, 'you ain't that strong yet, old chap, that you can take in more nor one additional shovelful today. Old Orlick he's been a bustin' open a dwelling-ouse.'

'Whose?' said I.

'Not, I grant you, but what his manners is given to blusterous,' said Joe, apologetically; 'still, a Englishman's ouse is his Castle, and castles must not be busted 'cept when done in war time. And wotsume'er the failings on his part, he were a corn and seedsman in his hart.'

'Is it Pumblechook's house that has been broken into, then?'

'That's it, Pip,' said Joe; 'and they took his till, and they took his cash-box, and they drinked his wine, and they partook of his wittles, and they slapped his face, and they pulled his nose, and they tied him up to his bedpust, and they giv' him a dozen, and they stuffed his mouth full of flowering annuals to prewent his crying out. But he knowed Orlick, and Orlick's in the county jail.'

By these approaches we arrived at unrestricted conversation. I was slow to gain strength, but I did slowly and surely become less weak, and Joe stayed with me, and I fancied I was little Pip again.

For the tenderness of Joe was so beautifully proportioned to my need, that I was like a child in his hands. He would sit and talk to me in the old confidence, and with the old simplicity, and in the old unassertive protecting way, so that I would half believe that all my life since the days of the old kitchen was one of the mental troubles of the fever that was gone. He did everything for me except the household work, for which he had engaged a very decent woman, after paying off the laundress on his first arrival. 'Which I do assure you, Pip,' he would often say, in explanation of that liberty; 'I found her a tapping the spare bed, like a cask of beer, and drawing off the feathers in a bucket, for sale. Which she would have tapped yourn next, and draw'd it off with you a laying on it, and was then a carrying away the coals gradiwally in the soup-tureen and wegetable-dishes, and the wine and spirits in your Wellington boots.'

We looked forward to the day when I should go out for a ride, as we had once looked forward to the day of my apprenticeship. And when the day came, and an open carriage was got into the Lane, Joe wrapped me up, took me in his arms, carried me down to it, and put me in, as if I were still the small helpless creature to whom he had so abundantly given of the wealth of his great nature.

And Joe got in beside me, and we drove away together into the country, where the rich summer growth was already on the trees and on the grass, and sweet summer scents filled all the air. The day happened to be Sunday, and when I looked on the loveliness around me, and thought how it had grown and changed, and how the little wild-flowers had been forming, and the voices of the birds had been strengthening, by day and by night, under the sun and under the stars, while poor I lay burning and tossing on my bed, the mere remembrance of having burned and tossed there came like a check upon my peace. But when I heard the Sunday bells, and looked around a little more upon the outspread beauty, I felt that I was not nearly thankful enough,—that I was too weak yet to be even that,—and I laid my head on Joe's shoulder, as I had laid it long ago when he had taken me to the Fair or where not, and it was too much for my young senses.

More composure came to me after a while, and we talked as we used to talk, lying on the grass at the old Battery. There was no change whatever in Joe. Exactly what he had been in my eyes then, he was in my eyes still; just as simply faithful, and as simply right.

When we got back again, and he lifted me out, and carried me—so easily!—across the court and up the stairs, I thought of that eventful Christmas Day when he had carried me over the marshes. We had not yet made any allusion to my change of fortune, nor did I know how much of my late history he was acquainted with. I was so doubtful of myself now, and put so much trust in him, that I could not satisfy myself whether I ought to refer to it when he did not.

'Have you heard, Joe,' I asked him that evening, upon further consideration, as he smoked his pipe at the window, 'who my patron was?'

'I heerd,' returned Joe, 'as it were not Miss Havisham, old chap.'

'Did you hear who it was, Joe?'

'Well! I heerd as it were a person what sent the person what giv' you the bank-notes at the Jolly Bargemen, Pip.'

'So it was.'

'Astonishing!' said Joe, in the placidest way.

'Did you hear that he was dead, Joe?' I presently asked, with increasing diffidence.

'Which? Him as sent the bank-notes, Pip?'

'Yes.'

'I think,' said Joe, after meditating a long time, and looking rather evasively at the window-seat, 'as I *did* hear tell that how he were something or another in a general way in that direction.'

'Did you hear anything of his circumstances, Joe?'

'Not partickler, Pip.'

'If you would like to hear, Joe—' I was beginning, when Joe got up and came to my sofa.

'Lookee here, old chap,' said Joe, bending over me. 'Ever the best of friends; ain't us, Pip?'

I was ashamed to answer him.

'Wery good, then,' said Joe, as if I *had* answered; 'that's all right; that's agreed upon. Then why go into subjects, old chap, which as betwixt two sech must be forever onnecessary? There's subjects enough as betwixt two sech, without onnecessary ones. Lord! To think of your poor sister and her Rampages! And don't you remember Tickler?'

'I do indeed, Joe.'

'Lookee here, old chap,' said Joe. 'I done what I could to keep you and Tickler in sunders, but my power were not always fully equal to my inclinations. For when your poor sister had a mind to drop into you, it were not so much,' said Joe, in his favourite argumentative way, 'that she dropped into me too, if I put myself in opposition to her, but that she dropped into you always heavier for it. I noticed that. It ain't a grab at a man's whisker, not yet a shake or two of a man (to which your sister was quite welcome), that 'ud put a man off from getting a little child out of punishment. But when that little child is dropped into heavier for that grab of whisker or shaking, then that man naterally up and says to himself, 'Where is the good as you are a doing? I grant you I see the 'arm,' says the man, 'but I don't see the good. I call upon you, sir, therefore, to pint out the good.'

'The man says?' I observed, as Joe waited for me to speak.

'The man says,' Joe assented. 'Is he right, that man?'

'Dear Joe, he is always right.'

'Well, old chap,' said Joe, 'then abide by your words. If he's always right (which in general he's more likely wrong), he's right when he says this: Supposing ever you kep any little matter to yourself, when you was a little child, you kep it mostly because you know'd as J. Gargery's power to part you and Tickler in sunders were not fully equal to his inclinations. Theerfore, think no more of it as betwixt two sech, and do not let us pass remarks upon onnecessary subjects. Biddy giv' herself a deal o' trouble with me afore I left (for I am almost awful dull), as I should view it in this light, and, viewing it in this light, as I should so put it. Both of which,' said Joe, quite charmed with his logical arrangement, 'being done, now this to you a true friend, say. Namely. You mustn't go a overdoing on it, but you must have your supper and your wine and water, and you must be put betwixt the sheets.'

The delicacy with which Joe dismissed this theme, and the sweet tact and kindness with which Biddy—who with her woman's wit had found me out so soon—had prepared him for it, made a deep impression on my mind. But whether Joe knew how poor I was, and how my great expectations had all dissolved, like our own marsh mists before the sun, I could not understand.

Another thing in Joe that I could not understand when it first began to develop itself, but which I soon arrived at a sorrowful comprehension of, was this: As I became stronger and better, Joe became a little less easy with me. In my weakness and entire dependence on him, the dear fellow had fallen into the old tone, and called me by the old names, the dear 'old Pip, old chap,' that now were music in my ears. I too had fallen into the old ways, only happy and thankful that he let me. But, imperceptibly, though I held by them fast, Joe's hold upon them began to slacken; and whereas I wondered at this, at first, I soon began to understand that the cause of it was in me, and that the fault of it was all mine.

Ah! Had I given Joe no reason to doubt my constancy, and to think that in prosperity I should grow cold to him and cast him off? Had I given Joe's innocent heart no cause to feel instinctively that as I got stronger, his hold upon me would be weaker, and that he had better loosen it in time and let me go, before I plucked myself away?

It was on the third or fourth occasion of my going out walking in the Temple Gardens leaning on Joe's arm, that I saw this change in him very plainly. We had been sitting in the bright warm sunlight, looking at the river, and I chanced to say as we got up,—

'See, Joe! I can walk quite strongly. Now, you shall see me walk back by myself.'

'Which do not overdo it, Pip,' said Joe; 'but I shall be happy fur to see you able, sir.'

The last word grated on me; but how could I remonstrate! I walked no further than the gate of the gardens, and then pretended to be weaker than I was, and asked Joe for his arm. Joe gave it me, but was thoughtful.

I, for my part, was thoughtful too; for, how best to check this growing change in Joe was a great perplexity to my remorseful thoughts. That I was ashamed to tell him exactly how I was placed, and what I had come down to, I do not seek to conceal; but I hope my reluctance was not quite an unworthy one. He would want to help me out of his little savings, I knew, and I knew that he ought not to help me, and that I must not suffer him to do it.

It was a thoughtful evening with both of us. But, before we went to bed, I had resolved that I would wait over tomorrow,—tomorrow being Sunday,—and would begin my new course with the new week.

On Monday morning I would speak to Joe about this change, I would lay aside this last vestige of reserve, I would tell him what I had in my thoughts (that secondly, not yet arrived at), and why I had not decided to go out to Herbert, and then the change would be conquered forever. As I cleared, Joe cleared, and it seemed as though he had sympathetically arrived at a resolution too.

We had a quiet day on the Sunday, and we rode out into the country, and then walked in the fields.

'I feel thankful that I have been ill, Joe,' I said.

'Dear old Pip, old chap, you're a'most come round, sir.'

'It has been a memorable time for me, Joe.'

'Likeways for myself, sir,' Joe returned.

'We have had a time together, Joe, that I can never forget. There were days once, I know, that I did for a while forget; but I never shall forget these.'

'Pip,' said Joe, appearing a little hurried and troubled, 'there has been larks. And, dear sir, what have been betwixt us—have been.'

At night, when I had gone to bed, Joe came into my room, as he had done all through my recovery. He asked me if I felt sure that I was as well as in the morning?

'Yes, dear Joe, quite.'

'And are always a getting stronger, old chap?'

'Yes, dear Joe, steadily.'

Joe patted the coverlet on my shoulder with his great good hand, and said, in what I thought a husky voice, 'Goodnight!'

When I got up in the morning, refreshed and stronger yet, I was full of my resolution to tell Joe all, without delay. I would tell him before breakfast. I would dress at once and go to his room and surprise him; for, it was the first day I had been up early. I went to his room, and he was not there. Not only was he not there, but his box was gone.

I hurried then to the breakfast-table, and on it found a letter. These were its brief contents:—

'Not wishful to intrude I have departured fur you are well again dear Pip and will do better without JO.

'P.S. Ever the best of friends.'

Enclosed in the letter was a receipt for the debt and costs on which I had been arrested. Down to that moment, I had vainly supposed that my creditor had withdrawn, or suspended proceedings until I should be quite recovered. I had never dreamed of Joe's having paid the money; but Joe had paid it, and the receipt was in his name.

What remained for me now, but to follow him to the dear old forge, and there to have out my disclosure to him, and my penitent remonstrance with him, and there to relieve my mind and heart of that reserved, secondly, which had begun as a vague something lingering in my thoughts, and had formed into a settled purpose?

The purpose was, that I would go to Biddy, that I would show her how humbled and repentant I came back, that I would tell her how I had lost all I once hoped for, that I would remind her of our old confidences in my first unhappy time. Then I would say to her, 'Biddy, I think you once liked me very well, when my errant heart, even while it strayed away from you, was quieter and better with you than it ever has been since. If you can like me only half as well once more, if you can take me with all my faults and disappointments on my head, if you can receive me like a forgiven child (and indeed I am as sorry, Biddy, and have as much need of a hushing voice and a soothing hand), I hope I am a little worthier of you that I was,—not much, but a little. And, Biddy, it shall rest with you to say whether I shall work at the forge with Joe, or whether I shall try for any different occupation down in this country, or whether we shall go away to a distant place where an opportunity awaits me which I set aside, when it was offered, until I knew your answer. And now, dear Biddy, if you can tell me that you will go through the world with me, you will surely make it a better world for me, and me a better man for it, and I will try hard to make it a better world for you.'

Such was my purpose. After three days more of recovery, I went down to the old place to put it in execution. And how I sped in it is all I have left to tell.

Chapter 58

The tidings of my high fortunes having had a heavy fall had got down to my native place and its neighbourhood before I got there. I found the Blue Boar in possession of the intelligence, and I found that it made a great change in the Boar's demeanour. Whereas the Boar had cultivated my good opinion with warm assiduity when I was coming into property, the Boar was exceedingly cool on the subject now that I was going out of property.

It was evening when I arrived, much fatigued by the journey I had so often made so easily. The Boar could not put me into my usual bedroom, which was engaged (probably by someone who had expectations), and could only assign me a very indifferent chamber among the pigeons and post-chaises up the yard. But I had as sound a sleep in that lodging as in the most superior accommodation the Boar could have given me, and the quality of my dreams was about the same as in the best bedroom.

Early in the morning, while my breakfast was getting ready, I strolled round by Satis House. There were printed bills on the gate and on bits of carpet hanging out of the windows, announcing a sale by auction of the Household Furniture and Effects, next week. The House itself was to be sold as old building materials, and pulled down. LOT 1 was marked in whitewashed knock-knee letters on the brew house; LOT 2 on that part of the main building which had been so long shut up. Other lots were marked off on other parts of the structure, and the ivy had been torn down to make room for the inscriptions, and much of it trailed low in the dust and was withered already. Stepping in for a moment at the open gate, and looking around me with the uncomfortable air of a stranger who had no business there, I saw the auctioneer's clerk walking on the casks and telling them off for the information of a catalogue-compiler, pen in hand, who made a temporary desk of the wheeled chair I had so often pushed along to the tune of Old Clem.

When I got back to my breakfast in the Boar's coffee-room, I found Mr Pumblechook conversing with the landlord. Mr Pumblechook (not improved in appearance by his late nocturnal adventure) was waiting for me, and addressed me in the following terms:—

'Young man, I am sorry to see you brought low. But what else could be expected! What else could be expected!'

As he extended his hand with a magnificently forgiving air, and as I was broken by illness and unfit to quarrel, I took it.

'William,' said Mr Pumblechook to the waiter, 'put a muffin on table. And has it come to this! Has it come to this!'

I frowningly sat down to my breakfast. Mr Pumblechook stood over me and poured out my tea—before I could touch the teapot—with the air of a benefactor who was resolved to be true to the last.

'William,' said Mr Pumblechook, mournfully, 'put the salt on. In happier times,' addressing me, 'I think you took sugar? And did you take milk? You did. Sugar and milk. William, bring a watercress.'

'Thank you,' said I, shortly, 'but I don't eat watercresses.'

'You don't eat 'em,' returned Mr Pumblechook, sighing and nodding his head several times, as if he might have expected that, and as if abstinence from watercresses were consistent with my downfall. 'True. The simple fruits of the earth. No. You needn't bring any, William.'

I went on with my breakfast, and Mr Pumblechook continued to stand over me, staring fishily and breathing noisily, as he always did.

'Little more than skin and bone!' mused Mr Pumblechook, aloud. 'And yet when he went from here (I may say with my blessing), and I spread afore him my humble store, like the Bee, he was as plump as a Peach!'

This reminded me of the wonderful difference between the servile manner in which he had offered his hand in my new prosperity, saying, 'May I?' and the ostentatious clemency with which he had just now exhibited the same fat five fingers.

'Hah!' he went on, handing me the bread and butter. 'And air you a going to Joseph?'

'In heaven's name,' said I, firing in spite of myself, 'what does it matter to you where I am going? Leave that teapot alone.'

It was the worst course I could have taken, because it gave Pumblechook the opportunity he wanted.

'Yes, young man,' said he, releasing the handle of the article in question, retiring a step or two from my table, and speaking for the behoof of the landlord and waiter at the door, 'I *will* leave that teapot alone. You are right, young man. For once you are right. I forgit myself when I take such an interest in your breakfast, as to wish your frame, exhausted by the debilitating effects of prodigygality, to be stimilated by the 'olesome nourishment of your forefathers. And yet,' said Pumblechook, turning to the landlord and waiter, and pointing me out at arm's length, 'this is him as I ever sported with in his days of happy infancy! Tell me not it cannot be; I tell you this is him!'

A low murmur from the two replied. The waiter appeared to be particularly affected.

'This is him,' said Pumblechook, 'as I have rode in my shay-cart. This is him as I have seen brought up by hand. This is him untoe the sister of which I was uncle by marriage, as her name was Georgiana M'ria from her own mother, let him deny it if he can!'

The waiter seemed convinced that I could not deny it, and that it gave the case a black look.

'Young man,' said Pumblechook, screwing his head at me in the old fashion, 'you air a going to Joseph. What does it matter to me, you ask me, where you air a going? I say to you, Sir, you air a going to Joseph.'

The waiter coughed, as if he modestly invited me to get over that.

'Now,' said Pumblechook, and all this with a most exasperating air of saying in the cause of virtue what was perfectly convincing and conclusive, 'I will tell you what to say to Joseph. Here is Squires of the Boar present, known and respected in this town, and here is William, which his father's name was Potkins if I do not deceive myself.'

'You do not, sir,' said William.

'In their presence,' pursued Pumblechook, 'I will tell you, young man, what to say to Joseph. Says you, "Joseph, I have this day seen my earliest benefactor and the founder of my fortun's. I will name no names, Joseph, but so they are pleased to call him up town, and I have seen that man."'

'I swear I don't see him here,' said I.

'Say that likewise,' retorted Pumblechook. 'Say you said that, and even Joseph will probably betray surprise.'

'There you quite mistake him,' said I. 'I know better.'

'Says you,' Pumblechook went on, '"Joseph, I have seen that man, and that man bears you no malice and bears me no malice. He knows your character, Joseph, and is well acquainted with your pig-headedness and ignorance; and he knows my character, Joseph, and he knows my want of gratitoode. Yes, Joseph,' says you,' here Pumblechook shook his head and hand at me, 'he knows my total deficiency of common human gratitoode. *He* knows it, Joseph, as none can. *You* do not know it, Joseph, having no call to know it, but that man do.'

Windy donkey as he was, it really amazed me that he could have the face to talk thus to mine.

'Says you, 'Joseph, he gave me a little message, which I will now repeat. It was that, in my being brought low, he saw the finger of providence. He knowed that finger when he saw Joseph, and he saw it plain. It pinted out this writing, Joseph. *Reward of ingratitoode to his earliest benefactor, and founder of fortun's*. But that man said he did not repent of what he had done, Joseph. Not at all. It was right to do it, it was kind to do it, it was benevolent to do it, and he would do it again.'

'It's pity,' said I, scornfully, as I finished my interrupted breakfast, 'that the man did not say what he had done and would do again.'

'Squires of the Boar!' Pumblechook was now addressing the landlord, 'and William! I have no objections to your mentioning, either up town or down town, if such should be your wishes, that it was right to do it, kind to do it, benevolent to do it, and that I would do it again.'

With those words the Impostor shook them both by the hand, with an air, and left the house; leaving me much more astonished than delighted by the virtues of that same indefinite 'it.' I was not long after him in leaving the house too, and when I went down the High Street I saw him holding forth (no doubt to the same effect) at his shop door to a select group, who honoured me with very unfavourable glances as I passed on the opposite side of the way.

But, it was only the pleasanter to turn to Biddy and to Joe, whose great forbearance shone more brightly than before, if that could be, contrasted with this brazen pretender. I went towards them slowly, for my limbs were weak, but with a sense of increasing relief as I drew nearer to them, and a sense of leaving arrogance and untruthfulness further and further behind.

The June weather was delicious. The sky was blue, the larks were soaring high over the green corn, I thought all that countryside more beautiful and peaceful by far than I had ever known it to be yet. Many pleasant pictures of the life that I would lead there, and of the change for the better that would come over my character when I had a guiding spirit at my side whose simple faith and clear home wisdom I had proved, beguiled my way. They awakened a tender emotion in me; for my heart was softened by my return, and such a change had come to pass, that I felt like one who was toiling home barefoot from distant travel, and whose wanderings had lasted many years.

The schoolhouse where Biddy was mistress I had never seen; but, the little roundabout lane by which I entered the village, for quietness' sake, took me past it. I was disappointed to find that the day was a holiday; no children were there, and Biddy's house was closed. Some hopeful notion of seeing her, busily engaged in her daily duties, before she saw me, had been in my mind and was defeated.

But the forge was a very short distance off, and I went towards it under the sweet green limes, listening for the clink of Joe's hammer. Long after I ought to have heard it, and long after I had fancied I heard it and found it but a fancy, all was still. The limes were there, and the white thorns were there, and the chestnut-trees were there, and their leaves rustled harmoniously when I stopped to listen; but, the clink of Joe's hammer was not in the midsummer wind.

Almost fearing, without knowing why, to come in view of the forge, I saw it at last, and saw that it was closed. No gleam of fire, no glittering shower of sparks, no roar of bellows; all shut up, and still.

But the house was not deserted, and the best parlour seemed to be in use, for there were white curtains fluttering in its window, and the window was open and gay with flowers. I went softly towards it, meaning to peep over the flowers, when Joe and Biddy stood before me, arm in arm.

At first Biddy gave a cry, as if she thought it was my apparition, but in another moment she was in my embrace. I wept to see her, and she wept to see me; I, because she looked so fresh and pleasant; she, because I looked so worn and white.

'But dear Biddy, how smart you are!'

'Yes, dear Pip.'

'And Joe, how smart *you* are!'

'Yes, dear old Pip, old chap.'

I looked at both of them, from one to the other, and then—

'It's my wedding-day!' cried Biddy, in a burst of happiness, 'and I am married to Joe!'

They had taken me into the kitchen, and I had laid my head down on the old deal table. Biddy held one of my hands to her lips, and Joe's restoring touch was on my shoulder. 'Which he warn't strong enough, my dear, fur to be surprised,' said Joe. And Biddy said, 'I ought to have thought of it, dear Joe, but I was too happy.' They were both so overjoyed to see me, so proud to see me, so touched by my coming to them, so delighted that I should have come by accident to make their day complete!

My first thought was one of great thankfulness that I had never breathed this last baffled hope to Joe. How often, while he was with me in my illness, had it risen to my lips! How irrevocable would have been his knowledge of it, if he had remained with me but another hour!

'Dear Biddy,' said I, 'you have the best husband in the whole world, and if you could have seen him by my bed you would have— But no, you couldn't love him better than you do.'

'No, I couldn't indeed,' said Biddy.

'And, dear Joe, you have the best wife in the whole world, and she will make you as happy as even you deserve to be, you dear, good, noble Joe!'

Joe looked at me with a quivering lip, and fairly put his sleeve before his eyes.

'And Joe and Biddy both, as you have been to church today, and are in charity and love with all mankind, receive my humble thanks for all you have done for me, and all I have so ill repaid! And when I say that I am going away within the hour, for I am soon going abroad, and that I shall never rest until I have worked for the money with which you have kept me out of prison, and have sent it to you, don't think, dear Joe and Biddy, that if I could repay it a thousand times over, I suppose I could cancel a farthing of the debt I owe you, or that I would do so if I could!'

They were both melted by these words, and both entreated me to say no more.

'But I must say more. Dear Joe, I hope you will have children to love, and that some little fellow will sit in this chimney-corner of a winter night, who may remind you of another little fellow gone out of it forever. Don't tell him, Joe, that I was thankless; don't tell him, Biddy, that I was ungenerous and unjust; only tell him that I honoured you both, because you were both so good and true, and that, as your child, I said it would be natural to him to grow up a much better man than I did.'

'I ain't a going,' said Joe, from behind his sleeve, 'to tell him nothink o' that natur, Pip. Nor Biddy ain't. Nor yet no one ain't.'

'And now, though I know you have already done it in your own kind hearts, pray tell me, both, that you forgive me! Pray let me hear you say the words, that I may carry the sound of them away with me, and then I shall be able to believe that you can trust me, and think better of me, in the time to come!'

'O dear old Pip, old chap,' said Joe. 'God knows as I forgive you, if I have anythink to forgive!'

'Amen! And God knows I do!' echoed Biddy.

'Now let me go up and look at my old little room, and rest there a few minutes by myself. And then, when I have eaten and drunk with you, go with me as far as the finger-post, dear Joe and Biddy, before we say goodbye!'

I sold all I had, and put aside as much as I could, for a composition with my creditors,—who gave me ample time to pay them in full,— and I went out and joined Herbert. Within a month, I had quitted England, and within two months I was clerk to Clarriker and Co., and within four months I assumed my first undivided responsibility. For the beam across the parlour ceiling at Mill Pond Bank had then ceased to tremble under old Bill Barley's growls and was at peace, and Herbert had gone away to marry Clara, and I was left in sole charge of the Eastern Branch until he brought her back.

Many a year went round before I was a partner in the House; but I lived happily with Herbert and his wife, and lived frugally, and paid my debts, and maintained a constant correspondence with Biddy and Joe. It was not until I became third in the Firm, that Clarriker betrayed me to Herbert; but he then declared that the secret of Herbert's partnership had been long enough upon his conscience, and he must tell it. So he told it, and Herbert was as much moved as amazed, and the dear fellow and I were not the worse friends for the long concealment. I must not leave it to be supposed that we were ever a great House, or that we made mints of money. We were not in a grand way of business, but we had a good name, and worked for our profits, and did very well. We owed so much to Herbert's ever cheerful industry and readiness, that I often wondered how I had conceived that old idea of his inaptitude, until I was one day enlightened by the reflection, that perhaps the inaptitude had never been in him at all, but had been in me.

Chapter 59

For eleven years, I had not seen Joe nor Biddy with my bodily eyes,— though they had both been often before my fancy in the East,—when, upon an evening in December, an hour or two after dark, I laid my hand softly on the latch of the old kitchen door. I touched it so softly that I was not heard, and looked in unseen. There, smoking his pipe in the old place by the kitchen firelight, as hale and as strong as ever, though a little grey, sat Joe; and there, fenced into the corner with Joe's leg, and sitting on my own little stool looking at the fire, was—I again!

'We giv' him the name of Pip for your sake, dear old chap,' said Joe, delighted, when I took another stool by the child's side (but I did *not* rumple his hair), 'and we hoped he might grow a little bit like you, and we think he do.'

I thought so too, and I took him out for a walk next morning, and we talked immensely, understanding one another to perfection. And I took him down to the churchyard, and set him on a certain tombstone there, and he showed me from that elevation which stone was sacred to the memory of Philip Pirrip, late of this Parish, and

Also Georgiana, Wife of the Above.

'Biddy,' said I, when I talked with her after dinner, as her little girl lay sleeping in her lap, 'you must give Pip to me one of these days; or lend him, at all events.'

'No, no,' said Biddy, gently. 'You must marry.'

'So Herbert and Clara say, but I don't think I shall, Biddy. I have so settled down in their home, that it's not at all likely. I am already quite an old bachelor.'

Biddy looked down at her child, and put its little hand to her lips, and then put the good matronly hand with which she had touched it into mine. There was something in the action, and in the light pressure of Biddy's wedding-ring, that had a very pretty eloquence in it.

'Dear Pip,' said Biddy, 'you are sure you don't fret for her?'

'O no,— I think not, Biddy.'

'Tell me as an old, old friend. Have you quite forgotten her?

'My dear Biddy, I have forgotten nothing in my life that ever had a foremost place there, and little that ever had any place there. But that poor dream, as I once used to call it, has all gone by, Biddy,—all gone by!'

Nevertheless, I knew, while I said those words, that I secretly intended to revisit the site of the old house that evening, alone, for her sake. Yes, even so. For Estella's sake.

I had heard of her as leading a most unhappy life, and as being separated from her husband, who had used her with great cruelty, and who had become quite renowned as a compound of pride, avarice, brutality, and meanness. And I had heard of the death of her husband, from an accident consequent on his ill-treatment of a horse. This release had befallen her some two years before; for anything I knew, she was married again.

The early dinner hour at Joe's, left me abundance of time, without hurrying my talk with Biddy, to walk over to the old spot before dark. But, what with loitering on the way to look at old objects and to think of old times, the day had quite declined when I came to the place.

There was no house now, no brewery, no building whatever left, but the wall of the old garden. The cleared space had been enclosed with a rough fence, and looking over it, I saw that some of the old ivy had struck root anew, and was growing green on low quiet mounds of ruin. A gate in the fence standing ajar, I pushed it open, and went in.

A cold silvery mist had veiled the afternoon, and the moon was not yet up to scatter it. But, the stars were shining beyond the mist, and the moon was coming, and the evening was not dark. I could trace out where every part of the old house had been, and where the brewery had been, and where the gates, and where the casks. I had done so, and was looking along the desolate garden walk, when I beheld a solitary figure in it.

The figure showed itself aware of me, as I advanced. It had been moving towards me, but it stood still. As I drew nearer, I saw it to be the figure of a woman. As I drew nearer yet, it was about to turn away, when it stopped, and let me come up with it. Then, it faltered, as if much surprised, and uttered my name, and I cried out,—

'Estella!'

'I am greatly changed. I wonder you know me.'

The freshness of her beauty was indeed gone, but its indescribable majesty and its indescribable charm remained. Those attractions in it, I had seen before; what I had never seen before, was the saddened, softened light of the once proud eyes; what I had never felt before was the friendly touch of the once insensible hand.

We sat down on a bench that was near, and I said, 'After so many years, it is strange that we should thus meet again, Estella, here where our first meeting was! Do you often come back?'

'I have never been here since.'

'Nor I.'

The moon began to rise, and I thought of the placid look at the white ceiling, which had passed away. The moon began to rise, and I thought of the pressure on my hand when I had spoken the last words he had heard on earth.

Estella was the next to break the silence that ensued between us.

'I have very often hoped and intended to come back, but have been prevented by many circumstances. Poor, poor old place!'

The silvery mist was touched with the first rays of the moonlight, and the same rays touched the tears that dropped from her eyes. Not knowing that I saw them, and setting herself to get the better of them, she said quietly,—

'Were you wondering, as you walked along, how it came to be left in this condition?'

'Yes, Estella.'

'The ground belongs to me. It is the only possession I have not relinquished. Everything else has gone from me, little by little, but I have kept this. It was the subject of the only determined resistance I made in all the wretched years.'

'Is it to be built on?'

'At last, it is. I came here to take leave of it before its change. And you,' she said, in a voice of touching interest to a wanderer,—'you live abroad still?'

'Still.'

'And do well, I am sure?'

'I work pretty hard for a sufficient living, and therefore—yes, I do well.'

'I have often thought of you,' said Estella.

'Have you?'

'Of late, very often. There was a long hard time when I kept far from me the remembrance of what I had thrown away when I was quite ignorant of its worth. But since my duty has not been incompatible with the admission of that remembrance, I have given it a place in my heart.'

'You have always held your place in my heart,' I answered.

And we were silent again until she spoke.

'I little thought,' said Estella, 'that I should take leave of you in taking leave of this spot. I am very glad to do so.'

'Glad to part again, Estella? To me, parting is a painful thing. To me, the remembrance of our last parting has been ever mournful and painful.'

'But you said to me,' returned Estella, very earnestly, 'God bless you, God forgive you!' And if you could say that to me then, you will not hesitate to say that to me now,—now, when suffering has been stronger than all other teaching, and has taught me to understand what your heart used to be. I have been bent and broken, but—I hope—into a better shape. Be as considerate and good to me as you were, and tell me we are friends.'

'We are friends,' said I, rising and bending over her, as she rose from the bench.

'And will continue friends apart,' said Estella.

I took her hand in mine, and we went out of the ruined place; and, as the morning mists had risen long ago when I first left the forge, so the evening mists were rising now, and in all the broad expanse of tranquil light they showed to me, I saw no shadow of another parting from her.

IS SHE HIS WIFE?

FOREWORD

Charles Dickens and Catherine Hogarth had been married on 2 April 1836, and had spent a one-week honeymoon at the cottage of a Mrs Nash, in Chalk, near Gravesend. Dickens was still working as a Parliamentary reporter, and he could only take a short time away from work, while the Houses were in Easter recess.

Ten months later, the couple was to return to the same cottage, this time for an entire month (Feb 1837). Things had changed. Two days before the marriage, the first number of *Pickwick Papers* had appeared, and in the time intervening, Dickens had quit his day job as a reporter, and had become one of the most popular writers in London. He was so busy, in fact, that when he went on this second honeymoon, he had to take some work along him, finish it off the first night (Sat 4 Feb), and send it back to London by priority mail.

What was this work? The actor J.P. Harley had wanted another play from Dickens, to follow the success of *The Strange Gentleman*. Dickens wrote to Harley: 'I have by me a little piece in one act called *Cross Purposes*, which I wrote long before I was Boz. It would admit of the introduction of any music; and if you think there is anything in it, it is at your service.' (Pilgrim 1:226). Dickens had first used the name 'Boz' for part two of *The Boarding-House* (Aug 1834), so, if he was being literal, the play was over two years old.

In *Pickwick Papers*, and in *Nicholas Nickleby*, several not-too-relevant short stories are dropped into the novels, and it's sometimes thought that these were older pieces pulled in to help with deadline problems. The case of *Cross Purposes*, presented below as *Is She His Wife?*, is the only time we know for certain that Dickens pulled such old material 'out of the trunk', and used work from the days before his success, to help meet the sudden demand for his writing. Such a practice would help to explain Dickens's phenomenal burst of productivity and activity at this time.

The storyline of *Is She His Wife?* involves a couple, married six months, with the husband restless, snappish, and bored from staying in the country, and both of the pair unhappy. Given the circumstances under which the play was revised, the storyline must, inevitably, raise eyebrows. But the piece is not autobiographical. The bulk of it had been written long before the Dickens marriage, and the revisions made in the honeymoon cottage, done for Harley, must have served to create or modify the role of his character, Felix Tapkins. The piece is too good-natured and frivolous to reflect any marital discord.

Charles and Caroline probably returned from Chalk in time to see the premiere of the short play. *Is She His Wife?* opened on Monday, 6 March, 1837; by 25 April it was on its nineteenth performance. It appeared on and off through the end of the season (31 May). A thirty-minute farce like this serves mainly as an extra attraction to supplement longer and more substantial dramas; we would not expect it to draw much in the way of crowds or attention. The name of Boz did not appear on the playbills until one week after the farce premiered, and without knowing that Dickens was involved, few papers bothered to review such a short slight piece. *The Sunday Times* called it 'a trifle, but a pleasant one, containing sufficient incident to interest the audience while it lasts'. *The Morning Chronicle*, Dickens's old employer, wrote: 'The few meagre incidents had not even the merit of novelty to recommend them, and the dialogue was singularly pointless with the exception of a few puns of venerable antiquity... It was well received, but whether the audience of another night will be so indulgent, is doubtful' (both quoted in Dexter). *Wife* has been revived, as a lunch-time pub production in London (1971), and by the Broadstairs Dickens Players (1975?), the latter winning local awards.

Is She His Wife? is Dickens's most risqué work. It features such racy material as extra-marital flirting, flippant jokes about adultery, and even a woman displaying her shapely ankle. *The Times* wrote that: 'The plot bordered on the dangerous, but it was so dexterously and delicately managed that its success was decided. We have rarely seen Harley to such advantage.' (quoted in Dexter, 254). Like all plays at this time, it was registered with the Lord Chamberlain for licensing, as required by law; but nothing was censored. Similarly, no deletions are indicated in the published copy. *The Village Coquettes* had undergone 'choppings and changings' (Pilgrim 1:246), in its passages about seduction, gambling, and subversion; but *Is She His Wife?* appears to have escaped unscathed.

In the past, *Is She His Wife?* has sometimes been of more interest to book collectors than to playgoers. A version of the comedy was published about the time of its production, but only one copy was ever known to exist—perhaps some kind of print test. The single copy was in the possession of James Ripley Osgood, one of Dickens's American publishers, when it was lost in a fire in Boston (1879). Luckily it had already been reprinted (1872?, 1877); these are among the rarest of Dickens early editions.

We are fortunate that the text of this play has survived. It would have been a shame to lose it. Deliberately loud and hammy, *Is She His Wife?* is a marvellous opportunity for actors to act daft, overact, and chew up the carpet. It follows the conventions of many theatre farces of the time, and strings together a series of contrived coincidences and implausible misunderstandings. Audiences liked and expected such things. Like all three of the St. James's Theatre plays, the best part is the 'low comic' character—in this case, Felix Tapkins, a good example of one of Dickens's eternal optimists. To Boz's new fans, Felix Tapkins in *Wife*, and Martin Stokes in *Coquettes*—both played by Harley—would have seemed like the most 'Dickensian' characters in those plays.

Just a few annotations should be noted, and then we can let anxious readers proceed to Dickens. 'Humane man-traps' are mentioned; these were intended to be just what they sound like; groundskeepers would sometimes set these out to prevent poaching. The Felix Tapkins character makes his entrance singing 'A hunting we will go'; this is the second verse of the song from Henry Fielding's ballad opera, *Don Quixote*; another case of Dickens alluding to two of his favourites—Cervantes and Fielding. Readers can understand the rest by themselves, with some application, so put all distractions aside, turn off your cell phones, and let the curtain rise.

IS SHE HIS WIFE?
OR, SOMETHING SINGULAR!
A COMIC BURLETTA
IN ONE ACT
[by Charles Dickens - 1837]

DRAMATIS PERSONÆ
AT ST. JAMES'S THEATRE, 6 MARCH 1837
ALFRED LOVETOWN, ESQ.
Mr FORESTER
Mr PETER LIMBURY
Mr GARDNER

FELIX TAPKINS, ESQ. (formerly of the India House, Leadenhall Street, and Prospect Place, Poplar; but now of the Rustic Lodge, near Reading)

Mr HARLEY.
JOHN (servant to Lovetown)
[name not given]

Mrs LOVETOWN
MISS ALLISON

Mrs PETER LIMBURY
MADAME SALA

IS SHE HIS WIFE?
OR, SOMETHING SINGULAR!

SCENE I.—*A Room opening into a Garden. A Table laid for Breakfast; Chairs, etc. Mr and Mrs* LOVETOWN, *C., discovered at Breakfast, R. H. The former in a dressing-gown and slippers, reading a newspaper. A Screen on one side.*

LOVETOWN (*L. H. of table, yawning*). Another cup of tea, my dear,—O Lord!

Mrs LOVETOWN (*R. H. of table*). I wish, Alfred, you would endeavour to assume a more cheerful appearance in your wife's society. If you are perpetually yawning and complaining of ennui a few months after marriage, what am I to suppose you'll become in a few years? It really is very odd of you.

LOVETOWN. Not at all odd, my dear, not the least in the world; it would be a great deal more odd if I were not. The fact is, my love, I'm tired of the country; green fields, and blooming hedges, and feathered songsters, are fine things to talk about and read about and write about; but I candidly confess that I prefer paved streets, area railings and dustman's bells, after all.

Mrs LOVETOWN. How often have you told me that, blessed with my love, you could live contented and happy in a desert?

LOVETOWN (*reading*). 'Artful impostor!'

Mrs LOVETOWN. Have you not over and over again said that fortune and personal attractions were secondary considerations with you? That you loved me for those virtues which, while they gave additional lustre to public life, would adorn and sweeten retirement?

LOVETOWN (*reading*). 'Soothing syrup!'

Mrs LOVETOWN. You complain of the tedious sameness of a country life. Was it not you yourself who first proposed our residing permanently in the country? Did you not say that I should then have an ample sphere in which to exercise those charitable feelings which I have so often evinced, by selling at those benevolent fancy fairs?

LOVETOWN (*reading*). 'Humane man-traps!'

Mrs LOVETOWN. He pays no attention to me,—Alfred dear,—

LOVETOWN (*stamping his foot*). Yes, my life.

Mrs LOVETOWN. Have you heard what I have just been saying, dear?

LOVETOWN. Yes, love.

Mrs LOVETOWN. And what can you say in reply?

LOVETOWN. Why, really, my dear, you've said it so often before in the course of the last six weeks, that I think it quite unnecessary to say anything more about it. (*reads*) 'The learned judge delivered a brief but impressive summary of the unhappy man's trial.'

Mrs LOVETOWN (*aside*). I could bear anything but this neglect. He evidently does not care for me.

LOVETOWN (*aside*). I could put up with anything rather than these constant altercations and little petty quarrels. I repeat, my dear, that I am very dull in this out-of-the-way villa—confoundedly dull, horridly dull.

Mrs LOVETOWN. And I repeat that if you took any pleasure in your wife's society, or felt for her as you once professed to feel, you would have no cause to make such a complaint.

LOVETOWN. If I did not know you to be one of the sweetest creatures in existence, my dear, I should be strongly disposed to say that you were a very close imitation of an aggravating female.

Mrs LOVETOWN. That's very curious, my dear, for I declare that if I hadn't known you to be such an exquisite, good-tempered, attentive husband, I should have mistaken you for a very great brute.

LOVETOWN. My dear, you're offensive.

Mrs LOVETOWN. My love, you're intolerable. (*They turn their chairs back to back.*)

Mr FELIX TAPKINS (*sings without*).

> 'The wife around her husband throws
> Her arms to make him stay;
> 'My dear, it rains, it hails, it blows,
> And you cannot hunt today.'
> But a hunting we will go,
> And a hunting we will go,—wo—wo—wo!
> And a hunting we will go.'

Mrs LOVETOWN. There's that dear, good-natured creature, Mr Tapkins,—do you ever hear him complain of the tediousness of a country life? Light-hearted creature,—his lively disposition and rich flow of spirits are wonderful, even to me. (*Rising*)

LOVETOWN. They need not be matter of astonishment to anybody, my dear,—he's a bachelor.

(Mr FELIX TAPKINS *appears at window, L.H.*)

TAPKINS. Ha, ha! How are you both?—Here's a morning! Bless my heart alive, what a morning! I've been gardening ever since five o'clock, and the flowers have been actually growing before my very eyes. The London Pride is sweeping everything before it, and the stalks are half as high again as they were yesterday. They're all run up like so many tailors' bills, after that heavy dew of last night broke down half my rosebuds with the weight of its own moisture,—something like a dew that!—reg'lar doo, eh?—come, that's not so bad for a before-dinner one.

LOVETOWN. Ah, you happy dog, Felix!

TAPKINS. Happy! Of course I am,— Felix by name, Felix by nature,— what the deuce should I be unhappy for, or anybody be unhappy for? What's the use of it, that's the point.

Mrs LOVETOWN. Have you finished your improvements yet, Mr Tapkins?

TAPKINS. At Rustic Lodge? (*She nods assent.*) Bless your heart and soul! You never saw such a place,—cardboard chimneys, Grecian balconies,— Gothic parapets, thatched roof.

Mrs LOVETOWN. Indeed!

TAPKINS. Lord bless you, yes,—green verandah with ivy twining round the pillars.

Mrs LOVETOWN. How very rural!

TAPKINS. Rural, my dear Mrs Lovetown! Delightful! The French windows, too! Such an improvement!

Mrs LOVETOWN. I should think they were!

TAPKINS. Yes, I should think they were. Why, on a fine summer's evening the frogs hop off the grass-plot into the very sitting-room.

Mrs LOVETOWN. Dear me!

TAPKINS. Bless you, yes! Something like the country,—quite a little Eden. Why, when I'm smoking under the verandah, after a shower of rain, the black beetles fall into my brandy-and-water.

Mr and Mrs LOVETOWN. No!—Ha! Ha! Ha!

TAPKINS. Yes. And I take 'em out again with the teaspoon, and lay bets with myself which of them will run away the quickest. Ha! Ha! Ha! (*They all laugh.*) Then the stable, too. Why, in Rustic Lodge the stables are close to the dining-room window.

LOVETOWN. No!

TAPKINS. Yes. The horse can't cough but I hear him. There's compactness. Nothing like the cottage style of architecture for comfort, my boy. By the bye, I have left the new horse at your garden-gate this moment.

Mrs LOVETOWN. The new horse!

TAPKINS. The new horse! Splendid fellow,—such action! Puts out its feet like a rocking-horse, and carries its tail like a hat-peg. Come and see him.

LOVETOWN (*laughing*). I can't deny you anything.

TAPKINS. No, that's what they all say, especially the—eh! (*Nodding and winking.*)

LOVETOWN. Ha! Ha! Ha!

Mrs LOVETOWN. Ha! Ha! Ha! I'm afraid you're a very bad man, Mr Tapkins; I'm afraid you're a shocking man, Mr Tapkins.

TAPKINS. Think so? No, I don't know,—not worse than other people similarly situated. Bachelors, my dear Mrs Lovetown, bachelors—eh! Old fellow? (Winking to LOVETOWN.)

LOVETOWN. Certainly, certainly.

TAPKINS. We know—eh? (*They all laugh.*) By the by, talking of bachelors puts me in mind of Rustic Lodge, and talking of Rustic Lodge puts me in mind of what I came here for. You must come and see me this afternoon. Little Peter Limbury and his wife are coming.

Mrs LOVETOWN. I detest that man.

LOVETOWN. The wife is supportable, my dear.

TAPKINS. To be sure, so she is. You'll come, and that's enough. Now come and see the horse.

LOVETOWN. Give me three minutes to put on my coat and boots, and I'll join you. I won't be three minutes.

[*Exit* LOVETOWN, R. H.]

TAPKINS. Look sharp, look sharp!— Mrs Lovetown, will you excuse me one moment? (*Crosses to L.; calling off.*) Jim,—these fellows never know how to manage horses,—walk him gently up and down,—throw the stirrups over the saddle to show the people that his master's coming, and if anybody asks what that fine animal's pedigree is, and who he belongs to, say he's the property of Mr Felix Tapkins of Rustic Lodge, near Reading, and that he's the celebrated horse who ought to have won the Newmarket Cup last year, only he didn't.

[*Exit* TAPKINS.]

Mrs LOVETOWN. My mind is made up,— I can bear Alfred's coldness and insensibility no longer, and come what may I will endeavour to remove it. From the knowledge I have of his disposition I am convinced that the only mode of doing so will be by rousing his jealousy and wounding his vanity. This thoughtless creature will be a very good instrument for my scheme. He plumes himself on his gallantry, has no very small share of vanity, and is easily led. I see him crossing the garden. (*She brings a chair hastily forward and sits R.H.*)

[*Enter* FELIX TAPKINS, *L. H. window.*]

TAPKINS (*singing*). 'My dear, it rains, it hails, it blows,—'

Mrs LOVETOWN (*tragically*). Would that I had never beheld him!

TAPKINS (*aside*). Hallo! She's talking about her husband. I knew by their manner there had been a quarrel, when I came in this morning.

Mrs LOVETOWN. So fascinating, and yet so insensible to the tenderest of passions as not to see how devotedly I love him.

TAPKINS (*aside*). I thought so.

Mrs LOVETOWN. That he should still remain unmarried is to me extraordinary.

TAPKINS. Um!

Mrs LOVETOWN. He ought to have married long since.

TAPKINS (*aside*). Eh! Why, they aren't married!—'ought to have married long since.'— I rather think he ought.

Mrs LOVETOWN. And, though I am the wife of another,—

TAPKINS (aside). Wife of another!

Mrs LOVETOWN. Still, I grieve to say that I cannot be blind to his extraordinary merits.

TAPKINS. Why, he's run away with somebody else's wife! The villain!— I must let her know I'm in the room, or there's no telling what I may hear next. (*Coughs.*)

Mrs LOVETOWN (*starting up in affected confusion*). Mr Tapkins! (*They sit.*) Bring your chair nearer. I fear, Mr Tapkins, that I have been unconsciously giving utterance to what was passing in my mind. I trust you have not overheard my confession of the weakness of my heart.

TAPKINS. No—no—not more than a word or two.

Mrs LOVETOWN. That agitated manner convinces me that you have heard more than you are willing to confess. Then why—why should I seek to conceal from you—that though I esteem my husband, I—I—love—another?

TAPKINS. I heard you mention that little circumstance.

Mrs LOVETOWN. Oh! (*Sighs.*)

TAPKINS (*aside*). What the deuce is she Oh-ing at? She looks at me as if I were Lovetown himself.

Mrs LOVETOWN (*putting her hand on his shoulder with a languishing air*). Does my selection meet with your approbation?

TAPKINS (*slowly*). It doesn't.

Mrs LOVETOWN. No!

TAPKINS. Decidedly not. (*Aside.*) I'll cut that Lovetown out, and offer myself. Hem! Mrs Lovetown.

Mrs LOVETOWN. Yes, Mr Tapkins.

TAPKINS. I know an individual—

Mrs LOVETOWN. Ah! An individual!

TAPKINS. An individual,— I may, perhaps, venture to say an estimable individual,—who for the last three months has been constantly in your society, who never yet had courage to disclose his passion, but who burns to throw himself at your feet. Oh! (*Aside.*) I'll try an Oh or two now,—Oh! (*Sighs.*) That's a capital Oh!

Mrs LOVETOWN (*aside*). He must have misunderstood me before, for he is evidently speaking of himself. Is the gentleman you speak of handsome, Mr Tapkins?

TAPKINS. He is generally considered remarkably so.

Mrs LOVETOWN. Is he tall?

TAPKINS. About the height of the Apollo Belvidere.

Mrs LOVETOWN. Is he stout?

TAPKINS. Of nearly the same dimensions as the gentleman I have just named.

Mrs LOVETOWN. His figure is—

TAPKINS. Quite a model.

Mrs LOVETOWN. And he is—

TAPKINS. Myself. (*Throws himself on his knees and seizes her hand.*)
Enter LOVETOWN, R. H.

Tapkins immediately pretends to be diligently looking for something on the floor.

Mrs LOVETOWN. Pray don't trouble yourself. I'll find it. Dear me! how could I lose it?

LOVETOWN. What have you lost, love? I should almost imagine that you had lost yourself, and that our friend Mr Tapkins here had just found you.

TAPKINS (*aside*). Ah! You always will have your joke,—funny dog! Funny dog! Bless your heart and soul, there's that immortal horse standing outside all this time! He'll catch his death of cold! Come and see him at once,—come—come.

LOVETOWN. No. I can't see him today. I had forgotten. I've letters to write,—business to transact,— I'm engaged.

TAPKINS (*to* Mrs LOVETOWN). Oh! If he's engaged, you know, we'd better not interrupt him.

Mrs LOVETOWN. Oh! Certainly! Not by any means.

TAPKINS (*taking her arm*). Goodbye, old fellow.

LOVETOWN (*seating himself at table*). Oh!—goodbye.

TAPKINS (*going*). Take care of yourself. I'll take care of Mrs L.

[*Exit* TAPKINS *and* Mrs LOVETOWN, C.]

LOVETOWN. What the deuce does that fellow mean by laying such emphasis on Mrs L.? What's my wife to him, or he to my wife? Very extraordinary! I can hardly believe that even if he had the treachery to make any advances, she would encourage such a preposterous intrigue. (*Walks to and fro.*) She spoke in his praise at breakfast-time, though,—and they have gone away together to see that confounded horse. But stop, I must keep a sharp eye upon them this afternoon, without appearing to do so. I would not appear unnecessarily suspicious for the world. Dissembling in such a case, though, is difficult—very difficult.

Enter a Servant, L. H.

SERVANT. Mr *and* Mrs Peter Limbury.

LOVETOWN. Desire them to walk in.

[Exit Servant, L. H.]

A lucky visit! It furnishes me with a hint. This Mrs Limbury is a vain, conceited woman, ready to receive the attentions of anybody who feigns admiration for her, partly to gratify herself, and partly to annoy the jealous little husband whom she keeps under such strict control. If I pay particular attention to her, I shall lull my wife and that scoundrel Tapkins into a false security, and have better opportunities of observation. They are here.

Enter Mr *and* Mrs LIMBURY, L. H.

LOVETOWN. My dear Mrs Limbury. (*Crosses to C.*)

LIMBURY. Eh?

LOVETOWN (not regarding him). How charming—how delightful—how divine you look today.

LIMBURY (*aside*). Dear Mrs Limbury,—charming,—divine and beautiful look today! They are smiling at each other,—he squeezes her hand. I see how it is. I always thought he paid her too much attention.

LOVETOWN. Sit down,—sit down.

(LOVETOWN *places the chairs so as to sit between them, which* LIMBURY *in vain endeavours to prevent.*)

Mrs LIMBURY. Peter and I called as we passed in our little pony-chaise, to inquire whether we should have the pleasure of seeing you at Tapkins's this afternoon.

LOVETOWN. Is it possible you can ask such a question? Do you think I could stay away?

Mrs LIMBURY. Dear Mr Lovetown! (*Aside.*) How polite,—he's quite struck with me.

LIMBURY (*aside*). Wretched miscreant! A regular assignation before my very face.

LOVETOWN (*to* Mrs LIMBURY). Do you know I entertained some apprehensions—some dreadful fears—that you might not be there.

LIMBURY. Fears that we mightn't be there? Of course we shall be there.

Mrs LIMBURY. Now don't talk, Peter.

LOVETOWN. I thought it just possible, you know, that you might not be agreeable—

Mrs LIMBURY. O, Peter is always agreeable to anything that is agreeable to me. Aren't you, Peter?

LIMBURY. Yes, dearest. (*Aside.*) Agreeable to anything that's agreeable to her! O Lor'!

Mrs LIMBURY. By the by, Mr Lovetown, how do you like this bonnet?

LOVETOWN. O, beautiful!

LIMBURY (*aside*). I must change the subject. Do you know, Mr Lovetown, I have often thought, and it has frequently occurred to me—when—

Mrs LIMBURY. Now don't talk, Peter. (*To* LOVETOWN.) The colour is so bright, is it not?

LOVETOWN. It might appear so elsewhere, but the brightness of those eyes casts it quite into shade.

Mrs LIMBURY. I know you are a connoisseur in ladies' dresses; how do you like those shoes?

LIMBURY (*aside*). Her shoes! What will she ask his opinion of next?

LOVETOWN. O, like the bonnet, you deprive them of their fair chance of admiration. That small and elegant foot engrosses all the attention which the shoes might otherwise attract. That taper ankle, too—

LIMBURY (*aside*). Her taper ankle! My bosom swells with the rage of an ogre. Mr Lovetown,— I—

Mrs LIMBURY. Now, pray do not talk so, Limbury. You've put Mr Lovetown out as it is.

LIMBURY (*aside*). Put him out! I wish I could put him out, Mrs Limbury. I must.

Enter SERVANT, hastily.

SERVANT. I beg your pardon, sir, but the bay pony has got his hind leg over the traces, and he's kicking the chaise to pieces!

LIMBURY. Kicking the new chaise to pieces!

LOVETOWN. Kicking the new chaise to pieces! The bay pony! Limbury, my dear fellow, fly to the spot! (*Pushing him out.*)

LIMBURY. But, Mr Lovetown, I—

Mrs LIMBURY. Oh! he'll kick somebody's brains out, if Peter don't go to him.

LIMBURY. But perhaps he'll kick my brains out if I do go to him.

LOVETOWN. Never mind, don't lose an instant,—not a moment. (*Pushes him out, both talking together.*)

[Exit LIMBURY.]

   (*Aside.*) Now for it,—here's my wife. Dearest Mrs Limbury—(*Kneels by her chair, and seizes her hand.*)

Enter Mrs LOVETOWN, C.

Mrs LOVETOWN (*aside*). Can I believe my eyes? (*Retires behind the screen.*)

Mrs LIMBURY. Mr Lovetown!

LOVETOWN. Nay. Allow me in one hurried interview, which I have sought in vain for weeks,—for months,—to say how devotedly, how ardently I love you. Suffer me to retain this hand in mine. Give me one ray of hope.

Mrs LIMBURY. Rise, I entreat you,—we shall be discovered.

LOVETOWN. Nay, I will not rise till you promise me that you will take an opportunity of detaching yourself from the rest of the company and meeting me alone in Tapkins's grounds this evening. I shall have no eyes, no ears for anyone but yourself.

Mrs LIMBURY. Well, well,— I will— I do—

LOVETOWN. Then I am blest indeed!

Mrs LIMBURY. I am so agitated. If Peter or Mrs Lovetown—were to find me thus — I should betray all. I'll teach my husband to be jealous! (*Crosses to L. H.*) Let us walk round the garden.

LOVETOWN. With pleasure,—take my arm. Divine creature! (*Aside.*) I'm sure she is behind the screen. I saw her peeking. Come.

[Exit LOVETOWN and Mrs LIMBURY, L. H.

Mrs LOVETOWN (*coming forward*). Faithless man! His coldness and neglect are now too well explained. O Alfred! Alfred! How little did I think when I married you, six short months since, that I should be exposed to so much wretchedness! I begin to tremble at my own imprudence, and the situation in which it may place me; but it is now too late to recede. I must be firm. This day will either bring my project to the explanation I so much desire, or convince me of what I too much fear,—my husband's aversion. Can this woman's husband suspect their intimacy? If so, he may be able to prevent this assignation taking place. I will seek him instantly. If I can but meet him at once, he may prevent her going at all.

[Exit Mrs LOVETOWN, R. H.]

Enter TAPKINS, *L. H. window.*

TAPKINS. This, certainly, is a most extraordinary affair. Not her partiality for me—that's natural enough,—but the confession I overheard about her marriage to another. I have been thinking that, after such a discovery, it would be highly improper to allow Limbury and his wife to meet her without warning him of the fact. The best way will be to make him acquainted with the real state of the case. Then he must see the propriety of not bringing his wife to my house tonight. Ah! here he is. I'll make the awful disclosure at once, and petrify him.

Enter LIMBURY, *L. H. window.*

LIMBURY. That damned little bay pony is as bad as my wife. There's no curbing either of them; and as soon as I have got the traces of the one all right, I lose all traces of the other.

TAPKINS (*R.*). Peter!

LIMBURY (*L.*). Ah! Tapkins!

TAPKINS. Hush! Hush! (*Looking cautiously round.*) If you have a moment to spare, I've got something of great importance to communicate.

LIMBURY. Something of great importance, Mr Tapkins! (*Aside.*) What can he mean? Can it relate to Mrs Limbury? The thought is dreadful. You horrify me!

TAPKINS. You'll be more horrified presently. What I am about to tell you concerns yourself and your honour very materially; and I beg you to understand that I communicate it—in the strictest confidence.

LIMBURY. Myself and my honour! I shall dissolve into nothing with horrible anticipations!

TAPKINS (*in a low tone*). Have you ever observed anything remarkable about Lovetown's manner?

LIMBURY. Anything remarkable?

TAPKINS. Ay,—anything very odd, and rather unpleasant?

LIMBURY. Decidedly! No longer than half an hour ago,—in this very room, I observed something in his manner particularly odd and exceedingly unpleasant.

TAPKINS. To your feelings as a husband?

LIMBURY. Yes, my friend, yes, yes;—you know it all, I see!

TAPKINS. What! Do you know it?

LIMBURY. I'm afraid I do; but go on—go on.

TAPKINS (*aside*). How the deuce can he know anything about it? Well, this oddness arises from the peculiar nature of his connection with— You look very pale.

LIMBURY. No, no,—go on,—'connection with—'

TAPKINS. A certain lady,—you know whom I mean.

LIMBURY. I do, I do! (*Aside.*) Disgrace and confusion! I'll kill her with a look! I'll wither her with scornful indignation! Mrs Limbury!—viper!

TAPKINS (*whispering with caution*) They—aren't—married.

LIMBURY. They aren't married! Who aren't?

TAPKINS. Those two, to be sure!

LIMBURY. Those two! What two?

TAPKINS. Why, them. And the worst of it is she's—she's married to somebody else.

LIMBURY. Well, of course I know that.

TAPKINS. You know it?

LIMBURY. Of course I do. Why, how you talk! Isn't she my wife?

TAPKINS. Your wife! Wretched bigamist! Mrs Lovetown your wife?

LIMBURY. Mrs Lovetown! What! Have you been talking of Mrs Lovetown all this time? My dear friend! (*Embraces him.*) The revulsion of feeling is almost insupportable. I thought you were talking about Mrs Limbury.

TAPKINS. No!

LIMBURY. Yes. Ha! Ha! But I say, what a dreadful fellow this is—another man's wife! Gad, I think he wants to run away with every man's wife he sees. And Mrs Lovetown, too—horrid!

TAPKINS. Shocking!

LIMBURY. I say, I oughtn't to allow Mrs Limbury to associate with her, ought I?

TAPKINS. Precisely my idea. You had better induce your wife to stay away from my house tonight.

LIMBURY. I'm afraid I can't do that.

TAPKINS. What, has she any particular objection to staying away?

LIMBURY. She has a very strange inclination to go, and 'tis much the same; however, I'll make the best arrangement I can!

TAPKINS. Well, so be it. Of course I shall see you?

LIMBURY. Of course.

TAPKINS. Mind the secret,—close—close—you know, as a Cabinet Minister answering a question.

LIMBURY. You may rely upon me.

[Exit LIMBURY, L. H., TAPKINS, R. H.]

SCENE II.—*A Conservatory on one side. A Summer-house on the other.*
Enter LOVETOWN *at L. H.*

LOVETOWN. So far so good. My wife has not dropped the slightest hint of having overheard the conversation between me and Mrs Limbury; but she cannot conceal the impression it has made upon her mind, or the jealousy it has evidently excited in her breast. This is just as I wished. I made Mr Peter Limbury's amiable helpmate promise to meet me here. I know that refuge for destitute reptiles (*pointing to summer-house*) is Tapkins's favourite haunt, and if he has any assignation with my wife I have no doubt he will lead her to this place. A woman's coming down the walk. Mrs Limbury, I suppose,— no, my wife, by all that's actionable. I must conceal myself here, even at the risk of a shower of black beetles, or a marching regiment of frogs. (*Goes into conservatory, L. H.*)

Enter Mrs LOVETOWN *from top, L. H.*

Mrs LOVETOWN. I cannot have been mistaken. I am certain I saw Alfred here; he must have secreted himself somewhere to avoid me. Can his assignation with Mrs Limbury have been discovered? Mr Limbury's behaviour to me just now was strange in the extreme; and after a variety of incoherent expressions he begged me to meet him here, on a subject, as he said, of great delicacy and importance to myself. Alas! I fear that my husband's neglect and unkindness are but too well known. The injured little man approaches. I summon all my fortitude to bear the disclosure.

Enter Mr LIMBURY *at top, L. H.*

LIMBURY (*aside*). Now as I could not prevail on Mrs Limbury to stay away, the only distressing alternative I have is to inform Mrs Lovetown that I know her history, and to put it to her good feeling whether she hadn't better go.

LOVETOWN (*peeping*). Limbury! What the deuce can that little wretch want here?

LIMBURY. I took the liberty, Mrs Lovetown, of begging you to meet me in this retired spot, because the esteem I still entertain for you, and my regard for your feelings, induce me to prefer a private to a public disclosure.

LOVETOWN (*peeping*). 'Public disclosure!' What on earth is he talking about? I wish he'd speak a little louder.

Mrs LOVETOWN. I am sensible of your kindness, Mr Limbury, and believe me most grateful for it. I am fully prepared to hear what you have to say.

LIMBURY. It is hardly necessary for me, I presume, to say, Mrs Lovetown, that I have accidentally discovered the whole secret.

Mrs LOVETOWN. The whole secret, sir?

LOVETOWN (*peeping*). Whole secret! What secret?

LIMBURY. The whole secret, ma'am, of this disgraceful— I must call it disgraceful—and most abominable intrigue.

Mrs LOVETOWN (*aside*). My worst fears are realized,—my husband's neglect is occasioned by his love for another.

LOVETOWN (*peeping*). Abominable intrigue! My first suspicions are too well founded. He reproaches my wife with her infidelity, and she cannot deny it,—that villain Tapkins!

Mrs LOVETOWN (*weeping*). Cruel—cruel— Alfred!

LIMBURY. You may well call him cruel, unfortunate woman. His usage of you is indefensible, unmanly, scandalous.

Mrs LOVETOWN. It is. It is, indeed.

LIMBURY. It's very painful for me to express myself in such plain terms, Mrs Lovetown; but allow me to say, as delicately as possible, that you should not endeavour to appear in society under such unusual and distressing circumstances.

Mrs LOVETOWN. Not appear in society! Why should I quit it?

LOVETOWN (*peeping*). Shameful woman!

LIMBURY. Is it possible you can ask such a question?

Mrs LOVETOWN. What should I do? Where can I go?

LIMBURY. Gain permission to return once again to your husband's roof.

Mrs LOVETOWN. My husband's roof?

LIMBURY. Yes, the roof of your husband, your wretched, unfortunate husband!

Mrs LOVETOWN. Never!

LIMBURY (*aside*). She's thoroughly hardened, steeped in vice beyond redemption. Mrs Lovetown, as you reject my well-intentioned advice in this extraordinary manner, I am reduced to the painful necessity of expressing my hope that you will,—now pray don't think me unkind,—that you will never attempt to meet Mrs Limbury more.

Mrs LOVETOWN. What! Can you suppose I am so utterly dead to every sense of feeling and propriety as to meet that person,—the destroyer of my peace and happiness,—the wretch who has ruined my hopes and blighted my prospects forever? Ask your own heart, sir,—appeal to your own feelings. You are naturally indignant at her conduct. You would hold no further communication with her. Can you suppose, then, I would deign to do so? The mere supposition is an insult!

[*Exit* Mrs LOVETOWN *hastily at top, L.H.*]

LIMBURY. What can all this mean? I am lost in a maze of astonishment, petrified at the boldness with which she braves it out. Eh! It's breaking upon me by degrees. I see it. What did she say? 'Destroyer of peace and happiness,—person—ruined hopes and blighted prospects—her.' I see it all. That atrocious Lovetown, that Don Juan multiplied by twenty, that unprecedented libertine, has seduced Mrs Limbury from her allegiance to her lawful lord and master. He first of all runs away with the wife of another man, and he is no sooner tired of her, than he runs away with another wife of another man. I thirst for his destruction. I—(LOVETOWN *rushes from the conservatory and embraces* LIMBURY, *who disengages himself.*) Murderer of domestic happiness! Behold hold your victim!

LOVETOWN. Alas! You speak but too truly. (*Covering his face with his hands.*) I am the victim.

LIMBURY. I speak but too truly!— He avows his own criminality. I shall throttle him. I know I shall. I feel it.

Enter Mrs LIMBURY *at back, L. H.*

Mrs LIMBURY (*aside*). My husband here! (*Goes into conservatory.*)

Enter TAPKINS *at back, L. H.*

TAPKINS (*aside*). Not here, and her husband with Limbury. I'll reconnoitre. (*Goes into summer-house, R. H.*)

LIMBURY. Lovetown, have you the boldness to look an honest man in the face?

LOVETOWN. O, spare me! I feel the situation in which I am placed acutely, deeply. Feel for me when I say that from that conservatory I overheard the greater part of what passed between you and Mrs Lovetown.

LIMBURY. You did?

LOVETOWN. Need I say how highly I approve both of the language you used, and the advice you gave her?

LIMBURY. What! You want to get rid of her, do you?

LOVETOWN. Can you doubt it?

TAPKINS (*peeping*). Hallo! He wants to get rid of her. Queer!

LOVETOWN. Situated as I am, you know, I have no other resource, after what has passed. I must part from her.

Mrs LIMBURY (*peeping*). What can he mean?

LIMBURY (*aside*). I should certainly throttle him, were it not that the coolness with which he refers to the dreadful event paralyses me. Mr Lovetown, look at me! Sir, consider the feelings of an indignant husband, sir!

LOVETOWN. Oh, I thank you for those words. Those strong expressions prove the unaffected interest you take in the matter.

LIMBURY. Unaffected interest! I shall go raving mad with passion and fury! Villain! Monster! To embrace the opportunity afforded him of being on a footing of friendship.

LOVETOWN. To take a mean advantage of his being a single man.

LIMBURY. To tamper with the sacred engagements of a married woman.

LOVETOWN. To place a married man in a disgraceful and humiliating situation.

LIMBURY. Scoundrel! Do you mock me to my face?

LOVETOWN. Mock you. What d' ye mean? Who the devil are you talking about?

LIMBURY. Talking about—you!

LOVETOWN. Me!

LIMBURY. Designing miscreant! Of whom do you speak?

LOVETOWN. Of whom should I speak but that scoundrel Tapkins?

TAPKINS (*coming forward, R.*). Me! What the devil do you mean by that?

LOVETOWN. Ha! (*Rushing at him, is held back by* LIMBURY.)

LIMBURY (*to* TAPKINS). Avoid him. Get out of his sight. He's raving mad with conscious villainy.

TAPKINS. What are you all playing at? I spy over my two acres of infant hay for?

LOVETOWN (*to* TAPKINS). How dare you tamper with the affections of Mrs Lovetown?

TAPKINS. O, is that all? Ha! Ha! (*Crosses to C.*)

LOVETOWN. All!

TAPKINS. Come, come, none of your nonsense.

LOVETOWN. Nonsense! Designate the best feelings of our nature nonsense!

TAPKINS. Pooh! Pooh! Here, I know all about it.

LOVETOWN (*angrily*). And so do I, sir! And so do I.

TAPKINS. Of course you do. And you've managed very well to keep it quiet so long. But you're a deep fellow, by Jove! You're a deep fellow!

LOVETOWN. Now, mind! I restrain myself sufficiently to ask you once again before I knock you down, by what right dare you tamper with the affections of Mrs Lovetown?

TAPKINS. Right! O, if you come to strict right, you know, nobody has a right but her husband.

LOVETOWN. And who is her husband? Who is her husband?

TAPKINS. Ah! To be sure, that's the question. Nobody that I know. I hope—poor fellow—

LOVETOWN. I'll bear these insults no longer! (*Rushes towards* TAPKINS. LIMBURY *interposes.* LOVETOWN *crosses to R. H. A scream is heard from the conservatory—a pause.*)

TAPKINS. Something singular among the plants! (*He goes into the conservatory and returns with* Mrs LIMBURY.) A flower that wouldn't come out of its own accord. I was obliged to force it. Tolerably full blown now, at all events.

LIMBURY. My wife! Traitoress! (*Crosses to L. H.*) Fly from my presence! Quit my sight! Return to the conservatory with that demon in a frock-coat!

Enter Mrs LOVETOWN *at top, L. H. and comes down C.*

TAPKINS. Hallo! Somebody else!

LOVETOWN (*aside*). My wife here!

Mrs LOVETOWN (*to* LIMBURY). I owe you some return for the commiseration you expressed just now for my wretched situation. The best, the only one I can make you is, to entreat you to refrain from committing any rash act, however excited you may be, and to control the feelings of an injured husband.

TAPKINS. Injured husband! Decidedly singular!

LOVETOWN. The allusion of that lady I confess my utter inability to understand. Mr Limbury, to you an explanation is due, and I make it more cheerfully, as my abstaining from doing so might involve the character of your wife. Stung by the attentions which I found Mrs Lovetown had received from a scoundrel present,—

TAPKINS (*aside*). That's me.

LOVETOWN. I—partly to obtain opportunities of watching her closely, under an assumed mask of levity and carelessness, and partly in the hope of awaking once again any dormant feelings of affection that might still slumber in her breast, affected a passion for your wife which I never felt, and to which she never really responded. The second part of my project, I regret to say, has failed. The first has succeeded but too well.

LIMBURY. Can I believe my ears? But how came Mrs Peter Limbury to receive those attentions?

Mrs LIMBURY. Why, not because I liked them, of course, but to assist Mr Lovetown in his project, and to teach you the misery of those jealous fears. Come here, you stupid little jealous, insinuating darling. (*They retire up L. H., she coaxing him.*)

TAPKINS (*aside*). It strikes me very forcibly that I have made a slight mistake here, which is something particularly singular. (*Turns up R. H.*)

Mrs LOVETOWN. Alfred, hear me! I am as innocent as yourself. Your fancied neglect and coldness hurt my weak vanity, and roused some foolish feelings of angry pride. In a moment of irritation I resorted to some such retaliation as you have yourself described. That I did so from motives as guiltless as your own I call Heaven to witness. That I repent my fault I solemnly assure you.

LOVETOWN. Is this possible?

TAPKINS. Very possible indeed! Believe your wife's assurance and my corroboration. Here, give and take is all fair, you know. Give me your hand and take your wife's. Here, Mr and Mrs L. (*To* LIMBURY.) Double L,—I call them. (*To* LOVETOWN.) Small italic and Roman capital. (*To* Mr *and* Mrs LIMBURY, *who come forward.*) Here, it's all arranged. The key to the whole matter is that I've been mistaken, which is something singular. If I have made another mistake in calculating on your kind and lenient reception of our last half-hour's misunderstanding (*to the audience*), I shall have done something more singular still. Do you forbid me committing any more mistakes, or may I announce my intention of doing something singular again?

Afterword

Felix Tapkins's closing address to the audience simply asks whether or not the crowd approved of the performance. Theatre managers would continue or terminate a play's run, based on such applause or hisses.

We must end now on an unhappy note. The most noted performance of *Is She His Wife?*—the evening of 6 May 1837—is known for the saddest of reasons, and for one of the great tragedies in Dickens's life. The story of how Dickens lost his beloved sister-in-law is well known to all Dickensians. Henry Burnett, an actor at the St. James's Theatre, and Dickens's future brother-in-law, played in another piece that same evening. Many years later, he remembered seeing Dickens and his family in the audience: 'As to Mary Hogarth, I can see her sweet face looking over the Box upon the Stage of the St. James's Theatre as it appeared the night she died...Dickens had a box on the night and with him were his Father, Mother, Wife and Mary Hogarth. My future Wife [Fanny Dickens] was nervous and could not go. There was some excitement, of course, for the House was very full. Mary was to sleep at her sister's house in Doughty Street. On her way back she fell ill—was carried in from the coach, and it was not long before her head was gently laid back on the pillow—a very spirit of sweetness—in her last sleep. The shadow from her grave darkened the sensitive life of Dickens for a long time, for he had the warmest brotherly love for her unaffected simplicity and the sweetness of her character and her beauty.' (Carlton, 71). Mary died in Dickens's arms the following afternoon (7 May 1837). She was only seventeen. When Dickens returned to the St. James Theatre, later the same year (12 Dec 1837), he asked for different seating: 'let us have either a pit or proscenium box on the same side as that in which we used to sit; but not a box on the same tier, or opposite. Old recollections make us shun our old haunts, or the sight of them.' (Pilgrim 1:343).

Dickens was never to write another play for the St. James Theatre. His first novel *Pickwick* was already a roaring hit, and was to be one of the most popular novels of the century. But his plays had met with only limited success, and even that was due in part to the fame of Harley and of *Pickwick*. *Coquettes* had been a critical failure and a disappointment. Dickens took the natural route and pursued the novels.

There exists one further letter from Dickens on the subject, in which he offers to write a two-act piece for the St. James—for one-hundred and fifty pounds. It was five times what he had received for *The Strange Gentleman* (Pilgrim 1:254). Nothing came of it. Dickens had become too popular and too expensive an author to continue as a playwright.

MASTER HUMPHREY'S CLOCK

Chapter 1

Master Humphrey, from His Clock-Side in the Chimney Corner

The reader must not expect to know where I live. At present, it is true, my abode may be a question of little or no import to anybody; but if I should carry my readers with me, as I hope to do, and there should spring up between them and me feelings of homely affection and regard attaching something of interest to matters ever so slightly connected with my fortunes or my speculations, even my place of residence might one day have a kind of charm for them. Bearing this possible contingency in mind, I wish them to understand, in the outset, that they must never expect to know it.

I am not a churlish old man. Friendless I can never be, for all mankind are my kindred, and I am on ill terms with no one member of my great family. But for many years I have led a lonely, solitary life;—what wound I sought to heal, what sorrow to forget, originally, matters not now; it is sufficient that retirement has become a habit with me, and that I am unwilling to break the spell which for so long a time has shed its quiet influence upon my home and heart.

I live in a venerable suburb of London, in an old house which in bygone days was a famous resort for merry roysterers and peerless ladies, long since departed. It is a silent, shady place, with a paved courtyard so full of echoes, that sometimes I am tempted to believe that faint responses to the noises of old times linger there yet, and that these ghosts of sound haunt my footsteps as I pace it up and down. I am the more confirmed in this belief, because, of late years, the echoes that attend my walks have been less loud and marked than they were wont to be; and it is pleasanter to imagine in them the rustling of silk brocade, and the light step of some lovely girl, than to recognize in their altered note the failing tread of an old man.

Those who like to read of brilliant rooms and gorgeous furniture would derive but little pleasure from a minute description of my simple dwelling. It is dear to me for the same reason that they would hold it in slight regard. Its worm-eaten doors, and low ceilings crossed by clumsy beams; its walls of wainscot, dark stairs, and gaping closets; its small chambers, communicating with each other by winding passages or narrow steps; its many nooks, scarce larger than its corner-cupboards; its very dust and dullness, are all dear to me. The moth and spider are my constant tenants; for in my house the one basks in his long sleep, and the other plies his busy loom secure and undisturbed. I have a pleasure in thinking on a summer's day how many butterflies have sprung for the first time into light and sunshine from some dark corner of these old walls.

When I first came to live here, which was many years ago, the neighbours were curious to know who I was, and whence I came, and why I lived so much alone. As time went on, and they still remained unsatisfied on these points, I became the centre of a popular ferment, extending for half a mile round, and in one direction for a full mile. Various rumours were circulated to my prejudice. I was a spy, an infidel, a conjurer, a kidnapper of children, a refugee, a priest, a monster. Mothers caught up their infants and ran into their houses as I passed; men eyed me spitefully, and muttered threats and curses. I was the object of suspicion and distrust—ay, of downright hatred too.

But when in course of time they found I did no harm, but, on the contrary, inclined towards them despite their unjust usage, they began to relent. I found my footsteps no longer dogged, as they had often been before, and observed that the women and children no longer retreated, but would stand and gaze at me as I passed their doors. I took this for a good omen, and waited patiently for better times. By degrees I began to make friends among these humble folks; and though they were yet shy of speaking, would give them 'good day,' and so pass on. In a little time, those whom I had thus accosted would make a point of coming to their doors and windows at the usual hour, and nod or courtesy to me; children, too, came timidly within my reach, and ran away quite scared when I patted their heads and bade them be good at school. These little people soon grew more familiar. From exchanging mere words of course with my older neighbours, I gradually became their friend and adviser, the depositary of their cares and sorrows, and sometimes, it may be, the reliever, in my small way, of their distresses. And now I never walk abroad but pleasant recognitions and smiling faces wait on Master Humphrey.

It was a whim of mine, perhaps as a whet to the curiosity of my neighbours, and a kind of retaliation upon them for their suspicions—it was, I say, a whim of mine, when I first took up my abode in this place, to acknowledge no other name than Humphrey. With my detractors, I was Ugly Humphrey. When I began to convert them into friends, I was Mr Humphrey and Old Mr Humphrey. At length I settled down into plain Master Humphrey, which was understood to be the title most pleasant to my ear; and so completely a matter of course has it become, that sometimes when I am taking my morning walk in my little courtyard, I overhear my barber—who has a profound respect for me, and would not, I am sure, abridge my honours for the world—holding forth on the other side of the wall, touching the state of 'Master Humphrey's' health, and communicating to some friend the substance of the conversation that he and Master Humphrey have had together in the course of the shaving which he has just concluded.

That I may not make acquaintance with my readers under false pretences, or give them cause to complain hereafter that I have withheld any matter which it was essential for them to have learnt at first, I wish them to know—and I smile sorrowfully to think that the time has been when the confession would have given me pain—that I am a misshapen, deformed old man.

I have never been made a misanthrope by this cause. I have never been stung by any insult, nor wounded by any jest upon my crooked figure. As a child I was melancholy and timid, but that was because the gentle consideration paid to my misfortune sunk deep into my spirit and made me sad, even in those early days. I was but a very young creature when my poor mother died, and yet I remember that often when I hung around her neck, and oftener still when I played about the room before her, she would catch me to her bosom, and bursting into tears, would soothe me with every term of fondness and affection. God knows I was a happy child at those times,—happy to nestle in her breast,—happy to weep when she did,—happy in not knowing why.

These occasions are so strongly impressed upon my memory, that they seem to have occupied whole years. I had numbered very, very few when they ceased forever, but before then their meaning had been revealed to me.

I do not know whether all children are imbued with a quick perception of childish grace and beauty, and a strong love for it, but I was. I had no thought that I remember, either that I possessed it myself or that I lacked it, but I admired it with an intensity that I cannot describe. A little knot of playmates—they must have been beautiful, for I see them now—were clustered one day round my mother's knee in eager admiration of some picture representing a group of infant angels, which she held in her hand. Whose the picture was, whether it was familiar to me or otherwise, or how all the children came to be there, I forget; I have some dim thought it was my birthday, but the beginning of my recollection is that we were all together in a garden, and it was summer weather,— I am sure of that, for one of the little girls had roses in her sash. There were many lovely angels in this picture, and I remember the fancy coming upon me to point out which of them represented each child there, and that when I had gone through my companions, I stopped and hesitated, wondering which was most like me. I remember the children looking at each other, and my turning red and hot, and their crowding round to kiss me, saying that they loved me all the same; and then, and when the old sorrow came into my dear mother's mild and tender look, the truth broke upon me for the first time, and I knew, while watching my awkward and ungainly sports, how keenly she had felt for her poor crippled boy.

I used frequently to dream of it afterwards, and now my heart aches for that child as if I had never been he, when I think how often he awoke from some fairy change to his own old form, and sobbed himself to sleep again.

Well, well,—all these sorrows are past. My glancing at them may not be without its use, for it may help in some measure to explain why I have all my life been attached to the inanimate objects that people my chamber, and how I have come to look upon them rather in the light of old and constant friends, than as mere chairs and tables which a little money could replace at will.

Chief and first among all these is my Clock,—my old, cheerful, companionable Clock. How can I ever convey to others an idea of the comfort and consolation that this old Clock has been for years to me!

It is associated with my earliest recollections. It stood upon the staircase at home (I call it home still mechanically), nigh sixty years ago. I like it for that; but it is not on that account, nor because it is a quaint old thing in a huge oaken case curiously and richly carved, that I prize it as I do. I incline to it as if it were alive, and could understand and give me back the love I bear it.

And what other thing that has not life could cheer me as it does? What other thing that has not life (I will not say how few things that have) could have proved the same patient, true, untiring friend? How often have I sat in the long winter evenings feeling such society in its cricket-voice, that raising my eyes from my book and looking gratefully towards it, the face reddened by the glow of the shining fire has seemed to relax from its staid expression and to regard me kindly! How often in the summer twilight, when my thoughts have wandered back to a melancholy past, have its regular whisperings recalled them to the calm and peaceful present! How often in the dead tranquillity of night has its bell broken the oppressive silence, and seemed to give me assurance that the old clock was still a faithful watcher at my chamber-door! My easy-chair, my desk, my ancient furniture, my very books, I can scarcely bring myself to love even these last like my old clock.

It stands in a snug corner, midway between the fireside and a low arched door leading to my bedroom. Its fame is diffused so extensively throughout the neighbourhood, that I have often the satisfaction of hearing the publican, or the baker, and sometimes even the parish-clerk, petitioning my housekeeper (of whom I shall have much to say by-and-by) to inform him the exact time by Master Humphrey's clock. My barber, to whom I have referred, would sooner believe it than the sun. Nor are these its only distinctions. It has acquired, I am happy to say, another, inseparably connecting it not only with my enjoyments and reflections, but with those of other men; as I shall now relate.

I lived alone here for a long time without any friend or acquaintance. In the course of my wanderings by night and day, at all hours and seasons, in city streets and quiet country parts, I came to be familiar with certain faces, and to take it to heart as quite a heavy disappointment if they failed to present themselves each at its accustomed spot. But these were the only friends I knew, and beyond them I had none.

It happened, however, when I had gone on thus for a long time, that I formed an acquaintance with a deaf gentleman, which ripened into intimacy and close companionship. To this hour, I am ignorant of his name. It is his humour to conceal it, or he has a reason and purpose for so doing. In either case, I feel that he has a right to require a return of the trust he has reposed; and as he has never sought to discover my secret, I have never sought to penetrate his. There may have been something in this tacit confidence in each other flattering and pleasant to us both, and it may have imparted in the beginning an additional zest, perhaps, to our friendship. Be this as it may, we have grown to be like brothers, and still I only know him as the deaf gentleman.

I have said that retirement has become a habit with me. When I add, that the deaf gentleman and I have two friends, I communicate nothing which is inconsistent with that declaration. I spend many hours of every day in solitude and study, have no friends or change of friends but these, only see them at stated periods, and am supposed to be of a retired spirit by the very nature and object of our association.

We are men of secluded habits, with something of a cloud upon our early fortunes, whose enthusiasm, nevertheless, has not cooled with age, whose spirit of romance is not yet quenched, who are content to ramble through the world in a pleasant dream, rather than ever waken again to its harsh realities. We are alchemists who would extract the essence of perpetual youth from dust and ashes, tempt coy truth in many light and airy forms from the bottom of her well, and discover one crumb of comfort or one grain of good in the commonest and least-regarded matter that passes through our crucible. Spirits of past times, creatures of imagination, and people of today are alike the objects of our seeking, and, unlike the objects of search with most philosophers, we can insure their coming at our command.

The deaf gentleman and I first began to beguile our days with these fancies, and our nights in communicating them to each other. We are now four. But in my room there are six old chairs, and we have decided that the two empty seats shall always be placed at our table when we meet, to remind us that we may yet increase our company by that number, if we should find two men to our mind. When one among us dies, his chair will always be set in its usual place, but never occupied again; and I have caused my will to be so drawn out, that when we are all dead the house shall be shut up, and the vacant chairs still left in their accustomed places. It is pleasant to think that even then our shades may, perhaps, assemble together as of yore we did, and join in ghostly converse.

One night in every week, as the clock strikes ten, we meet. At the second stroke of two, I am alone.

And now shall I tell how that my old servant, besides giving us note of time, and ticking cheerful encouragement of our proceedings, lends its name to our society, which for its punctuality and my love is christened 'Master Humphrey's Clock'? Now shall I tell how that in the bottom of the old dark closet, where the steady pendulum throbs and beats with healthy action, though the pulse of him who made it stood still long ago, and never moved again, there are piles of dusty papers constantly placed there by our hands, that we may link our enjoyments with my old friend, and draw means to beguile time from the heart of time itself? Shall I, or can I, tell with what a secret pride I open this repository when we meet at night, and still find new store of pleasure in my dear old Clock?

Friend and companion of my solitude! Mine is not a selfish love; I would not keep your merits to myself, but disperse something of pleasant association with your image through the whole wide world; I would have men couple with your name cheerful and healthy thoughts; I would have them believe that you keep true and honest time; and how it would gladden me to know that they recognized some hearty English work in Master Humphrey's clock!

The Clock-Case

It is my intention constantly to address my readers from the chimney-corner, and I would fain hope that such accounts as I shall give them of our histories and proceedings, our quiet speculations or more busy adventures, will never be unwelcome. Lest, however, I should grow prolix in the outset by lingering too long upon our little association, confounding the enthusiasm with which I regard this chief happiness of my life with that minor degree of interest which those to whom I address myself may be supposed to feel for it, I have deemed it expedient to break off as they have seen.

But, still clinging to my old friend, and naturally desirous that all its merits should be known, I am tempted to open (somewhat irregularly and against our laws, I must admit) the clock-case. The first roll of paper on which I lay my hand is in the writing of the deaf gentleman. I shall have to speak of him in my next paper; and how can I better approach that welcome task than by prefacing it with a production of his own pen, consigned to the safe keeping of my honest Clock by his own hand?

The manuscript runs thus:

Introduction to the Giant Chronicles

Once upon a time, that is to say, in this our time,—the exact year, month, and day are of no matter,—there dwelt in the city of London a substantial citizen, who united in his single person the dignities of wholesale fruiterer, alderman, common-councilman, and member of the worshipful Company of Patten-makers; who had superadded to these extraordinary distinctions the important post and title of Sheriff, and who at length, and to crown all, stood next in rotation for the high and honourable office of Lord Mayor.

He was a very substantial citizen indeed. His face was like the full moon in a fog, with two little holes punched out for his eyes, a very ripe pear stuck on for his nose, and a wide gash to serve for a mouth. The girth of his waistcoat was hung up and lettered in his tailor's shop as an extraordinary curiosity. He breathed like a heavy snorer, and his voice in speaking came thickly forth, as if it were oppressed and stifled by feather-beds. He trod the ground like an elephant, and eat and drank like—like nothing but an alderman, as he was.

This worthy citizen had risen to his great eminence from small beginnings. He had once been a very lean, weazen little boy, never dreaming of carrying such a weight of flesh upon his bones or of money in his pockets, and glad enough to take his dinner at a baker's door, and his tea at a pump. But he had long ago forgotten all this, as it was proper that a wholesale fruiterer, alderman, common-councilman, member of the worshipful Company of Patten-makers, past sheriff, and, above all, a Lord Mayor that was to be, should; and he never forgot it more completely in all his life than on 8 November in the year of his election to the great golden civic chair, which was the day before his grand dinner at Guildhall.

It happened that as he sat that evening all alone in his counting-house, looking over the bill of fare for next day, and checking off the fat capons in fifties, and the turtle-soup by the hundred quarts, for his private amusement,—it happened that as he sat alone occupied in these pleasant calculations, a strange man came in and asked him how he did, adding, 'If I am half as much changed as you, sir, you have no recollection of me, I am sure.'

The strange man was not over and above well dressed, and was very far from being fat or rich-looking in any sense of the word, yet he spoke with a kind of modest confidence, and assumed an easy, gentlemanly sort of an air, to which nobody but a rich man can lawfully presume. Besides this, he interrupted the good citizen just as he had reckoned three hundred and seventy-two fat capons, and was carrying them over to the next column; and as if that were not aggravation enough, the learned recorder for the city of London had only ten minutes previously gone out at that very same door, and had turned round and said, 'Goodnight, my lord.' Yes, he had said, 'my lord;'—he, a man of birth and education, of the Honourable Society of the Middle Temple, Barrister-at-Law,—he who had an uncle in the House of Commons, and an aunt almost but not quite in the House of Lords (for she had married a feeble peer, and made him vote as she liked),—he, this man, this learned recorder, had said, 'my lord.' 'I'll not wait till tomorrow to give you your title, my Lord Mayor,' says he, with a bow and a smile; 'you are Lord Mayor *de facto*, if not *de jure*. Goodnight, my lord.'

The Lord Mayor elect thought of this, and turning to the stranger, and sternly bidding him 'go out of his private counting-house,' brought forward the three hundred and seventy-two fat capons, and went on with his account.

'Do you remember,' said the other, stepping forward,—'*do* you remember little Joe Toddyhigh?'

The port wine fled for a moment from the fruiterer's nose as he muttered, 'Joe Toddyhigh! What about Joe Toddyhigh?'

'*I* am Joe Toddyhigh,' cried the visitor. 'Look at me, look hard at me,—harder, harder. You know me now? You know little Joe again? What a happiness to us both, to meet the very night before your grandeur! O! give me your hand, Jack,—both hands,—both, for the sake of old times.'

'You pinch me, sir. You're a-hurting of me,' said the Lord Mayor elect pettishly. 'Don't,—suppose anybody should come,—Mr Toddyhigh, sir.'

'Mr Toddyhigh!' repeated the other ruefully.

'O, don't bother,' said the Lord Mayor elect, scratching his head. 'Dear me! Why, I thought you was dead. What a fellow you are!'

Indeed, it was a pretty state of things, and worthy the tone of vexation and disappointment in which the Lord Mayor spoke. Joe Toddyhigh had been a poor boy with him at Hull, and had oftentimes divided his last penny and parted his last crust to relieve his wants; for though Joe was a destitute child in those times, he was as faithful and affectionate in his friendship as ever man of might could be. They parted one day to seek their fortunes in different directions. Joe went to sea, and the now wealthy citizen begged his way to London. They separated with many tears, like foolish fellows as they were, and agreed to remain fast friends, and if they lived, soon to communicate again.

When he was an errand-boy, and even in the early days of his apprenticeship, the citizen had many a time trudged to the Post-office to ask if there were any letter from poor little Joe, and had gone home again with tears in his eyes, when he found no news of his only friend. The world is a wide place, and it was a long time before the letter came; when it did, the writer was forgotten. It turned from white to yellow from lying in the Post-office with nobody to claim it, and in course of time was torn up with five hundred others, and sold for waste-paper. And now at last, and when it might least have been expected, here was this Joe Toddyhigh turning up and claiming acquaintance with a great public character, who on the morrow would be cracking jokes with the Prime Minister of England, and who had only, at any time during the next twelve months, to say the word, and he could shut up Temple Bar, and make it no thoroughfare for the king himself!

'I am sure I don't know what to say, Mr Toddyhigh,' said the Lord Mayor elect; 'I really don't. It's very inconvenient. I'd sooner have given twenty pound,—it's very inconvenient, really.'—A thought had come into his mind, that perhaps his old friend might say something passionate which would give him an excuse for being angry himself. No such thing. Joe looked at him steadily, but very mildly, and did not open his lips.

'Of course I shall pay you what I owe you,' said the Lord Mayor elect, fidgeting in his chair. 'You lent me—I think it was a shilling or some small coin—when we parted company, and that of course I shall pay with good interest. I can pay my way with any man, and always have done. If you look into the Mansion House the day after tomorrow,—some time after dusk,—and ask for my private clerk, you'll find he has a draft for you. I haven't got time to say anything more just now, unless,'—he hesitated, for, coupled with a strong desire to glitter for once in all his glory in the eyes of his former companion, was a distrust of his appearance, which might be more shabby than he could tell by that feeble light,—'unless you'd like to come to the dinner tomorrow. I don't mind your having this ticket, if you like to take it. A great many people would give their ears for it, I can tell you.'

His old friend took the card without speaking a word, and instantly departed. His sunburnt face and grey hair were present to the citizen's mind for a moment; but by the time he reached three hundred and eighty-one fat capons, he had quite forgotten him.

Joe Toddyhigh had never been in the capital of Europe before, and he wandered up and down the streets that night amazed at the number of churches and other public buildings, the splendour of the shops, the riches that were heaped up on every side, the glare of light in which they were displayed, and the concourse of people who hurried to and fro, indifferent, apparently, to all the wonders that surrounded them. But in all the long streets and broad squares, there were none but strangers; it was quite a relief to turn down a by-way and hear his own footsteps on the pavement. He went home to his inn, thought that London was a dreary, desolate place, and felt disposed to doubt the existence of one true-hearted man in the whole worshipful Company of Patten-makers. Finally, he went to bed, and dreamed that he and the Lord Mayor elect were boys again.

He went next day to the dinner; and when in a burst of light and music, and in the midst of splendid decorations and surrounded by brilliant company, his former friend appeared at the head of the Hall, and was hailed with shouts and cheering, he cheered and shouted with the best, and for the moment could have cried. The next moment he cursed his weakness on behalf of a man so changed and selfish, and quite hated a jolly-looking old gentleman opposite for declaring himself in the pride of his heart a Patten-maker.

As the banquet proceeded, he took more and more to heart the rich citizen's unkindness; and that, not from any envy, but because he felt that a man of his state and fortune could all the better afford to recognize an old friend, even if he were poor and obscure. The more he thought of this, the more lonely and sad he felt. When the company dispersed and adjourned to the ballroom, he paced the hall and passages alone, ruminating in a very melancholy condition upon the disappointment he had experienced.

It chanced, while he was lounging about in this moody state, that he stumbled upon a flight of stairs, dark, steep, and narrow, which he ascended without any thought about the matter, and so came into a little music-gallery, empty and deserted. From this elevated post, which commanded the whole hall, he amused himself in looking down upon the attendants who were clearing away the fragments of the feast very lazily, and drinking out of all the bottles and glasses with most commendable perseverance.

His attention gradually relaxed, and he fell fast asleep.

When he awoke, he thought there must be something the matter with his eyes; but, rubbing them a little, he soon found that the moonlight was really streaming through the east window, that the lamps were all extinguished, and that he was alone. He listened, but no distant murmur in the echoing passages, not even the shutting of a door, broke the deep silence; he groped his way down the stairs, and found that the door at the bottom was locked on the other side. He began now to comprehend that he must have slept a long time, that he had been overlooked, and was shut up there for the night.

His first sensation, perhaps, was not altogether a comfortable one, for it was a dark, chilly, earthy-smelling place, and something too large, for a man so situated, to feel at home in. However, when the momentary consternation of his surprise was over, he made light of the accident, and resolved to feel his way up the stairs again, and make himself as comfortable as he could in the gallery until morning. As he turned to execute this purpose, he heard the clocks strike three.

Any such invasion of a dead stillness as the striking of distant clocks, causes it to appear the more intense and insupportable when the sound has ceased. He listened with strained attention in the hope that some clock, lagging behind its fellows, had yet to strike,—looking all the time into the profound darkness before him, until it seemed to weave itself into a black tissue, patterned with a hundred reflections of his own eyes. But the bells had all pealed out their warning for that once, and the gust of wind that moaned through the place seemed cold and heavy with their iron breath.

The time and circumstances were favourable to reflection. He tried to keep his thoughts to the current, unpleasant though it was, in which they had moved all day, and to think with what a romantic feeling he had looked forward to shaking his old friend by the hand before he died, and what a wide and cruel difference there was between the meeting they had had, and that which he had so often and so long anticipated. Still, he was disordered by waking to such sudden loneliness, and could not prevent his mind from running upon odd tales of people of undoubted courage, who, being shut up by night in vaults or churches, or other dismal places, had scaled great heights to get out, and fled from silence as they had never done from danger. This brought to his mind the moonlight through the window, and bethinking himself of it, he groped his way back up the crooked stairs,—but very stealthily, as though he were fearful of being overheard.

He was very much astonished when he approached the gallery again, to see a light in the building: still more so, on advancing hastily and looking round, to observe no visible source from which it could proceed. But how much greater yet was his astonishment at the spectacle which this light revealed.

The statues of the two giants, Gog and Magog, each above fourteen feet in height, those which succeeded to still older and more barbarous figures, after the Great Fire of London, and which stand in the Guildhall to this day, were endowed with life and motion. These guardian genii of the city had quitted their pedestals, and reclined in easy attitudes in the great stained glass window. Between them was an ancient cask, which seemed to be full of wine; for the younger Giant, clapping his huge hand upon it, and throwing up his mighty leg, burst into an exulting laugh, which reverberated through the hall like thunder.

Joe Toddyhigh instinctively stooped down, and, more dead than alive, felt his hair stand on end, his knees knock together, and a cold damp break out upon his forehead. But even at that minute curiosity prevailed over every other feeling, and somewhat reassured by the good-humour of the Giants and their apparent unconsciousness of his presence, he crouched in a corner of the gallery, in as small a space as he could, and, peeping between the rails, observed them closely.

It was then that the elder Giant, who had a flowing grey beard, raised his thoughtful eyes to his companion's face, and in a grave and solemn voice addressed him thus:

First Night of the Giant Chronicles

Turning towards his companion the elder Giant uttered these words in a grave, majestic tone:

'Magog, does boisterous mirth beseem the Giant Warder of this ancient city? Is this becoming demeanour for a watchful spirit over whose bodiless head so many years have rolled, so many changes swept like empty air—in whose impalpable nostrils the scent of blood and crime, pestilence, cruelty, and horror, has been familiar as breath to mortals—in whose sight time has gathered in the harvest of centuries, and garnered so many crops of human pride, affections, hopes, and sorrows? Bethink you of our compact. The night wanes; feasting, revelry, and music have encroached upon our usual hours of solitude, and morning will be here apace. Ere we are stricken mute again, bethink you of our compact.'

Pronouncing these latter words with more of impatience than quite accorded with his apparent age and gravity, the Giant raised a long pole (which he still bears in his hand) and tapped his brother Giant rather smartly on the head; indeed, the blow was so smartly administered, that the latter quickly withdrew his lips from the cask, to which they had been applied, and, catching up his shield and halberd, assumed an attitude of defence. His irritation was but momentary, for he laid these weapons aside as hastily as he had assumed them, and said as he did so:

'You know, Gog, old friend, that when we animate these shapes which the Londoners of old assigned (and not unworthily) to the guardian genii of their city, we are susceptible of some of the sensations which belong to human kind. Thus when I taste wine, I feel blows; when I relish the one, I disrelish the other. Therefore, Gog, the more especially as your arm is none of the lightest, keep your good staff by your side, else we may chance to differ. Peace be between us!'

'Amen!' said the other, leaning his staff in the window-corner. 'Why did you laugh just now?'

'To think,' replied the Giant Magog, laying his hand upon the cask, 'of him who owned this wine, and kept it in a cellar hoarded from the light of day, for thirty years,—'till it should be fit to drink,' quoth he. He was twoscore and ten years old when he buried it beneath his house, and yet never thought that he might be scarcely 'fit to drink' when the wine became so. I wonder it never occurred to him to make himself unfit to be eaten. There is very little of him left by this time.'

'The night is waning,' said Gog mournfully.

'I know it,' replied his companion, 'and I see you are impatient. But look. Through the eastern window—placed opposite to us, that the first beams of the rising sun may every morning gild our giant faces—the moon-rays fall upon the pavement in a stream of light that to my fancy sinks through the cold stone and gushes into the old crypt below. The night is scarcely past its noon, and our great charge is sleeping heavily.'

They ceased to speak, and looked upward at the moon. The sight of their large, black, rolling eyes filled Joe Toddyhigh with such horror that he could scarcely draw his breath. Still they took no note of him, and appeared to believe themselves quite alone.

'Our compact,' said Magog after a pause, 'is, if I understand it, that, instead of watching here in silence through the dreary nights, we entertain each other with stories of our past experience; with tales of the past, the present, and the future; with legends of London and her sturdy citizens from the old simple times. That every night at midnight, when St. Paul's bell tolls out one, and we may move and speak, we thus discourse, nor leave such themes till the first grey gleam of day shall strike us dumb. Is that our bargain, brother?'

'Yes,' said the Giant Gog, 'that is the league between us who guard this city, by day in spirit, and by night in body also; and never on ancient holidays have its conduits run wine more merrily than we will pour forth our legendary lore. We are old chroniclers from this time hence. The crumbled walls encircle us once more, the postern-gates are closed, the drawbridge is up, and pent in its narrow den beneath, the water foams and struggles with the sunken starlings. Jerkins and quarter-staves are in the streets again, the nightly watch is set, the rebel, sad and lonely in his Tower dungeon, tries to sleep and weeps for home and children. Aloft upon the gates and walls are noble heads glaring fiercely down upon the dreaming city, and vexing the hungry dogs that scent them in the air, and tear the ground beneath with dismal howlings. The axe, the block, the rack, in their dark chambers give signs of recent use. The Thames, floating past long lines of cheerful windows whence come a burst of music and a stream of light, bears suddenly to the Palace wall the last red stain brought on the tide from Traitor's Gate. But your pardon, brother. The night wears, and I am talking idly.'

The other Giant appeared to be entirely of this opinion, for during the foregoing rhapsody of his fellow-sentinel he had been scratching his head with an air of comical uneasiness, or rather with an air that would have been very comical if he had been a dwarf or an ordinary-sized man. He winked too, and though it could not be doubted for a moment that he winked to himself, still he certainly cocked his enormous eye towards the gallery where the listener was concealed. Nor was this all, for he gaped; and when he gaped, Joe was horribly reminded of the popular prejudice on the subject of giants, and of their fabled power of smelling out Englishmen, however closely concealed.

His alarm was such that he nearly swooned, and it was some little time before his power of sight or hearing was restored. When he recovered he found that the elder Giant was pressing the younger to commence the Chronicles, and that the latter was endeavouring to excuse himself on the ground that the night was far spent, and it would be better to wait until the next. Well assured by this that he was certainly about to begin directly, the listener collected his faculties by a great effort, and distinctly heard Magog express himself to the following effect:

In the sixteenth century and in the reign of Queen Elizabeth of glorious memory (albeit her golden days are sadly rusted with blood), there lived in the city of London a bold young 'prentice who loved his master's daughter. There were no doubt within the walls a great many 'prentices in this condition, but I speak of only one, and his name was Hugh Graham.

This Hugh was apprenticed to an honest Bowyer who dwelt in the ward of Cheype, and was rumoured to possess great wealth. Rumour was quite as infallible in those days as at the present time, but it happened then as now to be sometimes right by accident. It stumbled upon the truth when it gave the old Bowyer a mint of money. His trade had been a profitable one in the time of King Henry the Eighth, who encouraged English archery to the utmost, and he had been prudent and discreet. Thus it came to pass that Mistress Alice, his only daughter, was the richest heiress in all his wealthy ward. Young Hugh had often maintained with staff and cudgel that she was the handsomest. To do him justice, I believe she was.

If he could have gained the heart of pretty Mistress Alice by knocking this conviction into stubborn people's heads, Hugh would have had no cause to fear. But though the Bowyer's daughter smiled in secret to hear of his doughty deeds for her sake, and though her little waiting-woman reported all her smiles (and many more) to Hugh, and though he was at a vast expense in kisses and small coin to recompense her fidelity, he made no progress in his love. He durst not whisper it to Mistress Alice save on sure encouragement, and that she never gave him. A glance of her dark eye as she sat at the door on a summer's evening after prayer-time, while he and the neighbouring 'prentices exercised themselves in the street with blunted sword and buckler, would fire Hugh's blood so that none could stand before him; but then she glanced at others quite as kindly as on him, and where was the use of cracking crowns if Mistress Alice smiled upon the cracked as well as on the cracker?

Still Hugh went on, and loved her more and more. He thought of her all day, and dreamed of her all night long. He treasured up her every word and gesture, and had a palpitation of the heart whenever he heard her footstep on the stairs or her voice in an adjoining room. To him, the old Bowyer's house was haunted by an angel; there was enchantment in the air and space in which she moved. It would have been no miracle to Hugh if flowers had sprung from the rush-strewn floors beneath the tread of lovely Mistress Alice.

Never did 'prentice long to distinguish himself in the eyes of his lady-love so ardently as Hugh. Sometimes he pictured to himself the house taking fire by night, and he, when all drew back in fear, rushing through flame and smoke, and bearing her from the ruins in his arms. At other times he thought of a rising of fierce rebels, an attack upon the city, a strong assault upon the Bowyer's house in particular, and he falling on the threshold pierced with numberless wounds in defence of Mistress Alice. If he could only enact some prodigy of valour, do some wonderful deed, and let her know that she had inspired it, he thought he could die contented.

Sometimes the Bowyer and his daughter would go out to supper with a worthy citizen at the fashionable hour of six o'clock, and on such occasions Hugh, wearing his blue 'prentice cloak as gallantly as 'prentice might, would attend with a lantern and his trusty club to escort them home. These were the brightest moments of his life. To hold the light while Mistress Alice picked her steps, to touch her hand as he helped her over broken ways, to have her leaning on his arm,—it sometimes even came to that,—this was happiness indeed!

When the nights were fair, Hugh followed in the rear, his eyes riveted on the graceful figure of the Bowyer's daughter as she and the old man moved on before him. So they threaded the narrow winding streets of the city, now passing beneath the overhanging gables of old wooden houses whence creaking signs projected into the street, and now emerging from some dark and frowning gateway into the clear moonlight. At such times, or when the shouts of straggling brawlers met her ear, the Bowyer's daughter would look timidly back at Hugh, beseeching him to draw nearer; and then how he grasped his club and longed to do battle with a dozen rufflers, for the love of Mistress Alice!

The old Bowyer was in the habit of lending money on interest to the gallants of the court, and thus it happened that many a richly-dressed gentleman dismounted at his door. More waving plumes and gallant steeds, indeed, were seen at the Bowyer's house, and more embroidered silks and velvets sparkled in his dark shop and darker private closet, than at any merchants in the city. In those times no less than in the present it would seem that the richest-looking cavaliers often wanted money the most.

Of these glittering clients there was one who always came alone. He was nobly mounted, and, having no attendant, gave his horse in charge to Hugh while he and the Bowyer were closeted within. Once as he sprung into the saddle, Mistress Alice was seated at an upper window, and before she could withdraw he had doffed his jewelled cap and kissed his hand. Hugh watched him caracoling down the street, and burnt with indignation. But how much deeper was the glow that reddened in his cheeks when, raising his eyes to the casement, he saw that Alice watched the stranger too!

He came again and often, each time arrayed more gaily than before, and still the little casement showed him Mistress Alice. At length one heavy day, she fled from home. It had cost her a hard struggle, for all her old father's gifts were strewn about her chamber as if she had parted from them one by one, and knew that the time must come when these tokens of his love would wring her heart,—yet she was gone.

She left a letter commanding her poor father to the care of Hugh, and wishing he might be happier than ever he could have been with her, for he deserved the love of a better and a purer heart than she had to bestow. The old man's forgiveness (she said) she had no power to ask, but she prayed God to bless him,—and so ended with a blot upon the paper where her tears had fallen.

At first the old man's wrath was kindled, and he carried his wrong to the Queen's throne itself; but there was no redress he learnt at Court, for his daughter had been conveyed abroad. This afterwards appeared to be the truth, as there came from France, after an interval of several years, a letter in her hand. It was written in trembling characters, and almost illegible. Little could be made out save that she often thought of home and her old dear pleasant room,—and that she had dreamt her father was dead and had not blessed her,—and that her heart was breaking.

The poor old Bowyer lingered on, never suffering Hugh to quit his sight, for he knew now that he had loved his daughter, and that was the only link that bound him to earth. It broke at length and he died,—bequeathing his old 'prentice his trade and all his wealth, and solemnly charging him with his last breath to revenge his child if ever he who had worked her misery crossed his path in life again.

From the time of Alice's flight, the tilting-ground, the fields, the fencing-school, the summer-evening sports, knew Hugh no more. His spirit was dead within him. He rose to great eminence and repute among the citizens, but was seldom seen to smile, and never mingled in their revelries or rejoicings. Brave, humane, and generous, he was beloved by all. He was pitied too by those who knew his story, and these were so many that when he walked along the streets alone at dusk, even the rude common people doffed their caps and mingled a rough air of sympathy with their respect.

One night in May—it was her birthnight, and twenty years since she had left her home—Hugh Graham sat in the room she had hallowed in his boyish days. He was now a grey-haired man, though still in the prime of life. Old thoughts had borne him company for many hours, and the chamber had gradually grown quite dark, when he was roused by a low knocking at the outer door.

He hastened down, and opening it saw by the light of a lamp which he had seized upon the way, a female figure crouching in the portal. It hurried swiftly past him and glided up the stairs. He looked for pursuers. There were none in sight. No, not one.

He was inclined to think it a vision of his own brain, when suddenly a vague suspicion of the truth flashed upon his mind. He barred the door, and hastened wildly back. Yes, there she was,—there, in the chamber he had quitted,—there in her old innocent, happy home, so changed that none but he could trace one gleam of what she had been,—there upon her knees,—with her hands clasped in agony and shame before her burning face.

'My God, my God!' she cried, 'now strike me dead! Though I have brought death and shame and sorrow on this roof, O, let me die at home in mercy!'

There was no tear upon her face then, but she trembled and glanced round the chamber. Everything was in its old place. Her bed looked as if she had risen from it but that morning. The sight of these familiar objects, marking the dear remembrance in which she had been held, and the blight she had brought upon herself, was more than the woman's better nature that had carried her there could bear. She wept and fell upon the ground.

A rumour was spread about, in a few days' time, that the Bowyer's cruel daughter had come home, and that Master Graham had given her lodging in his house. It was rumoured too that he had resigned her fortune, in order that she might bestow it in acts of charity, and that he had vowed to guard her in her solitude, but that they were never to see each other more. These rumours greatly incensed all virtuous wives and daughters in the ward, especially when they appeared to receive some corroboration from the circumstance of Master Graham taking up his abode in another tenement hard by. The estimation in which he was held, however, forbade any questioning on the subject; and as the Bowyer's house was close shut up, and nobody came forth when public shows and festivities were in progress, or to flaunt in the public walks, or to buy new fashions at the mercers' booths, all the well-conducted females agreed among themselves that there could be no woman there.

These reports had scarcely died away when the wonder of every good citizen, male and female, was utterly absorbed and swallowed up by a Royal Proclamation, in which Her Majesty, strongly censuring the practice of wearing long Spanish rapiers of preposterous length (as being a bullying and swaggering custom, tending to bloodshed and public disorder), commanded that on a particular day therein named, certain grave citizens should repair to the city gates, and there, in public, break all rapiers worn or carried by persons claiming admission, that exceeded, though it were only by a quarter of an inch, three standard feet in length.

Royal Proclamations usually take their course, let the public wonder never so much. On the appointed day two citizens of high repute took up their stations at each of the gates, attended by a party of the city guard, the main body to enforce the Queen's will, and take custody of all such rebels (if any) as might have the temerity to dispute it: and a few to bear the standard measures and instruments for reducing all unlawful sword-blades to the prescribed dimensions. In pursuance of these arrangements, Master Graham and another were posted at Lud Gate, on the hill before St. Paul's.

A pretty numerous company were gathered together at this spot, for, besides the officers in attendance to enforce the proclamation, there was a motley crowd of lookers-on of various degrees, who raised from time to time such shouts and cries as the circumstances called forth. A spruce young courtier was the first who approached: he unsheathed a weapon of burnished steel that shone and glistened in the sun, and handed it with the newest air to the officer, who, finding it exactly three feet long, returned it with a bow. Thereupon the gallant raised his hat and crying, 'God save the Queen!' passed on amidst the plaudits of the mob. Then came another—a better courtier still—who wore a blade but two feet long, whereat the people laughed, much to the disparagement of his honour's dignity. Then came a third, a sturdy old officer of the army, girded with a rapier at least a foot and a half beyond Her Majesty's pleasure; at him they raised a great shout, and most of the spectators (but especially those who were armourers or cutlers) laughed very heartily at the breakage which would ensue. But they were disappointed; for the old campaigner, coolly unbuckling his sword and bidding his servant carry it home again, passed through unarmed, to the great indignation of all the beholders. They relieved themselves in some degree by hooting a tall blustering fellow with a prodigious weapon, who stopped short on coming in sight of the preparations, and after a little consideration turned back again. But all this time no rapier had been broken, although it was high noon, and all cavaliers of any quality or appearance were taking their way towards Saint Paul's churchyard.

During these proceedings, Master Graham had stood apart, strictly confining himself to the duty imposed upon him, and taking little heed of anything beyond. He stepped forward now as a richly-dressed gentleman on foot, followed by a single attendant, was seen advancing up the hill.

As this person drew nearer, the crowd stopped their clamour, and bent forward with eager looks. Master Graham standing alone in the gateway, and the stranger coming slowly towards him, they seemed, as it were, set face to face. The nobleman (for he looked one) had a haughty and disdainful air, which bespoke the slight estimation in which he held the citizen. The citizen, on the other hand, preserved the resolute bearing of one who was not to be frowned down or daunted, and who cared very little for any nobility but that of worth and manhood. It was perhaps some consciousness on the part of each, of these feelings in the other, that infused a more stern expression into their regards as they came closer together.

'Your rapier, worthy sir!'

At the instant that he pronounced these words Graham started, and falling back some paces, laid his hand upon the dagger in his belt.

'You are the man whose horse I used to hold before the Bowyer's door? You are that man? Speak!'

'Out, you 'prentice hound!' said the other.

'You are he! I know you well now!' cried Graham. 'Let no man step between us two, or I shall be his murderer.' With that he drew his dagger, and rushed in upon him.

The stranger had drawn his weapon from the scabbard ready for the scrutiny, before a word was spoken. He made a thrust at his assailant, but the dagger which Graham clutched in his left hand being the dirk in use at that time for parrying such blows, promptly turned the point aside. They closed. The dagger fell rattling on the ground, and Graham, wresting his adversary's sword from his grasp, plunged it through his heart. As he drew it out it snapped in two, leaving a fragment in the dead man's body.

All this passed so swiftly that the bystanders looked on without an effort to interfere; but the man was no sooner down than an uproar broke forth which rent the air. The attendant rushing through the gate proclaimed that his master, a nobleman, had been set upon and slain by a citizen; the word quickly spread from mouth to mouth; Saint Paul's Cathedral, and every book-shop, ordinary, and smoking-house in the churchyard poured out its stream of cavaliers and their followers, who mingling together in a dense tumultuous body, struggled, sword in hand, towards the spot.

With equal impetuosity, and stimulating each other by loud cries and shouts, the citizens and common people took up the quarrel on their side, and encircling Master Graham a hundred deep, forced him from the gate. In vain he waved the broken sword above his head, crying that he would die on London's threshold for their sacred homes. They bore him on, and ever keeping him in the midst, so that no man could attack him, fought their way into the city.

The clash of swords and roar of voices, the dust and heat and pressure, the trampling under foot of men, the distracted looks and shrieks of women at the windows above as they recognized their relatives or lovers in the crowd, the rapid tolling of alarm-bells, the furious rage and passion of the scene, were fearful. Those who, being on the outskirts of each crowd, could use their weapons with effect, fought desperately, while those behind, maddened with baffled rage, struck at each other over the heads of those before them, and crushed their own fellows. Wherever the broken sword was seen above the people's heads, towards that spot the cavaliers made a new rush. Every one of these charges was marked by sudden gaps in the throng where men were trodden down, but as fast as they were made, the tide swept over them, and still the multitude pressed on again, a confused mass of swords, clubs, staves, broken plumes, fragments of rich cloaks and doublets, and angry, bleeding faces, all mixed up together in inextricable disorder.

The design of the people was to force Master Graham to take refuge in his dwelling, and to defend it until the authorities could interfere, or they could gain time for parley. But either from ignorance or in the confusion of the moment they stopped at his old house, which was closely shut. Some time was lost in beating the doors open and passing him to the front. About a score of the boldest of the other party threw themselves into the torrent while this was being done, and reaching the door at the same moment with himself cut him off from his defenders.

'I never will turn in such a righteous cause, so help me Heaven!' cried Graham, in a voice that at last made itself heard, and confronting them as he spoke. 'Least of all will I turn upon this threshold which owes its desolation to such men as ye. I give no quarter, and I will have none! Strike!'

For a moment they stood at bay. At that moment a shot from an unseen hand, apparently fired by some person who had gained access to one of the opposite houses, struck Graham in the brain, and he fell dead. A low wail was heard in the air,—many people in the concourse cried that they had seen a spirit glide across the little casement window of the Bowyer's house—

A dead silence succeeded. After a short time some of the flushed and heated throng laid down their arms and softly carried the body within doors. Others fell off or slunk away in knots of two or three, others whispered together in groups, and before a numerous guard which then rode up could muster in the street, it was nearly empty.

Those who carried Master Graham to the bed upstairs were shocked to see a woman lying beneath the window with her hands clasped together. After trying to recover her in vain, they laid her near the citizen, who still retained, tightly grasped in his right hand, the first and last sword that was broken that day at Lud Gate.

The Giant uttered these concluding words with sudden precipitation; and on the instant the strange light which had filled the hall faded away. Joe Toddyhigh glanced involuntarily at the eastern window, and saw the first pale gleam of morning. He turned his head again towards the other window in which the Giants had been seated. It was empty. The cask of wine was gone, and he could dimly make out that the two great figures stood mute and motionless upon their pedestals.

After rubbing his eyes and wondering for full half an hour, during which time he observed morning come creeping on apace, he yielded to the drowsiness which overpowered him and fell into a refreshing slumber. When he awoke it was broad day; the building was open, and workmen were busily engaged in removing the vestiges of last night's feast.

Stealing gently down the little stairs, and assuming the air of some early lounger who had dropped in from the street, he walked up to the foot of each pedestal in turn, and attentively examined the figure it supported. There could be no doubt about the features of either; he recollected the exact expression they had worn at different passages of their conversation, and recognized in every line and lineament the Giants of the night. Assured that it was no vision, but that he had heard and seen with his own proper senses, he walked forth, determining at all hazards to conceal himself in the Guildhall again that evening. He further resolved to sleep all day, so that he might be very wakeful and vigilant, and above all that he might take notice of the figures at the precise moment of their becoming animated and subsiding into their old state, which he greatly reproached himself for not having done already.

Correspondence to Master Humphrey

'Sir,—Before you proceed any further in your account of your friends and what you say and do when you meet together, excuse me if I proffer my claim to be elected to one of the vacant chairs in that old room of yours. Don't reject me without full consideration; for if you do, you will be sorry for it afterwards—you will, upon my life.

'I enclose my card, sir, in this letter. I never was ashamed of my name, and I never shall be. I am considered a devilish gentlemanly fellow, and I act up to the character. If you want a reference, ask any of the men at our club. Ask any fellow who goes there to write his letters, what sort of conversation mine is. Ask him if he thinks I have the sort of voice that will suit your deaf friend and make him hear, if he can hear anything at all. Ask the servants what they think of me. There's not a rascal among 'em, sir, but will tremble to hear my name. That reminds me—don't you say too much about that housekeeper of yours; it's a low subject, damned low.

'I tell you what, sir. If you vote me into one of those empty chairs, you'll have among you a man with a fund of gentlemanly information that'll rather astonish you. I can let you into a few anecdotes about some fine women of title, that are quite high life, sir—the tiptop sort of thing. I know the name of every man who has been out on an affair of honour within the last five-and-twenty years; I know the private particulars of every cross and squabble that has taken place upon the turf, at the gaming-table, or elsewhere, during the whole of that time. I have been called the gentlemanly chronicle. You may consider yourself a lucky dog; upon my soul, you may congratulate yourself, though I say so.

'It's an uncommon good notion that of yours, not letting anybody know where you live. I have tried it, but there has always been an anxiety respecting me, which has found me out. Your deaf friend is a cunning fellow to keep his name so close. I have tried that too, but have always failed. I shall be proud to make his acquaintance—tell him so, with my compliments.

'You must have been a queer fellow when you were a child, confounded queer. It's odd, all that about the picture in your first paper—prosy, but told in a devilish gentlemanly sort of way. In places like that I could come in with great effect with a touch of life—don't you feel that?

'I am anxiously waiting for your next paper to know whether your friends live upon the premises, and at your expense, which I take it for granted is the case. If I am right in this impression, I know a charming fellow (an excellent companion and most delightful company) who will be proud to join you. Some years ago he seconded a great many prize-fighters, and once fought an amateur match himself; since then he has driven several mails, broken at different periods all the lamps on the right-hand side of Oxford-street, and six times carried away every bell-handle in Bloomsbury-square, besides turning off the gas in various thoroughfares. In point of gentlemanliness he is unrivalled, and I should say that next to myself he is of all men the best suited to your purpose.

'Expecting your reply,
'I am, '&c. &c.'

Master Humphrey informs this gentleman that his application, both as it concerns himself and his friend, is rejected.

Chapter 2

Master Humphrey, from his Clock-Side in the Chimney-Corner

My old companion tells me it is midnight. The fire glows brightly, crackling with a sharp and cheerful sound, as if it loved to burn. The merry cricket on the hearth (my constant visitor), this ruddy blaze, my clock, and I, seem to share the world among us, and to be the only things awake. The wind, high and boisterous but now, has died away and hoarsely mutters in its sleep. I love all times and seasons each in its turn, and am apt, perhaps, to think the present one the best; but past or coming I always love this peaceful time of night, when long-buried thoughts, favoured by the gloom and silence, steal from their graves, and haunt the scenes of faded happiness and hope.

The popular faith in ghosts has a remarkable affinity with the whole current of our thoughts at such an hour as this, and seems to be their necessary and natural consequence. For who can wonder that man should feel a vague belief in tales of disembodied spirits wandering through those places which they once dearly affected, when he himself, scarcely less separated from his old world than they, is for ever lingering upon past emotions and bygone times, and hovering, the ghost of his former self, about the places and people that warmed his heart of old? It is thus that at this quiet hour I haunt the house where I was born, the rooms I used to tread, the scenes of my infancy, my boyhood, and my youth; it is thus that I prowl around my buried treasure (though not of gold or silver), and mourn my loss; it is thus that I revisit the ashes of extinguished fires, and take my silent stand at old bedsides. If my spirit should ever glide back to this chamber when my body is mingled with the dust, it will but follow the course it often took in the old man's lifetime, and add but one more change to the subjects of its contemplation.

In all my idle speculations I am greatly assisted by various legends connected with my venerable house, which are current in the neighbourhood, and are so numerous that there is scarce a cupboard or corner that has not some dismal story of its own. When I first entertained thoughts of becoming its tenant, I was assured that it was haunted from roof to cellar, and I believe that the bad opinion in which my neighbours once held me, had its rise in my not being torn to pieces, or at least distracted with terror, on the night I took possession; in either of which cases I should doubtless have arrived by a short cut at the very summit of popularity.

But traditions and rumours all taken into account, who so abets me in every fancy and chimes with my every thought, as my dear deaf friend? and how often have I cause to bless the day that brought us two together! Of all days in the year I rejoice to think that it should have been Christmas Day, with which from childhood we associate something friendly, hearty, and sincere.

I had walked out to cheer myself with the happiness of others, and, in the little tokens of festivity and rejoicing, of which the streets and houses present so many upon that day, had lost some hours. Now I stopped to look at a merry party hurrying through the snow on foot to their place of meeting, and now turned back to see a whole coachful of children safely deposited at the welcome house. At one time, I admired how carefully the working man carried the baby in its gaudy hat and feathers, and how his wife, trudging patiently on behind, forgot even her care of her gay clothes, in exchanging greeting with the child as it crowed and laughed over the father's shoulder; at another, I pleased myself with some passing scene of gallantry or courtship, and was glad to believe that for a season half the world of poverty was gay.

As the day closed in, I still rambled through the streets, feeling a companionship in the bright fires that cast their warm reflection on the windows as I passed, and losing all sense of my own loneliness in imagining the sociality and kind-fellowship that everywhere prevailed. At length I happened to stop before a tavern, and, encountering a Bill of Fare in the window, it all at once brought it into my head to wonder what kind of people dined alone in taverns upon Christmas Day.

Solitary men are accustomed, I suppose, unconsciously to look upon solitude as their own peculiar property. I had sat alone in my room on many, many anniversaries of this great holiday, and had never regarded it but as one of universal assemblage and rejoicing. I had excepted, and with an aching heart, a crowd of prisoners and beggars;

but *these* were not the men for whom the tavern doors were open. Had they any customers, or was it a mere form?—a form, no doubt.

Trying to feel quite sure of this, I walked away; but before I had gone many paces, I stopped and looked back. There was a provoking air of business in the lamp above the door which I could not overcome. I began to be afraid there might be many customers—young men, perhaps, struggling with the world, utter strangers in this great place, whose friends lived at a long distance off, and whose means were too slender to enable them to make the journey. The supposition gave rise to so many distressing little pictures, that in preference to carrying them home with me, I determined to encounter the realities. So I turned and walked in.

I was at once glad and sorry to find that there was only one person in the dining-room; glad to know that there were not more, and sorry that he should be there by himself. He did not look so old as I, but like me he was advanced in life, and his hair was nearly white. Though I made more noise in entering and seating myself than was quite necessary, with the view of attracting his attention and saluting him in the good old form of that time of year, he did not raise his head, but sat with it resting on his hand, musing over his half-finished meal.

I called for something which would give me an excuse for remaining in the room (I had dined early, as my housekeeper was engaged at night to partake of some friend's good cheer), and sat where I could observe without intruding on him. After a time he looked up. He was aware that somebody had entered, but could see very little of me, as I sat in the shade and he in the light. He was sad and thoughtful, and I forbore to trouble him by speaking.

Let me believe it was something better than curiosity which riveted my attention and impelled me strongly towards this gentleman. I never saw so patient and kind a face. He should have been surrounded by friends, and yet here he sat dejected and alone when all men had their friends about them. As often as he roused himself from his reverie he would fall into it again, and it was plain that, whatever were the subject of his thoughts, they were of a melancholy kind, and would not be controlled.

He was not used to solitude. I was sure of that; for I know by myself that if he had been, his manner would have been different, and he would have taken some slight interest in the arrival of another. I could not fail to mark that he had no appetite; that he tried to eat in vain; that time after time the plate was pushed away, and he relapsed into his former posture.

His mind was wandering among old Christmas days, I thought. Many of them sprung up together, not with a long gap between each, but in unbroken succession like days of the week. It was a great change to find himself for the first time (I quite settled that it *was* the first) in an empty silent room with no soul to care for. I could not help following him in imagination through crowds of pleasant faces, and then coming back to that dull place with its bough of mistletoe sickening in the gas, and sprigs of holly parched up already by a Simoom of roast and boiled. The very waiter had gone home; and his representative, a poor, lean, hungry man, was keeping Christmas in his jacket.

I grew still more interested in my friend. His dinner done, a decanter of wine was placed before him. It remained untouched for a long time, but at length with a quivering hand he filled a glass and raised it to his lips. Some tender wish to which he had been accustomed to give utterance on that day, or some beloved name that he had been used to pledge, trembled upon them at the moment. He put it down very hastily—took it up once more—again put it down—pressed his hand upon his face—yes—and tears stole down his cheeks, I am certain.

Without pausing to consider whether I did right or wrong, I stepped across the room, and sitting down beside him laid my hand gently on his arm.

'My friend,' I said, 'forgive me if I beseech you to take comfort and consolation from the lips of an old man. I will not preach to you what I have not practised, indeed. Whatever be your grief, be of a good heart—be of a good heart, pray!'

'I see that you speak earnestly,' he replied, 'and kindly I am very sure, but—'

I nodded my head to show that I understood what he would say; for I had already gathered, from a certain fixed expression in his face, and from the attention with which he watched me while I spoke, that his sense of hearing was destroyed. 'There should be a freemasonry between us,' said I, pointing from himself to me to explain my meaning; 'if not in our grey hairs, at least in our misfortunes. You see that I am but a poor cripple.'

I never felt so happy under my affliction since the trying moment of my first becoming conscious of it, as when he took my hand in his with a smile that has lighted my path in life from that day, and we sat down side by side.

This was the beginning of my friendship with the deaf gentleman; and when was ever the slight and easy service of a kind word in season repaid by such attachment and devotion as he has shown to me!

He produced a little set of tablets and a pencil to facilitate our conversation, on that our first acquaintance; and I well remember how awkward and constrained I was in writing down my share of the dialogue, and how easily he guessed my meaning before I had written half of what I had to say. He told me in a faltering voice that he had not been accustomed to be alone on that day—that it had always been a little festival with him; and seeing that I glanced at his dress in the expectation that he wore mourning, he added hastily that it was not that; if it had been he thought he could have borne it better. From that time to the present we have never touched upon this theme. Upon every return of the same day we have been together; and although we make it our annual custom to drink to each other hand in hand after dinner, and to recall with affectionate garrulity every circumstance of our first meeting, we always avoid this one as if by mutual consent.

Meantime we have gone on strengthening in our friendship and regard and forming an attachment which, I trust and believe, will only be interrupted by death, to be renewed in another existence. I scarcely know how we communicate as we do; but he has long since ceased to be deaf to me. He is frequently my companion in my walks, and even in crowded streets replies to my slightest look or gesture, as though he could read my thoughts. From the vast number of objects which pass in rapid succession before our eyes, we frequently select the same for some particular notice or remark; and when one of these little coincidences occurs, I cannot describe the pleasure which animates my friend, or the beaming countenance he will preserve for half-an-hour afterwards at least.

He is a great thinker from living so much within himself, and, having a lively imagination, has a facility of conceiving and enlarging upon odd ideas, which renders him invaluable to our little body, and greatly astonishes our two friends. His powers in this respect are much assisted by a large pipe, which he assures us once belonged to a German Student. Be this as it may, it has undoubtedly a very ancient and mysterious appearance, and is of such capacity that it takes three hours and a half to smoke it out. I have reason to believe that my barber, who is the chief authority of a knot of gossips, who congregate every evening at a small tobacconist's hard by, has related anecdotes of this pipe and the grim figures that are carved upon its bowl, at which all the smokers in the neighbourhood have stood aghast; and I know that my housekeeper, while she holds it in high veneration, has a superstitious feeling connected with it which would render her exceedingly unwilling to be left alone in its company after dark.

Whatever sorrow my dear friend has known, and whatever grief may linger in some secret corner of his heart, he is now a cheerful, placid, happy creature. Misfortune can never have fallen upon such a man but for some good purpose; and when I see its traces in his gentle nature and his earnest feeling, I am the less disposed to murmur at such trials as I may have undergone myself. With regard to the pipe, I have a theory of my own; I cannot help thinking that it is in some manner connected with the event that brought us together; for I remember that it was a long time before he even talked about it; that when he did, he grew reserved and melancholy; and that it was a long time yet before he brought it forth. I have no curiosity, however, upon this subject; for I know that it promotes his tranquillity and comfort, and I need no other inducement to regard it with my utmost favour.

Such is the deaf gentleman. I can call up his figure now, clad in sober grey, and seated in the chimney-corner. As he puffs out the smoke from his favourite pipe, he casts a look on me brimful of cordiality and friendship, and says all manner of kind and genial things in a cheerful smile; then he raises his eyes to my clock, which is just about to strike, and, glancing from it to me and back again, seems to divide his heart between us. For myself, it is not too much to say that I would gladly part with one of my poor limbs, could he but hear the old clock's voice.

Of our two friends, the first has been all his life one of that easy, wayward, truant class whom the world is accustomed to designate as nobody's enemies but their own. Bred to a profession for which he never qualified himself, and reared in the expectation of a fortune he has never inherited, he has undergone every vicissitude of which such an existence is capable. He and his younger brother, both orphans from their childhood, were educated by a wealthy relative, who taught them to expect an equal division of his property; but too indolent to court, and too honest to flatter, the elder gradually lost ground in the affections of a capricious old man, and the younger, who did not fail to improve his opportunity, now triumphs in the possession of enormous wealth. His triumph is to hoard it in solitary wretchedness, and probably to feel with the expenditure of every shilling a greater pang than the loss of his whole inheritance ever cost his brother.

Jack Redburn—he was Jack Redburn at the first little school he went to, where every other child was mastered and surnamed, and he has been Jack Redburn all his life, or he would perhaps have been a richer man by this time—has been an inmate of my house these eight years past. He is my librarian, secretary, steward, and first minister; director of all my affairs, and inspector-general of my household. He is something of a musician, something of an author, something of an actor, something of a painter, very much of a carpenter, and an extraordinary gardener, having had all his life a wonderful aptitude for learning everything that was of no use to him. He is remarkably fond of children, and is the best and kindest nurse in sickness that ever drew the breath of life. He has mixed with every grade of society, and known the utmost distress; but there never was a less selfish, a more tender-hearted, a more enthusiastic, or a more guileless man; and I dare say, if few have done less good, fewer still have done less harm in the world than he. By what chance nature forms such whimsical jumbles I don't know; but I do know that she sends them among us very often, and that the king of the whole race is Jack Redburn.

I should be puzzled to say how old he is. His health is none of the best, and he wears a quantity of iron-grey hair, which shades his face and gives it rather a worn appearance; but we consider him quite a young fellow notwithstanding; and if a youthful spirit, surviving the roughest contact with the world, confers upon its possessor any title to be considered young, then he is a mere child. The only interruptions to his careless cheerfulness are on a wet Sunday, when he is apt to be unusually religious and solemn, and sometimes of an evening, when he has been blowing a very slow tune on the flute. On these last-named occasions he is apt to incline towards the mysterious, or the terrible. As a specimen of his powers in this mood, I refer my readers to the extract from the clock-case which follows this paper: he brought it to me not long ago at midnight, and informed me that the main incident had been suggested by a dream of the night before.

His apartments are two cheerful rooms looking towards the garden, and one of his great delights is to arrange and rearrange the furniture in these chambers, and put it in every possible variety of position. During the whole time he has been here, I do not think he has slept for two nights running with the head of his bed in the same place; and every time he moves it, is to be the last. My housekeeper was at first well-nigh distracted by these frequent changes; but she has become quite reconciled to them by degrees, and has so fallen in with his humour, that they often consult together with great gravity upon the next final alteration. Whatever his arrangements are, however, they are always a pattern of neatness; and every one of the manifold articles connected with his manifold occupations is to be found in its own particular place. Until within the last two or three years he was subject to an occasional fit (which usually came upon him in very fine weather), under the influence of which he would dress himself with peculiar care, and, going out under pretence of taking a walk, disappeared for several days together. At length, after the interval between each outbreak of this disorder had gradually grown longer and longer, it wholly disappeared; and now he seldom stirs abroad, except to stroll out a little way on a summer's evening. Whether he yet mistrusts his own constancy in this respect, and is therefore afraid to wear a coat, I know not; but we seldom see him in any other upper garment than an old spectral-looking dressing-gown, with very disproportionate pockets, full of a miscellaneous collection of odd matters, which he picks up wherever he can lay his hands upon them.

Everything that is a favourite with our friend is a favourite with us; and thus it happens that the fourth among us is Mr Owen Miles, a most worthy gentleman, who had treated Jack with great kindness before my deaf friend and I encountered him by an accident, to which I may refer on some future occasion. Mr Miles was once a very rich merchant; but receiving a severe shock in the death of his wife, he retired from business, and devoted himself to a quiet, unostentatious life. He is an excellent man, of thoroughly sterling character: not of quick apprehension, and not without some amusing prejudices, which I shall leave to their own development. He holds us all in profound veneration; but Jack Redburn he esteems as a kind of pleasant wonder, that he may venture to approach familiarly. He believes, not only that no man ever lived who could do so many things as Jack, but that no man ever lived who could do anything so well; and he never calls my attention to any of his ingenious proceedings, but he whispers in my ear, nudging me at the same time with his elbow: 'If he had only made it his trade, sir—if he had only made it his trade!'

They are inseparable companions; one would almost suppose that, although Mr Miles never by any chance does anything in the way of assistance, Jack could do nothing without him. Whether he is reading, writing, painting, carpentering, gardening, flute-playing, or what not, there is Mr Miles beside him, buttoned up to the chin in his blue coat, and looking on with a face of incredulous delight, as though he could not credit the testimony of his own senses, and had a misgiving that no man could be so clever but in a dream.

These are my friends; I have now introduced myself and them.

THE CLOCK-CASE

A Confession Found in a Prison in the Time of Charles the Second

I held a lieutenant's commission in His Majesty's army, and served abroad in the campaigns of 1677 and 1678. The treaty of Nimeguen being concluded, I returned home, and retiring from the service, withdrew to a small estate lying a few miles east of London, which I had recently acquired in right of my wife.

This is the last night I have to live, and I will set down the naked truth without disguise. I was never a brave man, and had always been from my childhood of a secret, sullen, distrustful nature. I speak of myself as if I had passed from the world; for while I write this, my grave is digging, and my name is written in the black-book of death.

Soon after my return to England, my only brother was seized with mortal illness. This circumstance gave me slight or no pain; for since we had been men, we had associated but very little together. He was open-hearted and generous, handsomer than I, more accomplished, and generally beloved. Those who sought my acquaintance abroad or at home, because they were friends of his, seldom attached themselves to me long, and would usually say, in our first conversation, that they were surprised to find two brothers so unlike in their manners and appearance. It was my habit to lead them on to this avowal; for I knew what comparisons they must draw between us; and having a rankling envy in my heart, I sought to justify it to myself.

We had married two sisters. This additional tie between us, as it may appear to some, only estranged us the more. His wife knew me well. I never struggled with any secret jealousy or gall when she was present but that woman knew it as well as I did. I never raised my eyes at such times but I found hers fixed upon me; I never bent them on the ground or looked another way but I felt that she overlooked me always. It was an inexpressible relief to me when we quarrelled, and a greater relief still when I heard abroad that she was dead. It seems to me now as if some strange and terrible foreshadowing of what has happened since must have hung over us then. I was afraid of her; she haunted me; her fixed and steady look comes back upon me now, like the memory of a dark dream, and makes my blood run cold.

She died shortly after giving birth to a child—a boy. When my brother knew that all hope of his own recovery was past, he called my wife to his bedside, and confided this orphan, a child of four years old, to her protection. He bequeathed to him all the property he had, and willed that, in case of his child's death, it should pass to my wife, as the only acknowledgment he could make her for her care and love. He exchanged a few brotherly words with me, deploring our long separation; and being exhausted, fell into a slumber, from which he never awoke.

We had no children; and as there had been a strong affection between the sisters, and my wife had almost supplied the place of a mother to this boy, she loved him as if he had been her own. The child was ardently attached to her; but he was his mother's image in face and spirit, and always mistrusted me.

I can scarcely fix the date when the feeling first came upon me; but I soon began to be uneasy when this child was by. I never roused myself from some moody train of thought but I marked him looking at me; not with mere childish wonder, but with something of the purpose and meaning that I had so often noted in his mother. It was no effort of my fancy, founded on close resemblance of feature and expression. I never could look the boy down. He feared me, but seemed by some instinct to despise me while he did so; and even when he drew back beneath my gaze—as he would when we were alone, to get nearer to the door—he would keep his bright eyes upon me still.

Perhaps I hide the truth from myself, but I do not think that, when this began, I meditated to do him any wrong. I may have thought how serviceable his inheritance would be to us, and may have wished him dead; but I believe I had no thought of compassing his death. Neither did the idea come upon me at once, but by very slow degrees, presenting itself at first in dim shapes at a very great distance, as men may think of an earthquake or the last day; then drawing nearer and nearer, and losing something of its horror and improbability; then coming to be part and parcel—nay nearly the whole sum and substance—of my daily thoughts, and resolving itself into a question of means and safety; not of doing or abstaining from the deed.

While this was going on within me, I never could bear that the child should see me looking at him, and yet I was under a fascination which made it a kind of business with me to contemplate his slight and fragile figure and think how easily it might be done. Sometimes I would steal upstairs and watch him as he slept; but usually I hovered in the garden near the window of the room in which he learnt his little tasks; and there, as he sat upon a low seat beside my wife, I would peer at him for hours together from behind a tree; starting, like the guilty wretch I was, at every rustling of a leaf, and still gliding back to look and start again.

Hard by our cottage, but quite out of sight, and (if there were any wind astir) of hearing too, was a deep sheet of water. I spent days in shaping with my pocket-knife a rough model of a boat, which I finished at last and dropped in the child's way. Then I withdrew to a secret place, which he must pass if he stole away alone to swim this bauble, and lurked there for his coming. He came neither that day nor the next, though I waited from noon till nightfall. I was sure that I had him in my net, for I had heard him prattling of the toy, and knew that in his infant pleasure he kept it by his side in bed. I felt no weariness or fatigue, but waited patiently, and on the third day he passed me, running joyously along, with his silken hair streaming in the wind, and he singing— God have mercy upon me!—singing a merry ballad,—who could hardly lisp the words.

I stole down after him, creeping under certain shrubs which grow in that place, and none but devils know with what terror I, a strong, full-grown man, tracked the footsteps of that baby as he approached the water's brink. I was close upon him, had sunk upon my knee and raised my hand to thrust him in, when he saw my shadow in the stream and turned him round.

His mother's ghost was looking from his eyes. The sun burst forth from behind a cloud; it shone in the bright sky, the glistening earth, the clear water, the sparkling drops of rain upon the leaves. There were eyes in everything. The whole great universe of light was there to see the murder done. I know not what he said; he came of bold and manly blood, and, child as he was, he did not crouch or fawn upon me. I heard him cry that he would try to love me,—not that he did,—and then I saw him running back towards the house. The next I saw was my own sword naked in my hand, and he lying at my feet stark dead,—dabbled here and there with blood, but otherwise no different from what I had seen him in his sleep—in the same attitude too, with his cheek resting upon his little hand.

I took him in my arms and laid him—very gently now that he was dead—in a thicket. My wife was from home that day, and would not return until the next. Our bedroom window, the only sleeping-room on that side of the house, was but a few feet from the ground, and I resolved to descend from it at night and bury him in the garden. I had no thought that I had failed in my design, no thought that the water would be dragged and nothing found, that the money must now lie waste, since I must encourage the idea that the child was lost or stolen. All my thoughts were bound up and knotted together in the one absorbing necessity of hiding what I had done.

How I felt when they came to tell me that the child was missing, when I ordered scouts in all directions, when I gasped and trembled at everyone's approach, no tongue can tell or mind of man conceive. I buried him that night. When I parted the boughs and looked into the dark thicket, there was a glow-worm shining like the visible spirit of God upon the murdered child. I glanced down into his grave when I had placed him there, and still it gleamed upon his breast; an eye of fire looking up to Heaven in supplication to the stars that watched me at my work.

I had to meet my wife, and break the news, and give her hope that the child would soon be found. All this I did,—with some appearance, I suppose, of being sincere, for I was the object of no suspicion. This done, I sat at the bedroom window all day long, and watched the spot where the dreadful secret lay.

It was in a piece of ground which had been dug up to be newly turfed, and which I had chosen on that account, as the traces of my spade were less likely to attract attention. The men who laid down the grass must have thought me mad. I called to them continually to expedite their work, ran out and worked beside them, trod down the earth with my feet, and hurried them with frantic eagerness. They had finished their task before night, and then I thought myself comparatively safe.

I slept,—not as men do who awake refreshed and cheerful, but I did sleep, passing from vague and shadowy dreams of being hunted down, to visions of the plot of grass, through which now a hand, and now a foot, and now the head itself was starting out. At this point I always woke and stole to the window, to make sure that it was not really so. That done, I crept to bed again; and thus I spent the night in fits and starts, getting up and lying down full twenty times, and dreaming the same dream over and over again,—which was far worse than lying awake, for every dream had a whole night's suffering of its own. Once I thought the child was alive, and that I had never tried to kill him. To wake from that dream was the most dreadful agony of all.

The next day I sat at the window again, never once taking my eyes from the place, which, although it was covered by the grass, was as plain to me—its shape, its size, its depth, its jagged sides, and all—as if it had been open to the light of day. When a servant walked across it, I felt as if he must sink in; when he had passed, I looked to see that his feet had not worn the edges. If a bird lighted there, I was in terror lest by some tremendous interposition it should be instrumental in the discovery; if a breath of air sighed across it, to me it whispered murder. There was not a sight or a sound—how ordinary, mean, or unimportant soever—but was fraught with fear. And in this state of ceaseless watching I spent three days.

On the fourth there came to the gate one who had served with me abroad, accompanied by a brother officer of his whom I had never seen. I felt that I could not bear to be out of sight of the place. It was a summer evening, and I bade my people take a table and a flask of wine into the garden. Then I sat down *with my chair upon the grave*, and being assured that nobody could disturb it now without my knowledge, tried to drink and talk.

They hoped that my wife was well,—that she was not obliged to keep her chamber,—that they had not frightened her away. What could I do but tell them with a faltering tongue about the child? The officer whom I did not know was a down-looking man, and kept his eyes upon the ground while I was speaking. Even that terrified me. I could not divest myself of the idea that he saw something there which caused him to suspect the truth. I asked him hurriedly if he supposed that—and stopped. 'That the child has been murdered?' said he, looking mildly at me: 'O no! What could a man gain by murdering a poor child?' *I* could have told him what a man gained by such a deed, no one better: but I held my peace and shivered as with an ague.

Mistaking my emotion, they were endeavouring to cheer me with the hope that the boy would certainly be found,—great cheer that was for me!—when we heard a low deep howl, and presently there sprung over the wall two great dogs, who, bounding into the garden, repeated the baying sound we had heard before.

'Bloodhounds!' cried my visitors.

What need to tell me that! I had never seen one of that kind in all my life, but I knew what they were and for what purpose they had come. I grasped the elbows of my chair, and neither spoke nor moved.

'They are of the genuine breed,' said the man whom I had known abroad, 'and being out for exercise have no doubt escaped from their keeper.'

Both he and his friend turned to look at the dogs, who with their noses to the ground moved restlessly about, running to and fro, and up and down, and across, and round in circles, careering about like wild things, and all this time taking no notice of us, but ever and again repeating the yell we had heard already, then dropping their noses to the ground again and tracking earnestly here and there. They now began to snuff the earth more eagerly than they had done yet, and although they were still very restless, no longer beat about in such wide circuits, but kept near to one spot, and constantly diminished the distance between themselves and me.

At last they came up close to the great chair on which I sat, and raising their frightful howl once more, tried to tear away the wooden rails that kept them from the ground beneath. I saw how I looked, in the faces of the two who were with me.

'They scent some prey,' said they, both together.

'They scent no prey!' cried I.

'In Heaven's name, move!' said the one I knew, very earnestly, 'or you will be torn to pieces.'

'Let them tear me from limb to limb, I'll never leave this place!' cried I. 'Are dogs to hurry men to shameful deaths? Hew them down, cut them in pieces.'

'There is some foul mystery here!' said the officer whom I did not know, drawing his sword. 'In King Charles's name, assist me to secure this man.'

They both set upon me and forced me away, though I fought and bit and caught at them like a madman. After a struggle, they got me quietly between them; and then, my God! I saw the angry dogs tearing at the earth and throwing it up into the air like water.

What more have I to tell? That I fell upon my knees, and with chattering teeth confessed the truth, and prayed to be forgiven. That I have since denied, and now confess to it again. That I have been tried for the crime, found guilty, and sentenced. That I have not the courage to anticipate my doom, or to bear up manfully against it. That I have no compassion, no consolation, no hope, no friend. That my wife has happily lost for the time those faculties which would enable her to know my misery or hers. That I am alone in this stone dungeon with my evil spirit, and that I die tomorrow.

CORRESPONDENCE

Master Humphrey has been favoured with the following letter written on strongly-scented paper, and sealed in light-blue wax with the representation of two very plump doves interchanging beaks. It does not commence with any of the usual forms of address, but begins as is here set forth.

Bath, Wednesday night.

Heavens! Into what an indiscretion do I suffer myself to be betrayed! To address these faltering lines to a total stranger, and that stranger one of a conflicting sex!—and yet I am precipitated into the abyss, and have no power of self-snatchation (forgive me if I coin that phrase) from the yawning gulf before me.

Yes, I am writing to a man; but let me not think of that, for madness is in the thought. You will understand my feelings? O yes, I am sure you will; and you will respect them too, and not despise them,—will you?

Let me be calm. That portrait,—smiling as once he smiled on me; that cane,—dangling as I have seen it dangle from his hand I know not how oft; those legs that have glided through my nightly dreams and never stopped to speak; the perfectly gentlemanly, though false original,—can I be mistaken? O no, no.

Let me be calmer yet; I would be calm as coffins. You have published a letter from one whose likeness is engraved, but whose name (and wherefore?) is suppressed. Shall *I* breathe that name! Is it—but why ask when my heart tells me too truly that it is!

I would not upbraid him with his treachery; I would not remind him of those times when he plighted the most eloquent of vows, and procured from me a small pecuniary accommodation; and yet I would see him—see him did I say—*him*—alas! Such is woman's nature. For as the poet beautifully says—but you will already have anticipated the sentiment. Is it not sweet? O yes!

It was in this city (hallowed by the recollection) that I met him first; and assuredly if mortal happiness be recorded anywhere, then those rubbers with their three-and-sixpenny points are scored on tablets of celestial brass. He always held an honour—generally two. On that eventful night we stood at eight. He raised his eyes (luminous in their seductive sweetness) to my agitated face. '*Can* you?' said he, with peculiar meaning. I felt the gentle pressure of his foot on mine; our corns throbbed in unison. '*Can* you?' he said again; and every lineament of his expressive countenance added the words 'resist me?' I murmured 'No,' and fainted.

They said, when I recovered, it was the weather. *I* said it was the nutmeg in the negus. How little did they suspect the truth! How little did they guess the deep mysterious meaning of that inquiry! He called next morning on his knees; I do not mean to say that he actually came in that position to the house-door, but that he went down upon those joints directly the servant had retired. He brought some verses in his hat, which he said were original, but which I have since found were Milton's; likewise a little bottle labelled laudanum; also a pistol and a sword-stick. He drew the latter, uncorked the former, and clicked the trigger of the pocket fire-arm. He had come, he said, to conquer or to die. He did not die. He wrested from me an avowal of my love, and let off the pistol out of a back window previous to partaking of a slight repast.

Faithless, inconstant man! How many ages seem to have elapsed since his unaccountable and perfidious disappearance! Could I still forgive him both that and the borrowed lucre that he promised to pay next week! Could I spurn him from my feet if he approached in penitence, and with a matrimonial object! Would the blandishing enchanter still weave his spells around me, or should I burst them all and turn away in coldness! I dare not trust my weakness with the thought.

My brain is in a whirl again. You know his address, his occupations, his mode of life,—are acquainted, perhaps, with his inmost thoughts. You are a humane and philanthropic character; reveal all you know—all; but especially the street and number of his lodgings. The post is departing, the bellman rings,—pray Heaven it be not the knell of love and hope too.

Belinda

P.S. Pardon the wanderings of a bad pen and a distracted mind. Address to the Post-office. The bellman, rendered impatient by delay, is ringing dreadfully in the passage.

P.P.S. I open this to say that the bellman is gone, and that you must not expect it till the next post; so don't be surprised when you don't get it.

Master Humphrey does not feel himself at liberty to furnish his fair correspondent with the address of the gentleman in question, but he publishes her letter as a public appeal to his faith and gallantry.

Chapter 3

Master Humphrey's Visitor

When I am in a thoughtful mood, I often succeed in diverting the current of some mournful reflections, by conjuring up a number of fanciful associations with the objects that surround me, and dwelling upon the scenes and characters they suggest.

I have been led by this habit to assign to every room in my house and every old staring portrait on its walls a separate interest of its own. Thus, I am persuaded that a stately dame, terrible to behold in her rigid modesty, who hangs above the chimney-piece of my bedroom, is the former lady of the mansion. In the courtyard below is a stone face of surpassing ugliness, which I have somehow—in a kind of jealousy, I am afraid—associated with her husband. Above my study is a little room with ivy peeping through the lattice, from which I bring their daughter, a lovely girl of eighteen or nineteen years of age, and dutiful in all respects save one, that one being her devoted attachment to a young gentleman on the stairs, whose grandmother (degraded to a disused laundry in the garden) piques herself upon an old family quarrel, and is the implacable enemy of their love. With such materials as these I work out many a little drama, whose chief merit is, that I can bring it to a happy end at will. I have so many of them on hand, that if on my return home one of these evenings I were to find some bluff old wight of two centuries ago comfortably seated in my easy chair, and a lovelorn damsel vainly appealing to his heart, and leaning her white arm upon my clock itself, I verily believe I should only express my surprise that they had kept me waiting so long, and never honoured me with a call before.

I was in such a mood as this, sitting in my garden yesterday morning under the shade of a favourite tree, revelling in all the bloom and brightness about me, and feeling every sense of hope and enjoyment quickened by this most beautiful season of Spring, when my meditations were interrupted by the unexpected appearance of my barber at the end of the walk, who I immediately saw was coming towards me with a hasty step that betokened something remarkable.

My barber is at all times a very brisk, bustling, active little man,—for he is, as it were, chubby all over, without being stout or unwieldy,—but yesterday his alacrity was so very uncommon that it quite took me by surprise. For could I fail to observe when he came up to me that his grey eyes were twinkling in a most extraordinary manner, that his little red nose was in an unusual glow, that every line in his round bright face was twisted and curved into an expression of pleased surprise, and that his whole countenance was radiant with glee? I was still more surprised to see my housekeeper, who usually preserves a very staid air, and stands somewhat upon her dignity, peeping round the hedge at the bottom of the walk, and exchanging nods and smiles with the barber, who twice or thrice looked over his shoulder for that purpose. I could conceive no announcement to which these appearances could be the prelude, unless it were that they had married each other that morning.

I was, consequently, a little disappointed when it only came out that there was a gentleman in the house who wished to speak with me.

'And who is it?' said I.

The barber, with his face screwed up still tighter than before, replied that the gentleman would not send his name, but wished to see me. I pondered for a moment, wondering who this visitor might be, and I remarked that he embraced the opportunity of exchanging another nod with the housekeeper, who still lingered in the distance.

'Well!' said I, 'bid the gentleman come here.'

This seemed to be the consummation of the barber's hopes, for he turned sharp round, and actually ran away.

Now, my sight is not very good at a distance, and therefore when the gentleman first appeared in the walk, I was not quite clear whether he was a stranger to me or otherwise. He was an elderly gentleman, but came tripping along in the pleasantest manner conceivable, avoiding the garden-roller and the borders of the beds with inimitable dexterity, picking his way among the flower-pots, and smiling with unspeakable good humour. Before he was halfway up the walk he began to salute me; then I thought I knew him; but when he came towards me with his hat in his hand, the sun shining on his bald head, his bland face, his bright spectacles, his fawn-coloured tights, and his black gaiters,—then my heart warmed towards him, and I felt quite certain that it was Mr Pickwick.

'My dear sir,' said that gentleman as I rose to receive him, 'pray be seated. Pray sit down. Now, do not stand on my account. I must insist upon it, really.' With these words Mr Pickwick gently pressed me down into my seat, and taking my hand in his, shook it again and again with a warmth of manner perfectly irresistible. I endeavoured to express in my welcome something of that heartiness and pleasure which the sight of him awakened, and made him sit down beside me. All this time he kept alternately releasing my hand and grasping it again, and surveying me through his spectacles with such a beaming countenance as I never till then beheld.

'You knew me directly!' said Mr Pickwick. 'What a pleasure it is to think that you knew me directly!'

I remarked that I had read his adventures very often, and his features were quite familiar to me from the published portraits. As I thought it a good opportunity of adverting to the circumstance, I condoled with him upon the various libels on his character which had found their way into print. Mr Pickwick shook his head, and for a moment looked very indignant, but smiling again directly, added that no doubt I was acquainted with Cervantes's introduction to the second part of Don Quixote, and that it fully expressed his sentiments on the subject.

'But now,' said Mr Pickwick, 'don't you wonder how I found you out?'

'I shall never wonder, and, with your good leave, never know,' said I, smiling in my turn. 'It is enough for me that you give me this gratification. I have not the least desire that you should tell me by what means I have obtained it.'

'You are very kind,' returned Mr Pickwick, shaking me by the hand again; 'you are so exactly what I expected! But for what particular purpose do you think I have sought you, my dear sir? Now what *do* you think I have come for?'

Mr Pickwick put this question as though he were persuaded that it was morally impossible that I could by any means divine the deep purpose of his visit, and that it must be hidden from all human ken. Therefore, although I was rejoiced to think that I had anticipated his drift, I feigned to be quite ignorant of it, and after a brief consideration shook my head despairingly.

'What should you say,' said Mr Pickwick, laying the forefinger of his left hand upon my coat-sleeve, and looking at me with his head thrown back, and a little on one side,—'what should you say if I confessed that after reading your account of yourself and your little society, I had come here, a humble candidate for one of those empty chairs?'

'I should say,' I returned, 'that I know of only one circumstance which could still further endear that little society to me, and that would be the associating with it my old friend,—for you must let me call you so,—my old friend, Mr Pickwick.'

As I made him this answer every feature of Mr Pickwick's face fused itself into one all-pervading expression of delight. After shaking me heartily by both hands at once, he patted me gently on the back, and then— I well understood why—coloured up to the eyes, and hoped with great earnestness of manner that he had not hurt me.

If he had, I would have been content that he should have repeated the offence a hundred times rather than suppose so; but as he had not, I had no difficulty in changing the subject by making an inquiry which had been upon my lips twenty times already.

'You have not told me,' said I, 'anything about Sam Weller.'

'O! Sam,' replied Mr Pickwick, 'is the same as ever. The same true, faithful fellow that he ever was. What should I tell you about Sam, my dear sir, except that he is more indispensable to my happiness and comfort every day of my life?'

'And Mr Weller senior?' said I.

'Old Mr Weller,' returned Mr Pickwick, 'is in no respect more altered than Sam, unless it be that he is a little more opinionated than he was formerly, and perhaps at times more talkative. He spends a good deal of his time now in our neighbourhood, and has so constituted himself a part of my bodyguard, that when I ask permission for Sam to have a seat in your kitchen on clock nights (supposing your three friends think me worthy to fill one of the chairs), I am afraid I must often include Mr Weller too.'

I very readily pledged myself to give both Sam and his father a free admission to my house at all hours and seasons, and this point settled, we fell into a lengthy conversation which was carried on with as little reserve on both sides as if we had been intimate friends from our youth, and which conveyed to me the comfortable assurance that Mr Pickwick's buoyancy of spirit, and indeed all his old cheerful characteristics, were wholly unimpaired. As he had spoken of the consent of my friends as being yet in abeyance, I repeatedly assured him that his proposal was certain to receive their most joyful sanction, and several times entreated that he would give me leave to introduce him to Jack Redburn and Mr Miles (who were near at hand) without further ceremony.

To this proposal, however, Mr Pickwick's delicacy would by no means allow him to accede, for he urged that his eligibility must be formally discussed, and that, until this had been done, he could not think of obtruding himself further. The utmost I could obtain from him was a promise that he would attend upon our next night of meeting, that I might have the pleasure of presenting him immediately on his election.

Mr Pickwick, having with many blushes placed in my hands a small roll of paper, which he termed his 'qualification,' put a great many questions to me touching my friends, and particularly Jack Redburn, whom he repeatedly termed 'a fine fellow,' and in whose favour I could see he was strongly predisposed. When I had satisfied him on these points, I took him up into my room, that he might make acquaintance with the old chamber which is our place of meeting.

'And this,' said Mr Pickwick, stopping short, 'is the clock! Dear me! And this is really the old clock!'

I thought he would never have come away from it. After advancing towards it softly, and laying his hand upon it with as much respect and as many smiling looks as if it were alive, he set himself to consider it in every possible direction, now mounting on a chair to look at the top, now going down upon his knees to examine the bottom, now surveying the sides with his spectacles almost touching the case, and now trying to peep between it and the wall to get a slight view of the back. Then he would retire a pace or two and look up at the dial to see it go, and then draw near again and stand with his head on one side to hear it tick: never failing to glance towards me at intervals of a few seconds each, and nod his head with such complacent gratification as I am quite unable to describe. His admiration was not confined to the clock either, but extended itself to every article in the room; and really, when he had gone through them every one, and at last sat himself down in all the six chairs, one after another, to try how they felt, I never saw such a picture of good-humour and happiness as he presented, from the top of his shining head down to the very last button of his gaiters.

I should have been well pleased, and should have had the utmost enjoyment of his company, if he had remained with me all day, but my favourite, striking the hour, reminded him that he must take his leave. I could not forbear telling him once more how glad he had made me, and we shook hands all the way downstairs.

We had no sooner arrived in the hall that my housekeeper, gliding out of her little room (she had changed her gown and cap, I observed), greeted Mr Pickwick with her best smile and courtesy; and the barber, feigning to be accidentally passing on his way out, made him a vast number of bows. When the housekeeper courtesied, Mr Pickwick bowed with the utmost politeness, and when he bowed, the housekeeper courtesied again; between the housekeeper and the barber, I should say that Mr Pickwick faced about and bowed with undiminished affability fifty times at least.

I saw him to the door; an omnibus was at the moment passing the corner of the lane, which Mr Pickwick hailed and ran after with extraordinary nimbleness. When he had got about halfway, he turned his head, and seeing that I was still looking after him and that I waved my hand, stopped, evidently irresolute whether to come back and shake hands again, or to go on. The man behind the omnibus shouted, and Mr Pickwick ran a little way towards him: then he looked round at me, and ran a little way back again. Then there was another shout, and he turned round once more and ran the other way. After several of these vibrations, the man settled the question by taking Mr Pickwick by the arm and putting him into the carriage; but his last action was to let down the window and wave his hat to me as it drove off.

I lost no time in opening the parcel he had left with me. The following were its contents:

Mr Pickwick's Tale

A good many years have passed away since old John Podgers lived in the town of Windsor, where he was born, and where, in course of time, he came to be comfortably and snugly buried. You may be sure that in the time of King James the First, Windsor was a very quaint queer old town, and you may take it upon my authority that John Podgers was a very quaint queer old fellow; consequently he and Windsor fitted each other to a nicety, and seldom parted company even for half a day.

John Podgers was broad, sturdy, Dutch-built, short, and a very hard eater, as men of his figure often are. Being a hard sleeper likewise, he divided his time pretty equally between these two recreations, always falling asleep when he had done eating, and always taking another turn at the trencher when he had done sleeping, by which means he grew more corpulent and more drowsy every day of his life. Indeed it used to be currently reported that when he sauntered up and down the sunny side of the street before dinner (as he never failed to do in fair weather), he enjoyed his soundest nap; but many people held this to be a fiction, as he had several times been seen to look after fat oxen on market-days, and had even been heard, by persons of good credit and reputation, to chuckle at the sight, and say to himself with great glee, 'Live beef, live beef!' It was upon this evidence that the wisest people in Windsor (beginning with the local authorities of course) held that John Podgers was a man of strong, sound sense, not what is called smart, perhaps, and it might be of a rather lazy and apoplectic turn, but still a man of solid parts, and one who meant much more than he cared to show. This impression was confirmed by a very dignified way he had of shaking his head and imparting, at the same time, a pendulous motion to his double chin; in short, he passed for one of those people who, being plunged into the Thames, would make no vain efforts to set it afire, but would straightaway flop down to the bottom with a deal of gravity, and be highly respected in consequence by all good men.

Being well to do in the world, and a peaceful widower,—having a great appetite, which, as he could afford to gratify it, was a luxury and no inconvenience, and a power of going to sleep, which, as he had no occasion to keep awake, was a most enviable faculty,—you will readily suppose that John Podgers was a happy man. But appearances are often deceptive when they least seem so, and the truth is that, notwithstanding his extreme sleekness, he was rendered uneasy in his mind and exceedingly uncomfortable by a constant apprehension that beset him night and day.

You know very well that in those times there flourished divers evil old women who, under the name of Witches, spread great disorder through the land, and inflicted various dismal tortures upon Christian men; sticking pins and needles into them when they least expected it, and causing them to walk in the air with their feet upwards, to the great terror of their wives and families, who were naturally very much disconcerted when the master of the house unexpectedly came home, knocking at the door with his heels and combing his hair on the scraper. These were their commonest pranks, but they every day played a hundred others, of which none were less objectionable, and many were much more so, being improper besides; the result was that vengeance was denounced against all old women, with whom even the king himself had no sympathy (as he certainly ought to have had), for with his own most gracious hand he penned a most gracious consignment of them to everlasting wrath, and devised most gracious means for their confusion and slaughter, in virtue whereof scarcely a day passed but one witch at the least was most graciously hanged, drowned, or roasted in some part of his dominions. Still the press teemed with strange and terrible news from the north or the south, or the east or the west, relative to witches and their unhappy victims in some corner of the country, and the public's hair stood on end to that degree that it lifted its hat off its head, and made its face pale with terror.

You may believe that the little town of Windsor did not escape the general contagion. The inhabitants boiled a witch on the king's birthday and sent a bottle of the broth to court, with a dutiful address expressive of their loyalty. The king, being rather frightened by the present, piously bestowed it upon the Archbishop of Canterbury, and returned an answer to the address, wherein he gave them golden rules for discovering witches, and laid great stress upon certain protecting charms, and especially horseshoes. Immediately the towns-people went to work nailing up horseshoes over every door, and so many anxious parents apprenticed their children to farriers to keep them out of harm's way, that it became quite a genteel trade, and flourished exceedingly.

In the midst of all this bustle John Podgers ate and slept as usual, but shook his head a great deal oftener than was his custom, and was observed to look at the oxen less, and at the old women more. He had a little shelf put up in his sitting-room, whereon was displayed, in a row which grew longer every week, all the witchcraft literature of the time; he grew learned in charms and exorcisms, hinted at certain questionable females on broomsticks whom he had seen from his chamber window, riding in the air at night, and was in constant terror of being bewitched. At length, from perpetually dwelling upon this one idea, which, being alone in his head, had all its own way, the fear of witches became the single passion of his life. He, who up to that time had never known what it was to dream, began to have visions of witches whenever he fell asleep; waking, they were incessantly present to his imagination likewise; and, sleeping or waking, he had not a moment's peace. He began to set witch-traps in the highway, and was often seen lying in wait round the corner for hours together, to watch their effect. These engines were of simple construction, usually consisting of two straws disposed in the form of a cross, or a piece of a Bible cover with a pinch of salt upon it; but they were infallible, and if an old woman chanced to stumble over them (as not unfrequently happened, the chosen spot being a broken and stony place), John started from a doze, pounced out upon her, and hung round her neck till assistance arrived, when she was immediately carried away and drowned. By dint of constantly inveigling old ladies and disposing of them in this summary manner, he acquired the reputation of a great public character; and as he received no harm in these pursuits beyond a scratched face or so, he came, in the course of time, to be considered witch-proof.

There was but one person who entertained the least doubt of John Podgers's gifts, and that person was his own nephew, a wild, roving young fellow of twenty who had been brought up in his uncle's house and lived there still,—that is to say, when he was at home, which was not as often as it might have been. As he was an apt scholar, it was he who read aloud every fresh piece of strange and terrible intelligence that John Podgers bought; and this he always did of an evening in the little porch in front of the house, round which the neighbours would flock in crowds to hear the direful news,—for people like to be frightened, and when they can be frightened for nothing and at another man's expense, they like it all the better.

One fine midsummer evening, a group of persons were gathered in this place, listening intently to Will Marks (that was the nephew's name), as with his cap very much on one side, his arm coiled slyly round the waist of a pretty girl who sat beside him, and his face screwed into a comical expression intended to represent extreme gravity, he read—with Heaven knows how many embellishments of his own—a dismal account of a gentleman down in Northamptonshire under the influence of witchcraft and taken forcible possession of by the Devil, who was playing his very self with him. John Podgers, in a high sugar-loaf hat and short cloak, filled the opposite seat, and surveyed the auditory with a look of mingled pride and horror very edifying to see; while the hearers, with their heads thrust forward and their mouths open, listened and trembled, and hoped there was a great deal more to come. Sometimes Will stopped for an instant to look round upon his eager audience, and then, with a more comical expression of face than before and a settling of himself comfortably, which included a squeeze of the young lady before mentioned, he launched into some new wonder surpassing all the others.

The setting sun shed his last golden rays upon this little party, who, absorbed in their present occupation, took no heed of the approach of night, or the glory in which the day went down, when the sound of a horse, approaching at a good round trot, invading the silence of the hour, caused the reader to make a sudden stop, and the listeners to raise their heads in wonder. Nor was their wonder diminished when a horseman dashed up to the porch, and abruptly checking his steed, inquired where one John Podgers dwelt.

'Here!' cried a dozen voices, while a dozen hands pointed out sturdy John, still basking in the terrors of the pamphlet.

The rider, giving his bridle to one of those who surrounded him, dismounted, and approached John, hat in hand, but with great haste.

'Whence come ye?' said John.

'From Kingston, master.'

'And wherefore?'

'On most pressing business.'

'Of what nature?'

'Witchcraft.'

Witchcraft! Everybody looked aghast at the breathless messenger, and the breathless messenger looked equally aghast at everybody—except Will Marks, who, finding himself unobserved, not only squeezed the young lady again, but kissed her twice. Surely he must have been bewitched himself, or he never could have done it—and the young lady too, or she never would have let him.

'Witchcraft!' cried Will, drowning the sound of his last kiss, which was rather a loud one.

The messenger turned towards him, and with a frown repeated the word more solemnly than before; then told his errand, which was, in brief, that the people of Kingston had been greatly terrified for some nights past by hideous revels, held by witches beneath the gibbet within a mile of the town, and related and deposed to by chance wayfarers who had passed within ear-shot of the spot; that the sound of their voices in their wild orgies had been plainly heard by many persons; that three old women laboured under strong suspicion, and that precedents had been consulted and solemn council had, and it was found that to identify the hags some single person must watch upon the spot alone; that no single person had the courage to perform the task; and that he had been despatched express to solicit John Podgers to undertake it that very night, as being a man of great renown, who bore a charmed life, and was proof against unholy spells.

John received this communication with much composure, and said in a few words, that it would have afforded him inexpressible pleasure to do the Kingston people so slight a service, if it were not for his unfortunate propensity to fall asleep, which no man regretted more than himself upon the present occasion, but which quite settled the question. Nevertheless, he said, there *was* a gentleman present (and here he looked very hard at a tall farrier), who, having been engaged all his life in the manufacture of horseshoes, must be quite invulnerable to the power of witches, and who, he had no doubt, from his own reputation for bravery and good nature, would readily accept the commission. The farrier politely thanked him for his good opinion, which it would always be his study to deserve, but added that, with regard to the present little matter, he couldn't think of it on any account, as his departing on such an errand would certainly occasion the instant death of his wife, to whom, as they all knew, he was tenderly attached. Now, so far from this circumstance being notorious, everybody had suspected the reverse, as the farrier was in the habit of beating his lady rather more than tender husbands usually do; all the married men present, however, applauded his resolution with great vehemence, and one and all declared that they would stop at home and die if needful (which happily it was not) in defence of their lawful partners.

This burst of enthusiasm over, they began to look, as by one consent, toward Will Marks, who, with his cap more on one side than ever, sat watching the proceedings with extraordinary unconcern. He had never been heard openly to express his disbelief in witches, but had often cut such jokes at their expense as left it to be inferred; publicly stating on several occasions that he considered a broomstick an inconvenient charger, and one especially unsuited to the dignity of the female character, and indulging in other free remarks of the same tendency, to the great amusement of his wild companions.

As they looked at Will they began to whisper and murmur among themselves, and at length one man cried, 'Why don't you ask Will Marks?'

As this was what everybody had been thinking of, they all took up the word, and cried in concert, 'Ah! Why don't you ask Will?'

'*He* don't care,' said the farrier.

'Not he,' added another voice in the crowd.

'He don't believe in it, you know,' sneered a little man with a yellow face and a taunting nose and chin, which he thrust out from under the arm of a long man before him.

'Besides,' said a red-faced gentleman with a gruff voice, 'he's a single man.'

'That's the point!' said the farrier; and all the married men murmured, ah! that was it, and they only wished they were single themselves; they would show him what spirit was, very soon.

The messenger looked towards Will Marks beseechingly.

'It will be a wet night, friend, and my grey nag is tired after yesterday's work—'

Here there was a general titter.

'But,' resumed Will, looking about him with a smile, 'if nobody else puts in a better claim to go, for the credit of the town I am your man, and I would be, if I had to go afoot. In five minutes I shall be in the saddle, unless I am depriving any worthy gentleman here of the honour of the adventure, which I wouldn't do for the world.'

But here arose a double difficulty, for not only did John Podgers combat the resolution with all the words he had, which were not many, but the young lady combated it too with all the tears she had, which were very many indeed. Will, however, being inflexible, parried his uncle's objections with a joke, and coaxed the young lady into a smile in three short whispers. As it was plain that he set his mind upon it, and would go, John Podgers offered him a few first-rate charms out of his own pocket, which he dutifully declined to accept; and the young lady gave him a kiss, which he also returned.

'You see what a rare thing it is to be married,' said Will, 'and how careful and considerate all these husbands are. There's not a man among them but his heart is leaping to forestall me in this adventure, and yet a strong sense of duty keeps him back. The husbands in this one little town are a pattern to the world, and so must the wives be too, for that matter, or they could never boast half the influence they have!'

Waiting for no reply to this sarcasm, he snapped his fingers and withdrew into the house, and thence into the stable, while some busied themselves in refreshing the messenger, and others in baiting his steed. In less than the specified time he returned by another way, with a good cloak hanging over his arm, a good sword girded by his side, and leading his good horse caparisoned for the journey.

'Now,' said Will, leaping into the saddle at a bound, 'up and away. Upon your mettle, friend, and push on. Goodnight!'

He kissed his hand to the girl, nodded to his drowsy uncle, waved his cap to the rest—and off they flew pell-mell, as if all the witches in England were in their horses' legs. They were out of sight in a minute.

The men who were left behind shook their heads doubtfully, stroked their chins, and shook their heads again. The farrier said that certainly Will Marks was a good horseman, nobody should ever say he denied that: but he was rash, very rash, and there was no telling what the end of it might be; what did he go for, that was what he wanted to know? He wished the young fellow no harm, but why did he go? Everybody echoed these words, and shook their heads again, having done which they wished John Podgers goodnight, and straggled home to bed.

The Kingston people were in their first sleep when Will Marks and his conductor rode through the town and up to the door of a house where sundry grave functionaries were assembled, anxiously expecting the arrival of the renowned Podgers. They were a little disappointed to find a gay young man in his place; but they put the best face upon the matter, and gave him full instructions how he was to conceal himself behind the gibbet, and watch and listen to the witches, and how at a certain time he was to burst forth and cut and slash among them vigorously, so that the suspected parties might be found bleeding in their beds next day, and thoroughly confounded. They gave him a great quantity of wholesome advice besides, and—which was more to the purpose with Will—a good supper. All these things being done, and midnight nearly come, they sallied forth to show him the spot where he was to keep his dreary vigil.

The night was by this time dark and threatening. There was a rumbling of distant thunder, and a low sighing of wind among the trees, which was very dismal. The potentates of the town kept so uncommonly close to Will that they trod upon his toes, or stumbled against his ankles, or nearly tripped up his heels at every step he took, and, besides these annoyances, their teeth chattered so with fear, that he seemed to be accompanied by a dirge of castanets.

At last they made a halt at the opening of a lonely, desolate space, and, pointing to a black object at some distance, asked Will if he saw that, yonder.

'Yes,' he replied. 'What then?'

Informing him abruptly that it was the gibbet where he was to watch, they wished him goodnight in an extremely friendly manner, and ran back as fast as their feet would carry them.

Will walked boldly to the gibbet, and, glancing upwards when he came under it, saw—certainly with satisfaction—that it was empty, and that nothing dangled from the top but some iron chains, which swung mournfully to and fro as they were moved by the breeze. After a careful survey of every quarter he determined to take his station with his face towards the town; both because that would place him with his back to the wind, and because, if any trick or surprise were attempted, it would probably come from that direction in the first instance. Having taken these precautions, he wrapped his cloak about him so that it left the handle of his sword free, and ready to his hand, and leaning against the gallows-tree with his cap not quite so much on one side as it had been before, took up his position for the night.

Second Chapter of Mr Pickwick's Tale

We left Will Marks leaning under the gibbet with his face towards the town, scanning the distance with a keen eye, which sought to pierce the darkness and catch the earliest glimpse of any person or persons that might approach towards him. But all was quiet, and, save the howling of the wind as it swept across the heath in gusts, and the creaking of the chains that dangled above his head, there was no sound to break the sullen stillness of the night. After half an hour or so this monotony became more disconcerting to Will than the most furious uproar would have been, and he heartily wished for some one antagonist with whom he might have a fair stand-up fight, if it were only to warm himself.

Truth to tell, it was a bitter wind, and seemed to blow to the very heart of a man whose blood, heated but now with rapid riding, was the more sensitive to the chilling blast. Will was a daring fellow, and cared not a jot for hard knocks or sharp blades; but he could not persuade himself to move or walk about, having just that vague expectation of a sudden assault which made it a comfortable thing to have something at his back, even though that something were a gallows-tree. He had no great faith in the superstitions of the age, still such of them as occurred to him did not serve to lighten the time, or to render his situation the more endurable. He remembered how witches were said to repair at that ghostly hour to churchyards and gibbets, and such-like dismal spots, to pluck the bleeding mandrake or scrape the flesh from dead men's bones, as choice ingredients for their spells; how, stealing by night to lonely places, they dug graves with their fingernails, or anointed themselves before riding in the air, with a delicate pomatum made of the fat of infants newly boiled. These, and many other fabled practices of a no less agreeable nature, and all having some reference to the circumstances in which he was placed, passed and repassed in quick succession through the mind of Will Marks, and adding a shadowy dread to that distrust and watchfulness which his situation inspired, rendered it, upon the whole, sufficiently uncomfortable. As he had foreseen, too, the rain began to descend heavily, and driving before the wind in a thick mist, obscured even those few objects which the darkness of the night had before imperfectly revealed.

'Look!' shrieked a voice. 'Great Heaven, it has fallen down, and stands erect as if it lived!'

The speaker was close behind him; the voice was almost at his ear. Will threw off his cloak, drew his sword, and darting swiftly round, seized a woman by the wrist, who, recoiling from him with a dreadful shriek, fell struggling upon her knees. Another woman, clad, like her whom he had grasped, in mourning garments, stood rooted to the spot on which they were, gazing upon his face with wild and glaring eyes that quite appalled him.

'Say,' cried Will, when they had confronted each other thus for some time, 'what are ye?'

'Say what are *you*,' returned the woman, 'who trouble even this obscene resting-place of the dead, and strip the gibbet of its honoured burden? Where is the body?'

He looked in wonder and affright from the woman who questioned him to the other whose arm he clutched.

'Where is the body?' repeated the questioner more firmly than before. 'You wear no livery which marks you for the hireling of the government. You are no friend to us, or I should recognize you, for the friends of such as we are few in number. What are you then, and wherefore are you here?'

'I am no foe to the distressed and helpless,' said Will. 'Are ye among that number? Ye should be by your looks.'

'We are!' was the answer.

'Is it ye who have been wailing and weeping here under cover of the night?' said Will.

'It is,' replied the woman sternly; and pointing, as she spoke, towards her companion, 'she mourns a husband, and I a brother. Even the bloody law that wreaks its vengeance on the dead does not make that a crime, and if it did 'twould be alike to us who are past its fear or favour.'

Will glanced at the two females, and could barely discern that the one whom he addressed was much the elder, and that the other was young and of a slight figure. Both were deadly pale, their garments wet and worn, their hair dishevelled and streaming in the wind, themselves bowed down with grief and misery; their whole appearance most dejected, wretched, and forlorn. A sight so different from any he had expected to encounter touched him to the quick, and all idea of anything but their pitiable condition vanished before it.

'I am a rough, blunt yeoman,' said Will. 'Why I came here is told in a word; you have been overheard at a distance in the silence of the night, and I have undertaken a watch for hags or spirits. I came here expecting an adventure, and prepared to go through with any. If there be aught that I can do to help or aid you, name it, and on the faith of a man who can be secret and trusty, I will stand by you to the death.'

'How comes this gibbet to be empty?' asked the elder female.

'I swear to you,' replied Will, 'that I know as little as yourself. But this I know, that when I came here an hour ago or so, it was as it is now; and if, as I gather from your question, it was not so last night, sure I am that it has been secretly disturbed without the knowledge of the folks in yonder town. Bethink you, therefore, whether you have no friends in league with you or with him on whom the law has done its worst, by whom these sad remains have been removed for burial.'

The women spoke together, and Will retired a pace or two while they conversed apart. He could hear them sob and moan, and saw that they wrung their hands in fruitless agony. He could make out little that they said, but between whiles he gathered enough to assure him that his suggestion was not very wide of the mark, and that they not only suspected by whom the body had been removed, but also whither it had been conveyed. When they had been in conversation a long time, they turned towards him once more. This time the younger female spoke.

'You have offered us your help?'

'I have.'

'And given a pledge that you are still willing to redeem?'

'Yes. So far as I may, keeping all plots and conspiracies at arm's length.'

'Follow us, friend.'

Will, whose self-possession was now quite restored, needed no second bidding, but with his drawn sword in his hand, and his cloak so muffled over his left arm as to serve for a kind of shield without offering any impediment to its free action, suffered them to lead the way. Through mud and mire, and wind and rain, they walked in silence a full mile. At length they turned into a dark lane, where, suddenly starting out from beneath some trees where he had taken shelter, a man appeared, having in his charge three saddled horses. One of these (his own apparently), in obedience to a whisper from the women, he consigned to Will, who, seeing that they mounted, mounted also. Then, without a word spoken, they rode on together, leaving the attendant behind.

They made no halt nor slackened their pace until they arrived near Putney. At a large wooden house which stood apart from any other they alighted, and giving their horses to one who was already waiting, passed in by a side door, and so up some narrow creaking stairs into a small panelled chamber, where Will was left alone. He had not been here very long, when the door was softly opened, and there entered to him a cavalier whose face was concealed beneath a black mask.

Will stood upon his guard, and scrutinised this figure from head to foot. The form was that of a man pretty far advanced in life, but of a firm and stately carriage. His dress was of a rich and costly kind, but so soiled and disordered that it was scarcely to be recognized for one of those gorgeous suits which the expensive taste and fashion of the time prescribed for men of any rank or station.

He was booted and spurred, and bore about him even as many tokens of the state of the roads as Will himself. All this he noted, while the eyes behind the mask regarded him with equal attention. This survey over, the cavalier broke silence.

'Thou'rt young and bold, and wouldst be richer than thou art?'

'The two first I am,' returned Will. 'The last I have scarcely thought of. But be it so. Say that I would be richer than I am; what then?'

'The way lies before thee now,' replied the Mask.

'Show it me.'

'First let me inform thee, that thou wert brought here tonight lest thou shouldst too soon have told thy tale to those who placed thee on the watch.'

'I thought as much when I followed,' said Will. 'But I am no blab, not I.'

'Good,' returned the Mask. 'Now listen. He who was to have executed the enterprise of burying that body, which, as thou hast suspected, was taken down tonight, has left us in our need.'

Will nodded, and thought within himself that if the Mask were to attempt to play any tricks, the first eyelet-hole on the left-hand side of his doublet, counting from the buttons up the front, would be a very good place in which to pink him neatly.

'Thou art here, and the emergency is desperate. I propose his task to thee. Convey the body (now coffined in this house), by means that I shall show, to the Church of St. Dunstan in London tomorrow night, and thy service shall be richly paid. Thou'rt about to ask whose corpse it is. Seek not to know. I warn thee, seek not to know. Felons hang in chains on every moor and heath. Believe, as others do, that this was one, and ask no further. The murders of state policy, its victims or avengers, had best remain unknown to such as thee.'

'The mystery of this service,' said Will, 'bespeaks its danger. What is the reward?'

'One hundred golden unities,' replied the cavalier. 'The danger to one who cannot be recognized as the friend of a fallen cause is not great, but there is some hazard to be run. Decide between that and the reward.'

'What if I refuse?' said Will.

'Depart in peace, in God's name,' returned the Mask in a melancholy tone, 'and keep our secret, remembering that those who brought thee here were crushed and stricken women, and that those who bade thee go free could have had thy life with one word, and no man the wiser.'

Men were readier to undertake desperate adventures in those times than they are now. In this case the temptation was great, and the punishment, even in case of detection, was not likely to be very severe, as Will came of a loyal stock, and his uncle was in good repute, and a passable tale to account for his possession of the body and his ignorance of the identity might be easily devised.

The cavalier explained that a coveted cart had been prepared for the purpose; that the time of departure could be arranged so that he should reach London Bridge at dusk, and proceed through the city after the day had closed in; that people would be ready at his journey's end to place the coffin in a vault without a minute's delay; that officious inquirers in the streets would be easily repelled by the tale that he was carrying for interment the corpse of one who had died of the plague; and in short showed him every reason why he should succeed, and none why he should fail. After a time they were joined by another gentleman, masked like the first, who added new arguments to those which had been already urged; the wretched wife, too, added her tears and prayers to their calmer representations; and in the end, Will, moved by compassion and good nature, by a love of the marvellous, by a mischievous anticipation of the terrors of the Kingston people when he should be missing next day, and finally, by the prospect of gain, took upon himself the task, and devoted all his energies to its successful execution.

The following night, when it was quite dark, the hollow echoes of old London Bridge responded to the rumbling of the cart which contained the ghastly load, the object of Will Marks' care. Sufficiently disguised to attract no attention by his garb, Will walked at the horse's head, as unconcerned as a man could be who was sensible that he had now arrived at the most dangerous part of his undertaking, but full of boldness and confidence.

It was now eight o'clock. After nine, none could walk the streets without danger of their lives, and even at this hour, robberies and murder were of no uncommon occurrence. The shops upon the bridge were all closed; the low wooden arches thrown across the way were like so many black pits, in everyone of which ill-favoured fellows lurked in knots of three or four; some standing upright against the wall, lying in wait; others skulking in gateways, and thrusting out their uncombed heads and scowling eyes: others crossing and recrossing, and constantly jostling both horse and man to provoke a quarrel; others stealing away and summoning their companions in a low whistle. Once, even in that short passage, there was the noise of scuffling and the clash of swords behind him, but Will, who knew the city and its ways, kept straight on and scarcely turned his head.

The streets being unpaved, the rain of the night before had converted them into a perfect quagmire, which the splashing water-spouts from the gables, and the filth and offal cast from the different houses, swelled in no small degree. These odious matters being left to putrefy in the close and heavy air, emitted an insupportable stench, to which every court and passage poured forth a contribution of its own. Many parts, even of the main streets, with their projecting stories tottering overhead and nearly shutting out the sky, were more like huge chimneys than open ways. At the corners of some of these, great bonfires were burning to prevent infection from the plague, of which it was rumoured that some citizens had lately died; and few, who availing themselves of the light thus afforded paused for a moment to look around them, would have been disposed to doubt the existence of the disease, or wonder at its dreadful visitations.

But it was not in such scenes as these, or even in the deep and miry road, that Will Marks found the chief obstacles to his progress. There were kites and ravens feeding in the streets (the only scavengers the City kept), who, scenting what he carried, followed the cart or fluttered on its top, and croaked their knowledge of its burden and their ravenous appetite for prey. There were distant fires, where the poor wood and plaster tenements wasted fiercely, and whither crowds made their way, clamouring eagerly for plunder, beating down all who came within their reach, and yelling like devils let loose. There were single-handed men flying from bands of ruffians, who pursued them with naked weapons, and hunted them savagely; there were drunken, desperate robbers issuing from their dens and staggering through the open streets where no man dared molest them; there were vagabond servitors returning from the Bear Garden, where had been good sport that day, dragging after them their torn and bleeding dogs, or leaving them to die and rot upon the road. Nothing was abroad but cruelty, violence, and disorder.

Many were the interruptions which Will Marks encountered from these stragglers, and many the narrow escapes he made. Now some stout bully would take his seat upon the cart, insisting to be driven to his own home, and now two or three men would come down upon him together, and demand that on peril of his life he showed them what he had inside. Then a party of the city watch, upon their rounds, would draw across the road, and not satisfied with his tale, question him closely, and revenge themselves by a little cuffing and hustling for maltreatment sustained at other hands that night. All these assailants had to be rebutted, some by fair words, some by foul, and some by blows. But Will Marks was not the man to be stopped or turned back now he had penetrated so far, and though he got on slowly, still he made his way down Fleet Street and reached the church at last.

As he had been forewarned, all was in readiness. Directly he stopped, the coffin was removed by four men, who appeared so suddenly that they seemed to have started from the earth. A fifth mounted the cart, and scarcely allowing Will time to snatch from it a little bundle containing such of his own clothes as he had thrown off on assuming his disguise, drove briskly away. Will never saw cart or man again.

He followed the body into the church, and it was well he lost no time in doing so, for the door was immediately closed. There was no light in the building save that which came from a couple of torches borne by two men in cloaks, who stood upon the brink of a vault. Each supported a female figure, and all observed a profound silence.

By this dim and solemn glare, which made Will feel as though light itself were dead, and its tomb the dreary arches that frowned above, they placed the coffin in the vault, with uncovered heads, and closed it up. One of the torch-bearers then turned to Will, and stretched forth his hand, in which was a purse of gold. Something told him directly that those were the same eyes which he had seen beneath the mask.

'Take it,' said the cavalier in a low voice, 'and be happy. Though these have been hasty obsequies, and no priest has blessed the work, there will not be the less peace with thee thereafter, for having laid his bones beside those of his little children. Keep thy own counsel, for thy sake no less than ours, and God be with thee!'

'The blessing of a widowed mother on thy head, good friend!' cried the younger lady through her tears; 'the blessing of one who has now no hope or rest but in this grave!'

Will stood with the purse in his hand, and involuntarily made a gesture as though he would return it, for though a thoughtless fellow, he was of a frank and generous nature. But the two gentlemen, extinguishing their torches, cautioned him to be gone, as their common safety would be endangered by a longer delay; and at the same time their retreating footsteps sounded through the church. He turned, therefore, towards the point at which he had entered, and seeing by a faint gleam in the distance that the door was again partially open, groped his way towards it and so passed into the street.

Meantime the local authorities of Kingston had kept watch and ward all the previous night, fancying every now and then that dismal shrieks were borne towards them on the wind, and frequently winking to each other, and drawing closer to the fire as they drank the health of the lonely sentinel, upon whom a clerical gentleman present was especially severe by reason of his levity and youthful folly. Two or three of the gravest in company, who were of a theological turn, propounded to him the question, whether such a character was not but poorly armed for single combat with the Devil, and whether he himself would not have been a stronger opponent; but the clerical gentleman, sharply reproving them for their presumption in discussing such questions, clearly showed that a fitter champion than Will could scarcely have been selected, not only for that being a child of Satan, he was the less likely to be alarmed by the appearance of his own father, but because Satan himself would be at his ease in such company, and would not scruple to kick up his heels to an extent which it was quite certain he would never venture before clerical eyes, under whose influence (as was notorious) he became quite a tame and milk-and-water character.

But when next morning arrived, and with it no Will Marks, and when a strong party repairing to the spot, as a strong party ventured to do in broad day, found Will gone and the gibbet empty, matters grew serious indeed. The day passing away and no news arriving, and the night going on also without any intelligence, the thing grew more tremendous still; in short, the neighbourhood worked itself up to such a comfortable pitch of mystery and horror, that it is a great question whether the general feeling was not one of excessive disappointment, when, on the second morning, Will Marks returned.

However this may be, back Will came in a very cool and collected state, and appearing not to trouble himself much about anybody except old John Podgers, who, having been sent for, was sitting in the Town Hall crying slowly, and dozing between whiles. Having embraced his uncle and assured him of his safety, Will mounted on a table and told his story to the crowd.

And surely they would have been the most unreasonable crowd that ever assembled together, if they had been in the least respect disappointed with the tale he told them; for besides describing the Witches' Dance to the minutest motion of their legs, and performing it in character on the table, with the assistance of a broomstick, he related how they had carried off the body in a copper caldron, and so bewitched him, that he lost his senses until he found himself lying under a hedge at least ten miles off, whence he had straightway returned as they then beheld. The story gained such universal applause that it soon afterwards brought down express from London the great witch-finder of the age, the Heaven-born Hopkins, who having examined Will closely on several points, pronounced it the most extraordinary and the best accredited witch-story ever known, under which title it was published at the Three Bibles on London Bridge, in small quarto, with a view of the caldron from an original drawing, and a portrait of the clerical gentleman as he sat by the fire.

On one point Will was particularly careful: and that was to describe for the witches he had seen, three impossible old females, whose likenesses never were or will be. Thus he saved the lives of the suspected parties, and of all other old women who were dragged before him to be identified.

This circumstance occasioned John Podgers much grief and sorrow, until happening one day to cast his eyes upon his housekeeper, and observing her to be plainly afflicted with rheumatism, he procured her to be burnt as an undoubted witch. For this service to the state he was immediately knighted, and became from that time Sir John Podgers.

Will Marks never gained any clue to the mystery in which he had been an actor, nor did any inscription in the church, which he often visited afterwards, nor any of the limited inquiries that he dared to make, yield him the least assistance. As he kept his own secret, he was compelled to spend the gold discreetly and sparingly. In the course of time he married the young lady of whom I have already told you, whose maiden name is not recorded, with whom he led a prosperous and happy life. Years and years after this adventure, it was his wont to tell her upon a stormy night that it was a great comfort to him to think those bones, to whomsoever they might have once belonged, were not bleaching in the troubled air, but were mouldering away with the dust of their own kith and kindred in a quiet grave.

Further Particulars of Master Humphrey's Visitor

Being very full of Mr Pickwick's application, and highly pleased with the compliment he had paid me, it will be readily supposed that long before our next night of meeting I communicated it to my three friends, who unanimously voted his admission into our body. We all looked forward with some impatience to the occasion which would enroll him among us, but I am greatly mistaken if Jack Redburn and myself were not by many degrees the most impatient of the party.

At length the night came, and a few minutes after ten Mr Pickwick's knock was heard at the street-door. He was shown into a lower room, and I directly took my crooked stick and went to accompany him upstairs, in order that he might be presented with all honour and formality.

'Mr Pickwick,' said I, on entering the room, 'I am rejoiced to see you,—rejoiced to believe that this is but the opening of a long series of visits to this house, and but the beginning of a close and lasting friendship.'

That gentleman made a suitable reply with a cordiality and frankness peculiarly his own, and glanced with a smile towards two persons behind the door, whom I had not at first observed, and whom I immediately recognized as Mr Samuel Weller and his father.

It was a warm evening, but the elder Mr Weller was attired, notwithstanding, in a most capacious greatcoat, and his chin enveloped in a large speckled shawl, such as is usually worn by stage coachmen on active service. He looked very rosy and very stout, especially about the legs, which appeared to have been compressed into his top-boots with some difficulty. His broad-brimmed hat he held under his left arm, and with the forefinger of his right hand he touched his forehead a great many times in acknowledgment of my presence.

'I am very glad to see you in such good health, Mr Weller,' said I.

'Why, thankee, sir,' returned Mr Weller, 'the axle an't broke yet. We keeps up a steady pace,—not too sewere, but vith a moderate degree o' friction,—and the consekens is that ve're still a runnin' and comes in to the time reg'lar.—My son Samivel, sir, as you may have read on in history,' added Mr Weller, introducing his first born.

I received Sam very graciously, but before he could say a word his father struck in again.

'Samivel Veller, sir,' said the old gentleman, 'has conferred upon me the ancient title o' grandfather vich had long laid dormouse, and wos s'posed to be nearly hex-tinct in our family. Sammy, relate a anecdote o' vun o' them boys,—that 'ere little anecdote about young Tony sayin' as he *would* smoke a pipe unbeknown to his mother.'

'Be quiet, can't you?' said Sam; 'I never see such a old magpie—never!'

'That 'ere Tony is the blessedest boy,' said Mr Weller, heedless of this rebuff, 'the blessedest boy as ever *I* see in *my* days! of all the charmin'est infants as ever I heerd tell on, includin' them as was kivered over by the robin-redbreasts arter they'd committed sooicide with blackberries, there never wos any like that 'ere little Tony. He's alvays a playin' vith a quart pot, that boy is! To see him a settin' down on the doorstep pretending to drink out of it, and fetching a long breath artervards, and smoking a bit of firevood, and sayin', 'Now I'm grandfather,'—to see him a doin' that at two year old is better than any play as wos ever wrote. 'Now I'm grandfather!' He wouldn't take a pint pot if you wos to make him a present on it, but he gets his quart, and then he says, 'Now I'm grandfather!''

Mr Weller was so overpowered by this picture that he straightway fell into a most alarming fit of coughing, which must certainly have been attended with some fatal result but for the dexterity and promptitude of Sam, who, taking a firm grasp of the shawl just under his father's chin, shook him to and fro with great violence, at the same time administering some smart blows between his shoulders. By this curious mode of treatment Mr Weller was finally recovered, but with a very crimson face, and in a state of great exhaustion.

'He'll do now, Sam,' said Mr Pickwick, who had been in some alarm himself.

'He'll do, sir!' cried Sam, looking reproachfully at his parent. 'Yes, he *will* do one o' these days,—he'll do for his-self and then he'll wish he hadn't. Did anybody ever see sich a inconsiderate old file,—laughing into conwulsions afore company, and stamping on the floor as if he'd brought his own carpet vith him and wos under a wager to punch the pattern out in a given time? He'll begin again in a minute. There—he's a goin' off—I said he would!'

In fact, Mr Weller, whose mind was still running upon his precocious grandson, was seen to shake his head from side to side, while a laugh, working like an earthquake, below the surface, produced various extraordinary appearances in his face, chest, and shoulders,—the more alarming because unaccompanied by any noise whatever. These emotions, however, gradually subsided, and after three or four short relapses he wiped his eyes with the cuff of his coat, and looked about him with tolerable composure.

'Afore the governor vith-draws,' said Mr Weller, 'there is a pint, respecting vich Sammy has a qvestion to ask. Vile that qvestion is a perwadin' this here conwersation, p'raps the genl'men vill permit me to re-tire.'

'Wot are you goin' away for?' demanded Sam, seizing his father by the coat-tail.

'I never see such a undootiful boy as you, Samivel,' returned Mr Weller. 'Didn't you make a solemn promise, amountin' almost to a speeches o' wow, that you'd put that 'ere qvestion on my account?'

'Well, I'm agreeable to do it,' said Sam, 'but not if you go cuttin' away like that, as the bull turned round and mildly observed to the drover ven they wos a goadin' him into the butcher's door. The fact is, sir,' said Sam, addressing me, 'that he wants to know somethin' respectin' that 'ere lady as is housekeeper here.' 'Ay. What is that?'

'Vy, sir,' said Sam, grinning still more, 'he wishes to know vether she—'

'In short,' interposed old Mr Weller decisively, a perspiration breaking out upon his forehead, 'vether that 'ere old creetur is or is not a widder.'

Mr Pickwick laughed heartily, and so did I, as I replied decisively, that 'my housekeeper was a spinster.'

'There!' cried Sam, 'now you're satisfied. You hear she's a spinster.'

'A wot?' said his father, with deep scorn.

'A spinster,' replied Sam.

Mr Weller looked very hard at his son for a minute or two, and then said, 'Never mind vether she makes jokes or not, that's no matter. Wot I say is, is that 'ere female a widder, or is she not?'

'Wot do you mean by her making jokes?' demanded Sam, quite aghast at the obscurity of his parent's speech.

'Never you mind, Samivel,' returned Mr Weller gravely; 'puns may be wery good things or they may be wery bad 'uns, and a female may be none the better or she may be none the vurse for making of 'em; that's got nothing to do vith widders.'

'Wy now,' said Sam, looking round, 'would anybody believe as a man at his time o' life could be running his head agin spinsters and punsters being the same thing?'

'There an't a straw's difference between 'em,' said Mr Weller. 'Your father didn't drive a coach for so many years, not to be ekal to his own langvidge as far as *that*goes, Sammy.'

Avoiding the question of etymology, upon which the old gentleman's mind was quite made up, he was several times assured that the housekeeper had never been married. He expressed great satisfaction on hearing this, and apologized for the question, remarking that he had been greatly terrified by a widow not long before, and that his natural timidity was increased in consequence.

'It wos on the rail,' said Mr Weller, with strong emphasis; 'I wos a goin' down to Birmingham by the rail, and I wos locked up in a close carriage vith a living widder. Alone we wos; the widder and me wos alone; and I believe it wos only because we *wos* alone and there wos no clergyman in the conwayance, that that 'ere widder didn't marry me afore ve reached the halfway station. Ven I think how she began a screaming as we wos a goin' under them tunnels in the dark,—how she kept on a faintin' and ketchin' hold o' me,—and how I tried to bust open the door as was tight-locked and perwented all escape—Ah! It was a awful thing, most awful!'

Mr Weller was so very much overcome by this retrospect that he was unable, until he had wiped his brow several times, to return any reply to the question whether he approved of railway communication, notwithstanding that it would appear from the answer which he ultimately gave, that he entertained strong opinions on the subject.

'I con-sider,' said Mr Weller, 'that the rail is unconstitootional and an inwaser o' priwileges, and I should wery much like to know what that 'ere old Carter as once stood up for our liberties and wun 'em too,—I should like to know wot he vould say, if he wos alive now, to Englishmen being locked up vith widders, or with anybody again their wills. Wot a old Carter would have said, a old coachman may say, and I as-sert that in that pint o' view alone, the rail is an inwaser. As to the comfort, vere's the comfort o' sittin' in a harm-cheer lookin' at brick walls or heaps o' mud, never comin' to a public-house, never seein' a glass o' ale, never goin' through a pike, never meetin' a change o' no kind (horses or otherwise), but alvays comin' to a place, ven you come to one at all, the wery picter o' the last, vith the same p'leesemen standing about, the same blessed old bell a ringin', the same unfort'nate people standing behind the bars, a waitin' to be let in; and everythin' the same except the name, vich is wrote up in the same sized letters as the last name, and vith the same colours. As to the *h*onour and dignity o' travellin', vere can that be vithout a coachman; and wot's the rail to sich coachmen and guards as is sometimes forced to go by it, but a outrage and a insult? As to the pace, wot sort o' pace do you think I, Tony Veller, could have kept a coach goin' at, for five hundred thousand pound a mile, paid in adwance afore the coach was on the road? And as to the ingein,—a nasty, wheezin', creakin', gaspin', puffin', bustin' monster, alvays out o' breath, vith a shiny green-and-gold back, like a unpleasant beetle in that 'ere gas magnifier,—as to the ingein as is alvays a pourin' out red-hot coals at night, and black smoke in the day, the sensiblest thing it does, in my opinion, is, ven there's somethin' in the vay, and it sets up that 'ere frightful scream vich seems to say, 'Now here's two hundred and forty passengers in the wery greatest extremity o' danger, and here's their two hundred and forty screams in vun!'

By this time I began to fear that my friends would be rendered impatient by my protracted absence. I therefore begged Mr Pickwick to accompany me upstairs, and left the two Mr Wellers in the care of the housekeeper, laying strict injunctions upon her to treat them with all possible hospitality.

Chapter 4

The Clock

As we were going upstairs, Mr Pickwick put on his spectacles, which he had held in his hand hitherto; arranged his neckerchief, smoothed down his waistcoat, and made many other little preparations of that kind which men are accustomed to be mindful of, when they are going among strangers for the first time, and are anxious to impress them pleasantly. Seeing that I smiled, he smiled too, and said that if it had occurred to him before he left home, he would certainly have presented himself in pumps and silk stockings.

'I would, indeed, my dear sir,' he said very seriously; 'I would have shown my respect for the society, by laying aside my gaiters.'

'You may rest assured,' said I, 'that they would have regretted your doing so very much, for they are quite attached to them.'

'No, really!' cried Mr Pickwick, with manifest pleasure. 'Do you think they care about my gaiters? Do you seriously think that they identify me at all with my gaiters?'

'I am sure they do,' I replied.

'Well, now,' said Mr Pickwick, 'that is one of the most charming and agreeable circumstances that could possibly have occurred to me!'

I should not have written down this short conversation, but that it developed a slight point in Mr Pickwick's character, with which I was not previously acquainted. He has a secret pride in his legs. The manner in which he spoke, and the accompanying glance he bestowed upon his tights, convince me that Mr Pickwick regards his legs with much innocent vanity.

'But here are our friends,' said I, opening the door and taking his arm in mine; 'let them speak for themselves.— Gentlemen, I present to you Mr Pickwick.'

Mr Pickwick and I must have been a good contrast just then. I, leaning quietly on my crutch-stick, with something of a careworn, patient air; he, having hold of my arm, and bowing in every direction with the most elastic politeness, and an expression of face whose sprightly cheerfulness and good humour knew no bounds. The difference between us must have been more striking yet, as we advanced towards the table, and the amiable gentleman, adapting his jocund step to my poor tread, had his attention divided between treating my infirmities with the utmost consideration, and affecting to be wholly unconscious that I required any.

I made him personally known to each of my friends in turn. First, to the deaf gentleman, whom he regarded with much interest, and accosted with great frankness and cordiality. He had evidently some vague idea, at the moment, that my friend being deaf must be dumb also; for when the latter opened his lips to express the pleasure it afforded him to know a gentleman of whom he had heard so much, Mr Pickwick was so extremely disconcerted, that I was obliged to step in to his relief.

His meeting with Jack Redburn was quite a treat to see. Mr Pickwick smiled, and shook hands, and looked at him through his spectacles, and under them, and over them, and nodded his head approvingly, and then nodded to me, as much as to say, 'This is just the man; you were quite right;' and then turned to Jack and said a few hearty words, and then did and said everything over again with unimpaired vivacity. As to Jack himself, he was quite as much delighted with Mr Pickwick as Mr Pickwick could possibly be with him. Two people never can have met together since the world began, who exchanged a warmer or more enthusiastic greeting.

It was amusing to observe the difference between this encounter and that which succeeded, between Mr Pickwick and Mr Miles. It was clear that the latter gentleman viewed our new member as a kind of rival in the affections of Jack Redburn, and besides this, he had more than once hinted to me, in secret, that although he had no doubt Mr Pickwick was a very worthy man, still he did consider that some of his exploits were unbecoming a gentleman of his years and gravity. Over and above these grounds of distrust, it is one of his fixed opinions, that the law never can by possibility do anything wrong; he therefore looks upon Mr Pickwick as one who has justly suffered in purse and peace for a breach of his plighted faith to an unprotected female, and holds that he is called upon to regard him with some suspicion on that account. These causes led to a rather cold and formal reception; which Mr Pickwick acknowledged with the same stateliness and intense politeness as was displayed on the other side. Indeed, he assumed an air of such majestic defiance, that I was fearful he might break out into some solemn protest or declaration, and therefore inducted him into his chair without a moment's delay.

This piece of generalship was perfectly successful. The instant he took his seat, Mr Pickwick surveyed us all with a most benevolent aspect, and was taken with a fit of smiling full five minutes long. His interest in our ceremonies was immense. They are not very numerous or complicated, and a description of them may be comprised in very few words. As our transactions have already been, and must necessarily continue to be, more or less anticipated by being presented in these pages at different times, and under various forms, they do not require a detailed account.

Our first proceeding when we are assembled is to shake hands all round, and greet each other with cheerful and pleasant looks. Remembering that we assemble not only for the promotion of our happiness, but with the view of adding something to the common stock, an air of languor or indifference in any member of our body would be regarded by the others as a kind of treason. We have never had an offender in this respect; but if we had, there is no doubt that he would be taken to task pretty severely.

Our salutation over, the venerable piece of antiquity from which we take our name is wound up in silence. The ceremony is always performed by Master Humphrey himself (in treating of the club, I may be permitted to assume the historical style, and speak of myself in the third person), who mounts upon a chair for the purpose, armed with a large key. While it is in progress, Jack Redburn is required to keep at the farther end of the room under the guardianship of Mr Miles, for he is known to entertain certain aspiring and unhallowed thoughts connected with the clock, and has even gone so far as to state that if he might take the works out for a day or two, he thinks he could improve them. We pardon him his presumption in consideration of his good intentions, and his keeping this respectful distance, which last penalty is insisted on, lest by secretly wounding the object of our regard in some tender part, in the ardour of his zeal for its improvement, he should fill us with dismay and consternation.

This regulation afforded Mr Pickwick the highest delight, and seemed, if possible, to exalt Jack in his good opinion.

The next ceremony is the opening of the clock-case (of which Master Humphrey has likewise the key), the taking from it as many papers as will furnish forth our evening's entertainment, and arranging in the recess such new contributions as have been provided since our last meeting. This is always done with peculiar solemnity. The deaf gentleman then fills and lights his pipe, and we once more take our seats round the table before mentioned, Master Humphrey acting as president,—if we can be said to have any president, where all are on the same social footing,—and our friend Jack as secretary. Our preliminaries being now concluded, we fall into any train of conversation that happens to suggest itself, or proceed immediately to one of our readings. In the latter case, the paper selected is consigned to Master Humphrey, who flattens it carefully on the table and makes dog's ears in the corner of every page, ready for turning over easily; Jack Redburn trims the lamp with a small machine of his own invention which usually puts it out; Mr Miles looks on with great approval notwithstanding; the deaf gentleman draws in his chair, so that he can follow the words on the paper or on Master Humphrey's lips as he pleases; and Master Humphrey himself, looking round with mighty gratification, and glancing up at his old clock, begins to read aloud.

Mr Pickwick's face, while his tale was being read, would have attracted the attention of the dullest man alive. The complacent motion of his head and forefinger as he gently beat time, and corrected the air with imaginary punctuation, the smile that mantled on his features at every jocose passage, and the sly look he stole around to observe its effect, the calm manner in which he shut his eyes and listened when there was some little piece of description, the changing expression with which he acted the dialogue to himself, his agony that the deaf gentleman should know what it was all about, and his extraordinary anxiety to correct the reader when he hesitated at a word in the manuscript, or substituted a wrong one, were alike worthy of remark. And when at last, endeavouring to communicate with the deaf gentleman by means of the finger alphabet, with which he constructed such words as are unknown in any civilized or savage language, he took up a slate and wrote in large text, one word in a line, the question, 'How—do—you—like—it?'—when he did this, and handing it over the table awaited the reply, with a countenance only brightened and improved by his great excitement, even Mr Miles relaxed, and could not forbear looking at him for the moment with interest and favour.

'It has occurred to me,' said the deaf gentleman, who had watched Mr Pickwick and everybody else with silent satisfaction—'it has occurred to me,' said the deaf gentleman, taking his pipe from his lips, 'that now is our time for filling our only empty chair.'

As our conversation had naturally turned upon the vacant seat, we lent a willing ear to this remark, and looked at our friend inquiringly.

'I feel sure,' said he, 'that Mr Pickwick must be acquainted with somebody who would be an acquisition to us; that he must know the man we want. Pray let us not lose any time, but set this question at rest. Is it so, Mr Pickwick?'

The gentleman addressed was about to return a verbal reply, but remembering our friend's infirmity, he substituted for this kind of answer some fifty nods. Then taking up the slate and printing on it a gigantic 'Yes,' he handed it across the table, and rubbing his hands as he looked round upon our faces, protested that he and the deaf gentleman quite understood each other, already.

'The person I have in my mind,' said Mr Pickwick, 'and whom I should not have presumed to mention to you until some time hence, but for the opportunity you have given me, is a very strange old man. His name is Bamber.'

'Bamber!' said Jack. 'I have certainly heard the name before.'

'I have no doubt, then,' returned Mr Pickwick, 'that you remember him in those adventures of mine (the Posthumous Papers of our old club, I mean), although he is only incidentally mentioned; and, if I remember right, appears but once.'

'That's it,' said Jack. 'Let me see. He is the person who has a grave interest in old mouldy chambers and the Inns of Court, and who relates some anecdotes having reference to his favourite theme,—and an odd ghost story,—is that the man?'

'The very same. Now,' said Mr Pickwick, lowering his voice to a mysterious and confidential tone, 'he is a very extraordinary and remarkable person; living, and talking, and looking, like some strange spirit, whose delight is to haunt old buildings; and absorbed in that one subject which you have just mentioned, to an extent which is quite wonderful. When I retired into private life, I sought him out, and I do assure you that the more I see of him, the more strongly I am impressed with the strange and dreamy character of his mind.'

'Where does he live?' I inquired.

'He lives,' said Mr Pickwick, 'in one of those dull, lonely old places with which his thoughts and stories are all connected; quite alone, and often shut up close for several weeks together. In this dusty solitude he broods upon the fancies he has so long indulged, and when he goes into the world, or anybody from the world without goes to see him, they are still present to his mind and still his favourite topic. I may say, I believe, that he has brought himself to entertain a regard for me, and an interest in my visits; feelings which I am certain he would extend to Master Humphrey's Clock if he were once tempted to join us. All I wish you to understand is, that he is a strange, secluded visionary, in the world but not of it; and as unlike anybody here as he is unlike anybody elsewhere that I have ever met or known.'

Mr Miles received this account of our proposed companion with rather a wry face, and after murmuring that perhaps he was a little mad, inquired if he were rich.

'I never asked him,' said Mr Pickwick.

'You might know, sir, for all that,' retorted Mr Miles, sharply.

'Perhaps so, sir,' said Mr Pickwick, no less sharply than the other, 'but I do not. Indeed,' he added, relapsing into his usual mildness, 'I have no means of judging. He lives poorly, but that would seem to be in keeping with his character. I never heard him allude to his circumstances, and never fell into the society of any man who had the slightest acquaintance with them. I have really told you all I know about him, and it rests with you to say whether you wish to know more, or know quite enough already.'

We were unanimously of opinion that we would seek to know more; and as a sort of compromise with Mr Miles (who, although he said 'Yes— O certainly—he should like to know more about the gentleman—he had no right to put himself in opposition to the general wish,' and so forth, shook his head doubtfully and hemmed several times with peculiar gravity), it was arranged that Mr Pickwick should carry me with him on an evening visit to the subject of our discussion, for which purpose an early appointment between that gentleman and myself was immediately agreed upon; it being understood that I was to act upon my own responsibility, and to invite him to join us or not, as I might think proper. This solemn question determined, we returned to the clock-case (where we have been forestalled by the reader), and between its contents, and the conversation they occasioned, the remainder of our time passed very quickly.

When we broke up, Mr Pickwick took me aside to tell me that he had spent a most charming and delightful evening. Having made this communication with an air of the strictest secrecy, he took Jack Redburn into another corner to tell him the same, and then retired into another corner with the deaf gentleman and the slate, to repeat the assurance. It was amusing to observe the contest in his mind whether he should extend his confidence to Mr Miles, or treat him with dignified reserve. Half a dozen times he stepped up behind him with a friendly air, and as often stepped back again without saying a word; at last, when he was close at that gentleman's ear and upon the very point of whispering something conciliating and agreeable, Mr Miles happened suddenly to turn his head, upon which Mr Pickwick skipped away, and said with some fierceness, 'Goodnight, sir—I was about to say goodnight, sir,—nothing more;' and so made a bow and left him.

'Now, Sam,' said Mr Pickwick, when he had got downstairs.

'All right, sir,' replied Mr Weller. 'Hold hard, sir. Right arm fust— now the left—now one strong conwulsion, and the great-coat's on, sir.'

Mr Pickwick acted upon these directions, and being further assisted by Sam, who pulled at one side of the collar, and Mr Weller, who pulled hard at the other, was speedily enrobed. Mr Weller, senior, then produced a full-sized stable lantern, which he had carefully deposited in a remote corner, on his arrival, and inquired whether Mr Pickwick would have 'the lamps alight.'

'I think not tonight,' said Mr Pickwick.

'Then if this here lady vill per-mit,' rejoined Mr Weller, 'we'll leave it here, ready for next journey. This here lantern, mum,' said Mr Weller, handing it to the housekeeper, 'vunce belonged to the celebrated Bill Blinder as is now at grass, as all on us vill be in our turns. Bill, mum, wos the hostler as had charge o' them two vell-known piebald leaders that run in the Bristol fast coach, and vould never go to no other tune but a sutherly vind and a cloudy sky, which wos consekvently played incessant, by the guard, wenever they wos on duty. He wos took wery bad one arternoon, arter having been off his feed, and wery shaky on his legs for some veeks; and he says to his mate, 'Matey,' he says, 'I think I'm a-goin' the wrong side o' the post, and that my foot's wery near the bucket. Don't say I an't,' he says, 'for I know I am, and don't let me be interrupted,' he says, 'for I've saved a little money, and I'm a-goin' into the stable to make my last vill and testymint.' 'I'll take care as nobody interrupts,' says his mate, 'but you on'y hold up your head, and shake your ears a bit, and you're good for twenty years to come.' Bill Blinder makes him no answer, but he goes away into the stable, and there he soon artervards lays himself down a'tween the two piebalds, and dies,—previously a writin' outside the corn-chest, 'This is the last vill and testymint of Villiam Blinder.' They wos nat'rally wery much amazed at this, and arter looking among the litter, and up in the loft, and vere not, they opens the corn-chest, and finds that he'd been and chalked his vill inside the lid; so the lid was obligated to be took off the hinges, and sent up to Doctor Commons to be proved, and under that 'ere wery instrument this here lantern was passed to Tony Veller; vich circumstarnce, mum, gives it a wally in my eyes, and makes me rekvest, if you vill be so kind, as to take partickler care on it.'

The housekeeper graciously promised to keep the object of Mr Weller's regard in the safest possible custody, and Mr Pickwick, with a laughing face, took his leave. The bodyguard followed, side by side; old Mr Weller buttoned and wrapped up from his boots to his chin; and Sam with his hands in his pockets and his hat half off his head, remonstrating with his father, as he went, on his extreme loquacity.

I was not a little surprised, on turning to go upstairs, to encounter the barber in the passage at that late hour; for his attendance is usually confined to some half-hour in the morning. But Jack Redburn, who finds out (by instinct, I think) everything that happens in the house, informed me with great glee, that a society in imitation of our own had been that night formed in the kitchen, under the title of 'Mr Weller's Watch,' of which the barber was a member; and that he could pledge himself to find means of making me acquainted with the whole of its future proceedings, which I begged him, both on my own account and that of my readers, by no means to neglect doing.

Chapter 5

Mr Weller's Watch

It seems that the housekeeper and the two Mr Wellers were no sooner left together on the occasion of their first becoming acquainted, than the housekeeper called to her assistance Mr Slithers the barber, who had been lurking in the kitchen in expectation of her summons; and with many smiles and much sweetness introduced him as one who would assist her in the responsible office of entertaining her distinguished visitors.

'Indeed,' said she, 'without Mr Slithers I should have been placed in quite an awkward situation.'

'There is no call for any hock'erdness, mum,' said Mr Weller with the utmost politeness; 'no call wotsumever. A lady,' added the old gentleman, looking about him with the air of one who establishes an incontrovertible position,—'a lady can't be hock'erd. Natur' has otherwise purwided.'

The housekeeper inclined her head and smiled yet more sweetly. The barber, who had been fluttering about Mr Weller and Sam in a state of great anxiety to improve their acquaintance, rubbed his hands and cried, 'Hear, hear! Very true, sir;' whereupon Sam turned about and steadily regarded him for some seconds in silence.

'I never knew,' said Sam, fixing his eyes in a ruminative manner upon the blushing barber,—'I never knew but vun o' your trade, but *he* wos worth a dozen, and wos indeed dewoted to his callin'!'

'Was he in the easy shaving way, sir,' inquired Mr Slithers; 'or in the cutting and curling line?'

'Both,' replied Sam; 'easy shavin' was his natur', and cuttin' and curlin' was his pride and glory. His whole delight wos in his trade. He spent all his money in bears, and run in debt for 'em besides, and there they wos a growling avay down in the front cellar all day long, and ineffectooally gnashing their teeth, vile the grease o' their relations and friends wos being re-tailed in gallipots in the shop above, and the first-floor winder wos ornamented vith their heads; not to speak o' the dreadful aggrawation it must have been to 'em to see a man alvays a walkin' up and down the pavement outside, vith the portrait of a bear in his last agonies, and underneath in large letters, 'Another fine animal wos slaughtered yesterday at Jinkinson's!' Hows'ever, there they wos, and there Jinkinson wos, till he wos took wery ill with some inn'ard disorder, lost the use of his legs, and wos confined to his bed, vere he laid a wery long time, but sich wos his pride in his profession, even then, that wenever he wos worse than usual the doctor used to go downstairs and say, 'Jinkinson's wery low this mornin'; we must give the bears a stir;' and as sure as ever they stirred 'em up a bit and made 'em roar, Jinkinson opens his eyes if he wos ever so bad, calls out, 'There's the bears!' and rewives agin.'

'Astonishing!' cried the barber.

'Not a bit,' said Sam, 'human natur' neat as imported. Vun day the doctor happenin' to say, 'I shall look in as usual tomorrow mornin',' Jinkinson catches hold of his hand and says, 'Doctor,' he says, 'will you grant me one favour?' 'I will, Jinkinson,' says the doctor. 'Then, doctor,' says Jinkinson, 'vill you come unshaved, and let me shave you?' 'I will,' says the doctor. 'God bless you,' says Jinkinson. Next day the doctor came, and arter he'd been shaved all skilful and reg'lar, he says, 'Jinkinson,' he says, 'it's wery plain this does you good. Now,' he says, 'I've got a coachman as has got a beard that it 'ud warm your heart to work on, and though the footman,' he says, 'hasn't got much of a beard, still he's a trying it on vith a pair o' viskers to that extent that razors is Christian charity. If they take it in turns to mind the carriage when it's a waitin' below,' he says, 'wot's to hinder you from operatin' on both of 'em ev'ry day as well as upon me? You've got six children,' he says, 'wot's to hinder you from shavin' all their heads and keepin' 'em shaved? You've got two assistants in the shop downstairs, wot's to hinder you from cuttin' and curlin' them as often as you like? Do this,' he says, 'and you're a man agin.' Jinkinson squeedged the doctor's hand and begun that wery day; he kept his tools upon the bed, and wenever he felt his-self gettin' worse, he turned to at vun o' the children who wos a runnin' about the house vith heads like clean Dutch cheeses, and shaved him agin. Vun day the lawyer come to make his vill; all the time he wos a takin' it down, Jinkinson was secretly a clippin' avay at his hair vith a large pair of scissors. 'Wot's that 'ere snippin' noise?' says the lawyer every now and then; 'it's like a man havin' his hair cut.' 'It *is* wery like a man havin' his hair cut,' says poor Jinkinson, hidin' the scissors, and lookin' quite innocent. By the time the lawyer found it out, he was wery nearly bald. Jinkinson wos kept alive in this vay for a long time, but at last vun day he has in all the children vun arter another, shaves each on 'em wery clean, and gives him vun kiss on the crown o' his head; then he has in the two assistants, and arter cuttin' and curlin' of 'em in the first style of elegance, says he should like to hear the woice o' the greasiest bear, vich rekvest is immediately complied with; then he says that he feels wery happy in his mind and vishes to be left alone; and then he dies, previously cuttin' his own hair and makin' one flat curl in the wery middle of his forehead.'

This anecdote produced an extraordinary effect, not only upon Mr Slithers, but upon the housekeeper also, who evinced so much anxiety to please and be pleased, that Mr Weller, with a manner betokening some alarm, conveyed a whispered inquiry to his son whether he had gone 'too fur.'

'Wot do you mean by too fur?' demanded Sam.

'In that 'ere little compliment respectin' the want of hock'erdness in ladies, Sammy,' replied his father.

'You don't think she's fallen in love with you in consekens o' that, do you?' said Sam.

'More unlikelier things have come to pass, my boy,' replied Mr Weller in a hoarse whisper; 'I'm always afeerd of inadwertent captivation, Sammy. If I know'd how to make myself ugly or unpleasant, I'd do it, Samivel, rayther than live in this here state of perpetival terror!'

Mr Weller had, at that time, no further opportunity of dwelling upon the apprehensions which beset his mind, for the immediate occasion of his fears proceeded to lead the way downstairs, apologizing as they went for conducting him into the kitchen, which apartment, however, she was induced to proffer for his accommodation in preference to her own little room, the rather as it afforded greater facilities for smoking, and was immediately adjoining the ale-cellar. The preparations which were already made sufficiently proved that these were not mere words of course, for on the deal table were a sturdy ale-jug and glasses, flanked with clean pipes and a plentiful supply of tobacco for the old gentleman and his son, while on a dresser hard by was goodly store of cold meat and other eatables. At sight of these arrangements Mr Weller was at first distracted between his love of joviality and his doubts whether they were not to be considered as so many evidences of captivation having already taken place; but he soon yielded to his natural impulse, and took his seat at the table with a very jolly countenance.

'As to imbibin' any o' this here flagrant veed, mum, in the presence of a lady,' said Mr Weller, taking up a pipe and laying it down again, 'it couldn't be. Samivel, total abstinence, if *you* please.'

'But I like it of all things,' said the housekeeper.

'No,' rejoined Mr Weller, shaking his head,—'no'.

'Upon my word I do,' said the housekeeper. 'Mr Slithers knows I do.'

Mr Weller coughed, and notwithstanding the barber's confirmation of the statement, said 'No' again, but more feebly than before. The housekeeper lighted a piece of paper, and insisted on applying it to the bowl of the pipe with her own fair hands; Mr Weller resisted; the housekeeper cried that her fingers would be burnt; Mr Weller gave way. The pipe was ignited, Mr Weller drew a long puff of smoke, and detecting himself in the very act of smiling on the housekeeper, put a sudden constraint upon his countenance and looked sternly at the candle, with a determination not to captivate, himself, or encourage thoughts of captivation in others. From this iron frame of mind he was roused by the voice of his son.

'I don't think,' said Sam, who was smoking with great composure and enjoyment, 'that if the lady wos agreeable it 'ud be wery far out o' the vay for us four to make up a club of our own like the governors does upstairs, and let him,' Sam pointed with the stem of his pipe towards his parent, 'be the president.'

The housekeeper affably declared that it was the very thing she had been thinking of. The barber said the same. Mr Weller said nothing, but he laid down his pipe as if in a fit of inspiration, and performed the following manœuvres.

Unbuttoning the three lower buttons of his waistcoat and pausing for a moment to enjoy the easy flow of breath consequent upon this process, he laid violent hands upon his watch-chain, and slowly and with extreme difficulty drew from his fob an immense double-cased silver watch, which brought the lining of the pocket with it, and was not to be disentangled but by great exertions and an amazing redness of face. Having fairly got it out at last, he detached the outer case and wound it up with a key of corresponding magnitude; then put the case on again, and having applied the watch to his ear to ascertain that it was still going, gave it some half-dozen hard knocks on the table to improve its performance.

'That,' said Mr Weller, laying it on the table with its face upwards, 'is the title and emblem o' this here society. Sammy, reach them two stools this vay for the wacant cheers. Ladies and gen'lmen, Mr Weller's Watch is vound up and now a-goin'. Order!'

By way of enforcing this proclamation, Mr Weller, using the watch after the manner of a president's hammer, and remarking with great pride that nothing hurt it, and that falls and concussions of all kinds materially enhanced the excellence of the works and assisted the regulator, knocked the table a great many times, and declared the association formally constituted.

'And don't let's have no grinnin' at the cheer, Samivel,' said Mr Weller to his son, 'or I shall be committin' you to the cellar, and then p'r'aps we may get into what the 'Merrikins call a fix, and the English a qvestion o' privileges.'

Having uttered this friendly caution, the President settled himself in his chair with great dignity, and requested that Mr Samuel would relate an anecdote.

'I've told one,' said Sam.

'Wery good, sir; tell another,' returned the chair.

'We wos a talking jist now, sir,' said Sam, turning to Slithers, 'about barbers. Pursuing that 'ere fruitful theme, sir, I'll tell you in a wery few words a romantic little story about another barber as p'r'aps you may never have heerd.'

'Samivell!' said Mr Weller, again bringing his watch and the table into smart collision, 'address your observations to the cheer, sir, and not to priwate indiwiduals!'

'And if I might rise to order,' said the barber in a soft voice, and looking round him with a conciliatory smile as he leant over the table, with the knuckles of his left hand resting upon it,—'if I *might* rise to order, I would suggest that 'barbers' is not exactly the kind of language which is agreeable and soothing to our feelings. You, sir, will correct me if I'm wrong, but I believe there *is* such a word in the dictionary as hairdressers.'

'Well, but suppose he wasn't a hairdresser,' suggested Sam.

'Wy then, sir, be parliamentary and call him vun all the more,' returned his father. 'In the same vay as ev'ry gen'lman in another place is a *h*onourable, ev'ry barber in this place is a hairdresser. Ven you read the speeches in the papers, and see as vun gen'lman says of another, 'the *h*onourable member, if he vill allow me to call him so,' you vill understand, sir, that that means, 'if he vill allow me to keep up that 'ere pleasant and uniwersal fiction.''

It is a common remark, confirmed by history and experience, that great men rise with the circumstances in which they are placed. Mr Weller came out so strong in his capacity of chairman, that Sam was for some time prevented from speaking by a grin of surprise, which held his faculties enchained, and at last subsided in a long whistle of a single note. Nay, the old gentleman appeared even to have astonished himself, and that to no small extent, as was demonstrated by the vast amount of chuckling in which he indulged, after the utterance of these lucid remarks.

'Here's the story,' said Sam. 'Vunce upon a time there wos a young hairdresser as opened a wery smart little shop vith four wax dummies in the winder, two gen'lmen and two ladies—the gen'lmen vith blue dots for their beards, wery large viskers, oudacious heads of hair, uncommon clear eyes, and nostrils of amazin' pinkness; the ladies vith their heads o' one side, their right forefingers on their lips, and their forms deweloped beautiful, in vich last respect they had the adwantage over the gen'lmen, as wasn't allowed but wery little shoulder, and terminated rayther abrupt in fancy drapery. He had also a many hair-brushes and tooth-brushes bottled up in the winder, neat glass-cases on the counter, a floor-clothed cuttin'-room upstairs, and a weighin'-macheen in the shop, right opposite the door. But the great attraction and ornament wos the dummies, which this here young hairdresser wos constantly a runnin' out in the road to look at, and constantly a runnin' in again to touch up and polish; in short, he wos so proud on 'em, that ven Sunday come, he wos always wretched and mis'rable to think they wos behind the shutters, and looked anxiously for Monday on that account. Vun o' these dummies wos a favrite vith him beyond the others; and ven any of his acquaintance asked him wy he didn't get married—as the young ladies he know'd, in partickler, often did—he used to say, 'Never! I never vill enter into the bonds of vedlock,' he says, 'until I meet with a young 'ooman as realizes my idea o' that 'ere fairest dummy with the light hair. Then, and not till then,' he says, 'I vill approach the altar.' All the young ladies he know'd as had got dark hair told him this wos wery sinful, and that he wos wurshippin' a idle; but them as wos at all near the same shade as the dummy coloured up wery much, and wos observed to think him a wery nice young man.'

'Samivel,' said Mr Weller, gravely, 'a member o' this associashun bein' one o' that 'ere tender sex which is now immedetly referred to, I have to rekvest that you vill make no reflections.'

'I ain't a makin' any, am I?' inquired Sam.

'Order, sir!' rejoined Mr Weller, with severe dignity. Then, sinking the chairman in the father, he added, in his usual tone of voice: 'Samivel, drive on!'

Sam interchanged a smile with the housekeeper, and proceeded:

'The young hairdresser hadn't been in the habit o' makin' this avowal above six months, ven he en-countered a young lady as wos the wery picter o' the fairest dummy. 'Now,' he says, 'it's all up. I am a slave!' The young lady wos not only the picter o' the fairest dummy, but she was wery romantic, as the young hairdresser was, too, and he says, 'O!' he says, 'here's a community o' feelin', here's a flow o' soul!' he says, 'here's a interchange o' sentiment!' The young lady didn't say much, o' course, but she expressed herself agreeable, and shortly artervards vent to see him vith a mutual friend. The hairdresser rushes out to meet her, but d'rectly she sees the dummies she changes colour and falls a tremblin' wiolently. 'Look up, my love,' says the hairdresser, 'behold your imige in my winder, but not correcter than in my art!' 'My imige!' she says. 'Yourn!' replies the hairdresser. 'But whose imige is *that*?' she says, a pinting at vun o' the gen'lmen. 'No vun's, my love,' he says, 'it is but a idea.' 'A idea!' she cries: 'it is a portrait, I feel it is a portrait, and that 'ere noble face must be in the millingtary!' 'Wot do I hear!' says he, a crumplin' his curls. 'Villiam Gibbs,' she says, quite firm, 'never renoo the subject. I respect you as a friend,' she says, 'but my affections is set upon that manly brow.' 'This,' says the hairdresser, 'is a reg'lar blight, and in it I perceive the hand of Fate. Farevell!' Vith these vords he rushes into the shop, breaks the dummy's nose vith a blow of his curlin'-irons, melts him down at the parlour fire, and never smiles artervards.'

'The young lady, Mr Weller?' said the housekeeper.

'Why, ma'am,' said Sam, 'finding that Fate had a spite agin her, and everybody she come into contact vith, she never smiled neither, but read a deal o' poetry and pined avay,—by rayther slow degrees, for she ain't dead yet. It took a deal o' poetry to kill the hairdresser, and some people say arter all that it was more the gin and water as caused him to be run over; p'r'aps it was a little o' both, and came o' mixing the two.'

The barber declared that Mr Weller had related one of the most interesting stories that had ever come within his knowledge, in which opinion the housekeeper entirely concurred.

'Are you a married man, sir?' inquired Sam.

The barber replied that he had not that honour.

'I s'pose you mean to be?' said Sam.

'Well,' replied the barber, rubbing his hands smirkingly, 'I don't know, I don't think it's very likely.'

'That's a bad sign,' said Sam; 'if you'd said you meant to be vun o' these days, I should ha' looked upon you as bein' safe. You're in a wery precarious state.'

'I am not conscious of any danger, at all events,' returned the barber.

'No more wos I, sir,' said the elder Mr Weller, interposing; 'those vere my symptoms, exactly. I've been took that vay twice. Keep your vether eye open, my friend, or you're gone.'

There was something so very solemn about this admonition, both in its matter and manner, and also in the way in which Mr Weller still kept his eye fixed upon the unsuspecting victim, that nobody cared to speak for some little time, and might not have cared to do so for some time longer, if the housekeeper had not happened to sigh, which called off the old gentleman's attention and gave rise to a gallant inquiry whether 'there wos anythin' wery piercin' in that 'ere little heart?'

'Dear me, Mr Weller!' said the housekeeper, laughing.

'No, but is there anythin' as agitates it?' pursued the old gentleman. 'Has it always been obderrate, always opposed to the happiness o' human creeturs? Eh? Has it?'

At this critical juncture for her blushes and confusion, the housekeeper discovered that more ale was wanted, and hastily withdrew into the cellar to draw the same, followed by the barber, who insisted on carrying the candle. Having looked after her with a very complacent expression of face, and after him with some disdain, Mr Weller caused his glance to travel slowly round the kitchen, until at length it rested on his son.

'Sammy,' said Mr Weller, 'I mistrust that barber.'

'Wot for?' returned Sam; 'wot's he got to do with you? You're a nice man, you are, arter pretendin' all kinds o' terror, to go a payin' compliments and talkin' about hearts and piercers.'

The imputation of gallantry appeared to afford Mr Weller the utmost delight, for he replied in a voice choked by suppressed laughter, and with the tears in his eyes,

'Wos I a talkin' about hearts and piercers,—wos I though, Sammy, eh?'

'Wos you? Of course you wos.'

'She don't know no better, Sammy, there ain't no harm in it,—no danger, Sammy; she's only a punster. She seemed pleased, though, didn't she? O' course, she wos pleased, it's nat'ral she should be, wery nat'ral.'

'He's wain of it!' exclaimed Sam, joining in his father's mirth. 'He's actually wain!'

'Hush!' replied Mr Weller, composing his features, 'they're a comin' back,—the little heart's a comin' back. But mark these wurds o' mine once more, and remember 'em ven your father says he said 'em. Samivel, I mistrust that 'ere deceitful barber.'

Chapter 6

Master Humphrey, from His Clock-Side in the Chimney Corner

Two or three evenings after the institution of Mr Weller's Watch, I thought I heard, as I walked in the garden, the voice of Mr Weller himself at no great distance; and stopping once or twice to listen more attentively, I found that the sounds proceeded from my housekeeper's little sitting-room, which is at the back of the house. I took no further notice of the circumstance at that time, but it formed the subject of a conversation between me and my friend Jack Redburn next morning, when I found that I had not been deceived in my impression. Jack furnished me with the following particulars; and as he appeared to take extraordinary pleasure in relating them, I have begged him in future to jot down any such domestic scenes or occurrences that may please his humour, in order that they may be told in his own way. I must confess that, as Mr Pickwick and he are constantly together, I have been influenced, in making this request, by a secret desire to know something of their proceedings.

On the evening in question, the housekeeper's room was arranged with particular care, and the housekeeper herself was very smartly dressed. The preparations, however, were not confined to mere showy demonstrations, as tea was prepared for three persons, with a small display of preserves and jams and sweet cakes, which heralded some uncommon occasion. Miss Benton (my housekeeper bears that name) was in a state of great expectation, too, frequently going to the front door and looking anxiously down the lane, and more than once observing to the servant-girl that she expected company, and hoped no accident had happened to delay them.

A modest ring at the bell at length allayed her fears, and Miss Benton, hurrying into her own room and shutting herself up, in order that she might preserve that appearance of being taken by surprise which is so essential to the polite reception of visitors, awaited their coming with a smiling countenance.

'Good ev'nin', mum,' said the older Mr Weller, looking in at the door after a prefatory tap. 'I'm afeerd we've come in rayther arter the time, mum, but the young colt being full o' wice, has been' a boltin' and shyin' and gettin' his leg over the traces to sich a extent that if he an't wery soon broke in, he'll wex me into a broken heart, and then he'll never be brought out no more except to learn his letters from the writin' on his grandfather's tombstone.'

With these pathetic words, which were addressed to something outside the door about two feet six from the ground, Mr Weller introduced a very small boy firmly set upon a couple of very sturdy legs, who looked as if nothing could ever knock him down. Besides having a very round face strongly resembling Mr Weller's, and a stout little body of exactly his build, this young gentleman, standing with his little legs very wide apart, as if the top-boots were familiar to them, actually winked upon the housekeeper with his infant eye, in imitation of his grandfather.

'There's a naughty boy, mum,' said Mr Weller, bursting with delight, 'there's a immoral Tony. Wos there ever a little chap o' four year and eight months old as vinked his eye at a strange lady afore?'

As little affected by this observation as by the former appeal to his feelings, Master Weller elevated in the air a small model of a coach whip which he carried in his hand, and addressing the housekeeper with a shrill 'ya—hip!' inquired if she was 'going down the road;' at which happy adaptation of a lesson he had been taught from infancy, Mr Weller could restrain his feelings no longer, but gave him twopence on the spot.

'It's in wain to deny it, mum,' said Mr Weller, 'this here is a boy arter his grandfather's own heart, and beats out all the boys as ever wos or will be. Though at the same time, mum,' added Mr Weller, trying to look gravely down upon his favourite, 'it was wery wrong on him to want to—over all the posts as we come along, and wery cruel on him to force poor grandfather to lift him cross-legged over every vun of 'em. He wouldn't pass vun single blessed post, mum, and at the top o' the lane there's seven-and-forty on 'em all in a row, and wery close together.'

Here Mr Weller, whose feelings were in a perpetual conflict between pride in his grandson's achievements and a sense of his own responsibility, and the importance of impressing him with moral truths, burst into a fit of laughter, and suddenly checking himself, remarked in a severe tone that little boys as made their grandfathers put 'em over posts never went to heaven at any price.

By this time the housekeeper had made tea, and little Tony, placed on a chair beside her, with his eyes nearly on a level with the top of the table, was provided with various delicacies which yielded him extreme contentment. The housekeeper (who seemed rather afraid of the child, notwithstanding her caresses) then patted him on the head, and declared that he was the finest boy she had ever seen.

'Wy, mum,' said Mr Weller, 'I don't think you'll see a many sich, and that's the truth. But if my son Samivel vould give me my vay, mum, and only dis-pense vith his—*might* I venter to say the vurd?'

'What word, Mr Weller?' said the housekeeper, blushing slightly.

'Petticuts, mum,' returned that gentleman, laying his hand upon the garments of his grandson. 'If my son Samivel, mum, vould only dis-pense vith these here, you'd see such a alteration in his appearance, as the imagination can't depicter.'

'But what would you have the child wear instead, Mr Weller?' said the housekeeper.

'I've offered my son Samivel, mum, agen and agen,' returned the old gentleman, 'to purwide him at my own cost vith a suit o' clothes as 'ud be the makin' on him, and form his mind in infancy for those pursuits as I hope the family o' the Vellers vill alvays dewote themselves to. Tony, my boy, tell the lady wot them clothes are, as grandfather says, father ought to let you vear.'

'A little white hat and a little sprig weskut and little knee cords and little top-boots and a little green coat with little bright buttons and a little welwet collar,' replied Tony, with great readiness and no stops.

'That's the cos-toom, mum,' said Mr Weller, looking proudly at the housekeeper. 'Once make sich a model on him as that, and you'd say he *wos* an angel!'

Perhaps the housekeeper thought that in such a guise young Tony would look more like the angel at Islington than anything else of that name, or perhaps she was disconcerted to find her previously-conceived ideas disturbed, as angels are not commonly represented in top-boots and sprig waistcoats. She coughed doubtfully, but said nothing.

'How many brothers and sisters have you, my dear?' she asked, after a short silence.

'One brother and no sister at all,' replied Tony. 'Sam his name is, and so's my father's. Do you know my father?'

'O yes, I know him,' said the housekeeper, graciously.

'Is my father fond of you?' pursued Tony.

'I hope so,' rejoined the smiling housekeeper.

Tony considered a moment, and then said, 'Is my grandfather fond of you?'

This would seem a very easy question to answer, but instead of replying to it, the housekeeper smiled in great confusion, and said that really children did ask such extraordinary questions that it was the most difficult thing in the world to talk to them. Mr Weller took upon himself to reply that he was very fond of the lady; but the housekeeper entreating that he would not put such things into the child's head, Mr Weller shook his own while she looked another way, and seemed to be troubled with a misgiving that captivation was in progress. It was, perhaps, on this account that he changed the subject precipitately.

'It's wery wrong in little boys to make game o' their grandfathers, an't it, mum?' said Mr Weller, shaking his head waggishly, until Tony looked at him, when he counterfeited the deepest dejection and sorrow.

'O, very sad!' assented the housekeeper. 'But I hope no little boys do that?'

'There is vun young Turk, mum,' said Mr Weller, 'as havin' seen his grandfather a little overcome vith drink on the occasion of a friend's birthday, goes a reelin' and staggerin' about the house, and makin' believe that he's the old gen'lm'n.'

'O, quite shocking!' cried the housekeeper,

'Yes, mum,' said Mr Weller; 'and previously to so doin', this here young traitor that I'm a speakin' of, pinches his little nose to make it red, and then he gives a hiccup and says, "I'm all right," he says; "give us another song!" Ha, ha! "Give us another song," he says. Ha, ha, ha!'

In his excessive delight, Mr Weller was quite unmindful of his moral responsibility, until little Tony kicked up his legs, and laughing immoderately, cried, 'That was me, that was;' whereupon the grandfather, by a great effort, became extremely solemn.

'No, Tony, not you,' said Mr Weller. 'I hope it warn't you, Tony. It must ha' been that 'ere naughty little chap as comes sometimes out o' the empty watch-box round the corner,—that same little chap as wos found standing on the table afore the looking-glass, pretending to shave himself vith a oyster-knife.'

'He didn't hurt himself, I hope?' observed the housekeeper.

'Not he, mum,' said Mr Weller proudly; 'bless your heart, you might trust that 'ere boy vith a steam-engine a'most, he's such a knowin' young'—but suddenly recollecting himself and observing that Tony perfectly understood and appreciated the compliment, the old gentleman groaned and observed that 'it wos all wery shockin'—wery.'

'O, he's a bad 'un,' said Mr Weller, 'is that 'ere watch-box boy, makin' such a noise and litter in the backyard, he does, waterin' wooden horses and feedin' of 'em vith grass, and perpetivally spillin' his little brother out of a veelbarrow and frightenin' his mother out of her vits, at the wery moment wen she's expectin' to increase his stock of happiness vith another play-feller,—O, he's a bad one! He's even gone so far as to put on a pair of paper spectacles as he got his father to make for him, and walk up and down the garden vith his hands behind him in imitation of Mr Pickwick,—but Tony don't do sich things, O no!'

'O no!' echoed Tony.

'He knows better, he does,' said Mr Weller. 'He knows that if he wos to come sich games as these nobody wouldn't love him, and that his grandfather in partickler couldn't abear the sight on him; for vich reasons Tony's always good.'

'Always good,' echoed Tony; and his grandfather immediately took him on his knee and kissed him, at the same time, with many nods and winks, slyly pointing at the child's head with his thumb, in order that the housekeeper, otherwise deceived by the admirable manner in which he (Mr Weller) had sustained his character, might not suppose that any other young gentleman was referred to, and might clearly understand that the boy of the watch-box was but an imaginary creation, and a fetch of Tony himself, invented for his improvement and reformation.

Not confining himself to a mere verbal description of his grandson's abilities, Mr Weller, when tea was finished, invited him by various gifts of pence and halfpence to smoke imaginary pipes, drink visionary beer from real pots, imitate his grandfather without reserve, and in particular to go through the drunken scene, which threw the old gentleman into ecstasies and filled the housekeeper with wonder. Nor was Mr Weller's pride satisfied with even this display, for when he took his leave he carried the child, like some rare and astonishing curiosity, first to the barber's house and afterwards to the tobacconist's, at each of which places he repeated his performances with the utmost effect to applauding and delighted audiences. It was half-past nine o'clock when Mr Weller was last seen carrying him home upon his shoulder, and it has been whispered abroad that at that time the infant Tony was rather intoxicated.

I was musing the other evening upon the characters and incidents with which I had been so long engaged; wondering how I could ever have looked forward with pleasure to the completion of my tale, and reproaching myself for having done so, as if it were a kind of cruelty to those companions of my solitude whom I had now dismissed, and could never again recall; when my clock struck ten. Punctual to the hour, my friends appeared.

On our last night of meeting, we had finished the story which the reader has just concluded. Our conversation took the same current as the meditations which the entrance of my friends had interrupted, and The Old Curiosity Shop was the staple of our discourse.

I may confide to the reader now, that in connection with this little history I had something upon my mind; something to communicate which I had all along with difficulty repressed; something I had deemed it, during the progress of the story, necessary to its interest to disguise, and which, now that it was over, I wished, and was yet reluctant, to disclose.

To conceal anything from those to whom I am attached, is not in my nature. I can never close my lips where I have opened my heart. This temper, and the consciousness of having done some violence to it in my narrative, laid me under a restraint which I should have had great difficulty in overcoming, but for a timely remark from Mr Miles, who, as I hinted in a former paper, is a gentleman of business habits, and of great exactness and propriety in all his transactions.

'I could have wished,' my friend objected, 'that we had been made acquainted with the single gentleman's name. I don't like his withholding his name. It made me look upon him at first with suspicion, and caused me to doubt his moral character, I assure you. I am fully satisfied by this time of his being a worthy creature; but in this respect he certainly would not appear to have acted at all like a man of business.'

'My friends,' said I, drawing to the table, at which they were by this time seated in their usual chairs, 'do you remember that this story bore another title besides that one we have so often heard of late?'

Mr Miles had his pocket-book out in an instant, and referring to an entry therein, rejoined, 'Certainly. Personal Adventures of Master Humphrey. Here it is. I made a note of it at the time.'

I was about to resume what I had to tell them, when the same Mr Miles again interrupted me, observing that the narrative originated in a personal adventure of my own, and that was no doubt the reason for its being thus designated.

This led me to the point at once.

'You will one and all forgive me,' I returned, 'if for the greater convenience of the story, and for its better introduction, that adventure was fictitious. I had my share, indeed,—no light or trivial one,—in the pages we have read, but it was not the share I feigned to have at first. The younger brother, the single gentleman, the nameless actor in this little drama, stands before you now.'

It was easy to see they had not expected this disclosure.

'Yes,' I pursued. 'I can look back upon my part in it with a calm, half-smiling pity for myself as for some other man. But I am he, indeed; and now the chief sorrows of my life are yours.'

I need not say what true gratification I derived from the sympathy and kindness with which this acknowledgment was received; nor how often it had risen to my lips before; nor how difficult I had found it—how impossible, when I came to those passages which touched me most, and most nearly concerned me—to sustain the character I had assumed. It is enough to say that I replaced in the clock-case the record of so many trials,—sorrowfully, it is true, but with a softened sorrow which was almost pleasure; and felt that in living through the past again, and communicating to others the lesson it had helped to teach me, I had been a happier man.

We lingered so long over the leaves from which I had read, that as I consigned them to their former resting-place, the hand of my trusty clock pointed to twelve, and there came towards us upon the wind the voice of the deep and distant bell of St. Paul's as it struck the hour of midnight.

'This,' said I, returning with a manuscript I had taken at the moment, from the same repository, 'to be opened to such music, should be a tale where London's face by night is darkly seen, and where some deed of such a time as this is dimly shadowed out. Which of us here has seen the working of that great machine whose voice has just now ceased?'

Mr Pickwick had, of course, and so had Mr Miles. Jack and my deaf friend were in the minority.

I had seen it but a few days before, and could not help telling them of the fancy I had about it.

I paid my fee of twopence upon entering, to one of the money-changers who sit within the Temple; and falling, after a few turns up and down, into the quiet train of thought which such a place awakens, paced the echoing stones like some old monk whose present world lay all within its walls. As I looked afar up into the lofty dome, I could not help wondering what were his reflections whose genius reared that mighty pile, when, the last small wedge of timber fixed, the last nail driven into its home for many centuries, the clang of hammers, and the hum of busy voices gone, and the Great Silence whole years of noise had helped to make, reigning undisturbed around, he mused, as I did now, upon his work, and lost himself amid its vast extent. I could not quite determine whether the contemplation of it would impress him with a sense of greatness or of insignificance; but when I remembered how long a time it had taken to erect, in how short a space it might be traversed even to its remotest parts, for how brief a term he, or any of those who cared to bear his name, would live to see it, or know of its existence, I imagined him far more melancholy than proud, and looking with regret upon his labour done. With these thoughts in my mind, I began to ascend, almost unconsciously, the flight of steps leading to the several wonders of the building, and found myself before a barrier where another money-taker sat, who demanded which among them I would choose to see. There were the stone gallery, he said, and the whispering gallery, the geometrical staircase, the room of models, the clock—the clock being quite in my way, I stopped him there, and chose that sight from all the rest.

I groped my way into the Turret which it occupies, and saw before me, in a kind of loft, what seemed to be a great, old oaken press with folding doors. These being thrown back by the attendant (who was sleeping when I came upon him, and looked a drowsy fellow, as though his close companionship with Time had made him quite indifferent to it), disclosed a complicated crowd of wheels and chains in iron and brass,—great, sturdy, rattling engines,—suggestive of breaking a finger put in here or there, and grinding the bone to powder,—and these were the Clock! Its very pulse, if I may use the word, was like no other clock. It did not mark the flight of every moment with a gentle second stroke, as though it would check old Time, and have him stay his pace in pity, but measured it with one sledge-hammer beat, as if its business were to crush the seconds as they came trooping on, and remorselessly to clear a path before the Day of Judgment.

I sat down opposite to it, and hearing its regular and never-changing voice, that one deep constant note, uppermost amongst all the noise and clatter in the streets below,—marking that, let that tumult rise or fall, go on or stop,—let it be night or noon, tomorrow or today, this year or next,—it still performed its functions with the same dull constancy, and regulated the progress of the life around, the fancy came upon me that this was London's Heart,—and that when it should cease to beat, the city would be no more.

It is night. Calm and unmoved amidst the scenes that darkness favours, the great heart of London throbs in its giant breast. Wealth and beggary, vice and virtue, guilt and innocence, repletion and the direst hunger, all treading on each other and crowding together, are gathered round it. Draw but a little circle above the clustering housetops, and you shall have within its space everything, with its opposite extreme and contradiction, close beside. Where yonder feeble light is shining, a man is but this moment dead. The taper at a few yards' distance is seen by eyes that have this instant opened on the world. There are two houses separated by but an inch or two of wall. In one, there are quiet minds at rest; in the other, a waking conscience that one might think would trouble the very air. In that close corner where the roofs shrink down and cower together as if to hide their secrets from the handsome street hard by, there are such dark crimes, such miseries and horrors, as could be hardly told in whispers. In the handsome street, there are folks asleep who have dwelt there all their lives, and have no more knowledge of these things than if they had never been, or were transacted at the remotest limits of the world,—who, if they were hinted at, would shake their heads, look wise, and frown, and say they were impossible, and out of nature,—as if all great towns were not. Does not this Heart of London, that nothing moves, nor stops, nor quickens,—that goes on the same let what will be done, does it not express the city's character well?

The day begins to break, and soon there is the hum and noise of life. Those who have spent the night on doorsteps and cold stones crawl off to beg; they who have slept in beds come forth to their occupation, too, and business is astir. The fog of sleep rolls slowly off, and London shines awake. The streets are filled with carriages and people gaily clad. The jails are full, too, to the throat, nor have the workhouses or hospitals much room to spare. The courts of law are crowded. Taverns have their regular frequenters by this time, and every mart of traffic has its throng. Each of these places is a world, and has its own inhabitants; each is distinct from, and almost unconscious of the existence of any other. There are some few people well to do, who remember to have heard it said, that numbers of men and women—thousands, they think it was—get up in London every day, unknowing where to lay their heads at night; and that there are quarters of the town where misery and famine always are. They don't believe it quite,—there may be some truth in it, but it is exaggerated, of course. So, each of these thousand worlds goes on, intent upon itself, until night comes again,—first with its lights and pleasures, and its cheerful streets; then with its guilt and darkness.

Heart of London, there is a moral in thy every stroke! As I look on at thy indomitable working, which neither death, nor press of life, nor grief, nor gladness out of doors will influence one jot, I seem to hear a voice within thee which sinks into my heart, bidding me, as I elbow my way among the crowd, have some thought for the meanest wretch that passes, and, being a man, to turn away with scorn and pride from none that bear the human shape.

I am by no means sure that I might not have been tempted to enlarge upon the subject, had not the papers that lay before me on the table been a silent reproach for even this digression. I took them up again when I had got thus far, and seriously prepared to read.

The handwriting was strange to me, for the manuscript had been fairly copied. As it is against our rules, in such a case, to inquire into the authorship until the reading is concluded, I could only glance at the different faces round me, in search of some expression which should betray the writer. Whoever he might be, he was prepared for this, and gave no sign for my enlightenment.

I had the papers in my hand, when my deaf friend interposed with a suggestion.

'It has occurred to me,' he said, 'bearing in mind your sequel to the tale we have finished, that if such of us as have anything to relate of our own lives could interweave it with our contribution to the Clock, it would be well to do so. This need be no restraint upon us, either as to time, or place, or incident, since any real passage of this kind may be surrounded by fictitious circumstances, and represented by fictitious characters. What if we make this an article of agreement among ourselves?'

The proposition was cordially received, but the difficulty appeared to be that here was a long story written before we had thought of it.

'Unless,' said I, 'it should have happened that the writer of this tale—which is not impossible, for men are apt to do so when they write—has actually mingled with it something of his own endurance and experience.'

Nobody spoke, but I thought I detected in one quarter that this was really the case.

'If I have no assurance to the contrary,' I added, therefore, 'I shall take it for granted that he has done so, and that even these papers come within our new agreement. Everybody being mute, we hold that understanding if you please.'

And here I was about to begin again, when Jack informed us softly, that during the progress of our last narrative, Mr Weller's Watch had adjourned its sittings from the kitchen, and regularly met outside our door, where he had no doubt that august body would be found at the present moment. As this was for the convenience of listening to our stories, he submitted that they might be suffered to come in, and hear them more pleasantly.

To this we one and all yielded a ready assent, and the party being discovered, as Jack had supposed, and invited to walk in, entered (though not without great confusion at having been detected), and were accommodated with chairs at a little distance.

Then, the lamp being trimmed, the fire well stirred and burning brightly, the hearth clean swept, the curtains closely drawn, the clock wound up, we entered on our new story.

It is again midnight. My fire burns cheerfully; the room is filled with my old friend's sober voice; and I am left to muse upon the story we have just now finished.

It makes me smile, at such a time as this, to think if there were anyone to see me sitting in my easy-chair, my grey head hanging down, my eyes bent thoughtfully upon the glowing embers, and my crutch—emblem of my helplessness—lying upon the hearth at my feet, how solitary I should seem. Yet though I am the sole tenant of this chimney-corner, though I am childless and old, I have no sense of loneliness at this hour; but am the centre of a silent group whose company I love.

Thus, even age and weakness have their consolations. If I were a younger man, if I were more active, more strongly bound and tied to life, these visionary friends would shun me, or I should desire to fly from them. Being what I am, I can court their society, and delight in it; and pass whole hours in picturing to myself the shadows that perchance flock every night into this chamber, and in imagining with pleasure what kind of interest they have in the frail, feeble mortal who is its sole inhabitant.

All the friends I have ever lost I find again among these visitors. I love to fancy their spirits hovering about me, feeling still some earthly kindness for their old companion, and watching his decay. 'He is weaker, he declines apace, he draws nearer and nearer to us, and will soon be conscious of our existence.' What is there to alarm me in this? It is encouragement and hope.

These thoughts have never crowded on me half so fast as they have done tonight. Faces I had long forgotten have become familiar to me once again; traits I had endeavoured to recall for years have come before me in an instant; nothing is changed but me; and even I can be my former self at will.

Raising my eyes but now to the face of my old clock, I remember, quite involuntarily, the veneration, not unmixed with a sort of childish awe, with which I used to sit and watch it as it ticked, unheeded in a dark staircase corner. I recollect looking more grave and steady when I met its dusty face, as if, having that strange kind of life within it, and being free from all excess of vulgar appetite, and warning all the house by night and day, it were a sage. How often have I listened to it as it told the beads of time, and wondered at its constancy! How often watched it slowly pointing round the dial, and, while I panted for the eagerly expected hour to come, admired, despite myself, its steadiness of purpose and lofty freedom from all human strife, impatience, and desire!

I thought it cruel once. It was very hard of heart, to my mind, I remember. It was an old servant even then; and I felt as though it ought to show some sorrow; as though it wanted sympathy with us in our distress, and were a dull, heartless, mercenary creature. Ah! How soon I learnt to know that in its ceaseless going on, and in its being checked or stayed by nothing, lay its greatest kindness, and the only balm for grief and wounded peace of mind.

Tonight, tonight, when this tranquillity and calm are on my spirits, and memory presents so many shifting scenes before me, I take my quiet stand at will by many a fire that has been long extinguished, and mingle with the cheerful group that cluster round it. If I could be sorrowful in such a mood, I should grow sad to think what a poor blot I was upon their youth and beauty once, and now how few remain to put me to the blush; I should grow sad to think that such among them as I sometimes meet with in my daily walks are scarcely less infirm than I; that time has brought us to a level; and that all distinctions fade and vanish as we take our trembling steps towards the grave.

But memory was given us for better purposes than this, and mine is not a torment, but a source of pleasure. To muse upon the gaiety and youth I have known suggests to me glad scenes of harmless mirth that may be passing now. From contemplating them apart, I soon become an actor in these little dramas, and humouring my fancy, lose myself among the beings it invokes.

When my fire is bright and high, and a warm blush mantles in the walls and ceiling of this ancient room; when my clock makes cheerful music, like one of those chirping insects who delight in the warm hearth, and are sometimes, by a good superstition, looked upon as the harbingers of fortune and plenty to that household in whose mercies they put their humble trust; when everything is in a ruddy genial glow, and there are voices in the crackling flame, and smiles in its flashing light, other smiles and other voices congregate around me, invading, with their pleasant harmony, the silence of the time.

For then a knot of youthful creatures gather round my fireside, and the room re-echoes to their merry voices. My solitary chair no longer holds its ample place before the fire, but is wheeled into a smaller corner, to leave more room for the broad circle formed about the cheerful hearth. I have sons, and daughters, and grandchildren, and we are assembled on some occasion of rejoicing common to us all. It is a birthday, perhaps, or perhaps it may be Christmas time; but be it what it may, there is rare holiday among us; we are full of glee.

In the chimney-corner, opposite myself, sits one who has grown old beside me. She is changed, of course; much changed; and yet I recognize the girl even in that grey hair and wrinkled brow. Glancing from the laughing child who half hides in her ample skirts, and half peeps out,—and from her to the little matron of twelve years old, who sits so womanly and so demure at no great distance from me,—and from her again, to a fair girl in the full bloom of early womanhood, the centre of the group, who has glanced more than once towards the opening door, and by whom the children, whispering and tittering among themselves, *will* leave a vacant chair, although she bids them not,—I see her image thrice repeated, and feel how long it is before one form and set of features wholly pass away, if ever, from among the living. While I am dwelling upon this, and tracing out the gradual change from infancy to youth, from youth to perfect growth, from that to age, and thinking, with an old man's pride, that she is comely yet, I feel a slight thin hand upon my arm, and, looking down, see seated at my feet a crippled boy,—a gentle, patient child,—whose aspect I know well. He rests upon a little crutch,— I know it too,—and leaning on it as he climbs my footstool, whispers in my ear, 'I am hardly one of these, dear grandfather, although I love them dearly. They are very kind to me, but you will be kinder still, I know.'

I have my hand upon his neck, and stoop to kiss him, when my clock strikes, my chair is in its old spot, and I am alone.

What if I be? What if this fireside be tenantless, save for the presence of one weak old man? From my house-top I can look upon a hundred homes, in every one of which these social companions are matters of reality. In my daily walks I pass a thousand men whose cares are all forgotten, whose labours are made light, whose dull routine of work from day to day is cheered and brightened by their glimpses of domestic joy at home. Amid the struggles of this struggling town what cheerful sacrifices are made; what toil endured with readiness; what patience shown and fortitude displayed for the mere sake of home and its affections! Let me thank Heaven that I can people my fireside with shadows such as these; with shadows of bright objects that exist in crowds about me; and let me say, 'I am alone no more.'

I never was less so— I write it with a grateful heart—than I am tonight. Recollections of the past and visions of the present come to bear me company; the meanest man to whom I have ever given alms appears, to add his mite of peace and comfort to my stock; and whenever the fire within me shall grow cold, to light my path upon this earth no more, I pray that it may be at such an hour as this, and when I love the world as well as I do now.

The Deaf Gentleman from His Own Apartment

Our dear friend laid down his pen at the end of the foregoing paragraph, to take it up no more. I little thought ever to employ mine upon so sorrowful a task as that which he has left me, and to which I now devote it.

As he did not appear among us at his usual hour next morning, we knocked gently at his door. No answer being given, it was softly opened; and then, to our surprise, we saw him seated before the ashes of his fire, with a little table I was accustomed to set at his elbow when I left him for the night at a short distance from him, as though he had pushed it away with the idea of rising and retiring to his bed. His crutch and footstool lay at his feet as usual, and he was dressed in his chamber-gown, which he had put on before I left him. He was reclining in his chair, in his accustomed posture, with his face towards the fire, and seemed absorbed in meditation,—indeed, at first, we almost hoped he was.

Going up to him, we found him dead. I have often, very often, seen him sleeping, and always peacefully, but I never saw him look so calm and tranquil. His face wore a serene, benign expression, which had impressed me very strongly when we last shook hands; not that he had ever had any other look, God knows; but there was something in this so very spiritual, so strangely and indefinably allied to youth, although his head was grey and venerable, that it was new even in him. It came upon me all at once when on some slight pretence he called me back upon the previous night to take me by the hand again, and once more say, 'God bless you.'

A bell-rope hung within his reach, but he had not moved towards it; nor had he stirred, we all agreed, except, as I have said, to push away his table, which he could have done, and no doubt did, with a very slight motion of his hand. He had relapsed for a moment into his late train of meditation, and, with a thoughtful smile upon his face, had died.

I had long known it to be his wish that whenever this event should come to pass we might be all assembled in the house. I therefore lost no time in sending for Mr Pickwick and for Mr Miles, both of whom arrived before the messenger's return.

It is not my purpose to dilate upon the sorrow and affectionate emotions of which I was at once the witness and the sharer. But I may say, of the humbler mourners, that his faithful housekeeper was fairly heart-broken; that the poor barber would not be comforted; and that I shall respect the homely truth and warmth of heart of Mr Weller and his son to the last moment of my life.

'And the sweet old creetur, sir,' said the elder Mr Weller to me in the afternoon, 'has bolted. Him as had no wice, and was so free from temper that a infant might ha' drove him, has been took at last with that 'ere unawoidable fit o' staggers as we all must come to, and gone off his feed forever! I see him,' said the old gentleman, with a moisture in his eye, which could not be mistaken,—'I see him gettin', every journey, more and more groggy; I says to Samivel, 'My boy! The Grey's a-goin' at the knees;' and now my predilictions is fatally werified, and him as I could never do enough to serve or show my likin' for, is up the great uniwersal spout o' natur'.'

I was not the less sensible of the old man's attachment because he expressed it in his peculiar manner. Indeed, I can truly assert of both him and his son, that notwithstanding the extraordinary dialogues they held together, and the strange commentaries and corrections with which each of them illustrated the other's speech, I do not think it possible to exceed the sincerity of their regret; and that I am sure their thoughtfulness and anxiety in anticipating the discharge of many little offices of sympathy would have done honour to the most delicate-minded persons.

Our friend had frequently told us that his will would be found in a box in the Clock-case, the key of which was in his writing-desk. As he had told us also that he desired it to be opened immediately after his death, whenever that should happen, we met together that night for the fulfilment of his request.

We found it where he had told us, wrapped in a sealed paper, and with it a codicil of recent date, in which he named Mr Miles and Mr Pickwick his executors,—as having no need of any greater benefit from his estate than a generous token (which he bequeathed to them) of his friendship and remembrance.

After pointing out the spot in which he wished his ashes to repose, he gave to 'his dear old friends,' Jack Redburn and myself, his house, his books, his furniture,—in short, all that his house contained; and with this legacy more ample means of maintaining it in its present state than we, with our habits and at our terms of life, can ever exhaust. Besides these gifts, he left to us, in trust, an annual sum of no insignificant amount, to be distributed in charity among his accustomed pensioners—they are a long list—and such other claimants on his bounty as might, from time to time, present themselves. And as true charity not only covers a multitude of sins, but includes a multitude of virtues, such as forgiveness, liberal construction, gentleness and mercy to the faults of others, and the remembrance of our own imperfections and advantages, he bade us not inquire too closely into the venial errors of the poor, but finding that they *were* poor, first to relieve and then endeavour—at an advantage—to reclaim them.

To the housekeeper he left an annuity, sufficient for her comfortable maintenance and support through life. For the barber, who had attended him many years, he made a similar provision. And I may make two remarks in this place: first, that I think this pair are very likely to club their means together and make a match of it; and secondly, that I think my friend had this result in his mind, for I have heard him say, more than once, that he could not concur with the generality of mankind in censuring equal marriages made in later life, since there were many cases in which such unions could not fail to be a wise and rational source of happiness to both parties.

The elder Mr Weller is so far from viewing this prospect with any feelings of jealousy, that he appears to be very much relieved by its contemplation; and his son, if I am not mistaken, participates in this feeling. We are all of opinion, however, that the old gentleman's danger, even at its crisis, was very slight, and that he merely laboured under one of those transitory weaknesses to which persons of his temperament are now and then liable, and which become less and less alarming at every return, until they wholly subside. I have no doubt he will remain a jolly old widower for the rest of his life, as he has already inquired of me, with much gravity, whether a writ of habeas corpus would enable him to settle his property upon Tony beyond the possibility of recall; and has, in my presence, conjured his son, with tears in his eyes, that in the event of his ever becoming amorous again, he will put him in a strait-waistcoat until the fit is past, and distinctly inform the lady that his property is 'made over.'

Although I have very little doubt that Sam would dutifully comply with these injunctions in a case of extreme necessity, and that he would do so with perfect composure and coolness, I do not apprehend things will ever come to that pass, as the old gentleman seems perfectly happy in the society of his son, his pretty daughter-in-law, and his grandchildren, and has solemnly announced his determination to 'take arter the old 'un in all respects;' from which I infer that it is his intention to regulate his conduct by the model of Mr Pickwick, who will certainly set him the example of a single life.

I have diverged for a moment from the subject with which I set out, for I know that my friend was interested in these little matters, and I have a natural tendency to linger upon any topic that occupied his thoughts or gave him pleasure and amusement. His remaining wishes are very briefly told. He desired that we would make him the frequent subject of our conversation; at the same time, that we would never speak of him with an air of gloom or restraint, but frankly, and as one whom we still loved and hoped to meet again. He trusted that the old house would wear no aspect of mourning, but that it would be lively and cheerful; and that we would not remove or cover up his picture, which hangs in our dining-room, but make it our companion as he had been. His own room, our place of meeting, remains, at his desire, in its accustomed state; our seats are placed about the table as of old; his easy-chair, his desk, his crutch, his footstool, hold their accustomed places, and the clock stands in its familiar corner. We go into the chamber at stated times to see that all is as it should be, and to take care that the light and air are not shut out, for on that point he expressed a strong solicitude. But it was his fancy that the apartment should not be inhabited; that it should be religiously preserved in this condition, and that the voice of his old companion should be heard no more.

My own history may be summed up in very few words; and even those I should have spared the reader but for my friend's allusion to me some time since. I have no deeper sorrow than the loss of a child,—an only daughter, who is living, and who fled from her father's house but a few weeks before our friend and I first met. I had never spoken of this even to him, because I have always loved her, and I could not bear to tell him of her error until I could tell him also of her sorrow and regret. Happily I was enabled to do so some time ago. And it will not be long, with Heaven's leave, before she is restored to me; before I find in her and her husband the support of my declining years.

For my pipe, it is an old relic of home, a thing of no great worth, a poor trifle, but sacred to me for her sake.

Thus, since the death of our venerable friend, Jack Redburn and I have been the sole tenants of the old house; and, day by day, have lounged together in his favourite walks. Mindful of his injunctions, we have long been able to speak of him with ease and cheerfulness, and to remember him as he would be remembered. From certain allusions which Jack has dropped, to his having been deserted and cast off in early life, I am inclined to believe that some passages of his youth may possibly be shadowed out in the history of Mr Chester and his son, but seeing that he avoids the subject, I have not pursued it.

My task is done. The chamber in which we have whiled away so many hours, not, I hope, without some pleasure and some profit, is deserted; our happy hour of meeting strikes no more; the chimney-corner has grown cold; and MASTER HUMPHREY'S CLOCK has stopped forever.

TO THE READERS OF 'MASTER HUMPHREY'S CLOCK'

Dear Friends,

Next November we shall have finished the tale of which we are at present engaged, and shall have travelled together through twenty monthly parts and eighty-seven weekly numbers. It is my design when we have gone so far, to close this work. Let me tell you why.

I should not regard the anxiety, the close confinement, or the constant attention, inseparable from the weekly form of publication (for to commune with you in any form is to me a labour of love) if I had found it advantageous to the conduct of my stories, the elucidation of my meaning, or the gradual development of my characters. But I have not done so. I have often felt cramped and confined in a very irksome and harassing degree by the space in which I have been constrained to move. I have wanted you to know more at once than I could tell you; and it has frequently been of the greatest importance to my cherished intention, that you should do so. I have been sometimes strongly tempted (and have been at some pains to resist the temptation) to hurry incidents on, lest they should appear to you who waited from week to week, and had not, like me, the result and purpose in your minds, too long delayed. In a word, I have found this form of publication most anxious, perplexing, and difficult. I cannot bear these jerky confidences which are no sooner begun than ended, and no sooner ended than begun again.

Many passages in a tale of any length, depend materially for their interest on the intimate relation they bear to what has gone before, or to what is to follow. I have sometimes found it difficult when I issued thirty-two closely printed pages once a month, to sustain in your minds this needful connection: in the present form of publication it is often, especially in the first half of a story, quite impossible to preserve it sufficiently through the current numbers. And although in my progress, I am gradually able to set you right, and to show you what my meaning has been, and to work it out, I see no reason why you should ever be wrong when I have it in my power by resorting to a better means of communication between us to prevent it.

Considerations of immediate profit and advantage ought in such a case to be of secondary importance. They would lead me, at all hazards, to hold my present course. But for the reason I have just now mentioned, I have after long consideration, and with especial reference to the next new tale I bear in my mind, arrived at the conclusion that it will be better to abandon this scheme of publication in favour of our old and well-tried plan which has only twelve gaps in a year, instead of fifty-two.

Therefore my intention is, to close this story (with the limits of which I am of course by this time acquainted) and this work, within, or about, the period I have mentioned. I should add, that for the general convenience of subscribers, another volume of collected numbers will not be published until the whole is brought to a conclusion.

Taking advantage of the respite which the close of this work will afford me, I have decided, in January next, to pay a visit to America. The pleasure I anticipate from this realization of a wish I have long entertained, and long hoped to gratify, is subdued by the reflection that it must separate us for a longer time than other circumstances would have rendered necessary.

On 1 November, 1842, I purpose, if it please God, to commence my book in monthly parts, under the old green cover, in the old size and form, and at the old price.

I look forward to addressing a few more words to you in reference to this latter theme before I close the task on which I am now engaged. If there be any among the numerous readers of *Master Humphrey's Clock* who are at first dissatisfied with the prospect of this change—and it is not unnatural almost to hope there may be some— I trust they will, at no very distant day, find reason to agree with

September 1841   Its Author

POSTSCRIPT

Now that the time is come for taking leave, I find that the words I have to add are very few indeed.

We part until next November. It is a long parting between us, but if I have left you anything by which to remember me, in the meanwhile, with no unkind or distant feelings—anything by which I may be associated in spirit with your firesides, homes, and blameless pleasures— I am happy.

Believe me it has ever been my true desire to add to the common stock of healthful cheerfulness, good humour, and good-will, and trust me when I return to England and to another tale of English life and manners, I shall not slacken in this zealous work.

I take the opportunity for thanking all those who have addressed me by letter since the appearance of the foregoing announcement; and of expressing a hope that they will rest contented with this form of acknowledgment, as their number renders it impossible to me to answer them individually.

I bid farewell to them and all my readers with a regret that we feel in taking leave of Friends who have become endeared to us by long and close communication; and I look forward with truthfulness and pleasure to our next meeting.

November 1841

THE TRIAL FOR MURDER

I have always noticed a prevalent want of courage, even among persons of superior intelligence and culture, as to imparting their own psychological experiences when those have been of a strange sort. Almost all men are afraid that what they could relate in such wise would find no parallel or response in a listener's internal life, and might be suspected or laughed at. A truthful traveller, who should have seen some extraordinary creature in the likeness of a sea-serpent, would have no fear of mentioning it; but the same traveller, having had some singular presentiment, impulse, vagary of thought, vision (so-called), dream, or other remarkable mental impression, would hesitate considerably before he would own to it. To this reticence I attribute much of the obscurity in which such subjects are involved. We do not habitually communicate our experiences of these subjective things as we do our experiences of objective creation. The consequence is, that the general stock of experience in this regard appears exceptional, and really is so, in respect of being miserably imperfect.

In what I am going to relate, I have no intention of setting up, opposing, or supporting, any theory whatever. I know the history of the Bookseller of Berlin, I have studied the case of the wife of a late Astronomer Royal as related by Sir David Brewster, and I have followed the minutest details of a much more remarkable case of Spectral Illusion occurring within my private circle of friends. It may be necessary to state as to this last, that the sufferer (a lady) was in no degree, however distant, related to me. A mistaken assumption on that head might suggest an explanation of a part of my own case,—but only a part,—which would be wholly without foundation. It cannot be referred to my inheritance of any developed peculiarity, nor had I ever before any at all similar experience, nor have I ever had any at all similar experience since.

It does not signify how many years ago, or how few, a certain murder was committed in England, which attracted great attention. We hear more than enough of murderers as they rise in succession to their atrocious eminence, and I would bury the memory of this particular brute, if I could, as his body was buried, in Newgate Jail. I purposely abstain from giving any direct clue to the criminal's individuality.

When the murder was first discovered, no suspicion fell—or I ought rather to say, for I cannot be too precise in my facts, it was nowhere publicly hinted that any suspicion fell—on the man who was afterwards brought to trial. As no reference was at that time made to him in the newspapers, it is obviously impossible that any description of him can at that time have been given in the newspapers. It is essential that this fact be remembered.

Unfolding at breakfast my morning paper, containing the account of that first discovery, I found it to be deeply interesting, and I read it with close attention. I read it twice, if not three times. The discovery had been made in a bedroom, and, when I laid down the paper, I was aware of a flash—rush—flow—I do not know what to call it,—no word I can find is satisfactorily descriptive,—in which I seemed to see that bedroom passing through my room, like a picture impossibly painted on a running river.

Though almost instantaneous in its passing, it was perfectly clear; so clear that I distinctly, and with a sense of relief, observed the absence of the dead body from the bed.

It was in no romantic place that I had this curious sensation, but in chambers in Piccadilly, very near to the corner of St. James's Street. It was entirely new to me. I was in my easy-chair at the moment, and the sensation was accompanied with a peculiar shiver which started the chair from its position. (But it is to be noted that the chair ran easily on castors.) I went to one of the windows (there are two in the room, and the room is on the second floor) to refresh my eyes with the moving objects down in Piccadilly. It was a bright autumn morning, and the street was sparkling and cheerful. The wind was high. As I looked out, it brought down from the park a quantity of fallen leaves, which a gust took, and whirled into a spiral pillar. As the pillar fell and the leaves dispersed, I saw two men on the opposite side of the way, going from west to east. They were one behind the other. The foremost man often looked back over his shoulder. The second man followed him, at a distance of some thirty paces, with his right hand menacingly raised. First, the singularity and steadiness of this threatening gesture in so public a thoroughfare attracted my attention; and next, the more remarkable circumstance that nobody heeded it. Both men threaded their way among the other passengers with a smoothness hardly consistent even with the action of walking on a pavement; and no single creature, that I could see, gave them place, touched them, or looked after them. In passing before my windows, they both stared up at me. I saw their two faces very distinctly, and I knew that I could recognize them anywhere. Not that I had consciously noticed anything very remarkable in either face, except that the man who went first had an unusually lowering appearance, and that the face of the man who followed him was of the colour of impure wax.

I am a bachelor, and my valet and his wife constitute my whole establishment. My occupation is in a certain Branch Bank, and I wish that my duties as head of a Department were as light as they are popularly supposed to be. They kept me in town that autumn, when I stood in need of change. I was not ill, but I was not well. My reader is to make the most that can be reasonably made of my feeling jaded, having a depressing sense upon me of a monotonous life, and being 'slightly dyspeptic.' I am assured by my renowned doctor that my real state of health at that time justifies no stronger description, and I quote his own from his written answer to my request for it.

As the circumstances of the murder, gradually unravelling, took stronger and stronger possession of the public mind, I kept them away from mine by knowing as little about them as was possible in the midst of the universal excitement. But I knew that a verdict of Wilful Murder had been found against the suspected murderer, and that he had been committed to Newgate for trial. I also knew that his trial had been postponed over one Sessions of the Central Criminal Court, on the ground of general prejudice and want of time for the preparation of the defence. I may further have known, but I believe I did not, when, or about when, the Sessions to which his trial stood postponed would come on.

My sitting-room, bedroom, and dressing-room, are all on one floor.

With the last there is no communication but through the bedroom. True, there is a door in it, once communicating with the staircase; but a part of the fitting of my bath has been—and had then been for some years—fixed across it. At the same period, and as a part of the same arrangement,—the door had been nailed up and canvased over.

I was standing in my bedroom late one night, giving some directions to my servant before he went to bed. My face was towards the only available door of communication with the dressing-room, and it was closed. My servant's back was towards that door. While I was speaking to him, I saw it open, and a man look in, who very earnestly and mysteriously beckoned to me. That man was the man who had gone second of the two along Piccadilly, and whose face was of the colour of impure wax.

The figure, having beckoned, drew back, and closed the door. With no longer pause than was made by my crossing the bedroom, I opened the dressing-room door, and looked in. I had a lighted candle already in my hand. I felt no inward expectation of seeing the figure in the dressing-room, and I did not see it there.

Conscious that my servant stood amazed, I turned round to him, and said, 'Derrick, could you believe that in my cool senses I fancied I saw a—' As I there laid my hand upon his breast, with a sudden start he trembled violently, and said, 'O Lord, yes, sir! A dead man beckoning!'

Now I do not believe that this John Derrick, my trusty and attached servant for more than twenty years, had any impression whatever of having seen any such figure, until I touched him. The change in him was so startling, when I touched him, that I fully believe he derived his impression in some occult manner from me at that instant.

I bade John Derrick bring some brandy, and I gave him a dram, and was glad to take one myself. Of what had preceded that night's phenomenon, I told him not a single word. Reflecting on it, I was absolutely certain that I had never seen that face before, except on the one occasion in Piccadilly. Comparing its expression when beckoning at the door with its expression when it had stared up at me as I stood at my window, I came to the conclusion that on the first occasion it had sought to fasten itself upon my memory, and that on the second occasion it had made sure of being immediately remembered.

I was not very comfortable that night, though I felt a certainty, difficult to explain, that the figure would not return. At daylight I fell into a heavy sleep, from which I was awakened by John Derrick's coming to my bedside with a paper in his hand.

This paper, it appeared, had been the subject of an altercation at the door between its bearer and my servant. It was a summons to me to serve upon a Jury at the forthcoming Sessions of the Central Criminal Court at the Old Bailey. I had never before been summoned on such a Jury, as John Derrick well knew. He believed—I am not certain at this hour whether with reason or otherwise—that that class of Jurors were customarily chosen on a lower qualification than mine, and he had at first refused to accept the summons. The man who served it had taken the matter very coolly. He had said that my attendance or non-attendance was nothing to him; there the summons was; and I should deal with it at my own peril, and not at his.

For a day or two I was undecided whether to respond to this call, or take no notice of it. I was not conscious of the slightest mysterious bias, influence, or attraction, one way or other. Of that I am as strictly sure as of every other statement that I make here. Ultimately I decided, as a break in the monotony of my life, that I would go.

The appointed morning was a raw morning in the month of November. There was a dense brown fog in Piccadilly, and it became positively black and in the last degree oppressive east of Temple Bar. I found the passages and staircases of the Court-House flaringly lighted with gas, and the court itself similarly illuminated. I THINK that, until I was conducted by officers into the Old Court and saw its crowded state, I did not know that the murderer was to be tried that day. I THINK that, until I was so helped into the Old court with considerable difficulty, I did not know into which of the two Courts sitting my summons would take me. But this must not be received as a positive assertion, for I am not completely satisfied in my mind on either point.

I took my seat in the place appropriated to Jurors in waiting, and I looked about the court as well as I could through the cloud of fog and breath that was heavy in it. I noticed the black vapour hanging like a murky curtain outside the great windows, and I noticed the stifled sound of wheels on the straw or tan that was littered in the street; also, the hum of the people gathered there, which a shrill whistle, or a louder song or hail than the rest, occasionally pierced.

Soon afterwards the Judges, two in number, entered, and took their seats. The buzz in the court was awfully hushed. The direction was given to put the murderer to the bar. He appeared there. And in that same instant I recognized in him the first of the two men who had gone down Piccadilly.

If my name had been called then, I doubt if I could have answered to it audibly. But it was called about sixth or eighth in the panel, and I was by that time able to say, 'Here!' Now, observe. As I stepped into the box, the prisoner, who had been looking on attentively, but with no sign of concern, became violently agitated, and beckoned to his attorney. The prisoner's wish to challenge me was so manifest, that it occasioned a pause, during which the attorney, with his hand upon the dock, whispered with his client, and shook his head. I afterwards had it from that gentleman, that the prisoner's first affrighted words to him were, 'AT ALL HAZARDS, CHALLENGE THAT MAN!' But that, as he would give no reason for it, and admitted that he had not even known my name until he heard it called and I appeared, it was not done.

Both on the ground already explained, that I wish to avoid reviving the unwholesome memory of that murderer, and also because a detailed account of his long trial is by no means indispensable to my narrative, I shall confine myself closely to such incidents in the ten days and nights during which we, the jury, were kept together, as directly bear on my own curious personal experience. It is in that, and not in the murderer, that I seek to interest my reader. It is to that, and not to a page of the Newgate Calendar, that I beg attention.

I was chosen Foreman of the jury.

On the second morning of the trial, after evidence had been taken for two hours (I heard the church clocks strike), happening to cast my eyes over my brother jurymen, I found an inexplicable difficulty in counting them. I counted them several times, yet always with the same difficulty. In short, I made them one too many.

I touched the brother jurymen whose place was next me, and I whispered to him, 'Oblige me by counting us.' He looked surprised by the request, but turned his head and counted. 'Why,' says he, suddenly, 'we are Thirt-; but no, it's not possible. No. We are twelve.'

According to my counting that day, we were always right in detail, but in the gross we were always one too many. There was no appearance—no figure—to account for it; but I had now an inward foreshadowing of the figure that was surely coming.

The Jury were housed at the London Tavern. We all slept in one large room on separate tables, and we were constantly in the charge and under the eye of the officer sworn to hold us in safe-keeping. I see no reason for suppressing the real name of that officer. He was intelligent, highly polite, and obliging, and (I was glad to hear) much respected in the city. He had an agreeable presence, good eyes, enviable black whiskers, and a fine sonorous voice. His name was Mr Harker.

When we turned into our twelve beds at night, Mr Harker's bed was drawn across the door. On the night of the second day, not being disposed to lie down, and seeing Mr Harker sitting on his bed, I went and sat beside him, and offered him a pinch of snuff. As Mr Harker's hand touched mine in taking it from my box, a peculiar shiver crossed him, and he said, 'Who is this?'

Following Mr Harker's eyes, and looking along the room, I saw again the figure I expected,—the second of the two men who had gone down Piccadilly. I rose, and advanced a few steps; then stopped, and looked round at Mr Harker. He was quite unconcerned, laughed, and said in a pleasant way, 'I thought for a moment we had a thirteenth juryman, without a bed. But I see it is the moonlight.'

Making no revelation to Mr Harker, but inviting him to take a walk with me to the end of the room, I watched what the figure did. It stood for a few moments by the bedside of each of my eleven brother jurymen, close to the pillow. It always went to the right-hand side of the bed, and always passed out crossing the foot of the next bed. It seemed, from the action of the head, merely to look down pensively at each recumbent figure. It took no notice of me, or of my bed, which was that nearest to Mr Harker's. It seemed to go out where the moonlight came in, through a high window, as by an aerial flight of stairs.

Next morning at breakfast, it appeared that everybody present had dreamed of the murdered man last night, except myself and Mr Harker.

I now felt as convinced that the second man who had gone down

Piccadilly was the murdered man (so to speak), as if it had been borne into my comprehension by his immediate testimony. But even this took place, and in a manner for which I was not at all prepared.

On the fifth day of the trial, when the case for the prosecution was drawing to a close, a miniature of the murdered man, missing from his bedroom upon the discovery of the deed, and afterwards found in a hiding-place where the murderer had been seen digging, was put in evidence. Having been identified by the witness under examination, it was handed up to the Bench, and thence handed down to be inspected by the jury.

As an officer in a black gown was making his way with it across to me, the figure of the second man who had gone down Piccadilly impetuously started from the crowd, caught the miniature from the officer, and gave it to me with his own hands, at the same time saying, in a low and hollow tone,—before I saw the miniature, which was in a locket,—'I WAS YOUNGER THEN, AND MY FACE WAS NOT THEN DRAINED OF BLOOD.' It also came between me and the brother juryman to whom I would have given the miniature, and between him and the brother juryman to whom he would have given it, and so passed it on through the whole of our number, and back into my possession. Not one of them, however, detected this.

At table, and generally when we were shut up together in Mr Harker's custody, we had from the first naturally discussed the day's proceedings a good deal. On that fifth day, the case for the prosecution being closed, and we having that side of the question in a completed shape before us, our discussion was more animated and serious. Among our number was a vestryman,—the densest idiot I have ever seen at large,—who met the plainest evidence with the most preposterous objections, and who was sided with by two flabby parochial parasites; all the three impanelled from a district so delivered over to fever that they ought to have been upon their own trial for five hundred murders. When these mischievous blockheads were at their loudest, which was towards midnight, while some of us were already preparing for bed, I again saw the murdered man. He stood grimly behind them, beckoning to me. On my going towards them, and striking into the conversation, he immediately retired. This was the beginning of a separate series of appearances, confined to that long room in which we were confined. Whenever a knot of my brother jurymen laid their heads together, I saw the head of the murdered man among theirs. Whenever their comparison of notes was going against him, he would solemnly and irresistibly beckon to me.

It will be borne in mind that down to the production of the miniature, on the fifth day of the trial, I had never seen the Appearance in court. Three changes occurred now that we entered on the case for the defence. Two of them I will mention together, first. The figure was now in court continually, and it never there addressed itself to me, but always to the person who was speaking at the time. For instance: the throat of the murdered man had been cut straight across. In the opening speech for the defence, it was suggested that the deceased might have cut his own throat. At that very moment, the figure, with its throat in the dreadful condition referred to (this it had concealed before), stood at the speaker's elbow, motioning across and across its windpipe, now with the right hand, now with the left, vigorously suggesting to the speaker himself the impossibility of such a wound having been self-inflicted by either hand. For another instance: a witness to character, a woman, deposed to the prisoner's being the most amiable of mankind. The figure at that instant stood on the floor before her, looking her full in the face, and pointing out the prisoner's evil countenance with an extended arm and an outstretched finger.

The third change now to be added impressed me strongly as the most marked and striking of all. I do not theorize upon it; I accurately state it, and there leave it.

Although the Appearance was not itself perceived by those whom it addressed, its coming close to such persons was invariably attended by some trepidation or disturbance on their part. It seemed to me as if it were prevented, by laws to which I was not amenable, from fully revealing itself to others, and yet as if it could invisibly, dumbly, and darkly overshadow their minds. When the leading counsel for the defence suggested that hypothesis of suicide, and the figure stood at the learned gentleman's elbow, frightfully sawing at its severed throat, it is undeniable that the counsel faltered in his speech, lost for a few seconds the thread of his ingenious discourse, wiped his forehead with his handkerchief, and turned extremely pale. When the witness to character was confronted by the Appearance, her eyes most certainly did follow the direction of its pointed finger, and rest in great hesitation and trouble upon the prisoner's face. Two additional illustrations will suffice. On the eighth day of the trial, after the pause which was every day made early in the afternoon for a few minutes' rest and refreshment, I came back into court with the rest of the jury some little time before the return of the Judges. Standing up in the box and looking about me, I thought the figure was not there, until, chancing to raise my eyes to the gallery, I saw it bending forward, and leaning over a very decent woman, as if to assure itself whether the Judges had resumed their seats or not. Immediately afterwards that woman screamed, fainted, and was carried out. So with the venerable, sagacious, and patient Judge who conducted the trial. When the case was over, and he settled himself and his papers to sum up, the murdered man, entering by the Judges' door, advanced to his Lordship's desk, and looked eagerly over his shoulder at the pages of his notes which he was turning. A change came over his Lordship's face; his hand stopped; the peculiar shiver, that I knew so well, passed over him; he faltered, 'Excuse me, gentlemen, for a few moments. I am somewhat oppressed by the vitiated air;' and did not recover until he had drunk a glass of water.

Through all the monotony of six of those interminable ten days,—the same Judges and others on the bench, the same murderer in the dock, the same lawyers at the table, the same tones of question and answer rising to the roof of the court, the same scratching of the Judge's pen, the same ushers going in and out, the same lights kindled at the same hour when there had been any natural light of day, the same foggy curtain outside the great windows when it was foggy, the same rain pattering and dripping when it was rainy, the same footmarks of turnkeys and prisoner day after day on the same sawdust, the same keys locking and unlocking the same heavy doors,—through all the wearisome monotony which made me feel as if I had been Foreman of the Jury for a vast cried of time, and Piccadilly had flourished coevally with Babylon, the murdered man never lost one trace of his distinctness in my eyes, nor was he at any moment less distinct than anybody else. I must not omit, as a matter of fact, that I never once saw the Appearance which I call by the name of the murdered man look at the murderer. Again and again I wondered, 'Why does he not?' But he never did.

Nor did he look at me, after the production of the miniature, until the last closing minutes of the trial arrived.

We retired to consider, at seven minutes before ten at night. The idiotic vestryman and his two parochial parasites gave us so much trouble that we twice returned into court to beg to have certain extracts from the Judge's notes re-read. Nine of us had not the smallest doubt about those passages, neither, I believe, had anyone in the Court; the dunder-headed triumvirate, having no idea but obstruction, disputed them for that very reason. At length we prevailed, and finally the jury returned into court at ten minutes past twelve.

The murdered man at that time stood directly opposite the Jury-box, on the other side of the Court. As I took my place, his eyes rested on me with great attention; he seemed satisfied, and slowly shook a great grey veil, which he carried on his arm for the first time, over his head and whole form. As I gave in our verdict, 'Guilty,' the veil collapsed, all was gone, and his place was empty.

The murderer, being asked by the Judge, according to usage, whether he had anything to say before sentence of death should be passed upon him, indistinctly muttered something which was described in the leading newspapers of the following day as 'a few rambling, incoherent, and half-audible words, in which he was understood to complain that he had not had a fair trial, because the Foreman of the Jury was prepossessed against him.' The remarkable declaration that he really made was this: 'MY LORD, I KNEW I WAS A DOOMED MAN, WHEN THE FOREMAN OF MY JURY CAME INTO THE BOX. MY LORD, I KNEW HE WOULD NEVER LET ME OFF, BECAUSE, BEFORE I WAS TAKEN, HE SOMEHOW GOT TO MY BEDSIDE IN THE NIGHT, WOKE ME, AND PUT A ROPE ROUND MY NECK.'

THE LETTERS

THE LETTERS OF CHARLES DICKENS

1833 OR 1834, AND 1835, 1836

NARRATIVE

We have been able to procure so few early letters of any general interest that we put these first years together. Charles Dickens was then living, as a bachelor, in Furnival's Inn, and was engaged as a parliamentary reporter on *The Morning Chronicle*. The 'Sketches by Boz' were written during these years, published first in 'The Monthly Magazine' and continued in *The Evening Chronicle*. He was engaged to be married to Catherine Hogarth in 1835—the marriage took place on 2 April 1836; and he continued to live in Furnival's Inn with his wife for more than a year after their marriage. They passed the summer months of that year in a lodging at Chalk, near Gravesend, in the neighbourhood associated with all his life, from his childhood to his death. The two letters which we publish, addressed to his wife as Miss Hogarth, have no date, but were written in 1835. The first of the two refers to the offer made to him by Chapman and Hall to edit a monthly periodical, the emolument (which he calls 'too tempting to resist!') to be fourteen pounds a month. The bargain was concluded, and this was the starting of *The Pickwick Papers*. The first number was published in March 1836. The second letter to Miss Hogarth was written after he had completed three numbers of 'Pickwick,' and the character who is to 'make a decided hit' is 'Jingle.'

The first letter of this book is addressed to Henry Austin, a friend from his boyhood, who afterwards married his second sister Letitia. It bears no date, but must have been written in 1833 or 1834, during the early days of his reporting for *The Morning Chronicle*; the journey on which he was 'ordered' being for that paper.

MR HENRY AUSTIN

Furnivall's Inn, *Wednesday Night, past 12*

Dear Henry,

I have just been ordered on a journey, the length of which is at present uncertain. I may be back on Sunday very probably, and start again on the following day. Should this be the case, you shall hear from me before.

Don't laugh. I am going (alone) in a gig; and, to quote the eloquent inducement which the proprietors of Hampstead *chays* hold out to Sunday riders—'the gen'l'm'n drives himself.' I am going into Essex and Suffolk. It strikes me I shall be spilt before I pay a turnpike. I have a presentiment I shall run over an only child before I reach Chelmsford, my first stage.

Let the evident haste of this specimen of 'The Polite Letter Writer' be its excuse, and

Believe me, dear Henry, most sincerely yours,

Note: To avoid the monotony of a constant repetition, we propose to dispense with the signature at the close of each letter, excepting to the first and last letters of our collection. Charles Dickens's handwriting altered so much during these years of his life, that we have thought it advisable to give a facsimile of his autograph to this our first letter; and we reproduce in the same way his latest autograph.

MISS HOGARTH

Furnival's Inn, *Wednesday Evening, 1835*

My dearest Kate,

The House is up; but I am very sorry to say that I must stay at home. I have had a visit from the publishers this morning, and the story cannot be any longer delayed; it must be done tomorrow, as there are more important considerations than the mere payment for the story involved too. I must exercise a little self-denial, and set to work.

They (Chapman and Hall) have made me an offer of fourteen pounds a month, to write and edit a new publication they contemplate, entirely by myself, to be published monthly, and each number to contain four woodcuts. I am to make my estimate and calculation, and to give them a decisive answer on Friday morning. The work will be no joke, but the emolument is too tempting to resist.

THE SAME

Sunday Evening

I have at this moment got Pickwick and his friends on the Rochester coach, and they are going on swimmingly, in company with a very different character from any I have yet described, who I flatter myself will make a decided hit. I want to get them from the ball to the inn before I go to bed; and I think that will take me until one or two o'clock at the earliest. The publishers will be here in the morning, so you will readily suppose I have no alternative but to stick at my desk.

1837

NARRATIVE

From the commencement of *The Pickwick Papers*, and of Charles Dickens's married life, dates the commencement of his literary life and his sudden world-wide fame. And this year saw the beginning of many of those friendships which he most valued, and of which he had most reason to be proud, and which friendships were ended only by death.

The first letters which we have been able to procure to Mr Macready and Mr Harley will be found under this date. In January 1837, he was living in Furnival's Inn, where his first child, a son, was born. It was an eventful year to him in many ways. He removed from Furnival's Inn to Doughty Street in March, and here he sustained the first great grief of his life. His young sister-in-law, Mary Hogarth, to whom he was devotedly attached, died very suddenly, at his house, on 7 May. In the autumn of this year he took lodgings at Broadstairs. This was his first visit to that pleasant little watering-place, of which he became very fond, and whither he removed for the autumn months with all his household, for many years in succession.

Besides the monthly numbers of 'Pickwick,' which were going on through this year until November, when the last number appeared, he had commenced *Oliver Twist*, which was appearing also monthly, in the magazine called 'Bentley's Miscellany,' long before *Pickwick* was completed. And during this year he had edited, for Mr Bentley, 'The Life of Grimaldi,' the celebrated clown. To this book he wrote himself only the preface, and altered and rearranged the autobiographical MS. which was in Mr Bentley's possession.

The letter to Mr Harley, which bears no date, but must have been written either in 1836 or 1837, refers to a farce called *The Strange Gentleman* (founded on one of the 'Sketches,' called the 'Great Winglebury Duel'), which he wrote expressly for Mr Harley, and which was produced at the St. James's Theatre, under the management of Mr Braham. The only other piece which he wrote for that theatre was the story of an operetta, called *The Village Coquettes*, the music of which was composed by Mr John Hullah.

MR J.P. HARLEY

48, Doughty Street, *Saturday Morning*

My Dear Sir,

I have considered the terms on which I could afford just now to sell Mr Braham the acting copyright in London of an entirely new piece for the St. James's Theatre; and I could not sit down to write one in a single act of about one hour long, under a hundred pounds. For a new piece in two acts, a hundred and fifty pounds would be the sum I should require.

I do not know whether, with reference to arrangements that were made with any other writers, this may or may not appear a large item. I state it merely with regard to the value of my own time and writings at this moment; and in so doing I assure you I place the remuneration below the mark rather than above it.

As you begged me to give you my reply upon this point, perhaps you will lay it before Mr Braham. If these terms exceed his inclination or the ability of the theatre, there is an end of the matter, and no harm done.

Believe me ever faithfully yours

MR W.C. MACREADY

48, Doughty Street, *Wednesday Evening*

My Dear Sir,

There is a semi-business, semi-pleasure little dinner which I intend to give at The Prince of Wales, in Leicester Place, Leicester Square, on Saturday, at five for half-past precisely, at which only Talfourd, Forster, Ainsworth, Jerdan, and the publishers will be present. It is to celebrate (that is too great a word, but I can think of no better) the conclusion of my *Pickwick* labours; and so I intend, before you take that roll upon the grass you spoke of, to beg your acceptance of one of the first complete copies of the work. I shall be much delighted if you would join us.

I know too well the many anxieties that press upon you just now to seek to persuade you to come if you would prefer a night's repose and quiet. Let me assure you, notwithstanding, most honestly and heartily that there is no one I should be more happy or gratified to see, and that among your brilliant circle of well-wishers and admirers you number none more unaffectedly and faithfully yours than,

My dear Sir, yours most truly

1838

NARRATIVE

In February of this year Charles Dickens made an expedition with his friend, and the illustrator of most of his books, Mr Hablot K. Browne ('Phiz'), to investigate for himself the real facts as to the condition of the Yorkshire schools, and it may be observed that portions of a letter to his wife, dated Greta Bridge, Yorkshire, which will be found among the following letters, were reproduced in *Nicholas Nickleby*. In the early summer he had a cottage at Twickenham Park. In August and September he was again at Broadstairs; and in the late autumn he made another bachelor excursion—Mr Browne being again his companion—in England, which included his first visit to Stratford-on-Avon and Kenilworth. In February appeared the first number of *Nicholas Nickleby*, on which work he was engaged all through the year, writing each number ready for the following month, and never being in advance, as was his habit with all his other periodical works, until his very latest ones.

The first letter which appears under this date, from Twickenham Park, is addressed to Mr Thomas Mitton, a schoolfellow at one of his earliest schools, and afterwards for some years his solicitor. The letter contains instructions for his first will; the friend of almost his whole life, Mr John Forster, being appointed executor to this will as he was to the last, to which he was 'called upon to act' only three years before his own death.

The letter which we give in this year to Mr Justice Talfourd is, unfortunately, the only one we have been able to procure to that friend, who was, however, one with whom he was most intimately associated, and with whom he maintained a constant correspondence.

The letter beginning 'Respected Sir' was an answer to a little boy (Master Hastings Hughes), who had written to him as *Nicholas Nickleby* approached completion, stating his views and wishes as to the rewards and punishments to be bestowed on the various characters in the book. The letter was sent to him through the Rev. Thomas Barham, author of *The Ingoldsby Legends*.

The two letters to Mr Macready, at the end of this year, refer to a farce which Charles Dickens wrote, with an idea that it might be suitable for Covent Garden Theatre, then under Mr Macready's management.

MRS CHARLES DICKENS

Greta Bridge, *Thursday, 1 Feb. 1838*

My dearest Kate,

I am afraid you will receive this later than I could wish, as the mail does not come through this place until two o'clock tomorrow morning. However, I have availed myself of the very first opportunity of writing, so the fault is that mail's, and not this.

We reached Grantham between nine and ten on Thursday night, and found everything prepared for our reception in the very best inn I have ever put up at. It is odd enough that an old lady, who had been outside all day and came in towards dinner time, turned out to be the mistress of a Yorkshire school returning from the holiday stay in London. She was a very queer old lady, and showed us a long letter she was carrying to one of the boys from his father, containing a severe lecture (enforced and aided by many texts of Scripture) on his refusing to eat boiled meat. She was very communicative, drank a great deal of brandy and water, and towards evening became insensible, in which state we left her.

Yesterday we were up again shortly after seven a.m., came on upon our journey by the Glasgow mail, which charged us the remarkably low sum of six pounds fare for two places inside. We had a very droll male companion until seven o'clock in the evening, and a most delicious lady's-maid for twenty miles, who implored us to keep a sharp look-out at the coach-windows, as she expected the carriage was coming to meet her and she was afraid of missing it. We had many delightful vauntings of the same kind; but in the end it is scarcely necessary to say that the coach did not come, but a very dirty girl did.

As we came further north the mire grew deeper. About eight o'clock it began to fall heavily, and, as we crossed the wild heaths hereabout, there was no vestige of a track. The mail kept on well, however, and at eleven we reached a bare place with a house standing alone in the midst of a dreary moor, which the guard informed us was Greta Bridge. I was in a perfect agony of apprehension, for it was fearfully cold, and there were no outward signs of anybody being up in the house. But to our great joy we discovered a comfortable room, with drawn curtains and a most blazing fire. In half an hour they gave us a smoking supper and a bottle of mulled port (in which we drank your health), and then we retired to a couple of capital bedrooms, in each of which there was a rousing fire halfway up the chimney.

We have had for breakfast, toast, cakes, a Yorkshire pie, a piece of beef about the size and much the shape of my portmanteau, tea, coffee, ham, and eggs; and are now going to look about us. Having finished our discoveries, we start in a postchaise for Barnard Castle, which is only four miles off, and there I deliver the letter given me by Mitton's friend. All the schools are round about that place, and a dozen old abbeys besides, which we shall visit by some means or other tomorrow. We shall reach York on Saturday I hope, and (God willing) I trust I shall be at home on Wednesday morning.

I wish you would call on Mrs Bentley and thank her for the letter; you can tell her when I expect to be in York.

A thousand loves and kisses to the darling boy, whom I see in my mind's eye crawling about the floor of this Yorkshire inn. Bless his heart, I would give two sovereigns for a kiss. Remember me too to Frederick, who I hope is attentive to you.

Is it not extraordinary that the same dreams which have constantly visited me since poor Mary died follow me everywhere? After all the change of scene and fatigue, I have dreamt of her ever since I left home, and no doubt shall till I return. I should be sorry to lose such visions, for they are very happy ones, if it be only the seeing her in one's sleep. I would fain believe, too, sometimes, that her spirit may have some influence over them, but their perpetual repetition is extraordinary.

Love to all friends.

> Ever, my dear Kate,
> Your affectionate Husband

MR THOMAS MITTON

> Twickenham Park, *Tuesday Night*

Dear Tom,

I sat down this morning and put on paper my testamentary meaning. Whether it is sufficiently legal or not is another question, but I hope it is. The rough draft of the clauses which I enclose will be preceded by as much of the fair copy as I send you, and followed by the usual clause about the receipts of the trustees being a sufficient discharge. I also wish to provide that if all our children should die before twenty-one, and Kate married again, half the surplus should go to her and half to my surviving brothers and sisters, share and share alike.

This will be all, except a few lines I wish to add which there will be no occasion to consult you about, as they will merely bear reference to a few tokens of remembrance and one or two slight funeral directions. And so pray God that you may be gray, and Forster bald, long before you are called upon to act as my executors.

I suppose I shall see you at the water-party on Thursday? We will then make an appointment for Saturday morning, and if you think my clauses will do, I will complete my copy, seal it up, and leave it in your hands. There are some other papers which you ought to have. We must get a box.

Ever yours

MR SERJEANT TALFOURD, M.P

Twickenham Park, *Sunday, 15 July 1838*

My dear Talfourd,

I cannot tell you how much pleasure I have derived from the receipt of your letter. I have heard little of you, and seen less, for so long a time, that your handwriting came like the renewal of some old friendship, and gladdened my eyes like the face of some old friend.

If I hear from Lady Holland before you return, I shall, as in duty bound, present myself at her bidding; but between you and me and the general post, I hope she may not renew her invitation until I can visit her with you, as I would much rather avail myself of your personal introduction. However, whatever her ladyship may do I shall respond to, and anyway shall be only too happy to avail myself of what I am sure cannot fail to form a very pleasant and delightful introduction.

Your kind invitation and reminder of the subject of a pleasant conversation in one of our pleasant rides, has thrown a gloom over the brightness of Twickenham, for here I am chained. It is indispensably necessary that *Oliver Twist* should be published in three volumes, in September next. I have only just begun the last one, and, having the constant drawback of my monthly work, shall be sadly harassed to get it finished in time, especially as I have several very important scenes (important to the story I mean) yet to write. Nothing would give me so much pleasure as to be with you for a week or so. I can only imperfectly console myself with the hope that when you see 'Oliver' you will like the close of the book, and approve my self-denial in staying here to write it. I should like to know your address in Scotland when you leave town, so that I may send you the earliest copy if it be produced in the vacation, which I pray Heaven it may.

Meanwhile, believe that though my body is on the banks of the Thames, half my heart is going the Oxford circuit.

Mrs Dickens and Charley desire their best remembrances (the latter expresses some anxiety, not unmixed with apprehension, relative to the Copyright Bill, in which he conceives himself interested), with hearty wishes that you may have a fine autumn, which is all you want, being sure of all other means of enjoyment that a man can have.

I am, my dear Talfourd,
Ever faithfully yours

P.S.—I hope you are able to spare a moment now and then to glance at 'Nicholas Nickleby,' and that you have as yet found no reason to alter the opinion you formed on the appearance of the first number.

You know, I suppose, that they elected me at the Athenæum? Pray thank Mr Serjeant Storks for me.

MRS CHARLES DICKENS

Lion Hotel, Shrewsbury, *Thursday, 1 Nov. 1838*

My dearest Love,

I received your welcome letter on arriving here last night, and am rejoiced to hear that the dear children are so much better. I hope that in your next, or your next but one, I shall learn that they are quite well. A thousand kisses to them. I wish I could convey them myself.

We found a roaring fire, an elegant dinner, a snug room, and capital beds all ready for us at Leamington, after a very agreeable (but very cold) ride. We started in a postchaise next morning for Kenilworth, with which we were both enraptured, and where I really think we MUST have lodgings next summer, please God that we are in good health and all goes well. You cannot conceive how delightful it is. To read among the ruins in fine weather would be perfect luxury. From here we went on to Warwick Castle, which is an ancient building, newly restored, and possessing no very great attraction beyond a fine view and some beautiful pictures; and thence to Stratford-upon-Avon, where we sat down in the room where Shakespeare was born, and left our autographs and read those of other people and so forth.

We remained at Stratford all night, and found to our unspeakable dismay that father's plan of proceeding by Bridgenorth was impracticable, as there were no coaches. So we were compelled to come here by way of Birmingham and Wolverhampton, starting at eight o'clock through a cold wet fog, and travelling, when the day had cleared up, through miles of cinder-paths and blazing furnaces, and roaring steam-engines, and such a mass of dirt, gloom, and misery as I never before witnessed. We got pretty well accommodated here when we arrived at half-past four, and are now going off in a postchaise to Llangollen—thirty miles—where we shall remain to-night, and where the Bangor mail will take us up tomorrow. Such are our movements up to this point, and when I have received your letter at Chester I shall write to you again and tell you when I shall be back. I can say positively that I shall not exceed the fortnight, and I think it very possible that I may return a day or two before it expires.

We were at the play last night. It was a bespeak—'The Love Chase,' a ballet (with a phenomenon!), divers songs, and 'A Roland for an Oliver.' It is a good theatre, but the actors are very funny. Browne laughed with such indecent heartiness at one point of the entertainment, that an old gentleman in the next box suffered the most violent indignation. The bespeak party occupied two boxes, the ladies were full-dressed, and the gentlemen, to a man, in white gloves with flowers in their button-holes. It amused us mightily, and was really as like the Miss Snevellicci business as it could well be.

My side has been very bad since I left home, although I have been very careful not to drink much, remaining to the full as abstemious as usual, and have not eaten any great quantity, having no appetite. I suffered such an ecstasy of pain all night at Stratford that I was half dead yesterday, and was obliged last night to take a dose of henbane. The effect was most delicious. I slept soundly, and without feeling the least uneasiness, and am a great deal better this morning; neither do I find that the henbane has affected my head, which, from the great effect it had upon me—exhilarating me to the most extraordinary degree, and yet keeping me sleepy—I feared it would. If I had not got better I should have turned back to Birmingham, and come straight home by the railroad. As it is, I hope I shall make out the trip.

God bless you, my darling. I long to be back with you again and to see the sweet Babs.

Your faithful and most affectionate Husband

MASTER HASTINGS HUGHES

Doughty Street, London, 12 *Dec. 1838*

Respected Sir,

I have given Squeers one cut on the neck and two on the head, at which he appeared much surprised and began to cry, which, being a cowardly thing, is just what I should have expected from him—wouldn't you?

I have carefully done what you told me in your letter about the lamb and the two 'sheeps' for the little boys. They have also had some good ale and porter, and some wine. I am sorry you didn't say *what* wine you would like them to have. I gave them some sherry, which they liked very much, except one boy, who was a little sick and choked a good deal. He was rather greedy, and that's the truth, and I believe it went the wrong way, which I say served him right, and I hope you will say so too.

Nicholas had his roast lamb, as you said he was to, but he could not eat it all, and says if you do not mind his doing so he should like to have the rest hashed tomorrow with some greens, which he is very fond of, and so am I. He said he did not like to have his porter hot, for he thought it spoilt the flavour, so I let him have it cold. You should have seen him drink it. I thought he never would have left off. I also gave him three pounds of money, all in sixpences, to make it seem more, and he said directly that he should give more than half to his mamma and sister, and divide the rest with poor Smike. And I say he is a good fellow for saying so; and if anybody says he isn't I am ready to fight him whenever they like—there!

Fanny Squeers shall be attended to, depend upon it. Your drawing of her is very like, except that I don't think the hair is quite curly enough. The nose is particularly like hers, and so are the legs. She is a nasty disagreeable thing, and I know it will make her very cross when she sees it; and what I say is that I hope it may. You will say the same I know—at least I think you will.

I meant to have written you a long letter, but I cannot write very fast when I like the person I am writing to, because that makes me think about them, and I like you, and so I tell you. Besides, it is just eight o'clock at night, and I always go to bed at eight o'clock, except when it is my birthday, and then I sit up to supper. So I will not say anything more besides this—and that is my love to you and Neptune; and if you will drink my health every Christmas Day I will drink yours—come.

I am,
Respected Sir,
Your affectionate Friend.

P.S.—I don't write my name very plain, but you know what it is you know, so never mind.

MR W. C. MACREADY

Doughty Street, Monday Morning

My dear Macready,

I have not seen you for the past week, because I hoped when we next met to bring 'The Lamplighter' in my hand. It would have been finished by this time, but I found myself compelled to set to work first at the *Nickleby* on which I am at present engaged, and which I regret to say—after my close and arduous application last month—I find I cannot write as quickly as usual. I must finish it, at latest, by the 24th (a doubtful comfort!), and the instant I have done so I will apply myself to the farce. I am afraid to name any particular day, but I pledge myself that you shall have it this month, and you may calculate on that promise. I send you with this a copy of a farce I wrote for Harley when he left Drury Lane, and in which he acted for some seventy nights. It is the best thing he does. It is barely possible you might like to try it. Any local or temporary allusions could be easily altered.

Believe me that I only feel gratified and flattered by your inquiry after the farce, and that if I had as much time as I have inclination, I would write on and on and on, farce after farce and comedy after comedy, until I wrote you something that would run. You do me justice when you give me credit for good intentions; but the extent of my good-will and strong and warm interest in you personally and your great undertaking, you cannot fathom nor express.

> Believe me, my dear Macready,
> Ever faithfully yours.

P.S.—For Heaven's sake don't fancy that I hold 'The Strange Gentleman' in any estimation, or have a wish upon the subject.

MR W. C MACREADY

> 48, Doughty Street, 13 *Dec. 1838*

My dear Macready,

I can have but one opinion on the subject—withdraw the farce at once, by all means.

I perfectly concur in all you say, and thank you most heartily and cordially for your kind and manly conduct, which is only what I should have expected from you; though, under such circumstances, I sincerely believe there are few but you—if any—who would have adopted it.

Believe me that I have no other feeling of disappointment connected with this matter but that arising from the not having been able to be of some use to you. And trust me that, if the opportunity should ever arrive, my ardour will only be increased—not damped—by the result of this experiment.

> Believe me always, my dear Macready,
> Faithfully yours

1839

NARRATIVE

Charles Dickens was still living in Doughty Street, but he removed at the end of this year to 1, Devonshire Terrace, Regent's Park. He hired a cottage at Petersham for the summer months, and in the autumn took lodgings at Broadstairs.

The cottage at Alphington, near Exeter, mentioned in the letter to Mr Mitton, was hired by Charles Dickens for his parents.

He was at work all through this year on *Nicholas Nickleby*.

We have now the commencement of his correspondence with Mr George Cattermole. His first letter was written immediately after Mr Cattermole's marriage with Miss Elderton, a distant connection of Charles Dickens; hence the allusions to 'cousin,' which will be found in many of his letters to Mr Cattermole. The bride and bridegroom were passing their honeymoon in the neighbourhood of Petersham, and the letter refers to a request from them for the loan of some books, and also to his having lent them his pony carriage and groom, during their stay in this neighbourhood.

The first letter in this year to Mr Macready is in answer to one from him, announcing his retirement from the management of Covent Garden Theatre.

The portrait by Mr Maclise, mentioned to Mr Harley, was the, now, well-known one, which appeared as a frontispiece to *Nicholas Nickleby*.

MR W.C. MACREADY

Doughty Street, *Sunday*

My dear Macready,

I will have, if you please, three dozen of the extraordinary champagne; and I am much obliged to you for recollecting me.

I ought not to be sorry to hear of your abdication, but I am, notwithstanding, most heartily and sincerely sorry, for my own sake and the sake of thousands, who may now go and whistle for a theatre—at least, such a theatre as you gave them; and I do now in my heart believe that for a long and dreary time that exquisite delight has passed away. If I may jest with my misfortunes, and quote the Portsmouth critic of Mr Crummles's company, I say that: 'As an exquisite embodiment of the poet's visions and a realisation of human intellectuality, gilding with refulgent light our dreamy moments, and laying open a new and magic world before the mental eye, the drama is gone—perfectly gone.'

With the same perverse and unaccountable feeling which causes a heart-broken man at a dear friend's funeral to see something irresistibly comical in a red-nosed or one-eyed undertaker, I receive your communication with ghostly facetiousness; though on a moment's reflection I find better cause for consolation in the hope that, relieved from your most trying and painful duties, you will now have leisure to return to pursuits more congenial to your mind, and to move more easily and pleasantly among your friends. In the long catalogue of the latter, I believe that there is not one prouder of the name, or more grateful for the store of delightful recollections you have enabled him to heap up from boyhood, than.

My dear Macready,
Yours always faithfully

MR THOMAS MITTON

New London Inn, Exeter,
Wednesday Morning, 6 March 1839

Dear Tom,

Perhaps you have heard from Kate that I succeeded yesterday in the very first walk, and took a cottage at a place called Alphington, one mile from Exeter, which contains, on the ground-floor, a good parlour and kitchen, and above, a full-sized country drawing-room and three bedrooms; in the yard behind, coal-holes, fowl-houses, and meat-safes out of number; in the kitchen, a neat little range; in the other rooms, good stoves and cupboards; and all for twenty pounds a year, taxes included. There is a good garden at the side well stocked with cabbages, beans, onions, celery, and some flowers. The stock belonging to the landlady (who lives in the adjoining cottage), there was some question whether she was not entitled to half the produce, but I settled the point by paying five shillings, and becoming absolute master of the whole!

I do assure you that I am charmed with the place and the beauty of the country round about, though I have not seen it under very favourable circumstances, for it snowed when I was there this morning, and blew bitterly from the east yesterday. It is really delightful, and when the house is to rights and the furniture all in, I shall be quite sorry to leave it. I have had some few things second-hand, but I take it seventy pounds will be the mark, even taking this into consideration. I include in that estimate glass and crockery, garden tools, and such like little things. There is a spare bedroom of course. That I have furnished too.

I am on terms of the closest intimacy with Mrs Samuell, the landlady, and her brother and sister-in-law, who have a little farm hard by. They are capital specimens of country folks, and I really think the old woman herself will be a great comfort to my mother. Coals are dear just now—twenty-six shillings a ton. They found me a boy to go two miles out and back again to order some this morning. I was debating in my mind whether I should give him eighteenpence or two shillings, when his fee was announced—twopence!

The house is on the high road to Plymouth, and, though in the very heart of Devonshire, there is as much long-stage and posting life as you would find in Piccadilly. The situation is charming. Meadows in front, an orchard running parallel to the garden hedge, richly-wooded hills closing in the prospect behind, and, away to the left, before a splendid view of the hill on which Exeter is situated, the cathedral towers rising up into the sky in the most picturesque manner possible. I don't think I ever saw so cheerful or pleasant a spot. The drawing-room is nearly, if not quite, as large as the outer room of my old chambers in Furnival's Inn. The paint and paper are new, and the place clean as the utmost excess of snowy cleanliness can be.

You would laugh if you could see me powdering away with the upholsterer, and endeavouring to bring about all sorts of impracticable reductions and wonderful arrangements. He has by him two second-hand carpets; the important ceremony of trying the same comes off at three this afternoon. I am perpetually going backwards and forwards. It is two miles from here, so I have plenty of exercise, which so occupies me and prevents my being lonely that I stopped at home to read last night, and shall to-night, although the theatre is open. Charles Kean has been the star for the last two evenings. He was stopping in this house, and went away this morning. I have got his sitting-room now, which is smaller and more comfortable than the one I had before.

You will have heard perhaps that I wrote to my mother to come down tomorrow. There are so many things she can make comfortable at a much less expense than I could, that I thought it best. If I had not, I could not have returned on Monday, which I now hope to do, and to be in town at half-past eight.

Will you tell my father that if he could devise any means of bringing him down, I think it would be a great thing for him to have Dash, if it be only to keep down the trampers and beggars. The cheque I send you below.

MR GEORGE CATTERMOLE

Elm Cottage, Petersham, *Wednesday Morning*

My dear Cattermole,

Why is 'Peveril' lingering on my dusty shelves in town, while my fair cousin and your fair bride remains in blissful ignorance of his merits? There he is, I grieve to say, but there he shall not be long, for I shall be visiting my other home on Saturday morning, and will bring him bodily down and forward him the moment he arrives.

Not having many of my books here, I don't find any among them which I think more suitable to your purpose than a carpet-bagful sent herewith, containing the Italian and German novelists (convenient as being easily taken up and laid down again; and I suppose you won't read long at a sitting), Leigh Hunt's 'Indicator' and 'Companion' (which have the same merit), 'Hood's Own' (complete), 'A Legend of Montrose,' and 'Kenilworth,' which I have just been reading with greater delight than ever, and so I suppose everybody else must be equally interested in. I have Goldsmith, Swift, Fielding, Smollett, and the British Essayists 'handy;' and I need not say that you have them on hand too, if you like.

You know all I would say from my heart and soul on the auspicious event of yesterday; but you don't know what I could say about the delightful recollections I have of your 'good lady's' charming looks and bearing, upon which I discoursed most eloquently here last evening, and at considerable length. As I am crippled in this respect, however, by the suspicion that possibly she may be looking over your shoulder while you read this note (I would lay a moderate wager that you have looked round twice or thrice already), I shall content myself with saying that I am ever heartily, my dear Cattermole,

Hers and yours

P.S.—My man (who with his charge is your man while you stay here) waits to know if you have any orders for him.

MR J. P. HARLEY

Elm Cottage, Petersham, near Richmond,
28 *June 1839*

My dear Harley,

I have 'left my home,' and been here ever since the end of April, and shall remain here most probably until the end of September, which is the reason that we have been such strangers of late.

I am very sorry that I cannot dine with you on Sunday, but some people are coming here, and I cannot get away. Better luck next time, I hope.

I was on the point of writing to you when your note came, to ask you if you would come down here next Saturday—tomorrow week, I mean—and stop till Monday. I will either call for you at the theatre, at any time you name, or send for you, 'punctual,' and have you brought down. Can you come if it's fine? Say yes, like a good fellow as you are, and say it per post.

I have countermanded that face. Maclise has made another face of me, which all people say is astonishing. The engraving will be ready soon, and I would rather you had that, as I am sure you would if you had seen it.

In great haste to save the post, I am, my dear Harley,

Faithfully yours

MR WILLIAM LONGMAN

Doughty Street, *Monday Morning.*

My dear Sir,

On Friday I have a family dinner at home—uncles, aunts, brothers, sisters, cousins—an annual gathering.

By what fatality is it that you always ask me to dine on the wrong day?

While you are tracing this non-consequence to its cause, I wish you would tell Mr Sydney Smith that of all the men I ever heard of and never saw, I have the greatest curiosity to see and the greatest interest to know him.

Begging my best compliments at home,

I am, my dear Sir,
Faithfully yours

MR W. C. MACREADY

Petersham, 26 *July 1839*

My dear Macready,

Fix your visit for whenever you please. It can never give us anything but delight to see you, and it is better to look forward to such a pleasure than to look back upon it, as the last gratification is enjoyable all our lives, and the first for a few short stages in the journey.

I feel more true and cordial pleasure than I can express to you in the request you have made. Anything which can serve to commemorate our friendship and to keep the recollection of it alive among our children is, believe me, and ever will be, most deeply prized by me. I accept the office with hearty and fervent satisfaction; and, to render this pleasant bond between us the more complete, I must solicit you to become godfather to the last and final branch of a genteel small family of three which I am told may be looked for in that auspicious month when Lord Mayors are born and guys prevail. This I look upon as a bargain between us, and I have shaken hands with you in spirit upon it. Family topics remind me of Mr Kenwigs. As the weather is wet, and he is about to make his last appearance on my little stage, I send Mrs Macready an early proof of the next number, containing an account of his baby's progress.

I am going to send you something else on Monday—a tragedy. Don't be alarmed. I didn't write it, nor do I want it acted. A young Scotch lady whom I don't know (but she is evidently very intelligent and accomplished) has sent me a translation of a German play, soliciting my aid and advice in the matter of its publication. Among a crowd of Germanisms, there are many things in it which are so very striking, that I am sure it will amuse you very much. At least I think it will; it has me. I am going to send it back to her—when I come to Elstree will be time enough; and meantime, if you bestow a couple of hours upon it, you will not think them thrown away.

It's a large parcel, and I must keep it here till somebody goes up to town and can book it by the coach. I warrant it, large as it looks, readable in two hours; and I very much want to know what you think of the first act, and especially the opening, which seems to me quite famous. The metre is very odd and rough, but now and then there's a wildness in it which helps the thing very much; and altogether it has left a something on my mind which I can't get rid of.

Mrs Dickens joins with me in kindest regards to yourself, Mrs, and Miss Macready. And I am always,

My dear Macready,
Faithfully and truly yours

P.S.—A dreadful thought has just occurred to me—that this is a quadruple letter, and that Elstree may not be within the twopenny post. Pray Heaven my fears are unfounded.

MR W. C. MACREADY

40, Albion Street, Broadstairs,
21 *September 1839*

My dear Macready,

I am so anxious to prefer a request to you which does not admit of delay that I send you a double letter, with the one redeeming point though of having very little in it.

Let me prefix to the last number of *Nickleby*, and to the book, a duplicate of the leaf which I now send you. Believe me that there will be no leaf in the volume which will afford me in times to come more true pleasure and gratification, than that in which I have written your name as foremost among those of the friends whom I love and honour. Believe me, there will be no one line in it conveying a more honest truth or a more sincere feeling than that which describes its dedication to you as a slight token of my admiration and regard.

So let me tell the world by this frail record that I was a friend of yours, and interested to no ordinary extent in your proceedings at that interesting time when you showed them such noble truths in such noble forms, and gave me a new interest in, and associations with, the labours of so many months.

I write to you very hastily and crudely, for I have been very hard at work, having only finished today, and my head spins yet. But you know what I mean. I am then always,

Believe me, my dear Macready,
Faithfully yours

P.S.—(Proof of Dedication enclosed): 'To W. C. Macready, Esq., the following pages are inscribed, as a slight token of admiration and regard, by his friend, the Author.'

MR W. C. MACREADY

Doughty Street, Friday Night, 25 Oct. 1839

My dear Macready,

The book, the whole book, and nothing but the book (except the binding, which is an important item), has arrived at last, and is forwarded herewith. The red represents my blushes at its gorgeous dress; the gilding, all those bright professions which I do not make to you; and the book itself, my whole heart for twenty months, which should be yours for so short a term, as you have it always.

With best regards to Mrs and Miss Macready, always believe me,

My dear Macready,
Your faithful Friend

THE SAME

Doughty Street, *Thursday, 14 Nov. 1839*

My dear Macready,

Tom Landseer—that is, the deaf one, whom everybody quite loves for his sweet nature under a most deplorable infirmity—Tom Landseer asked me if I would present to you from him the accompanying engraving, which he has executed from a picture by his brother Edwin; submitting it to you as a little tribute from an unknown but ardent admirer of your genius, which speaks to his heart, although it does not find its way there through his ears. I readily undertook the task, and send it herewith.

I urged him to call upon you with me and proffer it boldly; but he is a very modest and delicately-minded creature, and was shy of intruding. If you thank him through me, perhaps you will say something about my bringing him to call, and so gladden the gentle artist and make him happy.

You must come and see my new house when we have it to rights. By Christmas Day we shall be, I hope, your neighbours.

Kate progresses splendidly, and, with me, sends her best remembrances to Mrs Macready and all your house.

Ever believe me,
Dear Macready,
Faithfully yours

1840

NARRATIVE

Charles Dickens was at Broadstairs with his family for the autumn months. During all this year he was busily engaged with the periodical entitled *Master Humphrey's Clock*, in which the story of 'The Old Curiosity Shop' subsequently appeared. Nearly all these letters to Mr George Cattermole refer to the illustrations for this story.

The one dated 9 March alludes to short papers written for *Master Humphrey's Clock* prior to the commencement of 'The Old Curiosity Shop.'

We have in this year Charles Dickens's first letter to Mr Daniel Maclise, this and one other being, unfortunately, the only letters we have been able to obtain addressed to this much-loved friend and most intimate companion.

MR GEORGE CATTERMOLE

1, Devonshire Terrace,
Monday, 13 January 1840

My Dear Cattermole,

I am going to propound a mightily grave matter to you. My now periodical work appears—or I should rather say the first number does—on Saturday, the 28 March; and as it has to be sent to America and Germany, and must therefore be considerably in advance, it is now in hand; I having in fact begun it on Saturday last. Instead of being published in monthly parts at a shilling each only, it will be published in weekly parts at threepence and monthly parts at a shilling; my object being to baffle the imitators and make it as novel as possible. The plan is a new one—I mean the plan of the fiction—and it will comprehend a great variety of tales. The title is: 'Master Humphrey's Clock.'

Now, among other improvements, I have turned my attention to the illustrations, meaning to have woodcuts dropped into the text and no separate plates. I want to know whether you would object to make me a little sketch for a woodcut—in indian-ink would be quite sufficient—about the size of the enclosed scrap; the subject, an old quaint room with antique Elizabethan furniture, and in the chimney-corner an extraordinary old clock—the clock belonging to Master Humphrey, in fact, and no figures. This I should drop into the text at the head of my opening page.

I want to know besides—as Chapman and Hall are my partners in the matter, there need be no delicacy about my asking or your answering the question—what would be your charge for such a thing, and whether (if the work answers our expectations) you would like to repeat the joke at regular intervals, and, if so, on what terms? I should tell you that I intend to ask Maclise to join me likewise, and that the copying the drawing on wood and the cutting will be done in first-rate style. We are justified by past experience in supposing that the sale would be enormous, and the popularity very great; and when I explain to you the notes I have in my head, I think you will see that it opens a vast number of very good subjects.

I want to talk the matter over with you, and wish you would fix your own time and place—either here or at your house or at the Athenæum, though this would be the best place, because I have my papers about me. If you would take a chop with me, for instance, on Tuesday or Wednesday, I could tell you more in two minutes than in twenty letters, albeit I have endeavoured to make this as businesslike and stupid as need be.

Of course all these tremendous arrangements are as yet a profound secret, or there would be fifty Humphreys in the field. So write me a line like a worthy gentleman, and convey my best remembrances to your worthy lady.

Believe me always, my dear Cattermole,
Faithfully yours

MR GEORGE CATTERMOLE

Devonshire Terrace, *Tuesday Afternoon*

My dear Cattermole,

I think the drawing most famous, and so do the publishers, to whom I sent it today. If Browne should suggest anything for the future which may enable him to do you justice in copying (on which point he is very anxious), I will communicate it to you. It has occurred to me that perhaps you will like to see his copy on the block before it is cut, and I have therefore told Chapman and Hall to forward it to you.

In future, I will take care that you have the number to choose your subject from. I ought to have done so, perhaps, in this case; but I was very anxious that you should do the room.

Perhaps the shortest plan will be for me to send you, as enclosed, regularly; but if you prefer keeping account with the publishers, they will be happy to enter upon it when, where, and how you please.

Faithfully yours always

MR GEORGE CATTERMOLE

1, Devonshire Terrace,
Monday, 9 March 1840

My dear Cattermole,

I have been induced, on looking over the works of the 'Clock,' to make a slight alteration in their disposal, by virtue of which the story about 'John Podgers' will stand over for some little time, and that short tale will occupy its place which you have already by you, and which treats of the assassination of a young gentleman under circumstances of peculiar aggravation. I shall be greatly obliged to you if you will turn your attention to this last morsel as the feature of No. 3, and still more if you can stretch a point with regard to time (which is of the last importance just now), and make a subject out of it, rather than find one in it. I would neither have made this alteration nor have troubled you about it, but for weighty and cogent reasons which I feel very strongly, and into the composition of which caprice or fastidiousness has no part.

I should tell you perhaps, with reference to Chapman and Hall, that they will never trouble you (as they never trouble me) but when there is real and pressing occasion, and that their representations in this respect, unlike those of most men of business, are to be relied upon.

I cannot tell you how admirably I think Master Humphrey's room comes out, or what glowing accounts I hear of the second design you have done. I had not the faintest anticipation of anything so good—taking into account the material and the despatch.

With best regards at home,
Believe me, dear Cattermole,
Heartily yours.

P.S.—The new (No. 3) tale begins: 'I hold a lieutenant's commission in His Majesty's army, and served abroad in the campaigns of 1677 and 1678.' It has at present no title.

MR S.A. DIEZMAN

1, Devonshire Terrace, York Gate, Regent's Park,
London, *10 March 1840*

My dear Sir,

I will not attempt to tell you how much gratified I have been by the receipt of your first English letter; nor can I describe to you with what delight and gratification I learn that I am held in such high esteem by your great countrymen, whose favourable appreciation is flattering indeed.

To you, who have undertaken the labourious (and often, I fear, very irksome) task of clothing me in the German garb, I owe a long arrear of thanks. I wish you would come to England, and afford me an opportunity of slightly reducing the account.

It is with great regret that I have to inform you, in reply to the request contained in your pleasant communication, that my publishers have already made such arrangements and are in possession of such stipulations relative to the proof-sheets of my new works, that I have no power to send them out of England. If I had, I need not tell you what pleasure it would afford me to promote your views.

I am too sensible of the trouble you must have already had with my writings to impose upon you now a long letter. I will only add, therefore, that I am.

My dear Sir,
With great sincerity,
Faithfully yours

MR DANIEL MACLISE

Broadstairs, *2 June 1840*

My dear Maclise,

My foot is in the house,
My bath is on the sea,
And, before I take a souse,

Here's a single note to thee.

It merely says that the sea is in a state of extraordinary sublimity; that this place is, as the Guide Book most justly observes, 'unsurpassed for the salubrity of the refreshing breezes, which are wafted on the ocean's pinions from far-distant shores.' That we are all right after the perils and voyages of yesterday. That the sea is rolling away in front of the window at which I indite this epistle, and that everything is as fresh and glorious as fine weather and a splendid coast can make it. Bear these recommendations in mind, and shunning Talfourdian pledges, come to the bower which is shaded for you in the one-pair front, where no chair or table has four legs of the same length, and where no drawers will open till you have pulled the pegs off, and then they keep open and won't shut again.

COME!

I can no more.

Always faithfully yours

MR GEORGE CATTERMOLE

Devonshire Terrace, 21 December

My dear George,

Kit, the single gentleman, and Mr Garland go down to the place where the child is, and arrive there at night. There has been a fall of snow. Kit, leaving them behind, runs to the old house, and, with a lanthorn in one hand and the bird in its cage in the other, stops for a moment at a little distance with a natural hesitation before he goes up to make his presence known. In a window—supposed to be that of the child's little room—a light is burning, and in that room the child (unknown, of course, to her visitors, who are full of hope) lies dead.

If you have any difficulty about Kit, never mind about putting him in. The two others tomorrow.

Faithfully always

MR GEORGE CATTERMOLE

Devonshire Terrace, *Friday Morning*

My dear Cattermole,

I sent the MS. of the enclosed proof, marked 2, up to Chapman and Hall, from Devonshire, mentioning a subject of an old gateway, which I had put in expressly with a view to your illustrous pencil. By a mistake, however, it went to Browne instead. Chapman is out of town, and such things have gone wrong in consequence.

The subject to which I wish to call your attention is in an unwritten number to follow this one, but it is a mere echo of what you will find at the conclusion of this proof marked 2. I want the cart, gaily decorated, going through the street of the old town with the wax brigand displayed to fierce advantage, and the child seated in it also dispersing bills. As many flags and inscriptions about Jarley's Wax Work fluttering from the cart as you please. You know the wax brigands, and how they contemplate small oval miniatures? That's the figure I want. I send you the scrap of MS. which contains the subject.

Will you, when you have done this, send it with all speed to Chapman and Hall, as we are mortally pressed for time, and I must go hard to work to make up for what I have lost by being dutiful and going to see my father.

I want to see you about a frontispiece to our first 'Clock' volume, which will come out (I think) at the end of September, and about other matters. When shall we meet and where?

I say nothing about our cousin or the baby, for Kate bears this, and will make me a full report and convey all loves and congratulations.

Could you dine with us on Sunday, at six o'clock sharp? I'd come and fetch you in the morning, and we could take a ride and walk. We shall be quite alone, unless Macready comes. What say you?

Don't forget despatch, there's a dear fellow, and ever believe me,

Heartily yours

MR GEORGE CATTERMOLE

22 December 1840

Dear George,

The child lying dead in the little sleeping-room, which is behind the open screen. It is winter time, so there are no flowers; but upon her breast and pillow, and about her bed, there may be strips of holly and berries, and such free green things. Window overgrown with ivy. The little boy who had that talk with her about angels may be by the bedside, if you like it so; but I think it will be quieter and more peaceful if she is quite alone. I want it to express the most beautiful repose and tranquillity, and to have something of a happy look, if death can.

2.

The child has been buried inside the church, and the old man, who cannot be made to understand that she is dead, repairs to the grave and sits there all day long, waiting for her arrival, to begin another journey. His staff and knapsack, her little bonnet and basket, etc., lie beside him. 'She'll come tomorrow,' he says when it gets dark, and goes sorrowfully home. I think an hourglass running out would help the notion; perhaps her little tilings upon his knee, or in his hand.

I am breaking my heart over this story, and cannot bear to finish it. Love to Missis.

Ever and always heartily

1841

NARRATIVE

In the summer of this year Charles Dickens made, accompanied by Mrs Dickens, his first visit to Scotland, and was received in Edinburgh with the greatest enthusiasm.

He was at Broadstairs with his family for the autumn, and at the close of the year he went to Windsor for change of air after a serious illness.

On the 17 January 'The Old Curiosity Shop' was finished. In the following week the first number of his story of 'Barnaby Rudge' appeared, in *Master Humphrey's Clock*, and the last number of this story was written at Windsor, in November of this year.

We have the first letters to his dear and valued friends the Rev. William Harness and Mr Harrison Ainsworth. Also his first letter to Mr Monckton Milnes (now Lord Houghton).

Of the letter to Mr John Tomlin we would only remark, that it was published in an American magazine, edited by Mr E. A. Poe, in the year 1842.

'The New First Rate' (first letter to Mr Harrison Ainsworth) must, we think, be an allusion to the outside cover of 'Bentley's Miscellany,' which first appeared in this year, and of which Mr Ainsworth was editor.

The two letters to Mr Lovejoy are in answer to a requisition from the people of Reading that he would represent them in Parliament.

The letter to Mr George Cattermole (26 June) refers to a dinner given to Charles Dickens by the people of Edinburgh, on his first visit to that city.

The 'poor Overs,' mentioned in the letter to Mr Macready of 24 August, was a carpenter dying of consumption, to whom Dr Elliotson had shown extraordinary kindness. 'When poor Overs was dying' (wrote Charles Dickens to Mr Forster), 'he suddenly asked for a pen and ink and some paper, and made up a little parcel for me, which it was his last conscious act to direct. She (his wife) told me this, and gave it me. I opened it last night. It was a copy of his little book, in which he had written my name, 'with his devotion.' I thought it simple and affecting of the poor fellow.'

'The Saloon,' alluded to in our last letter of this year, was an institution at Drury Lane Theatre during Mr Macready's management. The original purpose for which this saloon was established having become perverted and degraded, Charles Dickens had it much at heart to remodel and improve it. Hence this letter to Mr Macready.

REV. WILLIAM HARNESS

Devonshire Terrace, *Saturday Morning, 2 Jan. 1841*

My dear Harness,

I should have been very glad to join your pleasant party, but all next week I shall be laid up with a broken heart, for I must occupy myself in finishing the 'Curiosity Shop,' and it is such a painful task to me that I must concentrate myself upon it tooth and nail, and go out nowhere until it is done.

I have delayed answering your kind note in a vague hope of being heart-whole again by the seventh. The present state of my work, however (Christmas not being a very favourable season for making progress in such doings), assures me that this cannot be, and that I must heroically deny myself the pleasure you offer.

Always believe me,
Faithfully yours

MR GEORGE CATTERMOLE

Devonshire Terrace, *Thursday, 14 Jan. 1841*

My dear Cattermole,

I cannot tell you how much obliged I am to you for altering the child, or how much I hope that my wish in that respect didn't go greatly against the grain.

I saw the old inn this morning. Words cannot say how good it is. I can't bear the thought of its being cut, and should like to frame and glaze it in *statu quo* for ever and ever.

Will you do a little tail-piece for the 'Curiosity' story?—only one figure if you like—giving some notion of the etherealized spirit of the child; something like those little figures in the frontispiece. If you will, and can despatch it at once, you will make me happy.

I am, for the time being, nearly dead with work and grief for the loss of my child.

Always, my dear George,
Heartily yours

THE SAME

Devonshire Terrace, *Thursday Night, 28 Jan. 1841*

My dear George,

I sent to Chapman and Hall yesterday morning about the second subject for No. 2 of 'Barnaby,' but found they had sent it to Browne.

The first subject of No. 3 I will either send to you on Saturday, or, at latest, on Sunday morning. I have also directed Chapman and Hall to send you proofs of what has gone before, for reference, if you need it.

I want to know whether you feel ravens in general and would fancy Barnaby's raven in particular. Barnaby being an idiot, my notion is to have him always in company with a pet raven, who is immeasurably more knowing than himself. To this end I have been studying my bird, and think I could make a very queer character of him. Should you like the subject when this raven makes his first appearance?

Faithfully always

MR GEORGE CATTERMOLE

Devonshire Terrace, *Saturday Evening, 30 Jan. 1841*

My dear George,

I send you the first four slips of No. 48, containing the description of the locksmith's house, which I think will make a good subject, and one you will like. If you put the ''prentice' in it, show nothing more than his paper cap, because he will be an important character in the story, and you will need to know more about him as he is minutely described. I may as well say that he is very short. Should you wish to put the locksmith in, you will find him described in No. 2 of 'Barnaby' (which I told Chapman and Hall to send you). Browne has done him in one little thing, but so very slightly that you will not require to see his sketch, I think.

Now, I must know what you think about the raven, my buck; I otherwise am in this fix. I have given Browne no subject for this number, and time is flying. If you would like to have the raven's first appearance, and don't object to having both subjects, so be it. I shall be delighted. If otherwise, I must feed that hero forthwith.

I cannot close this hasty note, my dear fellow, without saying that I have deeply felt your hearty and most invaluable co-operation in the beautiful illustrations you have made for the last story, that I look at them with a pleasure I cannot describe to you in words, and that it is impossible for me to say how sensible I am of your earnest and friendly aid. Believe me that this is the very first time any designs for what I have written have touched and moved me, and caused me to feel that they expressed the idea I had in my mind.

I am most sincerely and affectionately grateful to you, and am full of pleasure and delight.

Believe me, my dear Cattermole,
Always heartily yours

MR JOHN TOMLIN

1, Devonshire Terrace, York Gate, Regent's Park,
London, *Tuesday, 23 Feb. 1841*

Dear Sir,

You are quite right in feeling assured that I should answer the letter you have addressed to me. If you had entertained a presentiment that it would afford me sincere pleasure and delight to hear from a warm-hearted and admiring reader of my books in the backwoods of America, you would not have been far wrong.

I thank you cordially and heartily both for your letter and its kind and courteous terms. To think that I have awakened a fellow-feeling and sympathy with the creatures of many thoughtful hours among the vast solitudes in which you dwell, is a source of the purest delight and pride to me; and believe me that your expressions of affectionate remembrance and approval, sounding from the green forests on the banks of the Mississippi, sink deeper into my heart and gratify it more than all the honorary distinctions that all the courts in Europe could confer.

It is such things as these that make one hope one does not live in vain, and that are the highest reward of an author's life. To be numbered among the household gods of one's distant countrymen, and associated with their homes and quiet pleasures; to be told that in each nook and corner of the world's great mass there lives one well-wisher who holds communion with one in the spirit, is a worthy fame indeed, and one which I would not barter for a mine of wealth.

That I may be happy enough to cheer some of your leisure hours for a very long time to come, and to hold a place in your pleasant thoughts, is the earnest wish of 'Boz.'

And, with all good wishes for yourself, and with a sincere reciprocation of all your kindly feeling,

I am, dear Sir,
Faithfully yours

MR R. MONCKTON MILNES

Devonshire Terrace, *Wednesday, 10 March 1841*

My dear Milnes,

I thank you very much for the 'Nickleby' correspondence, which I will keep for a day or two, and return when I see you. Poor fellow! The long letter is quite admirable, and most affecting.

I am not quite sure either of Friday or Saturday, for, independently of the 'Clock' (which for ever wants winding), I am getting a young brother off to New Zealand just now, and have my mornings sadly cut up in consequence. But, knowing your ways, I know I may say that I will come if I can; and that if I can't I won't.

That Nellicide was the act of Heaven, as you may see any of these fine mornings when you look about you. If you knew the pain it gave me—but what am I talking of? if you don't know, nobody does. I am glad to shake you by the hand again autographically,

And am always,
Faithfully yours

MR GEORGE CATTERMOLE

Devonshire Terrace, *Tuesday, 9 February*

My dear George,

My notes tread upon each other's heels. In my last I quite forgot business.

Will you, for No. 49, do the locksmith's house, which was described in No. 48? I mean the outside. If you can, without hurting the effect, shut up the shop as though it were night, so much the better. Should you want a figure, an ancient watchman in or out of his box, very sleepy, will be just the thing for me.

I have written to Chapman and requested him to send you a block of a long shape, so that the house may come upright as it were.

Faithfully ever

THE SAME

Old Ship Hotel, Brighton, *26 Feb. 1841*

My dear Kittenmoles,

I passed your house on Wednesday, being then atop of the Brighton Era; but there was nobody at the door, saving a solitary poulterer, and all my warm-hearted aspirations lodged in the goods he was delivering. No doubt you observed a peculiar relish in your dinner. That was the cause.

I send you the MS. I fear you will have to read all the five slips; but the subject I think of is at the top of the last, when the guest, with his back towards the spectator, is looking out of window. I think, in your hands, it will be a very pretty one.

Then, my boy, when you have done it, turn your thoughts (as soon as other engagements will allow) first to the outside of The Warren—see No. 1; secondly, to the outside of the locksmith's house, by night—see No. 3. Put a penny pistol to Chapman's head and demand the blocks of him.

I have addled my head with writing all day, and have barely wit enough left to send my love to my cousin, and—there's a genealogical poser—what relation of mine may the dear little child be? At present, I desire to be commended to her clear blue eyes.

Always, my dear George,
Faithfully yours

MR WILLIAM HARRISON AINSWORTH

Devonshire Terrace, *29 April 1841*

My dear Ainsworth,

With all imaginable pleasure. I quite look forward to the day. It is an age since we met, and it ought not to be.

The artist has just sent home your 'Nickleby.' He suggested variety, pleading his fancy and genius. As an artful binder must have his way, I put the best face on the matter, and gave him his. I will bring it together with the 'Pickwick' to your house-warming with me.

The old *Royal George* went down in consequence of having too much weight on one side. I trust the new 'First Rate' won't be heavy anywhere. There seems to me to be too much whisker for a shilling, but that's a matter of taste.

Faithfully yours always

MR G. LOVEJOY

1, Devonshire Terrace, York Gate, Regent's Park,
Monday Evening, 31 May 1841

Sir,

I am much obliged and flattered by the receipt of your letter, which I should have answered immediately on its arrival but for my absence from home at the moment.

My principles and inclinations would lead me to aspire to the distinction you invite me to seek, if there were any reasonable chance of success, and I hope I should do no discredit to such an honour if I won and wore it. But I am bound to add, and I have no hesitation in saying plainly, that I cannot afford the expense of a contested election. If I could, I would act on your suggestion instantly. I am not the less indebted to you and the friends to whom the thought occurred, for your good opinion and approval. I beg you to understand that I am restrained solely (and much against my will) by the consideration I have mentioned, and thank both you and them most warmly.

Yours faithfully

THE SAME

Devonshire Terrace, *10 June 1841*

Dear Sir,

I am favoured with your note of yesterday's date, and lose no time in replying to it.

The sum you mention, though small I am aware in the abstract, is greater than I could afford for such a purpose; as the mere sitting in the House and attending to my duties, if I were a member, would oblige me to make many pecuniary sacrifices, consequent upon the very nature of my pursuits.

The course you suggest did occur to me when I received your first letter, and I have very little doubt indeed that the Government would support me—perhaps to the whole extent. But I cannot satisfy myself that to enter Parliament under such circumstances would enable me to pursue that honourable independence without which I could neither preserve my own respect nor that of my constituents. I confess therefore (it may be from not having considered the points sufficiently, or in the right light) that I cannot bring myself to propound the subject to any member of the administration whom I know. I am truly obliged to you nevertheless, and am,

Dear Sir,
Faithfully yours

MR GEORGE CATTERMOLE

Devonshire Terrace, *Wednesday Evening, 28 July 1841*

My dear George,

Can you do for me by Saturday evening—I know the time is short, but I think the subject will suit you, and I am greatly pressed—a party of rioters (with Hugh and Simon Tappertit conspicuous among them) in old John Willet's bar, turning the liquor taps to their own advantage, smashing bottles, cutting down the grove of lemons, sitting astride on casks, drinking out of the best punch-bowls, eating the great cheese, smoking sacred pipes, etc. etc.; John Willet, fallen backward in his chair, regarding them with a stupid horror, and quite alone among them, with none of The Maypole customers at his back.

It's in your way, and you'll do it a hundred times better than I can suggest it to you, I know.

Faithfully always

MR GEORGE CATTERMOLE

Broadstairs, *Friday, 6 August 1841*

My dear George,

Here is a subject for the next number; the next to that I hope to send you the MS. of very early in the week, as the best opportunities of illustration are all coming off now, and we are in the thick of the story.

The rioters went, sir, from John Willet's bar (where you saw them to such good purpose) straight to The Warren, which house they plundered, sacked, burned, pulled down as much of as they could, and greatly damaged and destroyed. They are supposed to have left it about half an hour. It is night, and the ruins are here and there flaming and smoking. I want—if you understand—to show one of the turrets laid open—the turret where the alarm-bell is, mentioned in No. 1; and among the ruins (at some height if possible) Mr Haredale just clutching our friend, the mysterious file, who is passing over them like a spirit; Solomon Daisy, if you can introduce him, looking on from the ground below.

Please to observe that the M. F. wears a large cloak and a slouched hat. This is important, because Browne will have him in the same number, and he has not changed his dress meanwhile. Mr Haredale is supposed to have come down here on horseback, pell-mell; to be excited to the last degree. I think it will make a queer picturesque thing in your hands. I have told Chapman and Hall that you may like to have a block of a peculiar shape for it. One of them will be with you almost as soon as you receive this.

We are very anxious to know that our cousin is out of her trouble, and you free from your anxiety. Mind you write when it comes off. And when she is quite comfortable come down here for a day or two, like a bachelor, as you will be. It will do you a world of good. Think of that.

Always, dear Cattermole,
Heartily yours.

P.S.—When you have done the subject, I wish you'd write me one line and tell me how, that I may be sure we agree. Loves from Kate.

MR GEORGE CATTERMOLE

Devonshire Terrace, *Thursday, 13 August*

My dear Cattermole,

Will you turn your attention to a frontispiece for our first volume, to come upon the left-hand side of the book as you open it, and to face a plain printed title? My idea is, some scene from the 'Curiosity Shop,' in a pretty border, or scroll-work, or architectural device; it matters not what, so that it be pretty. The scene even might be a fanciful thing, partaking of the character of the story, but not reproducing any particular passage in it, if you thought that better for the effect.

I ask you to think of this, because, although the volume is not published until the end of September, there is no time to lose. We wish to have it engraved with great care, and worked very skilfully; and this cannot be done unless we get it on the stocks soon.

They will give you every opportunity of correction, alteration, revision, and all other ations and isions connected with the fine arts.

Always believe me,
Faithfully yours

MR GEORGE CATTERMOLE

Broadstairs, *19 August 1841*

My dear George,

When Hugh and a small body of the rioters cut off from The Warren beckoned to their pals, they forced into a very remarkable postchaise Dolly Varden and Emma Haredale, and bore them away with all possible rapidity; one of their company driving, and the rest running beside the chaise, climbing up behind, sitting on the top, lighting the way with their torches, etc. etc. If you can express the women inside without showing them—as by a fluttering veil, a delicate arm, or so forth appearing at the half-closed window—so much the better. Mr Tappertit stands on the steps, which are partly down, and, hanging on to the window with one hand and extending the other with great majesty, addresses a few words of encouragement to the driver and attendants. Hugh sits upon the bar in front; the driver sitting postilion-wise, and turns round to look through the window behind him at the little doves within. The gentlemen behind are also anxious to catch a glimpse of the ladies. One of those who are running at the side may be gently rebuked for his curiosity by the cudgel of Hugh. So they cut away, sir, as fast as they can.

Always faithfully

P.S.—John Willet's bar is noble.

We take it for granted that cousin and baby are hearty. Our loves to them.

MR W. C. MACREADY

Broadstairs, *Tuesday, 24 August 1841*

My dear Macready,

I must thank you, most heartily and cordially, for your kind note relative to poor Overs. I can't tell you how glad I am to know that he thoroughly deserves such kindness.

What a good fellow Elliotson is. He kept him in his room a whole hour, and has gone into his case as if he were Prince Albert; laying down all manner of elaborate projects and determining to leave his friend Wood in town when he himself goes away, on purpose to attend to him. Then he writes me four sides of paper about the man, and says he can't go back to his old work, for that requires muscular exertion (and muscular exertion he mustn't make), what are we to do with him? He says: 'Here's five pounds for the present.'

I declare before God that I could almost bear the Jones's for five years out of the pleasure I feel in knowing such things, and when I think that every dirty speck upon the fair face of the Almighty's creation, who writes in a filthy, beastly newspaper; every rotten-hearted pander who has been beaten, kicked, and rolled in the kennel, yet struts it in the editorial 'We,' once a week; every vagabond that an honest man's gorge must rise at; every live emetic in that noxious drug-shop the press, can have his fling at such men and call them knaves and fools and thieves, I grow so vicious that, with bearing hard upon my pen, I break the nib down, and, with keeping my teeth set, make my jaws ache.

I have put myself out of sorts for the day, and shall go and walk, unless the direction of this sets me up again. On second thoughts I think it will.

Always, my dear Macready,
Your faithful Friend

MR GEORGE CATTERMOLE

Broadstairs, *Sunday, 12 September 1841*

My dear George,

Here is a business letter, written in a scramble just before post time, whereby I dispose of loves to cousin in a line.

Firstly. Will you design, upon a block of wood, Lord George Gordon, alone and very solitary, in his prison in the Tower? The chamber as ancient as you please, and after your own fancy; the time, evening; the season, summer.

Secondly. Will you ditto upon a ditto, a sword duel between Mr Haredale and Mr Chester, in a grove of trees? No one close by. Mr Haredale has just pierced his adversary, who has fallen, dying, on the grass. He (that is, Chester) tries to staunch the wound in his breast with his handkerchief; has his snuffbox on the earth beside him, and looks at Mr Haredale (who stands with his sword in his hand, looking down on him) with most supercilious hatred, but polite to the last. Mr Haredale is more sorry than triumphant.

Thirdly. Will you conceive and execute, after your own fashion, a frontispiece for 'Barnaby'?

Fourthly. Will you also devise a subject representing 'Master Humphrey's Clock' as stopped; his chair by the fireside, empty; his crutch against the wall; his slippers on the cold hearth; his hat upon the chair-back; the MSS. of 'Barnaby' and 'The Curiosity Shop' heaped upon the table; and the flowers you introduced in the first subject of all withered and dead? Master Humphrey being supposed to be no more.

I have a fifthly, sixthly, seventhly, and eighthly; for I sorely want you, as I approach the close of the tale, but I won't frighten you, so we'll take breath.

Always, my dear Cattermole,
Heartily yours

P.S.—I have been waiting until I got to subjects of this nature, thinking you would like them best.

MR GEORGE CATTERMOLE

Broadstairs, *21 September 1841*

My dear George,

Will you, before you go on with the other subjects I gave you, do one of Hugh, bareheaded, bound, tied on a horse, and escorted by horse-soldiers to jail? If you can add an indication of old Fleet Market, and bodies of foot soldiers firing at people who have taken refuge on the tops of stalls, bulk-heads, etc., it will be all the better.

Faithfully yours always

MISS MARY TALFOURD

Devonshire Terrace, *16 December 1841*

My dear Mary,

I should be delighted to come and dine with you on your birthday, and to be as merry as I wish you to be always; but as I am going, within a very few days afterwards, a very long distance from home, and shall not see any of my children for six long months, I have made up my mind to pass all that week at home for their sakes; just as you would like your papa and mamma to spend all the time they possibly could spare with you if they were about to make a dreary voyage to America; which is what I am going to do myself.

But although I cannot come to see you on that day, you may be sure I shall not forget that it is your birthday, and that I shall drink your health and many happy returns, in a glass of wine, filled as full as it will hold. And I shall dine at half-past five myself, so that we may both be drinking our wine at the same time; and I shall tell my Mary (for I have got a daughter of that name but she is a very small one as yet) to drink your health too; and we shall try and make believe that you are here, or that we are in Russell Square, which is the best thing we can do, I think, under the circumstances.

You are growing up so fast that by the time I come home again I expect you will be almost a woman; and in a very few years we shall be saying to each other: 'Don't you remember what the birthdays used to be in Russell Square?' and 'How strange it seems!' and 'How quickly time passes!' and all that sort of thing, you know. But I shall always be very glad to be asked on your birthday, and to come if you will let me, and to send my love to you, and to wish that you may live to be very old and very happy, which I do now with all my heart.

> Believe me always,
> My dear Mary,
> Yours affectionately

MR W. C. MACREADY

Devonshire Terrace, *Tuesday, 28 Dec. 1841*

My dear Macready,

This note is about the saloon. I make it as brief as possible. Read it when you have time. As we were the first experimentalists last night you will be glad to know what it wants.

First, the refreshments are preposterously dear. A glass of wine is a shilling, and it ought to be sixpence.

Secondly, they were served out by the wrong sort of people—two most uncomfortable drabs of women, and a dirty man with his hat on.

Thirdly, there ought to be a box-keeper to ring a bell or give some other notice of the commencement of the overture to the after-piece. The promenaders were in a perpetual fret and worry to get back again.

And fourthly, and most important of all—if the plan is ever to succeed—you must have some notice up to the effect that as it is now a place of resort for ladies, gentlemen are requested not to lounge there in their hats and greatcoats. No ladies will go there, though the conveniences should be ten thousand times greater, while the sort of swells who have been used to kick their heels there do so in the old sort of way. I saw this expressed last night more strongly than I can tell you.

Hearty congratulations on the brilliant triumph. I have always expected one, as you know, but nobody could have imagined the reality.

Always, my dear Macready,
Affectionately yours

1842

NARRATIVE

In January of this year Charles Dickens went, with his wife, to America, the house in Devonshire Terrace being let for the term of their absence (six months), and the four children left in a furnished house in Osnaburgh Street, Regent's Park, under the care of Mr and Mrs Macready. They returned from America in July, and in August went to Broadstairs for the autumn months as usual, and in October Charles Dickens made an expedition to Cornwall, with Mr Forster, Mr Maclise, and Mr Stanfield for his companions.

During his stay at Broadstairs he was engaged in writing his 'American Notes,' which book was published in October. At the end of the year he had written the first number of 'Martin Chuzzlewit,' which appeared in January, 1843.

An extract from a letter, addressed to Messrs. Chapman and Hall before his departure for America, is given as a testimony of the estimation in which Charles Dickens held the firm with whom he was connected for so many years.

His letters to Mr H. P. Smith, for many years actuary of the Eagle Insurance Office, are a combination of business and friendship. Mr Smith gives us, as an explanation of a note to him, dated 14 July, that he alluded to the stamp of the office upon the cheque, which was, as he described it, 'almost a work of art'—a truculent-looking eagle seated on a rock and scattering rays over the whole sheet.

Of letters written by Charles Dickens in America we have been able to obtain very few. One, to Dr F. H. Deane, Cincinnati, complying with his request to write him an epitaph for the tombstone of his little child, has been kindly copied for us from an album, by Mrs Fields, of Boston. Therefore, it is not directly received, but as we have no doubt of its authenticity, we give it here; and there is one to Mr Halleck, the American poet.

At the close of the voyage to America (a very bad and dangerous one), a meeting of the passengers, with Lord Mulgrave in the chair, took place, and a piece of plate and thanks were voted to the captain of the *Britannia*, Captain Hewett. The vote of thanks, being drawn up by Charles Dickens, is given here. We have letters in this year to Mr Thomas Hood, Miss Pardoe, Mrs Trollope, and Mr W. P. Frith. The last-named artist—then a very young man—had made great success with several charming pictures of Dolly Varden. One of these was bought by Charles Dickens, who ordered a companion picture of Kate Nickleby, from the young painter, whose acquaintance he made at the same time; and the two letters to Mr Frith have reference to the purchase of the one picture and the commission for the other.

The letter to Mr Cattermole is an acknowledgment also of a completed commission of two water-colour drawings, from the subjects of two of Mr Cattermole's illustrations to 'The Old Curiosity Shop.'

A note to Mr Macready, at the close of this year, refers to the first representation of Mr Westland Marston's play, 'The Patrician's

Daughter.' Charles Dickens took great interest in the production of this work at Drury Lane. It was, to a certain extent, an experiment of the effect of a tragedy of modern times and in modern dress; and the prologue, which Charles Dickens wrote and which we give, was intended to show that there need be no incongruity between plain clothes of this century and high tragedy. The play was quite successful.

Messrs. Chapman and Hall

Having disposed of the business part of this letter, I should not feel at ease on leaving England if I did not tell you once more with my whole heart that your conduct to me on this and all other occasions has been honourable, manly, and generous, and that I have felt it a solemn duty, in the event of any accident happening to me while I am away, to place this testimony upon record. It forms part of a will I have made for the security of my children; for I wish them to know it when they are capable of understanding your worth and my appreciation of it.

Always believe me,
Faithfully and truly yours

MR THOMAS MITTON

Adelphi Hotel, Liverpool, *Monday, 3 Jan. 1842*

My dear Mitton,

This is a short note, but I will fulfil the adage and make it a merry one.

We came down in great comfort. Our luggage is now aboard. Anything so utterly and monstrously absurd as the size of our cabin, no 'gentleman of England who lives at home at ease' can for a moment imagine. Neither of the portmanteaus would go into it. There!

These Cunard packets are not very big you know actually, but the quantity of sleeping-berths makes them much smaller, so that the saloon is not nearly as large as in one of the Ramsgate boats. The ladies' cabin is so close to ours that I could knock the door open without getting off something they call my bed, but which I believe to be a muffin beaten flat. This is a great comfort, for it is an excellent room (the only good one in the ship); and if there be only one other lady besides Kate, as the stewardess thinks, I hope I shall be able to sit there very often.

They talk of seventy passengers, but I can't think there will be so many; they talk besides (which is even more to the purpose) of a very fine passage, having had a noble one this time last year. God send it so! We are in the best spirits, and full of hope. I was dashed for a moment when I saw our 'cabin,' but I got over that directly, and laughed so much at its ludicrous proportions, that you might have heard me all over the ship.

God bless you! Write to me by the first opportunity. I will do the like to you. And always believe me,

Your old and faithful Friend.

NARRATIVE

At a meeting of the passengers on board the *Britannia* steam-ship, travelling from Liverpool to Boston, held in the saloon of that vessel, on Friday, the 21 January, 1842, it was moved and seconded:

'That the Earl of Mulgrave do take the chair.'

The motion having been carried unanimously, the Earl of Mulgrave took the chair accordingly.

It was also moved and seconded, and carried unanimously:

'That Charles Dickens, Esq., be appointed secretary and treasurer to the meeting.'

The three following resolutions were then proposed and carried *nem. con.*:

'First. That, gratefully recognising the blessing of Divine Providence by which we are brought nearly to the termination of our voyage, we have great pleasure in expressing our high appreciation of Captain Hewett's nautical skill and of his indefatigable attention to the management and safe conduct of the ship, during a more than ordinarily tempestuous passage.

'Secondly. That a subscription be opened for the purchase of a piece of silver plate, and that Captain Hewett be respectfully requested to accept it, as a sincere expression of the sentiments embodied in the foregoing resolution.

'Thirdly. That a committee be appointed to carry these resolutions into effect; and that the committee be composed of the following gentlemen: Charles Dickens, Esq., E. Dunbar, Esq., and Solomon Hopkins, Esq.'

The committee having withdrawn and conferred with Captain Hewett, returned, and informed the meeting that Captain Hewett desired to attend and express his thanks, which he did.

The amount of the subscription was reported at fifty pounds, and the list was closed. It was then agreed that the following inscription should be placed upon the testimonial to Captain Hewett:

This Piece of Plate
was presented to
CAPTAIN JOHN HEWETT,
of the Britannia Steam-ship,

By the Passengers on board that vessel in a voyage from Liverpool to Boston, in the month of January, 1842,
As a slight acknowledgment of his great ability and skill under circumstances of much difficulty and danger,
And as a feeble token of their lasting gratitude.

Thanks were then voted to the chairman and to the secretary, and the meeting separated.

MR THOMAS MITTON

Tremont House, Boston, *31 January 1842*

My dear Mitton,

I am so exhausted with the life I am obliged to lead here, that I have had time to write but one letter which is at all deserving of the name, as giving any account of our movements. Forster has it, in trust, to tell you all its news; and he has also some newspapers which I had an opportunity of sending him, in which you will find further particulars of our progress.

We had a dreadful passage, the worst, the officers all concur in saying, that they have ever known. We were eighteen days coming; experienced a dreadful storm which swept away our paddle-boxes and stove our lifeboats; and ran aground besides, near Halifax, among rocks and breakers, where we lay at anchor all night. After we left the English Channel we had only one fine day. And we had the additional discomfort of being eighty-six passengers. I was ill five days, Kate six; though, indeed, she had a swelled face and suffered the utmost terror all the way.

I can give you no conception of my welcome here. There never was a king or emperor upon the earth so cheered and followed by crowds, and entertained in public at splendid balls and dinners, and waited on by public bodies and deputations of all kinds. I have had one from the Far West—a journey of two thousand miles! If I go out in a carriage, the crowd surround it and escort me home; if I go to the theatre, the whole house (crowded to the roof) rises as one man, and the timbers ring again. You cannot imagine what it is. I have five great public dinners on hand at this moment, and invitations from every town and village and city in the States.

There is a great deal afloat here in the way of subjects for description. I keep my eyes open pretty wide, and hope to have done so to some purpose by the time I come home.

When you write to me again—I say again, hoping that your first letter will be soon upon its way here—direct to me to the care of David Colden, Esq., New York. He will forward all communications by the quickest conveyance and will be perfectly acquainted with all my movements.

Always your faithful Friend

MR FITZ-GREENE HALLECK

Carlton House, *14 February 1842*

My dear Sir,

Will you come and breakfast with me on Tuesday, 22 at half-past ten? Say yes. I should have been truly delighted to have a talk with you to-night (being quite alone), but the doctor says that if I talk to man, woman, or child this evening I shall be dumb tomorrow.

Believe me, with true regard,
Faithfully your Friend

MR W.C. MACREADY

Baltimore, 22 March 1842

My dear Friend,

I beg your pardon, but you were speaking of rash leaps at hasty conclusions. Are you quite sure you designed that remark for me? Have you not, in the hurry of correspondence, slipped a paragraph into my letter which belongs of right to somebody else? When did you ever find me leap at wrong conclusions? I pause for a reply.

Pray, sir, did you ever find me admiring Mr ———? On the contrary, did you never hear of my protesting through good, better, and best report that he was not an open or a candid man, and would one day, beyond all doubt, displease you by not being so? I pause again for a reply.

Are you quite sure, Mr Macready—and I address myself to you with the sternness of a man in the pit—are you quite sure, sir, that you do not view America through the pleasant mirage which often surrounds a thing that has been, but not a thing that is? Are you quite sure that when you were here you relished it as well as you do now when you look back upon it. The early spring birds, Mr Macready, *do* sing in the groves that you were, very often, not over well pleased with many of the new country's social aspects. Are the birds to be trusted? Again I pause for a reply.

My dear Macready, I desire to be so honest and just to those who have so enthusiastically and earnestly welcomed me, that I burned the last letter I wrote to you—even to you to whom I would speak as to myself—rather than let it come with anything that might seem like an ill-considered word of disappointment. I preferred that you should think me neglectful (if you could imagine anything so wild) rather than I should do wrong in this respect. Still it is of no use. I *am* disappointed. This is not the republic I came to see; this is not the republic of my imagination. I infinitely prefer a liberal monarchy—even with its sickening accompaniments of court circulars—to such a government as this. The more I think of its youth and strength, the poorer and more trifling in a thousand aspects it appears in my eyes. In everything of which it has made a boast—excepting its education of the people and its care for poor children—it sinks immeasurably below the level I had placed it upon; and England, even England, bad and faulty as the old land is, and miserable as millions of her people are, rises in the comparison.

You live here, Macready, as I have sometimes heard you imagining! *You!* Loving you with all my heart and soul, and knowing what your disposition really is, I would not condemn you to a year's residence on this side of the Atlantic for any money. Freedom of opinion! Where is it? I see a press more mean, and paltry, and silly, and disgraceful than any country I ever knew. If that is its standard, here it is. But I speak of Bancroft, and am advised to be silent on that subject, for he is 'a black sheep—a Democrat.' I speak of Bryant, and am entreated to be more careful, for the same reason. I speak of international copyright, and am implored not to ruin myself outright. I speak of Miss Martineau, and all parties—Slave Upholders and Abolitionists, Whigs, Tyler Whigs, and Democrats, shower down upon me a perfect cataract of abuse. 'But what has she done? Surely she praised America enough!' 'Yes, but she told us of some of our faults, and Americans can't bear to be told of their faults. Don't split on that rock, Mr Dickens, don't write about America; we are so very suspicious.'

Freedom of opinion! Macready, if I had been born here and had written my books in this country, producing them with no stamp of approval from any other land, it is my solemn belief that I should have lived and died poor, unnoticed, and a 'black sheep' to boot. I never was more convinced of anything than I am of that.

The people are affectionate, generous, open-hearted, hospitable, enthusiastic, good-humoured, polite to women, frank and candid to all strangers, anxious to oblige, far less prejudiced than they have been described to be, frequently polished and refined, very seldom rude or disagreeable. I have made a great many friends here, even in public conveyances, whom I have been truly sorry to part from. In the towns I have formed perfect attachments. I have seen none of that greediness and indecorousness on which travellers have laid so much emphasis. I have returned frankness with frankness; met questions not intended to be rude, with answers meant to be satisfactory; and have not spoken to one man, woman, or child of any degree who has not grown positively affectionate before we parted. In the respects of not being left alone, and of being horribly disgusted by tobacco chewing and tobacco spittle, I have suffered considerably. The sight of slavery in Virginia, the hatred of British feeling upon the subject, and the miserable hints of the impotent indignation of the South, have pained me very much; on the last head, of course, I have felt nothing but a mingled pity and amusement; on the other, sheer distress. But however much I like the ingredients of this great dish, I cannot but come back to the point upon which I started, and say that the dish itself goes against the grain with me, and that I don't like it.

You know that I am truly a Liberal. I believe I have as little pride as most men, and I am conscious of not the smallest annoyance from being 'hail fellow well met' with everybody. I have not had greater pleasure in the company of any set of men among the thousands I have received (I hold a regular levée every day, you know, which is duly heralded and proclaimed in the newspapers) than in that of the carmen of Hertford, who presented themselves in a body in their blue frocks, among a crowd of well-dressed ladies and gentlemen, and bade me welcome through their spokesman. They had all read my books, and all perfectly understood them. It is not these things I have in my mind when I say that the man who comes to this country a Radical and goes home again with his opinions unchanged, must be a Radical on reason, sympathy, and reflection, and one who has so well considered the subject that he has no chance of wavering.

We have been to Boston, Worcester, Hertford, New Haven, New York, Philadelphia, Baltimore, Washington, Fredericksburgh, Richmond, and back to Washington again. The premature heat of the weather (it was eighty yesterday in the shade) and Clay's advice—how you would like Clay!—have made us determine not to go to Charleston; but having got to Richmond, I think I should have turned back under any circumstances.

We remain at Baltimore for two days, of which this is one; then we go to Harrisburgh. Then by the canal boat and the railroad over the Alleghany Mountains to Pittsburgh, then down the Ohio to Cincinnati, then to Louisville, and then to St. Louis. I have been invited to a public entertainment in every town I have entered, and have refused them; but I have excepted St. Louis as the farthest point of my travels. My friends there have passed some resolutions which Forster has, and will show you. From St. Louis we cross to Chicago, traversing immense prairies. Thence by the lakes and Detroit to Buffalo, and so to Niagara. A run into Canada follows of course, and then—let me write the blessed word in capitals—we turn towards home.

Kate has written to Mrs Macready, and it is useless for me to thank you, my dearest friend, or her, for your care of our dear children, which is our constant theme of discourse. Forster has gladdened our hearts with his account of the triumph of 'Acis and Galatea,' and I am anxiously looking for news of the tragedy. Forrest breakfasted with us at Richmond last Saturday—he was acting there, and I invited him—and he spoke very gratefully, and very like a man, of your kindness to him when he was in London.

David Colden is as good a fellow as ever lived; and I am deeply in love with his wife. Indeed we have received the greatest and most earnest and zealous kindness from the whole family, and quite love them all. Do you remember one Greenhow, whom you invited to pass some days with you at the hotel on the Kaatskill Mountains? He is translator to the State Office at Washington, has a very pretty wife, and a little girl of five years old. We dined with them, and had a very pleasant day. The President invited me to dinner, but I couldn't stay for it. I had a private audience, however, and we attended the public drawing-room besides.

Now, don't you rush at the quick conclusion that I have rushed at a quick conclusion. Pray, be upon your guard. If you can by any process estimate the extent of my affectionate regard for you, and the rush I shall make when I reach London to take you by your true right hand, I don't object. But let me entreat you to be very careful how you come down upon the sharpsighted individual who pens these words, which you seem to me to have done in what Willmott would call 'one of Mr Macready's rushes.' As my pen is getting past its work, I have taken a new one to say that

> I am ever, my dear Macready,
> Your faithful Friend

MR THOMAS MITTON

Baltimore, United States, *22 March 1842*

My dear Friend,

We have been as far south as Richmond in Virginia (where they grow and manufacture tobacco, and where the labour is all performed by slaves), but the season in those latitudes is so intensely and prematurely hot, that it was considered a matter of doubtful expediency to go on to Charleston. For this unexpected reason, and because the country between Richmond and Charleston is but a desolate swamp the whole way, and because slavery is anything but a cheerful thing to live amidst, I have altered my route by the advice of Mr Clay (the great political leader in this country), and have returned here previous to diving into the far West. We start for that part of the country—which includes mountain travelling, and lake travelling, and prairie travelling—the day after tomorrow, at eight o'clock in the morning; and shall be in the West, and from there going northward again, until the 30th of April or 1st of May, when we shall halt for a week at Niagara, before going further into Canada. We have taken our passage home (God bless the word) in the *George Washington* packet-ship from New York. She sails on the 7th of June.

I have departed from my resolution not to accept any more public entertainments; they have been proposed in every town I have visited—in favour of the people of St. Louis, my utmost western point. That town is on the borders of the Indian territory, a trifling distance from this place—only two thousand miles! At my second halting-place I shall be able to write to fix the day; I suppose it will be somewhere about the 12 April. Think of my going so far towards the setting sun to dinner!

In every town where we stay, though it be only for a day, we hold a regular levée or drawing-room, where I shake hands on an average with five or six hundred people, who pass on from me to Kate, and are shaken again by her. Maclise's picture of our darlings stands upon a table or sideboard the while; and my travelling secretary, assisted very often by a committee belonging to the place, presents the people in due form. Think of two hours of this every day, and the people coming in by hundreds, all fresh, and piping hot, and full of questions, when we are literally exhausted and can hardly stand. I really do believe that if I had not a lady with me, I should have been obliged to leave the country and go back to England. But for her they never would leave me alone by day or night, and as it is, a slave comes to me now and then in the middle of the night with a letter, and waits at the bedroom door for an answer.

It was so hot at Richmond that we could scarcely breathe, and the peach and other fruit trees were in full blossom; it was so cold at Washington next day that we were shivering; but even in the same town you might often wear nothing but a shirt and trousers in the morning, and two greatcoats at night, the thermometer very frequently taking a little trip of thirty degrees between sunrise and sunset.

They do lay it on at the hotels in such style! They charge by the day, so that whether one dines out or dines at home makes no manner of difference. T'other day I wrote to order our rooms at Philadelphia to be ready on a certain day, and was detained a week longer than I expected in New York. The Philadelphia landlord not only charged me half rent for the rooms during the whole of that time, but board for myself and Kate and Anne during the whole time too, though we were actually boarding at the same expense during the same time in New York! What do you say to that? If I remonstrated, the whole virtue of the newspapers would be aroused directly.

We were at the President's drawing-room while we were in Washington. I had a private audience besides, and was asked to dinner, but couldn't stay.

Parties—parties—parties—of course, every day and night. But it's not all parties. I go into the prisons, the police-offices, the watch-houses, the hospitals, the workhouses. I was out half the night in New York with two of their most famous constables; started at midnight, and went into every brothel, thieves' house, murdering hovel, sailors' dancing-place, and abode of villany, both black and white, in the town. I went *incog.* behind the scenes to the little theatre where Mitchell is making a fortune. He has been rearing a little dog for me, and has called him 'Boz.' I am going to bring him home. In a word I go everywhere, and a hard life it is. But I am careful to drink hardly anything, and not to smoke at all. I have recourse to my medicine-chest whenever I feel at all bilious, and am, thank God, thoroughly well.

When I next write to you, I shall have begun, I hope, to turn my face homeward. I have a great store of oddity and whimsicality, and am going now into the oddest and most characteristic part of this most queer country.

Always direct to the care of David Colden, Esq., 28, Laight Street, Hudson Square, New York. I received your Caledonia letter with the greatest joy.

Kate sends her best remembrances.

And I am always.

P.S.—Richmond was my extreme southern point, and I turn from the South altogether the day after tomorrow. Will you let the Britannia know of this change—if needful?

DR F.H. DEANE

Cincinnati, Ohio, *4 April 1842*

My dear Sir,

I have not been unmindful of your request for a moment, but have not been able to think of it until now. I hope my good friends (for whose christian-names I have left blanks in the epitaph) may like what I have written, and that they will take comfort and be happy again. I sail on the 7th of June, and purpose being at the Carlton House, New York, about the 1st. It will make me easy to know that this letter has reached you.

Faithfully yours

This is the Grave of a Little Child,

WHOM GOD IN HIS GOODNESS CALLED TO A BRIGHT ETERNITY
WHEN HE WAS VERY YOUNG.
HARD AS IT IS FOR HUMAN AFFECTION TO RECONCILE ITSELF TO DEATH IN ANY
SHAPE (AND MOST OF ALL, PERHAPS, AT FIRST IN THIS),
HIS PARENTS CAN EVEN NOW BELIEVE THAT IT WILL BE A CONSOLATION
TO THEM THROUGHOUT THEIR LIVES,
AND WHEN THEY SHALL HAVE GROWN OLD AND GRAY,
Always to think of him as a Child in Heaven.
'And Jesus called a little child unto Him, and set him in the midst of them.'
He was the Son of Q—— and M——THORNTON, christened
CHARLES JERKING.
HE WAS BORN ON THE 20 JANUARY, 1841,
AND HE DIED ON THE 12 MARCH, 1842,
having lived only thirteen months and twenty days.

MR HENRY AUSTIN

Niagara Falls (English Side),
Sunday, 1 May 1842

My dear Henry,

Although I date this letter as above, it will not be so old a one as at first sight it would appear to be when it reaches you. I shall carry it on with me to Montreal, and despatch it from there by the steamer which goes to Halifax, to meet the Cunard boat at that place, with Canadian letters and passengers. Before I finally close it, I will add a short postscript, so that it will contain the latest intelligence.

We have had a blessed interval of quiet in this beautiful place, of which, as you may suppose, we stood greatly in need, not only by reason of our hard travelling for a long time, but on account of the incessant persecutions of the people, by land and water, on stage coach, railway car, and steamer, which exceeds anything you can picture to yourself by the utmost stretch of your imagination. So far we have had this hotel nearly to ourselves. It is a large square house, standing on a bold height, with overhanging eaves like a Swiss cottage, and a wide handsome gallery outside every story. These colonnades make it look so very light, that it has exactly the appearance of a house built with a pack of cards; and I live in bodily terror lest any man should venture to step out of a little observatory on the roof, and crush the whole structure with one stamp of his foot.

Our sitting-room (which is large and low like a nursery) is on the second floor, and is so close to the Falls that the windows are always wet and dim with spray. Two bedrooms open out of it—one our own; one Anne's. The secretary slumbers near at hand, but without these sacred precincts. From the three chambers, or any part of them, you can see the Falls rolling and tumbling, and roaring and leaping, all day long, with bright rainbows making fiery arches down a hundred feet below us. When the sun is on them, they shine and glow like molten gold. When the day is gloomy, the water falls like snow, or sometimes it seems to crumble away like the face of a great chalk cliff, or sometimes again to roll along the front of the rock like white smoke. But it all seems gay or gloomy, dark or light, by sun or moon. From the bottom of both Falls, there is always rising up a solemn ghostly cloud, which hides the boiling cauldron from human sight, and makes it in its mystery a hundred times more grand than if you could see all the secrets that lie hidden in its tremendous depth. One Fall is as close to us as York Gate is to No. 1, Devonshire Terrace. The other (the great Horse-shoe Fall) may be, perhaps, about half as far off as 'Creedy's.' One circumstance in connection with them is, in all the accounts, greatly exaggerated—I mean the noise. Last night was perfectly still. Kate and I could just hear them, at the quiet time of sunset, a mile off. Whereas, believing the statements I had heard I began putting my ear to the ground, like a savage or a bandit in a ballet, thirty miles off, when we were coming here from Buffalo.

I was delighted to receive your famous letter, and to read your account of our darlings, whom we long to see with an intensity it is impossible to shadow forth, ever so faintly. I do believe, though I say it as shouldn't, that they are good 'uns—both to look at and to go. I roared out this morning, as soon as I was awake, 'Next month,' which we have been longing to be able to say ever since we have been here. I really do not know how we shall ever knock at the door, when that slowest of all impossibly slow hackney-coaches shall pull up—at home.

I am glad you exult in the fight I have had about the copyright. If you knew how they tried to stop me, you would have a still greater interest in it. The greatest men in England have sent me out, through Forster, a very manly, and becoming, and spirited memorial and address, backing me in all I have done. I have despatched it to Boston for publication, and am coolly prepared for the storm it will raise. But my best rod is in pickle.

Is it not a horrible thing that scoundrel booksellers should grow rich here from publishing books, the authors of which do not reap one farthing from their issue by scores of thousands; and that every vile, blackguard, and detestable newspaper, so filthy and bestial that no honest man would admit one into his house for a scullery door-mat, should be able to publish those same writings side by side, cheek by jowl, with the coarsest and most obscene companions with which they must become connected, in course of time, in people's minds? Is it tolerable that besides being robbed and rifled an author should be forced to appear in any form, in any vulgar dress, in any atrocious company; that he should have no choice of his audience, no control over his own distorted text, and that he should be compelled to jostle out of the course the best men in this country who only ask to live by writing? I vow before high heaven that my blood so boils at these enormities, that when I speak about them I seem to grow twenty feet high, and to swell out in proportion. 'Robbers that ye are,' I think to myself when I get upon my legs, 'here goes!'

The places we have lodged in, the roads we have gone over, the company we have been among, the tobacco-spittle we have wallowed in, the strange customs we have complied with, the packing-cases in which we have travelled, the woods, swamps, rivers, prairies, lakes, and mountains we have crossed, are all subjects for legends and tales at home; quires, reams, wouldn't hold them. I don't think Anne has so much as seen an American tree. She never looks at a prospect by any chance, or displays the smallest emotion at any sight whatever. She objects to Niagara that 'it's nothing but water,' and considers that 'there is too much of that.'

I suppose you have heard that I am going to act at the Montreal theatre with the officers? Farce-books being scarce, and the choice consequently limited, I have selected Keeley's part in 'Two o'Clock in the Morning.' I wrote yesterday to Mitchell, the actor and manager at New York, to get and send me a comic wig, light flaxen, with a small whisker halfway down the cheek; over this I mean to wear two night-caps, one with a tassel and one of flannel; a flannel wrapper, drab tights and slippers, will complete the costume.

I am very sorry to hear that business is so flat, but the proverb says it never rains but it pours, and it may be remarked with equal truth upon the other side, that it never *don't* rain but it holds up very much indeed. You will be busy again long before I come home, I have no doubt.

We purpose leaving this on Wednesday morning. Give my love to Letitia and to mother, and always believe me, my dear Henry,

Affectionately yours

MR HENRY AUSTIN

Montreal, Canada, *12 May 1842*

All well, though (with the exception of one from Fred) we have received no letters whatever by the *Caledonia*. We have experienced impossible-to-be-described attentions in Canada. Everybody's carriage and horses are at our disposal, and everybody's servants; and all the Government boats and boats' crews. We shall play, between the 20th and the 25th, 'A Roland for an Oliver,' 'Two o'Clock in the Morning,' and 'Deaf as a Post.'

MR THOMAS LONGMAN

Athenæum, *Friday Afternoon*

My dear Sir,

If I could possibly have attended the meeting yesterday I would most gladly have done so. But I have been up the whole night, and was too much exhausted even to write and say so before the proceedings came on.

I have fought the fight across the Atlantic with the utmost energy I could command; have never been turned aside by any consideration for an instant; am fresher for the fray than ever; will battle it to the death, and die game to the last.

I am happy to say that my boy is quite well again. From being in perfect health he fell into alarming convulsions with the surprise and joy of our return.

I beg my regards to Mrs Longman,

> And am always,
> Faithfully yours

MISS PARDOE

> Devonshire Terrace, York Gate, Regent's Park,
> *19 July 1842*

Dear Madam,

I beg to set you right on one point in reference to the American robbers, which perhaps you do not quite understand.

The existing law allows them to reprint any English book, without any communication whatever with the author or anybody else. My books have all been reprinted on these agreeable terms.

But sometimes, when expectation is awakened there about a book before its publication, one firm of pirates will pay a trifle to procure early proofs of it, and get so much the start of the rest as they can obtain by the time necessarily consumed in printing it. Directly it is printed it is common property, and may be reprinted a thousand times. My circular only referred to such bargains as these.

I should add that I have no hope of the States doing justice in this dishonest respect, and therefore do not expect to overtake these fellows, but we may cry 'Stop thief!' nevertheless, especially as they wince and smart under it.

> Faithfully yours always

MR H. P. SMITH

Devonshire Terrace, *Thursday, 14 July 1842*

My dear Smith,

The cheque safely received. As you say, it would be cheap at any money. My devotion to the fine arts renders it impossible for me to cash it. I have therefore ordered it to be framed and glazed.

I am really grateful to you for the interest you take in my proceedings. Next time I come into the City I will show you my introductory chapter to the American book. It may seem to prepare the reader for a much greater amount of slaughter than he will meet with; but it is honest and true. Therefore my hand does not shake.

Best love and regards. 'Certainly' to the Richmondian intentions. Always faithfully your Friend

MR HARRISON AINSWORTH

Broadstairs, Kent, *14 September 1842*

My dear Ainsworth,

The enclosed has been sent to me by a young gentleman in Devonshire (of whom I know no more than that I have occasionally, at his request, read and suggested amendments in some of his writings), with a special petition that I would recommend it to you for insertion in your magazine.

I think it very pretty, and I have no doubt you will also. But it is poetry, and may be too long.

He is a very modest young fellow, and has decided ability.

I hope when I come home at the end of the month, we shall foregather more frequently. Of course you are working, tooth and nail; and of course I am.

Kate joins me in best regards to yourself and all your house (not forgetting, but especially remembering, my old friend, Mrs Touchet), and I am always,

My dear Ainsworth,
Heartily yours

MR HENRY AUSTIN

Broadstairs, *Sunday, 25 September 1842*

My dear Henry,

I enclose you the Niagara letter, with many thanks for the loan of it.

Pray tell Mr Chadwick that I am greatly obliged to him for his remembrance of me, and I heartily concur with him in the great importance and interest of the subject, though I do differ from him, to the death, on his crack topic—the New Poor-Law.

I have been turning my thoughts to this very item in the condition of American towns, and had put their present aspects strongly before the American people; therefore I shall read his report with the greater interest and attention.

We return next Saturday night.

If you will dine with us next day or any day in the week, we shall be truly glad and delighted to see you. Let me know, then, what day you will come.

I need scarcely say that I shall joyfully talk with you about the Metropolitan Improvement Society, then or at any time; and with love to Letitia, in which Kate and the babies join, I am always, my dear Henry,

Affectionately yours.

P.S.—The children's present names are as follows:
Katey (from a lurking propensity to fieryness), Lucifer Box.
Mamey (as generally descriptive of her bearing), Mild Glo'ster.
Charley (as a corruption of Master Toby), Flaster Floby.
Walter (suggested by his high cheek-bones), Young Skull.
Each is pronounced with a peculiar howl, which I shall have great pleasure in illustrating.

REV. WILLIAM HARNESS

Devonshire Terrace, *8 November 1842*

My dear Harness,

Some time ago, you sent me a note from a friend of yours, a

barrister, I think, begging me to forward to him any letters I might receive from a deranged nephew of his, at Newcastle. In the midst of a most bewildering correspondence with unknown people, on every possible and impossible subject, I have forgotten this gentleman's name, though I have a kind of hazy remembrance that he lived near Russell Square. As the Post Office would be rather puzzled, perhaps, to identify him by such an address, may I ask the favour of you to hand him the enclosed, and to say that it is the second I have received since I returned from America? The last, I think, was a defiance to mortal combat. With best remembrances to your sister, in which Mrs Dickens joins, believe me, my dear Harness,

Always faithfully yours

MR W. C. MACREADY

Devonshire Terrace, *Saturday, 12 Nov. 1842*

My dear Macready,

You pass this house every day on your way to or from the theatre. I wish you would call once as you go by, and soon, that you may have plenty of time to deliberate on what I wish to suggest to you. The more I think of Marston's play, the more sure I feel that a prologue to the purpose would help it materially, and almost decide the fate of any ticklish point on the first night. Now I have an idea (not easily explainable in writing but told in five words), that would take the prologue out of the conventional dress of prologues, quite. Get the curtain up with a dash, and begin the play with a sledge-hammer blow. If on consideration, you should think with me, I will write the prologue heartily.

Faithfully yours ever

PROLOGUE

To Mr Marston's Play of 'The Patrician's Daughter.'

No tale of streaming plumes and harness bright
Dwells on the poet's maiden harp to-night;

No trumpet's clamour and no battle's fire
Breathes in the trembling accents of his lyre;
Enough for him, if in his lowly strain
He wakes one household echo not in vain;
Enough for him, if in his boldest word
The beating heart of man be dimly heard.

Its solemn music which, like strains that sigh
Through charmèd gardens, all who hearing die;
Its solemn music he does not pursue
To distant ages out of human view;
Nor listen to its wild and mournful chime
In the dead caverns on the shore of Time;
But musing with a calm and steady gaze
Before the crackling flames of living days,
He hears it whisper through the busy roar
Of what shall be and what has been before.
Awake the Present! shall no scene display
The tragic passion of the passing day?
Is it with Man, as with some meaner things,
That out of death his single purpose springs?
Can his eventful life no moral teach
Until he be, for aye, beyond its reach?
Obscurely shall he suffer, act, and fade,
Dubb'd noble only by the sexton's spade?
Awake the Present! Though the steel-clad age
Find life alone within the storied page,
Iron is worn, at heart, by many still—
The tyrant Custom binds the serf-like will;
If the sharp rack, and screw, and chain be gone,
These later days have tortures of their own;
The guiltless writhe, while Guilt is stretched in sleep,
And Virtue lies, too often, dungeon deep.
Awake the Present! what the Past has sown

Be in its harvest garner'd, reap'd, and grown!
How pride breeds pride, and wrong engenders wrong,
Read in the volume Truth has held so long,
Assured that where life's flowers freshest blow,
The sharpest thorns and keenest briars grow,
How social usage has the pow'r to change
Good thoughts to evil; in its highest range
To cramp the noble soul, and turn to ruth
The kindling impulse of our glorious youth,
Crushing the spirit in its house of clay,
Learn from the lessons of the present day.
Not light its import and not poor its mien;
Yourselves the actors, and your homes the scene.

MR W.C. MACREADY

Saturday Morning

My dear Macready,

One suggestion, though it be a late one. Do have upon the table, in the opening scene of the second act, something in a velvet case, or frame, that may look like a large miniature of Mabel, such as one of Ross's, and eschew that picture. It haunts me with a sense of danger. Even a titter at that critical time, with the whole of that act before you, would be a fatal thing. The picture is bad in itself, bad in its effect upon the beautiful room, bad in all its associations with the house. In case of your having nothing at hand, I send you by bearer what would be a million times better. Always, my dear Macready,

Faithfully yours

P.S.—I need not remind you how common it is to have such pictures in cases lying about elegant rooms.

MR W. P. FRITH

1, Devonshire Terrace, York Gate, Regent's Park,
15 November 1842

My dear Sir,

I shall be very glad if you will do me the favour to paint me two little companion pictures; one, a Dolly Varden (whom you have so exquisitely done already), the other, a Kate Nickleby.

Faithfully yours always

P.S.—I take it for granted that the original picture of Dolly with the bracelet is sold?

THE SAME

Devonshire Terrace, *17 November 1842*

My dear Sir,

Pray consult your own convenience in the matter of my little commission; whatever suits your engagements and prospects will best suit me.

I saw an unfinished proof of Dolly at Mitchell's some two or three months ago; I thought it was proceeding excellently well then. It will give me great pleasure to see her when completed.

Faithfully yours

MR THOMAS HOOD

Devonshire Terrace, *30 November 1842*

My dear Hood,

In asking your and Mrs Hood's leave to bring Mrs D.'s sister (who stays with us) on Tuesday, let me add that I should very much like to bring at the same time a very unaffected and ardent admirer of your genius, who has no small portion of that commodity in his own right, and is a very dear friend of mine and a very famous fellow; to wit, Maclise, the painter, who would be glad (as he has often told me) to know you better, and would be much pleased, I know, if I could say to him, 'Hood wants me to bring you.'

I use so little ceremony with you, in the conviction that you will use as little with me, and say, 'My dear D.—Convenient;' or, 'My dear D.—Ill-convenient,' (as the popular phrase is), just as the case may be. Of course, I have said nothing to him.

Always heartily yours,
Boz

MRS TROLLOPE

1, Devonshire Terrace, York Gate, Regent's Park,
16 December 1842

My dear Mrs Trollope,

Let me thank you most cordially for your kind note, in reference to my Notes, which has given me true pleasure and gratification.

As I never scrupled to say in America, so I can have no delicacy in saying to you, that, allowing for the change you worked in many social features of American society, and for the time that has passed since you wrote of the country, I am convinced that there is no writer who has so well and accurately (I need not add so entertainingly) described it, in many of its aspects, as you have done; and this renders your praise the more valuable to me. I do not recollect ever to have heard or seen the charge of exaggeration made against a feeble performance, though, in its feebleness, it may have been most untrue. It seems to me essentially natural, and quite inevitable, that common observers should accuse an uncommon one of this fault, and I have no doubt that you were long ago of this opinion; very much to your own comfort.

Mrs Dickens begs me to thank you for your kind remembrance of her, and to convey to you her best regards. Always believe me,

Faithfully yours

MR GEORGE CATTERMOLE

Devonshire Terrace, *20 December 1842*

My dear George,

It is impossible for me to tell you how greatly I am charmed with those beautiful pictures, in which the whole feeling, and thought, and expression of the little story is rendered to the gratification of my inmost heart; and on which you have lavished those amazing resources of yours with a power at which I fairly wondered when I sat down yesterday before them.

I took them to Mac, straightway, in a cab, and it would have done you good if you could have seen and heard him. You can't think how moved he was by the old man in the church, or how pleased I was to have chosen it before he saw the drawings.

You are such a queer fellow and hold yourself so much aloof, that I am afraid to say half I would say touching my grateful admiration; so you shall imagine the rest. I enclose a note from Kate, to which I hope you will bring the only one acceptable reply. Always, my dear Cattermole,

Faithfully yours